THE LAST
SHIP

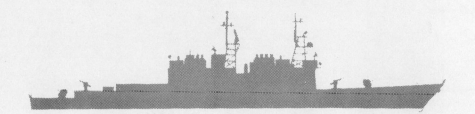

THE LAST
SHIP

.A NOVEL BY.

WILLIAM BRINKLEY

VIKING

FOR GORDON KINGSLEY

"A FRIEND MAY WELL BE RECKONED THE
MASTERPIECE OF NATURE."
—EMERSON

VIKING
Published by the Penguin Group
Viking Penguin Inc., 40 West 23rd Street, New York, New York 10010, U.S.A.
Penguin Books Ltd, 27 Wrights Lane, London W8 5TZ, England
Penguin Books Australia Ltd, Ringwood, Victoria, Australia
Penguin Books Canada Ltd, 2801 John Street, Markham, Ontario, Canada L3R 1B4
Penguin Books (N.Z.) Ltd, 182–190 Wairau Road, Auckland 10, New Zealand

Penguin Books Ltd, Registered Offices:
Harmondsworth, Middlesex, England

Second printing April 1988

Copyright © William Brinkley, 1988
All rights reserved

First published in 1988 by Viking Penguin Inc.
Published simultaneously in Canada

LIBRARY OF CONGRESS CATALOGING IN PUBLICATION DATA
Brinkley, William, 1917–
The last ship.
I. Title.
PS3503.R56175L37   1988   813'.54   87-40288
ISBN 0-670-80981-0

Printed in the United States of America by
Haddon Craftsmen, Scranton, Pennsylvania
Set in Avanta
Design by Ellen S. Levine

.CONTENTS.

CONTENTS

CONTENTS

BOOK VI: THE LAST WOMEN

BOOK VII: ASTARTE

BOOK VIII: *PUSHKIN*

.PROLOGUE.

THE SWORD OF
THE FLEET

In bravura beauty, no ship has ever come off a Navy ways to be compared with the destroyer and she was a fine example of a noble breed. Rakish and swift in the seas: 466 feet overall, beam of fifty-nine feet, draft of twenty-seven, of 8,200 tons displacement with full load, rated speed of 38 knots, nothing existing in any navy of the world that could overtake her on long waters. But most of all her worth was measured in what could not be seen, by what she carried in magazines deep within: She came armed with Tomahawk. She was named the *Nathan James* after a young ensign who had received the Navy Cross for valor in the Second Battle of the Philippine Sea in World War II.

A word about Tomahawk. It was fundamentally different from the big fat intercontinental ballistic missile. Powered by a small air-breathing engine rather than by huge rockets that lifted ICBM's above the atmosphere, Tomahawk "cruised" aerodynamically: a pilotless torpedo-shaped airplane, ingeniously preprogrammed to do all its own work, and of wondrous virtuosity; altogether, perhaps the smartest weapon yet contrived by the heartfelt genius of man. All we did was launch it. A "fire and forget" weapon, it totally guided itself from the moment it left the ship until the moment it found target. Initially it climbed and cruised at around 10,000 feet to conserve its fuel. As it made landfall, it activated its TERCOM (terrain contour matching) attribute, comparing the ground over which it flew with a map stored in its computerized brain, periodically correcting course. Because it was so small and flew so low, hugging the earth, often at treetop level, its own radar return one one-thousandth that of a B-52 bomber, equipped now also with both stealth technology and ECM (electronic countermeasures) to confuse or jam enemy radars, it was virtually impossible to detect, track or intercept. And finally its accuracy defied imagination, an order of magnitude more so than ballistic trajectories. Having flown a couple thousand miles or more, from a ship standing far at sea, it could have guided itself through a selected window in the Kremlin.

Its history had been a curiously sly one. It was with the Tomahawk cruise missile, sometimes it seemed with scarcely anyone noticing the fact, that matters began to get beyond all hope of control. It was almost as if it grew and flourished while people were looking the other way, attention focused on the more glamorous showcase ICBM, due to its enormous size, its silo fixed-residence, and its far smaller, treaty-restricted numbers quite easily verifiable; while all the time, in the back shop, these little things, free of any limitations whatever, were being turned out like sausages, by the thousands. Length twenty-one feet, diameter one foot nine inches, weight 3,200 pounds, wing span eight feet; by comparison with the ICBM, dirt cheap to manufacture ($1.5 million per missile). Until then a crucial premise had been that each side could employ satellites to count nuclear weapons the other deployed. But here now was a device entirely beyond any such reins. One woke up one morning and realized that a weapon had come into being and was proliferating wildly which was literally immune to restraint. By now cozily in place inside hundreds of movable ships, it had become impossible to count, much less to verify, by any system, any more than you could verify the number of chaff launchers, torpedoes, five-inch rounds—or, for that matter, loaves of bread—in the fleet; no way even to determine which Tomahawks were conventionally armed, as many were, which enclosed nuclear warheads, or which of the two a particular ship was carrying: Nothing told them apart. Counting— hence control—was now forever out of reach.

The astonishing thing was how little appreciation existed for what all this meant; for what Tomahawk could do. As if it had not penetrated human understanding that each of them could transport a 200-kiloton nuclear warhead and that ships carried them by the score; the circumstance scarcely realized that Tomahawk embodied a revolution not just in seapower but in warfare itself, to the extent one could fairly state that it made little difference any longer what happened to land weapons, whether they were banned or not. It is a hard thing to say but the fact was this: All of the talk concerning the restriction or elimination of land-based missiles constituted a historic charade, terrible in its meaning, its illusion. If the last one of these had been removed by such negotiations, nothing would have changed. It was almost as though people were being lulled into forgetting that there existed something called the sea: and that there are many seas, indeed that they occupy seven-tenths of the planet, and that there is no spot of land on it that cannot be reached by an object launched from some sea by a ship. People either did not know or could not grasp the fact that a single ship, such as ours, could fairly well exterminate a continent. And there were many ships.

The Navy's consciousness these matters had certainly penetrated, doctrinal writings soon quite accurately enshrining Tomahawk as "the sword of the fleet." We were fitted with two sixty-one-cell Mk 41 VLS's (Vertical Launch Systems) each including at the time of these events twenty-eight TLAM-N (Tomahawk Land Attack Missile-Nuclear) missiles for a total of fifty-six; each of these incarnating the 200-kiloton warhead for an aggregate of 11,200 kilotons. Employing the fission bomb dropped on the city of Hiroshima—yield 12½ kilotons—as a benchmark to determine our strike capability, the *Nathan James* constituted an 896-H ship. Put another way, we could inflict that number of Hiroshimas. Perhaps no one could be expected, in the sense of truly received knowledge, to comprehend this fact. The human mind seems curiously designed to contain the ability to invent such weaponry while in any effective manner lacking that to take in the reality of the force thus created. I, the captain of this ship, scarcely comprehended it myself.

I have often felt that the captain of a Navy ship is the last absolute monarch left on earth, as close to possessing the divine rights of kings as remains. A man-of-war is an autocracy to a degree scarcely explicable to those who dwell out their lives confined within the littorals of the world. Little has changed in this respect since John Paul Jones, under date of 14 September 1775, wrote the Naval Committee of Congress:

> A navy is essentially and necessarily aristocratic. True as may be the political principles for which we are now contending they can never be practically applied or even admitted on board ship, out of port, or off soundings. This may seem a hardship, but it is nevertheless the simplest of truths. Whilst the ships sent forth by the Congress may and must

fight for the principles of human rights and republican freedom, the ships themselves must be ruled and commanded at sea under a system of absolute despotism.

A letter, indeed, reasserted in all editions of Naval Leadership, the present-day bible in the education and making of officers of the United States Navy. On a vessel carrying nuclear missiles these elements of prepotency and authority reach levels suggestive of the limitless. No Caesar, no Alexander or Napoleon, ever had a fraction of the power of a single such ship's commander. The power to launch missiles on their own initiative was given solely to ship's captains, both of surface vessels and of submarines, who were freed of the elaborate system of safeguards—including electronic locks and fail-safe Go-Codes from the President—that presided over the launching of land-based missiles. The "fail-deadly" firing mechanism for ships operated in precisely the opposite manner; this remarkable autonomy considered necessary to insure retaliation after an enemy first strike in the event messages could not get through from National Command Authorities.

The Navy was by no means unaware of this circumstance. It did all, it seems to me, that it could do about it. Before being chosen for command, a captain of such a ship was put through a prolonged and cunning series of tests, not a few brutalizing in character, far beyond in their thoroughness those traditionally rigorous ones given prior to the same assignment to the identical ship conventionally armed, involving, I suppose, every means of prediction as to behavior of a given human being known to modern psychological and psychiatric science. All of it cloaked in every secrecy. Even the existence of the tests and their nature were matters of top-secret classification, even their location (the center happened to be situated in one of those not infrequent naval oddities, land-locked Kansas). It was a procedure of weeks, carried out by teams of ingenious and merciless examiners; examiners not there to determine one's qualifications for sea command—the Navy had already done that—but something quite different and infinitely more difficult of ascertainment.

I can remember feeling a sense of total mental and moral nakedness that I have not experienced before or since, a period associated in my memory with an unalloyed torment, a devastation of the spirit, which I do not enjoy recalling even today, the examiners at times appearing to me as medieval demons whose purpose was to break me. Yet the crucible, in my view, was entirely necessary: an attempt to determine the possession

4

in a single human being of two qualities on the face of it so utterly oppositive in nature as to be on the order of demanding of a man that he be both an atheist and believe absolutely in the existence of a Divine being. In this case, involving the extermination of a million souls, that he would (1) not conceivably of his own volition, having become momentarily crazed, send off the missile that would accomplish that deed and (2) not for a moment hesitate to do so if thus ordered. So far as one could tell a number of such creatures were found—myself among them; though no way ever of testing the matter to a certainty beforehand. The failure rate was high. I have had close friends, actual classmates of mine, men I knew with great intimacy from Annapolis days, who appeared to me the soul of dependability and calm, who were turned down for command of a nuclear-armed ship, no reason of course ever being given, who would have been considered eminently qualified for the captaincy of a vessel not so armed, as evidenced by the fact that they were normally then given such commands. At the end of it I can remember scarcely caring whether I was one of the chosen or not: and yet came that leap of pure joy in me when such became the case. The truth was, I wanted it dearly. Why is a mystery even to myself.

There follows the story of my ship, the *Nathan James*, DDG (guided missile destroyer) 80. I sometimes have wondered, as perhaps did every soul of the 282 men and twenty-three officers in ship's company, as to the extent to which what happened was affected by the fact that thirty-two of these—six officers, twenty-six enlisted—were women. What the difference might have been had they not been present and aboard.

.BOOK I.

THE ISLAND

.1.

LAND

The island lay alone in the sea, moored in tranquil waters of turquoise, embraced in a radiant stillness, trees rising from it beyond the sienna beaches, and no sign whatever of life.

"Right standard rudder," I said.

"Right standard rudder, aye, sir," the helmsman repeated.

I could feel the ship swerve under me, elegantly responsive. "Steady on course two two five."

"Steady on course two two five, aye, sir . . . Checking two two eight magnetic."

The words needed little more than whispers in the undivided quiescence that reigned everywhere. I stepped out on the starboard bridge wing, the ship brought now line abreast to the land. Not a breath of wind stirred the morning. The last stars paled in the sky, the silent waters stretched away in a vast mirror, glittering in the oncoming sunlight, bringing with it the softened sky of low latitudes, sea and sky so deliquescing into one that I would have had difficulty taking a sextant bearing, making a horizon. I brought my binoculars up and slowly glassed the one object that broke the endless blue. It stood flat on a bearing N.E. to S.W., then rose sharply to a curious, shelflike protuberance before falling off

9

again to the sea. The island was perhaps a dozen miles in length. The far side of the island was shrouded in low flocculent clouds, opaque cumulus, so that I could not make its breadth. I brought the binoculars down, returned to the pilot house, looked at the Fathometer, and gave the command to the lee helm.

"All engines stop."

"All engines stop, aye, sir." I heard the clank of the engine-order telegraph, then a slight shudder through the ship. Then she lay still in the water.

"You may resume the conn, Mr. Thurlow," I said to my navigator. "Let go the anchor."

"Aye, aye, sir."

I stepped back to the wing and looked over into the blue-green water, luminescent with sunlight. Then the anchor hit it in an explosion of turbulence. I could hear the long-drawn rumbling of the chain through the hawsepipe as the great cast-iron thing descended. Presently the ship gave another shudder, then settled, as the anchor payed out. I stepped back into the pilot house.

"Ship anchored, sir," Thurlow reported. "Seventy fathoms on deck."

"Mr. Woodward," I said to the JOOD. "Take the conn. Mr. Thurlow. Will you please prepare a landing party. Yourself. Chief Delaney. Silva, Preston. Eight hands, marksmen. And myself. Number Two boat— Meyer, Barker. Bring a shovel. An ax. We've got a couple of machetes?"

"Aye, sir. A couple."

"Officers to carry side arms. All others to sling carbines. Except Delaney and Travis."

"When will we be shoving off, Captain?"

"Immediately. Look alive, Mr. Thurlow."

"Yes, *sir.*"

He disappeared with a quickstep out the pilot house. I glanced once more at the island; from the ocean rising, it looked like an emerald of unimagined beauty, worn as an adornment by the sea simply to relieve its vastness, its impossible loneliness. I went below to my cabin and strapped on the web belt and the service .45 and joined the others at the accommodation ladder. On the hushed water the boat bobbed hardly at all below us. The men descended. Then the chief. Then Thurlow. Then myself. We came over the mile of lagoon, the boat's engine sounding shamelessly loud in the great stillness, and slid gently onto the sand. We debarked in reverse order, myself first. The Navy: officers last into the boat, first out, and by order of rank. We stood on the sand, feeling the immense strangeness of earth under our feet, saying not a word, regarding the island with

10

the careful, suspicious appraisal one gives a stranger, credentials unknown, with whom one is required to have dealings. I looked at my watch. 0745.

"Mr. Thurlow. Single-file, couple paces apart. Steady as you go, men. Look about. Chief. Come along with me, if you will."

Chief Gunner's Mate Amos Delaney had grown up on a Missouri farm and had known farming as a first love, the sea as a second. I think perhaps he loved both farm and sea in equal measure, as a man might reasonably two women, differing in aspect rather than degree, both of high charms. He played the fiddle, quite well, and on good evenings, with the ship running a gentle sea, the men liked to gather round him on the fantail and listen to the old songs. If the sea was calm enough I could hear the music faintly from the bridge, and sometimes the low lilt of sailor voices drifting out over the water, telling of hills and loves far away.

With Thurlow and Delaney alongside or directly behind me at the lead, we entered into the island and commenced our reconnoitering. Its denseness closed quickly around us as we moved through an abrupt chillness of air, not unpleasant, thicket, shrub, and the high clashing branches of trees blotting out the day, so that soon looking back, the men in their dungarees, I could see only the sailor's white hats strung out behind me through the foliage. Then a little farther on the curtain parted, the sunlight came leaping through the spiring trees in long dazzling white shafts, mote-sparkling, then sweet clearings, green grown as lawns, appeared, oases for a look at the cerulean island sky before plunging back into the forested caverns. In there seemed eerie, a mystery of hush; one wondered if man had ever before disturbed these dark silences. A seaman forgets: The myriad odors of the land sprang at us with a keen awareness after the long uniform smell of the sea. And in riotous flourishings the multicolors after the sea's single one. Everywhere, in tree and shrub, in jubilant fertility, flared the discrete greens, a queen's offering of shades, from yellowy lime to deepest tourmaline, and often the fragrance of strange flowers in lavish presentations, cerise, indigo, a royal lavender. It brought a soaring of my spirit to see the manner in which the men, in their state of debilitation not just physical but mental and emotional, too, were so marvelously lifted by all of this, by these sights, the smells, the sounds: that quick leap inside like an extra heartbeat when we saw the first bee, nuzzling into some bud, intent on its ancient business of pollination as if it were the most important work on earth. "Isn't that a pretty sight, Captain?" Delaney said as we paused and watched it almost reverentially.

Exploring as we went, feeling our way with due tenderness, I was leading us to the island's southmost end, our clear objective that shelflike eminence I had observed from the ship's bridge, for if the island had what

11

we were looking for it would in every likelihood have it there; or have it not at all. From within our darksome cover, we could hear just ahead a curious tinkling sound, not unlike wind chimes where no wind blew. We shouldered our way against the growth and broke through it onto a ravine that curled around the base of a hill.

A creek gleaming in the patches of shadow and light, the broken sunshine slanting through the trees that climbed the hillside, rippled through the ravine, clean and clear and washing over shining white and tan pebbles. I looked back and saw the men still single-filed. I motioned them up and we bunched around the creek and stood regarding it and listening to its gurgling sound as a kind of marvel. I kneeled, bent, and sipped. Then so did Delaney, then the men fell upon it, all of us lapping in the water with eager avarice.

"That is fine water," I said, straightening up. After living for so long on the ship's evaporator water, whose taste was that of a yet-to-be-discovered species of metal, it was nectar and achingly cold.

"As good as anything in the Ozarks," Delaney said. This was the gunner's mate's metaphor for all heavenly things. "There have to be springs up there, Captain."

We curved around the creek and started up, the sailors with their carbines slung loosely over their shoulders, through the stands of trees that held to the gently rising hillside, the shimmering bolts of sunlight penetrating the branches and seeming to draw us upward. Here and there we stopped at a tree and examined it. I called up Noisy Travis, the shipfitter and a first-rate carpenter. He was a tall, angular Maine man and so taciturn as to earn that nickname from the crew. But he communicated eloquently with wood. Delaney had spoken of the usefulness of stakes. And wood of a certain strength could have other employments.

With his ax Travis skillfully cut into the bark of a couple of the trees to reveal the white wood beneath and then cut into that. Into one the blade went much more deeply.

"Well, Noisy?" I said at last. He never volunteered information. You always had to ask.

"A kind of ash," he said of the harder one. "Like. Couldn't say the name. But it's working wood."

"I wonder if you could make a wheelbarrow out of that wood," I said.

Travis gave the wood a somber, thoughtful look. "Aye, sir. Make about anything out of that wood, Cap'n," he said.

We moved on, climbing slowly, inspecting various growths. Suddenly there appeared a large bush on which a small scarlet fruit hung in many clusters, at one of which a yellow-and-sapphire bird one could have enclosed in a hand hovered like a toy helicopter, wings flapping vigorously to keep him in place, long tail employed ingeniously as a rudder, while he pecked away at the fruit. We watched in rapt fascination, feeling the wonder and comic aspect of the sight. He seemed concerned not at all by our approach but continued pecking, independent as you please, as if he were not about to allow these vulgar and impolite newcomers to interfere with getting his fill. Having done so, he regarded us dismissively with his outsized orangeish eyes, emitted a burst of high-soprano song, and took his leave, sweeping swiftly upward through the trees. He had told us that the fruit was safe, and Delaney plucked one off and popped it in his mouth.

"Wild plum," he said. "Something like. We've got them back home. Try one, Captain."

He held it out. It had a lovely fresh tart taste.

"Why aren't you men helping yourselves?" I said.

With that the sailors descended upon the bush, tasting the fruit, then coming back for more until the bush was stripped as naked as if a whole flight of birds had fallen upon it.

"I can't remember the last time, Captain." The voice had the depth and resonance of the sea itself. "Something fresh like that."

It was Preston, boatswain's mate first, a man of the Old Navy. He was not a man one could simply glance at and ignore. It was not just his size, his armory of biceps, musculature, rock-hardness, and the vast reserves of strength these suggested. There was a certain nobility of bearing in him, a seaman's bearing—I think it would have been apparent to a stranger, perhaps in his case in a manner he did not understand, that here was a man apart. My feeling of this was of course bound up in the fact of his being the finest pure seaman we had aboard, as pure Navy as a man could be, a thirty-year man, knowing as much about those demanding, sentient structures called ships as it is possible to know. He had a deceptively sanguine face, as a roll call of liberty ports had discovered during my command of the ship. I had sometimes felt that the port itself should be warned that we were coming ashore with Preston, though in reality he was a gentle man unless aroused, and afterward, if at captain's mast, sincerely contrite that he had been forced by those shore people to use his extraordinary strength to straighten them out on something or other. Under his sailor's hat his shirt was open, and through the thick blackish hair I could view the full glory of the battle of Trafalgar. A delicately lettered "Sharon" was etched across a small heart in the great fold of a shoulder, and immediately above the nipples the artist had depicted two bluebirds, meant to guarantee that you would never drown: the bluebirds would bear you up. As Preston sometimes pointed out, he had never drowned. The Navy life had been the only one he had ever known, the sea his home as much as it was that of any fish, and only on the land did he have confrontational difficulties with his species, never with his ship-mates. It was as though the shore were alien to him and existed largely to provoke him. Partly because of his seaman's skills and partly because of his strength and his huge magnanimity concerning it—if anything heavy on the ship needed lifting someone would always say, "Get Preston"—I somehow counted on him in a special way in the times ahead. Looking at him now as he went for the fruit, I thought how that great body of his, as with the others, had been so depleted.

"Nothing could taste better, Boats," I said. "Let's see what's up there."

We pushed upward on a steepening grade, crested the hill, and came to an abrupt halt, as one man without the necessity of a command.

A sunlit plain, high above the sea, stood spread out before us, stretching to the island's end until halted by the blue, and covered entirely in a long and glistening silky lime-green grass. A good dozen acres of it, I calculated, plain and growth seeming altogether unlike the rest of the undulating, thick-grown island we had just traversed, a pasture of promise and orderliness perched above the jungle wilderness. From off the sea came a faint southeasterly freshening, setting the willowy grass singing in the wind and bearing on it a scent half sea and half the tart fructuousness of earth in growth.

"Well, what do you know," Delaney said.

We marched gingerly forward into it, the grass rustling around our shoe tops. Then the gunner's mate stopped, knelt, shoved back his hat, and began to pull away the grass until he had exposed a patch about a foot square. Then he took the shovel and plunged into it, turning over a large bladeful of earth of a chocolate-brown dampness. From it rose an odor pungent and parturient. The gunner's mate leaned nose to it.

"The smell is the first thing, Captain," he said. "To tell you what you've got. This one's farmer's perfume."

Delaney cupped a handful of earth. I was astonished to see him actually taste it, with the profound concentration of the winegrower sampling a new vintage. Then he let it dribble slowly out of his hand, squishing its texture with his fingers. When it was gone he held his hand straight up, like a man being sworn, to show how the soil clung to it.

"Porous. Moist. And notice how deep that shovel went with hardly no resistance, Captain?"

I knew nothing of the land but I had begun to learn. The gunner's mate looked around the shining expanse of grass, then at me.

"I'd say it would grow most anything. I mean, that grows in this latitude. What was that you were saying about the rains, Mr. Thurlow?"

"Most of the year about twenty minutes a day," the navigator said. He was an officer almost feverishly committed not just to the stars which guide ships but to geography, seasons, weather, the movement of waters, to all the permutations of the earthly system, a Vesalius of the planet. "By the clock."

"That explains," Delaney said. "That and the springs, that creek. And those bees. Nothing is as smart as a bee."

I could feel the men looking at one another. Sailors are slow to question a ship's captain but I could sense theirs as clearly as if they had spoken them aloud. Was it to be here? Delaney picked up another handful of earth and let it run through his fingers.

"It'll grow things, Captain," he said. "But it'll take a load of work. The hardest kind of work in the world, I mean." He paused a beat. "Stoop labor."

He looked at me rather intently as though, too delicate to put the matter directly, he was wondering whether I comprehended what was meant by those two words.

"I understand, Gunner," and said it back myself to make clear that that at least I knew: "Stoop labor."

"Aye, sir. It'll be the only way here." And once more like a couplet clap of somber bells: "Stoop labor."

Gently embracing us on either side was the sound of water, one way the creek on its course through the ravine, the other the murmuring sea. The former sound certified the first indispensable gift we asked of the island. We walked through the grass and came to where the island ended. A gentle cliff, itself like an immense dune, dropped down to clean beaches.

A sound startled us. We turned to see a white burst of birds, cawing and wings flapping, take flight. Some kind of tern. They caught a wind current and headed out, seaward.

"Let's have a look," I said.

We climbed along the top of the dunes and found their nests, tucked in astutely under the protecting ridges. Not all the terns had taken wing at our approach. Three remained on guard duty, looking entirely stalwart and competent, fussing furiously, snapping out savagely to stab at us with their respectable beaks and keep us off their nests. So there were creatures

15

approaching birth beneath them. Silva looked at me, eyes point-blank on mine, and then out to where the diminishing white shapes of the hunting terns could be seen flying in tight formation low above the blue.

"There are fish out there, Captain. The question is . . ."

Once Angus Silva had been a trawler fisherman, out of New Bedford, Massachusetts. He was a born sailor, almost literally so, having been in either boats or ships since he was seven. He had the burnished skin and chiseled features of generations of Portuguese ancestors who had known no livelihood save the sea, and curly hair, thick, black as licorice. Into that face his Scotch mother had inserted eyes as blue as the sea beyond soundings and they gave it a curious effect, to me a somewhat saintly one, as though above some altar. Silva would have been rightly startled to hear that. He, too, now would be counted on much beyond his rating of boatswain's mate second. I spoke to him.

"The question is," I said, "in what abundance."

"Aye, sir," he said soberly.

"Tomorrow morning: take a boat out. Very early." If I knew little of the land, I knew the sea and when fish ran. "We have to be certain, Silva. Very certain. Beyond any chance of mistake. You understand?"

"Aye, sir. I'll be over them before first light, Captain. If they're there."

We stood a few moments more, all of us, unspeaking, with our thoughts. One of these, an alleviation to the unpredictability that was never absent, surely was a kind of quiet exultation at seeing these living things. The hummingbird, the bee, the terns: they bespoke the island, a thing that lived, breathed. Another, certainly for me and doubtless for all, was a somber taking the measure of that willowy grass, which we continued to study like appraisers. We came back from the nests and I stood on the heights looking out into the vastness of the ocean reach. Beside it everything else had always seemed small to me, almost insignificant. I never really felt free ashore and cared little for what went on there. But now it was the shore I had to turn to, the land which offered sustenance, if such were to be found at all, though the sea would have to provide its share. The water stretched, great and silent as a painting, far as the eye took you, as virgin as at the first creation save only for the ship, slightly darker, sitting in regal stillness between pale azures; as though too painted there and seeming but to enhance the infinite loneliness. The destroyer: I had always loved them. I thought how lucky I had been to spend nearly all of my Navy life in them and luckiest of all, or so I felt at the time, finally to be given this one to command. Then I thought of her company and how they had thus far borne up, under trials, under calamity and horrors to test the most valiant of men. A fierce resolve filled me: to shield them from all further harm; to bring them through. Then as I looked at the ship, the pain came as it had so often, a quick, throbbing thing, an overpowering sense of loss, of the men taken from her. I had learned to be prepared for it. I waited, confronting it as an old enemy by now, forcing it down, burying it as I had learned to do, knew I must, until its next sure resurrection. I faced back, from sea and ship, and stood looking at the plateau of grass: another thought, one I was not prepared for, struck me like a blow. Had we not lost them, the food which that field might, with immense work and even more immense luck, yield, together with what we had aboard, could not have been enough, whereas with present size of ship's company we stood a chance. I stood shocked with a sense of shame that such a thought could occur to me.

Vertical sunshine now fell full on our plateau as the sun crossed over and brought a new awareness: the sun nourished; it would yet, on this latitude, add a sure fierceness to the struggle of parturition, of making this meadow yield to us what we wanted from it.

"Men, let's go back to the ship," I said.

We came down off the plateau and along the creek, through the trees and brush to the beach, and started along it toward the boat in the distance, sitting intrusively on the naked shoreline. The navigator and I walked a little behind the others, speaking in quiet tones.

"Well, Mr. Thurlow?"

"Favorable climate for it, you'd have to say, sir. Two rainy seasons of about two months apiece. November-December, May-June. Most days in the nonrainy season, just a twenty-minute shower as noted. Usually about thirteen hundred hours. We'll probably have today's before we get back." He looked at his watch. "In fact, almost any moment."

We stopped and studied the countenance of the island, trying to penetrate it with our minds, to break through its secretive demeanor. I looked north and then across it, where the low ledge of cumulus still preserved unrevealed the far western side. Were there people somewhere in there? I was on the verge of an hallucination. We had become accustomed to, experts in, hallucinations, in chimeras. I looked back to this side, where each way the land curved to form the U-lagoon. To the south the grassy plateau ended in the long ridge which sat like a sea lookout above the beach.

"That ridge," Thurlow said thoughtfully. "Nothing else but just that. Reminds me a touch of the coastline down toward Carmel. The way it sits up there, I mean, rather cockylike, looking down at the sea. Were you ever in Carmel, Captain?"

"Oh, yes, Mr. Thurlow. I was in Carmel."

We went on. Sure enough Thurlow's rain came up. Just out of nowhere. We stepped off the beach and stood under some trees and waited for it to finish. And sure enough, only about twenty minutes. A clean, straight fall, virtually soundless, gentle as dew. Then the sun was back out, just as though it had never happened. The island had taken a shower to refresh itself.

"Congratulations, Mr. Thurlow."

He looked at his watch. We started back up the beach. "Actually I was seven minutes off. Highly irregular, what?" Lieutenant Thurlow was a sort of defrocked Rhodes Scholar, with the distinction, he once told me, not without pride, of being the only grantee ever to be sent down from Oxford. For what transgression he never said. At least he had been there long enough to get fluent Russian out of it, a linguistic talent that had served us well beginning with that astonishing arrangement with the Russian submarine at Gibraltar. It was his conceit, and form of humor, at times to speak in mock British tones, phrases. It was not a type of wit I would ordinarily have appreciated but in Thurlow even I sometimes found it amusing, I never knew why. Maybe it was just Thurlow himself I found amusing, most of the time. He had an undeniable charm: off and on he was by way of being my court jester. No one aboard had been so . . . well, almost blithe about our circumstance; no one seemingly so little changed by it. This acted to give him an edge, an advantage. He was a truly gifted navigator, and, as I have said, knew a great deal concerning the earth's manifestations other than just stars. Within the limits of his one central interest, he was a sound thinker. If he had a fault, it may have been that when he ventured beyond that interest he sometimes thought too much. He understood things better than people. I had had little choice but to make him executive officer, the ship's assigned exec having been on emergency leave when we launched in the Barents. Still I would much rather have him than not have him. He had the far-ranging mind, inventive, out there on the frontiers. Qualities we would need, need now and later.

"No problem about showers," he was saying. "All hands can just strip and stand outside for twenty minutes."

"I don't think we can keep looking." I stopped and picked up a handful of beach. It was uncommonly fine sand, in texture and tint like a woman's face powder. I looked up to where, considerably down-beach from us now, high above the sea, stood the tableland of the silky grass. "Delaney seemed pretty sure it would give us, stand a good chance of giving us, what we need. Not easily. But nothing will be. Replenishment of stores." Food, we both understood. For some reason, perhaps because it was the final barrier, one tried not to say the word. "We're getting too close." Nor did I mention fuel.

I spoke without looking at him.

"That rainy-season pattern. Planting times in that kind of situation?"

Ignorant as I was of such matters, I imagined I knew that one, just by common sense, but Thurlow would know more.

"Right after the close of one rainy season. The drill is: get them in and out before the next one arrives."

"Do I understand you correctly? Another such calendar arrangement would not come again for five months?"

"That seems so if these calculations are accurate. And they have to be. My opinion, sir."

There would be hard work, brutal as work could be, in that sun, of a kind most of the men had never been near, knew nothing whatever of. Stoop labor. The phrase was not hard enough to convey the ferocity of it, especially in these latitudes. The men to endure it. Then the land up there to come through, that dozen acres to harbor a fecundity we in truth could only guess at. The contents of Delaney's shipboard greenhouse to take to their new home. The necessary luck, the gunner's mate had educated me, wherever growing things are in venture . . . if all that came together. We needed to be right the first time. The reserves for fail-and-try-again were simply not there.

"So we would have to move fast. Begin right now, in fact?"

"I'm afraid so, sir."

He stopped there, waiting. There would be no further help from that quarter. But none was really expected. I knew it and he knew it. It was not his part to take responsibility, not this one. He had learned well the old Navy lesson: Never stick your neck out an inch further than is required, lest it get chopped off at the collarbone. Not applicable to ship's captains, these not being chosen for their ability to avoid hard decisions.

"Then that would seem to settle it. We have no choice."

We stood silent on the strand. He said nothing but gave me a look that contained a question as to whether there was more. So I offered a little of it. A lie would not do. But vagueness, given things as they were, was acceptable, even imperative. A captain was allowed that in the name of his men's welfare. It was no time to get the other started as scuttlebutt. It could whip through ship's company, and as the most disturbing of elements, just when all our powers, physical, mental, emotional, were spoken for by the plain of grass.

"For the time being," I said. "For our immediate needs. Then we'll just have to see." I stopped there. Thurlow, or any other of ship's company, would get no more for now.

I looked seaward. "And of course out there will have to deliver. If we can trust those birds. Well, we can trust Silva. We'll know that part by tomorrow."

I turned and scanned the land again. "It's a pretty place," I said finally. I seemed to want to conclude it with an inanity.

This he safely agreed with. "That it is, Captain. A pretty place. When will you tell the others?"

"Soon, Mr. Thurlow. Soon."

"Oh, Captain?"

"Yes, Mr. Thurlow."

"The women, sir. Do you plan to bring the women ashore or leave them aboard?"

I turned, facing him. I saw his knowledge that even as he said the words he had gone too far.

"Who said I was planning to bring anybody ashore, Mr. Thurlow?"

I could hear the hardness in my voice, and it must have been in my look as well for I saw the sudden fear in his eyes, fear of me. Well, that was all right, too. If ever exactitude in matters of discipline, than which nothing else can hold a ship together, were demanded, it was in this.

"All I meant, sir, was if just possibly here or somewhere else . . ."

"Mr. Thurlow."

He stopped, I think truly aghast now that he had ventured there, in such forbidden waters. "Mr. Thurlow," I said, and heard the cold edge. "When I decide something, and then when I decide it is time to tell you of my decision, I will do so. Do I make myself clear?"

"Entirely, sir. My fault altogether. I was out of line, sir."

"Embark the men, Mr. Thurlow."

We came up to where they were waiting at the boat. They stood in a desultory silence, their eyes ranging slowly back and forth over the island. I looked down the beach at our many footprints, winding away and out of sight, violations of the chaste sand.

"Do you think men have been here before, Captain?"

I turned, somehow startled. It was Barker, seaman apprentice, coxswain striker, only eighteen, a boy from Texas, literally the last hand, joining the ship in Norway straight out of boot camp at Great Lakes; had not, before coming aboard, even set eyes on the sea; lean and supple of body, tall, in any other society but that of sailors to be considered almost wondrously handsome, radiating an exceptional air of innocence. The question was almost as if, had they not been, how could they intend to be here now?

"If they were, it was a long time ago, Billy." He was the one hand aboard everyone called by his Christian name, seeming that boyish, that young: nonetheless already on his way to becoming a fine seaman. My hand touched his shoulder, dropped. A gesture I would once not have made. "But—maybe it's us—wherever there's land somebody has to be first."

He spoke almost shyly. "Yes, sir. I guess that's so."

I followed the men into the boat and we made for the ship. She rose gray and gallant beyond the blue-green lagoon, lean and alert, seeming to strain against the leash of her anchor, as if telling us that she was ready to up anchor on a moment's notice. It was not so. The most brutal fact of all: so little fuel left. Still, she has done her job, I thought. She had brought us here, nearly a hundred degrees in latitude, from the frigid Barents to tropical seas, to all appearances sound in body and mind, if near, possibly, certain edges. Now I had to do mine.

All the rest of the day long, to the last of dusk, I kept the boats going back and forth from ship to shore, in a kind of series of liberty parties, such as they were, so that all hands could touch down on the island for an hour or so. So that all could feel the spectral, unreal thing I had felt: Land under our feet after four months on the oceans with only the decks of the USS *Nathan James*, DDG 80, guided missile destroyer, first of her class, beneath us. I stood watching the boats; stood looking, studying, in profound concentration, the stranger island, its plaintive scents drifting across to me, as if it should somehow be about to speak some counsel into my ears, saying either "Come and see" or "Stay away from me." The one or the other. Knowing that it would say neither, holding steadfast to its impregnable air of mystery; knowing that the answer could come only from where answers always must in a ship off soundings—from within a captain's secret all-lonely soul. Yet feeling surely it must be the former, how could it be otherwise: Remembering that moment when Lieutenant (jg) Selmon, gone ashore all alone with his instruments, staying overlong to make sure beyond all doubt of his findings, had finally returned, climbed the accommodation ladder to the quarterdeck where I stood awaiting him, and spoken in his quiet manner that imprimatur that took us awhile even to comprehend before belief set in: "Captain, the island is uncontaminated."

.2.

BAND OF BROTHERS

I: Morning

The memory so seared in my soul as to have become forever a part of me, as deep scars leave their rubrics upon the body; occasionally coming upon me suddenly, at unexpected times, but coming without fail at night, as ritualistically as the prayers children say on their knees before tumbling into bed; the very act of turning into my bunk presenting me with the terrible vision, clear as on a slide-viewer, of those four boats disappearing over the western horizon, swallowed up by the sea: 109 shipmates, two of these women, in a desperate, yes, in my view, fraudulent attempt to reach home, the mutiny led by an officer who I believed had deceived them. It was as if I had reached a compact with that remembrance to allow it its two minutes or so of daily reenactment if it then would allow me to find sleep; or perhaps a ship's captain's special knowledge that to permit it more was to surrender to it yet another victim, making it impossible for me to command. The tenacity of the memory was not altogether a negative thing, for it constituted also a warning that kept forever alert an absolute resolve on my part, exceeding all others, that it should never happen again with this of my ship's company that remained; the memory rendering the further service of causing me to bear indelibly in mind that grim truth I had so imprudently, in an almost criminal negligence, let slide before: most mutinies are led by officers.

■■■

Nothing is more deadly to a ship's company's confidence in its captain than undue hesitation or procrastination. Thus well I knew the urgency of making my initial will concerning the island known, quickly, decisively, for any trepidations could only build and fester if the captain were seen as irresolute. The island's first reconnoitering had implanted a cautious hope. I felt the prudence of a second appraisal. For that purpose I had sent Gunner's Mate Delaney off, accompanied by Lieutenant Thurlow, in the early morning for a final assay of the grassy plateau. Since sea as well as land must prove fecund for us, Silva also I sent forth, seaward in a boat long before daybreak. One thing more. I determined that it was insistent that I take an exact and meticulous inventory of the ship as of this our moment of crossover. Delaney and Silva not being due back until noonday or beyond with their findings, I began on this matter.

To assist me in the first part of the task I would require Lieutenant Girard, my supply officer, and the lieutenant's efficient if somewhat free-mouthed deputy, Storekeeper First Class Talley, and had so alerted them the night before. The three of us started on the task at 0600, when light was just appearing from beyond the east's horizon, casting its halo of rose over the dark island which sat impassively awaiting our decision. Not until the sun had reached its blazing zenith, six hours later, did we complete the grim labor of tabulating what we had brought out with us, to last us for—how long?

When the Navy not long ago first commenced assigning a few women to ships, I felt it to be one of those incalculable fundamental errors that seem to be made only by civilizations in decline, a lapse profound and past comprehension in both the most elementary morality and judgment. The idea that we should take these embodiments—harbors, repositories—of all that is gentle and of final value in life, and God and Nature's chosen instrument for the species' very survival, and place them where they would be caught up in the ancient rough-and-tumble of shipboard existence, where peril was one's daily bread, indeed where they might be maimed or slaughtered, and this act based on the concept that equality consisted in women doing exactly what men do: this seemed to me wicked to the point of malignancy, an abomination in the sight of the Lord and of pure reason, and a consummate fraud pulled off on half the human race by their own kind, abetted by a number of men masquerading as their champions. Besides these lofty moral considerations there lay a practical one. To add to the already immensely complex daily burden of operating a fighting ship a required ship's company mixture of female and male appeared to many of us charged with the task an aberration little short of madness, comparable to putting ammunition stores alongside engine-room boilers. There was even this: any true sailor has learned long since the first lesson of the sea: never trifle with it, lest it turn on you. The sea is a tyrannical place, ruthlessly unforgiving of man's frailties and miscalculations. I was not at all certain but that it might look upon this novelty—women aboard warships—as some kind of personal affront, a violation of the natural order, an act of hubris, an insolent challenge let loose upon its domain, not to be tolerated: and in its Olympian wrath in some fashion exact the terrible toll it never fails to levy for man's arrogance toward it.

However, since the deed was struck, I treated females, once they began to come aboard the *Nathan James,* exactly as I did the men and officers. If equality was what they wanted, equality I would give them. I was not prepared further to insult them by setting for them standards lower than those I enjoined on my other sailors.

I never changed a particle in my view that the placement of women on men-of-war was a fallacy grave in the extreme. In particular, all my ethical reasons against doing so stood. But, that aside, I must in fairness say that, where practical matters are concerned, it worked out considerably better than I had foreseen. The doom and gloom predicted by many Navy men, myself among them, for ships with "mixed crews" was not forthcoming. Certainly not on my ship, or on any ship of which I had knowledge. For, I believe, a number of reasons. To start with: As it is true, by a process akin to natural selection, that the very best men and officers in the Navy make certain that they go to sea while the worst just as diligently seek out a "dry" career, earnestly managing never to set foot off the land onto blue waters—an odd, forever incomprehensible sort of sailor to my mind—such was true also of the women when the Navy began to send a certain number of these to sea. We got the best.

Our stores relating to keeping the body well-functioning fell, I calculated, into these groups and in order of importance: first, food, canned, bulked, and refrigerated; second, clothing; third, medical supplies; fourth, toiletries and assorted incidentals. The first, second, and fourth were the charge of Lieutenant Girard, so we dealt with these. Medical stores I would inventory later with the ship's doctor. It was my feeling that an on-hands inspection might suggest ways to cut down further, to conserve, and tell us more directly where it was urgent we do so.

Hunger: No greater enemy exists. If it was not upon us it clearly had appeared on the horizon. Starting in the reefer deck in the bottom of the ship, we entered the dry provisions storeroom, the large compartment housing our canned and freeze-dried foods. We stood for a few moments in sober contemplation of how little there was left. Then Girard began to call out the item and the number of cases remaining while Talley checked them on her clipboard: lima beans, peas, potatoes, spinach, others. Moving on to flour, sugar, rice, beans, in hundred-pound bags. From that compartment, down the passageway to the bank of chill boxes, these the most diminished of all. Girard sounded forth and Talley registered the few boxes of beef, slabs of bacon, and the rest.

"Jesus-God, it's cold in here," popped out of Talley at one point. "We're going to freeze our buns off."

She was a butterball of a girl—less so now. She had a tendency to speak up, but with such a free-speech naturalness that it would have been like asking a macaw to shut up.

"That'll do, Talley," Lieutenant Girard said sharply.

Lieutenant Girard had of course been doing frequent calculations and reporting these to me. Now she said, speaking aloud thoughts we had unremittingly gone over, but with perhaps new elements now added:

"At continued reduced rations we can live off ship's stores for four months—allowing that for any kind of harvest ashore . . . figuring in an awful lot of fish . . ." Her voice bore down. "I mean a *lot* . . . I've checked all this with Palatti. He agrees."

Chief Palatti ran ship's messes. He concocted the best food I had yet to eat in the Navy, and in addition was a ferocious scrounger in ports we visited for the choicest local products to liven up the daily fare. The latter talent unfortunately was no longer exercisable by him, but I did not underestimate his ingenuity even in an island waste. Indeed, given our circumstances, I looked on him as one of our mainstays.

"If the fish come through . . ." She was looking straight at me.

"Fish," I repeated. The word seemed to stand in the air, as if representing salvation itself—or at least half of it. The other half of course being that southern plateau on the island. I waited a moment in the quietness. "Very well. We'll just have to see what Silva comes back with."

I regarded her gravely. "Thank you for doing these projections. I value initiative, Lieutenant."

"It's my job, Captain," she said axiomatically.

"Of course it is," I said, a bit briskly. "I still value it."

I moved quickly on.

"All right, Talley," I said. "You can now get them out of here. I wouldn't want you to freeze them off."

She grinned a bit sheepishly. "Aye, sir."

We were glad to move from the reefer cold, up to the second deck and back down past the watertight bulkhead into another compartment. We stood amid the small stores. Girard's voice had become a liturgical monotone . . . "Trousers . . . Shirts . . . Hats . . . Shoes . . . Skivvies . . ." She stepped across a space. "Pantyhose . . . Brassieres . . . Panties . . . Blouses . . . Hats . . . Shoes . . . Sewing kits . . ."

As she called out these items, my thoughts ranged away into areas somehow activated by watching her. In the past six months I had dealt with Lieutenant Girard and perhaps been more in her company than was the case with any other officer aboard; a natural, actually unavoidable thing: she was first our supply officer and, second, what the Navy calls "welfare and recreation officer," more explicitly, in present circumstances, morale officer: and on my list of concerns none stands higher than stores and morale. Indeed a subtle and indefinable bond had been created between us as we conferred daily over the diminishing nature of the one and the not infrequently changing nature of the other; meticulous labors, exhausting, fraying of both mind and nerves. Difficult enough to go through so almost incessantly with anybody, saved, I somehow felt, by her characteristics: a sardonic smile breaking at just the needed moment across her lips to relieve a tension; a simple, modulating look from level gray eyes. She combined inner toughness with clarity of insight—stalwart assets, being as she is, so to speak, in our most direct lines of fire: that the men eat, and that they bear up. She faced stern facts entirely absent of that visible and depleting emotion which itself adds formidably to matters already demanding; complex problems, some fiendishly so, each as something to be coped with and handled, with a coolness apparently unassailable. I have not mentioned another aspect that may be as important as any: her effect on others of ship's company. Her very steadiness as she went about her duties had the consequence of calming those more vulnerable than herself in our circumstances to problems of an emotional character; her self-possession acted to instill a similar state in her shipmates.

Beyond this litany of virtues lay other suggestions, possibly not altogether so seraphic, some apparent enough, some little more than presentiments and so in doubt. Some may have found a certain severity in her, an intimation of iron within, an excess of poise, a quiet knowingness that might at times seem to flirt with a felt superiority, a breath of loftiness. I knew of none of these carried, thus far, to the clearly intemperate. If she had a fault as an officer it may have been that in exactitude she was in some ways perhaps overly unbending. She carried that greatest of all handicaps that may befall a woman: She was simply too bright for most men of this world.

Something "remote" about her: In the two years since she had come aboard I felt I had learned nothing of what lay behind this composed, impregnable exterior except for one thing. I had discovered—mainly through reading her service record and reviewing her PQS (personal qualification standards) that accompanied her—that she had had as fierce a desire to go to sea as any man I had known; and being persistent, even exasperatingly so, in achieving her purpose and what she judged fair (with an adroit ability, one sensed, to equate the two)—something I gleaned also from the comments in these reports of her previous commanding officers—was one of the first women to do so. She had come straight out of Wellesley College (a scholarship student, the daughter of a small-town newspaper editor in North Carolina) into the Navy as an ordinary seaman recruit, at just the time the Navy had announced its imminent opening of the world's oceans to women, the latter act, I had an idea, strongly determining the former. She had gone through boot camp at Great Lakes, and after assignment to NAVSTA Norfolk, into Officer Candidate School. She had wanted gunnery. No such sea billets were then open to her gender. She had taken supply rather than mildew on the beach. Then two years aboard a cruiser as a junior supply officer. The moment one looked at her in uniform one saw an exceptional thing. She wore "water wings." They certified her as a surface warfare officer; meaning that in addition to fulfilling her supply duties she had mastered and passed the rigorous tests in every major combat system the ship carried, including standing actual watches in each. Two more years ashore, recurrent requests for further sea duty and at last aboard the *Nathan James* as supply officer. Her service record revealed another curious point at the time of but mild interest to me: she had specifically requested the duty she had got: a guided missile destroyer. However first-rate a supply officer, she had made certain that she qualified for gunnery. She was by now Navy as much as any man. I was suddenly aware, watching her on the ladder, that she had mastered with seeming ease something I had felt, since these matters began, to be among the most difficult of feats: at once to be a Navy officer and remain a woman.

There was no doubt in my mind that she possessed as something close to an absolute both the desire and the determination to get what she wanted. I had often felt this trait carried to her degree to be the very engine force of those possessing it; further felt it to be the Jekyll-and-Hyde of human personality characteristics: inherent in it, its accompanying drive capable of producing either the greatest good for others or the greatest harm. So far at least we had been beneficiaries of the former. And something else: However little exercised it was to date, I would have been disappointed if my judgment that she had something of the bitch in her was in error. I spoke of presentiments: In our daily sessions of late there had entered, though but now and then, a curious and puzzling tension, inexact as to source, clothed in a penumbra seeming to hang in the air; emerging, faintly disturbing, as if forerunner to . . . yes, I should say, to a testing of wills. Over what? That deeply submerged, unresolved, not yet even spoken, matter of the women? Or something else? I cannot know. It is at these moments—they are hardly more than that, seeming to pass as swiftly as they arise—that I seem to sense the presence of another quality: a considerable willingness for power; a lack of hesitation at outright ruthlessness to acquire it and apply it with maximum force should opportune circumstances present themselves and she in her view find it necessary. And then a thought that startled me: The reason I recognize that secluded strain of ruthlessness in Lieutenant Girard is that I have acquired it myself; we would not be here today had I not.

"Three hundred and ten men's skivvies," she finished up crisply, and turned back facing me.

"What's the drill on issuing these items, Lieutenant?"

"As requested by hands, sir." She had not missed a beat.

"Well, cease and desist on that. Henceforth I want to see a rationing schedule. A tough one."

"Yes, sir. I'll take care of it."

"Some of it isn't very practical in present latitudes."

"No, sir. All dress blues. The men would suffocate in them."

This was the blue woolen uniform worn in cold parallels; from our Barents duty, along with much other heavy-weather gear. "Men," in this context shipboard, as in others, along with most pronouns and possessives, meant women as well. "Persons" and similar degeneracies in speech, the Navy, with its ancient respect for language, found impossible to assimilate; radarwoman, sonarperson, helmsgirl: wisely the Navy steered away from this nonsense. It might have caused ships to collide, have ended up foundering the fleet. I never heard the women complain about it.

"They scratch," said Talley.

"Storekeeper Talley puts the matter clearly, sir. Possibly we could alter and adapt it in some way," Lieutenant Girard said. "Shall I see what I can come up with?"

"By all means, Lieutenant."

Suddenly, a shot out of nowhere square into the mind, came Selmon's admonition: the possibility, however remote, of a forced return to cold latitudes. I said nothing of this. I did say, "Put the actual alterations on hold."

"Aye, sir," she said without suspicion. "No point in doing them until present clothing runs out. With proper care that shouldn't be for some while. I'll recalculate for present latitude." She waited a moment. "If we're stopping here."

I cannot say if the last was a fishing expedition. Knowing Girard, I hardly thought so. In any event I ignored it.

"Yes, do these calculations, if you will."

"We don't need to wear much around here," Storekeeper Talley said. "That's for sure."

I looked at Lieutenant Girard. I thought her eyes rolled.

"Until you do," I said, "cease issuing all clothing. If someone asks for a new pair of pants—or pantyhose—lend him a sewing kit. *Lend.* Get it signed for."

"Yes, sir."

"I'm wearing mended pantyhose right now," Storekeeper Talley said.

"Belay it, Talley."

"Aye, ma'm."

"Can we get on with it?" I said.

Through another door and we were in the ship's store storeroom containing toiletries and so-called "crew comfort" items. Again on shelves reaching from deck to overhead the stacked cases stood. Again Girard sounded them out.

"Toothpaste . . . Toothbrushes . . . Bath soap . . . Razors . . . Razor blades . . ." A step. "Lipstick . . . Rouge . . . Mascara . . . Tampax . . ."

"Duration time?" I said.

"It'll be much shorter, sir. First to go will be the soap."

"Then let's start. Right now. On all of this. The tightest rations possible."

"Aye, sir."

I looked over at the shelves of cigarette cartons. We had gone over that list.

"Starting now," I said, "the cigarette ration will be one pack a week."

"One pack, sir?" Lieutenant Girard said.

"And no new smokers. At that ration, how long will the cigarettes hold out?"

She flipped through the clipboard. "Four months, sir. More or less. I'll get you a more precise figure."

We stepped back into the passageway. Tally opened a locker. Neatly arranged on shelves in battened racks to secure them in high seas was what sports equipment we had: a half dozen footballs, a dozen baseballs, a half dozen baseball bats, a catcher's mask, three volleyballs and a net and stanchions for it. Only the footballs appeared used.

"When's the next touch football game, sir?" the storekeeper said brightly.

"We're all aware you're the ship's star, Talley." Which happened to be the truth.

"That's for sure." The smallest pause. "Since you say so, sir."

We proceeded up to the first deck and the ship's library. I regarded the shelves for a few moments, in a way I had not extended to the other stores. There it was. There they sat. An assortment of fiction and non-fiction, from a standard list. Some of the names surprised me. I skimmed the authors. We had not done badly.

"The Navy did pretty well by us," I said.

"They give you a choice," Girard said. "The Navy can be flexible, sir."

"Is that a fact, Lieutenant? I'm delighted to learn about the Navy's flexibility."

"What I meant, sir," briskly, "was that they do supply a list. Then they give you what's called an optional choice. Up to five hundred volumes."

"You're saying you picked five hundred of these? I didn't realize that anything went on aboard this ship involving a figure of five hundred that the captain was unaware of."

"I felt it was an authority you would have wished delegated, sir."

"I never had the opportunity to delegate, did I, Lieutenant? Well, I suppose you acted within your authority."

"I thought so, sir."

I looked at her. No sarcasm. She never really used that. Merely getting the facts out. Altogether 985 books. Not a bad figure, and the quality quite high. We were very fortunate. I felt consolation. In addition, fifty complete Bibles. One hundred New Testaments, half of these red-letter versions for the words of Christ. Two copies of the Talmud. One hundred copies of the Army and Navy Hymnal and Order of Worship, all about exactly how to do it for Catholics, Protestants, Jews—by, in our case, one chaplain. Then I looked toward the overhead and a light came on in me. Parked on a long upper shelf was a complete set of the *Encyclopaedia Britannica.* I riffled it with my fingers, stopped at one—HER-MOUP-LALLY.

"These," I said, touching them. "I want the entire set put under lock and key."

She looked at me a moment, as though she might ask.

"Will do, sir," was all she said.

Here also were our music tapes—316 of them, it turned out. Not bad at all. Beethoven, Mozart, Bach. We had Handel's *Messiah.* Rock, jazz, country, folk. The Beatles. Woody Guthrie. Madonna, Bruce Springsteen, Whitney Houston. I wondered but did not ask whether a portion of these had also been selected by Lieutenant Girard, or all by the Navy. Also 500 videocassettes of American movies. Also our stores of paper and pens were here and my eyes drilled in on these with a special intensity, mind thoughtful, waiting in the stillness. Five dozen reams of 20-pound bond. Thirty thousand sheets of paper. One hundred dozen-sized boxes of ballpoints.

"Cease at once issuing paper and pens," I said, for some reason a bit sharply, to Girard. "To anyone. For any purpose."

"Aye, sir."

Six spare typewriters; 192 typewriter ribbons.

"What's the shelf life of these, would you say, Talley?"

"For a guess, sir, five years."

Five years: I made a mental note. We had finished.

"Thank you, Lieutenant," I said. "Talley." And added, meaning it: "In particular, for the anticipation you've shown."

"I'll get with the projections," the lieutenant said smartly. "More accurate ones. How long each specific item will last. Now that we're here. You should have them by zero eight hundred tomorrow. Will that do, Captain?"

"That'll do just fine, Lieutenant."

"Come along, Talley. We've got work."

"Aye, ma'm. That's for sure."

Just lately the first fringes of gray had begun to appear on the doctor's temples, rather suddenly. He lit a cigarette.

"That's it, Skipper," he said, handing it over. "Complete. Not exactly Bethesda Naval. But we're pretty well fixed."

Now I studied the list I had told him to have ready. Penicillin. Tetracycline. Aspirin. Maybe sixty other medicines. Shots for every disease conquered by man. Typhus, tetanus, typhoid. Plague. The narcotics, resident in a combination safe I could see on the bulkhead beyond him. The sick-bay medicines suffused the air around us in an odor of antisepsis. I had shut the door.

I tipped back in my chair. "The men, Doc. Would they be okay working here? Just a professional opinion. Any medical land mines I'm missing that you picked up?"

On my instruction he had been on the island starting at first light, applying his keen eye to it.

"Too early to tell completely, of course. I'd say we could have come out on far worse places. Fresh water. Not many colds, bronchial problems, on this parallel. We're well stocked. We've got enough penicillin to wipe out syphilis and clap in the Seventh Fleet. Of course we had in mind Alexandria, Port Lyautey, and *bella Napoli.* It's one plague we shouldn't have to worry about here. I should have specialized in tropical diseases. Not that the surroundings don't look healthy enough," he added quickly. "Nothing I saw that seemed to attack health directly—given the usual precautions. I suppose it depends on whether we're talking long-term or short-term."

Yes. Well, not even the doc was going to get it out of me. "It isn't just the usual hard work," I said. "In that sun. Stoop labor. That's the operable phrase. You know about it?"

"Well, I'm a city boy, of course. I may have seen a farm once flying over it. But yes, I comprehend."

"So?"

"Equator sun," he said. "It can fry a man and bake his brains. But we can protect against that. To a degree. It's more, well, enervation at one end of that spectrum; at the other, dizzy spells, prostration, maybe worse. Especially the shape these men are in. They've been on low rations too long. Go easy as you can at first, Skipper."

I looked hard at him. "Understood, Doc."

I looked around at the four sick-bay beds, consolingly empty, at the operating table. I looked over at the medical stores in their cabinets.

"I won't ask a stupid question such as how long will that stuff last. Depends on sick bay traffic, of course. How is that lately?"

"It's leveled off."

"Leveled off?"

"To what it was before. Situation normal."

"Real versus imaginary ailments?"

"Back to normal on that, too. More aspirin than anything."

"No serious malingering?"

"Again just the usual. Minimal. I'd feel disappointed if I didn't see an occasional one deciding this just isn't the particular day he feels like working."

I looked at him. Lieutenant Commander Samuel Cozzens, MC, USN. He was a lean and angular man, tall and floppy, his body narrow and sinewy to the point of frailty. One had the feeling that he needed to see a doctor. His head was adorned with thinning reddish hair, matched both by furry eyebrows and a benign oversized moustache, carroty growths on skin of an almost feminine whiteness, and with large eyes of a ridiculously light and childlike blue. They had always seemed to me slightly weary. Nothing in the behavior of men, they seemed to say, should be considered surprising, and therefore nothing was more a waste of time than to judge them or to be upset by their idiosyncrasies. If men were meant to be angels, they would have wings and fly about. Far from being cynical, this came out as the only sensible, even compassionate view of life, intellectually leaps beyond cynicism, which after all is such an effortless thing. I had never seen those eyes show shock or even wonder, only a kind of stolid and imperturbable appraisal. With them he could virtually look at a man and tell what was wrong with him. And of especial worth to a ship's captain, they were peculiarly acute at knowing quickly that nothing was. The men knew they couldn't fool him; some had to try now and then, otherwise it wouldn't be the Navy. Johns Hopkins, residency at Columbia Presbyterian, Ochsner Clinic, board internist, research at Rockefeller University—all matters I knew from his service record. His speech was in mensural tones, tinged with wryness, a declaration that life was above all a faintly comic thing, and was not that realization the only way to get through it? Everything about him was muted, as if to say that agitation of manner was the true enemy and that the secret to almost anything was to keep the noise down.

Though still Navy, the doctor rightly conceived it his peculiar function not to let excessive formalities stand in the way with the captain. He knew the captain wouldn't like that. Aboard ship, two only, doctor and chaplain, are permitted a latitude of frankness not generally granted others of ship's company.

"Aspirin will go first," he said. "We've got more of it than anything but then it's the treatment of choice, as we medical people like to say to impress the lay folks, for anything the doctors can't figure out. We never say that part. But the fact is, aspirin is the single best medicine man ever came up with. Of course all my remarks are directed to physical ailments."

Something picked up in me. "Physical ailments? Do we have any other kind? I'm talking of a pressing nature, of course." We all had had the other kind short of that. I had heard him from time to time use the term "intermittent neuroses."

He lit another cigarette. It occurred to me that the pack-a-week ration which I would announce tomorrow would hit him harder than anyone aboard. I wished I could make an exception. I could not. But I could not have anything happen to him.

"Not at present." He waited a beat, then spoke in that measured cadence. "The fact is, I'm out of my depth here. Off soundings. I'm afraid I possess an unfortunate gap in my medical education of never having believed in much of that stuff. I've often wondered which, psychiatry or religion, has done more damage. Between them, they about owned it all. I was just thinking up the line. But we shouldn't fish for trouble, should we? A medical adage."

I looked directly at him, and heard my voice harden.

"There's a Navy adage, too, the same: Don't stir still waters. I like that adage, Doc, medical or naval. Shall we stick with it?"

He was suddenly Navy. "Yes, sir. I'm certainly not trying to stir anything, Skipper."

Once on a signalman first named Chauncey, threatened with a bile peritonitis that could have killed him if not quickly acted upon, he had performed something called a bilary tract procedure. It's a difficult enough operation, as I had learned, in the Lahey Clinic but he had done it in a Beaufort 8 gale off the Hebrides. Two of our biggest men, Preston and Brewster, had held the doc's body steady to the deck while he slid the knife in. Chauncey had been lost since but not from that—overboard in the Barents. I spoke more softly.

"I know you're not, Doc. About the aspirin. Here's the word. Starting now, give it to a man only if you're personally convinced his head will fall off in your lap if you don't. Then only a couple. Under those conditions, how long will the aspirin last?"

"Seven . . . eight months. Depending on falling heads."

I glanced again at the list of medical supplies. "I want a daily report on my desk at zero eight hundred of all medicine used the day before. Including aspirin. That plus the binnacle list."

I waited a moment, made it casual, offhand. "The women. Anything special?"

Nothing of surprise reached his expression. Nothing would. Only that bland look of his, a hardly perceptible shrug of nonchalance, of what-do-you-know.

"Only this. Their health in every category—physical, mental, emotional—continues clearly better than the men's."

"How the hell do you account for that?"

He paused. "I don't understand it myself. Of course these are exceptional women. The Navy saw to that. Especially those sent to sea. But that couldn't explain it all. It has to be something else."

He gave that soft grin. I had had a problem separating when the doc was being serious and when he was not until I came to learn that, in one shading or another, he was always being the former.

"Maybe it's that women can get along without men a damn sight better than men can get along without women. And the fact that they know it. That alone gives them a big edge. In endurance, in whatever you want to call it. They know they'll win out in the end."

"Nobody is going to win out on this ship." I could hear the rather brusque edge in my voice.

"I was not predicting that, sir; only speaking of women in general terms. Home truths."

I looked into those eyes that, also, told nothing. Yet suddenly I knew full well that he knew it as I did—knew to the last intimacy what I was thinking, and would speak it aloud no more than would I. Neither dared, both feared to do so. We could only dance around it. It may have been right there and then that I first made a distinction. I did it without really thinking of what it meant, its significance, save perhaps the instinctive thought of numbers, the visceral protection in any ship's captain of what is in short supply.

"About the aspirin," I said. "Belay the rule for women. Give them what you think best."

Both of us waited a long moment more, our eyes locked, expectant. I felt I was looking into ancient pools of blue full of knowledge, and of a sudden apprehension that must be given language. But there came only a quiet, almost humorous, "Aye, aye, Skipper."

II: Afternoon

Finally, I needed Selmon's reading, my RO. I always did.

I had had chow, then stepped topside. The sun had crossed over and blazed down violently on a silent sea, pale blue merging with a synonymous sky to form a seamless horizon, a single vast and monochromatic universe, unoccupied by so much as a cloud, a bird. I scanned both ways. No sign of Silva to seaward. He must have gone far out in his search but

I was not uneasy. He knew the sea, reserved for it the ultimate in respect, and was not the man to test it unduly; knew small boats, and the water lay in glassy unmenacing repose, free of the slightest swell. Neither did the other direction give any sign of Delaney and Thurlow, who remained swallowed up in the island, which sat in sultry virescent silence beyond the glimmering lagoon, seeming a thing of eyes looking at us quite as much as we continued to look at it. I could see off-watch men standing about the decks, turned toward it in gazes of uncertain wariness. It was as though some sort of reluctant spell, attempting to overcome suspicions on both sides and to reach some sort of accommodation, were developing between the ship and the island. I alerted a lookout to tell me of the approach of either of our emissaries to land or sea, then went to my cabin. Melville and Selmon were standing just outside. We went in and I shut the door.

"Could it reach here?"

We sat in calm reflection. I spoke to the slightly built, wan-appearing young officer without whose consent we did nothing. Lieutenant (jg) Selmon, I thought. He possessed that Jewishness which is quietly confident of its superiority of intellect, by the same token far too smart to let his knowledge of the fact show through, realizing that to do so throws away half its power. No officer aboard had so ascended in importance.

"It could," he said thoughtfully. "But I don't think it will, Captain. I don't think the winds will bring it. Not with the westerly flow this time of year. We've got four months before the winds shift, the northerly currents begin . . ." He hesitated. "If the schedule holds, if something has not happened to throw off that, even . . . By then I calculate most of it will have settled wherever it's made up its mind to settle."

The winds, I thought. They now govern everything. I thought of a phrase from Milton: the felon winds.

"Unless it's added to," Selmon added judiciously. "That seems so improbable that . . . Wouldn't you say, sir?"

"I can't imagine who would do it. But if either of those two unlikelihoods happened—or both . . ."

The Navy taught you to figure out what was least likely to happen, and the worst thing that could, then count on it. He seemed almost to be speaking to himself.

"If there was still some left four months down the line; or if it had been added to; and came the shift of the winds . . ."

He stopped, needing to say no more. I looked at him and said quietly,

"Girard and I were doing the great inventory today. I was a tailor at one point. The idea was to alter our Barents clothing, somehow adapt it, to present latitude."

Selmon permitted himself a soft smile; memory taking him, I imagine, nearly a hundred degrees of parallel north from where the ship now lay at anchor to seas as bleak and fierce as earth held, gales of Beaufort 7 chronic, weatherdeck watches so thickly bundled only eyes showed, waters so appalling a hand overboard—it happened twice with us—would be claimed by the cold even before the sea could take him; from there back to this serene equatorial domain, these pale azures, ruled by the sun, with its own ferocity. The matter hung in the air as fully as if it had been stated. Were we to see the cold again, this time at the other end of latitude? The radiation officer had returned to that thoughtful, fully concentrated expression that was his manner at any proposed course.

"No," he said quietly. "I don't think I would. Not just yet. I'd leave Barents clothing as is. Wait and see, I'd say, sir."

"Wait and see," I repeated tonelessly.

He said: "If those things happened—or even one of them . . . There would be nothing to do but run before it. Get as far south in latitude as possible. And it might be necessary to go all the way. As conclusive as one can be in these matters, I can't believe it would ever reach there. Certainly it would be the last to go."

We had gone over it all, times without number; stopped always by, How did you exist there? I let the silence hold a moment; then turned my head fractionally; spoke to the hardest, coldest fact of all, bringing everything inside oneself to a kind of chill of finality: two months of running time left on the nuclear reactor cores containing the highly enriched uranium fuel which propelled the ship.

"Mr. Melville," I said. "We can go to Antarctica and back. Or we can go home, all the way, and back. Not both. Or: we can navigate Antarctica there and back; go home; but could not then return. Is all of that correct?"

"Affirmative, sir," the engineering officer said. "I've worked it out practically to the mile, Captain. All figures being calculated on slow-steaming basis. Not above twelve knots."

I could never have one of these conversations with Melville concerning our low fuel supply, and the unforgiving urgency of hoarding it, without my mind's flashing helplessly back to that final session with the Russian submarine commander in the Strait of Gibraltar, to our agreement: ourselves to undertake to find a habitable place for both of us, him to go where he believed the nuclear fuel still to be that would free us from the prison that any place we found and settled on was certain otherwise to become. There had been a time when I hardly knew whether to long for his arrival more than anything on earth, the fuel being the greatest gift that could be made us, enabling us to go anywhere without the desperate calculations on which we were even now engaged; or to dread that same arrival for the reason of the awesome complications sure to be attendant on the integration of his ship's company of 112 men into whatever community we might establish on whatever habitable space we might find, a difficult enough undertaking for ourselves alone; coming down at last on the former, believing we could somehow make it together; the matter long since become academic, his having vanished an almost forgotten time back from the frequencies on which we kept contact, presumably lost at sea in a manner we would never know. All of it seeming such a long shot even at the time that I had withheld the nature of his mission from all my officers save two, lest it distort our every planning. How wise that now seemed! Yet I still found my mind unwillingly admitting the thinnest possibility, catching myself at odd times gazing at the northern horizon to see if that immense low black profile known as the *Pushkin* would appear against it . . . the prospect of such an impossible bounty, a five-year fuel supply, making me for those instants hope's fool. A road to madness. I turned back to Selmon.

"This is contingency, from your data." I had to hear it again. "You don't think we'd be forced out of here?"

"Not by that. Barring those two changes, or perhaps even one of them, negative. In my department I couldn't imagine better atmosphere than right where we're presently anchored, Captain."

I waited again. I thought I heard the distant clatter. "What a pleasant change from your usual reports, Mr. Selmon."

The j.g. smiled back almost boyishly. "I try to please, sir."

"I never noticed it. Then, gentlemen," I said, "let us rest it there for the present."

Sure enough there was the ritualistic three knocks on the door. "Enter," I said.

The lookout stood there.

"Silva, Captain. Boat's coming alongside, sir."

"Captain, the terns were right. Sea birds always are. All I had to do was follow them. That ocean," he said, "is full of fish—great schools of fish . . ."

His blue Scot's eyes shone against his bronze Portuguese skin. The exaltation there reflected in myself. A sense of the most immense relief. We stood on the quarterdeck at the top of the accommodation ladder. Just looking at each other. Above the emotion in me I could just hear him going on.

"Cantwell here . . ." He indicated the ship's sailmaker who had followed him up the ladder from the boat " . . . says he can make casting nets from ship's lines. We can have the first in three days. Big nets. And when the fuel runs out he can make us sails . . ."

Then had come Delaney. On top of Silva, it was almost as if that single ingenuity decided me, its affirmation of our one true strength; the light of hope it lit; a thing so seemingly small but in truth saying everything about the men I had under me.

"Grapnels," the gunner's mate said, "sir."

His eyes filled with fervor.

"Captain, you'd be amazed how much like a harrow they are. Harrowing, sir, that's about the most important part of farming there is. And these grapnels here, we've got *fourteen* of them. I and Mr. Thurlow tried this one out."

Under the hot zenith sunshine we squatted on the fanfail, examining it, Silva there with us. Bits of island earth still clung to its flukes.

"Noisy says he can sharpen these flukes. Make them dig deeper."

He waited, then exclaimed it again, as a thing of a certain wonder.

"Aye, sir, grapnels."

It was simply a metal pole ending in a four-pronged anchor; an ancient tool of ships on the seas, little changed in thousands of years, with many and discrete uses; fishing objects—or people—off the bottom of the water; anchoring dories; in the old days of the sea, for holding an enemy ship alongside for hand-to-hand combat. I could not remember that ours had ever seen use, but somewhere in the holds of this ship Delaney had found them. I glanced at Thurlow. The navigator had something of the same look in his eyes, deriving from the excitement and astonishment, and the pure delight, one always feels at a device intended for one thing, or a series of things, being seen, possibly for the first time, by the intelligent mind—in this case, Delaney's—as having application to altogether another. He gave an affirming nod.

"Grapnels: They'll make all the difference," the gunner's mate was going on. "Fetched me up when I saw how much like they are to what our mules used to pull."

"Where do we get the mules, Delaney?" I knew of course. I wanted to hear him say it, and, more important, how he was working it out.

He looked up, his eyes moving across the decks at some of the crew engaged in the work of the ship.

"Why, the men, naturally, Captain," he said, as if I were a terribly ignorant person in these agricultural matters, a judgment which would not have been far off the mark. "Men like Preston. He may even be stronger'n a mule. Ship's lines rigged from the grapnels, hitched around a man's waist, shoulders. I been studying on it; begun a mule list already," he said soberly. "Besides grapnels . . . we got some *tools*, Captain. Like this here."

He pulled it from somewhere under him. Earth clung also to the blade.

"We got thirty-five of these entrenching tools." These were meant for digging protective cover against people eager to harm you; by, for example, a trapped shore party; again never used. "Short handles. Other'n that, good as any shovel—or hoe. A man would just have to bend down more. But for stoop labor a short handle's even better . . ."

The gunner's mate's bright-voiced zeal kept coming at me, bringing something like an exhilaration; outsized perhaps; almost certainly not that justified. But we had known so little of its portion of late that I let it flood in. He was going on. " . . . I thought I'd try in small patches, Captain. Everything we got plantings for in the greenhouse. See what takes. Then go for them . . ."

"Grapnels," I said. "Entrenching tools. Beating swords into plowshares, Delaney?"

"Aye, sir. Come to think of it. And spears into pruninghooks," the gunner said quietly, a touch of smile. "Isaiah 2:4, sir."

"You know your Bible, Gunner."

"The Bible's mighty big in the Ozarks, Captain."

It was the favorable facts, of course, an edge in our favor or at least the odds made more even, suddenly proffered, since on nothing else can decision be based. But as much, too, was the belief in what such men could do. I felt an immense surge in me, the greatest in time remembered. I looked silently at Thurlow, at Silva, at Delaney. Then stood up, they with me. As one we turned and gazed across the lagoon at the island, as one followed down it until our eyes came to rest on the plateau which rose high above the sea on its southerly end; stopped there awhile, eyes fixed profoundly on it, as if in some final assessment; the island, hushed across the blue water, radiant in its greenness, seeming to await our decision as to whether we proposed to take it on. I looked at the boatswain's mate then the gunner's mate. Thought suddenly, wryly: now Silva the fisherman, Delaney the farmer.

Then let's start," I said quietly. "Tomorrow."

As an afterthought I found Signalman Bixby and consulted her about her two goats. She also had had another look at the island.

"Best thing would be just to turn them loose over there for the time being," she said.

"You mean they can take care of themselves?" I said.

She looked at me with the unuttered expression of how little I knew about goats.

"Once they get ashore, Captain, it's the island that'd better watch out."

Somehow this seemed a further reassurance of the island's fecundity.

III: Night

I went out on deck. The sun sat, in immense fieriness, just above the horizon, the sea, glittering in great swatches of phosphorescent white, waiting to receive it. Then the blazing ball dived and was gone, swallowed in one big gulp by the hungry waters. Amazing how fast, once it got near it, the sun in these latitudes hastened into the sea. It was as though in such burning parallels it was anxious to take a dip and cool off, to wash down before showing itself again to us, pristine, fresh, at tomorrow's dawn. And amazing how, once that happened, darkness, real darkness came on so swiftly with hardly any twilight at all. Though in truth there was no mystery to it. It means you are near the equator where the sun's rays, falling more perpendicularly, bring on quicker real night. Only the sea, stretching before me to all horizons and beyond, seemed eternal, and somehow never more so than at this time between last light and true darkness when, having received the sun into its depths, it waits in majestic certainty the coming of the stars.

The ship rested in utter immobility, swinging not at all on her anchor, the air unstirred by the slightest breeze, the sea herself asleep. I stood aft by the lifeline in the great solitude and watched them as they came on in a rush, the constellations, old friends, never-failing guides of seamen, rendering themselves into their ancient choreography until the heavens stood filled with their numbers; studying, by habit, their arrangements I knew as a boy knows his school copybook, checking them out, as if to make certain they were where they were supposed to be. Red Antares, yellow Carina, on station, radiant in their assigned positions;

others I knew by name, for over long years they had guided me across many seas. Tonight they seemed to flicker and preen themselves in an exceptionally dazzling manner as though in a personal reassurance, signaling zealously to me as clearly as a signalman's blinker light, as if saying that in the dark loneliness, in the absolute silence which seemed to bring the load of oppressions pressing down on me as of some unbearable weight, I still had old and steadfast friends.

My eyes followed them down the sky and touched the top of the forward then the mainmast and moving, sought out our multiple articulation with the outside world: the top-hat antenna UHF, the two whip-antennas, the smaller VHF and the longest range of all, the big-whip HF, lingering there a moment; proceeded to the corresponding antennas for SATNAV, SATCOM, ESM and finally the radar antenna in its slow ghostly orbit; all unceasingly, almost ravenously, seeking some signature from beyond, some mute hail of life appearing as a green blip on a dark screen, a faint sound in a sailor's ear; for some response, almost any would do. Joining these profound devices in their mission, I scanned the far waters as though expecting something actually visible to the human eye to appear there, an apparition flung forth from the horizon's distant starlit curve. But nothing save our solitary ship broke the ocean vastness.

Gazing across it I thought how, far back as I could remember, to boyhood, I had wanted it. The sea, for herself, and to find what lay beyond her horizons, knowing full well that one never found it, that beyond each waited yet another horizon that would keep beckoning me. But that was the greatest summons of all; I would never run out of horizons to go to. Many who hear that call simply wish to leave behind the everlasting and immutable messinesses and clutter of the shore life. For these a wise Providence has provided the sea; otherwise I hardly know what would become of them. Even then I felt that life on the oceans was the only life worth living, the sea seeming to me, even at the earliest age—that surely but sensed dimly then, certainly put in no such grandiose terms; looking back I could but see the fledgling shoots for present, substantiated, full-grown certainty—to possess a purity, a simple straightforwardness, a rectitude, a scrupulousness, yes, a clear aristocracy, that stood in contradiction to the unnumbered corruptions of the churlish and plebeian land and the land life, with all its hustling, its tedious and incessant hype, its seemingly essential duplicities and deviousness, its insect busyness, its insatiable avarice, all in zealous pursuit of goals I did not judge worth having if, when, attained. I never hesitated and was off at the first chance, never looking back. Nothing that had happened since had shown wrong these early glimmerings, in any way of substance, any that mattered. That rare case perhaps where adult fact verifies boyish imagining. On present knowledge I would add this: The real call of the sea is in the life of the mind. I find myself unable to explain this. Perhaps it is that the mind, finding itself emptied of the unceasing flurry and enterprise, the all-devouring encumbrances of the shore, is simply rendered uncluttered and left free and pristine to explore, or merely to rest. The thoughts that the mind then engages may or may not be profound. The point is not to claim for sailors the musings of philosophers—the intelligences of seamen, as with other mortals, varies from the rudimentary to the exalted—rather it is to speculate that the mind is somehow rendered uncrippled, on its way to becoming healed, when the land is left behind and one is enclosed, on all sides, only by the immense and unfettered sea. From then on, of course, it is up to the individual man how he chooses to fill the space thus left empty. But perhaps this fact has to do with that other one: No place so surely brings self-discovery as a life at sea; so inescapably reveals to himself, and to others, what a man is made of.

And from the beginning also, the sweetest and most fervent of those longings had been to hold command of some ship that sailed the great waters, and now I had reached that pinnacle. In inner satisfaction, in the unqualified knowledge that this was right for me, that anything else would have been so wrong as to have tossed life away, it had all come out true as the long look ahead had envisioned it to be. I had liked commanding a ship. I was qualified for it. I was a good mariner. I knew the sea and her eternal inconstancy perhaps as well as a man ever can; that is to say, I was forever learning new things about her, with eagerness voracious and undimmed. I knew the ship on which I stood. I felt I knew my ship's company as only one can who wishes above all to protect them, to give them a sense of security, to care for them. Knew, I felt, when to be gentle with men, when to come down hard; in short, to be a ship's captain. Shipmates we were: In all the lexicon of the sea there is no word so sublime, so full of meaning. I do not believe there is any closer, more committed human relationship to be found on earth. The sea, the ship, the ship's company: They were all, they were one, and embraced in its bosom, I stood as fulfilled in that unity as it seemed to me a man could be. All of this surely enhanced by a particularized love for the *Nathan James* herself. I was a plank-owner, present during her building stage in the Litton/Ingalls Shipbuilding yard at Pascagoula, Mississippi, and three years aboard as her two-striped navigator; after two years of shore duty in Naples assigned as XO on another DDG, shore duty in Washington, then with that tremendous surge not short of exaltation the *James* given back into my hands as her commanding officer.

As to the power of it: It was not some piece of vanity to know that bringing this whole undertaking off, on this island and in any new life, counted greatly on their belief in me as their captain. I am tempted to say counted entirely. I can think of no body of men whose daily well-being or misery, and quite often safety or even survival, lies so fully in the hands of one man as does a ship's company. The reason for the perdurability of this sea sovereignty against the grain of history is simple: No way has ever been found that permits a fighting ship to function other than by this one-man rule. It is certain that if such a system existed, it would long since have been discovered and installed in a world where the plebiscitary, the "democratic," has been the onward wave. A rajah, a monarch of the seas. Of course, no ship's captain of the slightest worth ever thought in those terms. Such authority on the high seas confers less of arrogance than the sense of ultimate responsibility, each new day presented, for the fate of others, living quiet in the soul as one's very reason for being. Knowing also that this very coin of absolutism has its opposite side: the thin line trod every day by every ship's captain the seas over. To the very degree that he holds power over them, a captain must have his men's trust, which alone assures their love for the ship herself: Without this, his vessel can scarcely operate and danger lurks everywhere. And let that trust once be lost, it is never retrieved. It is lost forever. But no law of the sea, no good practice of ships decreed that the captain at every stage admit his crew into his soul. Indeed, the mind could without difficulty postulate circumstances wherein the blatancy of entire truth, the flaunting of full intentions, would be the worst treason of all toward them; an abject, even craven abdication of a captain's responsibility. For included in his duties is this one: not to shift onto them, as sources of anxiety and fear, the burden that is his alone lawfully to bear.

Here was the fine, infinitely fastidious line: A captain is permitted almost anything where the safety and survival of his ship and her company are at issue. Cunning, schemery, artifice, maneuverance, stratagem, stopping always short of outright deceit. But these must all be seen by ship's company not to be these things. They must take on, in that curious transmutation perhaps known only to seamen—deracinated as they are from the general world, a thing so remote as to be hardly existent, creatures of their indigenous ship-immured perceptions, canons, and indeed morality—the clothing of acts done by the captain solely in behalf of the ship and the men themselves, so that artifice becomes care, contrivance love for his men. And at the moment of announced decision, the course he chooses seen to be the only right course. The captain, fortressed in his deeds by the steel in him, seizing single-mindedly whatever befriends his one allegiance: that no harm within his power to prevent shall come to the company of his ship.

I had always accepted that power as part of being a ship's captain and when I got my command lived easily with it. Only of late had I begun to be attacked at odd hours by doubts, expressible to no one. For a ship's captain has also the loneliest job on earth or on all the seas, and the display of certain quite ordinary human emotions is entirely forbidden him. That divine despotic right unchallenged at sea: In truth it was not that I had become suspicious of its validity, other than wrestling with the enormity of 179 souls being in the hands of one man in the magnitude of present circumstances. It was rather that, in tremulous dialogue only with myself, I had begun to question whether that right, that power, already enhanced even further, would now hold fast, and even more so in realities certain to come. Unlike lesser dictators, a ship's captain has no bodyguards, no armies to shield him. He is gravely outnumbered, his only armament being the sea's ancient law of command and his own resolve. Therefore, the more crucial both the resolve and the unwavering assumption that it would be accepted wherever it might lead, whatever portend. Nelson's band of brothers, to be sure, but also his "If I give an order I expect it to be obeyed." Hence self-doubts of any kind were the very thing I must above all suppress. A calm presence, whatever tremblings I might feel inside. Calm presence: Sometimes I felt that in that considerable list of attributes indispensable to a ship's captain, this was the most important of all.

Only once on our odyssey had that rule felt serious challenge; for one terrible moment we had come to the very brink. I had stood it down by the only weapon I had. There was no assurance that that governance would not be tested again and this time more formidably. And if it came, the weapon would be no different. I had had to harden myself; the departure, loss, of over a third of ship's company on other seas affixing that indelible imprint—that absence of pause by which ruthlessness becomes but another resource where circumstances insist. In the end there is no substitute for will: Other men may have the choice of embracing that conviction, that banal option, or not. A ship's captain, none. For him it is immutable fact. If he loses that, he loses all: Nothing must be permitted to deny it.

I had decided on the island as a place on whose land and near waters we would seek sustenance. But reason, craftiness, said one step at a time. Beyond that manifestly my first essential cunning was to keep to myself those other intentions I had for it—and for them.

Turning slightly, I looked with purpose across the star-caught water to the dark recumbent island, which alone shared the sea with us; feeling somehow there was something of importance about it we did not know, some unrevealed essence, perhaps favorable, perhaps otherwise; knowing, whichever, we stood committed to its strangeness, its unknownness. Nothing came forth. It stayed as slumbering as the sea itself, wrapped in mystery, harboring its secrets, reluctant to part with a single one. Then something pleasant. A sibilance of wind stirred, its brief plaintive sound through the halyards like some nightly orison, and before it as quickly vanished bore to me from somewhere forward the faintest scent of one of them, a barely discernible whisper of perfume, mingling with the sea smell, even before I saw her shadowy form crossing up the ladder to the bridge. Navy directives, you must take my word, had something to say even on that matter: "in good taste." The Navy leaves nothing to chance. The affected hands had remained in line. Even so, to this day I had not become accustomed to that shipboard trace—the last thing from being unpleasant, only always still a surprise, that one should find it here of all places, on this man-of-war; the scents of women. Probably Seaman Thornberg, quartermaster striker, on her way to relieve the dog watch—yes, we kept a helmsman on watch even at anchor, by that unforgiving sea law that decrees that a ship must be ready to act instantly at any sign of danger, and to get underway at once. The quick intake of scent must have started it: I began consciously to think back over when it had begun, as though the history of that strange thing, turning inside out as it did the very texture of ships that had held from earliest voyages on great waters, might somehow now suggest an answer; a way through the hazardous difficulty that had begun to haunt me like a dark foreboding and whose tenacity seemed but to intensify, to resist all my mental efforts to stow it away until other, presumably more urgent, matters—food, for instance—were underway.

As I have recounted, I had strongly opposed their original admission into ships, for the rather high-flown reasons given; though in a more down-to-earth seaman's view fearful that their presence would screw up, complicate in a thousand ways, some explicitly envisioned in one's mind, some left to suspicious imagination, the already infinitely complex and delicate job of operating such a ship as this one. Now: In my heart of hearts I suppose I still stood opposed to it. At the same time I felt practically, as a ship's captain, that if anything they made for a better, more efficient ship; as skillful sailors as any man in the performance of their shipboard duties and, to my mind, in not a few instances superior; more—I will not say intelligent, perhaps the phrase is somewhat more fiercely dedicated to their respective jobs, ratings, skills. Some of this, I would expect, due to tougher Navy standards, first in the selection of the women it permitted to enlist, and second in those it allowed to go to sea (among those applying, in the first instance the acceptance rate was said to be one in ten, in the second one in a hundred), checked out as few sailors had ever been; some to the singleness of purpose that brought them here, and once aboard to being more determined to hack it, to prove they could do it. For whatever reasons, they performed as well as men. They brought a number of surprises. First of these was that the younger of these women sailors appeared to be distinctly more mature emotionally than men sailors of similar ages; whether this was due to the nature of women or to the mentioned Navy's stiffer selection process for them, especially those sent to sea, I did not know. They presented fewer disciplinary problems. They carried other advantages, some of them decidedly eso-teric, entirely unforeseen: one of these being—something as a seaman I found interesting as a novelty, rather charming, as a captain grimly de-lighted—their faculty, due to smaller physical dimensions, of getting through hatches more quickly. This is more important an asset than one might think in modern sea-battle conditions, where the ability to come swiftly to battle stations can quite conceivably make all the difference in outcome to a ship about to be attacked by today's weaponry, an extra second enabling her to dodge an SS-N-12 Sandbox missile instead of being blown up by it.

In practice, for a given task I soon ceased to be concerned, or even aware, whether it was a man sailor or a woman sailor doing something I wanted done. They were alike in executing their jobs. Of the other ways in which they were not at all alike, the Navy—which is the least naïve of establishments—had naturally been cognizant when it sent the women forth and in its ineffable wisdom promulgated a veritable typhoon of directives dealing with the correct behavior between these two kinds of sailors and further enjoining ship's captains, under severe penalties, to make certain of such conduct and giving them extraordinary powers to punish infractions. One specific Navy directive, NAVOP 87/249, read, and I quote verbatim now, "Women will not be addressed, either in general, or specifically, as 'broads,' 'fillies,' 'dolls,' 'girl,' or like phrases." (At the time I wondered what the "like phrases" were that the Navy didn't specify.) Fat chance of any of my men trying on for size any of those terms, considering the breed of women we had received on board, these being spirited to the last woman. They had not got here by being patsies. They got here because they were smart, because they could cope—and, yes, because they were, or had the makings of, first-class seamen.

Another directive dealt with the sternness of retribution should any "molesting" occur of such sailors. I had not heard that fine old word in that context since my early youth—it was either my mother or my father, I cannot remember which so that perhaps it was both, in separate sessions, to make certain beyond all doubt in a matter of such gravity that Thomas got the point and no mistake, who at the proper age meticulously instructed me that this was something that no boy ever did to any girl—and "molesting" became a court-martial offense (as it would have been for me in the form of a razor strop or worse). CNO directives flowed like the repeated tides of the sea, and were interesting studies in meticulous, to-the-point wording—the Navy has always been uncommonly gifted in the scrupulousness, the precision, of language, necessarily so considering that a misunderstood or ill-expressed command can bring instant disaster to a ship—impossible of any but the most exact interpretation, and yet withal with a certain intuitive delicacy. This one: "Overt displays of affection are out of line and will not be tolerated." That one: "Men and women on board ship are considered to be on duty at all times. Conduct is expected to meet traditional standards of decorum." (In other words, any sailor would instantly and correctly interpret, nothing funny off watch or on liberty either.)

But I do not think it was for the reason of this accumulation of threats dispatched over the frequencies to all fleets that the thing worked. Rather I believe it was the fact that the men and women themselves knew almost primally—as if the sea herself had spoken to them and told them in her stern no-nonsense tones, stronger than bookfuls of *Navy Regulations*, Navy directives, that it had to be so—the absolute, nonnegotiable imperativeness of this code and of rigorously abiding by it if the ship were not to be torn apart, something no true sailor wants, abhors above all else. Who chooses to upset the house where he lives and make it unlivable— especially if there is no way for him to exit it? In any event we had no difficulties in our normal operations. No sailor called a fellow sailor a doll or a filly and certainly none ventured anything, not on my ship, that could remotely be characterized as "molesting."

Sailors are correctly viewed by landsmen as human beings with tendencies to "let go" ashore. The reason they are such on the beach is that they are the exact opposite aboard ship. Shipboard they desire equanimity, discipline, even a certain rigidity, for the simple reason that they know as a first principle of life at sea that their welfare, even their survival, counts on the sure presence of these qualities, these rituals, throughout a ship's decks. The Navy could do what it wished (though goaded and compelled to it, and against its desires I shall always believe), introduce whatever new, strange, even bizarre ingredients it liked, and the sailors were not about to throw away the elements essential to their well-being and to the very functioning of the ship on which they to a man depended. The women became sailors, too, holding the same verities; sometimes, I had on occasion felt, holding them even more so. Furthermore, it was accomplished with a swiftness that to a landsman would not have seemed possible. Perhaps most important of all, the women became with the men what the latter were already with one another: shipmates.

All of this had been in the beginning. And it had worked and held fast. And now? Well, so far, so good. Nothing had happened—with that one exception, that derangement. Until now; until this present moment, up to and including it.

Before heading for my cabin and sleep I looked a final time at the heavens, as a sailor will before turning in. This time I sought out the Cross, standing in white majesty in the heavens. In the south, shimmering against the black sky, stood the Magellanic Clouds, stood constellations unknown to dwellers in the Northern Hemisphere. It was while looking at them that the thought—surely a random synchronism—occurred; seized me by the throat, as it were.

I thought that I knew men. Or at least men who go to sea. I knew seamen and their ways; a knowledge including, I believed, a reasonably indulgent appreciation of the weaknesses of men. No, I was not so modest but to feel that I had acquired this rather punctilious insight in considerable degree, than which nothing stood me better. But perhaps from being from an early age a sailor—an entire child of the sea, whose ways I had engaged to learn as fully as might be possible, an undertaking demanding an unconditional devotion of a nature little short of the monastic—I was remarkably untutored in women: they seemed to me to carry a secret code I was without either talent or experience to decipher, as labyrinthine as the mysteries of the sea. One cannot devote one's life to penetrating two of the great mysteries, one needs all of a lifetime to make a breach into one . . . Just because I had spent virtually my entire adult life at sea, I had known few women at all. If the word "known" be enlarged to mean the inner workings of another human being, the inner life, one could come very close to saying I had known none whatsoever. For all purposes I knew nothing about women.

Somewhere up above, in the vicinity of the bridge, I heard the quick, distant sound of girlish laughter. One hundred and fifty-two men, twenty-seven women, I thought. In the heavy heat of the equatorial night I felt a chill pass through me. I went on up to my cabin to seek sleep.

Standing orders for any deck watch aboard a U.S. Navy ship of the line are to awaken the captain if anything "unusual" occurs, the interpretation of that word being left to the officer of the deck and its latitude, in all my naval experience, being long and wide, but in practice generally interpreted on the side of caution. Any OOD would much rather face the irritation of an awakened captain, unpleasant as that might be, when the object floating two points off the starboard bow in the near distance turns out to be a bundle of used beer cans, than to face a court-martial if it should turn out to be a floating mine. To the general standing orders inherent on any ship I had added a particular one of my own. I was to be awakened if any signal, of whatever nature, even a presumed or possible one, were raised by the twenty-four-hour watch, with continuous transmission by us, I had established in the radio shack. I felt as if the great ape himself had seized me and my eyes came open. In the gleam of the flashlight I recognized the boatswain of the watch.

"I'm awake, Preston," I said. "You may stop shaking me. What time is it?"

The big boatswain's mate unhanded me. Preston, given his size and his hands, was one of the more aggressive waker-uppers.

"Sorry, Captain." The beam moved to my own cabin clock. "Zero two forty-four, sir."

"What is it, Boats?"

"Ears thinks she's raised something, sir."

I was instantly all awake, faculties in full gear.

"I'll be right down."

Preston was gone and I slid trousers over my skivvies, shoes over my feet, shirt around me, all more or less in one long habitual movement, popped out of my cabin, and swung down two ladders to the radio shack. An aura of another world here; through it came the sound of Ears tapping out something in Morse code. I put on the spare earphones and listened to the continuous-wave signal.

The crew called her Ears because Radioman Second Class Amy

Walcott had the best pair aboard; a special gift, incalculably valuable to any ship, hearing sounds that others did not. I leaned over her and waited until she had finished her keying. Something faint as the last fading echo off a canyon wall seemed to come through my earphones. She promptly keyed back. We waited again. Then an even fainter sound in return. She keyed back. Silence. Keyed again. Silence. Ten minutes of keying and only silence rolling back to us through the night. We removed our earphones. To better conform with these she kept her hair knotted back, moored by a sailmaker's splice, serving to emphasize the fragile girlish structure of her face.

"Was it any stronger earlier?" I asked.

"The first time, quite a bit stronger, Captain."

"A false echo? Atmospheric aberration?"

"Always possible, sir. But it sounded different."

Her whole being seemed calibrated to pick up the most minute nuances of sounds, detecting, separating, and classifying them across a wide and personal spectrum unknown to others, her world.

"Different?" I repeated.

"I know. Like those you heard, no code we know. But a different rhythm to it. The beat, even."

"Let's try some more."

I stayed with her, another half hour it must have been, while she tried and tried again to raise something out there, if something there was. She sat back in her chair.

"Sorry to have got you up for nothing, Captain. It came," she said sardonically, helplessly, "and now it has gone away. For nothing."

"No. Nothing might be something sometime. Any chance at all, always awaken me."

"Aye, sir." She cast a wan smile. "Hope you can get back to your dreams."

"They were pretty noisy anyhow. Walcott?"

"Sir?"

She had always seemed such a slight thing. But of late I felt I sensed something new, a certain frailty coming on, the beginnings of a wearing down from the endless listening hours, and a resolute struggle against it; something of the same concern I had had with a number of others in the crew, wondering, discussing the matter with the doc, whether it could be related to that terrible passage through the dark and the cold.

"I just want to say I'm mindful of what you're doing."

"Why, thank you, sir. Not at all."

She had volunteered, as the best we had, to stand watch and watch, four on and four off, rather than the customary four and eight. It had become an obsession of hers to find, raise, something out there.

"If it ever gets too much, you're to let me know, understood? I can't have you vanishing away from lack of fresh air."

"I *like* this air." Her head moved to take in the tiny, etheric, portless kingdom where she reigned. For all her slightness she could have a firm, no-nonsense, territorial tone in her voice and I heard it now. "Besides, when it happens I want to be the one."

"Yes. I know."

"When. Those who say if. I know it'll be when."

"Of course. Always wake me."

"Oh, I'll do that, sir."

I felt her soft smile, heard her voice. The latter was a thing of exceptional tenderness, a purring of barely audible sound. That way, I think, because listening the long hours was itself a quiet, soft matter, of great intensity and concentration, where loudness would have been an unwelcome, even perilous intruder.

"Good night, Walcott."

But her earphones were back in place and she could not hear me. I stood a moment at the door looking at the small figure in her sailor dungarees, intent, waiting, everlastingly hunched over her wizard's array of the most sophisticated electronic gear men had been able to devise. As I left I could hear her fingers resume their keying. Twenty-four hours, day and night, never stopping. Her or another operator.

I went topside, thoughtful. A party of four or five of the men was standing by the lifeline, in a pretense of being out for the night air but actually, both they and I knew, for something else. How swiftly word fled through a ship! I paused a moment, looking at them in the night shadows, at the mute question on their faces. I shook my head and went on by them.

I went back to my cabin, got down to my skivvies and into my bunk. If a man who follows the sea does not possess the unconditional ability to return to sleep after being jolted awake for various alarms, he will not for long follow it at all. He will crack and land on the beach. Especially a ship's captain. I had known more than one, some of them friends and two classmates, to whom that had happened. I think the trick was that I had long since mastered the First Commandment for those who would go on ships. Avoid, as you would the greatest of perils from the sea herself, two things: Anger. Irritation. I had further mastered that other counsel of my missionary father's: Worry is a sin. Or thought I had, though of late I had felt disturbances creeping insidiously into that skill, probing its defenses like the first building onset of heavy seas poised to strike a destroyer's plunging bow. Then I was asleep, my last conscious thoughts being of the grassy plateau on the stranger island, where lay our hopes and which we would attack on the morrow, sitting high above the blue.

.3.

THE SAILORS
IN THE FIELDS

It was perhaps two hours before first light, that spectral moment when the curtain of opaque cloud which had hid the western part of the island chose to lift itself briefly and to provide me with a surprise and a riddle. Not a rumor of breeze solaced the stifling air; it lay like some palpable weight pressing down on ship and sea. For a few moments I remained in the dimness of the decks, watching the dark recumbent island across the lagoon. How like a sleeping beast it looked, the profound stillness of the night, the unstirring waters in which it lay, that southerly ridge giving it the aspect of a Sphinx of the sea, and like it too in its emanation of mystery. Then, with all abruptness, I felt a land breeze come up from it, seeming almost a gesture of amity, whispering across the water and touching our few grateful figures on the deck like a welcome fan. It was the first true semblance of wind we had felt since coming to this place. I stayed a moment, savoring it and idly examining the stars hanging limply in the heat-hazed western sky. As I watched, the cloud bank below them, given a gentle push by that errant breeze, began to move, the curtain parted, and I beheld on the island's far side the dim phantasmic shape of what seemed a long spine of land, a surprisingly high, almost mountainous configuration, mountainous certainly for these latitudes. Then the clouds closed in again. It was like a fata morgana. Spirits, we are told, reside in the lofty places of the earth, on craggy heights. Of course it was the eeriness somehow of the night, the brooding island, the hush of the sea, the enigmatic cloudbank, impervious as a watertight door, the quick glimpse as of an apparition and a portent, given and taken away. Nonetheless, it was as though I were being presented a peek and a taunt: if you wish to know more, have a look. I decided on the spot where I would venture tomorrow.

But this in truth was no sudden decision: The spooky *coup d'oeil* but hastened the matter, set a date. From the first I had been aware that though our present side of the island appeared docile enough, it lay well open to the prevailing southeasterly winds, and that it was only a matter of time before high gales and even hurricanes would attack it, making it unsuitable to my other intention regarding the island and one I had zealously guarded even from intimation to my men. For that intention I would have to seek a lee shore. Whether the far side of the island provided as well certain other essentials also needed determination.

But this was for the morrow. This long day was fully spoken for: establishing, on the grassy plateau, the farming beachhead on which so much depended. I took one more look at our Sphinx—no answers, of course—then went on down to the wardroom for coffee.

If one were called upon to pick an existent body of men best equipped to begin life from nothing on an uninhabited piece of land, one would be hard pressed to come up with any superior to the ship's company of a U.S. Navy destroyer. In the first place, the destroyer, for its own functioning and operation, carries a complement of basic skills difficult to surpass for versatility. The very designations given to the various Navy ratings attest to this fact. Shipfitter, machinist's mate, molder, patternmaker, engineman, hospital corpsman; many others. In the second, from the very beginnings men who go to sea have come from every imaginable background. The notion that men who grow up by the sea constitute the principal source of those attracted to it as a livelihood is in error. The actual case is quite the opposite. It is the men who spend boyhood never having laid eyes there who are drawn, so many of them, to the idea of setting forth upon the great oceans. It is as though the call of the sea were heard most clearly not on the shores but on the farms and prairies of Iowa and Wyoming, far from any salt spray. So that in addition to the skills which they acquire in the Navy, sailors ofttimes bring with them other previous skills, not presently used but never forgotten. Of these, farming would be a prize example, and a numerous one. The great Navy fleets are full of farm boys; I never knew why so many turned up sailors and more often than not made very good ones, some of the best. It led one to wonder whether there existed some secret kinship between being a farmer and being a sailor.

Equal to, perhaps exceeding even the enormous asset of our diversity of skills, spanning virtually the entire spectrum needed to sustain men physically, we bring with us another capital.

It would appear that on coming of age a man is confronted with making one of two choices: the life of the imagination or the life of power. To these two I have sometimes felt that a third choice, so particularized is it, so discrete in virtually every respect, should be added: the life of the sea. I am not suggesting that this election is done necessarily in any directly conscious way, as, let us say, the way in which a religious takes vows. But I do feel the act to bear at least one similarity, in that, with so many sailors, it also proceeds from something deep and fundamental in them and against the grain of human life as practiced. Men who go to sea are different from men who stay ashore. To become a sailor, to choose the sea way, is more than anything else essentially to reject the values that drive so much of mankind. Sailors are almost entirely free of the smell of money, that aroma of avarice, that like some unpleasant body odor had come to afflict so much of human intercourse. The ritualized accumulation of possessions; that whole congeries of land barometers of "success" that goes under the general term of "material interests": These are not of first importance to a true seaman. Were they, he would never take ship, for no vocation save possibly the priesthood runs in such an opposite direction from their fulfillments. Some think sailors innocent or even naïve, like children, to leave behind such treasures, not comprehending that they leave behind also acquisitiveness, greed, covetousness, the manipulation for his own purposes one human being of another. Many see something almost unnatural in the choice: for example, in a man deliberately choosing to spend the great part of his life away from home. And they have a point. But it is one that itself marks sailors as men apart. And indeed there is a certain simplicity in naval sailors. But they are far from being naïve. In them resides a curious mixture of innocence and skepticism I have found nowhere else. They are remarkably discerning judges of character. Here it is impossible to fool them—no civilian, no shipmate, no captain can do so, and only a fool would attempt it. Seamen effortlessly see through pretense as through clear glass. It is a gift of the sea. They despise cant, hypocrisy, all insincerity, and can detect it in a moment. So precise is their perception in these matters that to this day I hardly understand why it should be so. It is as though in the act of rejecting certain normal or at least not infrequent human traits and motives for themselves, they had become experts at detecting them in others.

The replacement for land's icons—since men must value something—appears to me, after being among sailors for eighteen years now, to be an uncomplicated belief in, the giving of high marks to, two qualities: forthrightness in human dealings; and coping, simple and direct, with whatever his world, that being life at sea, presents. In the sailor's catechism, his articles of faith, this twain marks the man. The necessity for both are self-evident: the first in the fact that sailors live so closely together (a tiny example: Thievery is almost unknown on ships, looked upon as a capital offense, since there is not the slightest defense against it, and the rare occasion it occurs, however minor, can turn a ship upside down); the second in the inherent condition of a ship's isolation. The sea is a faithless thing: one never knows what she may bring, either in her ever-changing temperaments or as a bearer on or under her of forces with hostile intent toward one. Even with no assist from the sea, the hazards a distant ship on the waters may fall upon, within herself or her company, are numberless. Dealing with these, it is entirely common for a ship to come up short in this, that, or the other. This ever-present circumstance of their lives, itself against the grain since most men desire to store up every imaginable aid for every conceivable contingency, seems perversely to be a thing that attracts men of a certain kind to the sea and makes of them good sailors, Navy men. By nature sailors cope; by long experience they are virtuosos of making do with what is at hand, and if nothing is, creating it. It was a talent I counted greatly on in the times ahead. The other imperative is one that is never given a thought, being taken for granted in a sailor as much as is the fact that he has eyes, arms, legs: One assumes the possession of courage in a Navy man. Even if one had the opposite intention, or temptation, that of cravenness, of cowardice, there is no way to avail oneself of it: one may turn tail and run off a battlefield—this has been known; when harm comes calling, one part of a ship is as hazardous as another; one may not run off a ship without landing in the sea, which is very deep, and the shore customarily far away.

A ship is like no other kind of life: set apart, dissevered—physically, spiritually, root and branch—from all other experiences. She is all alone; an extrinsic incarnation moving over great waters, a tiny principality, possessing of her own codes and worths having little kinship with those of the shore. Inherent, in her company, a comradeship of an order I take to be indigenous, idiosyncratic, to ships; members of a ship's company being interlocked in a manner exceeding that even of families: from these one can also always walk away. On a ship only the same everlasting sea awaits. That mystic force: the feeling of shipmates for one another and for the ship that is, in sum entire, their home and life, their true country. Herein, it seems to me, lies the preeminent difference of all in the land and the sea way: that in the former, the graspings of men for their own interests are so often at the expense and even ill of others, almost, it would appear, necessarily so—if oneself is to rise, others must not; and that this process hardly exists on ships. Sailors are accustomed to thinking of the welfare of one's shipmates equally with that of oneself.

None of this is meant to claim the aspects of angels for men who go to sea. Far from it. Treachery has walked many a ship's decks; vileness; stupid men; worse, stupid and arrogant officers; worst of all, stupid and selfish captains. Indeed the sea would seem to divulge these attributes as fully as it does their opposites.

I have spoken at length about these matters, not because of their novelty (a thousand others, from Homer to Conrad, have said the same and legions of seamen know it in their blood), but in order to establish that nothing is more critical to our unknown future than this discrepant makeup of the body of men whom I lead into it. Their very nature, in character, in temperament, in everything that counts in the construction of that complex creature called a human being: Nothing sustains me more. There lies, however, another meaning in the same condition: the riddle which is not a riddle, the but seeming contradiction. By that nature also am I filled with my deepest foreboding; in the sense that, my best hope, it constitutes them as well able adversary—and a possibly dangerous one. Accustomed in the sea way to being ruled by captains with near sachemlike powers, they are paradoxically men of the most independent of minds. It is not by chance that man's noblest deeds have occurred on the seas of the planet, far from any land, on the ships that course the great oceans; or that on these same ships, and for the identical reason, that of isolation beyond the reach of other forces, have been committed acts among man's most profoundly evil. These antipodal directions for men to take seeming more potential in matters soon to be upon us.

First light was casting its glow, rose shading into carmine, over the island and across sky and waters, the annunciation of a tranquil day. I had sent upward of forty men chosen and indoctrinated by Gunner's Mate Delaney ashore first. Now I stood at the top of the accommodation ladder with the deck watch and Delaney stood at the bottom as the sailors, each with infinite solicitude carrying a tray of seedlings in cut-down five-inch casings, filed by me and started gingerly down the ladder into the first of the boats, Coxswain Rachel Meyer standing amidships at the wheel. On the glassy water the boat bobbed hardly at all.

"Steady as you go," I kept saying as the men passed by me. "Take an even strain."

As the sailor reached the platform on the ladder's bottom, Delaney received the tray from him, held it until the man had seated himself securely in the boat, then gave it carefully back. "Hold it with both hands, mate," I heard him say in his Ozark twang. "Straight up. In your lap."

Not until the entire boarding procedure had been completed but for one man did the gunner's mate yell up to me. "Captain, we're ready for another."

Thus the first boat filled with men, each with a tray of seedlings. "Stand off, Coxswain," I called down.

Meyer swung away smartly and the next boat came alongside. We filled three boats, including the farming gear—the grappling irons, the entrenching-tools, the lines—and then the flotilla got underway for the island lying half a league off.

Ever since we first raised the island that morning now less than a week back, both sea and lagoon had preserved an unruffled stillness. I was particularly glad that, carrying our fragile and priceless cargo, the same shiny patina of waters bore us this day. As we moved in, the quiescence of sea and island seemed to envelop us in a solitude in which even a voice was a jarring thing, the reigning peacefulness appearing to silence the men, leaving them with their thoughts; they sat very straight, exceptionally solemn, each grasping the tray in his lap with both hands. Delaney had put the fear of God in them about those seedlings. Our flotilla came on line abreast, so as not to have them troubled even by a boat's wake, and at one-quarter speed. Beyond the bow I could see the advance party standing on the beach, watching us approach, behind them the island's prideful green rising. Together, as if choreographed, the boats slid up gently out of the green-on-azure lagoon and onto the fine pinkish sand and Delaney hopped out, the first one. Again under the gunner's mate's nursing ministrations, the men first handed the seedlings out to the beach party, then each debarked himself and took back the tray that was his charge and responsibility. It was a wonder, the somber, tender ritual in which these sea-fashioned men moved, as if knowing all too well the preciousness of their lading. Then we off-loaded the farming gear.

The beach party picked up the gear and our company of sailors started off. Instead of cutting through the island with its tangled growth, which could trip a man carrying a tray of seedlings, we went straight down the beach, the sailors bearing the plants grouped in a body and the forty-odd shipmates behind and to each side, as though convoying them. Signalman Third Alice Bixby walked alongside me toting the portable signal light with which we could keep contact with the ship and they with us for any emergency or peril that might arise on sea or land. (As for the latter there had been murmurings among the crew, not entirely frivolous ones, that there might be eyes watching us from within the island's deep growth. I could only reassure them that if so, there was nothing we could do about it but hope that they were more curious than hostile, since I was not about to mount a land campaign to sweep the island of imaginary unfriendlies. We were too in a hurry to have time for that.) Southerly we moved until we came to a path opening from the beach, cleared by a crew a couple of days back, in accordance with Delaney's unstinting foresight, of the brush that blockaded the approach to the ridge. We went into it single file. Soon we were cutting around the clear-running stream where we could see the pebbles glistening on the bottom. We started up the hill and between the trees in the sweet early morning light, which nonetheless spoke of a crueler sun to come, and finally came out on the meadowlike plateau with its long silky lime-green grass, stirring ever so slightly now in a wisp of breeze coming over the duny cliff from the sea just beyond. There we could see our destroyer standing out, gray and motionless, the solitary mark on the endless ocean blue. Under a grove of green trees on ground which Delaney's men, on the preparatory mission two days back, had cleared and leveled for the purpose, the gunner's mate directed the men to place the trays gently down and soon they rested there, clusters in the shade of the trees. Their sailor-bearers sighed as if glad at last to be relieved of a fearsome responsibility. The seedlings stood safe and waiting alongside the soil which we hoped earnestly would accept them.

With the exactitude we might render to any naval operation, Delaney had planned this one. He took charge now, radiating a knowledge of farming as conclusively as he might, in another context, of naval gunnery, of nuclear missiles. The sailors, as sailors always are, seemed glad to follow a man who knew what he was doing. His instructions came with a crisp precision; under his superintendence the men turned to with a will.

First he made up four plowing teams, each astutely constituted. A pair of the biggest and strongest men in ship's company, previously chosen, were hitched to a grapnel plow fashioned to Delaney's specifications, navigated behind in each instance by a farm boy the gunner's mate had found among the crew. The heart of the rig was a pair of strong boards, essentially two-by-fours, cut by Noisy Travis, one laid across the backs, at waist level, of the pulling men, the other attached to the grappling iron itself; connecting the two, Boatswain's Mate Second Class Singer, who was a master of marlinspike seamanship, of moorings and hitches of all kind, secured and lashed lines around the pulling team's hips and shoulders thence to the plow. The big sailors in the hitches stood patiently for Singer's rigging, somber and curious as to their new employment. One of them was Boatswain's Mate First Class Preston, imposing as a Santa Gertrudis bull. Machinist's Mate First Class Andrew Brewster, an engine-room man as opposed to Preston's weather-deck domain, stood by him as his plowmate. Both were thirty-year Navy men. I felt quite certain neither had ever seen a farm, certainly not seen one worked.

"I'll be watching close to see that you pull your weight, Boats," Brewster said to his partner in the hitch. "Below decks, Preston, we know what to do with a man that caulks off."

Preston gave his shipmate a benign look. He was perhaps an inch taller. In weight and visible strength they could have been a matched pair. "I will pull like a mule," Preston said gently. "Looking at you, Brewster, I won't find it hard to imagine I'm hitched with one."

Waiting behind the improvised plow as Singer proceeded with his complex ritual of lashings and knots stood Jerome Hardy, a mere seaman apprentice and a farm boy who would be their driver. He was not much more than half the size of either man in his two-man hitch. None of this stopped him from putting in his word.

"Now, men," he said thoughtfully. "I'm not sure I'm going to permit you men in the ranks to talk. Might interfere with your pulling power. A little discipline here, if you please. Chief?"

"Yep?" the gunner said, hardly hearing any of this, engaged as he was with getting the operation underway. "What is it, Hardy?"

"In Georgia, if mules don't pop along proper, we give them a little tap on the hind end with a stick or switch. I take it we can do the same here. Only if necessary of course."

Preston and Brewster turned and looked balefully at Hardy, rather like real mules in harness rotating their heads to regard the human being behind them, to size up whether he knew what he was doing, and above all whether he knew about mules.

"We not anywhere near Georgia, son," Preston said. "Pay heed you remember that."

Singer was finished with his hitch.

"All right, men," Hardy said with loud authority. "Mind your rudder. Let's look alive there." And they were off.

The team started forward, Hardy skillfully dug in his grapnel plow, the soil under the willowy grass turned, and the first smell of parturience leapt from the earth. It was like attar. A distance away the same thing happened with the second team; then with the other two. Meanwhile Delaney, wasting no time, had put other men to following the plows, carrying off the grass, leveling the earth with their entrenching tools, used like hoes now, working backward so as not to trample the soil, the men bent over under the climbing sun. The stoop labor had begun.

Those sailors stripped to the waist, showing even more how much their bodies were weakened and wasted, their white hats perched at jaunty angles, some inverted in protection against the sun, their bodies pouring sweat as they moved slowly down the meadow, turning up the soil, and rearranging it: they seemed to me actually to be enjoying these labors, almost exuberant in the chance to commit their bodies to a useful purpose after the months of being cooped up on the ship, though as the day wore on enjoyment became determination; exuberance, doggedness. Some were farm boys and some city boys who knew almost nothing of how food was brought into being, but whichever, to a man they seemed eager to do their share, the only difference being that Delaney had to show what and how to the latter group. Some of these seemed if anything more zealous than their farm-boy shipmates. It was killing work. The figures of the seamen stooped repeatedly. Now and then a man would pause to mop the drenching sweat from his face, with a handkerchief, his hand, or his sailor's hat. Farm boys and city boys, I said. Meaning as well, of course, farm girls and city girls, for a half dozen of these were out there among the farming detail, men and women all, volunteers. No complaints rose from the field, even the cherished sailor's bitching missing. It would surely come later. At one point I was standing at the end of a row when the Preston-Brewster mule team approached before making a turn. As they strained and struggled forward, I could make out on one Nelson at Trafalgar, the tattooed sea wet as with waves real; on the other, an equivalent sweat gleaming from that majestic black chest; Preston from the deck crew, Brewster from the engineroom: they seemed determined to outdo each other in effort as their mighty bent bodies moved down the rows and the grappling iron behind them turned earth. As the sun climbed the sky, and burned brutally over the plateau, I had the men spell each other, rest in the shade of the trees, and sent them down to the clear stream below the ridge to refresh themselves. That cold running water was our gift from the Lord, our balm in Gilead; we would not have made it without. The morning went on, the transformation of the plateau proceeding, the proportion of turned earth increasing as that of the willowy grass diminished.

It was nearing 1200 when I looked and saw a figure waddling over the ridge. Chief Palatti was followed by a retinue of six hands carrying sacks. The chief stood panting from his exertions, his belly retrenched from formerly but still proudly protruding and going like a bellows.

"Chow down," he got out.

"Any word from Silva, Chief?" I asked. I had sent him and his crew seaward before first light to seek fish.

"Still not back, Captain."

Chief Palatti could do things even with processed-meat sandwiches. Mainly it was probably the fresh-baked bread. He had brought a cold lemonade kind of drink and the men sat cross-legged under the trees and had their chow. As I ate I tried to remember how much of the meat was left aboard, and how much of the flour. I could not have a meal without this awareness of our diminishing stores, a concern slightly abated by looking out over our meadow where now long rows of turned earth counted for about a fourth of the plateau, the soil rich-looking and pungent against the long grass yet unturned, its scent mingling with the scent of the sea in an almost erotic, comforting alchemy.

"A good morning's work, Captain," Delaney, sitting by me, said.

"Yes, Gunner. A good morning. Who would have thought sailors would make such farmers?"

"Well, it works the other way, don't it, sir?"

"That it does."

Gunner's Mate Delaney. Added to all his other knowledge of naval gunnery, he knew as much about missiles and their launching as the Navy could put into a man: a VLS (Vertical Launch System) gunner's mate, graduate both of the Martin Marietta training unit and the guided missile school at Virginia Beach, an elite 0981 classification. He was square and sturdy, emanating an almost planted look, and of an unhurried countenance. It may be the first requirement of a good seaman that he not have a low flash point. A ship, and especially a destroyer, is simply too intimate a place to have room for such a being. The trait itself represents danger. Considering his direct role in any missile launching, this most particularly stood true of Delaney. From the time our lives came together, I made it an especial point to know him. The quietness of the gunner's mate's personality somehow seemed to certify his dependability, his resolve.

I thought about the time, not that long ago, when I had summoned Delaney to my cabin and asked if he could start a vegetable garden on the ship. He selected the missile launcher maintenance shop, which we cleared out and refitted with wooden racks made by Noisy Travis to hold the plants; plants dug gently from the land along the sea-lanes of our odyssey in our incessant scrounging and placed in cut-down cans from the galley. The compartment had been chosen because it led conveniently by ladder to the after part of the weather deck and to the 61-cell vertical launch system which made an ideal setting for the plants to absorb the needed sunlight, protected there as they were by the fact that the salt spray which chronically blows down the length of the ship underway would have been relatively dissipated by the time it reached this area; the plants customarily remaining topside on the VLS except when inclement weather or seas prompted the gunner to stash them below. "Delaney's Garden," it was soon called. It was a popular attraction aboard ship. The men would stop by and look at it thoughtfully as at a botanical garden of rare flowers, though these were plain, even scrubby things with now and then timid green shoots beginning to sprout. Then the sailors, those of them not come from the farm, with expressions as if the growing of vegetables was a sacred mystery to which only Delaney held the key, would watch intently as the gunner's mate did his fussy sorcery, taking a single bean for example and causing it to germinate, watering the plants, when the time came employing a small trowel fashioned by Molder First Class A. J. Phayme to transplant the seedlings into larger pots, turning the seedlings daily to correct the sun's leaning effect and make for straight stems; finally when the plant bore, taking its multiple seeds and planting them in the five-inch casings, both abbreviated by and holes to allow water seepage drilled in their bottoms by Phayme, which the gunner's mate had discovered to be the exact size required. We even fired a considerable number of rounds at nothing to obtain the casings. I was one of the most frequent visitors, for I knew nothing of these things, and was keenly aware of my appalling ignorance of how the first essential to man's survival operated. Now, of course, knowing the urgency represented in those jury-rig flowerings, I was eager and anxious to make up for this neglect. I studied Delaney and his rituals and questioned him closely, for instance about such matters as growing seasons and time to maturation for different vegetables, as he went about his ceremonies with a mighty simplicity of purpose and that certain zeallike brightness in his eyes. Soon I had relieved the gunner's mate of all other shipboard duties, so that he might devote himself full-time to "Delaney's Garden."

Some of the men had finished lunch and the smokers among them were having one of their new ration, inhaling deeply, smoking the butts to the very end. Some shared a cigarette.

"It's going to be good soil, Captain," Delaney was saying. He sipped his lemonade drink. I could feel like a field of force the quiet exultation in him, of one happy to be back at the work he was born to, or perhaps exultant more from what he saw happening here, and mostly his handiwork it was, going back to that shipboard garden.

As we were finishing chow, the island's daily rain began to fall, thin and gentle, virtually soundless. Just started, without advance notice. Some of the men got up from under the trees and stood out in it, clothes and all, letting the rain cool and wash their bodies. Now and then the men turned their faces up to the falling misty water as one does in a shower. In almost exactly twenty minutes the rain stopped as if shut off by a spigot. Now you could smell even more strongly the rich fructuousness of the soil. I heard Delaney's quiet voice beside me.

"Captain, I been studying on it. You know what's going to make the difference here? It's this rain. Every day. It's like *irrigation*. It's what the Lord give this place to make sure things'll grow."

The gunner's mate paused a moment. "Yes, sir, it's this rain every day that makes this island so you could live on it."

I was startled, as though he had read my thoughts, knew. But no. His face said nothing of that. He was speaking only of agricultural matters. He spoke again, in a tone of somber conviction, looking out over the meadow.

"Aye, sir. I believe it's going to work, Captain. The Farm."

"The Farm," I repeated, looking at our meager beginnings on the plateau.

And after that, that is what we called it. The Farm.

The men began fetching the trays into the fields and under Delaney's meticulous management carefully removed the plants and commenced to imbed them down the laid-out rows, then with their hands spreading earth around them as he showed them. Also implanting the seeds which Delaney had brought along in bags.

"Gentle, mates," he kept saying, moving up and down the rows. "Sharp lookout where you walk."

A row of squash. Another of peas, black-eyed. Several of beans— navy, pinto, lima. Several of potatoes. Corn, onions, cabbage, lettuce. We would see what worked, what grew, and concentrate on those.

Plowing and planting. Boatswain's mates, enginemen, firemen, seamen; electrician's mates, electronic technicians; signalmen, sonarmen; torpedomen, missile technicians; radiomen, quartermasters. Deck men, engineroom men. All labored, all sweated. The ridge might have been a ship, one that needed certain attentions, ministrations, and from all hands, and right now, to make her do what she was supposed to do. All the afternoon under the violent sunshine, an incandescent ball blazing down mercilessly on the bent bodies of seagoing men. At 1700 I called a halt to it.

The sailors raised up in the fields, and for a moment did not move but stood strangely there in the earth in a tableaulike statuary, as if themselves planted. Then in curious, almost balletlike motions their bodies began to sway this way and that: to assuage sorenesses, stiffnesses, muscles not used by shipboard labors but called forth by pulling plows— by stoop labor. I knew now. The hardest kind of work in the world. Then they all stood silent and motionless, dirt-streaked, bathed in sweat, looking at the field they had half transformed. No need even to murmur a well done. But what an immense pride I felt in them! A kind of wonder and innocence was on their faces as they gazed around them now at the reclamation they had wrought, their own pride shining as from some fierce inner light through the brutal physical exhaustion.

"Let's go home, men," I said.

Facing the ship, Signalman Bixby stood on the edge of the cliff with her portable light and signaled the message I gave her, a letter at a time.

> STANDING DOWN FROM THE FARM SEND
> BOATS TO BEACH RENDEZVOUS FARM LOOKS
> GOOD CAPTAIN

I read the letters the ship's blinker sent back in white flickerings across the water.

> BOATS UNDERWAY SILVA BACK WITH FINE
> CATCH ENOUGH FOR ALL HANDS SILVA
> SAYS FISH AS GOOD AS CAPE COD SO MUST BE
> SOMETHING SINCE SILVA SAYS THAT'S
> WHERE GOD WAS BORN

I felt the surge of an immense relief. I had Bixby send this:

> WELL DONE TO SILVA AND CREW
> PROCEED TO GRILL FISH CAPTAIN

I glassed the destroyer and could see three boats move out from her and proceed toward shore. We prepared to descend.

"Captain," Delaney said, "do you reckon it would be all right to leave the gear here? Seems a lot of trouble to fetch it all back and forth every day. I been studying on it and I don't know who's going to steal it."

I looked around at the great solitude of the island and smiled a moment.

"Permission granted, Gunner."

So we stacked the gear—grappling irons now plows, entrenching tools now shovels, and the rest of it—neatly beneath the cover of the trees. Then, a company of seventy or so sailors, we started over the ridge. We went around the creek, along the cleared path, came out on the beach, and walked up it. Even before we got there we could see up ahead the boats beaching. The men looked bone-tired. They looked good, as though to say, we are seamen but if need be can learn land's ways. As we went up the beach Porterfield, the helmsman, got out his harmonica and began playing. It had always been one of his favorite songs.

Oh, Shenandoah, I long to hear you,
Away, you rolling river,
Shenandoah, I can't get near you,
Away, away, I'm bound away
'Cross the wide Missouri . . .

Some of the crew took up the words, singing as we went along, the lilting haunting strains of the men's and women's voices drifting out over the motionless lagoon . . .

Oh, Shenandoah, I love your daughter,
Away, you rolling river,
For her, I've crossed the stormy water,
Away, away, I'm bound away
'Cross the wide Missouri . . .

I looked back at the long trail of our footprints in the sand. By tomorrow they would be gone with the tide and we would make fresh ones. We got in the boats and headed out. I think we were all looking forward to Palatti's chow; hungry from God's hard labor. Stoop labor. Surely of all work done by men He must look with special mercy on those thus engaged since only the most needful of men do it. As we neared the ship, the sun which we had seen emerge from the sea that morning now was moving swiftly back into the same stilled waters. Then we could begin to see the lights of the ship come on and cast their glow across the sea, welcoming sailors home.

.4.

THE OTHER SIDE OF
THE ISLAND

For my inspection of the other side of the island I chose the boat that had Coxswain Meyer and Seaman Apprentice Billy Barker for its crew. She was our best boat handler and we might, in coming in close as I intended, be in tricky waters, for I had no notion of what was around there. I wanted to see. Of the three boats one was assigned permanently now to Silva and his fishing detail. The other two and a lifeboat towed behind one took the men into the Farm in the morning, and returned to the ship. Fishing and farming, both got started quite early, fishing at about 0400 and farming an hour later, that is, the boats shoving off for the island then, the early start meant to beat the heat a little. We cast off immediately after Coxswain Meyer had returned from taking our farm crew in. It was a little after 0530, with a certain pleasant, not coolness but lightness of air. From island and sea came the first fresh scents of morning.

We headed south, keeping fairly inshore, Coxswain Meyer, perched at the console amidships, standing easy and alert with her hand on the wheel, Barker, the boat hook, keeping a watch forward for any shoals or bars, and myself standing aft—no problem in a sea so polished we glided over it—scrutinizing the shoreline and the island, sometimes with the naked eye, sometimes with the 7x50 binoculars I had slung around my neck. My field of vision moved to the ship standing off and receding for

68

a last glimpse before we should make the turn for the other side. Contemplating her, I was taken again with that troubling wonderment I had each time she was about to leave my sight, as to whether she would be there when I got back. A silly foreboding, surely, and yet what a constant temptation it was and what a small party of hands it would take to accomplish the deed. It could be done while so many of ship's company were at the Farm and to sea fishing, while her captain was off, let us say, on a reconnoitering of the island's far side . . . If I had had plans for the ship, why should I think others would not? I put the thought down; realities were enough to deal with. I had no time for imaginings. But not before I found myself, hardly knowing I was doing so, lifting the binoculars and glassing the ship stem to stern and observing identifiable members of ship's company going about their normal shipboard tasks. Then I lowered the glasses quickly, feeling foolish and a bit embarrassed with myself over requiring this reassurance.

We came to the end of the island and looked up toward the plateau where we could see the small figures of our shipmates working the Farm. We waved and could make out their waves back. We began to round the island. Then, as we came about its southernmost end and veered on a northwesterly course, suddenly the boat was kicked up in the waters, the bow thrown high to starboard. I could see the sky above it from where I was flung against the gunwale, the sea crashing over the boat and myself. Forward I saw Barker pitched to the deck. Meyer had both hands grasping the wheel, coolly bringing the boat back to port while letting her ride through it. Then, as suddenly, we were in gentle waters. It had lasted a half minute, dampened Barker and myself considerably, and that was it. We had just learned that a tide rip separated the two sides of the island. I looked at Meyer riding steady at her perch.

"Nice job, Coxswain," I said.

"No problem, sir."

She took us on around. The sun dried us all, crew and boat, fast enough and we proceeded on our N. by N.W. bearing. Up ahead I could see a big bulge where the island fattened out around its midriff, so that presently we had to steer slightly more northwesterly, my having told the coxswain to keep us a half mile offshore at all times. I had not expected to find the island so wide. As a guess, I would have said seven or eight miles at that fat point, though a more exact measurement awaited a future land crossing. Then, as we moved over a composed sea, we were presented with further intelligences and surprises.

The aspect of the western side of the island could not have been more different from the eastern side where we had gone ashore and above which had started the Farm. We should have had much more difficulty doing so here. Just getting ashore, for one. The eastern side, with its unbroken beach of powdery sand and with the sea touching shore like a caress, and with that sunny silky-grassed plateau above it, was by comparison a place of welcome and invitation. Here was its opposite. All was forbidding, inhospitable; all said beware, especially to seamen. A shoreline continuously rocky, high jagged rocks, ascending in long stretches to cliff height, rising straight out of the sea, with waves slapping sharply against them, with no beach whatever save for an occasional tiny apron of sand indented in that rocky countenance. But it had a fierce beauty of its own. Rocks and cliff were of a granitic appearance, of a Pompeiian-red hue, lovely with a kind of warriorlike defiance in the morning sunlight that played off them, altogether formidable and saying so. The range of rock coast and cliffs stretched northwest as far as I could make out. As I minutely glassed this barrier, my first thought was that if storms came to the island it would be a far safer place to be. On two counts. First, as I have mentioned, the prevailing winds of the latitude were southeasterly, making the other side of the island the windward side: storms would bring the high winds and the big waves to attack that shore unopposed. Provided he could get established ashore here, the western part, being on the leeward side, would afford far more safety for man. The eastern side might look more inviting. The truth was, heavy enough weather, certainly anything resembling a hurricane, would almost surely sweep away everything present of a man-made character. Further, even if the odd westerly blow came, the rocks and cliffs on this side would present an ungiving fortress against which sea and wind could beat and break as long as they pleased.

I remarked that I wanted to see the other side of the island. It was for no casual reason. I wished to determine whether it held sites where we might build habitations ashore. It was an idea I had not so much as breathed to a single member of ship's company. I feared to do so too early. It was of the greatest imperativeness to prepare them for it. First, by getting them accustomed to the island, even friendly to it. Then by making them dependent on it—the Farm was part of that. Then perhaps I might, with the proper portions of firmness, care, and gentleness, safely broach the idea of habitations. The better so if I had found a place suitable for these. There was a time in my command of the ship when I would simply have ordered it done. Technically I still could. But it would be a very foolish captain who did that now. Far better, perhaps even necessary—I did not wish to test those waters—to have their consent. Better still, their willingness. Best of all, their eagerness.

Hence, a certain deliberateness: one thing at a time. Certainly not until the crops were underway. Let the crops be a step, a big one, to anchoring them to the island. Nothing so much as food sources tied down animals. Men were no different; hunger was man's strongest drive, as it was in any animal. He will not leave where there is food until he has assurance that it can be had at another place to which he goes. I had to bind them with that and if possible other ties before propounding anything like habitations. I stepped forward.

"I'll take the wheel, Coxswain. You may sightsee for a spell."

"Aye, aye, sir." Not with the greatest enthusiasm. I don't think she liked anyone, even her captain, taking over her boat, which she considered hers. That amused me and it bespoke a good sailor.

"Here, take this," I said, unslinging them.

With a natural, almost gibbonish, agility, at home in that boat more than in any room, she moved around out of her pulpit and took up a position forward, where she stood studying the island through the binoculars I had given her. As I brought the boat slightly inshore and then resumed our northwesterly course, paralleling the land, I looked alternately at the island and forward along the boat to the sea where she broke my line of sight, and thus necessarily at her. She was a small thing in her sailor's dungarees, sailor's white hat, less than a hundred pounds of her and probably managing the Navy minimum height of five feet with little to spare. She was at that crossover between girlhood and womanhood. She had an almond complexion, high-boned cheeks and impudent chin, and a flare of raven hair, kept rather short and bobbed but not so much so that I could not see some of it sticking out pertly from under her shoved-forward hat. If in some ways she was a girl yet, and you felt the dew still on her, in her trade of coxswain she was a full sailor. Anything concerned with that boat, she had a self-confidence bordering on the brazen, and wholly justified. She seemed almost permanently cross, as a guard and a tactic—don't mess with me, Buster!—in a way that inwardly—often, if not invariably—amused me. You had a feeling that if you poked her she might bite you. She possessed a derisive little laugh, prohibitively not at me. At times I found myself impatient or even annoyed with a quality she had mastered into an art of being stubborn without being insubordinate. The skill of her boat handling made up for about anything, a fact I fancied she was quite aware of.

Not far beyond her, along the length of the boat, I saw Barker in the bow keeping watch on the water just ahead. We were far enough out not to have concern over sandbars, unlikely anyhow on this side of the island with its rocky shore.

"Barker!"

His head snapped around.

"Sir!"

"You may stand down for the present."

"Aye, aye, sir."

He stepped from his perch and promptly came aft to join Meyer. She made no move to acknowledge his presence, but continued to inspect the island with absorbed interest through the glasses while he stood by her, rather as though in attendance, watching it through his naked eye. He stood a foot above Meyer, rail-lean, all limbs and bones. He had sun-streaked fair hair, a good-looking mouth likely to break into a sudden artless smile, and thoughtful, steady boyish eyes of sea blue. He was entirely placid and soft-spoken, not an unusual quality in apprentice seamen, except that I had the feeling Barker was that anyhow. A somewhat shy, almost somber young man, with an ingenuous face, the bones prominent everywhere, giving him rather the look of a novice Viking. There was something exceptionally unformed about him as yet, even allowing for his age; a high intelligence, yet a certain innocence of mind not only unacquainted with but unaware of the corruptibility of life. Meyer, who knew her own mind and where she was going, seemed light-years beyond him. His mind sometimes seemed off other places—I had no idea where, hers perpetually alert and on the matter at hand. She was twenty, he eighteen. Among her duties was to bring Barker, a striker for coxswain, along in his naval trade and I had every impression of a good tough taskmaster. For his part Barker, far from chafing at her strictness, appeared filled with a boyish eagerness to learn, and to be glad he had in Meyer an excellent teacher, to have a desire to please her.

Barker had one more attribute unusual and important to the ship. There is an official designation in the Navy that goes under the term "Expert Lookout." Not a rating, it denotes a talent so rare, indeed baffling, that even the Navy has never been able to explain it—only to have the sense to recognize that the gift exists and can be an immeasurable asset to a ship; a tribute to the possession of a set of eyes that seem above human in their ability to see things on the surface of the sea. One man on our ship, Barker, was so designated. At sea his watch-bill duty was always lookout. When we actually expected to see, or hoped to see, something of importance, he was assigned to the primary lookout post, on the open bridge atop the pilot house, wearing a pair of sound-powered headphones, a mouthpiece on his chest so that he could communicate instantly with the bridge concerning anything he raised on the vast plain of the sea. The skill had been tested times without number and the designation proved accurate beyond all question. If Barker said something was there it was there.

Finally without looking at him she passed Barker the binoculars. He employed them for about a minute, then dutifully passed them back to her. An odd thought occurred to me: I could just have been their father, had I married and had children. Once I had regretted above anything else in my life that I had not done both of these things a man must if he is to call his life full. Now I was glad that it had been so. Just as well, with what was facing me, not to have the thought of that tearing at my mind, attacking my resolve. Now I had no one. No one at all. Save my ship and my people.

"Meyer," I said.

The binoculars came down, the alert head around. "Sir."

"I want to take her in. See if you can find a place in all that rock."

I slowed us to one-quarter speed. She seemed to hesitate fractionally; then, leaning forward with the 7x50's, began to sweep the shoreline, slowly, intently, her body bent now almost double across the gunwale. Finally she downed the glasses and spoke back to me.

"Captain, I think I see a place. Doesn't look very good. But I don't make out anything else."

I stopped the boat. She came back and handed over the glasses. The boat rolled gently in the easy sea.

"About zero five zero, sir."

I looked through the binoculars, across the water, sunlit until it entered the lee of the high rocks where sweet dark shadows lay. A white patch of sand, appearing little more than a handkerchief, but even so, larger than anything we had encountered, sat tucked into the granite shore.

"Awfully small, isn't it, sir?" she said. I knew she was thinking of her boat.

"Why don't we have a look. It might accommodate us."

I gave her the wheel. "Take her in. Dead slow. We'll all have to look alive here. Barker!"

He had been staring desultorily shoreward. He came out of some reverie and his head popped around.

"Sir!"

"Up in the bow. Close watch on the bottom. Keep a sharp eye for underwater rocks. Sound back anything you see."

"Aye, aye, sir."

Coxswain Meyer brought the boat around cleanly and headed us inshore. Barker was flat on his belly in the bow, sticking well out so that he looked directly down into the sea. Intermittently he raised his head to sound back in a loud voice, "Clear, sir." We were closing the cliffs.

Barker's head came up from the sea. "Rocks to port!"

"Stop the boat, Coxswain."

"Aye, sir," and we came swiftly dead in the water.

I went forward, flopped down by Barker and stretched out over the bow. I could see the rock formation to port, mean and jagged looking, enough to stove in the bottom of something much stronger than our boat. Then I leaned far over and looked to starboard. All appeared clear. I raised up on an elbow.

"Nice eyes, Barker," I said. "Coxswain!"

"Sir!"

"Take her twenty degrees to starboard. Dead slow. Steady as you go."

"Twenty degrees to starboard," I heard come back. "Dead slow. Steady as she goes."

The boat turning, we crept in, both Barker and I sprawled alongside, our eyes hard and intent through the sea. The water showed cleanly to starboard until abruptly, beyond, loomed another rocky ridge. I raised up on my elbow and yelled back.

"Stop engine!"

The boat went instantly dead. I stuck my head out again and, with Barker, peered through the water. I could see the sand beginning to slope upward. It appeared we were in a tiny channel between two rocky protuberances. I raised back up.

"What do you think, Barker?"

"I think it'll take the boat, sir. Just."

"So do I. Coxswain! Ten degrees to port. Take her in."

"Ten degrees to port," came back at me and we inched in. My eyes and those of Barker tracked the bottom, Barker to port, myself to starboard, never leaving it. Then we could feel the boat bump up against the shore. We raised up. We saw ourselves perched on a patch of sand with the boat squeezed neatly between large rocks on either side, the beginnings of the underwater formations. Barker took a long breath.

"Just fits, sir."

"Make her fast," I said.

The sailor jumped out, taking the painter with him, and secured the boat to one of the rocks. I debarked onto the sandy apron. I looked the length of the boat at Meyer, still in her pulpit, hand on the wheel.

"A fine piece of work, Coxswain."

"Sure looks close enough." Her voice carried her disapproval still of this risk to her boat.

I stood and took a bearing on our surroundings. Up and down the beach, formations of high rock cliffs stretched far as eye could see. I looked upward at our own cliff, having to crane my neck far back to the hurting point to do it, for the cliff rose straight and high immediately above us, then near the top arched out to overhang us. I turned and looked to either side of the cliff. Northwest the cliff continued unbroken into the distance. On the other side, to the south, I could see where we were at a small break in the cliffline. Here a narrow ladder of earth went upward alongside the rock. I strained around and examined it. It looked steep, not much off the vertical, but trees grew from it, moderate-sized trees continuing to the heights. They could be our pulleys. I looked back at the boat.

It seemed secure enough there and I pondered. By rights I should leave someone with it: simply good seamanship. But for very particular reasons of my own, and ones I wished not to disclose, I wanted both of them with me. I wanted to see what it was like up there. But if it looked in any way possible, I wanted them to have seen it, too. Both of them. I wanted to get his reaction and I wanted to get her reaction. Possessives I seldom thought about in relation to my crew, except just of late. I had begun my careful and tricky preparations—how cunning does feed on itself! Nothing more quickly becomes a habit, a very way of life. I was finding that out. I think my ship's company would have every tendency to believe a report brought them by their captain. But such a report brought as well by their own: It would not hurt. I decided. The boat was not going to wedge itself out from between those rocks. I craned again, gazing up the cliffside; turned back.

"Let's all have a look up there," I said. "I think we can get up with the help of those trees."

Meyer looked surprised. I imagine she wanted to go. But she was coxswain of this boat. It was her boat.

"All of us, sir?"

"Yes, I know, Meyer. The boat will be all right. Let's shove off."

She looked still hesitant. When I give an order I expect it to be obeyed, not evaluated, and certainly not discussed.

"Did you hear me, Coxswain?" I said more sharply. "Let's move it."

"Aye, sir. May we give her another mooring, sir?"

"Very well," I said shortly. "If you must."

"Barker!" she snapped out. She was already throwing the line.

The startled Barker caught the line, having to jump to do it, and secured it to the opposite rock, affording the boat a double mooring.

"I suppose you'd like to put over the anchor, too," I said, not meaning it.

"A very good idea, sir." She scrambled around in the boat's bottom, came up with it, and heaved it astern, where it hit water with a loud splash.

"Are you satisfied, Coxswain?"

"I think probably she'll be all right now, sir."

I looked at her. "Actually you were right, Meyer," I said, a bit tersely. "Never leave a boat unattended. If you must, do everything to secure her."

"I thought so, sir."

I gave her a sharp look. She was straight-faced.

"Now shall we ascend?"

I led us around the cliff to the tree-laced earth just to its side. I started up. It was hard going, but the trees were sturdy enough and frequent enough that you could get ready purchases to pull yourself upward. I looked back to see Meyer just below me and Barker just below her. They were doing as I was doing, digging their feet hard into the angled earth, reaching out then for a tree, finding a handhold, pulling themselves to the tree, pausing there, digging their feet in, then passing themselves to the next tree. We hoisted ourselves up tree by tree. I could feel the sweat and the twitch in my thighs. Patches of broken sunlight came flickering down through the trees and I heard a bird squawk. They probably had nests in those rock cliffs. They had made them here rather than on the island's windward, unprotected side. Those tern nests on the eastern shore had been summer-house breeding nests. Their real homes were here. Birds had their own built-in Beaufort scales, better than anything man knew. They must have seen high winds, and doubtless hurricanes, on the island, and being sensible creatures had situated their homes where they were properly sheltered. I held to a tree, getting breath. I looked back and saw Meyer holding onto another tree below me. I could hear her quick breathing.

"Are you all right, Coxswain?"

I started to reach out a hand, but caught myself. Looking at her I knew it was not a thing to do.

"Just fine, sir," came back at me, quite briskly. "No problem."

She looked below her. "Barker?"

I could just make him out beyond her, also holding on to a tree.

"All's well down here," I heard him call up. His voice had a panting edge to it. "I think."

He stumbled momentarily and I saw her reach a hand quickly down to him.

"Come on, Billy," she said, and yanked him vigorously up. I was surprised at a number of things: the strength in that taut little body as she gave a hand to such a bigger one; the sudden softness of concern and of entreaty, if insistent, in her tone; and even the name she called him—it had always been "Barker!" usually with an exclamation point and a certain rasp.

We moved upward, through the darkness and toward the sunlight, quite slowly, sweating, climbing steadily, working our way as we sought tree holds, pausing and gasping from breath, then upward again. An odd matter of defenses crossed my mind: Anything up there would certainly be invulnerable to attack of whatever kind. It was almost by surprise that we found ourselves stepping out onto the top, and onto a broad smooth rocky shelf that surmounted the cliff like a pie plate. We stood there breathing hard. Straight down, far below, we could see the boat fastened snugly in her rocky moorings. Then, having regained breath, we looked up and down the island. Then, one on each side of me, together we gazed out to sea.

Sea and sky lay in an impossible solitude, in a comradeship of palest blues. Not a whisper of wind stirred, not the smallest strip of cirrus broke the towering vault of blue arching over the other mighty blaze of blue beneath. The sea stood naked: Not an object, not a speck flawed the surface, north, south or west to a horizon so distant you felt you could see the curve of the planet. Nothing, nothing but the infinity of blue, the great waters standing in awesome serenity, in all majesty, voiceless save for a lone and rhythmic susurration where they met the rocks below. You felt it must have been like this in the beginning, before God spoke to these waters and decreed earth. The sea looked the one immortal thing ever created, alone everlasting where all else, sooner or later, passed away; regnant, sacramental, only and true queen of the universe. I thought how the earth was seven-tenths ocean and that in that sense it belonged to sailors more than to anyone else, a thought which strangely lifted me. I felt I was gazing at eternity itself. Perhaps all along, from the beginning, only the sea had been meant to endure.

We stood there looking for what must have been minutes. Not a word was spoken and for that I felt an intense closeness to the two fellow seamen alongside me. But along with this came an overpowering sense of aloneness, as if there were only us on all the earth; an aloneness that seemed to speak to us, saying that all we had was ourselves and so must cling to and love one another, shipmates. And suddenly there was comfort, a kind of healing, in that. I thought one thing more, like a light of divination. The sight, what it gave to one, seemed an omen. Sailors believe strongly in omens. We must, with such as that, have come to a place meant for us.

"Let's have a look," I said.

We turned around. We stood facing a forest of high trees, a forest broad both ways down the cliffs, the trees standing in august and serried ranks as far as we could see into it, and ahead of us to a depth we could not make out. The trees, soaring toward the sky, were grander by far than anything on the eastern side of the island, shamelessly flourishing in their proud greenness and of a guardsman-like straightness. They had obviously stood here over unnumbered years, against any kind of weather. The sunlight flashed down through them, dancing off their emerald leaves, the long dazzling shafts of whiteness bathing their columns in a stateliness cathedral like.

"Let's see what's in there," I said.

"Oh, yes, let's," Coxswain Meyer said. There was such unaccustomed eagerness in her voice, such unwonted girlish excitement, that both Barker and I laughed. Under the checkered sunshine, spilling through the high branches, we walked into the radiant stillness, between the trees and through the forest, hearing our padded steps on the soft forest bed, Barker and myself bracketing the coxswain, hardly reaching to the shoulder of either of us. Now and then the trees broke, presenting sizable clearings of the forest floor, with patches of bright lime-green grass decorated here and there with small blue and yellow wildflowers. We stopped in one and looked up, the fulgor of light tumbling down on us from the lavish encircling green. I had a sense of pure beauty all around me, undefiled, healing in its texture, stilling troubled souls. Now into that deep peace came up, high overhead, a freshening of breeze from off the sea, surprising in its nature, telling us of a west wind on the island not before known to us that brought a gentle and palliating coolness across the high cliffs; a soughing wind, trembling the upmost branches and leaves, sending them singing sweetly in the stillness. Meyer's head was craned back, looking high into that green and sunlit vault. She had taken off her sailor's hat and her hair stirred in the wind, her upturned face softened, transfigured.

"I've never seen a place so lovely," she said, her voice soft, hushed in the green silence, a wonder in it. "Do you think anyone has ever been here, Captain? Could we be the first ever to see this?"

It was the same question Barker had asked on the beach on the other side when first we set foot on the island.

"I don't know. I'd guess yes."

And yet—there is a feeling one has about such things. In this instance, that men had been here, even been here recently. An eerie feeling one had in that direction. And something more, never stated—that they were still here somewhere in the dark breadth of this land, somewhere between the place we now stood and the other side of the island where the ship lay—jungle wilderness home to them, impenetrable to us. It was a daydream—or a nightmare. I put it away as nonsense. Certainly, whatever it was, it was the last thing I should trouble any of my crew with now.

"I don't think any human eye ever saw any of this," I said, quite firmly. "We're the first."

We moved forward again, farther into the forest. We could not have gone far when we first heard it, somewhere up ahead of us, a low murmuring of sound.

We stopped and looked at one another, all alert. The sound was too far in to be of the sea and besides it clearly came from ahead, not behind. No one spoke. Then we resumed walking, very slowly, instinctively bearing off a little to follow it, hearing it grow spectrally larger. Then, the sound still mounting though never truly loud but like a steady humming, the forest came to a break, the land appeared to end as if sliced off. We stood startled, and a bit shaken, rather more than less afraid, on an edge, looking far down.

"Good Lord," Barker said. "Captain."

Below us lay a sudden deep green valley.

"Look!" Meyer said, and her arm came up.

At what appeared to be the head of the valley, a waterfall, embraced in arms of green, shining white in the sunlight flashing off it, came tumbling over a cliff. It was not wide, perhaps twenty feet across, not loud and angry but rather curling over the high place in a kind of lulling sweetness of intonation and for a remarkable drop until it found earth, and there far below formed a circular pool. From the pool we could see a strong stream emerge, so clear-bottomed in the light glittering through the high trees that overhung it that we could see the shining rocks there, cutting its way, with a distant, gently rippling timbre, down the valley until it disappeared in the thickening forest. We looked back at the waterfall. Now and then a breath of sea breeze, sliding between the trees and through the forest, played across it, sending out a gentle spume. I looked back down the valley.

"That creek," I said.

"Sir?" Barker said.

"The creek. Below the Farm. This is where that creek comes from. That stream must go clear across the island."

We stood there in mute examination of it, for myself a catalogue of cold hard appraisals and facts rushing in a tumble through my head. The valley, the fall, the pool, the stream, the trees. I cannot say for how long. Suddenly up through the treetops I felt the declining light. I looked at my watch. I was startled at how late it was. It would not do for darkness to overtake us at sea. Especially after that tide rip—we might have to negotiate another on the island's northern passage. One tended to forget how fast night came on in these latitudes.

"We'd best get on," I said.

We went back through the forest, passing through occasional clearings, caught in the softly oblique luminescence of a descending sun. I think each of us was afraid to talk, wanting to absorb the strange feelings filling us, to digest these visual invasions rushing in from all sides on our contemplations. My own thoughts raced ahead into time and my mind's eye saw: habitations, built from those sturdy guardsman trees under the supervision of Noisy Travis; built in those clearings, these being far enough back so that, leaving standing those parts of the forest which stood between them and the sea, the habitations would have the added protection of the trees themselves, security entire; all the fresh water needed just at hand; even a more salubrious temperature, given that gentle westerly wind, than on the island's other side . . .

We reached the cliff and from the pie plate looked down at the boat, tucked in securely between her twin moorings.

We went around the cliff and started down, tree to tree on the deep descent, much faster this time, and came out on the apron beach. I told Meyer to get in, she hauled in the anchor, and with her at the wheel Barker and I, wading, pushed the boat out carefully from between the rocks, then pulled ourselves in over the gunwales. Meyer backed off until we stood well clear. We idled for a few moments, looking up across the darkening water at the cliff of Pompeiian red, fixed in a mystic beauty in the light of the fading afternoon sun. Seeming, to me, ancient and solid, a place of protection, a haven of serenity—of security. I saw again in vision what was behind that cliff. A great sense of stillness filled me. And suddenly I knew: I had found what I was looking for.

"Coxswain," I said, "let's go home."

"Home it is, sir," she said, with a bright air exceptional for her, and brought the boat sharply to port and bore off northwesterly. Soon up ahead we could see the end of the island. We went around it—in smooth waters, no tide rip on this end—and then were on the eastern side and it was as if it were a different island. The long beach stretched unbroken and the land lay gently beyond it. Then I could see the ship far off, standing in resplendent and rather haughty solitude on the blue, and felt an unaccountable relief that she was still there. We followed down the beach, still our half-mile offshore, Meyer at the wheel, Barker and I parked in the stern sheets near her. The sun was headed down the western sky, the huge hot ball hastening to reach the cooling sea.

"Just imagine, Captain," Meyer said from her coxswain pulpit. "A waterfall." She spoke as if still in the grip of a reverie, her voice soft, all a girl. "I can't remember that I ever saw a waterfall before. No, definitely not." And said it again, as if it were some holy wonder of nature. "A waterfall."

"Wasn't it a pretty place, though?" Barker said. His face was alight. "Who would ever have thought?"

We could see the ship coming closer.

"I can't wait to tell," Meyer said.

"I'm sure everybody would like to hear about it," I said.

I need now to record, sadly, that about this time we lost a member of ship's company. Most regrettably of all, a woman. Her name was Emily Austin. She was on the farm detail, having been the daughter of a dirt farmer from eastern Tennessee. She had literally run away to that sea which she had never seen—"Have you ever chopped cotton for ten hours, Captain?" was the rather jaunty explanation she once gave me. She was religious without being proselytizing. There was an attractive, authentic gaiety to her personality; one, however, I could feel being eaten away at during our passage through the dark and the cold. She apparently slipped away from the Farm one day. Neither Delaney or any others of the detail missed her at first, not until quitting time near twilight. Next day we knocked off everything and made a thorough search of the island. Nothing. She was bright as a tack, as anyone in her rating of operations specialist had to be. She was one of the air trackers who, sitting at their consoles, monitored our missiles to their destinations at Orel.

We had a service for her on the fantail. The Jesuit read one of the Psalms and Porterfield led ship's company in the singing of "Majestic Sweetness Sits Enthroned," a favorite hymn of hers.

.5.

POWER

Daily I inspected the Farm; some days, the fishing grounds as well. These were the normal duties of any ship's captain to determine the progress of important work. But they had an added purpose, which was to see how the men themselves were faring, apart from their work. As I have said, it is in the nature of seamen: the setting of a purpose and the accomplishing of it, with often little more in the way of tools than their ingenuity and single-mindedness. But there was something beyond the expected coping that I felt that morning, carefully scrutinizing these of my ship's company in the field. In their brutal labor under that violent sun, bathed in dirt-streaked sweat, spread out across that acreage above the sea, bodies bent to the earth so that only the tops of their white hats marked their movements, they seemed near obsessed in a determination to subdue the soil and bring sustenance from it by their sheer unceasing endeavor, and by their very will, which would permit of no other result. Even I could not have foreseen the fanaticism with which these bluejackets toiled. We were paying the expected price: three men thus far victims of prostration, confined to sick bay, their places taken by ready volunteers. The furrowed soil now stretched in long black rows to the cliffside and the blue beyond, neat Bristol-fashion rows considering that both plowmen and mules had been men of the sea; rows harboring carefully imbedded

82

seeds and plants which we had reason to believe were flourishing, helped along immeasurably by the island's daily twenty-minute rain quota provided as if on standing watch order by some angel in charge of agriculture, or perhaps of sailors. Besides the promise of food, all of this went to further what I devoutly desired, a stake on the part of ship's company in the island itself.

I started down through the trees. It was a day of luminous serenity, the sunlight shimmering through the branches, a very sweetness in the island's air. Soon below I could hear the pleasing, now-familiar sound of the creek that flowed along the bottom of the ridge below the Farm, the creek that I now felt certain originated far across the island in that forest atop the cliffs. I began to feel borne upward in spirit, having just viewed the men so zealous at their labors; a sense of well-being filled me, seeing how the work was going—how the promise grew; I felt an increasing confidence that I could bring them along with me in that most final of all steps. Working my way down the hill I glimpsed, just visible through the trees, something that drew me up. Two sailors were kneeling at the brook, their mouths to the running water. There was nothing unusual about this. The sailor-farmers often came down off the ridge to drink of that cold water, its fresh pure taste a splendid and reviving thing after the hard going above. I was about to go on when a voice, rising faintly upward through the trees, caught my ear. Something in it made me wait.

It was a girl's voice, which also was not unusual—a few women sailors, I have said, worked on the Farm—but there was something in the timbre and tone of it. Then I heard a certain lilting laughter. I looked through the trees, feeling uncomfortably like a voyeur spying on my own people. Their heads were now raised, but they stayed on their knees and I saw them look at each other for a moment. Regarded one way, it was a charming tableau, a girl and a boy kneeling at a brook, their faces wet from the tasting of it. (Of course I knew their names.) Nothing whatsoever happened. But there was a quality in the scene itself, in the very configurations of their facing genuflected forms, a sense of something like intimacy, that made something terrible strike at my heart. I moved quickly on, wanting to get away from it. Surely it was nothing. But whether it was or not, for the present I did not wish to know, cowardly perhaps, and I certainly didn't want to get the information in that clandestine manner, spying through trees. I cleared the woods, faster than usual, and walked up the beach to my boat waiting on the sand. I decided to put the matter out of my mind as the meaningless thing it in all likelihood was.

I told Coxswain Meyer to take me out to the fishing grounds, today,

I knew, on the western side of the island which Silva also had discovered and found that the fish more often than not ran better there than on the eastern. "Fish like rocks," he said, and I had cautioned him about these, never to venture inshore without a close bow lookout. Our boat began to round the island. By now we knew well to make that transit farther out so as to avoid the rather vicious tide rip that formed closer inshore where the currents coming from the two sides of the island met. I had carefully warned Silva and his fishermen about that, too. Having brought us smartly around the island's tip, Meyer gave the wheel over to Barker while she monitored him closely and now and then furnished him a brisk pointer on boat handling, bringing him along in his Navy trade.

From the cloudless azure vault of sky sunlight fell on the cliffs that rose, majestic fortresses boldly confronting the sea, the light playing across their Pompeiian red, the water a polished mirror all the way in until it met the patient rocks and threw up now splashes, now fountains of white spume. My mind seldom left those cliffs, and now that they were in sight turned to what lay unseen just beyond them: that verdant forest of the guardsman trees, the good timber at hand, the sweet clearings in the forest bed, the fall of eternal fresh water. It put itself together to form a place I had never ceased, since first I saw it, to think of as surely God-given for our purposes, and if there was an angel of agriculture perhaps there was also an angel of housing and he had brought us, wandering seamen, here. To get a second opinion after the angel's, it now occurred to me that I might take Noisy Travis there tomorrow for a professional look at those trees.

A burst of laughter from aft startled me from these reveries. Youthful laughter that fell like a clear-striking ship's bell on the still morning and out across the silent sea. It was nothing at all, only that I had not heard it before between them. The relationship between the coxswain and the seaman as I had observed it was that strictly of a fine craftsman and one in the apprenticeship of that craft, and no nonsense. But now the laughter was curiously like that I had heard from the brook: that particular and special laughter of youth, girl and boy, the secret language of the young, something that in the right circumstances would have been pleasing and brought a tolerant smile in an older hearer. I looked back and saw them standing close alongside each other, chatting. Then the laughter again. Perhaps, with my constant use of this boat, they had become accustomed to their captain's presence and went about their business as they did in my absence. Nonetheless a ripple of foreboding as to whether it might be speaking of something new between them shot through me. This time I at least had the decent sense immediately to wonder, not as to whether it was already beginning to happen in my ship's company, but whether it was happening only in the mind of a prurient, voyeuristic captain, possibly too alert for signs of what he so deeply feared. We bore more to seaward and soon up ahead could see Silva's boat, motionless on the mirroring waters. As we came nearer we could see the men seize the large net, fling it back and skyward in a parabola, and then cast it wide and flowing into the sea where it fell gently as a tern's feather before settling to gather in its harvest. It was a lovely sight, full of skill and grace, an artistry almost moving in it, the modern nuclear sailors mastering the art as done in the days of Galilee. As if man, having moved forever forward into time, now had come about, 180 degrees so, and was setting a course backward through the ages of time and across ancient seas; as if progress the other way had after all been too hurried and haven lay where he had come from.

"Ahoy, Silva," I called as we drew near. "How goes the catch?"

Back came his exultant shout. "Captain, come see for yourself."

"Heave to, Coxswain," I spoke back to Meyer, who had retaken the wheel.

"Aye, aye, sir," she sang out. Coxswain Meyer had a voice clear and clean as a bird's call. Then came the snap in it.

"Barker! Stand by with the lines!"

The sailor leapt to her command. This time I felt a smile on my lips.

As far back as I can remember, on unnumbered waters of the world and in all manifestations of the sea's unending repertory of moods, whether placid as some inland lake or stormy enough to roll one's body back and forth, port and starboard, with the ship herself while one clutched hard the volume, I have read a half hour before bed, sitting up in my bunk, before marking my place and reaching up and snapping off the overhead light. I have often wondered how anyone who does not read, by which I mean daily, having some book going all the time, can make it through life. Indeed if I were required to make a sharp division in the very nature of people, I would be tempted to make it there: readers and nonreaders of books. (The second would be seamen and landsmen.) It is astonishing how the presence or absence of this habit so consistently characterizes an individual in other respects; it is as though it were a kind of barometer of temperament, of personality, even of character. Aside from that, for me it constituted something like sanity insurance. I made it a point, in that half hour, that what I read should have nothing whatever to do with my duties as a naval officer, or, now, ship's captain, but would bear me away into other realms, kingdoms of the mind and spirit, accessible only between bindings. That night the book happened to be *The Kreutzer Sonata*, one of the 985 we had brought out as I had discovered in the inventory of our possessions with Lieutenant Girard—how immeasurably grateful I was for these! I could feel the cloaking night around me, the stillness of the ship. Then, reading, my mind unaccustomedly kept slipping off, making its own steerageway, as if perversely determined to take away the one half hour of the day I felt I could call my own and forget every worry and concern, the whole agenda of anxiety. Until it fetched me up, like a fast-reverse, freeze-frame film, and displayed again to its unwilling viewer the twin sights: the two sailors by the brook; the two sailors in the whaleboat.

Then I pushed it back, locked it up again, as I had long since learned to do, as a matter of personal survival, with it and its great company of other problems, matters to be confronted, dealt with, in the broad light of day. As the book absorbed me and went into me and became a part of me, so that it was something I would always have, I began only to possess the book, and the book to possess me. Until at last I reluctantly marked my place in *The Kreutzer Sonata*, thanked Mr. Tolstoy, and reached up and snapped off the overhead light. Falling asleep thinking, what might the Jesuit know. Or Girard.

Before Lieutenant Girard came to me today I sat in my cabin, renewedly disturbed, if but faintly so, more nagging than acute, from a cause undetermined, imprecise in nature, a captain's sense of recent origin of a certain restiveness abroad on the ship; giving rise in turn to an apprehension, if still not one of major force, or unduly pressing, seeming to intensify as the days went by, and thought suddenly of a conversation of three months or so ago, on another sea. It was I who in these sessions on stores and morale—her twin responsibilities as an officer—generally put the questions. But on that occasion in the Mediterranean which I now sat bringing back in reflective recall, she came up with a question—a request—after we had finished up our routine daily matters, one that caught me totally offguard.

Looked at one way, the request was not all that unusual, presented as it was as being but an addition to a program we had already commenced. In fact it was Girard herself, acting as morale officer, who had suggested the program to me in the first place. I thought it an excellent idea, promptly okayed it, and in her fashion, she had begun at once and with characteristic efficiency and thoroughness to implement it. This while we continued to search for a place. A program to occupy the crew in various pursuits both educatory and enjoyable, the unstated purpose being to keep their minds off other things, to give them something of interest and stimulation on which to fasten their thoughts, and to have a little fun while doing it. While none of it was compulsory, there was scarcely a member of ship's company who did not enroll in one or another of the classes, and quite a number who enrolled in two or three. The eclectic curriculum included, on the physical side, boxing lessons taught by the Jesuit, a onetime Georgetown varsity boxer; fencing lessons offered by Sedgwick, who had been on the Academy fencing team (he had actually brought foils along to keep his hand in, and even a brace of épées, his specialty); Selmon providing a rudimentary course in gymnastics on some makeshift rings and bars; on the intellectual, Girard herself teaching a course in English literature (the nineteenth century, which had been her college major); Thurlow, a French class; Porterfield giving guitar lessons; myself a course in celestial navigation and shiphandling (student body principally women . . .). Some of the courses were purposefully designed to master skills we should urgently need in any future life: Delaney's course in farming methods fell in that category. There were two or three others. The crew's forthright eagerness for this impromptu school surprised me. Soon some were themselves suggesting new courses. It was my observation, and Girard's, that the program already had been of considerable worth. These activities and studies appeared to have a relaxing effect on the men, and to lift them out of a certain brooding which had reached a level that had begun to concern me. The new item that day was presented more or less in the context of an addition to this program.

I think I may have mentioned somewhere that Girard came to us fully qualified in gunnery, but due to her sex had been denied the billet at sea; indeed in her absolute determination concerning sea duty she then became a supply officer. That day, as we were finishing up, she asked me mildly if she might instruct the women in small-arms use. I remembered that I felt—nothing that could be called a suspicion—only a certain surprise.

"Why?" I responded.

She gave a mild shrug and smiled. "Something to help keep them occupied. Like the other courses. To acquire a skill."

She had made it sound so routine, her manner altogether offhand. I could simply think of no reasonable objection I could make, and so, I believe intelligently, made none. I shrugged myself.

"Of course. Why not? We are already gatherers." I was referring to our scavenging along the shorelines of our course for items that might be useful to our future: wheelbarrows and the like. "We could become hunters. It may come in handy, who can tell?"

"It may," she said with the same mildness, and a smile. "I'd like to make the instruction in both the .45 and the M-16. If the captain has no objection."

She said the last as if there could not possibly be any.

"The captain has no objection," I said.

It—the request, all of it—had seemed at the time altogether innocent. And had seemed so ever since. The astonishing, unexpected—the troubling thing was not the fact of the matter itself but that it should reappear now in my memory, for no discernible reason, nothing I could put my finger on. Perhaps—the mind's linkages forever a source of mystery—it was simply the wry thought that from teaching women how to use M-16's she had graduated to being in direct charge of our entire weaponry, from ASROCs to Tomahawks, "in addition to her other duties," in the Navy phrase; being now combat systems officer, my so designating her as the logical choice after the previous occupant had led his company of men off the ship; though in our present circumstances the position was largely nominal—the last thing we were likely to do was send off more missiles—except for that one aspect of her now holding the key necessary, in addition to my own, to launch the missiles.

From this excursion, whether detour or not I had no idea, my mind returned to course.

A Navy ship's company rarely confronts its captain with something, and if it ever does, it will be too late. He is alert for half-coded signals: a look, a word, even a gesture, the merest glance, will do it, these things constituting a kind of language of the sea. In that manner I had of late felt, sensed, as a sure fact, that muted perturbation aboard, an amorphous but unmistakable disturbing element, without being in any way certain as to its source. I had thought initially that it could only have been at the awaited decision in respect to the island, this something to be expected. Then it occurred to me as I sat waiting for her that this vague disquietude could have another origin. Forbidden as the subject was, perhaps, I thought, the time had come for a kind of reconnaissance on the perimeters of it, making careful soundings as I went, prepared to stop at the first sign of shallows. This surely could not be harmful; perhaps would give me a helpful signal. Indeed I felt I had no other choice but to proceed.

I heard the knock on my cabin door and glanced at the bell clock. Prompt to the second.

Out the port I could see the island and the green rising from it. The ship at anchor lay in perfect stillness, under wind-free skies; ship, sea, island seeming to stand in a harmonious and fraternal accord, a kind of understanding among themselves, in the peacefulness that held to all horizons.

We never talked about it anymore. I was therefore instantly alerted when she brought it up.

"The men," she said. "They wonder what happened to them."

It was not even necessary to identify the "them." I sensed an unaccustomed hesitancy in her, whose method it was never to hold back, especially bad news.

"Come on, Lieutenant," I said, rather sharply. "Let's have it."

"Some wish now they'd gone in the boats, with the others."

"With the mutineers?" I said harshly.

"They think of them more as shipmates."

"Don't quibble over words with me, Miss Girard."

"Sorry, sir. They think they may have made it home." She waited a moment, looked directly at me, a curious look. "Do you think they could have? In those open boats? Across five thousand miles of ocean?"

"Oh, yes. I think they could have made it home all right," I said, a certain detached note in my voice. "There were plenty of good seamen in those boats. Starting with Chatham. Chief Quartermaster Hewlitt, a first-class navigator. Yes, I think they could have made it home."

Again I thought she hesitated. "You don't have any doubts? I mean about conditions back there?"

The question astonished me. "Jesus Christ, Lieutenant. We went over that a thousand times. Our own failures to raise anything that would have affected the decision. Selmon's projections. The Russian sub commander. Even that dead French radioman. The evidence couldn't have been more conclusive. No one agreed with it more than yourself. What the hell's happening here? Have you just received a telegram from back there? New information you've discovered and for some reason are keeping to yourself?"

She smiled sardonically. "Negative to both, sir. No, I know the facts," she said more firmly. "I was just trying to convey the thinking of the men. Actually we're talking about a very few hands. No reason for concern, I'd say, sir. I thought it my duty to mention it."

"And so it was." I settled back a bit, seemed almost to speak more to myself than to her. "They were my shipmates, too."

"I understand, sir."

"Not a day passes that I don't wonder what happened to them. And hope they made it, are alive somewhere . . ."

My voice trailed off into the impossibility of it.

"Except for Lieutenant Commander Chatham. Whatever he got he deserved, and a few hells left over."

I waited a bit, spoke then, quietly, reflectively, yet looking at her with a keen directness she would at once understand.

"I blame myself for what happened. If I'd acted earlier . . . maybe would have stopped it. So something bothers me about this conversation. You're not suggesting there's enough discontent among the men to cause something like that again? If so, spit it out, Lieutenant."

She waited a moment, the words getting through to her all right, careful to frame her response.

"I would, sir. I think you know that. It's not anything like that, Captain. This is just talk."

"The other started in *talk*. I want to be kept minutely informed. Is that clear?"

"As always, sir," she said, a slight rebuke in her voice, as if she had ever done any other.

"Now let's leave it. What else?"

"Food inventories," she said promptly. "We're beating the schedule a little, Captain. We have the fish to thank. Aren't the men looking better though!"

It was good beyond measure to have such a rare thing happening: something to be actually increasing—we were freezing surplus fish—where all else was in slow, inexorable diminution. Especially those stores: Anyone who has been through it knows that it is not ideals but food that constitutes the thin blue line standing between men and horror. I had seen hunger, real hunger, once in my life and what it did—I mean did morally—to its victims was seared in my memory in a resolve that above all else this should not happen to my ship's company. I could feel the satisfaction of both of us.

"Any complaints? Of the palate, I mean. From so much of it."

"None I know of." Lieutenant Girard spoke now as the ship's morale officer. "It's very good fish. Then, of course, there's Chief Palatti, who works wonders. I haven't heard, Talley hasn't heard any grousing beyond the normal. So far anyhow."

Where Girard's morale duties were concerned, her enlisted assistant served, I had always felt certain, essentially as the lieutenant's spy among the crew. I never inquired about this but somehow knew it, and anyhow it was a favorable thing. I seemed now to want to dwell a bit on the unusual favorable turn in our supplies, to take some needful sustenance and comfort from the fact, before moving on to perhaps less promising matters. Also, the truth was, I seemed increasingly in these sessions to desire to keep Lieutenant Girard on a little longer. I felt a pleasure in her company, something that had surprised and to an extent perplexed me, an intellectual, almost esthetic thing—the kind of satisfaction in another human being that can be difficult for a ship's captain to come by, with the necessary barriers standing sternly between him and ship's company, so that when available, he tends to seek it out, and to treasure it. Heedful always of the inherent danger: favoritism as between a captain and any individual officer is one of the foremost of that multitude of pitfalls lying constantly in wait for a ship's captain, perceived and resented quickly by all officers not thus favored, to be avoided at all costs. Nevertheless, bearing that proscribed thing constantly in mind, I could proceed within limits. Even a ship's captain must relax, come down now and then and be a normal human being for a bit, a matter almost of mental balance.

"I'm not surprised. Once when I was sixteen, I put in a summer as a dragger fisherman off Cape Cod, out of a place called Wellfleet, Massachusetts."

"Did you?" she said with a bright air, her eyes lighting up, accommodating herself to her captain's patent desire for a few moments off all problems. "I went to school in Massachusetts. But I always thought you were an inlander."

"So I was. But I had an uncle up there. Anyhow I learned that it's true. I had never had it before—I mean literally never—but I learned. A fish caught the day you ate it: Well, there's no better food I know of a man can have."

She looked out the port at the blue, gleaming in the early morning light, that sensuous amalgam of scents, the sea and island vegetation, reaching fragrantly into the cabin.

"So we both were in Massachusetts," she said, turning back to me, as though that were some newly discovered fact of life.

Her voice had a lightness of inflection, soprano but soft in modulation. Her eyes as she talked bore a remarkable aliveness, a fine luster. Of course I had come to realize long since that that controlled demeanor was an important part of her tactic, of dealing with the world. Behind it a surely potent arsenal of strategem and schemery, held in reserve but quite readily available for skillful use if occasion for its application should arise; to me it issued from there as clear as some pennant of warning hoisted on a ship's halyards. I liked the quality, so long as it was on my side, or subject to my control and orders. I should not want it arrayed against me.

"Hardly at the same time," I said. "My time would have been, oh, about three years before you were born." I unexplainably felt a desire, right at that moment, to remind her of our considerable age difference. "I haven't had occasion to check your fitness reports and service record just lately, with all their facts and opinions about you, but I expect it would figure out at about that."

Eighteen years, I thought. The ascending sun sent a shimmering path of white across the lagoon and lancing softly into the cabin.

"Facts and opinions," she said, and a sort of mauve smile passed across her face. "Well, to save you the trouble of looking it up, sir, it's twenty-seven."

Fifteen years, I thought, and for some reason felt better.

"Well, I hadn't really planned to look it up."

Having started, my mind fled back across the years and fetched up at the precise moment: when I heard for the first time that low majestic roar like none other, that voice of deep waters. A boy, a long way from home, farther still from what life had thus far presented him—though that had been only a good thing, a thing he liked, still treasured: the Indian country of Oklahoma, his list of important matters measured in cow ponies, in his only friends the Cherokee children of his father's parishioners (his best friend, Ralph Walkingstick, later going to Dartmouth while he went to Annapolis, both seeming so infinitely far away worlds, both, unimaginably different from ours); now, never so much as having seen ocean before, standing in the dragger's bow watching in awe and wonder the mighty incoming line of waves, having completed their journey of three thousand miles from Europe's littorals, striking the wild desolation of Peakèd Hill Bars, there forming a plain of foaming white as far as eye could see, up and down that wilderness strand. One wave succeeding another, endlessly, coming home, as the waves would forever. He had seen, heard, nothing like it; had not so much as imagined the overpowering intensity of its existence, the consuming magnificence. It was like the light recounted in the Acts of the Apostles appearing suddenly on the road to Damascus, the boy a young Saul of Tarsus. Suddenly, the sea speaking to him in private conversation, the thing happening and in an instant of time that was to chart the boy's course forever. Summoning him: It was on the order of what my preacher forebears termed getting the call. My father, who had brought the good news of the Gospel to the Cherokees, had wanted another missionary to carry forward what he had started. But, loving his son, he was not a man to do battle with a thing he could see was so settled. After all—I remember his soft, faintly mocking smile—had it not happened on the road to Damascus?

She was asking—real interest I felt, not mere politeness—some question about the boats, how they worked.

"Very simple. You go along at about four knots, dragging the net behind you. Mouth held open by buoys, weights and boards. That's all there was to it."

"How big—the boats?"

"About the size of our gig. Forty-footers or a bit more. The Provincetown draggers. Came back in every day—those big Boston trawlers could stay out a lot longer. We'd come in, if we were lucky, with a load of, say, yellow-tail flounder, which doesn't run often so carries a fancy price tag, caught that day, and there'd be those big refrigerated semis on the pier ready to take them straight off the dragger and overnight to New York. Fulton Fish Market. So that a Boston fish may have been two weeks old even though it was right off the boat, a Provincetown fish you knew came out of the sea just a few hours before. That was why it brought a premium at Fulton. Nice. We worked on shares."

I paused, caught and held in memory's grip, painful and joyous.

"Those dragger boats off the Cape. It was the first time and that was all it took. That was when I knew it had to be the sea . . . Nothing else mattered."

I suddenly realized it was a kind of conversation we had never had, indeed that I could not remember ever having with a living being. I caught myself. I was letting her into my soul and a captain must never do that. It is not permitted him. I was aware of the stillness in the cabin, something anticipatory and oddly fervent in it, aware suddenly of a remarkably percipient human being listening intently, perhaps too intently. For a moment it was almost as if another young woman than the one I knew as Lieutenant Girard sat there. It was time to bring it back and I briskly did so.

"Let's get out of Massachusetts. Anything else, Lieutenant?"

And she was herself again, too, just as quickly, the subordinate naval officer attentive to the wishes and needs of her captain.

"That's it, sir." She invariably, and with the small, rather humorous sigh that came now, employed that phrase to end our discussion and always, such was my confidence in this officer, I felt that we had covered all important matters, that there was none, however formidable the problem, she would let slip through. She prepared to go. I waited a moment before dismissing her.

I sat back in my chair. I had hesitated. Too much so, I decided. A captain must move into a matter. The job is not meant for timid souls. I decided to test these waters, but with discretion, by a necessary indirection.

"Lieutenant," I said casually, "you wanted gunnery, didn't you? And qualified for it."

"Affirmative to both, sir. The sea billet wasn't available."

"Why gunnery?"

Always unruffled, never failing to appear in effortless control of herself, she now seemed mildly surprised, as if it were an intimate question I had asked. But she also appeared rather pleased than otherwise at the question, and a little whimsical.

"I guess because I thought that was what a Navy ship was all about. To use those guns; those missiles. Whatever I went into, I wanted to be in the center of it, of what was important, why the thing was there in the first place. I hope that doesn't sound too . . ." she hesitated and with that faint, almost mocking smile, used a strange word: " . . . pushy."

"Pushy? Well, to be in the middle of something . . . the best reason I can think of. Of course you wanted to get to sea even more."

"Aye, sir."

And so I made this peripheral talk, all the while pondering her; so artful in picking up the least signal sent in her presence, certain to see that I had something on my mind, perhaps even to see what it was. But I had been unable to think of a way to bring the matter forth naturally, without carrying suggestion itself. The words would not come to my lips.

There obtained an additional constraint. Aboard ship certain things must not be blurted out as probable facts or even likely surmise until one has arrived at a resolute certainty, the reason being that in the tight and enclosed world of a vessel at sea, where words spread like wildfire, until a thing presents itself in the form of some actual outbreak among the crew, some tangible incident, the very act of articulation can serve to create what was not there; for talk itself is the most dangerous enemy of all to the well-being of a ship, where words come back only as echoes, with no outside world to check against for an independent judgment, to correct perhaps an unstable one. One learns to treat language with care, as in the handling of lethal ammunition stores; in the present matter one felt the caution insistent in the extreme. It was in these devilish latitudes that I now navigated, and her with me. The very last thing I should do was to ask direct questions. It is almost always a mistake and now would be a foolish, stupid, even dangerous thing to do. A captain who has to ask has already lost control. A general question. I could safely put that. (If she wished to make a connection between the mention of gunnery and the next matter, that was up to her.) I decided to make the question rather abrupt after all—as if in that way to keep off it any sense of urgency, of undue import, to make it, insofar as possible, extraneous, something off an agenda, an inquiry a ship's captain might make, for instance, as to the length of a binnacle list.

"How are the women doing, Lieutenant?"

"The women, sir?" I felt immediately an equivocation. In her role of morale officer we had often discussed the welfare of ship's company in general; had never discussed the women as women.

"Why, they're doing fine, sir," was all the answer I got, seeming a deliberate inanity and thus, coming from her, almost bewildering. "Did you have something specific in mind, Captain?"

Something hung in the air, withheld in the suddenly tense hush; something new. I looked into those cool gray eyes. I felt they saw everything and told, now, nothing; that she knew to the last shading what I meant. Still she had to pretend otherwise. Just as did I. Or perhaps she had simply determined not to let me get away with it; to force it back upon me. And so she had murmured—with entire design it seemed to me—the question she knew full well I could not answer.

"No, Lieutenant. It was only a general question," I said.

"Why, sir," she said, curiously brightening, "the women are doing like the men are doing. Carrying on."

This astonished me. It seemed a dodge, a blatant circumvention.

"No better, no worse?" I smiled thinly. I could hear the different tone in my voice, moving to meet this change, dry, an edge in it. "Than the men, I mean."

"Well, if you put it that way, sir. I would say slightly better." Said almost as if they had resources unknown to other sailors. Now it was she who gave a soft, almost evanescent smile, of a kind I was left to make of what I might. I did not like the answer; liked even less what she then added oddly, with its faint touch of the superior. "The women will be all right, Captain."

This statement increased a kind of angry wariness I could feel as having appeared within myself, bringing with it suddenly a sense of danger lying just below the surface, something about it infinitely threatening. Apart from having the highest rank, she was a natural leader of the women. The women in their rigorously segregated quarters must talk over any number of things. There was nothing to keep them from talking over anything, and no man's ear ever hearing. It was not inconceivable that they might, in present circumstances, come to consider their first allegiance to themselves, to their own fraternity of womanhood. The very idea of the possible existence of such an entity, never having remotely occurred to me until this instant, was itself deeply unsettling; further, wholly inadmissible. Not only can it not be recognized, given any official standing whatsoever; nothing is more expressly, categorically forbidden aboard ship than cliques of any kind. And I could think of none more unacceptable, striking at the very functioning of the ship, than one consisting only of women; I would come down on it instantly, ruthlessly, with every force and power I possessed. The further idea that Lieutenant Girard might be the active leader of such a body . . . my mind moving backward to cast into suspicions matters that at the time had seemed routine, innocent, now appearing perhaps done with every intent, pondering the training of the women in small-arms usage . . . I stopped this. I did not remotely know any of these things as facts; had no manifest basis for suspecting them as such; they barely qualified as speculations; fearful suddenly of suspicion itself, another of those elements that can perilously flower and prosper, and in a peculiarly virulent manner, in the intimacy of shipboard life; once it starts, separating the real from the imagined becoming an authentic problem of its own. Any captain knows to be vigilant against the latter, and quickly to discard it unless tangible cause can be found. And I did so here. The hostility which I perhaps concealed at her answer, at these ambiguities in general, remained; indeed I could feel it growing, that impatience when I could not get what I felt was due me as captain of this ship, my voice close to the caustic, replying to her "The women will be all right."

"That's good to hear."

"Is that all, sir?" The question itself: Customarily, in the Navy way, she waited for me to dismiss her. Now it was as if she were anxious to get away before I should probe her further.

I sat vastly vexed with this blurry imprecision, the indeterminateness—something I had never got from her—I was ending up with; feeling the strain, merging into distress, that had by now invested the cabin; aware of having gotten exactly nowhere. I sat frustrated—thwarted and displeased, even on the edges of outright displayed anger, suppressing it only by the reminded conviction I had long held that of all tools anger is the stupidest; I had rarely seen it serve any useful purpose; generally only paralyze the intelligence. Steadying myself inwardly, I had about given up hope in the matter for today, with the intention either of coming at Girard at another time or of approaching the Jesuit, with his devices including the confession box, lately overcrowded and sometimes available to me by a highly circumspect indirection. Abruptly I dismissed her.

"That's it, Miss Girard," in those words hearing now a distinct curtness.

"Then until tomorrow morning, sir."

Perhaps it was her seeing of these things in me—the sum of my displeasure—that made it happen; perhaps that had no effect at all and she had simply decided that her strategy now called for her to take one positive step. I would never know. In any event, having half risen to go, she sat back and spoke.

"There is one thing, Captain. The women?" she said, with a curiously interrogatory note, as if speaking of some different, possibly higher species. She looked at me. "Well, sir . . ." She hesitated and then said: "The women are beginning to feel . . . well, outnumbered."

It was as though General Quarters had sounded in the pit of my stomach. I had been looking out the port at the lagoon, perhaps seeking some lenitive effect from its own benign peacefulness, perhaps just looking deliberately away from her, to show my dissatisfaction with this turn in our conversation. My head snapped around. I waited, letting things come very still in me, my mind bringing all its power to bear on that strange word. In the tense silence I spoke with a deliberate quiet; but just as intentionally with a hard and insistent edge in my voice.

"Outnumbered? What in the world does that mean, Lieutenant? Has something happened? Something specific? You must tell me at once."

"No, sir," she said. Her voice was undisturbed, in no way intimidated; equally, in no way aggressive. "Nothing specific. It's a feeling, sir."

I had had enough of this. I looked out once more at the lagoon; back at her, where her eyes awaited mine; and looking full into them spoke more sharply, coldly, than ever I had to her.

"It's difficult for a captain to act on feelings, Miss Girard. I would like a straight answer."

"I'm not asking you to act, sir. I thought it my duty to convey to you . . . I am morale officer."

My tone of voice, my manner, found no echo in hers, continuing to speak with all her wonted self-possession, her impregnable composure, on the outside; and yet, something I seemed to feel within her, a certain intensity I had not sensed there before. It was almost as if she were trying to give me a warning, urgent in nature, if I had ears to hear.

"Of course it is. Of course you are. Is there anything else you wish to say?"

"Just that, sir."

It was all very well to say you were supposed to treat them the same. What a stupid idea that was; for starters: Harshness with a woman simply makes her close down. I tried to speak more softly, not certain as to how much I succeeded in doing so. Something also in myself telling me I should pursue the matter no further with her today; come down on her no harder; not make demands, not insist on something more definite; not in the heat of this atmosphere; not anymore at all today.

"I'm glad you mentioned it. You were quite right to do so. You will continue to keep me informed, is that clear? Especially of anything remotely substantive."

"Aye, sir. It's clear."

If any residue of hostility remained, it appeared to be exclusively in myself. She walked to the door, taking her inviolate serenity—and, it seemed, her sureness of something undefined—with her. Her body and her way of carrying it were pliant and without effort, eurythmic, a grace by second nature, as though it were something she never had to give a thought to; impossible of making an awkward movement. I could see the shimmering water of the lagoon beyond, seeming to backdrop, and to outline, her woman's figure. But I was not looking at the lagoon. I was looking first at the back of her head and the pure grain of wheat-light hair, then all down her body, slender and cool, across her seat, down her legs, the clean white smartness of the uniform seeming to enhance as it were her womanhood; whilst I did, having the eerie conviction that she knew I was doing so. Then she was gone and I sat looking out at only the unobstructed lagoon. Feeling a tremor through all my being, a dampness breaking out all over me as from a fever. In this male stronghold of ships I felt suddenly enveloped in femininity, in its impenetrable mysteries, its unknown and perhaps unknowable secrets, its very scents—its snares, its traps. And then I knew.

I stepped through the opposite door onto the small catwalk perch, holding room for hardly more than one person, that the ship's designers had placed immediately outside the captain's cabin and made accessible only from it; a private place, a tiny quarterdeck, extending outward enough to fulfill its purpose of giving the ship's captain a view along the entire starboard length of the ship, of the Number 1 missile launcher and the five-inch gun forward, of the 20mm Phalanx and the Number 2 launcher aft, then straight down to the sea itself directly below where one stood. From it the captain could take in at a glance the physical state of the ship and yet not himself be seen unless some hand aft—he could not be seen at all from forward—consciously raised his head and looked up there, which none ever did. I had stood on that catwalk, the sea rushing past beneath me, ten thousand times, a thing that normally filled me with both comfort and exhilaration, for nowhere did I feel ship and sea—the lords of my life—more. Now in the late morning warmth of the climbing sun I gazed at the island, at the pure beauty of it, and felt only the onset of a dark and all-encompassing foreboding.

The unspoken power the women were beginning to gain over us. Without the slightest effort on their part to acquire it. None necessary. Simply by their presence, nothing else. The knowledge, too, that every day that passed that power increased. And then I knew something more. They were aware of all of this in the most meticulous way, to the most refined exactitude, like a navigational fix accurate to the degree, minute, and second; with that sensory apparatus, so exquisitely calibrated, they possess that exceeded by far our best radar, our finest sonar gear.

So long in doing so, it now arrived in merciless brutality, revealing in all fullness every particular of the fearful prospect as does the great lightning the night ocean. In that naked and defenseless illumination I seemed to stand on the shore of a dark and unknown sea, looking at an unventured horizon; without the least idea in the world of how to proceed; knowing only the certainty of the most treacherous shoals ahead, whatever the course I decided upon; shoals, given the terrible mathematics of the matter, I could see no way whatsoever of either going over or around.

I looked across the sea. The waters, in a profound reach of blue, stretched far and away in the tranquillity that held everywhere. And yet something premonitory seemed to hang in the air, as if some elemental and unspecified peripeteia awaited us that all my unending anticipation of everything that might happen to us had yet failed to foresee; the very serenity, the pellucid emptiness, pressing down on me. I stood a moment more in the tense quiescence. Suddenly a sheer of wind came up, flapping the halyards, then faded away. The breathless stillness returned. Standing on the captain's catwalk high above the sea, I felt an actual physical dizziness as though teetering on the very rim of the precipice.

.6.

MATHEMATICS AND GAMOGENESIS

Perhaps, needing time, I had pretended dangerously that the problem did not even latently exist; of distinctions suddenly beginning to assert themselves where there had been none, not allowed. Refusing almost to recognize the apprehension which surely had for so long now been in me. Still, I was not so innocent as to believe the matter would never arise, in present circumstances, to think that Navy directives in these areas would forever and in every respect hold fast. It reposed always in a special vault of my soul, having taken up a permanent residence there, waiting patiently and in its turn, so I supposed, locked up, ready to be brought out and dealt with at a time of my choosing. Not that it did not, now and then, and more recently than formerly, pop out of that safekeeping, briefly but tormentingly, to confront me, fill me with foreboding, and to ask me what I was going to do about it. Each time knowing I was fathoms deep, no nearer to answering that question, solving that vast riddle, than when first I began to consider it. It was not even that I did not want it to happen. Quite the opposite; coming to know even before we raised the island, as in some epiphany that changes everything, not only that it would, but that it must; yes, that I had some kind of ultimate responsibility to see that it did. It was rather that I had my hands quite full, and so had wished to put it off until such time as other urgencies—

food, finding a place for us, building thereon habitations—were attended
to and I could give the matter something like the full attention I was
certain it would require. But now that captain's inner compass that I had
learned long since on many seas to be guided by, and which seemed to
function independently of myself, veered: It can wait no longer; time is
running out. What if after all our strivings, our hardships met and overcome, our devotion to one another not without valor and the very limits
of selflessness that might be expected of men . . . if after all that we should
shipwreck on such secondary shoals as these! (I felt even an unreasoning
anger at the women themselves, as if they had deliberately brought the
matter on, when every known fact made clear that their guilt consisted
solely of their being members of ship's company.) The idea was intolerable. And at a time when our every resource, physical, mental, and emotional, was summoned for the task ahead, itself filled with every
uncertainty, with far greater trials and vicissitudes sure to come than any
we had thus far vanquished. Confront the matter now (said that guide),
lest, given its nature, the failure to do so imperil all other plans. Turn men,
until now brothers, shipmates, against one another. One could not but
think in terms of unspeakable—impermissible—horrors. A house divided
against itself: The old truth stands a thousandfold more certain for a ship,
which has no exit, no place to escape from the divisiveness. The voice had
begun to pound in my ears: Solve it by the authority that lies in you as
a ship's captain; the matter will only worsen and in exact step with the
time you delay. And with final urgency: Nothing will work if that does
not; if some way is not found. A taunt more than a voice. That great gulf
of numbers: What solution, what arrangement, could there possibly be?

The matter now emerged from its hidden, rather cozy refuge, my
mind having turned fervently to it through troubled days and awakened
nights, a kind of unceasing anguish of incessant thinking, figuring . . . the
combinations I came up with, the variety, in their infinity, of schemes,
systems—solutions! All of them foolish. Knowing that I had no higher
duty than to solve something I was in no way qualified to solve—but what
man would be? What *man.* Suddenly the mind made a movement to
dwell on certain general speculations, not for their originality or profun-
dity, aware even as I did so that they were entirely banal reflections,
matters obvious to anyone with a claim to thinking, but rather as one who
had learned long since not just that there is a great deal of necessary
banality in the Navy but that the realization of the fact, if one attended
to it, not infrequently curiously shines a way through a difficulty, like the
banal lighthouse standing on a shoal-ridden shore.

Knowing little about women, I had nonetheless over the years come to one conclusion as a truth. Women will stick together. Their bonds due to one another in their femaleness were as strong as anything I had seen. A thing absolutely their own, unique. Nothing like it is known in the general world of men. Standing together simply for the reason that they are women, nothing else, a supreme, a wonderfully functioning and unshakable instinct that binds them to the interests of womanhood. And where more than in this matter, their domain, their vocation: had not Nature decreed it so? The furtherest thing from my mind, therefore, should be to attempt to break up this invincible loyalty, as I first hastily thought. Rather that swift solidarity, with all its strengths, should be used. How stupid I had been not to have seen it! Perhaps it was that that Girard had been telling me all along.

Suddenly it all came together: I felt I knew the only way that might stand a remote chance of working. One, to be sure, filled with great hazard, with every difficulty the sea herself proffers in her endless moods, her cunning snares without number: these would be present also, aggressively so. Even so, I felt there was no other which would not lead us straight on a course fully capable of disintegrating us, foundering us as a ship founders. Thereafter always coming back to it, still with profound trepidations and misgivings, as the only way acceptable (what we called civilized), always returning as after a circumnavigational voyage round and round on some vast and infinitely baffling meridian—moral or practical, I hardly knew which, and scarcely cared so long as I could devise a method, any method, that would either subdue or accommodate that force in its immensity, that would *work,* stand a chance of working—to the one authority even a captain could not usurp, the only one not conferred on him, however sublimely confident he might be in his abilities in all other matters to arrange men's lives for them. Only one source had that authority. And almost instanteously with it a decision, a first step. I would give this candidate one week of all the full attention I could manage within the other demands on me; and during that period observe discreetly, furtively: the men, the women, in a way I never had, a different way, as of different persons from those I had so long now commanded; different beings in the sense of now being ambushed by thoughts, prospects, possibilities, hitherto forbidden; spend it also reconnoitering the matter in its every aspect. Then if the idea firmed, came resolutely whole, I would speak with the Jesuit. Looking not for balm but for a species of concordat or even dispensation; even, via him, for Providence's approval on top of mine. I did not disallow the possibility that my greatest trouble might come from this powerful quarter.

Simultaneous with the decision on this matter I made another. At the moment of execution of the other course I would begin at once the building of our habitations ashore. Before it was too late; before more restiveness—or worse—was permitted to form and magnify, even—such a possibility stood always just behind my shoulder, looking over it—reach a point beyond all control, the matter taken from my hands, with results no man could foretell.

Before proceeding I further needed to talk with Lieutenant (jg) Selmon.

We were in my cabin, the door closed. I waited a few moments and then spoke in tones only of reflection, studious, uncompulsive.

"We have picked up a certain amount ourselves, of course."

"Yes, sir. Couldn't be helped. Especially in that long passage through the dark and the cold. There's a great deal we don't know about it, as we've so often discussed. So I can only make a best guess, which is: not enough at one time, or cumulatively enough, to put us at risk. Chances I'd say considerably above fifty-fifty that we, or at least most of us, should be okay as far as our own lives are concerned."

It seemed a curious phrase. I picked up on it.

"Our own lives?"

"Sir?"

At times Selmon had a touch of the *distrait,* the far-away-in-another-world about him. I found this quite normal, given that world. He must have drifted off momentarily into some part of it. My question brought him back.

"I was referring to, well . . . just speaking in general terms. I sometimes find myself speculating about that branch of it. The possibilities. The endless permutations! Almost a philosophical hobby of mine you might say. Nothing more. The genetics of the thing. Gamogenesis. Can be rather fascinating to someone like myself—being in the field, you know." He laughed, slightly, almost with embarrassment. "Frankly, sir, taking some rather far-out hypothesis—wondering, for example, if I could produce a baby now and what it would be like. Whether or not I would want to take the chance. Whether it might be an altogether different result if I waited until whatever present level I've absorbed had gone down in me; or whether it is just the opposite: that the longer one waits the less the prospects for a favorable result. An ocean of unknowns . . ." He laughed again, sheepishly. "That mythical baby, for instance—figuring out the possibilities, the chances, the probabilities. Excuse the woolgathering, sir."

"The chances? Go ahead. Let's talk a little about your hobby."

"Well, sir, there's not very much to talk about. Very little was ever discovered for certain about it. Only the most elementary things really. For the simple reason that people hadn't experienced it on enough of a scale to draw any hard conclusions. There simply wasn't enough data—and no way to accumulate it. There are two questions essentially—we're talking only about safe people, of course—safe themselves but having absorbed certain amounts. One is whether such people can reproduce at all. The other is: if so, what they might pass on."

"You mean defects? Mutations?"

"It's just possible, sir. But, of course, not in everybody."

He paused a moment, in a concentration of analytical thought, mindful, I could sense, to exclude any amount of interfering sentiment, unhurried: all this a useful, perhaps urgent, mode in a profession accustomed to encountering as a matter of course the startling and often the forbidden. Some time since he had manifestly installed his own personal emotional dosimeter; seeing always to it that that private instrument, at least, remained steadily at a level nonperilous to his work; no major fluctuations permitted. He spoke with that deliberation now.

"That in any event was the best conclusion arrived at. No way to tell which was which. Nothing strange about that part of it, of course—I mean, scientifically speaking. People have always reacted differently to different . . . germs, viruses, whatever. Just in the same way, different individuals vary quite widely in their response to equivalent exposures. We know that much. In one, it might take very little to tip the scale, genetically speaking, what a given individual will pass on. Another individual might not be affected at all."

"And no way to find out? Which is which I mean."

"No, sir. Not without actually trying—experimenting, in individual cases. Of course there was scarcely any way to do that with human beings."

A breeze, sweet and gentle, stirred through the open port. I looked out, then back at the young officer sitting across the desk from me.

"That would mean—is this correct—that every exposed individual, though unharmed himself, would fall into one of three categories. He, she, could not reproduce at all; could reproduce mutated offspring; could reproduce normal offspring?"

"That's about it, sir. The best guess. To the extent of our knowledge. The rats in the laboratories told us that much. But even with them, it was hard to draw a precise line—that is to say, what exact dosage or accumulation put them in which of the three categories you mention. Far too much of a variance spectrum to speak in predictabilities. And, of course, people not being rats, it could be quite different with humans. They were able to calculate with a great deal of precision what dosages were lethal for the individual, what dosage was not lethal at the moment but put him at risk down the years, what dosage would be unlikely to cast any effect at all on his own years of living . . . That's why we're making it now, of course . . . But as to what that last one might pass on, or whether he could pass on anything, they never got very far. We have no way of knowing. Not surprising . . ." Then came that phrase that had become a byword to our lives, the ultimate in apothegms: "Considering we're dealing with something that's never happened before. But yes, that was the best guess they came up with, the nearest to anything solid: those three categories."

"Let us say, for example, that the woman could reproduce normally and the man fell into one of the first two categories."

"There would be a possibility of no fertilization or the risk of a mutated one. If the 'best guess' is right."

"In any group of people, to find the 'healthy' man and the 'healthy' woman—assuming one of each was present at all—would involve both risk and experimentation. Using various combinations of the individuals. Is that correct?"

"A great deal of both, sir. Unless you just happened to luck out in the early going. Normal reproduction becoming 'Russian roulette,' they used to call it at the laboratories where they sent us—part of the RO course."

"What a name for it."

"All the studies we were shown!" he said in a rare exclamation. "Everybody was making a study, it seemed. Nearly all of them so futile, I always thought—so little data available, no way to accumulate it. Now and then one of them had a little sense to it. One of our own internal Navy studies, for instance—classified top secret, if you can believe it— concluding that submariners would be the next fathers of mankind—if there was to be mankind."

"Absence of exposure? Sounds reasonable," I said idly, my mind beginning to reach beyond these intellectual explorations.

In this reflective mood, I heard myself say something unexpected even to my own ears.

"Nature cares little for men. Would you agree, Mr. Selmon?"

He looked at me first with surprise, this not a subject normally on our agenda. Then, comprehending, returned a faint smile.

"That would seem to be beyond argument, sir. If it came to that, matters could go on with very few men. If nature rather than the Navy had been doing it, she would just about have reversed our numbers of each."

This was getting into territory where I did not wish to venture. I waited a moment and then decided to say something that really didn't need saying. There were a couple of things about Selmon. Ship's captains adore straight answers and value hugely men who habitually give them. They value also men who keep their mouths shut. He had enough fear of me, I imagine, to take care of that. That was fine. But by nature also he was the last thing from being a peddler of scuttlebutt. Finally, from the beginning there was the recognition that what went on between us behind the closed door of my cabin was to go not a whisper further. In all this I trusted him without question whatever. Nevertheless, given the nature of this newest matter, I decided to say it.

"Mr. Selmon."

"Sir?"

"You are not to speak of this matter to the crew, any member of it. Do I make myself understood?"

He looked at me in what seemed a special way, speaking the unspoken.

"You make yourself understood, Captain."

I told the Jesuit I wanted to see him in my cabin the following day, Sunday, immediately after religious services on the fantail.

.7.

THE HIGHER PURPOSE

My father, himself a missionary, first taught me, and myself on my own came to believe, that the very best and the very worst men in history have been religious men; the noblest deeds in history performed by the believing; and the vilest. And not just had been: It was still going on. While not about to canonize him, I was prepared, at least thus far, to place my chaplain solidly in the first genus.

There was a mystery of some magnitude to Thomas Cavendish, S.J. Cavendish had all the right, the elegant chips. Georgetown, the American College in Rome, chancellor to the cardinal of one of the great U.S. archdioceses: facts all, gleaned not from him but from his service record. I could not imagine purlieus where he would not have stood with thoughtless ease. I had sometimes idly speculated why he had chosen to enter a service where he would spend his life ministering to the spiritual requirements of 300 men, most of them not even Catholic, surely few of these ripe subjects for conversion to Holy Mother Church—sailors are the most set of men in their ways; and this on a ship spending a fair amount of her time pitching, rolling, fighting the sea, while standing prepared at an instant's signal from afar to unleash a power of cataclysmic properties, and himself permitted to have no part whatever in any of these purposes; a supernumerary, some might have said. He seemed the last man on earth to be content with letting the days of his life run out so, his gifts seeming vastly to outmatch the job; also his seeming less a contemplative than a man of action. True, he had become as indelibly a blue-water sailor, in the realest sense, as any hand aboard, making it his business to master matters chaplains ordinarily do not: celestial navigation, aspects of ship-handling and the like. But that sea love which had brought me there—brought many others aboard, Girard for example: I never felt that this irresistible star was the thing that lighted his soul. Why was he here? Why was he aboard this ship? But of all questions that is the one never asked a shipmate, and the Jesuit had never so much as volunteered a scrap, talked even remotely in the direction of an answer. Mystery, it seemed, it must remain.

The Navy believes in God. The church pennant, blue cross on white field, hoisted during religious services aboard, is the only flag ever to fly above the Stars and Stripes on a man-of-war, as if to proclaim, One thing, and one only, the Lord God above, is superior to the United States Navy. The Navy is ecumenical, but by logistical necessity. Unable to see its way, from a manpower standpoint, to carrying in a single ship's company a Protestant minister, a Catholic priest, and a Jewish rabbi, the Navy cannily, and with spiritual economy, requires the one chaplain allotted to a ship to be versed in administering the assorted rituals to all faiths. While his ship plows the high seas, a Jewish sailor wearing a black skullcap may find himself seeking Talmudic counsel and solace from a Catholic priest wearing a reverse Roman collar, and, what is more, getting it. But there was something different now, as to the men. While the Jesuit had always conducted services so encompassing that all believers in a Divine Being could participate, normally only Catholics entered his confession box. This had changed dramatically. Of late, a goodly number of Protestants, even two of the four Jews in ship's company, and a fair number of those professing nothing noticeably of a religious character had discovered this institution. His confession box was crowded. The fact did not escape me; to say it aggrandized his importance was to mention only the beginning of its significance.

It was almost a habit of his to be both wise and perceptive, and, most important, to the point, without the numbing verbosity that sometimes afflicted the newer breed of holy people, and concerning the men I consulted him often. Not of course as to what explicit confessions they might have made to him in line of his duties, since even to the Navy that was a privileged matter, but as to their overall state of being, leaving to him any comments, even suggestions, he might choose to offer either in general or in any individual cases. He felt free to raise with me matters that another officer might not. In this respect he stood to me somewhat as did the doc, perhaps rather more so. A captain is well advised to establish this relationship with these special billets aboard his ship, and to give them quite a loose rein in discourse. Not to do so would simply be willfully, and to my mind stupidly, to deprive himself of two rich sources, available in none others aboard, concerning the welfare and thinking of his men. Sailors will say to priests and to doctors what they will not say to their other officers, much less their captain.

Lieutenant Commander Thomas Cavendish embodied those two institutions perhaps of all earthly ones not born yesterday: He was as versed in the ways of the Navy as in those of the Jesuits, no small feat itself, each having its own unswerving and labyrinthine complexities and insistences, rubrics forever baffling to outsiders, sometimes even to insiders, both aged in time and trial. He was a learned man, in the old, almost forgotten sense of the word, in matters both secular and clerical, though one could go years without fully realizing the extent of the first since, not being a professional intellectual, he did not push it off on you. Most of our dialogues concerned ship's company, problems one or more might have. But sometimes they concerned nothing at all; sometimes we spoke of matters far distant from the Navy, spoke about ideas; intellectual nourishment I suppose you would call it. For a captain who feels need of it, sometimes in his loneliness starved for it as from absence of food, difficult always to find, immutable barriers intervening; lucky there, too, to have the Jesuit aboard. I really had nothing like that with any other on the ship. Girard had offered some of it of late, but was still a distant second; so that I had reason to cherish him personally. Ship's company liked him to a noteworthy degree, with a clear fondness undiluted by their knowledge that he could be as firm as a rock with them if a matter he deemed in his jurisdiction so warranted. So that in the latter area his personal popularity was complemented by a considerable influence among the crew, not without its element of fear of invisible punishments at his command, as restraining in their way as the visible ones available to a ship's captain.

He was six feet two or thereabouts, as an undergraduate had been a boxer with the Georgetown varsity, light-heavyweight division, and remained as lean and fit as he would have had to have been then. Kept himself so by boxing still, with a few of the crew interested in this sport. He had hair of rich abundance and striking in its raven blackness above a delicate, pale face chiseled with strong, distinctly boned features. He had an almost unwilling animal magnetism of a kind one suspected would be curiously beckoning, even hypnotic, to women of lustful inclinations; the startling physical looks actually, I was sure, an important handicap in his profession, if not at present only because of the location of his post. It was easy for one to imagine that in his pre-Navy years this attribute had given him problems with the occasional female parishioner and equally easy to conclude that, being above all else a man who knew himself— Jesuits more than most—as much as any man can at a given stage of his life, he would have been aware of the faculty, and would have long since mastered, as a necessity of his vocation, the ritual of turning away any such probings with a skilled gentleness that doubtless only increased the ardor while at the same time keeping it firmly at bay. I had even wondered once or twice whether such possibilities had something to do with his presence aboard, his having actually sought duty in then womanless ships in part at least to escape the devil's persistent temptation: yes, a sea captain is at times as subject to bizarre fancy, in those recurrent mentally unoc- cupied moments coursing the endless deep, as is any other man who follows the sea.

He was the only soul aboard with whom I could speak openly, in an absolute sense; for that matter, he to me the same. We were locked together in an indissoluble embrace, its nature the most simple and straightforward first principle: that no hurt should reach the men that we could prohibit. All secrets of a surety were safe with the priest. But I had never explicitly raised the matter even with him. We had had only a general discussion, I certainly, and, I felt quite sure, he as well deliberately orbiting the matter, both of us making short, covert forays into it and then each stepping back, as if in fear of pronouncement, myself becoming almost as much of a Jesuit as was he. On my part I felt the first intimations of a future chasm arising between us, a parting of ways, a coming even of overt battle I wished to avoid—I did not hesitate to judge I preferred him greatly as ally over foe. In either role he would be a formidable force. He had made a glancing reference, even so unusual for him since he looked upon piety as a matter the articulation of which profaned and even invalidated it, to the question of God's grace, as something—this at least was my understanding of what he was saying—obviously given to us for reasons and purposes unknown (but surely later to be revealed) and there- fore obliging us to be deserving, worthy, of it. He had spoken, without aggression, of the men being under his "spiritual care," paused and added, "and these women"; immediately the brief smile, disarming, surely meant to be so, "How pompous that sounds. I meant only the office, with such ability as I possess," which I loosely interpreted to mean we both were stuck with our responsibilities; had spoken, with somewhat more firmness and rather to my astonishment, of what he called "the necessity of moral survival." I had had in mind to say, "Try that on hungry and deprived men, Father." Instead I had kept my peace, perhaps making a murmured, almost dismissive, "Of course, Chaplain." Two could play this game.

Even so, he had not really come at me, nothing on the order of laying down limits beyond which we dared not venture. The approach was characteristically oblique, almost as if he were speaking home truths on the assumption that I of course would agree with him—and with them. In any event I was not prepared, at the moment, to take on heavy seas from that quarter. Later, if it came to that, I would face the matter and deal with it as I had dealt with other turbulences. Concerned with ever-pressing ones, I had not the luxury of handling problems until they overtly rose and insisted on prompt answers. They must get in line. I had my own firm and sustaining guide, and one which never varied, inflexible, single-minded, my one sure compass, viewing but one matter truly urgent: to bring my ship's company through, by whatever means might prove necessary. Nothing else really entered. As regards him, I intended, of course, to have my way, as with any other force or person that might stand between myself and my objective. If the Jesuit was responsible to the Almighty, he also was responsible to me. I counted that he would not forget that—if he did, I was prepared to remind him of the fact—and that it would be his part, not mine, if the occasion arose, to work out any seeming conflict in allegiance to his twin deities. He was, after all, a Jesuit.

And now the moment had come.

The rain, holding off as though by a direct meteorological intervention of Providence just long enough for the completion of religious services, started just as he entered my cabin. Not the island's regular twenty-minute daily shower but a real rain. After the ever-recurrent days of solemn and unrelenting heat, it was a welcome visitor. We stood at the ports watching its sibilant fall. Then as the rain grew and became an opaque curtain falling between us and the island, lashing the ship and entering the cabin, I battened down the ports and we sat a while more hearing the rain drill the ship. It was a pleasant, invigorating thing after the long sullen calm of the island. Sailors like weather. I was just as glad it was the Sabbath, which we continued to observe as a day of rest so that the men were not at the Farm or at sea fishing. My only concern was the crops, but the rain, while lively, did not seem virile enough to do them real harm—anyhow they were not at present at such a vulnerable stage as to make that a likely worry, Gunner's Mate Delaney had assured me in his arcane and deliberative way when we had discussed the matter while contemplating the rain's approach high and far away in darkening skies.

He sat, his lanky body seeming almost awkwardly too much for any chair, waiting in an invulnerable serenity for whatever it was I had summoned him to say. If some men are all men and some men, the best (and strongest) I have always felt, both—mostly man, but part woman—then he belonged to the latter category. A strangely compelling inner force emanated from him. His method was to let you render the thought, idea, or concern in fullness, not to jigger it along. If you stumbled, he did not rush in. He waited, with no sense of hurry or impatience, for you to collect yourself and proceed. I think it was his way of making sure it came to him wholly uncontaminated, even by himself. It was a neat trick, remarkably efficacious in its simplicity. It had the effect of making you meticulously conscious of what you were saying. It had as well a certain devilish quality. It permitted your own words to turn on you, since no others were being said. So while he sat in silence, regarding me with those thoughtful, introspective eyes, with a listening so acutely active as to make me aware of it, I carefully described to him the site I had found on the far side of the island, atop the red cliffs. Why, first of all, it was the place of choice for us because of the way the winds flowed here, the island vulnerable on this side, shielded on that lee shore from the high Beauforts and hurricanes sure to attack it in time. For he was a sailor, too. Of its favorable aspects otherwise. The water supply. The tall trees, timber for habitations. The existent clearings for these.

The purpose of this rather punctilious explication was not to seek his imprimatur. It was rather to give the idea its final test. If he did not come down on it, it would not necessarily mean that it had his fullest blessing; he did not judge it his province to go around bestowing that with any promiscuity on his captain nor did I go around seeking it out before making a captain's decisions. But it would mean that an intelligent man saw no active objection to the proposed course. When I had finished, he waited a few moments, merely, I think, to make certain that I had no more to say.

"So it's to be here," he said simply. "This island."

"At least for now."

"Just for now?"

"It will give us a place," I said, not answering his question directly.

"An abode. A favorable setting for habitations, for living—for life. At the worst, a fallback position. If things change, we reassess. If we hear anything, pick up any viable, valid transmission, we evaluate. We still have the ship. Meantime, we have a *place*. Who knows, Chaplain," I said cunningly, "maybe God led us to it."

"Maybe He did. We'll find out soon enough."

That was blessing enough. We both waited in a rather long and meditative silence, only the rain commanding any sound at all. It reached us as a kind of symphony rainstorm concert, Beethovenish, with its varying wind-aided volumes and tonalities, now lashing at the ship, now coming straight down on it in a steady drumbeat, now slackening into an arpeggio of that poignant sound that occurs when rain and sea meet; silent we sat, taken with something I could not have said what, perhaps, now that it was upon us, simply the sense of the quite possibly irreversible step at last about to be taken, with its heartstruck-ness and its forebodings. The thing that comes after a long search, the acute awareness of . . . well, the beginning of a beginning. We had been through it all together. For so long our ship's company had been—the priest had been quite apt about that—as the Israelites of the Old Testament, seeking a home—the difference being that they knew where theirs was and had only to seize it, ancient in their blood, whereas we had to discover ours somewhere on all the lands of the earth, something new and alien to us, unknown in entirety. His head was tilted slightly downward, almost bowed, in that visible inward assessment which seemed like a graven part of him but was in no way forbidding: On the contrary it suggested a mind concentrated to the exclusion of all else on the needs of the one now before him, ready to receive them and perhaps to point out dangerous shoals, like some sonar man of the spirit.

I listened to the rain come down, a staccato cadence at present. My decision in respect to the habitations was by now a firm, even inflexible one. Its promise only grew: in the last week I had taken Noisy Travis to that far side of the island and the taciturn and not easily impressed shipfitter, after meticulous examination, applying his ax freely to one of those stately trees, had certified the building material as being acceptable; indeed, when pressed, of the first class. Yes, we would build. Now I had that one other matter, one that had come more and more to appear as the very cornerstone of the one we had just been about. I waited for the resolved issue to finish its movement in the mind, only the variant sounds of the rain violating the cabin's poised stillness. The matter seemed no longer willing to rest patiently within me, submerged, unspoken. Restless, it demanded release from the solitary confinement of my very soul; some-how using a form of address rare in our dialogues.

"Father," I said.

He looked up at me. His eyes were his most inescapable feature. Large and grave, meditative, of an anthracitic cast, deep-set in an embra-sure of salient cheekbones. All the tribulations of man seemed to rest like a chosen burden in their deep pools, in their lustrous blackness, as if they had seen everything that could happen to that creation of God's, his sins, pains, woes, imperfections, turpitudes, follies beyond imagination, and been led by them to one unshakable and all-guiding belief that formed the answer to all, to every single question and to all questions: Were these not what made up, constituted man, were his very essence? And was he still not God's creation? It followed that it was God's wish that man be as he was, full of frailties and impairments, invested with every malice, executant of iniquities endless in their variety, routinely activist of appall-ing transgressions, evildoings beyond comprehension—so why should these ever surprise us and who were we to quarrel with God's obvious intent as to man's nature? He alone disturbs the planet's intrinsic equanimity, balance. He alone is not wanted here—except by God, who has not seen fit either to tell us why or to alter him. Is not that enough? I sometimes thought how identically he and the doc viewed the creature man in his endless fallibility, but from what different ends of the tele-scope! The eyes waited, ready now in their profound heedfulness to see one more. An interlude faint, andante, came in the rain's progression. I went on, rather softly.

"I think I know real trouble when I see it. I don't think we are there, in any immediate sense."

The long-established habit of our talks, as opposed to the asking of direct questions, was rather to give him openings into which he could move or not, as he deemed fit. Our drill required that I not seem vulgarly to be probing his confession box. This served the purpose of permitting his own readings and exclusive sources of intelligence to be made available to his captain, always only to the extent he chose, without compromising his religious vows in respect to the sanctity of the revelations of his sailor flock. On this occasion he chose silence as a reply—he was a virtuoso of silence; a very tool of his, I felt. I moved on.

"But it has come over the horizon."

I waited again, heard the rain's acceleration. "It's going to happen," I said quietly. "The fact is, I believe it's already begun."

In this fashion I had just voiced a seeking of confirmation, but a readiness—more, an eagerness—to embrace the opposite if that be the fact. All of this he would know, and what we, captain and priest, were about here. If he felt surprise or trepidation it was concealed. But he was a professional at that, a master of concealment—or rather, a master at preserving his own concealments whilst penetrating those of another. He did not even ask me why I thought so. Simply acceptance of a palpable fact. Reality, consisting principally of man's unchanging and unchangeable, seemingly compulsive agitation of things and fellow men around him, man forever determined not to let good things be, obliged by his essence to stir them up, beheld harmony but a stimulant to create disharmony, was a thing neither to be argued with nor lamented over—that was work for a fool—only to be leavened, if possible controlled, guided, steered as by a clever helmsman, by hands both gentle and rock-firm, along God's ways and routes. Perhaps he had seen the evidence also, or sensed, heard—this was a clear probability—through those confessional devices possessed only by himself. Though these he could not pass along directly even to me, his silence was confirmation enough. Then I became aware of something strange: he had not seemed all that disturbed at the development. I heard a faint, distant rumble of thunder. I decided to try something.

"We are like a Noah's Ark. Except that Noah possessed the foresight to board one female for every male. Given the choice, I would have followed that biblical sailor's example, at least on present knowledge. Do you think it ever occurred to the Navy to take that balance into account?"

"Knowing the Navy, I doubt it, Captain. The Navy would have been quite critical of that Ark; probably found everything about it unacceptable. Starting with seaworthiness. Never make it."

So he was deflecting that matter of mathematics, simply declining to reconnoiter it, turning it back on me. I waited a moment, then spoke against the rain.

"It's begun. And I know this. We can't just stand by, let happen what might happen, what *would* happen. Pretend it isn't there. It would blow us out of the water." I waited, hearing the crescendoing downpour. "I had given thought to this—I've given thought to a lot as you may imagine: to keep the women on the ship, put the men in the habitations ashore."

His thick black eyebrows came up like question marks.

"Rather an idea."

"A bad one," I said. "I recognized that. First of all, I don't think the men would stand for it. Not for any outright separation like that.

But much worse . . . the women—well, the women could take the ship away . . ."

"What's that?" he said. "What are you saying, Captain?"

"Don't we have a tendency to forget that? Well, if I know these women . . . first-class seamen; also smart, and inventive as hell. Left alone on her, they could take the ship. They could navigate her, handle her underway, conn her . . . just barely but they could do it. I don't think they would—unless things occurred . . ." I waited for the phrasing, wanting to be Navy-careful with words in such a matter; the Navy, like Jesuits, both interstitially Byzantine, nonetheless values the greatest precision of language when it comes to the point . . . "Unacceptable things, demands made of them they could not endure." Feeling a certain repugnance at my own words, I hurried on from this. "But they have the skills to do it. It is my judgment that they would have the will if it came to that . . . simply to cast off one propitious day. Maroon the men on the island. The last one of us."

I think it may have been the first time I had ever seen him show anything like actual startlement; certainly the nearest I had seen him display agitation. A kind of revealed wonder, a glimpse into a hitherto unimagined eventuality—yes, horror, as he obviously saw it, took possession of his face. Against the tattooing rain his air of disturbance—it was that rare a thing—seemed of a sudden to inhabit and fill the cabin.

"So they could," he said slowly. "Yes. One tends to forget. Then under any circumstance, no. Not to separate them. Not with that risk," he said, with that unflinching tone he reserved for matters unthinkable, not for a moment to be considered. "No."

He sat a moment in a reflective pause, as if seeking to comprehend the dimensions of such a catastrophe. I waited, amazed at the extremeness of his reaction, at its abruptness. Taken together with his seeming acceptance over what I—obviously he as well—judged clearly was beginning between the women and the men, it seemed enigmatic; leaving me with a feeling strangely troubling in nature, its cause seeming right here, in this cabin. His sudden laugh then startled me.

"You're right about them, of course. In respect to the ship. They would not hesitate, given the right conditions—something they didn't like. They are far sturdier than men. They have much more resolve; tenacity. Men are innocents, children, by comparison. If it comes to it—to their own interests—they are far more brutal."

The word seemed to constitute such an unexpected turn in our dialogue that I simply in my surprise echoed it.

"More brutal?"

He looked at me, as though from ancient eyes, and as if in surprise himself at my innocence. He smiled distantly.

"Oh, indeed. You must know that, Captain. May I say something?"

"Could I stop you?"

"Just this. You regard women too highly."

Spoken lightly, with that touch he had, light and almost whimsical, yet never without intent. I gave the same back to him.

"You must forgive my clumsy ignorance in these matters, Chaplain. I'm just a poor homeless sailor. I've spent nearly all of my life at sea. I haven't had much opportunity to regard them one way or the other."

The Jesuit smiled, continued in those tones of rather spiked humor. "My experience has taught me that few things are more dangerous than overidealizing them. It is a mistake to expect from them the properties of angels."

"I shall try hard not to do so, Chaplain. Actually I don't expect to see many angels of any kind until we all get to heaven, as the old Protestant hymn goes."

"I am reassured to hear you say so."

"Though perhaps it's true, what we've always been told. About women's endurance. Resilience."

"I don't think there's any question about it," he said. "I imagine the Lord saw to that."

"Then He knew what He was doing."

"He usually does," he said dryly. "Emotionally—emotionally they can take so far much more than men. Almost as if they were a different species. One would come to envy them, if envy were not a sin. Short of being—well, physically overpowered, their weapons for dealing with life, especially in its hard-going phases, are altogether the superior ones to anything possessed by us. By men. We see that in present circumstances."

I felt a certain astonishment listening to this. He was saying something on the surface similar to what the doc had delineated, yet here it came out as something both more and different, vaguely suggestive of some imprecise idea, even resolve, in respect to the women; something absent from the doc's more casual and clinical commentary. At the same time it seemed unwonted coming from the Jesuit; an uncalled-for discursiveness; a detour away from the explicit I sought. Unlike him. Then, as in an illumination, I felt that this sudden outpouring of lightly spoken philosophy, almost homilies, dangerously close to platitudes, was both a cover and a signal. He was not a man to ramble, to speak in wearying and pronounciatory largenesses; unless perhaps to shield the specific, words being quite often used for that purpose. Even the phrase "physically overpowered" jumped out to stab at me.

It was a remarkable conversation to be having, dissecting the nature of women and their imputable variances; there was something almost anthropological about it. We had never had a discussion anything like it. For the very good reason that the basic assumption held the opposite. That was why they were on this ship. Indeed, it had occurred to me, our problem lay exactly there: Operating hereto—all this I have made clear elsewhere—on the canon that there should not be and could not be differences—those of which we spoke or any others; that we were to treat them infallibly, sedulously, the same: that had been the whole idea. And now, the sudden reassertion that there were not only differences but that they were so vast and fundamental as to constitute our chief difficulty. It was not without a kind of wicked irony, a monstrous joke played on us by some miscreant god; or perhaps by simple nature. And, of course, it was precisely those differences which were not supposed to exist that had everything to do with the decision I had reached. It was time to announce it. My week, as I have said, was up. Especially heedful now to keep out of my voice any taint of the mystical or the abstruse; to make it a straightforward thing, altogether pragmatic, a captain seeking only to make things work.

"However that may be, I soon rejected the ship thing; the separation. But I have reached a decision . . ."

I waited, listening to the rain; then began, seeming as much a hearer as speaker of my own words.

"I don't wish to make too much of this. It is very natural that all sorts of thoughts should . . . these days. One looks around everywhere . . . for whatever might help. My mind—somehow it keeps fastening on the women. They are here. Well . . . a feeling that they are the key . . . the way through . . . that . . ." I hesitated. "This odd sense that . . ." I hesitated again, trying somewhat desperately, I was now aware, not to make the statement sound hopelessly extravagant, above all not a paean, that being the last thing from my intent . . . "Well, that our fate may be in their hands . . . that the women will—could—save us."

I could feel not just the entire calmness with which he received this pronouncement but an immediate interest altogether different from our previous talk, and quite distanced from my purpose; this one seeming chiefly of intellectual curiosity, as if I had just set forth an interesting proposition, a perhaps bold theorem, though quite possibly a naïve and certainly excessive one, being so entirely untested and unproved, even unprovable; as though he and I were about to explore together a nonetheless fascinating subject of metaphysical and rather abstract character, residing in the higher philosophy, not meant for practical application, and one to challenge and hone the mind, which is always a pleasure. He said, almost as though catchechizing me:

"In what way?"

I could play this, too, simply by coming off of what had been, whatever its other shortcomings, however awkwardly set forth, a serious, even heartfelt, statement. "Perhaps through all those admirable qualities you enumerate, Chaplain."

"All right, Captain." Granting me the thinnest of smiles.

Having started, I could not abandon it now—indeed, felt no wish to do so; plunged on.

"Well, this. I do not know. Women heal. They can heal anything. I suppose it starts with that . . . that hypothesis? The simplest of theorems: Men who have women are better than men who don't." Instantly I felt I was on dangerous ground with him, the very ground where I judged our eventual conflict would arise. I immediately sheered off from it. "Beyond that . . . just the feeling—and the wondering, yes, just as you say . . . how, in what manner. That if I could find the answer to that, I would have the answer to a great deal of our difficulty. Assuming the thought has any validity to begin with: the women will save us. Then the corollary: Where such power resides, the two must come always together—part and parcel, inseparable. The gift of saving must carry with it also the ability to destroy. Even with God, He has, has to have, both powers. The women will be our salvation . . . or our downfall. The thought . . . that the way in which we handle the fact of their presence will determine everything, one way or the other. They will either save us or tear this ship apart . . . The women . . ."

I stopped a moment and said this: "This sudden power the women have gained over us . . . their awareness of it. Of course, if any of this have the slightest substance, one asks in prudence: What will their price be? I don't doubt they will have one. Maybe they are waiting for the price to go up. That is usually what happens, one can hardly blame them . . ."

Now I came to a true full stop, shocked that I could have gone so far, fearing that it had come out half apotheosis, half fear of the subject;

altogether too grandiose, gone overboard. I sat alarmed at my own prolixity, knowing that I myself had entered, for the second time, whether led by his really rather sinister skill or by the absolute necessity to escape if only for a few moments from my anguished solitude, his confession box; whether I wished to be there or not; aware of the intensity of listening there just by me. And heard only the now-gentle rain, no sound otherwise, only the hush—as though he felt his own absolute silence was at this moment his greatest gift—or perhaps clever tactic. After all, no one could have been more experienced in confessions, in extracting talk from men. I said it then with all abruptness, in rather a softened tone, one that would speak to him of finality.

"The decision I have reached is to let the women decide."

It was hardly more than a murmur from him. "Of course, Captain. No other way."

Few things in life are more shocking than complete acceptance where one expected formidable, forceful opposition; one feels a certain sense of collapse within oneself; certainly, hearing that response, I felt the full anticlimax that such a situation brings. (I even half expected a demurral, or at least a considerable surprise, of a naval not a priestly nature—after all he was officer as well as priest—that I, the captain, was prepared to throw over Navy legalities in the matter; there was not the least.) It also brought an abrupt cessation, a weird halt. To, it seemed, everything. We simply waited, mute as ghosts. Though it was not yet noon, the diminishing light through the ports, chattering with rain, left the cabin in shadows. I reached over and switched on the lamp. It made an ungodly noise. I could hear somewhere beyond and above the iterative screeching of rainstorm wind. Then the wind passed in gusts and our concert of the heavens, the fugue developing, once more modulated all around us into that mournful, almost portentous metronome of rain entering the sea. A heavy sense of finality, embracing the decisions both as to the habitations and the women, seemed to reach down and lay hold of us both; of no turning back. At last the priest spoke into that rain-laden silence, and—eerie in its precision of accuracy—into my thoughts.

"Tom . . ." He waited. He was one of the two officers aboard, the other being the doc, who in a matter unwritten anywhere was granted the license, by myself, if he wished so to address me in private. Neither of them often used it. The Jesuit and I, by the way, shared the same first name. And each of us, too, I believe, with our portion of the famous quality ascribed to our apostolic namesake. Doubting Thomases, both

. . . "I fear we are headed into heavy seas. Worse, uncharted waters. Heading where men have not been."

He stopped there, looking at me, and again a silence hung. I could hear returning the quick spasms of rain, drumming the ship:

"And so we have been all along."

"Not like this. This is something more."

Yes, looking at him, surely I must have expected something else, adjurations, perhaps, homilies, recourse if not to *Navy Regulations*— which, after all, were my province and concern, and which I had just announced I stood prepared to sweep aside, at least on this matter, then to divine regulations—which were his. It could only be that he had thought the matter through with the same exhaustiveness, and doubtless wakefulness, too, I had given it myself and reached a conclusion identical in its major premise, the only one that held promise, something that would be a nonnegotiable requirement were it to have his blessing, of combining the two, the moral and the practical: The resignation, almost compliance, on his face as before the one now admitted inevitability in our existence told me that; perhaps, I was not so foolish as to think otherwise, our shared conclusion varying only in its details of execution. Those divine regulations we should of a certainty see presently. But I got none of the other major assaults which he was always prepared to mount at once on any proposition where his heart—his God—so dictated. Again I wondered, almost idly, with a faint gnawing suspicion, why not. The prudent thing was to turn away from that, from any questionings it might suggest, to be grateful for his acceptance so far; knowing how much I would need him; therefore use him to the hilt.

"Father," I said.

Something in my voice. I could sense him look toward me.

"Yes, Tom? What is it?"

I could hear my voice come hard. "Not a day passes but what I think of something. The mutiny, which cost us one hundred and nine hands, two of them women. That passage through the dark and the cold, which cost us fifteen, including three women. Emily Austin. The following is for your confession box. Do you know, I think more about the loss of the six women than I do of the one hundred and twenty-one men?"

"I can understand that."

"So I don't intend to lose one more woman. It may come to the point where I have to bargain certain things, in a manner ship's captains customarily do not. I am prepared for that; up to a point; to give at least consideration to almost anything, coming from any hand aboard. Except for one thing. Can we agree as one matter nonnegotiable that whatever happens . . . whatever it takes . . . the women must be protected?"

I heard his voice against the murmuring rain; as if he sensed, too, that here must be dispensed with all indirection, all equivocation; all obliquity; with every firmness, in unshakable resolve, cold and hard as stone.

"As an article of faith, Captain," he said. "They are our most precious possession. Not the slightest harm can be allowed to come to a single one of them."

Said as a declaration so lapidary as to require no further discussion.

"I think the men know, know why," I said. "They are good men. I don't think they would let anything—well, bad, happen to the women . . . if anyone should try . . . They value them as much as do you or I."

He spoke as though that, in this matter, went for nothing.

"They may come to value them too much. In the wrong way." He paused. "The Bixby affair."

"An aberration," I said, even as that awful memory flashed through me. "Nevertheless . . ." I sat back and looked at him, this time on a level of eyes. I spoke as a ship's captain.

"The small arms. I put them under lock and key before the trouble. They still are. I retain the key."

He received that piece of intelligence as if he were being told the most obvious of details of a routine thing, of proper housekeeping, as though any other procedure would have been not only strange but criminally negligent; his acceptance of the measure so immediate as to make me for a moment wonder if he had heard something that he felt made the action imperatively prudent.

I shrugged. "Unnecessary, I'm sure. These are good men." I wondered why I had said that again. "Another thing. If anything happens, retribution will be swift and hard. Not reprimand. Not captain's mast. Not a summary or a special. But a general court-martial. You may feel free to make that clear, along with your gentler methods, at your discretion. If at all necessary, I shall myself."

He said wryly, yet with that same hard inflexibility in his voice, "Added to the Navy's, I shall remind them of the Lord's GCMs."

I then turned away from it. I found such thoughts distasteful at best—at worst, unworthy, undeserved by a ship's company as steadfast as had been this one, not once failing to do what was asked of them, and in circumstances to try the hardest of men's souls. I wanted to finish up. A course had been set. So get on with it; cast off. I felt a hush even within the sounds of wind and rain, a corner of stillness in which we waited, expectant, as though for a last word, a final thought. I wanted to say, to finish off with: "The numbers are what bother me. The mathematics of it." And then did not, that being the area where above all others I expected difficulty with him—where realistic details of execution were concerned, not for a moment did I judge that the matter had even begun to be settled. Having arrived at a sort of naval-clerical *pax*, I thought to leave well enough alone, to save for another time that matter of infinite complexity, the one most likely to breed head-on confrontation. Much better not to rush in; to wait, to build on present affinity, however imperfect. I spoke in a voice of accord, of all hope.

"Knowing they will decide it themselves. It should—well, settle, calm the women. I don't have the evidence but I suspect . . . a certain disquiet among them. Who can say why? Perhaps the idea that these decisions about them were going to be made for them. This should handle that. Knowing that choice, if any, will be in their hands alone." I waited and said quietly, as something beyond which there was no more to say, "The women are here."

His reply was as if not articulated, uninterruptive, a whisper of insertion slipping through the rain:

"If you believe in a functioning Providence . . ."

He stopped there and a silence hung. My sensory radar moved at once into an extra state of alertness. His was a voice of shadings, of subtle inflections, of certain varying timbres even, each I had long since discovered meant to convey discrete information, intelligence, judicious appraisal, sidelong suggestion, and to all of which I was carefully attuned, checked out, as to a private cipher. Into it now had come, to my wariness, something the opposite of some of the earlier oppression of our talk. I became aware of a subtle yet distinct change in him. Anxiety—now that the matter had been decided—replaced by anticipation—by, it seemed to me, something akin to eagerness, even fervor. Almost, it seemed, to my astonishment bordering on alarm, a hurry to get on with it. It was my own lurking doubts, these various suspicions, without discernible basis, that I could not understand. I should have been grateful to him—and was; but gratitude mixed with a palpable unease, a question as to motive, as to intent: bringing this hard disquiet into me, its source difficult to identify. I seemed to see a signal flashing danger as clearly as that pennant run up on a ship's halyard, quickening into alert attention the blood of any seaman. I had the clear conviction of the presence in him of a thought, even of an express design of his own, that he was not choosing to share with me in fair exchange for my putting all of this out in front of him; perhaps only a natural caution at our too-easy agreement. I had never denied him cunning.

"If you believe in a functioning Providence," he had said.

"They are here," I said as if he had not spoken.

I was aware that the rain had stopped and I could hear only the immense silence returning. And then suddenly I knew. Why he had raised no objections, floated no divine regulations; that flashing instant when I had felt, and thought my judgment had flown out the port, that he was actually pleased by what was happening; his unaccustomed startlement and dismay that the women, using their seagoing knowledge, might even attempt to depart; his not just willing but rather zealous acceptance of my decision when I had been prepared for perhaps forceful opposition. I knew. The higher purpose.

Light, I became aware, was returning through the ports, and I reached over and switched off the lamp. I realized that he had stood up to go. I looked up to where his tall, angular figure hovered over me in the shadows. The thought hardly occurring when confirmed. The quiet-spoken, almost murmured, "Captain, why do you think God put them aboard this ship?" "I didn't know He had. I thought that was the Navy's doing." The irreverence bringing but a soft smile. A ship's captain may at times require help but does not wish it to be of an insistent character; he is by nature jealous of his authority. Suddenly, an amendment to the feeling of thanksgiving for his support, I was taken with an unsettling wonderment as to the role he expected himself, almost in a taken-for-granted manner, to perform in the matter we had been discussing; one for which I was not at all sure I had a place in my plans, my own intentions, and especially if the role contemplated was that of playing the Almighty, or any facsimile thereof. On this tropical latitude, a tremor went through me. I felt his hand touch my shoulder. I hardly knew whether to be reassured by it or to feel the terror of God.

That very afternoon I called Lieutenant Girard to my cabin and, forcing the matter out into the open, doing all the talking while she did all the listening, told her of the decision I had reached. I asked—authorized, directed—her to convene a meeting of the women of ship's company in their own quarters, themselves only present, to inform them of it. To give them a week to determine if they could come up with a decision of their own. During that time to have as many closed meetings as they liked, sitting like some all-powerful court of last resort, its deliberations secret, sacrosanct from all men, while reaching toward a decision it knew would be as canon, apodictic, not subject to appeal; ratified, whatever it might turn out to be, in advance by ship's captain with all the weight of his sovereign authority. Then to report back to me. It was a colloquy calm, mannered, almost sacerdotal, on both of our parts. She received all of this as if hearing from her captain some routine order, dealing perhaps with the uniform of the day, which she would then proceed to carry out to the letter.

The week passed while preparations on the island went forward. To the day she made her appointment. I closed the door to my cabin. She sat and came at once to the point.

"Captain, the women have reached a decision." She spoke in her clean-run way, her voice unemphasized, forever unshrill, easy as always on the ear, quietly self-assured. "There remain many details to be worked out; for these we will need further time. But they have considered everything carefully and have drawn up . . ." She paused momentarily, as if searching for the exact identifying phrase. ". . . their overall basic decision in this matter. I have had Talley type it up. The paper, you will note, is signed by all the women."

Swift solidarity. She handed me the single sheet. I sat back and began to read.

When she had left I stayed awhile in the loneliness, still holding the piece of paper. Suddenly a remembrance came at me without warning, and as is often the case with remembrance, whether with connection or not it was impossible to tell; a thought that I seldom permitted myself these days pressing its way into my mind in a single word. *Pushkin.* Of the Russian submarine with whose captain I had struck that prodigious deal off Gibraltar; the matter now seeming beyond any reasonable conjecture, so long since the submarine had disappeared from our radio bands. Despite every resolve I found myself from time to time, hardly knowing I was doing so, still helplessly scanning the northern horizon as if that long black shape might suddenly come in sight, breaking the vast and never-ending emptiness, bringing that gift beyond price: a five-year supply of fuel, enabling us to go anywhere, freeing the *James* from the chains now binding her: changing everything. Customarily this exercise in the abstract conveniently stopping there before it got to my part of the compact and which, caught up as in some epiphany with the contemplation of what the fuel would mean, I sometimes forgot, which was to take him and his ship's company into our society should he make it through and ourselves find a place that would accept us, as we now had done. Remembering that half of the deal, which even now I scarcely knew whether to term an angel's or a devil's bargain, speculating yet again with myself whether that remarkable vessel was the last thing I wished to see manifest itself on the horizon. Never being able to decide: one moment praying for her coming; the next dreading it.

I shook my head involuntarily, almost violently, as though to dispel it of such dangerous divarications, such exorbitant reveries, arrival of any kind now so beyond admissibility; knowing that for those instants I had become that most precarious of all things for a ship's captain ever to permit himself to be, hope's fool. I came back to course. Read that single sheet of paper yet again.

Quite enough to fetch me back to concerns as far from the abstract as could be, to that most brutal of realities, whether we should construct on this island a decent community of men or see ourselves torn apart in a manner that did not bear thinking of; knowing in a chilling fullness for the first time, now that we were dead up against it, what I held in my hand telling me so, that the answer to this question would be resolved more than by any other single element by the matter that piece of paper addressed, by how we dealt with that frightening perversity in numbers. I seemed to stand at some sort of crossroads of time, where memory went one way and a future to which I had neither chart nor compass the other; and to know, little as I might wish to do so, I must travel the first in some way to help me reach a decision about the second, as to the ship's company, as to the ship herself, as to the proposal set forth by Lieutenant Girard and the women that now seemed to send through me a literal shudder of the flesh. And so, knowing not where any answer lay, or even if there be answer at all, feeling somehow that the only hope of finding one lay in what had served me well before, I allowed memory to take me backward to when it all began. In the way the mind measures time, seeming an epoch ago; in real time, a scant eight months. Exacting as it went memory's standard toll charge. Starting with simple numbers. Once we had been 282 men and twenty-three officers. The figures now were 160 men, eighteen officers. Expressed another way, 152 men, twenty-six women.

.BOOK II.

OUR CITY

1. Our City

In those days every ship of our capability in what was known as the retaliatory forces—variously submarines, cruisers, destroyers, frigates—had a fixed target city—or cities, depending on the number and type of missiles carried—and was deployed in one of nine bodies of water: the North Sea, the Baltic Sea, the Norwegian Sea, the Barents Sea, the Mediterranean, the Arabian Sea, the Indian Ocean, the North Pacific, and the Sea of Okhotsk. The Navy had used the waters of the world, free and unsovereign to all under ancient laws of the sea, effectively to surround the enemy on virtually all points of the compass. We felt actually lucky to have a city at all. The total capability had become so considerable that there were not enough cities to go around so that there developed something of a continuing bureaucratic battle in the armed services for target cities. Not only that, there was further such bureaucratic fighting within the services themselves for the assignments. In the Navy, for example, one ship alone, the nuclear submarine USS *Ohio*, carried an even two dozen multiple-warhead missiles—enough in one vessel to obliterate every major and medium-sized city on the enemy's surface. And the *Ohio* was but one of ten Trident submarines with seven of these on patrol in the North Pacific at all times; not to mention other missile-armed submersibles regularly patrolling other seas, all within range of targets. So that there arose a competition even within the Navy itself—for example, between the admiral in Washington commanding submarines and the admiral commanding destroyers—as to the allocation of cities.

The submarines, perhaps fairly, considering their relative invisibility, got most of them, but a few were reserved for the guided-missile destroyers, of which we, the USS *Nathan James*, were one. There were compelling reasons. Despite all our famous technology, unlike surface ships there was a good deal of unpredictability attached to communications between distant nations and their submarines. True, much progress had been made of late with VLF (very low frequency) channels, but the problem was still there. No one in far-off national command centers could be certain of reaching across long waters, then down into the deep to a submerged submarine, and especially in atmospheric conditions made twisted, distorted, as conflict would of a surety do. Why our ship was in the Barents in the first place could be said in a single word, one of those strange and omnipotent words, quite awful but apparently essential, which in the latter part of the century seemed eerily to change and darken the very nature of language itself. Redundancy. Redundancy, survivability, options, backups: These, not without cause, considering that the enemy was guided by the identical nomenclature, became the operable terms; if one system failed there would be another which would work. But perhaps the most mandatory reason of all for including surface ships in land-attack forces was the following: The submarine went principally armed with the ballastic missile, the surface ship with the cruise missile, which though slower was much more marvelously versatile; infinitely more accurate, far more difficult of detection; the fact furthermore that, due to limited magazine space, submarines could not carry anything like the quantity of missiles of a surface ship. Altogether, there was no escaping the fact that surface ships embraced many factors of reliability in regard to reaching target not present with the submersible fleet. All the same, considering the competition for them, we counted ourselves fortunate to be given a city. Its name was Orel, situated at latitude 36°00′ N., longitude 53°10′ E., 1,040 miles from the cold shores of the Barents Sea.

On our ship—and I have an idea that something of the sort was true of other vessels—the city that was assigned us became over time as familiar to us, almost in a familial sense, as is a "sister-city" in the kind of relationship that cities of different nations sometimes have with one another, in those cases most often because there is something to connect them—a city in Michigan, for example, keeping up a relationship with a city in Holland from which many of its citizenry had originally come, exchanging visits and holding welcoming festivals over the years and the like. We exchanged no such visits, but nevertheless the relationship became a strong and binding one on our part. We came to think of it as "our city" and grew to know it quite fondly. At first we knew little more than the population—311,656 by the latest available census, but in time we picked up, accumulated, in the nature of a research hobby, a good deal of information concerning it. The fact that its name translated as "eagle" and that it had been established in 1564 during the reign of Ivan the Terrible. Its status as the district capital and an important railway junction, situated at the confluence of the Oka and Orlik rivers. Its principal industries—manufacture of agricultural and roadmaking machinery and of food products. The item that the city boasted a small but exceptionally fine ballet company. Actually, in our case, as in most, the target of course was not the city itself but the installation located near it, in this instance the even dozen SS-18 missile silos, housing the great "heavy" ten-warhead ICBM, set not far beyond the city's perimeter on the road to a place called Spasskoye.

It was not that we needed any of these facts (except the last-named) in connection with our mission but rather that man being an inquisitive creature, it was natural that that curiosity in this case should be directed toward the one place on earth with which we were so inextricably linked, the city that indeed constituted the entire reason for our existence, though none of us had ever seen it or in all probability ever would. Except, by pure chance, one member of our ship's company, Lieutenant Thurlow, our navigator. Thurlow had undertaken Russian studies as a Rhodes Scholar at Oxford and had been in Orel once after Michaelmas term. As we patrolled, now in the Norwegian Sea, now in the Barents—thirty days in those often turbulent waters before being relieved by our sister ship, the USS *Cantwell*, and heading back to our base in Norway for ten days of liberty and upkeep before once more standing out to sea and returning north to station—we had many random conversations on Orel, with Thurlow telling us all he knew, and otherwise wondering, picturing in our minds, what the city that lay beyond those dark waves might be like on a given day, the people going about their business, market days on a summer Saturday, a church scene on a January Sunday with people approaching the church in astrakhans, bundled up as in a Tolstoy novel, and shaking the snow from their garments before entering to worship. Thurlow even furnished us with its name and description: Church of the Archangel Michael, located on a street interestingly named Sacco and Vanzetti. I think the loneliness and isolation of duty on those bleak and tossing waters also assisted the Orel studies by giving us something to be

131

interested in. Thurlow's freely proffered elucidations included the particular that local enthusiasts were accustomed to call the city the literary capital of Russia and that many of the streets were named for writers and poets who indeed were born and lived there, including Turgenev, Andreyev, Bunin, Granovsky, Fet, Prishvin, and Leskov, the last named setting forth the claim that the city "nourished for the motherland more Russian writers than any other Russian town." To few aboard were these names known except, by a certain number, that of Turgenev; Thurlow then going on to elaborate on the considerable Turgenev family estate, now a national shrine, and the datum that it lay forty miles north of the city at Spasskoye, where the writer grew up and, returning after years abroad, there accomplished some of his more illustrious writing including the completion of *Fathers and Sons;* the navigator fluently mentioning a letter penned by the writer in France to a Russian friend, "When you are next in Spasskoye give my regards to the house, the grounds and my young oak tree—to my homeland," adding offhandedly that he had observed on his own visit to the estate that Turgenev's oak tree was still to be seen. As a consequence of this tutelage, we went so far, at the navigator's instigation, as to procure this author's works for our library and enough of the crew, men and officers alike, read them as to make me feel safe in asserting unreservedly that the *Nathan James* numbered in her company more Turgenev scholars than any other vessel on the United States Navy's entire roster of ships.

As to our ship's strike capability, ourselves alone carrying weapons able to erase millions of souls, we scarcely ever alluded to the fact, much less discussed it. To converse on such a matter: there are things that to discuss seems an exercise in puerility before immutable fact, unalterable by men. One might as well have discussed why stars exist—or, perhaps more aptly, why wars. To do so is not the habit of sailors. Our ASWO (anti-submarine warfare officer), Lieutenant (jg) Rollins, happened to be a ballet aficionada. Once Rollins did comment briefly that a famous dancer by the name of Kalganov whom she had been fortunate enough to see perform in Houston, Texas, during a leave in her home state, had for a number of years lived in Orel as a member of its celebrated ballet before defecting to the United States and remarked oddly, "I'm glad he's not in Orel anymore." It didn't seem to occur to anybody where this famous dancer now was, New York, or that all of the earth's seas flow two ways. On a rare occasion someone might mention that if we had this almost affectionate relationship with Orel, surely one of theirs had a similar relationship with, say, the American city from which the speaker came, say Boston. But that sort of parenthetical interjection in our Orel conversations was a seldom thing, almost never picked up, certainly not encouraged. We preferred to dwell on the characteristics of Orel. It sounded altogether an interesting city. Not a hand aboard but who would have liked to have shore liberty there.

2. Aquavit and Rose-Tinted Cheeks

I always felt us fortunate in having as our home base the small town of Husnes, situated on the west coast of Norway, set on blue waters between blue mountains inside the Hardangerfjord. (The base's existence itself made possible by a change two years previously of a provision in that country's constitution forbidding any stationing of foreign troops on its soil.) The Norwegians are a marvelous people, a beautiful people in both body and spirit; their women as lovely as any I have scrutinized in my many visitations of ports the world over and characterized by a knowing femininity and a self-assured inner strength (the two traits perhaps con-sanguineous), not to mention the unsurpassed rich cream of their flesh, their rose-tinted cheeks; their men brave, heartily forthcoming, and entirely devoid of that compulsion to prove their manhood every hour or so that afflicts lesser men. Seafaring is bred in their bones, and they have in their hearts an especial place for the seaman breed of whatever nationality or origin. From the first they took us into their lives—and their homes. To the latter they invited us at Christmastime and even made it a point to discover our indigenous holidays such as Thanksgiving and, if we happened to be in port, have us to dinner then (yes, with turkey and all the trimmings, so fine, in their desire to please us, had been their research into our native ways). In turn we quite often had Norwegians as guests in wardroom and crew's mess, and once we delighted the whole town by turning up the identity of their great festival, Mid-Summer's Day (or St. John's Day), June 24, a day of very little darkness, and holding aboard ship a twenty-four-hour open-house celebration, beginning as the Norwegians do on St. John's Eve, with pickup music provided by members of ship's company who knew instruments, dancing on the fantail below the after missile cells, surprisingly elegant even dainty hors d'oeuvres prepared by our resourceful Chief Palatti, and even local spirits procured by us in direct violation of the Navy regulation, known infamously throughout the fleet as the Josephus Daniels Edict (he being the Secretary of the Navy who proclaimed it) and unique to the United States Navy among all navies

133

of the world, which specifies that no alcoholic beverages shall ever be available aboard ship other than for medicinal purposes. I was prepared to use this pretext if necessary, calculating that such diversions were the best of medicine for my crew after a month of Barents duty. It was a memorable party, one of the highest spirits and camaraderie, for both the crew and our Norwegian guests. On our ship any member of her company asked to name the world's most potent drink would instantly have responded Norwegian aquavit.

In sum the relationship with the townsfolk and these American bluejackets could not have been one of more warmth—both ways honestly given, honestly received—and between the two an amity rich and kindly reigned. So much so that three of our men—Brinton, signalman first; Hubbard, a boatswain second; and Hewlett, chief quartermaster— in time married Norwegian girls, all the ceremonies being held in the little Saint-Peter's-of-the-Sea Lutheran church in Husnes, situated not far from the water and whose charming steeple was the last thing we saw standing out to sea and the first returning from patrol, where I stood up as best man for these of my crew who had decided on this ultimate fraternization with the Norwegians. It may seem peculiar to some but the fact was, nothing was ever said in our agreeable intercourse with the sweet people of Husnes concerning the reason for our being home-ported in their town in the first place. In point of fact this was not strange. Seamen traditionally do not engage land people in shoptalk. Another factor may have been that there seemed no reason why one would choose such a subject to talk about.

Then, after one more sojourn of pleasant liberty, just after first light we headed out to relieve the *Cantwell* and commence another routine patrol. Besides the wives, a goodly number of other townsfolk were at the pier as always to see us off, even at that early and cold hour. As the ship stood out and receded into the Hardangerfjord toward the Norwegian Sea they waved to us and we waved back across our wake, frost-white in the intense blue of those waters, in that ancient, somehow forever poignant parting, however temporary and however routine the voyage, of the sea people and the land people. Paling the last stars, winter's dim vermilion sun was just coming up from that east where we were bound to proclaim a new day for both, to preside over another departure of a ship for the sea, and whatever surprises it may hold for those who would seek it out, and to cast into waving silhouettes the good-wishers huddled against the keen temperature on the pier. We waved back until even the silhouettes were no more and, soon turning, set a course N. by N.E. for the Barents. The date was December 3. We would be gone until after the New Year, meaning that that year we would be enjoying no Christmas festivities with our Norwegian friends. Not a hand aboard who didn't regret that, for Norwegian Christmases may be the most joyous of all.

3. Four Hours

I used to wonder why all of our capability, consisting of 896 Hiroshima equivalents, in the form of 56 Tomahawks, each carrying a 200-kiloton nuclear warhead, should be reserved for one target. A small part of it would have served the purpose. Or, alternatively, we could have been allocated a number of targets. Principally, I believe, the matter had to do with the all-ruling "mix" principle, in this case concentrating one ship on one target (for all I know even ourselves with some sort of backup, should anything prevent us from fulfilling our mission); a philosophy made possible by the aforementioned shortage of targets in comparison with the total capability. It had always been my judgment that in respect to that target, if it ever came to that, we would be ordered to send off but a small portion of our vertical capability, leaving us diminished scarcely at all, with the major portion of the missiles available for whatever undefined, indeed unforeseeable purpose they might be needed.

It had always been judged—a fact naturally known to the last hand aboard, reference never made to it—that once we fired our missiles, eliminated our target, our own ship was essentially not just at high risk but quite reasonably forfeit, one ship with a complement of 305 in exchange for a dozen SS-18 missile silos and parenthetically 311,656 of theirs, being considered not a bad trade-off. There was, however, one fortuitous circumstance that constituted, having launched, our chief chance of escape: the slowness of the Tomahawk itself, granting us four free hours from the time it left the ship until it hit target. And on all the high seas, than ours there was no faster ship.

The range of the Tomahawk missile was 2,500 miles. When the ice packed up in the Barents, we slid back down into the Norwegian Sea and when and if it packed up there, into the Baltic. Sometimes moving among them purely to reduce detection. Taken together with the Tomahawk range, the three bodies of water gave us a truly great amount of sea room over which to roam, immensely enhancing our own security. But whether in the Barents, Norwegian, or Baltic seas, our cruising patterns kept us at all times within a range not to exceed 1,500 miles from our city. Generally we were considerably nearer.

4. The Barents

Moving out from the Hardangerfjord, we crossed effortlessly the Musken Strauen, possibly the most celebrated whirlpool on any of the earth's waters, once believed to suck under every vessel within a wide radius, and giving the word "maelstrom" to the language. From there on a heading north by northeast through the Norwegian Sea, hugging the coast of Norway, staying at all times eastward of the warm North Cape current, one of those enticing permutations the sea, as of a gift, is forever proffering those who venture on it, being a continuation of the Gulf Stream and which, among other bounties, keeps the port of Murmansk ice-free the year long. Within this protective flow, nearing the Barents Trough, and eastward of it entering that sea.

For eighteen years now I have been a deep-water sailor and have stood watch on every sea the planet holds and on not a few of her gulfs, bays, and estuaries. In no other body of water have I had so full a consciousness of the ship under me being locked in mortal combat with the sea. The ship riding, during the long nights of the Barents winter, down into those troughs so deep that it seemed the ravenous waters would swallow her whole and she would never arise from them, the waves striking her with vicious, hammering blows which made her hull strain and tremble, the massive seas boarding her at will and racing toward the superstructure, smashing with a fearsome roar against the pilot house, splitting to hurl in angry force down both sides of the ship port and starboard; then through the wet darkness seeing dimly from the bridge the ship's bow ascending with infinite slowness through the raging waves before taking another plunge. This in endless succession across a dark and endless seascape.

It was a fray which exacted a profound toll on ship's company, the pitch of the ship slamming into the hollows attacking incessantly not only the vessel herself but also the men. Staying physically aboard the ship became a problem. Lines rigged fore and aft for men to hold onto and pull themselves along, work their way to their watch stations, over a route where, after each pitch the shipping seas bringing tons of water down on him in a merciless rhythm, any oncoming wave arrived fully capable of sweeping a man overboard however tenacious his grip, knowing if it happened that the ship could have no hope of stopping for him. By the time she came about in the raving violence of those waters, assuming we could ever find a lone man in them, and got to where the man appeared to have gone overboard, he would long since have been claimed by the cold, thirty seconds the average was said to be for this asphyxiation by freezing, even as the hungry sea pulled him under. Two men we lost that way. Seaman Apprentice Gibson and Signalman First Chauncey. I set out fairly long handwritten letters, one to Chauncey's wife in Marblehead, Massachusetts, one to Gibson's parents—the boy was but nineteen—in a small town called Buena Vista, Tennessee—trying, with what anguished feebleness I was aware even as I put the words to paper, to convey some shred of solace in the intimation that husband and son went quickly in the freezing deep.

Four hours of watch, then a collapse of one's sore and violated body into a bunk where often one had to buckle oneself in with the straps with which every bunk on the ship was rigged for Barents duty, hoping at best for snatches of sleep. Grateful for that: There were whole nights when not a soul got a wink. And the cold! I find it difficult to convey the cold, the desperate, appalling, cruel cold, of those latitudes but fifteen degrees distant from the top of the world. Even encased thickly in the warmest clothing provided by the Navy, shielded to where through a thin slit only the eyes of a man showed and one sometimes had to ask a shipmate one knew as well as a brother to whom he was speaking . . . no clothing ever devised could hope to keep out the piercing cold, abetted as it was by the instant drenching one got on the weather decks from the unceasing seas raking the ship and accompanied ofttimes by sleetlike rain, borne on screaming winds, savage and icy north winds arriving directly from Arctic wastes, that the Barents heavens seemed so fond of contributing to our discomfort, as if the sea below it needed any help in that undertaking. On watch one was at best only uncomfortable, at worst seized in the stranglehold of a numbing misery of body and mind, a physical and mental exhaustion that left one poised on the far edge of collapse, whilst straining with all one's will to concentrate solely on assisting the ship in her battle with the besieging sea, a battle on occasion for her very steerageway.

Thus our only enemy then: the sea, the remorseless, heartless sea. The thundering combers coming at us in a wild and senseless malevolence, in barbarous extortion, day after day—night after night would put it better in a latitude and time of year in which one seemed to exist in a world of blind blackness, the ship proceeding through black and tumultuous waters under black skies from which the very stars had fled into seemingly permanent hiding; daylight measured in four hours or three,

137

even these generally of a weakened and wan sun which appeared on the point of extinguishing itself at any moment like a candle fluttering in one of the Force 8 or 9 gales which the sea sometimes enlisted as ally. Sea and elements then conspiring to shake the ship from keel to truck in a paroxysm of ferocity, turning her normal inner workings into an anarchic chaos—all living spaces in a wanton, heedless shambles, crew's quarters and wardroom places of desolation; the simplest act, eating, sleeping, standing, become a tormenting problem. A sea of an unappeasable rage, intent, it seemed, on destroying everything, living and inanimate alike, it could reach, obsessively eager to take, gulp down this intruder—and during the two years of this duty, while never achieving that final triumph, inflicting on us wounds which, if not mortal, at times required considerably extensive repairs when once our thirty days were up and we charted a course for our Norwegian-port home. A list of wounds which would have included a ship's gig smashed to kindling wood in her davits, a dismantled mast, even an anchor torn away from its housing by a sea which seemed to gobble up that object with a particular relish, as if taking a big and especially satisfying bite out of us, an anchor being so precious to a ship. Wounds, some of them, severe enough to require dry-dock time in that facility the Navy had towed all the way across the Atlantic to the town— tribute enough to the Barents—where it waited as a kind of intensive-care unit for ships back from Barents duty. The lacerating sea inflicting wounds aplenty, too, on ship's company, a man thrown violently against a bulkhead, a simple stanchion become hazardous in those infuriate waters; cracked ribs, a smashed kneecap, huge livid bruises, the doc and the hospital corpsmen having to stand an almost continuous watch. The Barents. An avenging sea, of a monstrous fury, bent seemingly on punishing us for the very presumption of entering her domain.

We never entered her lightly. We came prepared, or as much so as any ship could. Above all, by the vessel we came on. No ship constructed by man, by her very lines, by her making from keel upward, sets forth better able to do battle with the deep. The destroyer! First warrior of the seas. Sometimes as she plunged headlong into those valleys so steep I could see from the bridge the gleaming crests of waves so high above me on either side as to seem to embrace the ship in a death-clasp, the sea laying as though a final siege to her, a sea gone berserk, frenzied, the ship attacked in brute force from every side so that she both rolled and pitched in a violent convulsion, and then saw, as if in surprise, her stem ride up, I had a feeling that she did so in a kind of wild and ferocious glee of her own, before plunging back eagerly for more. Absorbing the murderous battering as if she liked a good fight and desired to show the stuff she was made of. Then it was that through the brutal fatigue, the anguish of mind and body, would come what sustained me: the profound emotion, transcending, unrivaled, I felt toward that ship, a pride and something close to exaltation that it had been given me to be her captain; indivisible from it (for a ship and her company are one thing) a love discrete, idiosyncratic, perhaps known but to few men, and for all I know all of them ship's captains, a kind of safeguarding affection, deeper by far than anything my life had found, for those 305 enduring, uncomplaining souls aboard her, not one fainthearted, whose destinies along with mine were sealed into her, with no escape hatch, no exit, dependent utterly on one another and on the ship, and whose entire care, whose very lives, had been given into my hands. In the end I came to care for no one but them, and for them a care, a concern, complete, absolute.

Then, with sheer abruptness, after long days and longer nights of fighting off the assaulting waters in a madness it seemed would go on forever, the sea took a respite and we came out of it with, through the utter physical depletion, the infinite weariness, a kind of giddy exhilaration, vertiginous, a dazed and heady sense, grimly comic in its way, not of triumph but simply of having once more come through; of still being there—all afloat! Bloodshot and sleepless, vacant eyes, unbelieving, suddenly presented with a startling sight: tranquillity, quiescence. Good and simple things. Men could sit at tables and eat a hot meal instead of standing up holding to a stanchion while trying to time bites out of a cold sandwich to the ship's pitch. A cup of coffee would not jump from one's grip to scald the hands. A sweetness of sustained and unbuckled sleep became possible. Then it was that the Barents chose to display in brief cunning her other side, as for our edification, a species of reward for having endured her maniacal temper; as though declaring we had passed our true candidatures for seamen, Barents men, and thus stood worthy to be briefly reprieved by the mercy of the sea. The sea settling into an unearthly calm. Seeming to sit back for a moment to regard its adversary in thoughtful admiration for the fight she had put up, or perhaps only to take her measure in preparation for a fresh onslaught. A truce. The very heavens shutting down their winds and presiding in a hush of stainless azure over a surface turned eerily placid. By day the waters held in an untrembling stillness of deepest blue, resplendent, shimmering in the pellucid crystalline light of the few hours granted the sun in those latitudes of the high north. By night, with its twenty-hour allotment, the reappearing stars looking down with a lustrous whiteness I have witnessed in no other skies on a sea of a magisterial blackness I have beheld in no other waters.

After the incontinent fury of those same waters, it was a preternatural sight, a feeling of phantasm. The only sound that of the ship moving with a gentle sibilance through the dormant waters, a cathedral of a sea, her crew themselves caught up in that devout cold-purified serenity, in those dazzling and etheric silences, so that going about the weather decks men who had had to shout to be heard against the roar of gale and wave spoke as though in whispers, stood by the lifeline to stare in mute wonder at a seascape impassive, sublime. A spooky thing, pregnant with awe, with wonder, mothering other-worldly thoughts. At such times the sea looming across its lambent motionless surface under the soundless sky as though a crossing-over place, between this world and some other world of eternity set on forever receding shores just beyond it, another world whether of heaven or Hades one presumably would never know. I take no sea lightly—no seaman of any experience does—but on the Barents I felt myself in the presence of something that stands alone among the seas of my memory, the waters of the globe, something at once godlike and terrible, equally of a malevolent ferocity and a deathly beauty, exuding some profound and fearsome mystery; something unspeakable, forbidden; her very fury, returning always after those short-lived pacific interludes, a day or a couple, dependent seemingly on her whim, appearing acts of rage for our insolence in seeking out her dark secrets, or perhaps for using her for our own purposes.

Thus, there at the top of the world, we crossed and recrossed the cold sea on a course intentionally every-varying. Just waiting, I would think later. To be summoned only if someone far away, by some species of reasoning not to be shared with us, for whatever cause, real or imagined, got it in his head to summon us. Never, save for some occasional oblique allusion, quickly set aside, unpursued, this not being our province, really discussing why we were doing this; besides, a more useless topic of conversation, leading nowhere, being hardly conceivable. Just waiting, going back and forth as though we would do so forever, doing what fate in her unfathomable ways had decreed we should do, if one believes in that manner. Not truly believing we would ever be doing anything else. Had I been asked about the chances, I could scarcely have answered. Or rather, I would say the answer would have varied immensely, and even from moment to moment, the odds swinging more widely than on any wager one could ever imagine placing. Depending, I suppose, on what came over the radio bands bringing news of the goings-on in what was forever to us not just the outside world, but a world so distant, so foreign, and ourselves so severed, deracinated, from it, so on our own, in our coursings over those dark waters, it was as though we were hearing news from another sphere, seeming, much of it, to consist of the incomprehensible, the irrational, acts performed by a species hardly known to much less the same as ourselves; we not unlike men with noses pressed against the glass gazing into some luxurious restaurant at opulent diners, yet not with envy of them but more of astonishment, of wonder, at a life of such strange ease. Yet it was from these sumptuous-living souls that the summons, if ever it came at all, would issue.

The odds depending on the outside news accorded us—and perhaps also on our inner state, our emotions and our fatigues at any given time, our ups and our downs, for these, too, swung widely as the range of a magnetic compass and seemingly as out of our control; whether we felt high or low from the hard lonely fight with the sea. Not even knowing whether the high represented a devout hope never to be called upon to do it and the low a tiny, secret, utterly private desire that we would get to do it, if for no other reason than to bring reprieve from the terrible monotony—this not being the horror it might appear, since men stretched far enough in monotony, at least of sailors I believe firmly this to be true, are like men stretched far enough in hunger, in that just as in the second case they are capable of doing anything to allay it, in the first they can suffer momentary flashes of a desire to have that malady relieved, and by almost anything, so intense as to appear, indeed be, almost deranged—or whether that it was just the reverse, that that represented the high and the other the low. Perhaps even that changed about on the barometer of our emotions and our fatigues. And finally, as their captain to me the most solemnly unspeakable of all, I once or twice went so far in my meditations in that loneliest of seas as to speculate, in regarding the men under me—to wonder if I sensed distantly even the seed of such a thing—whether there existed at times a whisper of a wish, deep in those fathomages of men's souls where inadmissible secrets, the most shielded of longings, are kept under the strongest of locks, never to be let out, even to one's shipmates, to do it simply so that all our work and all our hardship would not have been wasted, would not have been in vain. Such, however quickly dismissed as themselves aberrant, were thoughts that only the long and claustral nights going endlessly back and forth on those dark waters could fetch up from the cognate darkness of the soul. I found then and find now none of this particularly strange, nor I think would anyone who has spent much time at sea in circumstances inherent of potential enemy conflict. Ourselves on a duty so profoundly lonely, so utterly isolated as to make us feel at times, not in hallucination but quite literally, alone on the planet, that other world so far away as to be hardly existent. Surely it was for this same reason that we felt more unseverably bound to one another than is usual even on a good ship. Bound to each other and to no one else.

Thus back and forth we coursed, waiting for the summons if ever it should come. Thinking, now and then, rather fondly, almost longingly, of our city, picturing how it must be at the moment and what her people might be about, their daily tasks, the market shopping they might be doing, the glittering ballet attending, the ice skating on her parks' frozen ponds, our city lying beyond the harsh waves of the Barents; locked in an indissoluble embrace of ship and city. Waiting. Deep inside us, knowing, I doubt not, all of us, what would happen one day. It would have taken an inconceivably ignorant person not to know, there being no rule of life or of all his recorded history more immutable. To know this: What man invents, man uses.

5. Valid Messages

Both the cryptography ordering it and the methods of actual execution were laced at every step with an exactitude designed with one purpose in mind, to avoid "falseness"—the official, all-embracing demon word adopted by the Navy—of whatever kind. As to the former: An exchange of three messages was required, employing as many different ciphers, known as TSP (Trinity Security Procedures), all three changed every twenty-four hours, each so top secret as not to be held even by the communications officer and reserved for one matter alone; in the case of two of these the cipher being in the possession only of the captain and the decoding and the encoding having to be done personally by him; and as a final precaution (against the captain) the third cipher in this deliberate and inexorably ascending chain being divided into two halves, one held by the captain and the other by the combat systems officer, so that the code using it could not be broken without their joint participation. The essential speed was achieved by a highly advanced communications channel termed VHSI (very high speed integrated-circuit) and a remarkable, almost instant-acting cryptographic machine, itself top secret and unlike any other aboard ship, designed for this usage alone, housed in the captain's cabin in a safe to which only he held the combination. As for actual launching, again the captain and the combat systems officer each held in his sole possession a key, and the launch could not be accomplished without each inserting his key on consoles placed far enough apart that no one person could reach both, then both turning keys simultaneously, all within a time frame of ten seconds. The Navy, I can state zealously from my own experience, had done everything it seemed the mind of man could conceive to avoid aberrations of whatever nature, whether by accident, rogue signals, human derangement, or anything else that might menace a valid order.

Shortly after 1300 on December 21, on a day of only gentle swells on the Barents, and not long from the expiration of our routine thirty-day patrol and return to our Norwegian port home, Ensign Martin, an assistant communications officer, brought to me a message in a code to which her department did not possess the deciphering mechanism. I happened at the time to be working on the annual task of filling out officers' fitness reports, not the least trying of a captain's chores. Laying these aside, I instructed her to stand by outside, closed my cabin door, alerted my CSO Lieutenant Commander Chatham on the intercom, stepped to the aft bulkhead, and, using the combination, unlocked a door, exposing the machine, actually a microcomputer known simply as Verify. From the safe I also brought forth a sealed envelope, opened it, determined the key for the twenty-first of December, fed the message into the computer, and then punched in this designated cipher. The message emerged instantly on a tiny screen.

SOURCE: NCA   211059Z

FLASH

FM: CINCLANTFLT NORFOLK VA

TO: USS NATHAN JAMES

BT

TOP SECRET

SUBJ: OPERATION ARCHANGEL

1. (TS) LAUNCH ORDERS

    A. TIME—IMMEDIATE

    B. NUMBER—TWELVE

    C. TARGET PACKAGE—SABLE 1-12

2. (TS) LAUNCH VERIFICATION—YV1.

   REPEAT YANKEE VICTOR ONE

3. (U) CONFIRM RECEIPT VIA CKT CHARLIE

BT

Employing the differentiated unlocking cipher for the same day, obtained also from the envelope, I fed into Verify the following message which the device brought back in two forms, plain and encoded.

```
FLASH          211104Z
FM: USS NATHAN JAMES
TO: CINCLANTFLT NORFOLK VA
BT
TOP SECRET
SUBJ: OPERATION ARCHANGEL
A. CINCLANTFLT NORFOLK VA 211059Z
1. (TS) CONFIRM REF A., LAUNCH
    ORDERS
        A. TIME: IMMEDIATE
        B. NUMBER: TWELVE
        C. TARGET PACKAGE: SABLE 1-12
2. (U) TOR: 211102Z
BT
```

I opened the cabin door, handed the encoded sheet to the communications officer waiting there with instructions to send it at once on the channel reserved exclusively for this series of messages, its VLF arteries believed through a further top-secret process to be ironclad invulnerable to contamination from whatever source. Standing alongside her was the CSO, who now entered my cabin. I closed the door, showing him in plain the message I had received and the one I had sent. I stepped to the safe and removed a second sealed envelope and turned to see him standing with an identical envelope in his hand, extracted I knew from a safe in his own stateroom to which he alone, even the captain excluded, held the combination. This had scarcely been done when Martin was back. She handed me an encoded message and again took up her position of attendance just outside the cabin. I closed the door and fed in the message, the CSO and I each opened his envelope, each looked at the designated separate cipher key it contained, and each punched his into Verify, which at once gave us the following:

```
SOURCE: NCA        211109Z
FM: CINCLANTFLT NORFOLK VA
TO: USS NATHAN JAMES
BT
```

TOP SECRET

SUBJ: OPERATION ARCHANGEL

A. CINCLANTFLT NORFOLK VA 211059Z

1. (U) REF A CONFIRMED, VERIFY EXECUTION
   IMMEDIATELY

2. (U) ARGONAUT, ARGONAUT, ARGONAUT

BT

all times being given in Greenwich mean.

The last word was the one that leapt out at us, forming a direct and unswerving line between itself and our resolutely attentive eyes. It also was changed daily, held within the highest secrecy of all, and was the final and incontrovertible seal and imprimatur, meant to remove any remaining shred of doubt a ship's captain might harbor that he had been the victim of an accident, or of mental derangement in the message's sender, or that it was a rogue message or any other species of falseness—that it was anything other than a valid order to execute; its thrice-repeated use being a further part of this assurance. I had already determined in the sealed envelope the correct operable word, and the CSO the same in his separate sealed envelope. We now showed these to each other and once more looked at the message on the screen, our eyes focused in unison on its single final word. The ultimate trinity of verifications was in place, in accord.

All of this procedure had been accomplished in less time that it takes to tell it here. During it Chatham and I spoke scarcely a word, conserving all of our faculties solely for the task unfolding. We simply worked, calm in the entire I believe, knowing the unforgoable necessity for the orderly, for concord, for the exclusion of the extraneous, links as we were in a fastidious procedure, impervious to interruption, into which we, the ship and her company, were now inescapably locked, a procedure not subject to consideration or even thought, each door we went through shutting behind us like a watertight door with the lock then slung, each step requiring its own precision and making all steps before it irreversible unless halted by a final callback procedure as secret as the others. I may once have caught Chatham's eyes—if it were so, I found there only a stolid if alert impassiveness, devoid of all comment whatsoever, free of the disturbed, a honed and imperturbable naval officer concerned with the one thing and nothing else of carrying out the series of measures for which he had in every respect been so meticulously trained and conditioned; I had not even the thought that I could have expected anything other than this essential composure. Indeed, looking back, I can think only of the professional naval coolness and competence, by all hands, the concentration in absolute on the matter itself, with which the ladder of steps was executed from the start. It was not just that this was possible; it was that it was ordained and anything other would have been the surprising, the aberrant, the unthinkable; ordained by one implacable fact: that, this being our sole reason for existence, we had been through the punctiliously undeviating procedure countless times on dummy runs. These were intensely familiar transactions to us, unalien in entire. So that our faculties now behaved to a cellular circumspection, in a manner almost prelapsarian, as during the functions we all had performed so often. With one difference, a new species of tension quickly to appear; distinct yet suppressed, felt throughout the entire crew, even from the ship herself, in the unspoken awareness that we were about to do what we had spent our lives trained to do and hoped we would never have to do: that it was going to happen. The act about to be committed itself bearable in the companion realization that it was out of our hands, out of our control. Myself working with the same consonant, almost removed attention to the task as did all other hands, with the possible exception only of a distant consciousness of one possibility stuck undisturbingly in a far corner of my mind: that there could yet be a callback. This had no effect whatsoever on my systematic, scrupulous actions. Immediately I had read the message I turned and spoke to the bridge through my cabin intercom.

"Mr. Sedgwick, sound Launch General Quarters."

The ship had been rigged with not just the usual General Quarters devised for bringing men to battle stations but also with a second system, readily distinguishable in sound from the first and both instantly identifiable to ship's company through regular drills. The first was the familiar GQ klaxon used by all naval vessels for the emergencies which traditionally men-of-war encounter in peril on the seas: hostile ships or aircraft sighted, the sonar picking up a possible submarine, an attack in extremis from the sea herself. The second was reserved solely to bring hands to launching stations. Even as the honking sound with its pulsating beat commenced throughout the ship, the CSO and I proceeded down two ladders and entered CIC amidships. We inserted our keys in the weapons control console. I said, "Three-two-one-Mark," and we turned the keys simultaneously. He remained there in attendance on the keys while I returned topside to the pilot house and went through it to the chartroom. My navigator, Lieutenant Thurlow, was already there, holding his parallel rulers, bent over the chart table, the Mercator projection of the region, sea and land, laid out under a bright light from overhead. He was just finishing up his plotting of cross-penciled lines on the compass rose. His work had nothing to do with the imminent flights of the missiles. Tomahawk did not have to be pointed at its target. We could launch it from any position, then it was on its own. All that was required before booster ignition was that the ship's fire-control system correspond the missile with our present position and set the gyroscope in the missile's inertial navigation system: procedures already underway beginning with our coming to launching GQ. No, Thurlow was engaged in something else altogether: plotting the most direct and advantageous course out of the Barents. It was urgent to get this matter settled and ourselves on the desired heading before matters concerned with the launch began to consume us. Under the harsh light I leaned over and with him studied it. I said, "Very well, Mr. Thurlow" and stepped into the pilot house and looked at the gyro repeater.

"Come left twenty degrees, Mr. Sedgwick," I said to the officer of the deck.

"Left twenty degrees rudder," he said to the helmsman, Porterfield.

"Left twenty degrees rudder, aye, sir," I heard Porterfield repeat. I felt the ship swerve with easy assurance to port, then Porterfield: "Rudder is left twenty degrees, sir."

Sedgwick: "Steady on course two nine zero."

Porterfield: "Steady on course two nine zero, aye, sir. Checking two nine four magnetic."

I said to the OOD: "All ahead one-third, Mr. Sedgwick."

Sedgwick spoke to Seaman Thornberg at the lee helm. "All engines ahead one-third. Indicate three zero revolutions for five knots."

Thornberg: "All engines ahead one-third. . . . " I heard the clank of the engine-order telegraph as she pushed it over then felt the ship pliantly slow down . . . "Engine room answers all ahead one-third. Indicating three zero revolutions for five knots, sir."

Both accomplished, the ship already on a course out of the Barents, the slower speed most favorable for launching set, after which we would go to flank. I stepped out to the starboard bridge wing and picked up the 21MC intercom from beneath the coaming of the bulwark. The air was cold, a piercing blue December day, the wind-free sky pristine, the waters offering us a spondaic series of soft swells which gave a gentle roll and pitch, so synchronized as to make the ship seem for once in fraternal rapport with the sea and to move through it with a serene swish. The sea all about lying in a melancholy splendor, a luminous stillness, the universe seeming held in hands of tranquillity. I looked down first toward the after launcher, then the forward one, both standing silently in the wintry sun, in full loneliness. The launchers would be controlled, their tasks performed, from below, by men who could not see them. Indeed the launchers and I stood in a solitude complete, not a soul else anywhere on the weather decks. I lifted the speaker to my mouth and spoke to CIC. Abruptly, with no premeditated intent, or even thought, I diverged from the prescribed procedure in an act not provided for in it but from which I decided no harm could follow. No, not that. I knew harm, in a proceeding such as this, could come from any variation, however slight. Tiny as it was—a matter of five seconds—it could have brought me to general court-martial, justifiably so, constituting as it did a change in an operation of utmost consequence, whose processes had been worked out long since by men of care to a final and infinitely painstaking precision and perfection of detail which counted on the scrupulous absence of all divagations whatever. I did it nonetheless.

"Mr. Bainbridge?" I spoke to the communications officer. "The captain speaking."

"Bainbridge here, sir."

"No callback?"

"Negative, sir. No callback received."

"Very well." I had committed my criminal five seconds. I spoke to the tactical action officer, Lieutenant Commander Coles.

"Commence launch preparation."

"Aye, sir. Commence launch preparation."

I could overhear the dialogue between him and Lieutenant Polk, the weapons control officer.

TAO: "WCO, TAO. Select cell number one, aft launcher."

WCO: "Cell one, aft launcher, aye."

I looked down at the launcher and watched the armored cell door spring open. I continued to listen.

WCO: "Launcher ready, sir. Missile targeting data entered. Ready in all respects for launching." Polk's voice had a Louisiana cadence. "Repeat. Ready in all respects for launching."

One had trained oneself, and ship's captains tested exhaustively, brutally, in this respect before being given command of such a ship as this, to block out emotion, even thought itself; that talent as essential in this instance as that of navigation, of shiphandling. If I had chosen to look into some far, submerged corner of my mind, I might have found there a grateful numbness impounding the feeling that something had gone monstrously wrong that it should have come to this: by which I would have meant something not in what had been happening in the past days to bring it about, but rather something a good deal further back; something fundamentally wrong as of a literal species mutation in the mind and in the spirit of man that this should be; beyond that, only the sense of irrefragable inevitability; none of this scarcely worthy of the label of conscious thought. If I felt anything active it was of an immense solitude, a loneliness absolute; perhaps for an instant a dangerous solipsism, at once overpowered by the sense of the needed care upcoming for my men and for the ship—a grim determination already, a kind of inward hardness, that we should make it, should survive—this flashing through my mind in the fraction of a moment, delaying nothing. The voice of the TAO now reaching through to me.

"Request weapons free, Captain."

"Weapons free," I said. "Commence launch."

"Commence launch, aye, sir," emerged in a clear and steady voice, like an echo, into my ears.

A deafening sound shattered the air as the first Tomahawk emerged from its cell, ascended out of its pool of fire the width of the ship and forty feet high into the radiance fashioned by the cold delicate sunlight of the high latitudes and moved upward over the impassive waters of the Barents into the chaste heavens, its spiraling tail stretching quickly a mile or more high from the ship to itself and topped with its ornament of bright white fire against the satin blue. Then from both launchers a vast eruption, eleven more missiles departing their cells in immense fiery bursts. I followed each with my naked eye until it had disappeared out of my sight and beyond the horizon. I looked at my watch. From first message to execution it had taken just under twenty-four minutes. It was as good as we had ever done in dummy runs.

6. Standing Orders

I stepped back into the pilot house and through the 21MC instructed the communications officer to send a previously prepared message, which I knew he was standing by so to do and the contents of which I knew by heart.

FLASH   211125Z
FM: USS NATHAN JAMES
TO: CINCLANTFLT NORFOLK VA

BT
TOP SECRET
SUBJ: OPERATION ARCHANGEL
A. CINCLANTFLT NORFOLK VA 211059Z
1. (U) MISSION REF A COMPLETE TIME
    211123Z, TWELVE ANGELS EXPENDED
2. (U) UNODIR PROCEEDING IAW
    STANDING ORDERS. REQUEST ACK
BT

I turned to the officer of the deck.

"Mr. Sedgwick," I said, "steady on course two nine zero. All engines ahead flank."

Even as I returned to the bridge wing, there visually to check empty skies, empty waters, I heard him repeat the series of commands to helmsman and lee helm. The ship, unleashed, leapt forward, flying through the sea at her rated speed of thirty-eight knots, at which nothing that floats could overtake us, the ship racing ahead of a wide and churning white wake on her fleeing westerly course. I returned to the pilot house and instructed the OOD to sound General Quarters, bringing the ship to maximum alert as in expectation of attack: all weapons systems, ASROC, Harpoon, Phalanx; all sensors, radar, ESM, sonar, manned and ready. I was about to go below to CIC when I became aware that the communications officer was standing beside me holding a message form. I took it and read:

FLASH   211130Z
FM: CINCLANTFLT NORFOLK VA
TO: USS NATHAN JAMES
BT
SECRET
SUBJECT: OPERATION ARCHANGEL
A. USS NATHAN JAMES 211125Z
1. (S) REF A ACKNOWLEDGED.
    REPORT BY FLASH MSG TIME OF TOUCHDOWN
BT

I proceeded down two ladders to CIC and stood observing at their NTDS consoles the air trackers monitoring the progress of the twelve Tomahawks toward their destinations. All in sailor dungarees; all wearing baseball-type caps, this not an idle fashion whim, rather the bills—the Navy had tested even this matter—serving to shield their eyes, improving concentration on the ever-changing light flashes on their screens; two of the trackers women. At the outset the room was dominated by an implacable silence, the sense of the fixed attention of those at their controls. All enclosed, the blue-darkened portless compartment, its every essence that of a space sacredly intact, paramount to the ship, situated in her most secure part amidships and below the damage control deck, no inessential words to be spoken, in that sense reverential as a chapel; now, with the ship granted a softened sea, the trackers not having to use the seat belts which were provided for these same operations in stormy waters, this sense of hush enhanced, we waited as the twelve fliers headed toward the coastline. The moment arrived.

The first beeping, a signal passed back to us by the first missile's radar altimeter, announcing to us: It had left the sea and crossed "the gate" into land; was performing its first update; measuring precisely the terrain below its flight path. Presently joined by the identical voices of eleven more also departing the waters and making landfall. They went on as a kind of chorus, not overloud, in the tenor register, metronomic, but holding a complete sway over the blue darkness of the room, as their authors steadily penetrated the land on their ineluctable courses. Launch to target, it would be four hours, this slowish time actually to the good, as mentioned, allowing us as it did to be well on our way out of the Barents by the time they touched down, the missiles ever proceeding even as we got the hell out of there, underway now as we were at flank speed.

Later I was to think of those four hours that they were both as an eternity and seemed to pass in the twinkling of an eye. The missiles guiding themselves in entirety, ourselves mere spectators, as though watching wondrously gifted virtuosos, we heard the sounds, the missiles talking to us, informing us of their positions at all times, the inertial navigation system of each guiding it, putting it through dives, turns, varying rates of climb and descent, zigzaggings, maneuvers designed to decrease still further chances of detection, avoiding known concentrations of enemy defenses, each maneuver followed by a fix to bring the Tomahawk back on its route to target, a precision of navigation determined by using maps internally stored in the missile's computer's memory, for accuracy this navigation system updated many times in flight for each, making correction for drift, for winds which would push the missile off the intended path; the missile, radar-avoiding, hugging the earth mile after reiterate mile. All these things I knew to the finest particular were happening, absorbing my technical attention as I followed the flights. The beepings seemed in addition to take on almost a visual quality in some separate part of the mind even as not infrequently does music to the absorbed ear. One's imagination seeing the implacable procession of missiles, their numbers twelve, keep low over the flatlands, move upward as they approached a hill, climb the hill, then descend as the earth descended, the missiles generally staying a hundred feet above it; followed them as they passed over lonely fields in the oncoming early twilight of the high north; passed now and then (mind's eye saw) over peasants tending them; over houses nearby where women went about preparations for the night's supper. One stayed with the missiles.

The TAO monitoring the time-of-flight of each Tomahawk commencing from the moment of its particular ejection from the launcher, if one wished one could look at the various timepieces and see how far a given missile was into its flight, how much farther it had to go; quite as one might, with a trace of anticipation or impatience, glance at one's watch on a plane to note the time remaining to one's destination. I found myself disciplining this impulse, not looking too often, just as on a routine plane flight, and for the same reason, to make time pass faster. A certain natural strain in oneself, and silently communicated osmotically from all, in no way excessive, never permitted to take charge; a hoarding of oneself, one's feelings, one's thoughts, one's reserves, out of a stern inner recognition of the absolute urgency of dispassion, chiefly in order that one remain fit to deal with events certain presently to be upon us. Not a hand aboard this ship but who had been tested rigorously for stability, men visceral in the knowledge that where they tread calm itself is the most indispensable quality of all, for success, for preservation, for survival itself; that and a fixed code of conduct, shipmates, held us together. Here again, in the CIC, reigned a quiet and concentrating exactitude of performance, of actions liturgistic, almost sacramental, only those crisp and pulsing sounds returned from the missiles commanding the air as from that pale-lit room the men at the ship's computers with sure steadiness tracked the Tomahawks' inexorable progress. As a redundant check, one not of great necessity, on the safe touchdown of the missiles, we had one of our radio frequencies tuned to an Orel civilian station, set on low volume, faintly heard as a backdrop to the other activities in CIC. We had long known the station, listened to it often, a source of entertainment; like many other Russian stations it played an extraordinary amount of classical music. It was in no way unusual that over these hours it was offering a Tchaikovsky program—at the beginning, on air, his symphonic poem *Romeo and Juliet*

I recognized. Later the first piano concerto, a portion of the ballet *Swan Lake,* other works.

After the twelve had made landfall I alternated my personal geography between CIC and the bridge, staying mostly in the former and making certain to be there as the fourth hour counted down. As each missile now reached its assigned fix, the digital scene-matching area correlator, with which it was equipped for hard targets, took over: the computer simply comparing a stored "picture" from its memory with the target. Then it came. Came in muteness, an intelligence passed to us by the first missile itself: it ceased beeping. It had found home. The blue dark seemed deepened to an intolerable quiescence as we waited, listening to the remaining beeps, now eleven; soon ceased the second; the third; the fourth; finally, the last. One by one they simply went off the air. At each, nothing but the distinctly articulated reports of the WCO at his console, the repeated word said twelve times in succession over a time frame of approximately four minutes. Impact.

The last beep from the last Tomahawk expired, over the room came a pause, one moment of transcendent stillness. A stillness of realization, felt in oneself, felt equally through a process of transference in those around one, palpable, merciful in not requiring, not permitting, speech. Somewhere in the back of my mind I became aware as an additional verification of success that the civilian radio station had gone off the air, in the middle of a violin concerto, at the impact of the second or third missile, I could not be certain which, only that it was not after the first. Then: I felt from all about only what I would describe as a professional satisfaction, in nature quiet. Men and officers having accomplished what they had been trained to accomplish; so I felt it, too; for them—yes, for myself, as captain of this ship. A natural, unvoiced kind of uplift, outwardly contained, communicating itself one shipmate to another. Just that. Nothing more. Then it vanished, other urgent duties being upon us. Bainbridge remaining all the time at my side, I instructed him to release at once another previously prepared message.

FLASH   211527Z
FM: USS NATHAN JAMES
TO: CINCLANTFLT NORFOLK VA
BT
SECRET
SUBJ: OPERATION ARCHANGEL
A. CINCLANTFLT NORFOLK VA

1. (S) TOUCHDOWN TIME 211523Z. ALL
   ANGELS MISSION COMPLETE
2. (S) PROCEEDING AT BEST SPEED TO
   NORTH SEA. REQ ADVISE FURTHER ORDERS
BT

I went topside. I do remember with what gratitude I escaped from the imprisonment of CIC into the fresh sea air. I paused on the starboard bridge wing, looking about. Out of the stillness a sudden ululant wind passed over the sea, the ship, like a benediction; a redemptive moment. I heard above me high on the mainmast a flapping of the halyards, the first freshening of wind, seeming strangely a gift of emollience, the clean sea smell it brought clearing the mind, strengthening one. I looked above the mast and saw heavy magenta clouds commence to take command of the heavens, hanging low over a darkening sea to all horizons, and they, too, seemed welcome as though arriving to hide us. I stepped into the pilot house and through it into the chartroom where Thurlow was waiting, leaning over the chart table. Proceeding on the standing instructions, we were now headed into the Norwegian Sea. I was studying our position when I heard a voice behind me.

"Captain."

I turned to see Ensign Martin holding a message form. I took it, brought it under the light and read:

FLASH   211540Z
FM: CINCLANTFLT NORFOLK VA
TO: USS NATHAN JAMES
BT
TOP SECRET
SUBJ: SAILING ORDERS
A. USS NATHAN JAMES 211527Z
1. (TS) REF A ACKNOWLEDGED. MODIFY
   DESTINATION. PROCEED AT FLANK SPEED
   TO LAT XY$.9* A1Z4$;/?&

The message stopped there, a garble. As if making some ghastly joke. I turned savagely to the communications officer.

"What is this, Miss Martin?"

"That was all that came in, Captain." I thought I detected a slight tremor, the faintest modulation of something like fear in her voice. "It stopped there. Sir."

"Repeat the message. And request a repeat of theirs."

"We've already done that, Captain. Nothing. A blank, sir."

"Then do it *again*, Miss Martin. And *keep* doing it."

"Aye, aye, sir."

She turned and was gone as if anxious to get out of my presence. We sent the last message without cessation, sent it over every frequency we possessed, sent it over a stretch of twelve hours, during which time I never left the bridge except to go below periodically to CIC to harangue the communications people. It seemed obvious: There had been an Electromagnetic Pulse blackout of communications. Still proceeding on the standing instructions, we had entered the Norwegian Sea and reached a position of 72°15′ N. latitude and 15°30′ E. longitude, not far south by southwest of Bear Island. No reply to our unremitting messages having been received, I then detailed the new course with the navigator, Mr. Thurlow, and the officer of the deck, now Lieutenant Bartlett, the three of us in the chartroom looking down on the spotlighted Mercator projection, just behind us Hewlett, the chief quartermaster, as Thurlow applied his dividers and made his cross-penciled marks for the course I had given him. I noted a slight hesitancy of this skilled navigator in the routine procedure. A course S. by S.W., one which would take us through the Norwegian Sea, proceeding down the west coast of Norway, crossing over the Musken Strauen, and continuing into the North Sea. We straightened up.

The two officers looked at me under the shaded light. I could feel their surprise, close to astonishment.

"Not back to Norway, sir?" Thurlow said.

"That's not what the standing orders say," I said. These I held in my hand, having obtained them, many hours back now, from yet another sealed envelope in my cabin safe. I indicated but did not show these to the two officers. "The standing orders say the North Sea."

I heard a sound, a strange sound, something between a croak and a gasp, and looked up to where Hewlett stood in the shadows. The thought flashed across the edges of my mind that he had a wife in Husnes. "Sorry, Captain," he said. "It's okay, Chief," I said quietly.

"But the message. . . ." Thurlow began, puzzlement in his voice. "Sir, the message said the standing orders were changed."

I spoke evenly. "The message *broke off*, Mr. Thurlow. It didn't say what the change was."

"The North Sea," he said in a mechanical voice, going on. "Then what, sir?"

"We will devoutly hope communications will open up in the North Sea."

"And if not . . ."

I had had enough of this. I looked sharply at the navigator, heard the hardness in my voice come down on him.

"If we haven't heard at that point, the captain will decide, Mr. Thurlow. And then so inform you and the others of ship's company. Is that understood?"

I stood looking at him. I did not think he had been shaken. It was more a matter of perplexity.

"Sorry, sir," he said. "I was out of line. Aye, sir. It's understood."

I touched the navigator's shoulder, squeezed it for a moment as though to steady him. The questioning, from him or any other officer aboard, was without precedent. I turned to the assistant communications officer standing just behind us.

"Miss Martin," I said, "you will continue to send the message on all frequencies and in constant repetition until I give orders to the contrary. From now on, in the clear."

"In the clear, sir?" she said, surprise in her voice, making sure she had heard correctly.

"In the clear, Miss Martin," I repeated matter-of-factly, and she was gone.

I turned to the watch officer. "Mr. Bartlett, you will proceed on our designated course. Reduce to two-thirds speed. Wake me if a reply to our message comes in. Wake me if you sight anything. Or for any other reason in your judgment. Wake me in any case in two hours."

"Aye, aye, sir. Two hours."

"Course one two four . . . all engines ahead two-thirds," were the last words I heard as I left the bridge. They and the clank of the engine-order telegraph.

I went to my sea cabin directly below and, removing nothing save my shoes, fell into my bunk and into the sleep of the dead.

.BOOK III.

THE SEARCH

.1.

LAND'S END

It was a stretch of 700 nautical miles from the Barents into the Norwegian Sea and a point almost exactly astride the meridian of Greenwich, from which all mankind calculates time, where I knew I would have to decide. Running with all engines full, ahead of the gathering mountainlike black clouds which seemed as if they were chasing us, I debated with myself all the way down what to do when I got there. Continuing on course would take me straight between the Danish Faeroe Islands to starboard and the Shetlands to port, thence beyond the Outer Hebrides into the Atlantic. Wreathed as they were in swirling deep gray masses, visible a great distance ahead across the cold waters and of a particularity I had never seen in all my eighteen years at sea observing weather, I dared not stop at any of these places and longed for the open sea. But the more I argued with myself about it, the more I knew that, although as a seaman I wished to reach the free ocean, another course was first required of us. And that unless we went there to discover for ourselves, we would remain in a realm of doubt and ignorance which might lead us to commit selfish or dangerous or even mortal acts. I felt we had to have, in this matter, a knowledge from which the last shred of incertitude had been removed. Almost as if this were the justification required for taking ourselves completely and single-mindedly into our hands. Added to this, or rather in point of fact preceding it, a sense of plain duty dictated what we should do. Therefore, on reaching the meridian, I ordered a course change and put us on a S. by S.W. heading. We came down out of the Norwegian Sea and crossing over the outer limits of the continental shelf entered the North Sea. We crossed over Viking Bank, over the 130 fathoms of Dogger Bank, over Southwest Patch and the Outer Dowsing, over Kentish Knock—all waters I knew with great intimacy—and at first light on the twenty-fourth of December passed Chapman's Light shining strongly through the mists, at slow speed entered the lower reaches of the estuary and stood in to Gravesend.

Lieutenant (jg) Aaron Selmon constituted a new breed of naval officer. He stood about five feet three inches and I don't believe he weighed more than 125 pounds. His age was twenty-five. He looked so out of place in the uniform of a United States naval officer as to make one, regarding him in it, have to suppress a smile. He had about him a distinctly undernourished look. His head appeared considerably too large for the tenuous pedestal that supported it. His whole body presented an image of boniness, topped by a bony, angled face with a milky-pale complexion that appeared never to have felt salt spray, eyebrows so blond-pale as to be invisible, and sandy hair starting to thin prematurely. His appearance, suggesting something close to delicacy, was deceiving. I was to learn from his service record that he had been a gymnast good enough to earn a spot on the war-canceled Olympic Games in Buenos Aires in his specialty of the stationary rings, the gymnastic event above all others requiring pure strength. He wore a perpetual look of seeming just on the point of smiling, at life in general, one presumed. His voice was monotonic and gentle, in the tenor registry, and he never raised it. A kind of aura of sobriety, even shyness, enveloped him, which made one as relaxed in his company and often as unaware of it as one would be with a favorite hound dog. He knew little more of ships as such, or the sea, or anything nautical, than did the most abject landlubber. But he knew one thing. He knew how much radiation men could tolerate, and for how long. Every ship of our capability had this new officer billet aboard. He was our Radiation Officer, or RO. He lived in a world of figures, and of rems and rads. To assist him he had some of the most sophisticated instruments the ship carried. Two principal ones. One was situated in the combat intelligence center and could take the readings of the outside through highly acute sensors placed at various points on the weather decks, with, on the bridge, set alongside the binnacle, a repeater much like that for the master gyro established in the hull of the ship. In addition, should we require it, he had the most advanced portable rem (roentgen equivalent man) counter made, which similarly measured levels of radiation in the air and could further determine such levels in food or drink. He had been the subject of good-natured ridicule from the other officers as being an officer with no duties, with no one to command, a seaman who knew nothing of the sea, and it was true that you could go weeks without realizing he was aboard. He took it amiably enough. One looked around for jobs for him to do—movie officer, shore relations officer, bagatelle tasks which he performed cheerfully. Maybe deep within him, behind that soft incipient smile, he was simply biding his time, awaiting his moment, with a secret scorn for all of us, thinking just you wait and see. And now it had come. Suddenly there was no more important officer aboard.

It was a river like none other in the world, a seaman's river. I looked beyond the ship's bow and thought, as I had every time I came in here, how from this river the greatest continuous generations of seafarers the world has ever known had set forth to every corner of the earth, to trade, to do battle, to make mighty voyages of discovery. From here had issued Nelson in *Victory*, destined for Trafalgar and glory; from here Drake in the *Golden Hind*, bound for the first English circumnavigation of the globe; from here sailed the *Beagle*, with a young naturalist named Darwin aboard. I had taken the conn myself from Lieutenant Sedgwick, with Selmon standing quietly at my side and in front of his repeater. I had gone over the plan in detail with him and achieved his consent: to do what his instrumentation permitted us to do—provided always we proceed with deliberation, ready at any moment to turn about. We went in at dead slow under a visibility scarcely 200 feet. This in itself was not all that unusual: I had conned this same ship up this river with no greater maneuvering arc in the rolling fogs that chronically swept in from the sea, immersing the land and making that white curtain the ship's chief foe in a passage up the river. But there was a difference in the fog that the ship now slowly breached.

The fog was mixed with something else. Something sooty, immense drifts of swirling vapors soiling the air and combining with the fog to form a viscous pall that shielded the very geography of the parallel. Over all a profound and sombrous silence reigned as of a place entombed. I had ordered all unnecessary personnel below decks, all hatches battened, and only the bridge watch was topside—and the lookouts. A double bow lookout and also along both sides of the ship forward. They could have seen but little. The vapor devoured all. I stepped out onto the starboard wing. The substance eddied in mute whorls, cold and blackish, around the ship, the vile and mephitic fumes seeming to invest the earth around us, flowing in tenebrous seizure over the Essex marshes to starboard, of which between the opaque billows I occasionally was granted a glimpse as onto a River of Woe.

I looked down at the green gleam of the starboard light—I had ordered our running lights turned on—and saw an astonishing thing: It grew dimmer. By the chronometer we were approaching day but it was as if it were just the opposite, that we were entering upon nightfall. It was as though time had been turned upside down. Not the faintest sound came from anywhere around us; only the soft swish of the slowed-down ship slicing through the river into the dark void. The mass of clotted air thickening with our trespass into it, the swirling darkness between bridge and bow, I felt even the ship hesitated, not the hesitation of a coward, but in a reluctance to confuse recklessness with boldness, a pause as before the most imminent peril. I kept expecting to hear from beyond that shroud of teeming silence the cries of human beings. I listened hard. I heard nothing. I felt then a strange, etheric sensation. As of disembodied voices from the shore, of souls already crossed over, whispering in hoarse and throaty injunction their threnody, *turn back.* I stepped into the pilot house.

Selmon was looking rigidly at his illuminated repeater in the swelling murk which now penetrated the wheelhouse. I think I knew before he spoke that it was no use. When he did it was quite matter-of-factly. I had said only:

"Yes, Mr. Selmon?"

He took his eyes off his counter and turned toward me. We simply looked at each other through the gloom in the immensity of a shared knowledge. It was at that moment, I believe, that without exchanging a word we first entered into that other knowledge, that henceforth salvation, if available at all, could only take the form of preserving a totally unwarranted steadiness of comportment, the outward naval composure which had always served ships and their seamen so well. I was grateful to him—hysteria, panic, was but a step away and here could translate into only one thing for the ship and her company, disaster—and also for the first time, through that reeking vapor that filled the pilot house, began to be aware that, never mind appearances, I had in this nonseaman a naval officer. I knew the figures by now as well as did he and hearing them, I felt an emotion whose nature startled me: An intense wave of loneliness moved through me. He had said the one word: "Captain."

"Yes, Mr. Selmon, I know. Let's get the hell out of here."

I spoke to the helmsman, Porterfield.

"Left full rudder."

"Left full rudder, aye, sir."

The ship began to turn, to swing and come broadside to the upstream, still swinging.

"Steady on course one one five."

"Steady on course one one five, aye, sir." I felt the ship come about and stand downstream. "Checking one one nine magnetic."

As the ship receded I stepped out onto the bridge wing and in the cold and bone-chilling air peered aft through the miasmic pall. Its wretched breath, acrid and nauseant, seemed to scratch my very eyes. That lurid, anthracitic mask: it hung there now virtually immobile, obscuring all. Then, as I stared into it, the veil seemed to part now and then, if only in the slightest degree, a penumbra, as if teasing and tantalizing us, as though pondering whether, as a consideration for all our efforts, to give us some glimpse of what lay behind its dark cerements. Quickly I pulled the cover off Big Eyes and squinted through. The sullen haze held again, impenetrable. A trick. Then abruptly it broke once more, and I felt an icy chill that seemed to move up out of the ship's decks into and through my body and to quiver it, a lingering shudder of the flesh. By a conscious effort I held still the trembling hands on the glasses.

My eyes straining to the edges of pain, I saw the lineaments of what appeared to be, or to have been, a thin tall structure of some sort, but now with large chunks gouged out of it, and what remained charred to where it appeared something like a smokestack in ruins. A tower. My eyes kept tracking it fiercely upward until halted by the murky turmoil that swirled around its top almost as if belched from the form itself. As I stared and held fast, the pall seemed for a moment to lift as a shutter lifts and I beheld an apparition. A clock. I peered hard, straining to read it. Then it was as if the very hands of the clock reached down with clear intention into the binoculars and slammed into my eyes. Twelve forty-eight. The clearing lasting long enough so that I could see that the clock had stopped. Then the shutter came down, the dark infestive billows licked across it and swallowed it up and I saw no more. I let the Big Eyes drop.

For a moment something like a seizure, a paroxysm, of nervous trembling, accompanied by a choking sensation, took me. I felt as though a terrible chasm were opening under my feet, beyond all soundings, of a depth greater than that of any sea. I reached out to the bridge-wing shield to steady myself, fighting, it seemed, for my very reason, until something welled up in me to stop it, some distant resource—who could ever know

from where?—perhaps that of a ship's captain's surfacing inner knowledge of the awful consequence for his men and his ship, to whom his every
allegiance belonged, if he did not; a moment in which all of our lives
seemed ludicrously to hang in the balance, dependent on such a simple
thing as my control of myself. I became aware of the ship moving downstream. I stepped back into the pilot house. I think it was out of the
remnants of that daze that I spoke, or heard myself to speak and as if to
myself only, in hoarse tones—that foul and putrid vapor had begun to
attack one's very voice.

"Anyhow, we found something out. The exact time. It had to have
been just after the noon hour. Everyone must have been Christmas
shopping. Big Ben."

In the swarthy gloom of the pilot house I could see only Selmon's
face, dimly lighted by the ghostly glitter of the binnacle light and of that
other repeater. He was looking at me strangely.

"What did you say, sir?"

"Nothing, Mr. Selmon. Nothing."

I turned to the officer of the deck.

'Mr. Sedgwick, secure all lookouts. Then activate the washdown
system."

"Aye, aye, sir. Lookouts stand down." I could hear the echoing words
of the 1MC announcing system pierce the swirling darkness between
bridge and bow. Then presently the ship was enveloped in an erupting
high fountain of water from that special device created for ships of our
mission. The coursing water washing her vigorously fore and aft, coating
her weather surfaces with the object of carrying away any particles which
may have fallen on her, filling her cracks and crevices so that the particles
could not settle into them. As the ship washed down, I could see us
beginning to come out of the river. Then we were clearing it and entering
the channel. I spoke to Porterfield.

"Right standard rudder."

"Right standard rudder, aye, sir."

The ship turned sharply.

"Steady on course two seven zero."

"Steady on course two seven zero, aye, sir. Checking two seven two
magnetic."

The ship stood down-channel. I spoke to Lancaster at the lee helm.

"All engines ahead flank. Indicate two zero nine revolutions for
thirty-eight knots."

"All engines ahead flank . . . " I heard the clank of the engine-order telegraph, then Lancaster's voice. "Engine room answers all ahead flank. Indicating two zero nine revolutions for thirty-eight knots, sir."

The ship leapt beneath us, as if she, too, wanted to get out of there. I had felt something like a brutal note in my voice giving out the familiar cadence of commands to remove us from that place, the echo of an inner rage and desolation, of having touched a madness the recognition much less contemplation of which attacked one's own sanity: a rage I knew I must subdue lest the madness take me, too. I stepped out onto the starboard wing.

Beyond the ship's wide white wake, stretching from channel to sky in the chill stillness, it hung like an enormous shroud over the Isles. I put our position simply. We did not know if somewhere behind that eclipse, moving, staggering, lurching about, there were live people or not. And there was no way to find out without finding our own doom in the act of discovery. I stood and permitted the ship to continue to go away from there. I turned my back on them. I had not—no, not remotely near it—done a more wrenching thing in my life. Never experienced the naked feelings of a coward. A terrible thing filled me, an overpowering self-loathing. Then by a conscious effort of will I let everything in me go limp, blanked out. Nothing was more urgent than not to think. I stepped back into the pilot house.

"Mr. Sedgwick, take the conn."

"Aye, sir. I have the conn," he said in a clear voice so that all the watch could hear.

All the way down we ran, the ship opened up, rushing to put the stench and peril of the land behind us, keeping well out, far across the water the shield of drifting black vapors to starboard continuing to hold the Isles in its funerary grasp, rendering invisible the tolling roll call of shorelines we passed, of Kent, of Sussex and the Isle of Wight, of Devon, Plymouth, and Cornwall. Engines all ahead flank, ripping at thirty-eight knots through the Channel, until finally we were approaching Land's End and the Isles of Scilly. Land's End! How the very name leapt up to thrill us. Then there it was. Twin azures: Stretching in an endless blaze of blue beneath the unblemished vault of a pale blue sky, her far horizon about to receive a hazeless sun, stood the great Atlantic; there as it had forever been: the clean and open sea. It was as if we had come home, found, by grace or fortune, our way back to the one safe refuge.

The first thing I decided was that we would go on half-rations.

■■■

I brought us a goodly distance out, fifty miles, then put us on the southerly course, staying always out of sight itself of the land. For it was during that run down the Channel that I had decided something else. Not a difficult decision, for in truth no other rational choice offered itself. One fact lay in our favor and dictated the decision: the pattern of Europe's winds.

Not until the midwatch change did I go below, pausing a moment in the port wing to look with immense thanksgiving across the cleanness of the waters, where Selmon's counters showed no corruption whatsoever, bearing us southward, the solitary inhabitant of the vast sea. No, not quite solitary, I stood thinking in the greatest thanksgiving of all, the knowledge having gone swiftly to all hands: Earlier we had sighted schools of dolphin, joining us, their timed leaps as they escorted us for a while sending a lift of something like exultation through the ship in their certification that the sea yet remained, in health, in well-being. Now I stood under the glorious array of stars still in their courses, I felt comforted to observe—I caught myself checking on the positions of a number. The keeping to the routine of the ship; nothing would be more important.

"It's a pretty night, Mr. Adams," I said to the oncoming officer of the deck as I might have at any other time.

"Aye, sir," he said, his voice as equable as my own. "A pretty night."

For one knew as from an unfailing inner compass that we could survive only by not talking of it. If from that moment we had all begun to fight for our soundness of mind, it would have to be a silent fight, at least for the time being. We had not the luxury of unproductive speculations and hypotheses, of useless conjectures. Our deadliest enemy, at least for the foreseeable future, would be to give expression to our horrors and anguishes, to hold any colloquy whatsoever on them; talk now would only put at risk reason. This, to the last hand, we knew as the most crucial imperative of all. One felt it in one of those unspoken understandings, a silent shared consent, surer than declared vows, that move so mysteriously through a ship. As for thinking, that would have to be left to each hand aboard, to deal with as best he could. I felt this in our favor: The seaman's work of attending to the needs of the ship, simply of keeping her moving through the waters, would come as a profound blessing: A ship underway at sea is the most demanding of creatures, requiring the mind's full resources in precision and concentration, leaving no room for extraneous probings and larkings. A ship at sea stands always in peril. The men know this; so they would do their job toward her as always.

I heard eight bells strike. I left the usual word to be awakened for any reason and in any case in two hours—the longest period I felt I could now be absent from whatever might be in the course of developing—and went on below to my cabin and was down to my skivvies and into my bunk and had found oblivion, hardly knowing the sequence of these rituals until I dreamed of bees in their hives and awakened to the buzzing of the sound-powered phone that connected the bridge with the top of the bunk. I heard the voice of the OOD.

"Captain, Rollins has picked up what she thinks is a sub. Following us, we believe."

"Sound General Quarters, Mr. Adams. Commence standard zigzagging."

"Aye, aye, sir."

The pulsating beat of the klaxon filled the air and broke out over the silent sea, through which the ship had already begun to execute her shrewd and graceful turns. I quickly pulled on trousers, shoes, hat, and swung my way down to CIC. I felt hardly any surprise at all. It was as though I had expected it. My only doubt lay in whose she was, theirs or ours.

.2.

THE COMPANION

It was such a night, had the angels chosen to tell sailors of the news, as they might have been hastening across the waters to Bethlehem. The thought was stirred in me surely by the Christmas time and by the profusion and particular glittering aspect of the white stars in the clear wintry night shining down upon an untroubled sea empty save for our solitary vessel making south toward the Pillars of Hercules. From the starboard bridge wing I leaned over and watched the bow phosphorescence enhanced by the huge underwater sonar dome lighting the ship's path. I turned and looked aft to the serene dark waters beneath which she lay cozily invisible to all save our detection gear. I stepped into the pilot house and assumed the conn.

It was the easiest thing in the world to determine if the submarine had simply stumbled across us by chance or if she was in fact stalking us. I spoke through the 21MC to Lieutenant (jg) Rollins, the ASWO, in the combat information center.

"The Captain here. Bearing and range to the contact."

"Aye, sir. Bearing zero seven five." I heard her steady voice. "Range ten thousand yards. Course estimate one eight zero, speed one five."

The sub was off my quarter and paralleling the *James.* I gave the command to the helmsman.

"Right ten degrees rudder."

"Right ten degrees rudder, aye, sir." In the shadows of the pilot house, the only light that cast by the binnacle and the engine-order telegraph, I was aware of Porterfield gently putting the ship over. She swerved expertly into the turn. "Rudder is right ten degrees, sir."

"Steady on course one nine five."

"Steady on course one nine five, aye, sir. Checking one nine eight magnetic."

I waited fifteen minutes to give our chaperon time and leaned to the 21MC.

"Sonar, report the contact."

"Bearing zero seven three. Range eleven thousand yards."

"Keep on her."

For an hour and a half I zigzagged under ten-degrees turns, now to port, now to starboard. She stayed resolutely in my wake, zigzagging as I did with a precision that stirred my seaman's admiration. I came back on my original course, determined that she was still with us at near the same bearing and range. I spoke to Garber at the lee helm. I had decided to string her out.

"All engines ahead full. Indicate one two zero revolutions for twenty-five knots."

I could hear the sharp clank as she put the engine-order telegraph through the notches, then the clear voice of Seaman Garber. "Engine room answers all ahead full. Indicating one two zero revolutions for twenty-five knots, sir."

The ship leapt through the night. Five minutes passed. I spoke into the 21MC.

"Range."

"Range eleven thousand five hundred, sir."

"Bearing."

"Bearing zero seven two, sir."

"Stay with her."

"Stay with her, aye, sir."

So she was nuclear, like myself. She was able to stay with us and she intended doing so. I brought us back down.

"All engines ahead standard. Indicate zero seven two revolutions for fifteen knots . . ."

It was no surprise when presently she reduced speed to accommodate ours. I stepped out onto the bridge wing and once more looked aft across our wide wake gleaming white to match the constellations above, across the sea beyond to where she came trailing us. No destroyer captain can

be happy with a sub in the vicinity and unhappiest of all is he if he knows
one is following him with some undeclared intent. I still might be able
to outrun her; I had not opened us up to flank. I decided I didn't want
to do that just now. For the time being I did not want to shake her,
assuming I could. For I had a great curiosity about her. We were being
stalked and I wanted to find out by whom and why. But as much as we
were being stalked, we were leading her. My thoughts went through the
night and across to the far star-fraught horizon and down through the sea's
surface and into the vessel, coursing like some immense fish of unknown
and unimagined striking power through the hidden depths, into her
captain's mind; penetrated there, in absolute concentration, striving to
probe his intentions. The possibilities appeared these:

1. He might not know that it was all over, given the difficulties by their
    nations in reaching submarines that I have mentioned elsewhere.
    And if he heard it from us, he might well choose not to believe it.
    He might look upon any such communication with the greatest of
    suspicion, a trick to avoid his sinking us and to give us a maneuvering
    edge to sink him. I must tread here with the greatest delicacy lest
    I arouse a quiescent tiger and he come bounding after us. He would
    carry nuclear torpedoes as we carried nuclear ASROCs and I did not
    wish that these should be unleashed against one another.

2. He might not know that it had started, much less that it was over.
    In that case he might simply be stalking us with no intent to do us
    harm. Merely using us to practice his following skills and perhaps
    teasing us, having his sport with us, as well. We had gone through
    that ten thousand times with them, and they with us, on many seas
    of the world, from the Gulf of Mexico to the Sea of Okhotsk, over
    many years. Indeed I think the sailors on both sides rather enjoyed
    the game, a break in the endless watchful monotony. Not knowing
    anything, he could be playing the old jolly sport. He hadn't heard.
    But this made no sense. Submarines, both ours and theirs, followed
    almost religious communications schedules.

The stars shone down in those multitudes and with that brilliance which
they seem to reserve for winter's night on quietened seas, the serene ocean
vastness conveying a blessed and restorative peace. Only our sonar gear
dispelled the illusion. Throughout the night it continued to feed us its
metronomic and warning *ping* as she clung to us with the tenacity of
metal to magnet. When we altered course, she altered course. When we
changed speed, she changed speed. Staying always on the same bearing
from us, the same range of six to seven miles. It did begin to get on the

nerves; standing as we were throughout at full GQ battle stations; ASROC poised in its mount. We began to have to fight back the impatience to do something. So that finally, after a long night of it, I did. The stars had begun to pale and first light was just appearing from behind an invisible Europe across the water to port when I decided to send her a simple message in a top-secret U.S. Navy code she would possess if she were American. Using our powerful active sonar as an old-fashioned signaling device we queried:

> WE ARE THE AMERICAN VESSEL USS NATHAN JAMES. PLEASE IDENTIFY YOURSELF.

No reply came back. Winter's clean sun rose and began to light the water and we continued to send the message. I looked across the windless sea aft, trying again to get inside the vessel trailing us below the unruffled horizon and into her commander's head. I began to add further possibilities to my list:

3. His radio gear could be knocked out.
4. For the first time another possible explanation for his curious behavior occurred to me: He may be in distress. His compressors, his piping, or God knows what else of the profoundly complex systems of a submersible may have been rendered inoperable, perhaps by some fearful underwater concussion during these recent times, so that, assuming he is nuclear, something of which I have every certainty, he may be caught in a terrible doom, condemned to remain forever in the deep, never to come up but to continue helplessly to roam the underseas until his food supplies run out—or perhaps his crew goes mad in their living tomb. In that case he would certainly latch on to the first surface ship that came along, friend or foe. In pure desperation. Not knowing of any solution to his problem but having nothing to lose and, the hopes of the hopeless and alone kept alive by the nearness of others of their kind, by their awareness of his predicament, even perhaps imagining that between them the seamen below and those above, with the ingenuity of their breed, could somehow together work out something, some device, some method, that would extricate them from the grave. So that he was not so much stalking us as clinging importunately, frantically, a mortal cripple, to us, as his only distant forlorn hope of help, and by his very silence sending out an imploring Mayday stating that he could neither answer nor surface, was marooned in the deep.

171

And then I added two more variations:

5. His ship could be crippled and he could be doomed himself. But was determined to take someone of an enemy character with him. Those about to die sometimes desire company.

6. His radio and his ability to surface could both be disabled. In his extremis he is seeking my help. Especially mine. He received my message and decoded it, could not answer, but knows by it that we are as himself. American. And in his mute plea for succor counts on my powers of reasoning, such as I am engaging right now, so to interpret matters and to assist not attack him: comes no closer for fear none of this has got through to my mind and that if he approaches I will blow him out of the water; and by his very nonapproach is signaling me that he is without hostile intent; himself needs every help. The thought was enough to stay the hand of the most eager destroyer captain.

And finally:

7. Treachery. Its presence, any man-of-war sailor allowed for that, was always possible, in some fashion all my thinking on the matter had been unable to divine.

Southward we moved, a troubled ship ourselves. For suddenly I found warring in me a fear of attack and a consciousness of the most imminent danger versus that profoundly ingrained and ineradicable feeling of compassion and desire to render all help to those in peril on the seas which runs strong in every sailor and nowhere more so than toward fellow seamen of whatever origin or nationality. There is this: We had almost a need now to show compassion if we could find someone to show it on.

In the end I decided to wait. Just barely. I will lead the submarine, to see if she will follow us through the Strait. Then, if she does so, do it then and there, one or the other, depending on conclusions reached at that time from her behavior: either turn and attack her or seek some way of determining if she is indeed a supplicant, crying out for us somehow to raise her from the monstrous fate closing over her; at least to make the effort. A method for ascertaining the latter occurs to me: to enter waters too shallow for her to follow, for instance the lee of Gibraltar, then if she comes stationary send a boat directly over her with the hope of communicating with her from there. *If* she should come stationary: as her captain's intelligent instinct should tell him to do based on my action— after all it was up to him to divine my intention as well as to myself to divine his, it would take two ship's captains conducting this silent dialogue, if this thing were to work, to bring it off. Looking across the waters aft I began to have the sensation, or hope, that just possibly he and I had begun to speak to each other.

Suddenly, while I was attempting to sort out the riddle, the sullen sea made its own decision; perhaps to call our distracted attention to itself. I had known before these waters westerly of the Bay of Biscay to possess their own peculiar temperament. As if in consultation, all the elements closed in; screaming winds escorting the whitecapped waves hammering into our pitching bow and lashing rain across our decks, the short, steep seas beginning to board the ship, leaving us unbefriended either by the sun by day or the stars by night, the dark and cumbersome heavens hanging low over one visible and one invisible ship driving on a single course south through assailing seas to the Mediterranean. Us not knowing who she is and perhaps even her not knowing who we are if truly her surfacing gear be disabled so that she cannot rise even to periscope depth to have her look at us. Something easier to do without detection in these turbid seas. I made certain our sonar watch kept a wary eye on her to see to it that she kept the distance I had allotted her.

Then she simply vanished from our sonar. Next day, about the time we were preparing to make our turn. It came as an actual shock. I could not make out whether I was relieved or despondent, felt a gain or a loss. And I felt something of the same uncertainty toward the matter in ship's company. A sense of renewed loneliness seemed to come over us, even as we stood down from the long General Quarters. It was entirely strange, a matter of perplexed astonishment—and about as unnatural a thing as I can imagine, destroyer men rightly looking upon submarines as their sworn enemy. Then I felt I knew why. The vessel which was following us was in a way actually good news: It meant that there were others.

But not for an instant did I have any conviction that she had disappeared into the deep. Quite the opposite. I had the distinct feeling that she would come back again, appear one day on our sonar screen, at a time of her own choosing. I even felt she had a message for me, if she could find a way to deliver it, or I one to extract it from her.

.3.

THE PILLARS OF
HERCULES

As regards the major air masses of the planet, in the Northern Hemisphere they move and wheel in a clockwise fashion, in the Southern Hemisphere in a counterclockwise one, all in accordance with the familiar Coriolis force known to all properly educated schoolchildren. These simple twin facts determine man's life to a degree perhaps not all realize and the first in particular had profound implications for our present circumstances. The mainland of Europe surely had received the worst of the contamination but it was also true that Europe's winds would in due time—though not, of course, until it had done its deadly work—send back to the east, upon the place that had sent it forth, the very poisoning itself, and no doubt had already commenced to do so. Whether this matter had been worked out by some god of Mars concerned with fair rules of warfare or by some angel of irony concerned only with that specialty I had no time to speculate.

My interest was that out of this fact and a couple of others a ship's captain could reason prudently the following series of probabilities. Our best chance and hope would seem to be to get below the targeted northern mainland of Europe. This meant the Mediterranean. The thing appeared to be to enter it, determine its status, i.e., whether it had escaped entirely, had suffered a temporary or partial alteration, or had suffered something of a more lasting character—I speak of habitability; if favorable, seek a haven there; if otherwise, proceed on the same plan, that is to say, moving always on an easterly course, on the course on which the contamination would move but would eventually stop and hence somewhere beyond that point surely permit us to find some sort of safety. One would pray that this consummation would occur well before then, specifically on the shores of the Mediterranean itself; that is, assuming the region had not been a direct target, the Coriolis might see to it that no serious after-fallout would reach it. If matters proved otherwise, there was a good deal of world left, or very possibly left.

Perhaps it requires Barents sailors fully to appreciate the simple benevolence of the sun. As we gained the Mediterranean latitudes, its very warmth, flooding wantonly down from a vault of pale blue upon stilled sapphire waters, seemed to commence an interim of healing. From the bridge wing I could see, whether I looked to fantail or fo'c'sle, off-watch crew sunbathing, the ship herself seeming to bask voluptuously in the joyous sunshine. Coursing through the ship like some deep-reaching balm I could feel the immense lift in our hearts as we stood eastward on a course which would take us directly between the Pillars and into a body of water perhaps blessed and special beyond all others, seeming the sea of the Divine; and supremely the sea of seamen. And altogether mine.

There was not a true sea on the planet I had not coursed with the decks of a ship beneath me. It was as though I had loved many women— the seas of the earth—but that one stayed fairest in my heart. That peculiar and idiosyncratic love I harbored for the Mediterranean was something that was never seriously contested, a sea alluring, beguiling in a mystery all its own, holding an unrivaled lavishness of earth's delights. I felt the sea even carried in its breath a scent different from other waters, as though a certain elusive and tantalizing spice hung in the air, in the winds that stirred over it. The sea of Homer and Ulysses, of Pindar and Aeschylus, of the Roman Caesars and of St. Paul . . . of Columbus and mighty Nelson . . . of great sea battles, Salamis, Actium, Lepanto, the Nile. Beyond all others, a seaman's sea; of bold seafarers. From here Phoenician sailors, so said Herodotus, circumnavigated Africa. From here Pytheas of Marseille voyaged to Britain and perhaps Iceland. Here Ptolemy published his *Geographia,* momentous to all seamen. From here da Gama set forth to find a sea route to India, Vespucci to find the New World was not Asia, Magellan to circumnavigate the globe. A sea standing sublime among the waters of the earth. From her shores came man's philosophies, his mathematics, his music, his painting and his sculpture, his architecture, his writings. Came the great and discrete civilizations that had arisen on its every littoral since man first made appearance on the planet. Spanish, French, Roman, Greek, Turkish, Arabian, Jewish, Egyptian, Carthaginian, the wondrous Moors—to take them clockwise, each leaving its distinct and priceless legacy. No place on earth, one felt, had the Almighty so singled out to favor, planting there what seemed his personal garden, one of such riotous intellectual variety, of so many differing peoples, ways of life, ideas and ideals, as to seem to encompass all the possibilities inherent in His supreme creation, man. And yet something kindred in them all, the first of which surely was their common belief, expressed in such diverse and fascinating ways, in the One who had placed them there: the Christians, the Jews, the Mohammedans, and a hundred offshoots of each, all raising their voices in praise to Him—often, too, raising their swords against one another in a manner, a zeal of hatred, which must have perplexed Him, as if one could ever chop off the head of one of His children and ascribe the act to His direct orders.

Never mind. The Mediterranean holds a reserved and glowing place in the secret heart of any sailor who knows its waters. And incidentally— to descend from such lofty matters—it holds also, I feel confident most sailors would agree, the most luscious liberty ports on all the seas: Marseille with its spicy and inventive French women, Naples with its saucy and knowing Italian ones, Tangier with the variegated and luxuriant flesh of a dozen races and nationalities, to name but a few. We had all been here before. We were all filled with a voracious eagerness to enter its gates again. Even the mighty and fitting name given to those guardians of its portals, Gibraltar and Jebel Musa: the Pillars of Hercules, for seamen one of the great signposts of the world of waters. I stepped into the pilot house and looked at the engine-order telegraph. It showed two-thirds. Ten knots.

"Mr. Sedgwick," I said to the OOD, "we appear to be dawdling. I think it's time we gave her a little exercise. Open her up. If you please."

"Aye, aye, *sir*," Sedgwick said. "All engines ahead full," he spoke brightly to the lee helm.

"All engines ahead full," Garber repeated in the same jaunty air.

The ship shot through the water with an exuberance of her own, as if she knew full well into which sea she was bound. I stepped back out to the port wing. Over the bow the waters split and gave way before her, the seas rushing back along her sides, coalescing in a wide and throbbing alabaster wake. She, too, had been through those gates. Three times. Fleet maneuvers twice. Once on an alarm of trouble in the chronically troubled Middle East, when it appeared we might be putting troops ashore, some place or another, in yet another outburst of that incessant and insensate snarling frenzy and rage by those shore peoples, the nature or cause of which I could no longer remember. It had happened too often—and then always matters had settled for a spell and once again we had returned to our Norwegian base and the somber and melancholy Barents. I kept peering eastward through the radiant sunshine.

The ship raced on. I had my binoculars up, alert for the first thrilling glimpse of it to appear over the horizon like a ship's mast. I saw nothing. But then I began to see land.

I climbed up to the open bridge. Below me I could see what seemed the entire crew, certainly all those off watch, lining the port lifelines and straining as was I for its first appearance. Now I could make out clearly the unfolding continents. Africa off the starboard bow, Europe off the port. The fifteen miles of water between them shining in the sunlight, majestic in the entire silence of sea and sky. Then I could begin to detect far off the very coastlines of the two great land masses unrolling before me and holding this sea of marvel as though in a protective embrace. We could be but eight or ten miles from the entrance. I found my eyes fastened on the land to port, to the European side. And remaining there, as the miles counted down. I spoke through the voice tube to the pilot house below.

"Mr. Sedgwick!"

"Sedgwick here, sir."

"Slow ahead."

"Slow ahead, aye, sir."

Even his voice had changed. As the ship came down to a crawl and made her approach between the two continents, I was aware of the men below, of hundreds of pairs of eyes looking, straining at one fixed spot, and felt a profound silence settle over the ship.

I lifted the binoculars, just to be sure. It was no longer there.

.4.

ON THE AMALFI ROAD

The fact that the ship was nuclear-powered did not mean that we could run the seas forever. We had remaining enough nuclear fuel—highly enriched uranium fuel, on which the reactor cores ran—to last us for approximately seven months based on low-to-medium cruising speeds. Seven months may seem a goodly time for a ship but there was much to be done before the expiration date of our reserves would bring us forever dead in the water, unable to move, marooned on the ship herself— barring, of course, the infinitely remote possibility of obtaining new cores. I could not afford aimless cruising. Sightseeing, even if one had been so inclined, was out of the question. Even the enormous curiosity as to what had happened had to be suppressed. All must be ruthlessly subjugated to the first requirement of finding a place for us before the fuel ran out. I conceived a plan. The disappearance of Gibraltar told me almost to a certainty that the great U.S. naval base at Rota in Spain, with its immense facilities including nuclear submarine pens, had been the object of a direct and massive strike—in military terms, it would have been criminally negligent, so to speak, if it had not—and that in consequence the entire western Mediterranean waist from the late Pillar of Hercules through Spain and France had most likely been rendered uninhabitable. On the other hand, sticking out as it did deep into the Mediterranean, essentially

178

a narrow peninsula of land embraced by seas, there was at least the outside chance that Italy had been partially spared, enough so to take us in. This hypothesis carried sufficient possibility to enable me to reach the following decision: I would first steer a straight-line course across the Mediterranean to the mid-portion of the Italian boot and reconnoiter there. If it also was gone I would then "sweep" the northern shore of the Mediterranean east to west, stopping only if something favorable presented itself, and if it did not, if nothing acceptable was found, cross the Strait of Gibraltar and commence another sweep from Tangier clear across the northern coast of Africa to Suez. If Europe was gone, Africa, with the Mediterranean as a buffer between them, might yet remain; or a part of it. Beyond that I did not at this juncture plan, or even allow myself to contemplate. For now everything pointed to Italy. I set a course for Naples.

I felt I understood a little more now about the submarine which had followed us so tenaciously then dropped abruptly from our sonar screen. It must have been based at Rota and have got away, though damaged. Another possibility was that she could have been returning from patrol when the base was hit and thus intelligently come about and headed out to sea. These speculations assumed she was American. A third possibility occurred. The submarine was not American at all. It was she who had destroyed the base and much of the Mediterranean coast with it. Whomever she belonged to, I felt to a certainty that we had not heard the last of her.

Only our navigational readings informed us that we were on the latitude of Naples. The city lay invisible across the waters, hidden in the familiar shroud of towering dark vapors, dense, gritty, and whirling in their trademark vortices, stretching from sea to firmament. That sight told us that it was the last place we should venture in. If further proof were needed it was furnished by Selmon's readings, which certified that even the atmosphere above the waters leading to the city was unacceptably threatening, so that we could approach no closer than some twenty nautical miles, and passing by could only stare across the sea at the city's somber funeral pyre. I was not altogether surprised. The NATO command for the entire Mediterranean basin. I had been stationed there. I decided to continue southward toward Amalfi, to as far as Calabria and the boot's toe, then if the approaches were still barred to us to come about, make a northerly heading up the Tyrrhenian, then at the top of the boot set a westerly course and conduct my sweep of the Mediterranean coast in accordance with my original plan.

I had kept lookouts posted as if we were in a war zone. Forward and aft, port and starboard sides of the ship, each constantly glassing his designated arc—no greater than forty-five degrees, each overlapping his mates'—and an extra lookout on the port bridge wing, this one peering through our most powerful sighting instrument, Big Eyes, with instructions to keep sweeping the shore smartly whenever we were in sight of it. Barker, our expert lookout, was one of the two who manned the position on watch-and-watch, and two hours instead of the customary four, it being such intense work. It was he at the time. Thurlow was officer of the deck and I was on the open bridge alternately scanning the shoreline with binoculars and gazing northeasterly at the retreating darksome and sinister substance shielding that joyously Byzantine city in which I had spent two years of my life. The black vapors had diminished appreciably as we moved on our southerly course, enabling us, with the permission of Selmon's counter, to steer closer in. We were some eight miles offshore, running a parallel course, and not far below Amalfi, when that thrilling cry sang out, surging across the weather decks and electrifying all in earshot.

"People on the beach."

I slid down the ladder to where Barker stood on the bridge wing, eyes riveted to his shore-pointed Big Eyes. I could feel the tremor in him as he stepped aside for me. I bent and peered through. The first thing that occurred to me was to let all hands see it. I stepped in the pilot house and spoke through the 1MC.

"This is the captain speaking. All hands not on watch report topside on the double. We have people ashore."

I could not keep the high exhilaration out of my voice. I turned to the watch officer. "Mr. Thurlow," I said, "I'll take the conn. Left full rudder," I said to the helmsman, Seaman Fletcher.

"Left full rudder, aye, sir."

I felt the ship respond eagerly under me. "Steady on course zero nine five."

"Steady on course zero nine five, aye, sir. Checking zero nine six magnetic."

We came about, perpendicular to the shore. I spoke to the lee helm, Seaman Keith. "All engines ahead two-thirds. Indicate five zero revolutions for ten knots."

Then Keith's voice: "Engine room answers all ahead two-thirds. Indicating five zero revolutions for ten knots, aye, sir."

Steadily and ardently on we came, the ship pointed straight for the beach. Looking down, I could see the men crowding the lifelines, their zealous eyes straining landward. From them, from throughout the ship, I felt the pulse of the most immense excitement running, a great and exultant fervor. I spoke to Lieutenant (jg) Selmon, standing by me as always.

"Mister Selmon, I want continuous readings. Any change. Start now."

"Aye, aye, sir." He looked at his bridge repeater, gave me the reading.

As we proceeded shoreward and the cluster on the beach began to take on recognizable shapes, the unmistakable lineaments of such as us, that emotion that had seized us from Barker's first sighting flowered and built into a field of force that filled us with its unbounded sense of rejoicing, its huge wonder: the discovery of one's own. Presently I heard Selmon's voice near me. I felt a mild surprise that it had gone up quite that rapidly. I spoke to the lee helm.

"Stop all engines."

"Stop all engines, aye, sir."

The ship lay dead in the water, at some four thousand yards offshore. The Mediterranean stretched away, a vast and untroubled mirror returning the ship's reflection. Across the water I could see them standing there. Beyond and above them rose the gentle hills of the Amalfi coast riding above the sea, indented, I knew, by small beaches all the way up the road to Naples, with a little town set above each beach, each tiny cove. I could not see any of this but I had driven down that road and I had stopped in some of the towns: had swum in some of those coves; many had underwater caves, things of delight and marvel. A bizarre and reflective sailor's thought, irrelevant as could be, crossed my mind: the invention of the mariner's compass is attributed to Gioja of Amalfi. 1302. My eyes came back down from the hills and rested on the small cluster standing on the sand, apparently not having moved an inch. I felt the thing leap anew in me, and the anxiousness to get with it.

"Mr. Jennings," I said to the JOOD, "take the conn. Mr. Thurlow."

"Sir."

"Prepare Number Two boat for lowering: eight hands. The doc. Mister Selmon. Yourself. Miss Girard. Also Palatti." He spoke the language of his forefathers. "The chaplain. I'll come along."

"The men under arms, Captain?"

I waited a moment. "No, Mr. Thurlow. No arms."

Soon we were climbing down the Jacob's ladder into the boat where Meyer and Barker awaited us.

"Slow in, Coxswain," I said.

"Slow in, aye, sir," she said from her helm.

We moved at circumspect speed toward the beach and directly toward them. I decided on a change.

"Put us in downbeach from them, Coxswain," I said. "Fifty yards."

Her wheel moved. "Fifty yards downbeach, aye, sir."

The boat slid in gently on the easy sand and we got out and stood on the beach. We could see the ship standing patiently out, gray-blue and immobile, sole lord of a gray-blue sea.

"Captain?"

I turned. He was looking at his counter. "What is it, Mr. Selmon?"

"We have one hour, sir."

I looked at him steadily, startled. In the warm sun I felt a chill touch me. I pushed it back. We did not know anything yet.

"Let's go, men," I said. "Soft and steady will do it."

I led the way slowly up the beach toward them. I was able to count them roughly as we came near. Thirty souls or thereabouts.

They stood in the bright sunshine, motionless figures in the sand, looking at us with a kind of staring vacancy. They seemed scarcely of this world, as though having crossed over into a world all their own, a nether world but recently invented and belonging neither to the living nor to the dead but to new beings in between. Phantoms, apparitions, they seemed, except for the faint and indistinct sounds that came from somewhere within that cluster and from the expressions that could be made out on those with sufficient faces left to form expressions. These were not those of phantoms. They stood as though holding secret and whispering intercourse with themselves, in solemn appraisal of these approaching figures from the sea.

It was a pretty day, a gentle warmth flowing down from the azure across which a few white billows of fat cumulus coursed lazily, the heavens standing serene, unspeaking, as if watching our enterprise. At first as we approached, having intentionally come in downbeach from them, they had actually begun to back away from us in seeming fright, as if we must have been the ones who had brought them to their present state and now had arrived in person to finish off the job. The Jesuit speaking softly to them in their language brought them warily to a stop in the sand and we came on, slowly so as not further to alarm them, as one might approach shy birds, to a distance of perhaps twenty feet away before halting ourselves. The two parties, the men from the sea and these shore people, stood looking across that space at each other.

They varied greatly in how far they were gone. But for the most part their bodies appeared to be—well, decomposing; in a process of disfigurement which seemed an ongoing thing; in diverse stages of disintegration, a state of decay: gouged-out places on their figures as though some great claw had simply torn hunks of flesh away at random and was continuing to do so; charred, blackened areas; bleedings everywhere, in various of them, from the flesh, from the gums, from all bodily orifices; livid crenulations of the flesh; immense and festering sores. In the hot brilliance of the Mediterranean sun, some seemed afflicted with an uncontrollable trembling; one was aware here and there of a ceaseless fluttering of hands, of bodies. From some, blood seeped from under rudimentary bandages or from fresh wounds which—and this was startling—seemed to inflict themselves on their bodies even as we watched them. The illusion was that their substance, their very flesh was still in the process of being slowly consumed, literally eaten away, before our eyes, by some feasting and cannibalistic creature, invisible, insatiable. Their faces carried puzzled expressions, seemingly permanent, looks of bewilderment, of indelible stupefaction, as if what had happened to them was the most immense mystery, a vast enigma, forever indecipherable and therefore hopeless and foolish to probe; they appeared to huddle close to one another, in the cruel loneliness of the abandoned. One wanted to apologize for watching them; it seemed an outrageous and intolerable invasion of privacy. Even our dress seemed an affront. We had come in our clean seaman's whites to confront figures whose clothing, torn, shabby, stained and clotted in filth, they seemed to have worn forever. The bleeding may have been the worst; the drops dripping with an infinitely slow and silent heaviness from their frail and meager figures and staining in blackish crimson patches the pristine sand. Many were losing hair, some quite obviously young ones among them beginning to turn bald. Some were blind. Almost all appeared to have had their vision affected in greater or lesser degree, as evidenced by the manner in which they patently had difficulty seeing us with any great definition, even across the short distance their eyes squinting, some holding a shading hand over them the better to focus on these arrivals from the great waters now no more than ten feet away. For we had edged cautiously nearer, trying not to alarm them. Close in, they had the look in the sullen stillness of the utterly forsaken, their figures cast in attitudes of agony and despair. A trancelike glaze lay over their staring eyes, a bulging glitter almost incandescent, pools of perplexity, gleams of something riveting and rapt, perfervid, as though they counted on their eyes to state what their voices could not, pitiless and merciless looks from inside a devouring torment: There was a great light in their eyes, the immobile and shining pupils seeming to look at once deep into our souls and, as if they struggled in the toils and turmoil of violent nightmares and epic horrors, to look far away into some unknown distance, beyond us, beyond the sea, beyond all horizons—to where? At things not seen before? Things now forever their sole and commanding possession, impossible to pass on to those who had not been present? One felt one gazed into the very soul of outer darkness.

For a moment, aware of the piercing fixity of their stares upon us, I had felt the fear that they blamed us for what had happened, seeing we were whole men. But had this been so, surely they would have come beating at us. They stood rather in an immense silence, as if blaming no one; stood infinitely resigned, in a fabulous acquiescence, a voiceless submissiveness, beyond all bitterness, all hatred, as though such human feelings were no longer available to them, that in the same precise sense in which they had been deprived of the right to use previously possessed physical attributes, so had they been deprived of the privilege of either feeling or expressing previously possessed human emotions. They stood in the bright stream of sunlight as though all was night within them; in a reclusion complete and impregnable, unbroken by the slightest whisper of hope, whatever they may have had left of moments or hours, weeks or months, rolling on in an impenetrable gloaming. They did almost no moving about, as if they knew they must hoard every drop of strength, for the most part standing mutely—though some were too weak even for that and simply sat in the sand. Those that did attempt now to move nearer us shuffled noiselessly over the sand, with a spastic effort taking two staggering short steps or three and then halting, as if giving profound consideration to the immense question of whether they might after all be able to manage one step more, or two, then simply collapsing in the sand before pushing themselves up again. They put one in mind of toddlers learning to walk. In that manner some came very near and then stopped and stood staring at us, eyes turning slowly in their sockets, focusing hard on us, at this intense almost point-blank range, with feverish concentration, as though in poignant wonder at seeing complete people. The stench of their bodies, of their flesh! I will not speak of that. Among them was a young woman as yet still possessed of shining long black hair about whom there was a suggestion that once she may have had great beauty—part of her face was gone, part . . . she still wore a pretty earring on the one that remained . . . I can no longer put down the words to describe her; I abandon myself to the reader's indulgence.

Sounds now began to stir from within them. Their voices seemed to come from afar. At first, the faintest of murmurs. Then from some a sort of gurgling, now a species of choking, a fight against strangulation, now a convulsive catching of the breath, as though in search of language, a paroxysmal soblike noise, incoherent stammerings, sounds like none we had ever heard, from lips swollen and blackened, lips that trembled. They emitted cries almost inaudible, distant moanings, something that was neither talking nor sobbing but that partook of both. An aphasia, plaintive and deadened, a sound of wonderment, a mournful resonance of voices, confused throaty vibrations. A rising murmur both gentle and powerful, both immense and faint, seemed to emanate from them. A kind of keening, as from a distant chorus. This was almost the hardest part of all for us to bear, for the gulf it put between us. A private inaccessible and unlearnable language it seemed, known only to themselves: It made them seem off in some great and inarticulate solitude which we could never enter, from which they could never be reached, to place them standing on some far shore, inadmissible to ourselves, forever outsiders.

All the time the doc was going from one to the other of them, assisted by the two hospital corpsmen, Lockridge and Hicks, her face and his both a controlled blankness, digging into bags, working silently, almost automatically, the compulsive work of those who know that all their best professional efforts will avail little, will at most bring but moments of anodyne before the thing that was devouring their patients resumed its steady irreversible business. As they worked, we—that is, the three of us who spoke their formal language, the Jesuit, Palatti, and myself—undertook to converse with them, to penetrate their mystery and their secret, to make some sort of headway against the boundless ignorance of which we felt ourselves victims. Tried to get information on what had happened. We got almost none beyond what we had already surmised. They stood or shuffled in the sand in a kind of daze of bewilderment at these strange and absurd interrogations. Their answers were as though having to make their way through some deep and darksome mist, full of haziness and confusions, of a riddlelike vagueness, an elusive disconcertion that seemed less to answer questions than to pose more, answers whose imprecision seemed less of deliberateness than of a profound incapacity to deal with the matter, a hopelessness at translation not of language but of experienced event, forever recondite to those who had not known it, without terms whatsoever of reference, not subject to the revelatory. Out of their murmurings and babblings, their dronings and susurrations, we could just piece together their efforts to tell us that their land was made sterile, would not produce growing things, their field animals stricken in any case, cows producing no milk (there were intimations of other human beings alive in the hills behind them, less fortunate than themselves, unable entirely to make the journey to the shoreline), and so they had come to stand on the beaches, for no other reason than that that was where the land ran out. It made great sense: They had not lost their power to reason. The land was nothing now, offered no refuge, relief, or sustenance: That they were able to convey. It was as though the land had rejected men, had said to them, Out! Begone! The only possible place of safety remaining was the sea, so their objective had been to get as close to it as possible; also from there they could mount lookout with what sight they had left for help from the sea. If any help were to come at all it had to come from the sea. There was no assurance that it would come. But there was nothing else left. Nothing but to go to the beach that lined the sea; to go where the land ended; there to stand, to wait.

I do not mean to suggest that they gave us these gleanings of events, these scraps of facts, with the logic perhaps suggested above. Their voices spoke in fragments, in hushed incantations, incoherencies, discordancies, seeming to come groping out from within some void previously unjourneyed by humans in which they stood, breathed, and lived yet. The air was filled with allusions, with contradictions, with obscurities in which they seemed mortally unable to keep their attention focused for more than the briefest period. A single simple question would send them into a long and agonizing meditation, followed by a huddling consultation among themselves, a shrill clamor, an abrupt babble of discursiveness and disputation. Sometimes at a question they simply turned and stared wordlessly at each other in profound distraction. We made a desperate effort to penetrate their meanings; it was infinitely painful going. But we could discern enough from their sounds, a clear word here, another there, to construct this plausible synthesis. It was like putting together the pieces of a ghastly puzzle, the essence of which was that their towns and their villages had not received any direct hit but, being not far south of Naples, where a great light as of a thousand suns had been seen from afar followed by the night darkness and black vapors of giant clouds, had been accorded the peculiar and idiosyncratic mercy of becoming side effects as opposed to intentional targets. After a while it seemed to us cruel to go on questioning them, heartless and brutal to exploit them in that fashion, and so we stopped it. What right indeed had we to use them as sources of information? To ask them anything? And what interest could they possibly have in giving it? They were beyond all information. Whatever the accurate information was, it no longer mattered in the least. Information itself had

186

become useless, senseless, even obscene. Information had ceased to exist.

"Captain?"

I turned, startled to hear a simple coherent word.

"Yes, Mr. Selmon."

He looked up from his counter meter. "Sir, it's time. We should clear out."

We left them some food Girard had brought and some medicine. It was so little. And we might need the stores for our own survival. But we had to do something. It would only prolong it and that but for a brief time. But we had to leave something. It was for ourselves really, not for them. Because they had once been what we were. They were of us. And we left these oblations also because of a curious thing in us for which one felt only shame. Seeing them made one feel intensely alive.

.5.

THE LAND PEOPLE

Aboard ship I went to my cabin, closed the door, and broke down sobbing. It was the first time I had done that, and the last. With the responsibilities, the burden, that lay upon me, I knew one thing above all. Anguish had become a sin.

It was as though I had crossed over some great divide, some immense and agonizing moral chasm, separating me from all that was not my affair, and turning all my thinking, all my resolve and dedication, to the one thing that was; a resolve almost brutal in its ferocity. From that time forward I thought of nothing but my ship's company and the ship, the two of course being indivisible. It was not so strange really. Given two sets of human beings, one for whom one can do nothing and the other of a quite survivable character, even humanity itself dictates that one's efforts be consecrated to the latter, a moral choice. The fact that these were my own, of my blood in the most profound way, that of a ship's captain to those given unto his care, immutable as any bond between father and sons and daughters, of course immeasurably strengthened this resolve. To this end, the first thing needed with some urgency, I felt, was simply to remove us physically from the imminent danger. Thus it was that I made straight out for sea. Not until we were actually out of sight of land did I set a course back to the north, proceeding in that direction according to the original plan of determining habitability along the upper Italian littoral. At a much-reduced speed, the ship progressing with solitary slowness through the water, chiefly to give us time to collect ourselves, only with the most thoughtful gentleness troubling the unruffled blaze of the sea that favored our course. Indeed, during nearly our whole voyage in what was to follow, the Mediterranean held to that tranquillity, of mirrorlike waters luminescent under ardent sunshine and perfect azure skies, so often pictured in those splendid cruise posters, though by no means omnipresent, as her sailors know, in these waters in which one quite often experiences high Beauforts lashing raging seas.

From the first our ship's company was possessed of one supreme knowledge as of an unvoiced sacred vow, the rigorous adherence to which, as I have mentioned, I believe carried our very salvation: We could survive only by not speaking of it. Those who had remained aboard did not ask the dozen of us who had gone ashore what we had seen there. I suppose it was our faces that told them what they needed to know. I did make up my mind to one thing: On our subsequent stops, should we raise other human life on the shore, I would vary the personnel of the beach party until I had gone through the entire crew. This was for two reasons. I felt I did not want to expose the crew to more than one experience of that sight (not to speak of the potential emotional and mental dangers, several of those who had gone ashore were violently ill for short periods once they returned to the ship, nausea, vomiting, fevers, states of depression, and the like)—except of course for Selmon, whom we had to have along for our own safety to take the readings; the doc, whom we had to have for professional purposes; and finally the Jesuit, both for his priestly office and the fact that, something of a linguist, he added fluent French to his Italian. And the second, opposite reason, that I actually wanted all aboard to see it once. And I accomplished this. Before we were through, every hand had made that trip ashore. To see the land people.

So began our "sweep" of the Mediterranean, up past Civitavecchia and Castiglione, past Livorno and Viareggio, north to Genoa, then on a westerly course off the beaches and shorelines of France and Spain, making for Gibraltar. First along the shores of the northern Tyrrhenian, then along the Côte d'Azur, small clusters of human beings stood on the beaches looking seaward. But what were they doing standing there? What could it be save to hope that some ship, such as ours, would come along and rescue them. Take them aboard. But we could not do that. First of all, we simply hadn't the space. And even if we had, their illnesses, their infections, their contaminations, possibly of a nature no medical knowledge or pharmaceuticals we possessed could deal with, might easily spread to us, make of us a diseased and doomed ship and crew, take us, one by one, down with them. I counted, as I have noted, that my duty was owed to my crew and my ship. The land people would only bring more problems, more emotions, aboard. We would do well to survive with our own present sum of problems and emotions.

At first we stopped and sent a beach party ashore in a boat, for two purposes: to do what we could to help them by way of leaving medicines and food; and to attempt to solicit information. (A selfish altruism, in Proust's phrase.) Our visits ashore were of varying duration, depending on Selmon's readings, which were always high. We simply stood and dealt with them until Selmon said, "It's time, Captain," the phrase, instantly to be obeyed, he had adopted. Sometimes he allowed us two hours ashore, sometimes as little as a half hour. What we found: Essentially, for all purposes, it was everywhere the same. Oh, the conditions of the shore people varied in degree: some better than those we had encountered below Amalfi; some worse. Some charred more, some less. Some stops with more blind ones, some with fewer. Some more profoundly afflicted with areas of invaded and desecrated flesh: rampant sores, ravaging lesions and ulcerations, tumorous growths, diverse stigmata and mortifications; some less so. Some with more of their bodies remaining in their possession and control, some with less. Hair loss varying. Loss of gums and teeth varying. Degrees of overt bleeding varying. But every stop one thing was the same: They assumed that we were going to take them aboard; indeed that we had stopped for that express purpose. Their expectant looks mutely articulated the fact. At every stop the most dread moment of all for us came to be that moment when it was time for us to leave and the people saw with disbelief that they were not to accompany us to the ship standing off. As the great fact became clear to them, they responded in an almost instantaneous changefulness which we at no time could predict. Sometimes they were utterly mute, standing there in the sand, only their gleaming and entreating eyes following us as we headed for the boat, with timorous and expectant gazes, in them the desolation of those who, knowing only suffering and pain, see departing their last and only hope; just the silence and the disbelief, standing in dumb immobility, only their feverish eyes judging us, these alone speaking to us of their horror and incredulity at this desertion; eyes full now of longing, now of appeal, full now of hate. It was not an easy thing to feel those eyes upon you as you prepared to step into the boat and make for the ship waiting there in the distance with her security, with her cleanness, her safety: her food, her medicines, her clothing; above all her mobility. Sometimes abruptly turning abject and imploring, a sobbing and a wailing of lamentation filling the air, tearful entreaties, some dropping to their knees, falling at our feet, clutching and pulling at our legs and trousers, begging us to take them with us. We had to disengage ourselves from these seizing hands. Sometimes with no warning turning hostile and menacing, their frail and depleted forms toiling across the sandy space between us, facing off to us and overwhelming us with a sudden and savage rage, an accusatory litany of noises raving and shrieking in which we seemed to detect that they held us, being warriors, responsible for everything that had happened to them and that we owed it to them as some small measure of atonement to take them aboard ship.

We would have been fearful for our safety had they been whole human beings. At one place, seeing we were not going to take them, they shouted at us that one word that is the most vile in the language to a sailor. "Cowards!" At another—a small fishing village between Nice and Antibes, by name Saint-Laurent-du-Var—on becoming aware of this same fact, that they were not to accompany us, they picked up rocks, shells, anything on the sand they could lay hands on, and began to throw them at our beach party. They were so feeble that most of the rocks fell pitifully short. Then they rushed us. As they came upon us we needed only to push them back, almost gently, as one would a child, and they immediately collapsed like rag dolls onto the sand. We got in the boat and started out. Some of them waded out and tried to climb into the boat and we had to push these away also with the same gentleness, to pry their fingers off the gunwales, as they fell back into the water and we headed back to the ship standing in the distance. After that incident we began to approach the beach more cautiously. And also to go armed in order if necessary to repel those who might try to board our boat. The weapons were never needed, so weakened and wasted of body were the shore people, hardly fit to attack anything.

They were the land people. We were the sea people. That now was become the great distinction. Of course, it had always been a large difference, that between these two kinds of people. But it had never been so vast a gulf as now. They, the land people, now lived where they were not wanted—the land no longer desired human beings. They were not welcome. We, the sea people, lived where what was beneath us tolerated us as it always had. So that all of those standing on the beaches now longed desperately to be where we were. And, of course, we could not take them. This itself began to do something to the men. I could see it. In differing ways. Some it hardened in a determination that we should not let one soul of them aboard lest we endanger ourselves. Some of these even expressed something like contempt for the land people: They had made their bed, let them lie in it. These resented even our giving them anything at all from our stores. Others of the crew it brought to the very limits of compassion, that we must try to do something for them. And we did. For a while we gave them food, medicine, clothing. As we began to pass by some of the clusters on the beaches, rather than stopping at each, some of the compassionate ones even tried to sneak stores ashore on little ingenious hand-made floats which they cast on the incoming tide to the land people. Then such compassion, such generosity, began, looking far enough ahead, to endanger our own stores, our own survival.

Indeed it was two of my officers whom I considered as essentially among the most compassionate of human beings who came to me and insisted, in tones as aggressive as I had ever heard from them, that I put a stop to it. One was Lieutenant Girard. "Captain, we just cannot afford to give any more food away," she said, looking at me out of some reluctant inner ruthlessness. The doc used almost identical language, speaking of our medical stores. So that I had to issue strict orders against it, post notices, captain-signed, that anyone found giving any of ship's stores to the land people would be subject to the severest discipline. Some of the compassionate ones even wanted to take the land people aboard. "And when the ship begins to sink because of their numbers?" I asked them. "What then?" Brutally. "Or if they begin to contaminate us all so that we have what they have—what then?" Then finally I had enough of it. I said to the compassionate ones: "Very well. If you want them aboard so much, any one of you may trade places with any one of them. A human being for a human being. You pick which one when the ship stops at the next beach. Then get ready to stop ashore yourself." It was a bluff but that put a stop to it. No, it didn't, not quite. At the little port of Cavalière, Hurley, seaman apprentice, tried to do just that. Picked out a child who was hanging on to his sailor's dungarees and turned to me. "Captain, take her. I'll stay." I just looked at him. "No, Hurley," I said. "You will not. Get into the boat." When he didn't I ordered the men to seize him and place him there. They had to drag him away from the child.

It had become so bad I began actually to fear that it would destroy the crew, tear the ship apart. The shore people: their pleading, their exhortations, their begging one moment, in their utter abasement falling to their knees, humbling and prostrating themselves as before gods, with clasped hands beseeching us to take them aboard, clutching our persons in their convulsive sobbing, their violent outbursts of grief, their desperate kisses on our trouser legs, their falling tears on our shoe-tops. Some even pressed futile, pitiful, absurd gifts upon us; men pulling out wallets and emptying them of money, wadding this worthless stuff into our hands; women offering jewelry, rings, earrings, bracelets—offering themselves; casting off every restraint, sometimes pushing their children forward as if at least surely we would take these. The next moment coming at us with a gleaming ferocity, a screeching fury, literally clawing at us in their frenzy, screaming at us the most loathsome imprecations as if we were demons, monsters, directly responsible for their condition, full of every obligation to take them aboard. These were shaking experiences, taking a fearful toll on the crew; it was getting to the men, decimating them, tearing them apart in onsets of agonizing dismay. I knew I had to stop it for the salvation of ship's company itself; if I were to save ourselves— from corruption, from sin, from disaster. So I ceased stopping at any beaches whatsoever, passing by all clusters of human beings.

By now all ship's company had seen at least once the people on the shore, according to my intentions. We stopped going in altogether. So that at last that question which had kept recurring like a pounding and terrible metronome in our minds and which seemed to shake the ship, "What is there to be done for them?" gave back its nonappealable answer, "Nothing, nothing, nothing." In sure finality can come a kind of solace. Sometimes we were signaled from the shore by people waving white flags that looked like bedsheets as if to suggest that they could not possibly harm us and were seeking only a parley between land and sea people. Sometimes sending out their cries for help which drifted distantly and feebly over the water as we passed by. Sometimes, waving nothing, they just stood motionless on the beach, looking to seaward. Certainly we had established that there was no habitability to be found here, anywhere on the Mediterranean littoral. Not once did any of Selmon's readings even approach a definition of that state, and as for the sought information, everything we were able to extract from those on all these strands agreed on one thing: that behind the shorelines matters were far worse; this fact indeed being the stimulus that drove the people to the beaches, they being the able ones, unlike those they left behind, competent, if often barely, to make the journey. We passed by these pitiful souls, these specters on the shore, and continued our journey; finally, so as to free ourselves of cries and supplications to which we had no answer, I ordered a course that kept us out of sight of the land entirely, increasing our speed, the destroyer slicing cleanly through the cobalt waters of the Mediterranean. We had to move along. For another reason, our diminishing nuclear fuel. I have no idea how much of it we will need to find a home.

More and more between watches, men may be seen topside, sometimes in twos or threes, more often alone, gazing at the empty sea, staring into its immense solitude from the equal solitude of the ship moving through it. Wrapped in those two solitudes, ship and sea, which define our existence. Seemingly looking at nothing. But in reality, I know, looking, with all intention, for the appearance of another ship to break that nakedness, nothing seeming more strange than the fact we have encountered none thus far; that we should have the sea all to ourselves. Above all they appear to long to see company, other ships, manned by fellow sailors, whatever nationality making no difference at all. Simultaneously, a curious, a remarkable thing from those excursions on the beaches. One sensed, for the first time, a kind of sexual tension move powerfully through the ship. It was almost as though ship's company, seeing only human beings no longer capable of anything, could combat that pervasiveness everywhere of the darkness and the dying, of the horror, by one means only, asserting the life force which remained all-vigorous in themselves and which is the supreme gift of the carnality of men and women. A tension tangible, startling, yes, something primitive and frightening about it. A sexual strain, approaching urgency, which rose and fell, day by day, on its own barometer. Then the sighting itself seemed to dissolve it, or more accurately to put it back into its secret lair, but only with a further ominous sense one had of its certain reappearance at another time with an impulse to take a more active form.

For lo, as if to reward all our scanning, every hand, officer and bluejacket, at one time or another having become a voluntary and eager lookout: Not far S. by S.W. of Marseille, we raised our first surface vessel.

.6.

THE FRENCH RADIOMAN

"Thirty minutes, Captain," Lieutenant (jg) Selmon said, facing me on the quarterdeck. He had gone over first and come back. "She's pretty hot."

We had raised her on the endlessly empty blue plain of the sea just as the sun was reaching down the western sky bound for evening waters. From the beginning I had ringed the ship with lookouts and it was one of these who, sighting but a speck on the far horizon, had given the word into the speaker attached to his chest, "Ship on the starboard bow." I was on the bridge at the time and stepped out to the wing and removed the cover from Big Eyes and saw her standing white and solitary on the blue. I swung to her stern, looking for the white wake of a ship underway: she showed none at all. She stood motionless upon the sea. I stepped back into the pilot house and looked at the gyro repeater.

"She lays thirty degrees to starboard, Mr. Thurlow," I said to the officer of the deck. "Come to course two eight five. Standard speed."

"Course two eight five, aye, sir. Standard speed."

As the ship heeled and made through the water I stepped back to the wing and, leaning to Big Eyes, studied her with methodical meticulousness as we approached. First up the mast where the tricolor hung limply in the languid air. From there I followed downward and forward and could make out the large script in royal blue on her bow, *Bonne-fille*. I swept her. About four hundred feet overall, a white ship with pretty lines, a somewhat low freeboard for her size—especially noting that—with davits for seven lifeboats on the starboard side, on which we were closing her, and presumably the same number on the port side. All that I could see snug in their cradles. I slowly swept the deck fore to aft and back again, then a third time, raking her with my eyes. Everywhere, stem to stern, she appeared shipshape, lines coiled properly, things in their places, Bristol-fashion, a smartly tended ship. Not a soul stood on her weather decks. I went back to the bow to reconfirm: Her anchor was housed. She lay still in the sea, with no sign even of drift, only because the Mediterranean itself was caught up in one of her times of consummate peacefulness. From the clean and cloud-free heavens not a breath of wind stirred the silent waters, which lay below unblemished by wave or ripple, sea and sky one almost perfectly matching pale-blue color, a departing sun casting its last dimming light over all. I stepped back into the pilot house.

"Mr. Thurlow," I said. "I want us alongside, no closer than five hundred yards. Stern to stern. Slow speed."

"Alongside, five hundred yards. Stern to stern. Slow speed, aye, sir."

"And have Mr. Selmon report to the bridge."

As the ship commenced her maneuvers I stepped into the chartroom and pulled down *Lloyd's Register* from a shelf and found her: 370 feet overall, 4,000 tons, French registry, French-manned, a luxury yacht-vessel engaged in the enterprise of passenger cruises through the Greek islands. I replaced the volume, picked up the loud hailer in the pilot house, and along with Selmon went back to the bridge wing. Below us I was aware of the many hands who had come topside, lining the lifelines, to look at her in quiet solemnity across the water. As we slowly closed, together Selmon and I stood observing her intently. She stood immaculate and gleaming in her smartness, pristine, untouched. I conferred with Selmon and he approved the course I suggested, subject to his first reconnoitering.

"Four men," I said. "With that freeboard I think you can get aboard her from the stern. Take Preston for your ladder. Meyer and Number Two boat."

As he went below to see to it and as we came on I began to call her through the hailer in the language of her registry. *"Bonne-fille! Nous sommes le vaisseau américain U.S.S. Nathan James. Bonne-fille! . . ."* hailing her repeatedly, turning the hailer up to maximum volume so that my voice boomed out across the interval of sea separating us. Only the reply of silence came back across the stilled waters.

Thurlow was bringing us smartly around until we stood five hundred yards away and abruptly the ship stopped in a faultless maneuver: Man-of-war and yacht stood, our port to her starboard, sterns on line; even on except for our extra hundred feet of length. Below me I could see Number 2 boat being lowered away and our Jacob's ladder dropped, then Selmon with four hands and Preston descending, the boat starting across, making for her stern. Then the boat idling there; Preston standing on the gunwale; Hardy climbing up the big boatswain's mate as he would a tree until he stood on his shoulders; a quick leap; presently I saw him standing firmly aboard her. The three others climbed up Preston and stood alongside Hardy. The four of them moving smartly along the deck as the boat swung away and followed slowly along the ship's side to where the four hands had reached midships; then doing their job of getting the short accommodation ladder over the low freeboard. Even as they did so I was astonished to see Selmon, ignoring the ladder, make a quick jump, grasp the ship's rail, and hoist himself quite easily up and over on to her. Then my memory fetching up a line from his service record that he had been an Olympic-class gymnast. I smiled. It had been a rather fond bit of showboating. I watched him moving around the deck, taking his readings. They came back and I had Selmon's report: Thirty minutes he would allow us. The others waited with me on the quarterdeck. "Chief Delaney. Four men, under sidearms," I had told Sedgwick. "Also the doc." I hesitated and added, "And Chaplain Cavendish." I followed the others down the ladder into the boat and we made across the water for her. We came alongside and I led the way up the accommodation ladder and stood on the quarterdeck, the men around me.

"We'll stay together," I said. Even a quiet voice sounded loud in the hush of ship and sea. "No straying. Keep your hands off things, understood? Look sharp. Steady as she goes, men."

It was as though the ship were a tableau in microcosm of the most familiar and ordinary habits of the human species caught and frozen in a moment of time. The entire ship oozed the luxuriance of a routine and accepted moneyed elegance. In the dining room, which we first entered, the men were in dinner clothes, the women in evening gowns which spoke of the fashionable and the expensive as matters of course. Perhaps seventy-five of these sat at tables, set in clear munificence with silver and fine china, the diners variously in the attitudes which occur during the eating of a meal. At the table nearest us on which all our gazes now rested a man and a woman were turned, leaning toward each other as though in a moment of whispered even secretive conversation, their heads almost touching.

One of the woman's hands held carelessly to her wineglass, the other touched the sleeve of her dinner companion, while the man's hands were affixed absently to a knife and fork in the position of cutting food, their ardent eyes staring steadfastly into each other's in an oblivion to all else. It seemed a moment of planned assignation; made one think of a later, more important rendezvous. Across from them at the round table seating eight, a man's head was thrown back in a manner suggesting that he had uttered an interesting remark, perhaps a witticism, at which he had just laughed, from the way his teeth were bared, all other faces at the table, save for the conspiratorial couple, being turned in expectant attentiveness toward him. On the raconteur's starched white front lay a thin layer of brownish or tannish substance which somehow suggested a woman's face powder of an exceptional fineness. Behind him and to his left—he appeared rather to be presiding over this particular party—stood a side table graced by a quartet of bottles of Bordeaux, lined up like files on parade, one empty, one half-empty, the others full but uncorked. I peered and read; all were Mouton-Rothschild, all vintage 1975. The diners had already passed the point at which substantial clues as to age remained save only for the color of hair that lay across their heads, from which the flesh, obviously with an infinitely unhurried leisurelessness, had begun to fall away in bits and pieces, in grayish-black strips, sprinkling table and food, in some instances the first evidences of bone structure beginning to appear. They made four couples, evenly divided as to men and women. Three of the men had gray or white hair, one of the women; another of the women reddish hair. Across this sedate and confidently formal scene the pure Mediterranean air, entering through the many opened ports, wafted in soft murmur, touching these terminal postures in a benison of final tranquillity; bringing also with it an almost essential assuagement for its viewers the living. But for that gentle evening breeze which had sprung up we would surely have found difficulty in standing there making our silent observations; as it was, hindrance enough that some of the men had pulled out handkerchiefs to clutch over their faces. We wandered among the tables, looking, as mute as they, at these various passengers who had boarded ship to witness the mighty and ancient artifacts of the Greek islands, the amphitheaters and the shrines, the marble temples, and to sail the wine-dark seas of the Aegean of Homer. There was a strangely gracile air of composure to the scene, a quality almost sacramental, as if the diners were waiting with a certain anticipation for the next course to be served, in the meantime well able to amuse themselves with lively conversation. Assorted nationalities surely? I tended, perhaps incorrectly, to think of such cruises as largely for Americans and kept looking for evidences. There was no way remotely to tell. Nationality, race, color, all had vanished in the common shared fate which with such evenhanded dispensation obliterates the last one of such distinctions. Though a few of those of possession, accumulation, of the ascendancy of material interests in these voyagers, as yet remained: A shaft of sparkling light flared into one's eyes which followed it to a woman wearing an immense diamond choker which had caught and reflected a last scrap of sunlight entering through a port and which now, at the particular stage she had reached, hung considerably more loosely than when it had been fitted, the same oblique rays striking as well above the glistening jewels and directly into staring lusterless eyes which did not blink. Moving among the tables, one's gaze rested a moment on this figure, that. A youngish-seeming woman with a Louise Brooks hairstyle and with a modeling of shoulders that seemed to mandate the unashamed display of proud nakedness extending to the line of her breasts before the blue gown began, this expanse now strewn delicately with that recurring, infinitely fine dust of Roman umber which clung everywhere. From every side their eyes regarded us, enormous and vacant in sunken sockets, the fixity of their stares in no way hostile, more of anticipation at the arrival of fresh and perhaps amusing company—one half-expected to be asked to pull up a chair. A certain languor, an unresentful indifference, lay over the entire setting. As one looked, eyes moving with an inexplicable wariness over these figures, a feeling of disconcertion as from a source unknown began to come over one, the riddlelike sense of a small mystery requiring elucidation. Their huge and ardent eyes seemed to look back at one as if about to wink. It seemed the last one of them had been grinning and even laughing uproariously when the moment arrived, as though the entire room had been caught at one instant in some universal merriment which had swept through and delighted the last table and the last diner . . . Then one became aware, in a monstrous chill of revelation, of nonexistent lips, smiles now made eternal as at some huge joke played on them and as it were on the human race . . . One then ceased to look anymore directly at individual faces.

Reaching the far end of the dining room, we stood surveying the curious pageantlike forcibleness of the scene, spell-like in its final immobility, its taciturn serenity, its company with their bared teeth joyous yet contemplative in their progressing emaciation, held in a kind of impenetrable, imbecilic beatitude, a splendid carelessness clung to in the face even of the invisible vandals that had attacked their ship and them with such ferocious stealth, the terrible plague that was even now ravaging them; felt, one did, an unreasoned moment of admiration for the manner in which they had met their fate, as if there had been choice; stood, our sailor company, looking at the scene's insistent formality as at a world of the distantly privileged and elect, but without envy even at their previous lives or any desire for it; stood immensely hushed, feeling ourselves caught up in the great solitude of the living—we seeming more victims of loneliness than this loyally united company whom nothing could now ever separate. Only the plaintive trembling of the Mediterranean sea breeze through the ports troubled the profound stillness.

I turned to Selmon. "It doesn't make sense."

He seemed as perplexed as the rest of us, studious, mind working to solve a mystery. Then in tones of deliberation:

"I think they must have been closer to shore, sir, to a blast . . . the ship drifted here . . . Perhaps . . . " His voice trailed off in reflective uncertainty. There was an almost imperceptible shrug. "There's so much we don't know. People have never experienced anything remotely like that much radiation in one dose." His eyes brightened with the possibility of solution. "It could have been a neutron bomb. Kills people. Leaves things alone."

We weren't there to solve mysteries, these, as Selmon said, unsolvable anyhow, and inexpressibly unimportant. Besides, I had in mind something that was important. Selmon as well had left the past, the irredeemable, the speculative, to return briskly to the present, where all our duties and allegiance lay. He looked up from his counter meter.

"Twenty minutes, Captain."

I turned without a word and heard the steps of the others follow me down a passageway. I opened two or three doors to find staterooms emptied, beds turned down for the night with a precise neatness; in one a woman in the universal black and white of maid's clothing, maid's bonnet, maid's white lace apron, seemed to have been in the act of doing so while the diners dined, her figure fallen like a rag doll, hunched, crumpled, face down, on the bed. I opened another and saw a couple in their nightclothes lying in twin beds, for some reason having retired at dinner time. Perhaps they were feeling ill, perhaps the sea had been a trifle rough for landsmen of their age. Perhaps simply they had dined at a first sitting. Only their heads were visible, their bodies otherwise sheeted to the neck. These were both propped up on double pillows, a manner of sleeping favored by some, and perhaps from being clearly elderly were at a stage of decomposition somewhat further along than was the case with any of the diners. From them white sparse hair sprung, like sprouting

snow upon the sooty field which in thin and fine layer spread across the
white pillows, spread across all. As with joint intention their eyes bulging
from concaved sockets seemed to stare directly and with unspeakable
outrage at this intruder who had dared burst into their bedroom with not
so much as a knock and disturb their sleep. I closed the door, leaving them
to resume it, and continued down the passageway, opened another. No
one asleep here. Two naked bodies, one astride the other, not elderly at
all. On a chair hung, neat and shipshape, the uniform jacket of an officer
of the French merchant service—the single stripe, the leanness of des-
sicating loins of the topside nude figure authenticated his youth. Coition
during the dinner hour! When least likely to be disturbed, caught at it.
How I admired the French, their unfailing shrewd pragmatism. In all of
these I backed out of the doorway and closed the door in quick silence,
to shield my men from sights, and went on down the passageway, opening
no more doors.

Eating, sleeping, screwing, the things men do, I thought, with a
certain unaccountable viciousness, a savage anger at something I knew not
what. Fat, dumb, and happy, as they said in the Old Navy. I led the way
up the ladder to the bridge. The binnacle light still weakly burned, casting
the pilot house in spectral shadows in the oncoming twilight. The form
of the steersman was slumped over the helm, which his hands, his whole
body seemed rapturously to embrace, glued as if hanging on for life.
Around him on the deck lay four bodies additionally in the uniforms of
the French merchant marine, appearing simply to have toppled over
where they were, two landing by chance pitched forward and face down,
two, including the captain with his four sleeve stripes, sprawled on their
backs, their officers' hats surviving on their heads though now seeming
markedly too large, just below the brims the quartet of eyes staring lividly
up at us in a perpetual astonishment and seeming bigger than men's eyes
could ever be. I heard something start in one of the men behind me, a
rasping noise as of a low moaning, a kind of rattling in the throat. I
stepped out onto the bridge wing, the men following me.

The world stood in radiant silence. The bright evening star of Venus
had appeared to announce the approach of night, other stars less brilliant
following in attendance to look down in their benevolence on the hushed
sea, amaranthine and glittering in the light of eventide; to look down, too,
on lost sailors; not the dead ones—they had found harbor, there was
nothing there to console—but on us, the living. I stood in the engulfing
stillness, in the peace of sky and sea, looking at our ship standing gray and
alone across the near water, lights beginning to flicker on in her as if

beckoning us, saying come home. I had already forgotten the dead. They were gone and they were strangers. I had no time or thought even for the horror. I was thinking of my people. I was thinking what else a ship such as this was certain to have on her, in richly bulging storage compartments below where we stood, and how terribly much we could use it—how desperately we might come to need it. Above all, food. This in mind from the moment of boarding, I had sent Selmon and the doc below to search out the food stores and the medications. They now stood before me, waiting.

"Loaded, Captain," Selmon said. "Chill rooms: sides of beef, lamb, veal, ham, fresh vegetables and fruits—the works. These people planned to eat." He paused and offered a rare inane reflection. "The French. Excuse me, sir. Food lockers," he hurried on. "Nearly all the food packaged just like ours: freeze-dried . . . "

"Very well," I interrupted. Freeze-dried: It was the way nearly all seagoing food now came. Something lifted in me, something almost fiercely voracious.

"What we will do is go back to the ship. Start tomorrow at first light. And loot this thing, stem to stern. Send over quick raiding parties, different men each time to allow for the exposure dose. No hand more than one trip. No one to stay aboard more than . . . What's the allowance?"

"Thirty minutes, sir. On safety's side. But sir . . . "

Something was wrong. I glared at him. "Well?"

Nothing, not even his captain, could breach his equanimity or intimidate him in his sovereign field. Nothing even alter the impregnably mensural cadence of his voice. There had been an entire metamorphosis in this officer. From the shy and retiring, virtually invisible officer before it happened, one then with no real duties aboard, he had become, now that we could not make a move without his approval, one wholly self-assured.

"That part would be safe enough, sir—with the men working quickly, no party aboard more than a half hour." He hesitated, a moment of weighing thought. "But everything aboard this ship is hot, sir, in greater or less degree. The meats: I ran the counter over some of them . . . "

"Then we'll leave the meats." I had turned with a certain tension of sternness to the radiation officer, unreasonably irritated, I suppose, that even I, the captain, had to have the j.g.'s permission; could hear the testiness in my voice, overly importunate I knew even as I spoke. "Just the sealed food."

"Sir, I metered them as well. Nothing protecting them but aluminum foil. Alpha and beta particles are almost certainly already through those packages. Not terribly high. But it would be a risk. I could not promise what would happen to anyone who ingested their contents." His voice had taken on the faintest but unmistakable tones of insistence. "Other items: found considerable cigarette stores. Countered them also . . . To smoke one of those cigarettes, it could . . . " He paused there, not wishing to say the word, and no need to. "Even to bring these articles aboard . . . I would have to strongly, fully, recommend against it, sir."

"The *medications?*" I snapped the word at the doc. He shrugged, as to higher authority. Selmon spoke.

"Captain, given the extremely high energy levels of a neutron bomb—if that is what it was, and we don't know otherwise—the medications especially could have been altered in some ways we could not even speculate on. They're the last thing you'd want to use on anybody already sick."

With that, of course, there was not the slightest question but that we must not dream of appropriating these stores, of introducing the contamination into our own ship. It would be the worst kind of folly. I cursed myself for a fool for even thinking of it—tempted into avariciousness myself, and if it were for the men, no less inexcusable, considering that possibly to do them such unpredictable harm was no favor. I looked straight at him for a moment, then turned, feeling again what I knew to be an intemperate anger—at the luxury of the dead, at their arrogance, their hubris, their eternal smug and insatiable greed in having taken with them their very stores of food, of medications, useless any longer to themselves, stores which might end up making the difference for us.

"Let's get the hell off this thing," I said savagely.

We went below, going down two inside ladders on a route that would take us back to the quarterdeck. I had come to the bottom of the second one when I noticed the sign on a closed door. *Communications de Radio.* Something made me hesitate. Some impulse pulled me in there.

"Chief, take the men on to the quarterdeck. I'll be along directly. Mr. Selmon."

The others proceeded through a watertight door and were gone. The RO standing beside me in silence, I opened the door. By now one found on opening doors what one expected to find, a familiar sight. A body, in this case slumped over the paraphernalia of his watch, wearing a rating's uniform. A small space embraced in gloom and darkness save for one faint light burning down on the table at which that stilled figure sat. A thought struck at my mind that possibly the radio operator had not been taken at the same moment as had the diners—shielded, perhaps, for an hour or so, maybe longer, by his enclosed, portless space inside the ship as opposed to the admitting ports-open freedom of the dining room. I stepped forward through the shadows—it was no more than a couple of paces—and stood over him. His head had fallen forward and lay bowed on his working table. I looked and saw attached to it a set of earphones which seemed on the point of dropping off due to the diminution of the flesh which held them in place. I followed the curve of the right sleeve of his French merchant marine uniform until I came to, emerging from it, a hand stretched forward, in an advanced state of decay, bone structure beginning to appear through the elongated fingers, yet these still clutching something. A piece of paper; just beyond it on the table, a writing pen. I bent closer and made out a radio communications form, covered with the fine umber dust that we had seen everywhere, enough so that I could not make out whether it was simply a blank form or something otherwise. I leaned quite close and pursing my lips as one does in blowing bubbles directed onto the paper an abrupt stream of air which sent most of the dust flying. Then pried the paper with a gentle force from the skeletal fingers, shook it quite vigorously so that the last particles fell away. I held it under the faltering light and discerned writing. Bending closer, I read a few lines, read a few more—then broke off. My heart stopped still. I felt as though the very hairs on the back of my neck rose. For a moment I fought for my composure. Then turned, striving to control the trembling of the hand that held the paper, back to Selmon. We stepped out and I closed the door. We stood in the passageway, looking speechlessly at each other.

"Mister Selmon, I should like very much to take this paper with me. I don't plan to eat it."

He smiled thinly. I held it out to him, concentrating to make my hand steady, and he took it, making no effort to inspect its writing, and ran his counter over it in a silence broken only by the minute emissions of the instrument. He handed it back.

"Low-grade, Captain. One piece of paper. It should do no harm."

I folded it and placed it in my shirt pocket.

"Mr. Selmon."

He turned. "Sir?"

"You will say nothing of this paper to anyone. Of its existence or of my possession of it. Is that understood?"

He looked at me, his eyes steady and still. "Understood, sir."

"Let's join the others."

We went aft and made our way to the quarterdeck, where our people stood waiting at the top of the accommodation ladder. Below us the boat with Meyer and Barker waited in turn, the boat hardly bobbing in the water.

"Captain?" the Jesuit said.

"Very well, Father. We've got about a minute."

He had brought his kit. In quick motions he sprinkled holy water over the quarterdeck, meant, by that choice of place, for the beneficence of all and whomsoever the ship carried in her spaces; all crew, all passengers; that crumpled maid; that steersman sprawled over the helm, that captain sprawled on the bridge; those diners one and all; that fornicating couple. Then bowed his head—us with him—and in the thinly starred dusk said a few words of prayer. I recognized them, from long back, from a childhood funeral, no doubt, as the entreaty to the Almighty for the repose of souls. "Come to their assistance, ye Saints of God, meet them, ye Angels of the Lord, receiving their souls, offer them in the sight of the Most High . . . ," the words falling clean and firm over the ship, over its entombed voyagers, over us, over the stilled sea. We went, hurrying a bit, down the accommodation ladder, into the boat, across the darkening waters—Meyer opened her up without having to be told to do so—and back aboard our safe home. Night was coming on fast. I ordered us underway at once. I somehow had a great passion to get us away from that ship, out to the clean and open sea.

We sighted a few more derelicts of ships scattered across the Mediterranean, nearly all freighters, of sundry registries, drifting aimlessly, another vagabond, another stray, crewless, rudderless things, drifting with a spectral gentleness, a certain careless majesty, wherever wind and wave took them, through the great peace of the sea. In each case we closed the vessel enough to hail her. From none came back to us the voice of a live human being. Always we took a long, hard look at their davits. With some, the boats were all still there, in their cradles, telling us, along with the silence in response to our calls through the hailer, that the ship's people were still aboard. With others, the davits were lowered, the boats gone, informing us that the crew had had time to abandon ship. In one instance, some of the boats remained in davits, other davits were in lowering-away position and empty. We did not go aboard any of these vessels. We dared not loot them. And we had none of curiosity's taste. I would allow no more boardings—because of what it did to the crew. It was simply too dangerous. I am not speaking of the danger of radiation infection, sickness—we could avoid that by staying within the limits dictated by Selmon's instruments. There was another danger almost as great. Horror. I felt the crew could not take any more of that. Every man has his limits of the amount of horror, of moral nausea, he can accommodate. I did not wish to test these limits further. Besides, it would serve no purpose. We continued across the Mediterranean, Gibraltar-bound.

Meantime, periodically, behind the closed doors of my cabin, I turned the combination of my safe and removed the single sheet of paper and studied and restudied the words taken down in those last hours or minutes by my French comrade of the sea. I deliberately never committed its translation to paper, only, over and over again, reading the words in French. By now I have them virtually committed to memory. He got down quite a bit, considering—a man of a certain courage and resolve, he must have been, to stick to it with the world coming apart around him; perhaps, recognizing just that, knowing himself in the throes of his last conscious act, he had a bit of the recording angel in him, as a radioman might, knowing as such do that someone, some random fellow sailor, would at some point come along. Oh, nothing in great detail had he got down, but the general lines of what happened. Not just to his ship with its last hand, its last passenger. To everything. Yes, including America.

And so, finding nothing habitable, we came back to rockless Gibraltar and proceeded across the Strait toward Jebel Musa to commence our sweep of the North African coast. To determine if matters were any different there, whether perhaps the Mediterranean had been wide enough to serve as a protective barrier between that continent and the continent from which—save for the even dozen blacks in ship's company—the blood of every last soul aboard had originally come and which we now left behind forever.

It was off the tip of Morocco, near a place called Punta Almina, that it happened. Barker's sure sighting. First, the periscope. Then, even as General Quarters sounded its pulsating beat throughout the ship, the immensely long thing, instead of diving, slowly rose from the deep with a certain dark majesty and as we watched in rapt bewitchment came still in the water. Stood wakeless, recumbent in the sea. Stood no more than a thin line across flawless waters, mirroring heavy clouds of mauveine in the oncoming twilight. I raised my glasses, where I had joined Barker on the starboard bridge wing, studying her as she lay, seeming to deliquesce into the darkening protective horizon, standing squarely across our path. Assured of our eventual arrival, knowing cunningly that we would be back; knowing to a dead certainty what we would find in our tour of those

Mediterranean shores that would force our return, so that she needed only to stand by for a bit. I felt a strange calmness in the fact that I was not all that surprised; indeed would have been so only if she had not been there; expecting her to be there, waiting for us; there seeming a kind of weird inevitability in her return. (I hardly gave thought to the possibility that it was a different vessel from that which had clung to us on Brittany seas.) I immediately ordered all engines stopped and presently we as well stood motionless in the stilled sea.

I swept her meticulously bow to stern, knowing her captain to be doing the same to me, staring point-blank at each other across some five miles of water. Above anything else I was anxious to determine her nationality. Saw nothing. Swept again. Then as my eyes came to rest on her sail I observed there, limp in the windless air but unmistakable, that startling ensign, apparently just raised—felt an instant wariness in that fact, a consideration as to fraudulent identity: Why so late in hoisting?

I raised up and immediately issued two commands: one bringing our anti-ship weaponry into firing position, the other instructing Signalman Bixby to blinker the message even as I fed the words to her verbally. Every fiber of the ship hair-trigger tense in the waiting, a Harpoon missile poised in its vertical cell launcher, its fire control system manned in CIC, I watched as the light flashes shot across the void of the Mediterranean. Not five minutes had passed before the answer came blinkering back over the stretched-taut zone of water between us—the flashes much slower than Bixby's had been, almost stuttering in execution, as though sent by a not altogether experienced hand, infiltrating further doubts, Bixby sounding them out and a seaman writer taking them down but the words known to me as, letter by slow letter, I also read the flashes; when it was over standing in a moment of astonishment and wonder, laced yet with a cold, hard streak of suspicion, scarcely realizing anyone was around me when I became aware that Thurlow, the OOD, was standing there and heard him say, "Sir?"

Startled, I turned, looking at him as at an apparition in the oncoming darkness, somehow aware of the first star having appeared, pale in the eastern sky. I waited a moment, during which the decision seemed not so much to have been made by myself as dictated from elsewhere: almost as though something was telling me it was a last chance, that if we rejected it there would not be another; as if saying that an excess of caution and skepticism can be fully as dangerous as its opposite: that the moment, and the ineluctable risks it carried with it, must be seized: this conviction fortified by a sly and slender intimation within, held all along, perhaps only false hope, still not to be resisted, that he had a message for me and for reasons unknown would deliver it only in person.

"Stand down the Harpoon, Mr. Thurlow," I said. "Lower the Jacob's ladder and Number Two boat."

In the shadows I felt the disconcertion in him, felt him hesitate fractionally. Then he turned and disappeared in the pilot house to carry out my orders.

For myself the course admitted no dispute. I had to find out about him. I had also not to risk the ship. Rather than the peril of taking the ship any closer, this appeared simply the safest method to accomplish my objective.

Having traded blinkers again, it was no more than ten minutes before I was stepping into the boat, having left the most explicit of contingency instructions. Barker's boat hook came out and gently shoved us away. The boat heeled as Meyer, standing high in her pulpit, swung the wheel and we started across the long interval to the low profile in the distance. Suddenly there appeared atop her sail area the yellow "flasher" above the masthead light mandated in peacetime under international maritime rules for surfaced submarines, commencing its sequential empiercements of the darkening waters, spectral and yet affording a grasp of assurance to a seaman's heart. I looked back and saw what I expected to see: my own ship's riding lights come on as if in amicable answer, Thurlow's smart doing. I turned back, from where I sat in the stern sheets, steadfastly watching the other vessel. Coming on was a night of a haunting beauty. The sun gone to the waters, taking with it whatever day breeze remained, no sound whatever save that of the low churn of the boat as we advanced, slowed down, seeming to glide over a sleeping sea, parting gently to permit our passage through the fervent stillness. The earlier cloud cover now stood peeled back to make way for the impatient stars. Only these, coming on in alacrity, beginning to fill the hushed heavens in their multitudes, looked on as our boat closed the long slender shape dead ahead, affording just enough light that, with the added aid of the flasher, I could begin to make out a few dark shapes standing at the submarine's Jacob's ladder, ready to receive me aboard.

.BOOK IV.

ABANDONMENT

The responsibility of an officer commanding at sea is unparalleled by that of any other relation in which man may stand to man. Both wisdom and humanity dictate that from the peculiarity of his position, a sea-officer in command should be clothed with a degree of authority and discretion inadmissible in any master ashore.

—Melville, *White Jacket*

.1.

NO EXIT, NO ENTRANCE

Prone in a blue sea, her low black shape coiled and menacing, she stood facing us across five miles of water. It was the immensity of the thing. It looked as if it would never submerge and if it did that it surely could never come up. I thought how her captain had shown me everything, stem to stern, seemingly holding back nothing; other than the curiosity of having my first look inside a Russian submarine, not too many surprises other than a certain astonishment at the amount of firepower she carried. I would not have estimated it as so much: twenty-six SS-N-20 Seahawk ballistic missiles, each packing eight 500-kt multiple independently targetable reentry vehicles—MIRV's—for a total of 104,000 kilotons; as measured by the Hiroshima 12½-kiloton divisor, an 8320-H vessel as originally constituted, as against our 896-H—each arsenal only slightly diminished by recent expenditures. He had pointed out the holes left by the launchings in the vast space extending upward through two decks—a full two-thirds of the submarine—reserved for the missiles. The unfathomable power remaining registered now but dully as a curiosity, there being nothing to use them on; they stood like worthless antiques, castrated dinosaurs, impotent for want of targets; something almost pathetic about them. I was far more interested in something else he had also shown me, his complement—intact, none used to date—of thirty-two C-533 nuclear torpedoes, as they designated them, virtually identical to our own Mk 48's, except for the warhead—this no coincidence, their having stolen the specifications from us, he had remarked almost prankishly. After that visit aboard, one close to cordial in tone, I had had to remind myself that, after my departure, a couple of these were of a certainty locked in on us. With good reason. Both our Harpoon antisurface missiles and our ASROC depth charges, the ASROC nuclear-armed, were ready, with the fire control watches fully manned, and in the case of the Harpoons the bearing of two-nine-zero set. We stood like two men shaking hands with one hand while the other rested on a cocked pistol.

I took one more look at her. *Pushkin.* One wondered at the thinking that had led them to name a class of submarines, and the largest ever built, after writers; for not very clear reasons one admired it. Turning, I climbed down the ladder and entered the wardroom to relate the particulars of my visit, and what I had been told, to my waiting officers, gathered expectantly around the long table with its green felt pool-table cloth.

"Very well, Mr. Selmon," I said. "You may proceed."

The most important thing I had done on my return to the ship was to brief this officer in meticulous detail on the Russian captain's report, giving him also my own translation of the French radioman's transcribed message, lifted from the doomed *Bonne-fille,* removed from my cabin safe where I had kept it, awaiting just such a time as had now come. The former by far the more extensive, almost voluminous: I had been surprised at first, the reason later made clear, that the submarine commander had prepared for me English translations of the considerable number of messages he had picked up dealing with events—these I had brought back for Selmon's intense perusal, applying all his knowledge on the subject, along with an as keenly analytical brain as I had come across in the Navy. He was ready with his interpretations. He proceeded straightaway, first with a preface directed at myself.

"This assumes the accuracy of our two sources, sir."

"They're all we have, Mr. Selmon," I said, a bit shortly. "Together they add up to a reasonable certainty in what you're about to tell us, wouldn't you say?"

"Fortified by the negative nature of our own communications efforts; taken also with our direct experience—the beaches on the north shore . . ." He meant the Mediterranean. "Very close to an unqualified certainty, sir."

"Then let's get on with it, Mr. Selmon," I said briskly.

"Aye, sir."

He had affixed to the wardroom bulletin board a simple Mercator projection of the United States and as he talked, addressing the officers at large, he flicked a pointer over it, pecking at regions as he referred to them, at individual states.

"The littorals . . . Maine, Massachusetts, Maryland . . . Virginia, the Carolinas, Georgia, Florida. The Eastern seaboard, all of it: One could not so much as set foot on the beach. Levels grossly intolerable. Pacific coast the same," he said almost as an afterthought. "Well inland—the Dakotas, an example" . . . the pointer flicked out . . . "Oklahoma . . . " flicked again, "—holding on a while longer, disallowing their being active targets, the information not absolute on that point. Irrelevant in any case: these also effectively gone by now, target or not. Considerable possibility of pockets here and there the substance did not reach—leaving a few gatherings of human beings in isolated parts of the country's deep interior. Likely talking about a few hundreds of people. These random enclaves, refuges, not apt to remain so for long, being subject to arriving waves of contamination that would remove their present rather fragile hold on habitability . . . "

Selmon's invulnerable equanimity, his tenor-voice pitch by nature pedantic, had existed from the first, an asset to the ship of major proportions: we could not have functioned, conducted our affairs, without it. He proceeded carefully, with that characteristic air of his of leaning always to the conservative, that is to say favorable, assessment.

"We've moved now into a degree of speculation: There may be a few thousands of human beings instead of a few hundreds. There may even . . . Some freak congruence of circumstances: example, the winds carrying the material missing altogether some truly deep-shielded patches in, say, a remote valley of the Appalachians . . . Kentucky, West Virginia . . . a coal mine might turn out to be something extremely useful to have at hand . . . some such combination might enable survival for a few dozens— a few hundreds—more or less permanently. I would not rule it out. Personally, I'd be surprised if the place were totally without people."

He paused as though on a hopeful note, and altogether like a professor giving his class time to absorb what had been thus far presented before proceeding with fresh material; attention absolute, silence total; continuing then in that cadence of his, something about it almost liturgistic.

"However. To our purpose. In absence of communications of any kind, absence also of all usual means of transport—cars, trains, planes, horses—it might take years of exploration simply to ascertain the where-abouts of these enclaves, assuming they exist. Even if the land lying between them and the seashore were traversable. As it is, what's hap-pened back there—the most massive nuclear-warhead throwweight, al-most certain meltdown of a considerable number of those hundred of nuclear power plants we were building including up and down both coasts . . . the likeliest situation is that an actual radioactive wall block-ing entrance to the country is in place—from Bar Harbor, Maine, to Key West, from Puget Sound, Washington, to San Diego. Megacuries of radiation released in such amounts that no reasonable man would even attempt to put a figure on it. Therefore no possibility exists of getting across that distance of fully corrupted terrain, through that prohibitive atmosphere—we're talking about true saturation readings—to wherever people may be, if they are. One could think of them as being imprisoned in a kind of oasis, if one may use such a term, ghetto might be a better one, surrounded on all sides by wasteland lethal to pass over; for us, for them, for anybody. No movement possible into or out of it. No exit, no entrance."

An almost imperceptible sigh, the last thing from being callous: rather, a viewpoint that one's sole duty lay in unhesitant embracement of whatever the mind's most unsparing analysis, based on the best available evidence, suggested the realities to be; any other course to be reserved for fools, or worse, certainly not for naval officers.

"Of course, no reason in the world to try to reach them; no reason other than curiosity. If, as I say, they exist at all. Even if one could get to them—one could not—the last thing they would welcome is new arrivals with whom to share what few resources for survival they may have remaining. Newcomers more likely to be met by shotguns than by open arms. Hypothesis reaching a futility here. Forgive the digression, sir."

Selmon shot a glance at me, obviously fearful he had stepped over that line he so punctiliously maintained between his role of explicator, concerned only with facts or probable facts, and his captain's of decision-making—never speaking to the latter unless specifically asked for his recommendations.

"That's about it, sir. As to the basic situation."

He stopped. It had been a shade eloquent for Selmon, understand-ably so given the subject matter: nothing being more crucial in directing the course of our future actions, and the literal course of the ship, than the matters he had just set forth. Remorse, desolation, the possible on-slaught even of panic: In all who heard (and who watched severally, with the most fixed attention, as Selmon's roving pointer touched down on one's own region of the nation), with no exceptions, I think I can say that, however present in human souls these might be, by efforts almost sublime they were there sealed away, for the most irreducible, unforgiving of reasons: we simply could not afford them; proscribed as constituting the most extreme peril. We stood in a nonnegotiable insistence of the last ounce of our faculties, emotional fully as much as mental; of calm most of all; to give way would have been not short of craven: 305 in ship's company, including themselves, mortally dependent on an unfailing adherence to this code of behavior. I was grateful for the company, the sure sustenance of such officers. Sitting quietly now for a bit, each of us with his thoughts, knowing as through a sure instinct given straight from the Lord that these could not be spoken—let that dam, with its inflexible constraint, be breached it would sweep us all away; each mind left to deal with his own; this unspeakable loneliness given a measure of emollience by the presence around one of shipmates known to be in identical suffering, identical pain. Beyond all of this, you felt that nothing you could say would reach the seat of the agony. Better by far to say nothing as regards that. A faint breeze entered through the ports. Looking up and out one of them, I could see the slightest of stirrings on the blue face of the sea. It was oddly solacing. I spoke to Selmon.

"South America?" It would at least be the nearest, forays to the north perhaps possible from there in time. "Assuming no direct hits."

"By now that would have made little difference, sir. Considering the massive nature of the direct trauma in the north. The winds will have delivered it there. If we were permitted to have a look at the two places, say by a flyover, there would be but one prevailing difference immediately apparent. Structures all standing in the south where there were only heaps of stones in the north. As for the occupants of the two—I should say the absence of occupants—no difference at all to amount to anything. By now the winds will have leveled that aspect out: so close by after all as winds move. Insofar as approachability is concerned, the situation in the two by now has to be effectively the same. Due again to wind patterns, the eastern ones—Colombia, Brazil, Argentina—going before those on the continent's western side—Peru and the others—forgive me, sir, the geography there has slipped my mind for the moment. In the deep interiors, possibility of those same mentioned pockets here and there, leaving a few parties of human beings as in the north; these too likely soon to follow, remote chance for the noted aberrant exception making it through, again speaking in terms of a few hundreds, a few thousands at most; maybe deep

215

in the Amazon, potential protection of extremely thick vegetation, if one were to hazard a guess."

He stopped again, like that. He had finished.

"Well, Mr. Melville." I turned promptly to the engineering officer, sitting at my left at the wardroom table. Him also, before this officers' meeting, I had directed to have ready findings for various courses. He spoke with a quiet professionalism.

"Sir, at fuel-conserving speeds not to exceed twelve knots, we have a few days short of six months of steaming time left on the core. If we make a direct heading at that speed—the coast of Virginia, my calculations are based on—reaching Hampton Roads . . . " He looked down at a clipboarded sheet covered with figures. "Calculated also on running time provided by Mr. Thurlow, at that juncture, sir, we would have expended approximately five thousand steaming miles."

"Captain?"

"Yes, Miss Girard?"

"I must mention, sir. The slower we proceed the more food supplies we consume."

"I take your point, Miss Girard. We're caught between rocks and shoals. For the time being we have to come down on the side of fuel. The men can fast for a while if it comes to that. The ship cannot." I turned back to the engineering officer. "Allow, say, two thousand more for reconnoitering. Atlantic coastline . . . " I waited a moment, figuring something myself . . . "Having completed our sweep Maine to Florida, we are standing off Key West. Fat, dumb, and happy. The Panama Canal is gone. So we continue down the longitude, keeping well off South America. Around the Cape . . . " I stopped, looked straight at him.

Lieutenant Commander Melville inevitably suggested an academic, not strange since he had been one, a bright one, a theoretical physicist at Georgia Tech, bound upward in his sheltered career when he abruptly abandoned it for the chance to work hands-on with nuclear reactors and cores on a seagoing missile ship. A body supple and hard, not an ounce of fat on it, in that respect looking rather like the 100-yard-dash man he had once been; his lean good looks, brown thoughtful eyes that looking at one made one think he was a step ahead of you but not at all vain of the fact, perhaps not even aware of it: All these seemed to be the exactly ordered up adjuncts to the rest of him; a man of rituals, of mansuetude entire, a graciousness of manner so marked as to seem almost to constitute a throwback, living out his life without the slightest seeking of drama. He looked at his clipboard.

"Sir, going that course, we could just about make it into the Pacific," he said in those soft Southern, almost courtly tones. "I'm not certain the exact fix. In any case, not far up the longitude. Dead in the water except for emergency reserves."

That brought a kind of shock moving outward from Melville and both ways around the table, like a sudden rogue ocean wave encompassing all. I suppose the engineering officer wanted to finish off the report neatly. He had always been a precise officer on fuel matters, as in tending his domain of nuclear propulsion devices; in those regions terrible penalties awaited any who were not.

"Dead in the water," I heard someone say softly, as if to himself.

We sat awhile, not a word spoken, sipped our coffee: slowly these days it seemed to me, coffee, that sailor's standby, rationed to two cups a day now. The only sounds the tinkling rattle of these, the murmur of the sea through the ports. I turned back to my officers, ranged on both sides of me down the table.

"Thank you, Mr. Melville, for those calculations. Let us leave these considerations for the time being. They require digestion in any case. I'd like now to report further matters arising out of my conversation with the Russian captain. He had a rather interesting suggestion."

I had their attention and I waited in the silence of it for a bit, then gave it to them all in one shot.

"He told me that he explicitly wanted us to see the beaches of Italy and France, the human beings there, knowing we would go there, find what we found, and that when we did would come back to the Strait, where he would be waiting for us, come back ready to deal with him."

A period of absolute stillness—the winds whispering through the ports no louder than moments before but now sounding almost noisy—held the wardroom. Every head lifted, all eyes looking up the table at me. Waiting.

"The deal being: for him to accompany us. To join forces. To look for a new place together."

A long pause. "Let's hear it." I opened it to reactions, opinions.

"What did you tell him, Captain?" Thurlow's voice, the softest of interrogatories.

It was the first time "a new place" had entered our considerations but, to my gratitude, it slipped by in the attention directed to the other proposition, which seemed to dumbfound them.

"Nothing. I turned noncommittal." I spoke rather absently, with the purpose of feeling my way with the utmost care in these waters; then more direct seriousness of tone: "I wished to consult my officers."

I sipped the coffee's last dregs, shoved the cup away from me, marched on in an explanatory and also probing fashion. "I suppose the idea was that if we ran into trouble, two ships are always better than one. No naval doctrine older than that. If that captain is anything, he is a navy man; my impression: a first-rate sailor. A destroyer and a submarine operating in tandem: I'm not sure that's ever been done. I can see it would make for a rather formidable force."

Girard said, "The Russian is not going home, sir?"

"To what? His answer. They've made their decision on that one."

"That part—the keeping together—would seem to make a good deal of sense." Thurlow spoke in a kind of slow thoughtfulness, in tones of reflection, almost as if to himself, as though uncertain about it but trying to move ahead into the various implications of such a proposal. No one aboard had a more open mind—whatever the subject—than did the navigator. "We might be able to help each other."

"How?" It was the unmistakable voice of Chatham, the combat systems officer; rather curt, the single syllable, in his usual challenging tone. It brought Thurlow up.

"Why, I don't rightly know, Henry." By habit amiable in temperament, a man of give-and-take in addressing any proposition, the navigator was nonetheless able to give as good as he got if poked. "I can't read the future. Especially these days. Perhaps you can, Henry."

"I can read this much. He's got to have something up his sleeve. He's a Russkie."

"Up his sleeve?" Thurlow repeated the phrase as if there was something impossibly childish, even idiotic in it; his voice now moving up a notch, headed toward the acerb; was about, I think, to make this semantic assessment of his quite explicit to Chatham; instead, smiled softly and sighted up the table at me. "You feel any ulterior motives there, Captain? I mean in this *Russkie?*" this time letting his feeling of something like distaste as to Chatham's use of such phrases, in the circumstances, come through clearly.

"I don't think so. Unless I was too stupid to catch them. Always a possibility, of course. I can't promise but I had no feeling he was any more devious than the average captain," I said rather slyly myself. "Not a practicing philanthropist; looking out for his own ship's interests, of course—like any captain. That allowed for, I think it was an honest suggestion; a straightaway sailor's suggestion; something he felt might be good for both of us. Stronger—in whatever difficulties we might encounter, these being quite unforeseeable—the two of us navigating together than one of us alone. I should mention one thing."

I stopped there a moment, with intention. "Mr. Chatham may have a point. When he took me through that monster of his . . . so far as I could tell we didn't miss a compartment . . . well, when we got into the stores spaces, I began to notice a lot of empty spots. There was no way you could miss them. It was easy to judge his food supplies were lower than ours, appreciably lower. Of course they have far less space for stores, even with that size—so much of it's for missiles and nuclear torpedoes, more of both than on any submersible of ours I ever saw. And, of course, they have a smaller ship's company. Still, when we got back to his wardroom and I was sipping the tea he offered me—damned fine tea—I simply asked him. He wasn't the least bit coy. Just smiled, sort of, at the question. Then said right off, 'Two months.' "

"There you have it," Chatham said, not without triumph. "He wants us to feed him."

"Two months' food supplies?" Girard said. She spoke in a sharp tone. "Against seven for us. Anything like that . . . it wouldn't be fair to the men, sir. Especially considering it's because of their being on half-rations all this time that we've got that many months left."

"No, it wouldn't," I said. "When I asked him, I think he detected what I was thinking so he asked me about ours and I gave him the seven-months figure. You know what he said? He said, 'Captain, assuming we don't find anything first, if we do join forces, go in company, we'll have one hard rule: we make it on our food supplies; you make it on yours.' "

"Has to be some kind of trick," Chatham said.

"Maybe. I don't know," I said. "I think it's pretty hard for one sailor to lie, straight off, face to face, to another sailor and get away with it. I think we'd agree on that. I don't care what the nationalities involved. But it's possible. Especially with the stakes."

Why I could not tell—perhaps it was brought on by this exercise in assessment of the Russian captain's character, integrity—but it was right then that my thoughts went to that particular moment that ever since had nagged troublingly at me, more so than any other in my conversation with him; it seeming to him, and thus to me, even in its inexactness, this appearing to me deliberate, to be the most important part of all in our interchange; none of this communicated in direct language but intimating, to my mind unmistakably, his intentions in wishing that we join up more truly than any of the motives which Chatham was attributing to him. I tried now as best I could to suggest something of this to my own officers; aware of the difficulty of conveying secondhand any solid meaning in a few phrases not clear even to myself who had heard them spoken.

"There was something else—this sensed rather than expressed between us . . . something in the idea that the known existent human beings should stay together. That we had something like a responsibility to do so."

This seemed to pass like a piece of indecipherable code, if not gibberish, over the ship's officers—or maybe it was simply that their minds had no space left for anything but what Selmon had told them; save for one. Somehow I was not surprised that as I paused it was Girard's voice I heard.

"Responsibility, sir?" was all she said. But I felt more in it than that echoing inflected question of the single word coming out of that steady poise of hers; felt the first faint beginnings of comprehension, a dawning on her part, this in turn seeming to validate my own perceptions as to what the Russian had in mind. Of course, all of this could have been an excessively grasping imagination—one felt unsure of anyone's words, not to mention thoughts, these days. The Russian's, Girard's, even one's own. Seeing meanings where none existed, an aggrandizement of a randomly uttered idea, of an intimation as to something else entirely . . . one could not know. Still, wagering, I would have placed strong money that I was right on this one, at least as to the purpose of the Russian captain . . . Suddenly a desire, bordering on urgency, to get away from it before Girard, or some other officer, come alert, should pursue the matter, pin me down; feeling distinctly that she was on the point of asking for elaboration, for my own interpretation of that strange word; beginning to have her own. So I cut away—hard right rudder—back to the course we had been running.

"I suppose Mr. Chatham has in mind that he's thinking of jumping us at some point, getting to our provisions. I can't chart his mind. I don't possess that kind of Fathometer, for exact depth readings. Unless someone else present here does, I suggest that we not anticipate. Myself, I'm not of a mind right now either to accept his proposal or turn it down out of hand. Much too early for either. We need time to consider—told him that. I'm going to want every officer's views. Think hard about the implications. Say, for instance, if we say nothing doing and he decides to come along anyhow, trail us, what do we do about that?" Someone started to speak. "Not now. Let's sleep on it. I'll have more thoughts of my own after I see him again. One more thing for now."

There is no way for a ship's captain to avoid slyness. He would be crippled without it; a necessary weapon and I had my share; still one to employ with great caution, and restraint; otherwise a weapon capable shipboard, where such devices run much less shielded, much more naked, than is the case on the shore, of turning in an instant dangerous, pointed, dagger's edge, at oneself. I knew that I was utilizing this resource and felt I was staying within those limits. Having deliberately held it back, now was the precise time, I decided, to hit them with it. I spoke in the most judicious of tones.

"I should point out that all the balances don't strike one way; it wouldn't be exactly a handout. We have seven months' food supplies to his two. On the other hand, in respect to nuclear fuel, of which Mr. Melville has just told us we have six months remaining . . . well, he has two years' running time left on his cores."

"Two years!" came from the engineering officer. I could not remember his ever making a like exclamation.

"He showed me everything required to support that figure; showed me through his engineering plant—reactor hours in the log. I spent a time checking it out—more there than any other single place on the sub, except for that long discussion in the wardroom. He was very up front with me. I'd call the two-years figure firm."

I spoke carefully into the abrupt hush. "When this ship stops moving, his will have a year and a half steaming time left on her. Speaking of having something up one's sleeve, it might be worthwhile on our part to take that fact into our considerations as to his proposal."

The point needed no elaboration now nor the implications; not to nuclear sailors. On that score comprehension was complete and instant in every officer present. Expressions alone said that. Nothing I had brought back from my visit aboard the Russian sub, other than that other terrible news, was anything like so important. An awesome new element had entered the equation. One felt something like a fear in all even to give voice to the enormity of the resource so suddenly appearing on our horizon: beyond all valuation. I moved—slyly—on.

"Just a thought, a possible trade-off: our sharing our food stores with him if it becomes necessary; in return his sharing the fact of having a long-fuel-reserve vessel under him if that becomes necessary; if ours runs out before we find something . . . if it came down to that." I stopped it there.

"Are you saying, sir . . . " Bainbridge, the communications officer, his words a kind of gasp, part chill, part a lifting hope as to immeasurable betterment of our circumstance.

"All I'm saying, Mr. Bainbridge, is that if we ran out of fuel, the land so far being as is, uninhabitable, I would rather have a ship alongside me that could still navigate than to have only an empty sea."

221

I could see Thurlow's mind working: "Captain, what did you say was the size of his crew?"

"One hundred and twelve officers and men."

The navigator came down on it directly. "I have in mind personnel accommodations—if things ever reached that stage."

"Well, no, he doesn't have that kind of space now. Not for all of us. I suppose if he cleared out his missiles—two-thirds of the ship—he could take on a good many more. Still not all of us . . . perhaps a half of ship's company . . . " It was time to sheer off; frightening possibilities lay just beyond, one dared not so much as approach them; my purpose achieved, give the idea itself time to take hold. "These matters are far on the horizon. I want it understood that I have not discussed any such contingencies with the Russian captain. To suggest to him that he jettison his missiles, for instance: Speaking of someone else's suspicions, he might throw me off his ship. I wouldn't blame him. However, if we ourselves should come to lean affirmatively toward his proposal—joining company, you may be sure I would open up everything . . . extract the firmest of stipulations before any agreement was entered into. No doubt he'll have a few of his own. Best to think about all this for a spell. I simply wanted that resource of his—his nuclear fuel—factored in. Now let's leave this matter for the time being. Other questions?"

They caught their breath for a bit from that last element, then came on, randomlike. Girard:

"Captain, with all that fuel, wouldn't you think he'd spend some of it having a look at his own place? At Russia? He doesn't have our problem of choices."

"Yes, Miss Girard, I would. I mentioned that. One reason only, he said. He was afraid that if he approached it . . . no matter what the rem readings . . . he was afraid some of the crew—maybe even most of them—would simply jump ship—pop off into the water, trying to make it ashore. May not be so farfetched. It doesn't take a great stretch of the imagination to see some of ours, in the same situation, doing the same thing."

"Jesus-god," Girard said.

"Captain?"

The voice hesitant: It was Ensign Jennings, a junior officer of the deck, seated furthest down on the left, in the lowliest chair; the first time he had spoken. At twenty-two he was the youngest officer aboard, the most junior in rank; married a week before the ship last sailed from Charleston harbor; home Tulsa, Oklahoma, one of those "deep interiors"

222

of which Selmon had spoken. Of all the officers, there was none about whom I had been more concerned.

"Yes, Mr. Jennings?"

"Does that fuel of his mean we might do both?"

"Both?"

"Sir, I mean take a look at home—and still have enough left to look for—look for . . . " He almost stuttered. "Some new place . . . "

So that idea had at last penetrated their consciousness. I spoke gently. "I don't think the logistics would work out that way. Many reasons: the first being I don't believe the Russian captain's idea of going along together would extend to making that kind of heading. If he won't go to his own home he certainly won't go to ours."

"Captain, you say this is the same sub that followed us off Brittany?" From down the table, Chatham again. "Did he say what he was doing there?"

"Indeed he did. He'd taken out our submarine base at Rota. Also the three SAC bases around Zaragoza. He described these actions to me straight off. Do you have a point, Mr. Chatham?"

"I just wanted that made clear. What he's already done to us."

I dealt fast with this. "Clear as what we've done to them."

"Sir, I'm having this problem of when we started believing Russians. I'm talking about the report itself—the one Mr. Selmon has so neatly based all his projections on."

This statement, the questioning of all the assumptions, seemed to ripple down the table, past all officers, layering a residue of tangible disquiet. Suggesting a lurking eagerness even with them to reject or at least permit doubts as to the thing evidence suggested, believe the thing it went against; so strong was the pull. So dangerous was this, for a moment the words were on my lips to slap it down, to come back at him. I hove to. It was not the time for it. A wrong step could only stoke schism. Besides, all opinions must be here allowed. I looked thoughtfully down the table at him a long moment; making certain to speak quietly; at the same time to move away from it.

"Yes. Well, of course you have a right to your opinion, Mr. Chatham. I think that's about it. We'll talk again when I've seen him next. Oh, yes. I almost forgot. In the meantime he did offer us one thing we don't have. A dentist."

"Did you say dentist, sir?" the doc said.

"He was surprised we didn't carry one. A little smug about his ship's superiority in that respect, I think. I don't know whether Russians have more problems with their teeth—I suggested as much as my comeback—but there it is. *Pushkin* carries a dentist in ship's company. The captain offered his services for any dental problems we might have."

"I'd like the first appointment." Bainbridge spoke up. The communications officer had had recurrent dental troubles.

"Doc?"

"I'd say about a dozen cases in the crew, Captain. I mean needing dental attention quite badly."

"Send him a signal, Doc," I said. "He's expecting it. Make arrangements to take the men over."

"Will do, sir."

"Anything else for the present? I don't want to keep the men waiting."

"Captain, I'd like to say something."

"Say ahead, Mr. Chatham. Make it as brief as possible."

"Speaking as CSO, and giving a general reaction, I have to be a shade alarmed about these . . . let us say, affiliations, interchanges. How do we know he's not using them as a cover; planning to blow us out of the water?"

"I suppose in the same way he knows we're not planning to blow him out of the water."

"Is that good enough, sir?"

"I'm afraid it'll have to be, Mr. Chatham. Unless our first priority is to blow each other up."

"That wasn't what I had in mind, sir."

"I know what you have in mind, Mr. Chatham." I spoke more sharply. I was trying in every way to remain open but I had had about enough for one day of the combat systems officer. "Even if it made any sense—it doesn't—it wouldn't work. He'd have a nuclear torpedo—he has quite a large supply on board, I inspected them . . . he'd have one of those C-533's into our belly by the time the Harpoons landed on his sail area. He's got lookouts all over, you may be certain of that, watching us, just as we have lookouts all over watching him. All his electronic gear zeroed in on us, exactly as ours is on him. He's at point-blank range. His would be on its way a second after ours. They'd probably pass each other en route."

"As a matter of fact," Chatham said, "I was thinking of something else. We've got the superior forces. Deck firepower, no comparison. It's just possible we might do it so as not to sink but capture him, with that fuel reserve. I think there are ways to pull it off, surprise him. I have in mind a plan, if I have the captain's permission . . . "

"You do not have it," I said. "Leave it, Mr. Chatham."

"Henry, if you're going to do anything like that," Thurlow said, "let me know first, will you? I'd like to get off."

For a moment Chatham's line of thought had injected a certain tension in the air, and of a different kind than that before. It was not unnatural. Destroyer men and submariners: no more congenial mortal enemies exist on the seas, each committed to the annihilation of the other. Suspicion would die hard: it had by no means died in myself; though since preferring it to remain muted for the time being in order to give unfettered consideration to the Russian's proposals, I was glad for Thurlow's interjection, which broke the tension. I heard some small laughter from around the table. But it did not make Chatham himself happy.

"I'm sure that's very witty, Mr. Thurlow. Myself, I think we're being a little too much of the buddy-buddy with this Russkie. Or since that expression seems to bother you, is it comrade-comrade?"

"Jesus Christ, Henry!" the navigator suddenly exploded, turning hard in his chair on his fellow officer. "Does it make any difference? Now?"

"Of course I don't have your advantage," Chatham said in that quiet, rasping voice of his which when he turned it on could have made saints growl, "of having spent all that time in Russia."

"Too bad you didn't, Henry," Thurlow shot right back. "Might have loosened your bowels."

From down the table I heard something between a smirk and a giggle from Lieutenant Girard.

"Come on, Mr. Chatham," she said in that condescending air she employed seldom but often to great effect when she did. "They're not going to eat us."

"Not me, anyhow," Chatham said, no slouch at this sort of thing himself. "You'd probably be their first course, Miss Girard . . . "

My hand hit the table, hard—coffee cups jumped.

"Gentlemen," I said. "Miss Girard. That's enough. Nobody's being buddy-buddy here. We're not simpletons. But nobody's going to launch any ASROCs or Harpoons and we're not going to mount any 'surprise' attacks either. Since we're also not fools."

"I still say instead of this cozening, we ought to be thinking about how to get him before he gets us."

That did it. Unable any longer not to strike back—point-blank range myself, with all my authority, I looked straight down the table at him. I could hear my own voice, steely-quiet.

"I'll say this just once, Mr. Chatham. You are to cease and desist: any such thinking. Starting right now. I don't want to hear one more word in that direction. That's an order. Is that clear to you, sir?"

Giving praise, it should be done in front of others; dressing an officer down, in private. It was a cardinal rule for a ship's captain. Perhaps I should have taken him aside, afterward. I must have decided that the course he was pursuing had to be stopped, brought dead in the water, even that it had to be done in the presence of the other officers, since that was where he had raised the idea, lest they, or some of them, pick up on it; this in turn then spreading a virulence, an active hostility, in this ship toward the one lying so near, render us unable even to give thought to possible advantage in some kind of arrangement with her. Later I was to think that something had hardened in Lieutenant Commander Chatham at that moment; though, perhaps in self-assuagement, I judged it was bound to have happened in any case. For now I was aware of the taut air that had suddenly filled the wardroom; then Chatham's response, one I never liked.

"As you say, sir."

My own tone quiet and firm as before. "Let all officers understand exactly what our position is. If they mean us harm we'll be ready for them. We'll keep on full alert. Full manning of all sensors; extra lookouts. That's it. No more, no less. He's the only ship we've met, for God's sake. The only one not full of corpses," I said with a kind of cold savagery. "Those on that submarine are men, like us. They are human beings. Now let's see what's in that fact for us. For all of us. There aren't enough around even to think about knocking each other off, for God's sake. End of discussion."

I was on the point of rising when Girard asked another question, in a voice that fell the more deeply after that exchange, for its softness of tone.

"Sir, did the Russian captain say how it started?"

For a moment I didn't know what she meant. When I realized, I suppose I was faintly surprised; even startled. Of all the questions on our minds, I expect that was the one in which we had come to have the least interest; hardly a matter even of intellectual interest by now, grossly unimportant; become banal, I would say, to men intensely occupied with more pressing matters.

"Why, no, Miss Girard. He didn't." I seemed to speak as softly as had she. "I'm not sure the subject ever came up. With everything else, I guess we just never got around to it. I'll try to remember to ask him next time; if he knows."

"I was just wondering," she said, almost apologetically.

"Right. Well, now. Let's go," I said, getting up. "Time to tell the men."

They stood, every hand except the most minimal of watches (extra crew, however, keeping eyes both visual and electronic locked on the Russian submarine), crowded into the largest free space on the ship, the fantail; gazing up at me where I had mounted the after missile launcher. To a sailor no more deep-felt word exists in the language, and I used it now as my first.

"Shipmates," I said.

I waited, gathering my thoughts. I had to tell it; there was no question as to that, of giving them anything other than the straight substance of it. The question facing me was rather whether to offer precisely the same report as that Selmon had the officers, in those same unrelenting terms. The only reason for not doing so was my fear that a certain number, enough so as to affect the welfare and even the operation of the ship, hearing it might cross over that line I was beginning to feel was already stretched dangerously thin, and becoming more so, with an increasing number of the crew, the line separating ability to function as men and as sailors and . . . I hardly dared say even to myself what lay on the other side of that line. I had come to this decision: to give them enough to understand what had happened, but not to assault them with the last brutal detail, not now. They were not a hundred percent without preparation: the failure of all our communications efforts to raise others had done an amount of that; by the same token had left the door of hope, by their nature close to inextinguishable, open. But here now were proclamations up by an order of magnitude: direct, positive reports asserting what had happened as opposed to the negative ones of silence. I further had a momentary hesitation as to how, thinking of simple tactics, to begin. Specifically, whether with the Frenchman or the Russian; deciding on the former; for a period of several minutes then, in the simplest way, recounting to them the information, the intelligence, contained in the two sources.

As I talked it seemed to me the silence only grew, became more piercing; deepened further, it may have been, by the total peace and silence of approaching eventide, the ship standing serenely, swinging not at all on her anchor, no wash even against her, the sea stretching away in a manner that first caught the ship's image as in a looking glass and then mirrored out to all horizons: to Europe in the distance (the absence of the great landmark Gibraltar seeming strange, almost disorienting, to

227

sailors who had been here before, nevertheless embraced by now in that ruthless acceptance which, greatest of gifts, had become part of us and—so far—kept steadfast); nearer, by the line of the north African strand sliding eastward toward Suez; a single object breaking those otherwise bereft waters, the Russian submarine lying visible to all five miles to the north-northwest. My words sounding bell-clear in that quietness, falling on ears, seemingly on the listening sea itself. When I had finished I waited, caught in a helpless caesura, looking down at them: their faces deliquescent with unutterable pain, assuaged only by bewilderment; frozen in the rictus of suppressed agony; a kind of slow-motion horror. I spoke to them.

"Of course we want to go home. The last one of us wants that."

The stillness maintained, heightened now to levels almost intolerable, a stillness as if not made of this world, rising from among them and cannonading back upon me like a field of force. I waited some seconds more and then came on hard, not hard in my voice, which I made certain did not change, in tone, in manner, but hard inside, hard as spirit could be, as strengthening not of them but of myself, to say what had to be said.

"We have many things to consider. Some of these are: All the evidence is that there is nothing to go home to. No home as we knew it to which we can go back. What basis is there for that determination? First, the simple fact that we have not been able to raise anyone there . . ."

I saw at once the fallacy of the argument. It was too late. The first response came in.

"But, Captain, you said yourself that communications have been knocked out so that whoever's there—home, I mean—couldn't tell us even if they were okay . . . " The voice stuttered, stumbled, in it a kind of tremor, half confusion, half despair, thin but almost defiant portion of hope one could not help but admire, while being instantly disturbed by it. "If some of them were okay."

"That's true," I said. "But we have the Russian sub commander's report."

"Since when . . . " It was another voice . . . "have we started trusting Russians?"

It was the same idea and for a moment—surely I was mistaken—I thought the same voice as in the wardroom. I could feel something swelling, a kind of undertone slipping through the men, moving upward, coming on at me. I heard an edge in my voice.

"What about the French?" I said. "Can we trust them? We have the *French* radioman's report saying pretty much the same thing. Some natural discrepancies from the Russian's. But essentially the same. And on the point we're talking about there is no disagreement at all."

"The Frenchman could have got it wrong." Still another voice from out there. I could not tell where or whom, and it didn't matter. "With all that was going on. Or some one could have deliberately fed him the wrong information . . . "

I brought everything in me to bear to keep patient. "A lot of ifs . . . " My voice hardening unwillingly . . . "to place against firm reports. Are we not to believe anybody?"

It had arrived, like ominous seas boarding a ship, what I had wanted above all else to avoid: Men simply refusing to believe what they did not choose to believe; told what I—and, all important, Selmon—judged to be the most solid information, short of what eye had beheld . . . this leaving the everlasting question of whether that final evidence would be required despite all . . . the awful sense rising cruelly in one that nothing short would in this lone instance ever satisfy them . . . The thing was to check it hard before it grew, took hold. I made my voice come back down.

"Shipmates, the point is, we can't afford to be wrong. If we went there and found nothing . . . no one to take us in . . . no land we could stay upon . . . no place we could stop ashore . . . we would have brought our fuel to a dangerous level. Mr. Melville has figured core reserves practically to the nautical mile and I have to tell you that those are the facts. Fuel we need to find a place that will accept us. We would have used up a large portion of it, so that if we found nothing there . . . It would be a desperate gamble . . . "

"Some of us are ready for desperate gambles . . . " For a moment I thought I knew whose voice that was; could not be certain, one soul speaking out of a packed assemblage of 300 . . . "What is this right now, if not the desperate?"

Something worse. The voice seemed almost to be speaking, not to me, the captain, but to the others around him, in tones of entreaty, of persuasion. I could hear the firmness in my own move up another notch.

"Listen to me. Listen well. Desperate now? I have to tell you that it can be far more so."

The tense stillness returned—men wary, but waiting, watching me with the eyes of lookouts; many—what number there was no way of telling—adversarial not to me, I felt, but to the news I brought; aware that the two could merge swiftly, indiscernibly, into a single hostile force. I spoke as though to each individually; no more loudly than before; but each sentence, each word, clear and hard as bullets aimed, in my own desperation, at a target I must not miss: their reason.

"At present we have the ship. The ship is the only home we've got and there is no other in sight; you have seen, all of you, what it is like on the beaches. But we will not always have the ship. When the fuel goes, she goes. And when the ship is gone, we will have no home. We have got to use the ship while we have her, while she can get us around. We have an amount of food. Neither is it unlimited. When the fuel is gone and the food is gone and we are still on the seas, having found nothing . . . We must not let that happen. We must use them both to one purpose: to find some place that will take us in. Otherwise we will simply come dead in the water one day; food running out; marooned on the sea. You know all of these things. Why have you forgotten them?"

I stopped. I had spoken with every intent of shocking them into their senses. That same intolerable silence again. Then a voice.

"I'm with the captain there. We can't afford sightseeing."

"Sightseeing?" The word came instantly back from somewhere. "You call it sightseeing to check out how things are . . . *home?* Well, by God. All these secondhand reports. Do we know?"

It came like a flash fire. I could only think: The men must not be set against one another. It was time to shut this down.

I spoke into the tenseness, in tones of reassurance.

"Shipmates," I said, "let us take an even strain. We are far from being without hope. The same fact of this ship beneath us: We have every right to think in terms of fair prospects. I have not decided against going home. I haven't decided our course at all. It is too early to do so. That land you see beyond the bow . . . " My head turned toward the line of the African continent. "We have not even begun to explore it. It may offer us a place, a habitable place, where we can dig in for a while, wait, perhaps in time hear directly from home . . . " I felt I was coming close to the line of offering too much, drew back from it . . . "If neither of these happens, when we reach Suez we will take a new look. Above all, we will not lose hope. There is no reason to do so. Hope—and fortitude . . . they will see us through."

I paused a few seconds, looking at them, they at me, in the great silence, broken only by the soft wash of the sea against the ship. I did it quickly. Feeling that the very fact of their staying assembled like this together would touch off something. I told them of the Russian submarine's proposals that we join forces, go in company, that I had not decided as to it. And wanting, I think, to leave them with a little shock, added, a bit brutally: "By the way. The Russians are not going home. They have the sense to know they cannot. Just something for you to be thinking about. That is all. Let us stand down for now. Ship's company dismissed."

For a moment they remained where they were; then began, with infinite slowness, as of men unresolved, men full of immense, all-baffling quandary, to disperse. As I stepped down from the launcher and started through them, I heard a low voice: "Why can't we take a vote on it?" I snapped around; a movement purely reflexive. Only silence. I was on the point of asking who had said that; realizing that was the worst thing I could do; dangerous at that moment even to challenge it; turning back, continued on. The men broke ranks to let their captain through. As I passed through them, it was as though on a swelling of silent murmurings, things unspoken but heard, as of a ghost wind, itself mute but audible as are all winds, beginning to freshen ominously through the ship's stilled halyards; certifying one thing only in its discrete and unmistakable texture, its sole scent, indigenous, detectable by any sea captain, none so dread to a ship off soundings; combining with it a thought that brought the mind hard and still: that last voice was the same as before.

The sea keeping to its sacramental stillness under skies unstirred by a breath of wind, I stood on the starboard bridge wing in the lateness of night, watching her across the water, her huge length silhouetted under pale stars against the western horizon. Somehow the sea seemed less lonely, the darkness itself less solipsistic, with her sitting there, a live ship, with 112 well and breathing souls in her; seeming in the night's great peace that held everywhere more reassurance than threat; comforting, the nearness of fellow sailors. Seamen, I thought, are closer than nationalities. As if in validation, the yellow beacon of surfaced submarines in peacetime struck brightly from her sail area, one flash per second for three seconds, followed by a three-second off period, harmonic as a chord of music, endlessly repeating itself, the long spectral pattern of illumination piercing far into the night and across the five miles of water between us; striking us rhythmically in a contact itself of amicable nature, so intended, I felt, nothing requiring him to comply. Just above me, our communications sweep antennas on the mainmast: suddenly I was aware of it; looked up. I looked back at *Pushkin* across the water. A small doubt infiltrated. Why had he been able to raise people, ourselves not? If anything our own communications gear was more sophisticated than his, though it was true he had special devices installed in submarines with their greater difficulty in that area. When I had asked to listen in on his equipment, he had said that the messages came no more, not from anywhere, and seeing my skepticism led me then to his communications room—where operators always on duty, as on our ship, tried every frequency for me without result; myself listening in with spare earphones all the while. Idly now I trained my nightscope on her during the beacon's three-second off periods. Nothing. Then as I watched, I saw his antenna mast rise, startling me: something normally done by a submarine when some prearranged communication is to be made. It did not in itself mean that: He might simply be undertaking some general effort to raise others, quite as we did endlessly ourselves. Nevertheless, remembering his noting that all returns had long ceased, suspicion set in. It seemed possible even that the beacon flashes which I had judged turned on as a friendly act might have been meant instead to obscure the raising of the antenna—it was only by chance, and with the aid of the powerful starlight scope, that I had picked up the movement in one of the three-second off interims. I looked at my watch—was further disturbed to see its hands just passing straight up 2300; exactly. It was not unusual for such efforts as between two distant parties to be laid on at a precise on-the-even-hour. Thoughts tumbled in on me: Was Chatham right all along; something up his sleeve, as he put it? I could not believe it, having talked with the man. I did not like to believe I could be conned, and certainly not now, not on this; least of all by another ship's captain. Nevertheless I would ask him about that antenna mast: I would want an explanation.

Whether or not brought on by these misgivings, some sort of falsehood, surreptitiousness, some kind of duplicity at work, seemed to stain the pure sea air; the sense of danger about; a foreboding felt, untraceable as to source, as I continued to study the long shape across the water. Treachery? Always a possibility. By nature sailors trusted; by compensation, a sense of smell for true danger to themselves and their ship, whether from the sea or otherwise, was given to them highly astute. Accordingly I set about calmly, methodically, to think it through.

If we should go in company with him, and if the time, God stay it, should arrive that we came hove-to in the water, all engines stopped forever: at that point we would appear to be at his mercy. He would have under him a fueled, navigating ship; ourselves sitting aboard a dead one. He could refuse to take us aboard—yes, it was my intention that he do that, if matters so evolved; could simply leave us, make for the horizon; abandon us to our fate. I did not think he would do so. First, because I didn't believe he had that kind of surprise in mind; trust. One seaman's trust of another. Second: if the thought should occur to him I didn't imagine he had any great wish for his crew to starve. By that time he would be living off our food supplies. Coming down to this: each of us with a club held over the other: his, fuel; ours, food. I liked that. In an unknown situation it was always pleasant, a source of comfort, to have trust backed up by a good strong heavy weapon, the more lethal the better; it would be difficult to imagine a more effective one in that category than food. The mind gave up its conclusion: We could run safe with him. Mind, not quite resting, worked on a bit: presented another element to reassure: that other thing that had seemed to, well, almost stop the Russian in our dialogue—the moment it had come out, quite parenthetically, that we had women aboard, members of ship's company; his look of astonishment supplanted by a kind of wonder, a mixture on his face of awe and calculation, or so I judged it. His desire for our joining forces, going together, seeming then to me subtly to augment. It was at that point, without directly connecting the two, that he had mentioned it. I tried now to reproduce in my mind his precise language, this, I think: "Isn't that our chief responsibility, Captain? Isn't anything else trivial by comparison?" What a curious word it had seemed for him to use. "Responsibility." Then I thought: It was not strange that it should have been Girard who alone among the officers appeared to have got it: being not just a naval officer; being also a woman. The thing might appear too shadowy in the entire; but as I shut it down, leaving it in the penumbra in which it dwelled, it somehow seemed finally to lay treachery at rest.

These matters then passed and I had stood rather in peace, the healing power of the sea reaching in to me; the stars appearing exceptionally bright and wondrous, in their great multitudes filling clean skies; looking up now and then to study a constellation, check its position with a navigator's eye, a gesture always remedial; when that other long-familiar thing said it was now its turn, rose from that deep inside where I habitually kept it under the most infrangible of seals, breaking with all ease through these defenses to make one of its periodic visits; myself never knowing when that would be, its coming at me at times of its own choosing, whim, with no decipherable schedule. I looked far out across the dark plain of the sea. One sometimes felt madness like a shadow stalking one. One felt one had a different mind now from the one that had accompanied oneself through life; it spoke to me now, in all temptation. The earth simply could not be empty out there, beyond those horizons; some vast mix-up, collusion even, in all the reports; perhaps we should go home; find out. I realized with a shock that I was beginning myself to doubt the evidence; stepped back in horror from the thought. I felt an actual physical dizziness, as though teetering on the utmost edge of the abyss; looked over the bridge wing shield, straight down at the sea; *there* was the abyss. To just slip into it—the sea would probably throw back in rage any sailor who tried that. Certainly a ship's captain. With a sudden spasm of the body as from some unspeakable cowardice, I came back from it, slamming, as by an actual violent physical movement, the demon once again back into that quarantine from which he had for a moment escaped; came back for my soul's sake—for the souls of my ship's company, given everlastingly into my hands. I realized I was breathing hard; reached up and felt sweat on my brow in the cool night. Then all came calm again. Sanity speaking, its clear intent to put a little spine into me, who had blabbered of fortitude, to face the one question I knew to be free of all imaginings, as real as the sea all around me, as the stars above: Will ship's company not let their captain take the ship and them anywhere but home? Aware that my captaincy hung in the balance.

.2.

TURGENEV

We had reached, after more exchange visits, his coming to the *James*, my going to *Pushkin*, an agreement that cleverly—on both our parts, I felt, each captain precisely aware of what the other was up to, the object of each being identical, never saying so—postponed the question of whether we should join forces, go together, with an immediate plan of operations that seemed to both of us prudent in itself. He would explore the west coast of Africa. We would reconnoiter the north coast (as we had intended, in any case). Keeping in communication on an arranged frequency; if either found a habitable place, he would so inform the other; though no commitments as to merging forces made even so, this topmost matter deliberately left in suspension, unresolved. And during the exchanges, one great gift he had brought me. Suez was open. It was a stunning piece of news. I pressed him.

"There must be no mistake about this," I said. "We are low on fuel. It could greatly affect our course."

"We went ourselves to its mouth." He shrugged, utterly nonchalant. "Obviously for some reason our side wanted to spare it. Your side wanted to spare it." I thought: "Sides." He shrugged again. "More likely, just that there was no particular reason to take it out." He gave a sardonic grin.

"Of course, they could just have overlooked it on the list—it was a pretty long list."

Whatever the reason, it was an incandescently precious bit of knowledge I hoarded in my innermost heart.

Otherwise: I was satisfied with this arrangement. It felt right. So were my officers when I presented it to them—even Lieutenant Commander Chatham. Nothing could be lost by it. It would give us time to decide as to the larger matter. One was nagged by amorphous feelings, making for irresolution. As if we were missing some element, so far elusive, needed to make the final decision. The interlude, besides allowing time to appraise and reflect, seemed also to offer an opportunity to test the Russian's bona fides: constituted somehow in his mission to West Africa. Surely on his part for him to test ours as well; none of this voiced, the negotiations being conducted on both sides with a subtlety, an obliqueness, that would have done honor to the Jesuit; but unmistakably understood by both of us. Chatham, while concurring, had by no means sanctified the Russians: "Captain, he may follow us clandestinely. We know the Russians had got pretty far up the road to perfecting a silent propulsion system." He had a point. Still, I had sighed. "We'll see, Mr. Chatham. We'll see. I have great faith in our sonar gear—I always felt we stayed a step ahead of their progress in that respect." Thurlow, at the mention of this at the officers' meeting, had suggested lightly that as a protection against such deception, Chatham be assigned liaison duty in the submarine. The combat systems officer was not amused. At all events it was a decision that seemed right, as I have said, so felt by all; leaving as it did all options as to any kind of conjunction open as could be.

Then, on my last visit, meant as a courtesy call more than anything, we reached, almost fortuitously, it seemed at the time, almost by a chance remark of his which he might very well not have made, another arrangement which embodied commitment, however dependent on an eventuality which I felt remote, certainly more remote than did he; which contained, in fact, the seed for changing everything and which I chose to keep secret from all of my officers save two; in part because of the long odds as I saw them; more important, because I felt even its possibility might weigh too heavily in our decision of where to go; distort, perhaps even lead to the wrong decision. Fortuitously, I said. Later I was to think there was nothing of chance to it, that he had shrewdly planned it, perhaps from the beginning, or more likely from the first moment of learning the distinct nature of the ship's company of the *Nathan James;* the very fact of saving it until the last, springing it, seeming to validate this notion.

Before that I had had something of my own to get out of the way and came right to it. We were alone in his cabin, having a farewell cup of that excellent tea of theirs. I looked very carefully at him. Then sprang it myself, watching his eyes as I did.

"Captain, what was your antenna doing being raised at twenty-three hundred two nights ago?"

There was no change at all in his expression. "We were running a drill," he said.

"Oh, I see. Good to keep the crew on their toes, isn't it?"

"I find it so."

He refilled teacups from a pot on the small table. I started to . . . then thought no. Give him any benefit of doubt on this one. It was not the time to question his word. Certainly not on such scant evidence, little more than suspicion; don't back him into a corner. We came away from it, relaxing a bit. Matters then suddenly quiet, the bond of the sea seeming to bring us together; beyond that, that special and peculiar affinity between ship's captains, of whatever nationality, all beset by the loneliness of command, none able to talk with unfettered fullness to anyone on his own ship; infinitely rewarding, a treasure often sought out when available, ships in port, to speak freely with one in the identical circumstance, under the identical burden; and now many other unvoiced things as well binding us, the chief of these being: how many of us remained, anywhere? We both spoke quietly, without constraint.

"Where is your home, Captain?"

"Insofar as I have one—Charleston, South Carolina."

He smiled softly. "I've seen it—through a periscope."

"Yours?"

"A place called Orel. You probably never heard of it."

My heart skipped a beat.

"Wasn't it Turgenev's home?"

"Why, yes," he said, the note of surprise, not, patently, that I had read Turgenev but that I knew of these origins.

For a moment I thought I might. I was too cowardly. I sipped my tea.

"In addition to Turgenev I believe you had a few SS-18 silos there."

"True. Until last November. They were moved."

Perhaps—who can say as to these things? . . . perhaps even that . . . surprise . . . was to lead in some way not immediately apparent to what followed; who can ever know what will be a catalytic agent to the unexpected, trigger the otherwise not-to-be? For the moment I was concerned only with, yes, personal control of myself. I looked at my hand on the teacup. I was afraid to lift the cup; afraid fingers would tremble. An actual dizziness seized me. I knew only that I must get away from it. Maybe that realization leading to the next thought and it leading in turn in its mysterious and circuitous way to his proposal. I cannot say. In any event, almost desperate to remove myself from the trap that had suddenly reached out for me, mind said: Why not that? Why not say to him, a fellow captain, what I could not say to a soul aboard my own ship; unburdening itself can clear the undecided mind for action, and a rare opportunity for that luxury sat before me.

"If Africa fails us . . ." I hesitated ". . . I haven't decided whether to take the ship to America."

"America?" He looked at me as if I had taken leave of my senses; sipped his tea before speaking. "Captain, you will forgive me—that is madness. As it would be for me to make a course for my own country. In either case: It would be like stepping into a furnace."

I looked at him, searching his eyes. I thought I had never seen eyes so blue, honest eyes, if I could judge men. The more I had come to know him, the more I thought it just possible that we could run together. By now, the matter postponed, as noted, we had an unspoken pact not to refer again to that possibility; everything we said as though the idea of joining forces had not been discussed, was not among the available choices; inside, each never forgetting it was. For that reason alone, I think we never ceased that other and perhaps more critical matter going on below the surface of our conversation, of estimating, appraising, each the other.

I sipped tea also. "The men may demand it."

The quick nod from him. Both absolutely understanding two things difficult to convey to landsmen: a captain's vast powers; yet the extreme risks. The latter especially applying now.

He would not ask, though it would have been obvious. But I decided, in this new burst of confession, to say it anyhow.

"If not that, it'll be the Pacific. By the most direct course. We have enough for that one thing. Just barely."

"Fuel," he repeated, and waited. I thought for a moment the word was almost a cruel taunt, his having so much, ourselves so little. If so, the word as said seemed more than that as well; one sensed a door opening a crack. He waited, some moments now, again filled our teacups; sat back and regarded me thoughtfully.

"Captain, have you ever heard of a place called Karsavina?"

I knew with great intimacy the names, purposes, and resources of

238

their bases, as well as he knew ours, particularly their bases on the northern tier, the Barents and the Siberian seas, anywhere in the region of what had been our stalking ground, in reach of the *James*'s own missiles. This one I did not know. I shook my head.

"It may have been the one secret place, I mean absolutely secret." He gave a small laugh. "Not just from you. Even from us, for whom it was meant as the last lifeline. Listen to this. . . ."

I could hear his voice going on, something hypnotic about it, as though the words were casting a spell over me, something also nostalgic in them . . . a sailor's tone . . .

"I was a dozen miles off it once, not knowing then. In the Laptev Sea, making the run in summertime from Murmansk to Kamchatka. You know what was officially there? A research station for polar bears. I remembered later how you couldn't see a thing, only a couple of small buildings on frozen tundra, summer ice. A couple of thousand miles from anything. It must have been quite an engineering feat, building that thing underground through the permafrost. Oh, yes, we didn't steal everything, Captain," he said slyly. "We had a few brains of our own. Then after this . . ." His hand made an odd sweeping gesture. ". . . after the missiles . . . when the pulse hit, the EMP, all contact lost . . . a sealed envelope in my cabin safe to open if that happened. Its name—its purpose. That we could replenish there." He leaned forward on his elbows on the table so that his face was a couple of feet from mine. "A storage place for rods of highly enriched uranium fuel, Captain. It may be the only such remaining anywhere."

He stopped and we found ourselves looking quietly at each other in the great silence of the cabin; looking into each other's souls. One knew without words. Some kind of underlayer of unspoken language and knowledge that had been operating between two ship's captains, each able to see ahead to the other's purpose, intent. Then the words themselves, but confirmatory, heard like a siren song through the tumult of thoughts welling up in me, the unspeakable implications. The words going on . . . He had a remarkably soft voice, never raised, its effect now being to make it the more insinuating, persuasive without seeming to be . . .

"After West Africa—frankly, Captain, I don't really expect anything there—that's where I'm setting course. I'd be very surprised if your side ever had the idea of hitting Karsavina." He laughed mirthlessly. "After all, your country and mine, we were able to reach an agreement to save the polar bears, if not anyone else. If it's intact—and the odds ought to be at least even—I will pick up rods for the *Pushkin* to recore my reactors . . ." He was talking rapidly now, even a bit feverishly, as if on to ideas so transcendent in nature that all must give way before them . . . "I could pick up some for you. For the *Nathan James.*"

He stopped again, this time with an abruptness that seemed intentional, as if to let the idea hit in as hard as possible; sipped his tea and spoke more deliberately—did I detect a certain slyness in his voice as well? "Well, now, Captain. There is no reason I could not then proceed through the Bering Strait, around Vladivostok and Kamchatka—that is to say, where they were—straight down the longitude. I've checked positions on the charts." So he had prepared, none of this was impromptu as I had so naïvely judged, I thought, as what seemed like a barrage, myself all vulnerable, kept coming at me . . . "Should bring us out just about where you would be. We could . . ." He paused again, said the two words: ". . . join you. Bringing our little present for you. Some more tea?"

That was all. I was suddenly aware as not before of the personality with which I was dealing and it seemed at once more admirable and more frightening; more complex, certainly ever so much more formidable. And yet I had no feeling that it was an overreaching personality, concerned only with greed, exclusively with self-interest. Nothing more said from across the table. No more was needed. No vulgar quid pro quo, no crass bargain. Bargain there would be if I but said the word. The thoughts, the implications once again, all of them, in all their turbulence, fled through my mind in an instant as on some fast-forward time machine, implications at once dreadful and glorious, simultaneously all-enticing and flashing the most insistent danger signal. The deal, the exchange. Participation in the settlement—including surely, in the women. I sat there stunned, trying to grasp the meaning of it.

"That is quite an offer, Captain." He said nothing, a man not interested in axioms, waiting in all patience for my true reply.

During all of our passage I had not found myself full of particularly noble thoughts. My one thought rather had been to bring my ship's company through. Nor will I attach that encomium to the thought I had then. Rather I believe it was a natural process of reasoning, of logic, of natural sequitur almost, that this thought should follow that other overwhelming idea of their actually coming in with us to make together a single community—yes, though he had said not a word as to that, nothing could have been more clear. That "responsibility" he had earlier spoken of: I wish I could say that the decision I presently reached was based on such elevated perceptions, dealing as they did with something so transmundane, speaking as they did of some infinite and supreme duty; that a loftier man than I might have judged as overriding even that supposedly utmost allegiance to men whose fate he had so absolutely in his hands. It was not. Oh, perhaps there was something of this: It was but natural that the only known ones left should cling to one another. Otherwise: To speak of self-interest: I was thinking only of my ship's company, and of nuclear fuel—how it would free us from the prison, even the tomb, the death ship, that the *Nathan James* was soon certain to be, come forever dead in waters unknown; permit us to check out home, come back to some island then if we wished or were forced to; enable us to explore just about everywhere. There seemed no price too excessive to pay for that. Indeed it would be accurate to say that, save for that brief ferment, I was oblivious, even blinded, to what the price would be; refused to think about it in the face of such unassessable bounty. The price will lay over. Get the fuel; then deal with whatever there may be to deal with. I could think no other way.

There was another thing. Something told me as of an absolute, something about the very essence of the man I was coming to realize I was dealing with across the table, that the deal must be made now; now or not at all. That discussion—starting with how the thing was to work— would only open the door to such vast and impervious complications, such an immensity of obstacles, even traps, in the idea as to kill it from their very weight: the deal, the offer, even withdrawn; snatched back. Once suspicion got in the door, it would corrupt the entire cabin. The idea— offer—must be taken in its purity—or refused point-blank; complex negotiations left for another time, another sea; for the reason that the offer's essential was trust, on both sides, and without that there would be no reason to proceed in any case. Hardly realizing I was saying it, seeming as much listener to as speaker of my own words, I said:

"Let's do it, Captain. Yes, I'll have some more tea."

What followed was simply two seamen at work in the most methodical, emotionless fashion. We might have been a couple of young navigation officers bent over a compass rose plotting the most favorable course between, say, Charleston and Bermuda. An actually enjoyable interlude, both of us natural sailors, liking hands-on work, especially the marvelous art of navigation. Teacups placed aside, charts brought out, spread, pored over; the two separate routes, for submarine and destroyer, sketched in; the most pragmatic working out of details, as to communications, as to frequencies. Even prescribed times laid on for his surfacing, raising antennae to receive, as I had seen him do two nights ago. He would report progress; as would I. My explaining to him that I intended to keep the matter secret from my ship's company in order not to raise false hopes should he come up empty, his messages would be sent in Russian. Thurlow—whom I had brought along on some of my visits to the submarine—himself sworn to secrecy, bringing them directly to me, doing the translations. Each would keep the other informed of his position; of what he found; ourselves, if the Mediterranean yielded nothing, headed on a S. by S.E. course for the Pacific (kept submerged in my consciousness, other than that one allusion, the one great incertitude of whether ship's company would take choice out of my hands); *Pushkin*, having completed the West Africa reconnoitering, setting a course N. by N. by N.E., up through the North Atlantic into the Norwegian Sea; the Barents; the East Siberian Sea—and Karsavina. Already become a hallowed word to me, I first saw the place then on the charts. It seemed in all truth a place in nowhere. Actually looking at it, it seemed the center of the universe. I was almost carried away, had to fight back the soaring emotion of the idea. Finally even working out a code word should he in fact find the nuclear fuel. It appeared a very obvious, natural choice. Turgenev.

We talked a little more. I prepared to go; came back to civilities.

"Captain, I want to thank you for the dental work," I said. "Those nine men, three women—they're enjoying life considerably more now. Oh, yes: if you can wait for our boat before casting off."

"Your boat?" he said, not understanding.

"It'll be alongside in a half hour."

I stood up, he with me. It came out of me, suddenly, quietly.

"What went wrong, Captain?"

He waited. Then a hand came up and touched my shoulder, rested there for a moment, fell away. An almost wistful smile.

"Who was ahead of whom?"

"It didn't make much difference, did it?"

"None at all."

He waited a moment. "Captain, together we could start the world over."

Cigarettes. I had discerned that this was what they missed more than anything. They were completely out. I could help but little. Cutting into our precious stores by twelve cartons—a pack for each hand aboard the sub. Our boat carrying them returned, hoisted aboard; he had blinkered his thanks as we stood away from each other, each vessel heeling gently. A rain had begun to fall and I could see his long gray shape beginning to move through the mists, the flashing light just decipherable. Then he was gone, headed around Morocco's curve on his course down the west coast of Africa. Then over the top of the world . . . Karsavina. Then I was thinking about another Russian place-name. Orel. The crew must never know; know what a waste it was.

As I said, other than Thurlow, I told but one officer of all this in regard to the nuclear fuel, that one sworn to secrecy. I informed Lieutenant Girard. I felt almost, as leader of the women, that she had a right to know. Otherwise I alerted Lieutenant Bainbridge, my communications officer, to the fact that we would be keeping contact with the *Pushkin* and gave him the frequency, doing all this in a routine matter, his patent acceptance that it was but natural that the two ships should do so; as to the Russian's course, the cover story he and I had come up with to explain the points on his journey from which we would be hearing from him, and now passed on to Bainbridge, was that he had decided after all to take a look at his homeland. Aside from all that, the high emotion at the prospects: These I felt dampening down, perhaps my making them do so, in the more somber realization, now that I was back on the *Nathan James,* of the outside chance of the thing.

Nevertheless, the deal having been made concerning a place called Karsavina . . . this, and perhaps even more, the idea of another ship out there: the world seemed a less lonely place.

We stood east toward Suez.

.3.

THE COMBAT SYSTEMS OFFICER

Shipboard, that intact palatinate bounded so tightly by the forbidding walls of the great sea, more than most places minds can imagine things, a condition compounded in an order of magnitude by present circumstances, where even the outright hallucination is not entirely stranger to us. Nevertheless, a captain's tendency is to err on the side of caution. There are so many necessary risks to take at sea—why take unnecessary ones? It was something I had had in mind for some time to see done, recent events somehow seeming to instill in me an urgency about it; not to put it off any longer. Propelled, I felt, into the decision by two particulars not in any way connected in my mind. One, a captain's sense of the beginnings of a certain disquietude abroad on the ship, the possibility that it might enhance, heading in directions no one could predict in the tight world of a ship at sea, notably one in our situation. The other, something in his behavior that kept nagging at me. The last-named stimulus for the action of course never to be communicated to him by the slightest hint, a scrap of intimation. Among other reasons, that all my thoughts concerning him and that subject were imprecise as could be, conjectures as to causes and possible intent quite likely imaginary—"imaginary" things were virtually endemic in ship's company these days, and even a ship's captain was by no means immune, nothing in the remotest tangible to support them. Nevertheless, I would ask him—in effect order him to do it. He would not like it. When that was the case, my method had always been to make it short and sweet, to the point, a direct order.

He was an unlikely leader of dissenting men. Yet if it ever came, I thought, it would come from him; the only officer I in any way looked upon as dangerous: some of this deriving from the fact that, short only of the captain, he was the most powerful officer aboard. Combat systems officer. Some to that captain's compass, that inner voice which in my years of command I had learned to listen to as to the sounds of the sea itself, in respect to a ship's company and conditions aboard my ship; both giving off signals, scents, intimations as to imminent behavior.

He was a man virtually without humor; rather difficult to talk with on any subject outside his field. But there, in his specialty—immensely complex, replete with consummate dangers, some esoteric in the extreme—he was an absolutely first-rate officer. I felt all the luck in the world to have him on the *Nathan James*. I had always given him the highest fitness reports the Navy allows, always recommending accelerated promotion. He seemed not to like or at least to enjoy people very much—not necessarily an absolutely negative trait. Perhaps as replacement, he clearly had a feeling kindred to love for the missiles, using the word in the sense applied to some men who might love to a certain obsession gardening or a particular sport, extending in his case, I had sometimes felt, to harboring an almost prescriptive right to them as belonging in fee simple to himself, a touch of arrogance in his proprietorship; something I had once found vaguely disturbing, even ominous, before deciding it was but a fancy of mine, nonsense in fact, facilely interpreting a necessarily meticulous and commendable care as a somehow sinister or suspect fondness, attachment, to them. As I continued to observe Chatham at his duties, I had come full about from this view to one of being profoundly grateful that they were the direct charge of one so immersed in their behavior and every aspect, a dedication which included the resolve that their presence—sometimes they seemed like sentient members of the crew—should not be allowed to threaten others of ship's company. In part due surely to his superlative mastery of his field, the enlisted men appeared to have a special respect for him—a common circumstance aboard men-of-war at work here, and one little known outside the seagoing world. One of the most distinguishing aspects of the shipboard life from the land life is that sailors care far less than do landsmen about the so-called "popular" aspects of the people set over them. The tradition is deep and ancient, for a reason: In the sea way, a man's very life often depends directly on an officer's ability, and there has never been a sailor but who, given the choice of a captain or an officer with somewhat hard-nosed "tight ship" tendencies who knows his seamanship and an excessively lenient and pleasing one who does not, will instantly choose the former. Lieutenant Commander Chatham was a superbly qualified sea officer, a natural leader of men.

Chatham, among naval officers of my acquaintance, had been one of the most vigorous in his opposition to the introduction of women into ships. This was not anything against him, or in any way unusual. If there had been a fleet-wide plebiscite on the matter, no woman would have got within a thousand leagues of a ship, and she would have had to swim that. So had I been counted in their number. My attitude after they had been aboard awhile had become more complex than formerly. Chatham, I was certain, had changed not in the smallest degree in this matter. On the other hand—and this was much to his credit—once they arrived, he had neither said nor done anything against them; in the realization, I felt, that their being here at last and nothing in the world to be done about it, however stupid the entire idea, not to accept it and work with the fact would threaten, perhaps disastrously, the welfare and even the mission of the ship. He was much too much a sailor to allow himself to behave in that direction; and especially embodying as he did that mission on this particular ship more than any other single officer. One could observe in him no difference whatsoever between his conduct toward the men and the women officers aboard, or in his treatment of the men and the women enlisted personnel; if anything, aware of them, perhaps compensating for his own now-suppressed opinions, being less abrupt with the latter than he sometimes was with the former. So circumspect was he in the matter of the women—the bending over to be fair, to display no antagonism toward them that might be taken as related to the fact of their not being men, almost as if to say they couldn't help that—that I was as certain as I could be of anything that the dislike Chatham and Girard had, and just of late, taken to each other had nothing to do with their gender difference.

As to its actual cause I had given little thought, had but indifferently wondered why. A ship's captain is a busy man. He has little time for nonsense. Such dislikes, as a rule temporary, between members of a ship's company, especially officers, enlisted men being much more sensible in this area, are not all that unusual, may crop up from time to time in the best of ships, often as not from unbelievably trivial causes, as suddenly disappear. A captain's wisest course is often not to interfere, to let the matter work itself out—until if and when it begins to affect the operations, the essential harmony of the ship. If that happened, you undertook to straighten it out by bringing the two officers together in your cabin, closing the door, and knocking their heads together: That, in my experience, usually put a stop to it. If that didn't work, you saw to it that one or both were transferred. Hardly an available option now.

I had commenced by telling him that I wished to go over the inventory of all the weaponry, the armory and ammunition list, from sidearms to missiles, in his books and also on-site inspections, a routine duty of a ship's captain to be carried out from time to time, not done lately due to the press of circumstances, and had set a date. We had completed the on-site part. It was late in the day, the sun moving down the sky and not far from its nocturnal home in the expectant waters. We were about to return to my cabin, over the weather decks rather than down to the main deck and inside. For no reason we paused a moment to gaze at the after missile launcher, its honeycomb of blast doors closed, its capability scarcely touched, only six cells empty. Fifty-five missiles—Tomahawks, ASROCs, Harpoons, Standard SM-2's—remaining. The same with the forward missile launcher. We continued forward to the cabin. I shut the door and we settled in.

When one thought of Chatham physically the adjective "round" immediately occurred: moon-faced, imbedded in it close-set eyes seeming also perfectly round and as unrevelatory as an owl's, a ball of a head on which grew a burry meadow of buff-colored needles kept always so close-cropped as each individual hair to seem razor-sharpened, atop a body whose further suggestion of roundness probably came from the feeling that he could lose twenty pounds of weight. That part, anyhow, had begun to change lately, as it had with all of us, I thought as I looked at him, on the reduced rations I had instituted. That decidedly circular appearance further accentuated by his being distinctively short. He was one of those men who carry through life the high advantage of looking much less intelligent than they actually are; the gift of appearing far less formidable than is in fact the case. In Navy terms he would be thought of as an officer who went by the book; while fair, an officer not to be messed with. If matters came to that, ready to hit back about twice as hard as he had received. He was as much of a loner as life on a destroyer will permit. Where other officers off-watch might be found in the wardroom shooting the breeze, Chatham was likely to be in his stateroom or the department office, studying tactics or systems, always attending everlastingly to his lethal charges. Even on liberty—when we had had that luxury—where both officers and bluejackets customarily go ashore in pairs or more, he went alone if he went at all, and as to whether his destination in Naples, for example, was the Museo Nazionale or a whorehouse off the Galleria I don't think anyone on the ship could have said. He was not easy company. I often had no idea what he was thinking. And never the slightest notion of what his inner life might be; his cautious air, not infrequently verging on the hubristic, effectively shutting off any remote view of such a territory. He projected a sense of seeming a rather uncomplicated, readable human being where I knew the opposite to be the case. I had long since given up on insofar as "knowing" him as I did my other officers. He was not to be known. Talking with him one had the feeling that he himself knew exactly what was in his own mind; that he was thereby entirely freed up to concentrate exclusively on what was going on in yours, your purpose, with the object of turning matters, whatever they might be, to his own preferences. He was unusually successful at these intricate, talent-requiring exercises. I got right to it.

"The small arms," I said. "I note how accessible they are, ready to use."

"Accessible? Yes, sir." Chatham had a habit of repeating the operable word one had just used. "So they can be got at in an emergency. To repel invaders. Hostile boarding parties."

I could hear my voice modulate if only a notch from ease to firmness.

"Hostile boarding parties?" I said. I decided, rather small-mindedly, to use it on him. What an odd phrase it seemed anyhow, I thought, in respect to any members of the race of human beings thus far encountered—for some reason a memory of those helpless wretches on the beaches of Amalfi for a moment stabbing at me. "I don't think we'll have many of those to repel. I want the small arms put under lock and key. Along with the ammunition. Remove them from the ready service lockers and put them in the high security lockers in the armory."

I could see the quick startlement in his eyes, a flash of anger, both as quickly, consciously, it seemed, quelled, return to impassive countenance. One advantage of being a captain is that one does not have to give reasons.

"As you say, sir."

I wished he did not say, "As you say, sir." Somehow it came across as a faintly reluctant compliance, especially so in that uninflected, monotonic voice he possessed that drilled in a kind of inflexible droning on the ear. It occurred to me how petty I was becoming in regard to Chatham, and made a note to watch that.

"When you've done that," I said, "bring me the locker keys."

It lasted but a moment, came and went as lightning does. But during it something malignant seemed to hang in the air, naked, a palpable tenseness, suggestive of something anarchic not just here but loose on the ship, exhaling the scent of menace, and but personified by the officer across from me. The response not coming with quite the automatic alacrity to which ship's captains are accustomed. For one suspended instant I felt he might be about to step across that most rigid of all Navy lines, insubordination. Not the first time for this series of impressions, of speculations—suspicions—from this same source, but more intense, stronger now, than ever before. I should have known better. Whatever lay in him, Chatham would never be the one to act rashly, let anger betray him into letting out a thing before the time he, not another, chose for it to be let out; far too self-controlled—and shrewd—an officer for that. I had caught myself fancifying, I decided. It was not exactly the kind of order any officer would find excessively pleasing. His reaction was but a natural one. He said only, "As you say, sir."

For that moment the cabin had been filled with a tense atmosphere so discernible as to surprise me. Then it was I who, sensing the possible high danger an inch away, pulled back from it. I added, wanting actually to soften it for him, to bend in his direction by a gesture of emollience, to give him a perfectly plausible and false reason for my action, face-saving for himself: "I intend that the keys shall at all times be in the custody of the officer of the deck. If needed suddenly."

He remained solemn; unspeaking; fooled, I knew, not in the slightest.

Keys. Perhaps reaction from that inner stab, perhaps partly from his attitude, his suppressed belligerence, it came surging up then from my mind. Other keys. That fact that only he held in his possession the key necessary to launch our missiles, jointly with myself, the familiar dual-key system, protection alleged against derangement or accident. And that in respect to those we carried for a total now of 704-H's, and whose fate and disposition I had not yet decided upon . . . I would not want them to come under Lieutenant Commander Chatham's control. For one implosive moment I fancied to ask for that second essential key; then stepped back, astonished at having it, frightened myself of the thought. That shared custody: It stood protected by the most inflexible of Navy directives, so that even for his captain to make such a request—demand—would be unthinkable, and should he do so, he entirely in his right to refuse—indeed, would normally face a GCM if he did not; and himself wholly aware of this circumstance. I dared not risk the confrontation. I was too certain that, the matter put to him, refuse he would. Indeed it would take a general court-martial instituted by myself to separate him from the key; some extreme act on his part, nothing remotely like any he had shown. I was startled to hear him say:

"Would the captain object if we ran a missile drill?"

As if reading my thoughts. This was a routine exercise, running through the complex procedure, identical in every detail to the real thing save only for the actual launching, the final instant, which we normally conducted about once a week; suspended by myself due to circumstances: other pressing matters, high unlikelihood of any imminent real application. The suggestion for renewal of the exercise might itself be taken as alerting the mind to something. It was almost as though Chatham, in riposte to my order concerning the small arms—an order about which he could do nothing—were reasserting, specifically to remind me of it, his other legal joint control of the missiles as something about which, in the exact same manner, I could do nothing. To remind me that he had most considerable power already, and of a nature untouchable by myself. He now added, almost in educatory tones:

"Otherwise the missile crew is certain to get rusty." His voice curiously tilted then, in it the faintest touch of condescension. "And we don't want that, do we, Captain?"

I looked at him steadily. "I hardly think we'll be sending anything off in the way of missiles in the immediate future, Mr. Chatham."

"With all respect, Captain. Is that the point?"

I did not even think of the impertinence. I was too occupied with a horrible unaccustomed feeling of being trapped, pushed into a corner by a subordinate reminding his captain of Navy doctrine, in this case that no one could predict in these matters what might happen even tomorrow, even today; hence, eternal state of readiness, indispensable to this condition what he was now suggesting.

"Very well, Mr. Chatham." I could feel a tightness in my voice; feel he was out-maneuvering me; felt helpless, decidedly not in the habit of feeling so, not at all liking it. I spoke crisply.

"Presently all hands are going to be too busy for drills of any kind for a while. With extensive lookout and other duties down this African coast. So make it tomorrow. So we can have done with it."

After all, my key canceled his. He could do nothing without it. I knew this was not a solace I would forever be content with; meantime feeling myself, by way of the keys each worthless without the other, locked inside a single, no-exit cage with Lieutenant Commander Chatham, with no visible or imagined means of either of us ever escaping this life's sentence of confinement with each other.

At least from this encounter I was about to acquire that other key, to the small-arms armory. Even that achievement was diluted by the clear sense I had that the very asking for it had alerted that exceptionally cunning mind of his to what was going on in my own; this in turn seeming to give him some unspecified advantage he had not had when this session began.

"As you say, sir."

There was one other thing I had been meaning to attend to. Now seemed suddenly an excellent time to do it. My voice had a captain's tone.

"By the way, Mr. Chatham. You and Lieutenant Girard. Whatever problem it is the two of you have, it's beginning to show, if you understand my meaning. It would be best all around if you worked it out. In fact, I shall expect you to do so, by which I mean sooner rather than later. I don't have to know what the problem is unless you wish to talk about it."

He smiled that smile of his that I sometimes thought was the worst part about him.

"Well, sir. As a general comment I'd say she figures everything out too closely for my taste. A calculating, uppity bitch I always had her in my book—if I may say so only to yourself, sir. I never liked uppity bitches, in uniform or out. Otherwise, in brief: It has to do with her keeping her nose out of other divisions' business. Specifically that of combat systems. I would have thought supply and morale should keep her quite busy. Beyond that I'd prefer you ask her."

"As you say, Mr. Chatham. I shall do so."

.4.

AFRICA

Foraging

Nothing. The destroyer creeping in toward shore, a lookout having fancied he may have noticed a suggestion of a movement through the Big Eyes, the 20-powered binoculars—a human being, an animal perhaps, a bird—where the white strand ends and the vegetation line begins; a stirring of the branches and leaves of trees by the wind it must have been. We return to the parallel course, generally staying close inshore. The ship ringed with lookouts; on the starboard side, the shore, for signs of life; on the port, the sea, for other ships. Steaming as we have been for days now at a bare six knots, a crawl for this destroyer, the better to pick up life to starboard; the ship's propulsion system muted like all else as she parts the stilled waters. The speed also fuel-saving, our reserves a matter on which my consciousness increasingly dwells with every turn of the twin screws. Slow ahead for another unrevealed reason: to give me all time possible to reach the decision that has laid siege to me, never truly ceasing to torment me out of that pool of anguish which has taken up a permanent abode in my soul. The continent passes by, voiceless both as to human sound and to any of that immense repertoire of sounds made by animals, by birds, in this land more blessed by their varieties than any on earth; a silent land, even the winds and the mirroring sea hushed in

252

a sympathetic quiescence; one listens for a heartbeat from it, as one might from a patient hovering between life and death.

Our interest, however, extends beyond animal life. We have begun to think in terms of objects useful to our future. The drill is, if a lookout spots anything appropriate, we stop the ship, lower a boat, a small party goes in, accompanied always by Lieutenant (jg) Selmon, who must first vet the object with his counter as not having an unacceptable level since above all we must not introduce contamination into the ship—Selmon, without whom we now go nowhere, anymore than a blind man would leave behind his seeing-eye dog; if approved, the bluejackets loading the item into the boat and returning, the boat hoisted back aboard, the ship getting underway again. The first acquisition a wheelbarrow near Temou-shant. Since then, among other objects, near Tetouan a bicycle, Mos-taganem a windlass and some rubber tires, El Asnam a canvas umbrella, Mers-el-Kebir beach chairs and table. And most important of all our foragings, these: Chief Gunner's Mate Delaney, having started his ship-board garden, whenever we stop, for whatever purpose, goes ashore and spends the time scouring the near countryside. Plants, when found prom-ising and provided they have passed Selmon's counter, he meticulously uproots and places in cut-down cans from the galley, carefully loads into the whaleboat, sees them aboard, and installs them in his growing racks.

Our full attention now turned to Africa's north shores. Any hopes we had as to these being hospitable to us are being rapidly dispelled on Selmon's counters, forays in the boat continuing to show prohibitive readings for any stay. I suppose I should have known. It is only that hope—and without that we cannot continue—so often gets in the way of confronting the probabilities. I should have known—perhaps I simply blocked the fact out—that the great oilfields would be near the top of somebody's list, deserving of the most massive treatment: Whose list is now hardly an object even of curiosity. The only thing of importance is that the further easterly the ship moves, the higher the readings.

Still, generally Selmon's readings have been no higher than were those on the European side of the Mediterranean. Why then have we seen no human beings, even standing on the beaches?

Amelioration

It was about 1700 hours, the sun moving steadily down a blue sky deco-rated prettily here and there with long streaks of cirrostratus, about to present us with twilight. We were proceeding on our parallel course, four thousand yards offshore, somewhat beyond Sidi Lakdar in Algerian waters.

Barker had the Big Eyes watch on the starboard bridge wing. I had stepped out there from the pilot house to study the shore, idly almost by now, as I nevertheless continued to do, seeming to spend more of my time than anywhere on the starboard wing simply tracking it as the ship moved slowly by. I saw Barker raise his head.

"Captain, would you take a look here?"

I bent and looked through. I raised up.

"Keep an eye on him, Billy."

His tall lean frame bent slightly to the glasses. I stepped to the pilot house door and spoke to the OOD.

"Mr. Sedgwick, we have a leopard ashore. Hard right rudder; bring the ship on a course dead-on to the beach. Reduce speed to minimum necessary to keep steerageway. Sharp watch on the Fathometer." I spoke to the entire bridge watch. "All hands keep quiet."

I stepped back to the wing, picked up the hand speaker attached to the bulwark shield.

"Mr. Selmon, this is the captain. Report immediately to the bridge." I waited a moment. "All hands not occupied on ship's duties report topside. Quiet ship."

The ship swinging with a graceful quickness in the water, we headed stealthily at rpm's at which she seemed barely to move, virtually wakeless, directly for shore and for him. The leopard had been simply standing there, all alone, looking out to sea. Now he appeared to look directly at the approaching ship, aware one felt that this object had made some sort of change of movement that was bringing it immediately toward him, however slowly. One felt he did not so much as blink an eye, but only watched. Barker still had the Big Eyes on him, myself 7x50 binoculars, but he was soon visible enough with the naked eye. I could hear the Fathometer watch sounding out depths to the OOD. Fifty fathoms, forty-five, thirty, twenty . . . We must have been no more than three hundred yards off when he next spoke.

"Fifteen fathoms showing, sir. Repeating, fifteen fathoms."

"Now," I said to Sedgwick.

"Stop all engines," he said.

I heard the clank of the engine-order telegraph by the lee helm: presently, "All engines stopped, sir."

We stood dead in the water, the ship seeming planted, swinging not at all in the stilled sea. Ship and leopard looking point-blank at each other. He stood there on the sand in absolute stillness; of a remarkable size; fawn colored with his black spots, his stately head, his powerful body; all grace, all beauty; motionless; waiting, fearless. I thought I had never seen a more magnificent creature. Below me, crowded along the lifelines, I could see the large numbers of ship's company come topside; watching with fascination and a quietness equaling that of the leopard's. We talked in hushed tones without lowering our binoculars.

"He looks a very healthy animal to me, Mr. Selmon."

"So he does, Captain."

"What's the reading here?"

He let the binoculars come to his chest, stepped into the pilot house and looked at the repeater, stepped back and gave me the figures.

"Allowing us?"

"Two hours ashore, sir. Without harm."

"If longer?"

"A man could live pretty well for anywhere from two to four weeks there. Downhill rather rapidly after that."

"He looks too healthy for that."

"He's a leopard, sir."

"I've already figured that out, Mr. Selmon."

"Sorry, sir. I simply meant that different animals have different tolerances."

"And that of a full-grown extremely healthy adult leopard?"

"I'm not certain anyone ever found out as to that particular animal, sir. I know I never did."

Suddenly as we were discussing him, he turned and walked slowly, soundlessly, majestically, across the sand and into the trees until the bush had swallowed him up. We returned to our parallel course four thousand yards off. Somehow the hearts of all ship's company lifted.

A Nice Outing

The schedule of our Jesuit chaplain, who must minister to Catholics, Jews, and Protestants, and in their own discrete rituals, had grown quite busy, as I have indicated, there having been an increased interest in religion aboard ship. Quite a number of the men have taken to reading the Bible. Fortunately we brought out more Bibles than anything, for use in regular Sunday church services. The Navy has always had a regard for the religious desires of its men; indeed that pennant bearing the Cross, as mentioned, is the only flag ever to fly atop the national ensign, during those services. The other day a delegation of the men came to me and asked if they could hold a short daily service and I granted the request. It takes place at 0600 on the fantail just about the time we are sailing toward the morning star and the sun is lifting from the sea. The number of sailors attending it slowly grows. It is a simple service. A reading of a few verses of Scripture, sometimes by the Jesuit, sometimes by a bluejacket or officer, standing on the vertical missile launcher, which makes a convenient pulpit. This is followed by a hymn or two . . .

A mighty fortress is our God,
A bulwark never failing;
Our helper He, amid the flood
Of mortal ills prevailing. . . .

To the voices of the sailors, accompanied by Delaney's fiddle, Porterfield's guitar, rising softly over the weather decks from aft, sometimes rather vigorously, as in this old Luther hymn, a favorite of mine, we have now become accustomed as heralding a new day of our search. It seems somehow not a bad way to start it, there being something reassuring, speaking of hope, in the music and lyrics of the old hymns. You can hear the service quite clearly from the bridge wing if you step out there to scan the waters. The Jesuit also quite often calls on Porterfield to give the homily, the helmsman having been a ministerial student before he turned mysteriously to the Navy.

Recently the chaplain came to me with the word that some of the men had asked for a baptismal service. Might we stop the ship somewhere in order to accomplish this purpose? I looked at him in astonishment.

"Did I hear you say baptismal service? And did I hear you say stop the ship?"

"Yes, Captain. You heard both precisely."

"Good Lord, why can't it be done aboard? Fantail, where you have services."

"They want to be immersed," he said.

"I didn't know Jesuits did immersions."

"A Navy Jesuit does. These particular sailors want it done like it was first done. To Jesus, by John the Baptist, in the River Jordan."

"Yes, I know, Chaplain."

He laughed. "I never doubted it, sir."

"Too bad it doesn't empty into the Mediterranean. We could take the ship there and make the thing complete."

"Any place the water's not over my head would do," he said.

I waited. "Do you really think that'll do any good?" I said then.

"Yes, I think it will, and I'm not thinking of the baptism."

I gave a sigh. "Very well," I said, "we'll do it."

Today we found a likely place. A strip of sandy beach, near a place called on the charts Zuwarah, not far into Libya. Selmon went in first and did his readings, which allowed us two hours ashore. A score of candidates had offered themselves for baptism. We went in in two boats, carrying them and some of their shipmates who wanted to witness the event.

We stood, all of us, in the stillness of the scene, meditative and attentive, on the white strand, the sea touching it with the barest of murmurs, while the Jesuit conducted a short service before the actual proceedings, commencing with a reading from the Gospel according to Saint Mark . . .

And it came to pass in those days, that Jesus came from Nazareth of Galilee, and was baptized of John in Jordan.

And straightaway coming up out of the water, he saw the heavens opened, and the Spirit like a dove descending upon him:

And there came a voice from heaven, saying, Thou art my beloved son, in whom I am well pleased.

The words drifted out over the water, reaching up toward a windless sky. Porterfield played on his guitar and the men who knew the words joined in the singing of the baptismal hymn . . .

Shall we gather at the river,
Where bright angel feet have trod,
With its crystal tide forever
Flowing by the throne of God . . .

Then the Jesuit and the candidates, all wearing their best sailor-whites, walked down into the transparent water and one by one he immersed them. First saying in a firm clear voice:

"I baptize thee in the name of the Father, the Son, and the Holy Ghost."

Said as a Baptist preacher would say it. Then with handkerchief held over the sailor's nose and mouth, bringing him (or her) backward until he was fully submerged, then raising him back up in the symbol of the Resurrection, the one-word pronouncement, spoken with a clear-sounding and unmistakable authority into the silence of the watching sailors.

"Amen."

Then the next sailor stepped forward for his turn. I was surprised at the Jesuit's skills in a ritual to which he was unaccustomed—it somehow seemed neither inconsonant nor heterodox to see one in reverse-collar priestly garb performing it—and not an undifficult one physically; but then he was a man strong in physique, once, as noted, a Georgetown varsity boxer in the light-heavyweight division and still in excellent shape, recently had taken to giving boxing lessons to the men, to help, I think, soothe them. It was a pretty day, the bounty of an unclouded heaven looking down in seeming blessing on our band of sailors gathered on the shore, a gleaming catena of sunlight stretching across the water to our ship standing off, the only remission to the far horizon in the vast blue solitude of the Mediterranean. We stood enveloped in a radiant silence, a certain strange and indecipherable serenity seeming to touch all around, to lay upon the waters, the beach, upon all of us present. A distinct tang of chillness hung in the air. If any of the immersed minded the cold, it was not apparent; there was no shivering of the dripping figures. Twenty of ship's company the Jesuit baptized, three of them women sailors: Radio-man Parkland, Seaman Salinas, Yeoman Kramer. In the name of the Father, the Son, and the Holy Ghost, all were baptized. It was a benignant and somehow particularly satisfying undertaking and one curiously of a shipmate character, drawing the men together. When it was over, the drenched score, their dry shipmates, and the Jesuit wet to his waist stood on the beach while Porterfield played one last chorus of the hymn, of which all the twenty and the previously baptized who knew the words joined in . . .

> Yes, we'll gather at the river,
> The beautiful, beautiful river,
> Gather with the saints at the river
> That flows by the throne of God . . .

As the last lines faded away, Selmon looked from his counter to me. "It's time, Captain."

We embarked in the boats, a little rapidly, and headed back out to the ship. Everybody seemed to have a good feeling. Preston put it best as we were nearing the ship.

"Captain," he said, "wasn't that a nice outing."

I was sitting next to the soaked chaplain.

"Why, so it was, Boats," I said. "A very nice outing."

"By God, if I don't think I'll do it myself next time if we have another one. Begging your pardon, Chaplain."

"Not at all, Boats," the Jesuit said. "Any time. I shall await your pleasure in the matter."

"Very good of you, sir," the boatswain's mate intoned gravely. "I'd like to think it over a bit."

"Of course, I offer either sprinkling or immersion, as desired."

"Very thoughtful of you I'm sure, sir."

"Immersion's pretty damned cold if you ask me." The chaplain had begun to shiver a bit. "Still, the Baptists claim no one ever caught anything from an immersion even if they had to break ice to do it. I trust the record remains unbroken. Sprinkling's simpler naturally. You can do it shipboard."

The boatswain's mate seemed to be pondering these matters of varying religious practices, of manifest choices presented one.

"If I do it I think I'll go for the full thing," he said after a moment. "They seemed pretty satisfied with it. Of course, if I decide I don't know when there'll be another chance."

I looked at Preston, mildly shocked by these considerations he was contemplating. Through his partially opened blouse I could see on his chest a segment of Nelson's great victory at Trafalgar. The boatswain's mate sat in solemn thoughtfulness.

"Boats," I said, "if you decide to be born again, I'll stop the ship and have another baptism just for you."

.5.

BY THE LIFELINE

Restiveness

As we pass by Africa's silent shores, a curious air seems increasingly to permeate the ship. Sailors as they live out their lives on ships are not traditionally a loud or noisy group of human beings. It is as though the lordly and unceasing sound of the sea had taught them that the human voice is a thing not best habitually raised. That tendency now seeming greatly enhanced as they go about their shipboard tasks; an excessive stillness, seeming to speak even in lowered, almost whispered tones, as if to disturb the soundlessness of the universe the least possible amount. A sense oddly almost of peace, approaching serenity. Of peace. Yet a tense quiescence.

Feelings move mysteriously throughout a ship at sea. Not merely from scuttlebutt either. More almost from that remarkable and precise sense sailors have of what is going on around them. It is as though some magnification of insight were granted them, in their own world contained entirely in their ship, an ability to see directly into the minds of their shipmates they know so well from this inescapable twenty-four-hour living with one another, to see even to a considerable degree into the mind of their captain however unrevelatory he may attempt to preserve his demeanor. Sometimes as I move about the decks, I find the eyes of one or more resting solemnly on me, a quiet look, neither hostile nor friendly, rather interrogatory, as if trying to penetrate what is taking place within me; now and then a sudden chill runs down me under those furtive glances. Of course, there is a great deal of all-too-available reality attached to these voiceless questionings. They can figure out for themselves, and no doubt have done so, that the Mediterranean being closed to us thus far, if it continues so, reaching Suez we will have to make one of two irreversible choices, cannot make both. And as the brutal knowledge slowly fills their consciousness, I have become aware of something foreboding in the air, a vague dread borne on fleeting, almost imperceptible signs. One can fear apparitions, fancy ghosts in our circumstances, but its persistence argues something more substantial. A sense of huge danger almost emergent; defining itself unmistakably as that greatest of all imperilments on the open sea: a ship becoming more and more divided against itself. The very stillness contributes to this feeling, giving it that same magnification. A sense of lurking expectancy. Of a grace period—for the ship's captain, for myself, one with some unspecified, but of a certainty not interminable, time limit. And whichever course chosen, a considerable part of ship's company by no manner to rest content with it. Though if ours were a society where votes were cast to determine decisions, and the vote taken today, I have little doubt where it would come down. The ship would have to make a 180-degree turn.

As if to help me in making the decision. With the doc, alone in sick bay.

"Could anything have happened to us? To *us?*"

He looked at me. "It's possible. Personally I don't think so. But we're on seas where men have not been, Skipper."

"Without chart or compass."

"Yes."

"There's only one way to find out?"

"Only one, Skipper."

I waited, made an abrupt change of course.

"Those 'intermittent neuroses' you spoke about. What a term."

"Isn't it?" he said rather jauntily, with a disdain for his own jargon. "Not absolutely absent with the women. But again, far more incidence with the men."

Home

With Girard in my cabin, the door closed. She spoke as morale officer.

"One new thing, Talley tells me. Quite a number have men-

261

tioned we're lucky to be at sea. They're with the ship more than ever. A good time to have a ship. To be a sailor. They know that. Especially since . . ."

She stopped, not having to say it. The people on the beaches.

"They couldn't be more right."

"Home." The word lingered, isolate. "It's always been that, I guess. Never so much so as now. The ship is home." She paused, quietly: "The word has the other meaning, too."

I waited. "If, when it does happen . . ."

I paused a beat, looking at her; heard her finish it for me.

"It'll come all at once, I'd say, sir. It may just explode."

I sat back and made myself relax. "As long as they feel that way about the ship . . . I count on that. The ship: She will hold us together. Most of us anyhow. The others . . . We'll handle that then, when it happens." I said again, "What else?"

"Reading way up. Those nine hundred and eighty-five books we brought out. A major blessing, I'd say."

"What are you reading?"

"Fathers and Sons."

"I'm going straight through Dickens. *Bleak House* at the moment. How did we happen to bring all of him? Rather hoggish of Dickens."

"Well, we couldn't leave Dickens behind."

The moment passed. I returned to business, to . . .

"What else?"

"They talk about their hometowns. Quite a few do."

Something strange in the way she said this, picked up by her from my expression.

"No, not in that way. Those that do—as if they were still there. The nice places they've always been. Some even talk about going back in one of the small boats."

I felt something grab at me, the pit of my stomach.

"The others . . . they don't talk about hometowns at all. Even walk away when someone else starts it."

Again, "What else?"

"Shanley. EW third. I'm not sure he's going to make it. He talks about going over the side. The chaplain, the doc, myself—we've all talked with him."

"I'll talk with him."

"Thornberg," she said.

"Thornberg?" She was a lee helmsman, striker for quartermaster. "I haven't noticed a thing on watch."

"Not there. In women's quarters. Cries a lot. She's coming around."

"I can see her."

She paused but a moment. "Not necessary, I think, sir. We're handling it."

For some reason the last—the "we" made me look quickly at her; suppress a comment.

"Anyone else in particular?"

"Among the men?" She meant women as well.

"Among anybody, Miss Girard," I said, a bit sharply.

She looked down at her lap, up at me. "Negative, sir. That's it."

I decided I might as well spring it on her. I wanted it handled.

"What's this about you and Mr. Chatham?"

"That?" She wasn't thrown for a moment, her voice easy, fluent, her eyes gray and cool, a glint of malice in them. "Of course, personally I sometimes get a feeling of nausea around him but that's not it. Goes back to a time in the wardroom, some of us shooting the breeze. I mentioned that perhaps we ought to be thinking about jettisoning the missiles—that is, Tomahawk land-attack ones at least, not necessarily anything else. I said something to the effect I couldn't possibly imagine any use we'd ever have for them now and of course they have a certain danger in themselves. He took it personally I think. Since you mention it, sir, I sometimes get the idea Mr. Chatham rather thinks he owns the missiles."

"You were out of line, Lieutenant." My voice was hard enough. "Not because it's his department, although incidentally he's the best combat systems officer I've ever known. But because it's *my* department. Anything as important as the question of jettisoning the missiles is not a proper subject for wardroom scuttlebutt. Is that understood?"

"It's understood, sir."

"I've given him the word. I now give you the same one. I want it knocked off. Both. The thing between you. And any more talk of that kind. The captain will decide what is and what is not to be jettisoned on this ship. I should hate to have to jettison an officer or two. Do you take my meaning, Miss Girard?"

"Perfectly, sir."

Carrot and Stick

The emotional state of the ship: It varies widely, hand to hand. And even with one individual, it may be quite different at different times. Thinking, brooding, contemplation: I sense that these grow. Only a very few cannot, at least temporarily, stand watches at all. I choose different ways of dealing with these, as I think will work or is merited. Debating first with myself whether to be tough, to charge the man with malingering; or whether to be gentle. The gentleness consists generally in talking with the man quietly for a while, then leaving him alone for a few days while waiting to see what happens. The toughness, as with Yeoman Third Logan, is to come down hard. He had complained simply that he did not feel like working, speaking of vague ills. I had before me the doc's report. The man faced me sullen, dangerously close to surly. I looked at him and said:

"Why are you different from the rest of us? You think you're the only one suffering?"

"I've got these pains, Captain," he almost whined.

"We've all got pains, Logan. The doc says you've got the exact same pains as the rest of us. No more, no less. You should be ashamed of yourself. For God's sake show a little spine, man."

With Machinist's Mate Second Jorgans, more gently, when he complained:

"But back there I have," he said, "a wife and two kids."

The present tense. Jorgans broke into tears, a convulsive sobbing. I stepped around him and shut my cabin door. Coming back I placed my hand on his shoulder.

"Rainey," I said quietly—he is a signalman—"has a wife and four children. . . . He hasn't missed a watch."

Somehow these altogether simplistic and direct approaches seem in the main to work. Only two men—Seaman Drexel and Cryptologic Technician Templeton—actually have I relieved, for the time being, of all watch-standing, to give them a chance to recover as from any illness, as a man is allowed to do aboard ship. One week limit on that indulgence. Then I call the man in and tell him quite sternly that he will have to shape up, that every hand must do his share. This also seems to work. So far. So far indeed the men are proving themselves intrepid, yes, gallant, in the main.

The Ship at Night

Previously most had appeared to be employing that remarkable ability of which I have spoken to put their minds on a sort of hold in respect to events and to continue their regular shipboard duties and lives, as if they had come to an agreement with themselves, a sort of solemn inner concordat, to probe into them at some unspecified future date. Now this fortification has to an increasing extent been breached by the disclosures to ship's company of the French radioman's report, the report from the Russian submarine commander. One senses a deep, inward contemplation. Pulsing in an unceasing torment through them this question: Are the reports to be believed? A struggle for their souls.

I have taken to prowling the ship at night, as I think through, never really stopping doing so, our choices as to course. I listen to the sea in its polyphony of voices, as if she might whisper some wondrous counsel in my ears; gaze up at the stars which guide us as if that direction might extend to other than navigational matters; as if they in their ageless wisdom might have a word of advice for a ship's captain, perhaps a suggestion or two, based on the ancient and fond friendship between themselves and seamen. From sea and stars no answers come, other than a seeming reminder concerning on whose shoulders these matters fall.

But mostly I go to be among the men. And for them to see me, to have my accessible presence. Sailors do not approach a ship's captain lightly—if they feel something genuinely urgent requires his attention they go through chief petty officers, through their division officers. It is my purpose by these coursings of the weather decks to convey a certain opening, enlargement, of the usual channels of command. I go for a further reason which I hardly dare admit to myself. I have never before asked myself such a thing concerning those I commanded, feeling I knew sailors, and especially that I knew, having long ago, on assuming command of this ship, made it my first order of business, those whose sworn duty it is to obey my orders; as much as I thought I understood my ship's company, I feel increasingly uncertain of the answer to a single question: What are they thinking? What is going on inside them? It is this really that turns me to these noctivagations. I go to attempt to determine whether there be any beginning telltale, any sign, any signal, however oblique, of that most fateful of all the affairs of ships on the ocean seas and before which the strongest captain's heart may tremble, of revolt beginning to stir in his men. Immense as are his powers, any ship's captain yet pauses before pitting his will against an authentic rebellion, if it have any basis of validity at all, subscribed to by a large number of his men. While stubbornness may be a virtue in a commander, unreasoning obstinacy may bring the heavens crashing down, take a ship under as surely as the sea herself has done uncounted times. No good captain has any problem distinguishing between the two. He knows the fineness of the line he must trod. He cannot forget that he is alone on that ship with them, cut off from the world. Vastly outnumbered, he has only his will and the ancient law of the sea to back him up, and while it is my business to attend to the first, the latter is now peculiarly vulnerable. I go to learn.

More and more between watches, in the hours of dark, men may be seen topside, sometimes in twos or threes, more often alone, sitting on the bitts or standing by the lifeline, gazing at the empty sea, staring into its immense solitude from the equal solitude of the ship moving through it, over the emptied blue plain of the Mediterranean. Wrapped in those two solitudes, ship and sea, which define our existence. Quite often, as I stand by the lifeline myself, a man will approach and stand by me and we talk. Usually about idle matters, not always. Once Bigelow, a missile technician, standing by me awhile in the darkness, then actually pulling at my sleeve, saying, "I've got to go home, Captain." I put my hand over the one now gripping my arm and held it hard. "Lad, we all want to go home." We just stood there in the dark, saying nothing. Until his low sobs stopped and I took my hand away. Sometimes I touch the dark shape of a man and move on. Other times I simply pass by, sensing that he does not wish to be disturbed. Sometimes I have a feeling when I come upon a man that he might be thinking about going over the side. Always then I stop and talk with him. Never, of course, about that. But about random things. But making it a point, too, to speak of the future, my purpose being to plant reassurance throughout the crew that there is a future—even possibly a decent future, not just one of survival, of mere existence. Nothing, as I have suggested, is more important than that the captain of a ship preserve at all times a calm presence, to the point even of serenity, and especially in the most trying of times. No matter the turmoils, even torments, that may be underway within himself: He must not fail to suppress them; they must never know it. It is the first commandment of captaincy. So much does a ship's company take its signal, its tone, its very emotions from its captain, and often augments them: Fear in a ship's captain can in an instant become panic in a ship's company; alarm, terror. But so also can fortitude in him find its mirror image in his men: endurance—mental and physical—and without a word of complaint through deprivation and hardship, even horror, that would seem beyond the ability of men to bear, deeds extending to the unhesitating risk of their lives for those of their shipmates: These are almost common virtues among sailors properly led.

Iowa

She was a young pony of a girl, the sailor's dungarees, sailor's hat seeming but to accentuate the fresh radiance of her mind and body, a naturalness, a spontaneity about her that echoed within oneself. She could have been my daughter; nineteen. The fact that at that age she had already made signalman third vouched for her brightness. I remembered her once telling me with mock solemnity as of a great distinction that she was from Odebolt, Iowa, "the popcorn capital of the world."

"Isn't it a pretty night, Captain?"

"Yes, Bixby. A lovely night."

High and glittering stood the stars guiding us eastward. Swarming in the heavens they looked down on a sea untroubled to the far horizon, the fullness of moon, riding a cloudless sky, joining them to light the waters and fashion a wide and radiant stream of white which followed us with mathematical precision; the dazzling stillness in command everywhere save for that steady low-pitched duet, the whisper of the sea, the heartbeat of the ship. We stood by the lifeline.

"I couldn't sleep," she said. "It's the moonlight. I always figured you should never waste a full moon on sleep."

I felt my own silence would best encourage the softness, tenderness of that voice. Her eyes traced a pattern from the zenith to the waters stretching endlessly away.

"I can't make up my mind whether it looks prettier over the sea or over wheat fields. A full moon." She paused as before a difficult choice; looked across to the beam horizon. "The way that path of light follows us. We move and it doesn't. I can never get over that. You don't get that in the wheat fields. Naturally, because you're not moving yourself. Mostly you're on a porch."

"Wheat fields? I thought it was corn, Bixby. In the song. Tall corn."

She laughed a little, a girlish laugh that fell like a small jewel into the quiet of the night. "Well, sir, we had that, too. But in our family, *our* farm, it was mostly wheat. Iowa."

She said the word as if to herself, somehow the three tiny syllables, the single word, full of the deepest meaning. I looked across the shimmering seascape, the very stars above seeming to hover attendant, eavesdropping on our conversation. Only at sea, the horizons unblocked by ridges of land, can the stars be seen in all their teeming multitudes, all their glory. Lately it seemed I had begun to hear increasing talk of a certain pattern; nothing of any directness, but a passing reference, the name of a state dropped into a conversation, of a town, of the many states and towns from which ship's company came; the names of home, their immense variety spanning augustness, pride, charm, and even comedy to form a mighty nomenclature, full of every meaning, everything held dear; almost, too, this stabbing into one, twisting like a knife, as if they stood there across the seas as untouched and beckoning as ever. As I pondered my decision, it seemed almost that they were being invoked like some ominous litany, swelling and merciless, that had begun to repeat itself over and over in my ears, rising at times to something like throbbing. The word "Iowa" fell into the silence and seemed to hover there for a moment, as if asserting its claim and its strength, before she went on. I almost feared the question, and from a signalman third, but if it had been on her mind to ask she turned away from it, with a relief so considerable on my part as itself to disturb me. I was aware somehow of the flurry of curls on the nape of her neck under her sailor's hat, the peacefulness of her youthful figure: the peace of the night seeming to envelop us, make whispers of our voices.

"But," she said with girlish firmness, "I think I've decided it looks prettier over the sea." The brief, young laugh again. "I guess it's a good thing I went in the Navy. I was going to be a veterinarian. Is it true that the earth is two-thirds ocean?"

"A bit more, I think. Seven-tenths."

"Seven-tenths sea!" She paused a beat, her voice quizzical, gentle as a note of music. "There must have been a reason for that. By God—or whoever," she added, seeming not to want to sound particularly religious.

"I think someone wrote long ago that the reason had to be that God—or whoever—had a preference for sailors. Probably a sailor wrote that."

I could sense the smile. Mixed with the salt-air smell of the sea was the elusive scent of her perfume, her femininity, where she stood beside me, motionless in the moonlight. We fell into a silence, listening to the reiterant wash of the sea, shipmates. At one point I thought she looked up high on the mainmast at our communications antennas. She may have been looking only at stars.

After a bit, she said quietly, "Good night, Captain." She turned to go below to women's quarters.

"Good night, Bixby."

The Navy, or the Iowa farm, or both, had given a girl now called Bixby—not Alice—something. I lingered under the stars; something unaccountable and strong I felt, communicated without speech from her to myself: There was something indomitable in her. A special gentleness seemed to come through—and a good toughness. Sometimes the comfort, the reassurance, went the other way. She was with the ship. And yet: Iowa.

Moses

Under Arabian stars, their silhouettes heavily lighted, we stood along the starboard lifeline studying the dunes, spectral and undulating, foreboding, magisterial, across the few miles of resting sea. We had been running a parallel course. With me a seaman apprentice, James Hurley, a striker for coxswain, being brought along by Preston. He is from a small town called

Dundee, Florida. He started telling me about the citrus groves. Then:

"It looks very bare over there, doesn't it, sir?"

"It should. It's all desert."

"I wonder what the desert's like. Just sand, I guess."

"They say it can be very beautiful, too."

"Didn't someone cross the desert following the star to see the baby Jesus when he was born?"

"I think so. I'm not sure about the desert part. But yes, I believe so."

The low, short laugh. "On a camel, of course."

We waited, watching sea and desert beyond go by; the sea seeming a familiar friend; the desert strange and phantasmal, somehow menacing, as though watching us with suspicion across the water; sea and desert yet combining to form an engulfing solitude, lessened a bit, I felt, by our sharing of it. We had stood for so long in the luminescent stillness of the night, in a kind of voiceless communion.

"Also there was something about Moses."

"Moses?"

"Wandering in the desert. Forty years if I remember."

Something in the voice made me turn sharply toward him. Then I dismissed it. Too alert for signs.

"Yes. That part I know," I said. "I think the Ten Commandments came along not much after that."

Sweetness

In the afternoon it had rained but now the rain had gone, leaving behind a low mist lying over the sea. He had just come off the first watch and must have seen me standing there in the dark. He joined me and we stood awhile, mostly silent, as much so as the night itself, a mute sea, the air drugged into utter windlessness; now and then a word or two.

Lieutenant Thurlow, the navigator, would have won any contest we should have had aboard having to do with being a dedicated "womanizer," a fact established conclusively years back on visits to various port cities on two continents. It was beyond me how he had ever ended up in the Navy. Some latent intense love of the science of navigation, I felt, in a pure sense; finding himself most happy doing things connected with navigation, when not doing things connected with women. The first must have won out over the second in a close contest. Ship life certainly gave him all the opportunity to drench himself in the former, though limiting the latter to those shore excursions. We both looked up. A few stars had broken through the cover.

"Sometimes I'm sorry things like loran even came along," he said. "Any idiot can do it. Rather glad it's gone now. Star-shooting, dead reckoning—more fun. And serves the purpose."

I was really becoming rather fond of him. For one thing, his enduringly untroubled air, seeming little altered by events. He seemed to come down on the side of harmony, the lessening of tensions, a welcome gift. When not engaged in his profession, where his exactness as to degrees, minutes, seconds, of latitude, longitude; as to star-sights; as to anything dealing with the present course or position of the ship you could take as gospel, no verification required—away from all that, a kind of splendid carelessness about him. Despite this, in some ways I looked upon him as our most vulnerable officer. His voice often took on an extraordinary sweetness as he talked, as now, and said, startling me:

"One thing, in the Pacific, I'd get to see the Southern Cross. I'd like to do that sometime before I check out."

It was spoken casually, lightly, not thinking of decisions; of immense choices; only of the stars he loved. The silence held again, a pleasant absence of compulsion. Then, before we both turned to go below, his quiet murmur of a voice, the words falling like inevitability itself, full of poignancy and an unspeakable heartbreak, though spoken offhandedly, carelessly, upon the stillness of the night.

"Actually, I don't have anybody back there anyhow," the words piercing my soul. Paused a beat. Then:

"I'll go where the ship goes. That's my preference."

Orel

Tonight standing by the lifeline with young Ensign Jennings, a junior OOD, the youngest officer aboard by a considerable margin. He suddenly said to me:

"Captain, those three hundred and eleven thousand people—that was the figure, wasn't it, sir?"

It would have been no use pretending I didn't know what he was talking about.

"Something like that," I said.

"That's about a thousand per man in ship's company," he said.

I waited in the abrupt tension. Then: "Do you believe in hell, Captain?"

"I don't know that I believe in hell for anything. And I certainly don't believe in it for what we have done." I waited a moment. Then said quietly, "Leave it, lad."

270

Dominoes

He had recently started his Garden.

"You liked farming, didn't you, Chief?"

The predicate seemed too mild.

"Oh, yes, sir. Delaneys have been farmers in those hills—well, just about forever, I reckon. Aye, sir. I liked it all right. I guess you like anything you grew up with. Most times, anyhow."

"I suppose you do. Then why the sea?"

"Five boys, sir. Somebody had to go. It wasn't that big a farm. We drew lots for it."

I turned and looked at him. "You drew lots?"

"Actually we each drew a down domino after my dad had shuffled them." He laughed shortly. "On the kitchen table. One night after supper."

I thought, my God, dominoes. I asked: "Then why the Navy? After you drew the one domino."

"Two was the lowest."

He paused then, to make sure, I think, that he was answering his captain with a scrupulous accuracy, just as he had about the domino; or perhaps to sort out himself a rather complex question. He spoke in his quiet manner.

"Well, sir." He paused again. "I've not studied on it too much. But I guess it was kind of this way. I had a mind there were maybe two things a man could get close to: worth a man's putting his life into. I'd had one. It was the other. I didn't know the first thing about it. I'd never even seen the sea. Never even been out of Missouri. Cricks was about all the water I'd ever seen. So I don't know where the idea came from. Anyhow that's the way I figured it. The land or the sea. I don't put it real well, sir."

"You put it all right. Would you go back—given the chance?"

The question seemed almost to shock him. "Oh, no sir. I like both, but negative, sir. I'd never go back. One time I might of. Boot camp I might of. But now . . . That farm thing. I guess it'll always be there. But to go back. Not now." He paused and said, as if that said it all: "I guess I'm a sailor now."

"Yes, I guess you are."

Crew of Number 2 Boat

Two entirely separate conversations, an hour or so apart on the same night; neither, I was certain, realizing the other had spoken to me.

"What a pretty night, sir. Better than the Barents."

He stood tall and loose-limbed over me, hovering it seemed.

"Aye, Billy. What sea isn't."

Barker gave his boyish laugh. "Yes, sir." A pause. "Both a long way from Bronte, Texas."

"Interesting name. There were two pretty well-known English novelists by that name."

"Yes, sir. Ours was named for Charlotte. Wrote *The Professor, Shirley, Villette.* And, of course, *Jane Eyre.*"

I looked at him in astonishment.

"Naturally the town library had everything written by the lady it was named for. Incidentally, there's a tradition in Texas of naming towns for ladies. Don't know why. Bronte's only got nine hundred and eighty-seven people. I'd like you to see it sometime, sir. It's a pretty little town."

"I'd like that," I said. *How we always speak in the present tense,* I thought. *Even I do it.* I could hear his voice going on, seeming not much beyond a choirboy's.

"About as small as a town can come, I reckon. Mom used to tell people visiting us the first time, relatives from off somewhere needing to be told how to get there, that we lived just beyond Resume Speed."

I laughed. "Sometimes I think everybody in the Navy came from a farm or a small town. I don't know why. It just seems I almost never meet a Navy man from a big city. You like it?"

"Like what, sir?"

"The Navy. You like being in the Navy?"

"That I do, sir. I don't know why either."

We both laughed softly at that. Suddenly I made a decision. I figured it might help my thoughts. I turned a little toward him, looking upward.

"Billy. I want a straight answer on something."

"I'll sure try to give you one, sir."

"Where do you really want to go?"

"Want to go?" As though the question was such a strange one to him.

"Want to go?" he repeated it. "Why, wherever the ship goes, sir. Doesn't make that much difference really. Wherever the ship goes will be four-oh with me, sir."

Just like Thurlow, I thought; but for what a different reason. I had found out something. We were silent then, comfortable in watching the sea.

"You should be up for your rating soon, Billy," I said then. "How do you like Coxswain Meyer for a teacher?"

"Well, sir, she must be just about the best coxswain there is. I'm pretty lucky to have her, I reckon. Yes, sir. Also she's . . . well, isn't Coxswain Meyer fun though, sir?"

"Fun?" The word shot out before I had thought. It was the last I would have used to characterize Meyer. I could think of a few others. He must see her with different eyes. I looked out at the sea, peaceful under the stars. Perhaps he had not noticed. "Oh, indeed she is. A lot of fun."

An hour or so later, Meyer. So diminutive, so slight alongside, I almost had to bend my head for conversation.

"Barker," I said. "Is he going to be ready for his coxswain exams soon?"

She was cautious. "He's coming along. But he needs some more work in approaching. Maybe when we put into port. Practice taking liberty parties ashore. Provided we anchor out rather than pier up."

"Yes, that'll help."

As with Billy, I thought I would try something, and for the same reason, to help my thoughts.

"For example, some of those Pacific islands that haven't got piers."

"They would do just fine," she said analytically, nothing of my intent registering on her. "He wouldn't get any practice with the ship docked in Charleston Harbor. Or New York." She gave a raucous little laugh. "Do you realize Barker has never even *seen* New York. A regular hayseed. Actually I don't think he was ever out of Texas before he got in the Navy. Would you believe it? Eighteen years old and had never been out of *Texas,* for God's sake. An absolute hayseed. But he's not bad. At least he's *teachable.* I'm bringing him along," she said firmly.

"You grew up in New York?"

"Grew up in New York?" she said, as if it were a dumb thing to ask and anything to the contrary out of the question. She spoke in those feisty tones of hers. "Absolutely."

She wasn't through with Billy.

"Yep. Very immature in some ways. Would you believe it? Actually quoted something to me out of the Bible the other day."

I smiled in the dark. "Are you serious?"

"I'd swear to God if I weren't an atheist. But he'll make a good coxswain—when I get through with him."

"I'm sure he will, Meyer. When you get through with him."

"I just wish he'd stop quoting the Bible to me. Well, Captain, I'm going below. Shut-eye time, you know."

It was almost as if she were dismissing me.

"Of course, one mustn't underrate Billy almost anywhere. You might want to ask him some time about *Jane Eyre.*"

Poker

Standing alone by the lifeline, mind searching always for something favorable, I thought of the reports we had been receiving steadily from *Pushkin;* proceeding off the coast of West Africa from Rabat as far south as Cap Blanc, finding no habitability, deciding then to come about and strike a course for Russian waters. Routine, but messages of reassurance where that virtue was in short supply, and they lifted me as I tracked her course: All went well with her. My reports back that thus far North Africa would not admit us and that we continued to stand toward Suez. Visualizing him surfaced to receive these. Something forgiving, somehow greatly comforting in the fact of another ship out there and of our two ships being able to feel each other out through the great imponderable; mind quietened by these thoughts.

So windless was the air as the *James* moved through the great continuing silence, so light her wake at the reduced speed I had ordered, that I could hear every word of the singing coming from the small group assembled on the fantail. It happens every night the weather is fair. Gathered around Porterfield and his guitar, assisted ofttimes by Gunner's Mate Delaney and his fiddle, songs from the hills, hymns, songs Porterfield and Delaney grew up with; the gently pitched voices falling plaintively out over the Mediterranean . . .

> Down in the valley,
> The valley so low,
> Hang your head over,
> Hear the wind blow . . .

The voices of the men sailors blending with those of women sailors to Porterfield's sweet guitar . . .

> Hear the wind blow, dear,
> Hear the wind blow,
> Hang your head over,
> Hear the wind blow . . .

You would never think it to look at him, what an exceptional helmsman is Seaman Porterfield. He is tall and gangly and if you saw him moving around you might well deem him awkward, floppy as a bird dog. But once at that wheel, his lean and embracing figure bent over, almost cradling it as if cradling the ship herself and crooning to her a coaxing lullaby, his elongated and bony fingers moving over the spokes with the attuned precision and mutual understanding of a virtuoso of music and his instrument, immaculately synchronized to her every swerve and movement, his reflexes instantaneous: There he is all helmsman. The ship seems somehow to perform better for him, to respond with more alacrity to his ministrations, as if expressing a distinct preference for him over others aboard in the intimacy of ship and steersman; it is as though there was a special communion between them. I would want him there in any storm at sea, and in any tight maneuvering, and so he has been on countless occasions, in many seas. He is from Kentucky, out of the hills. There is a rather astonishing fact about Seaman Porterfield. He has been in the Navy five years. He has an intelligence well above the average, more than sufficient to take him into petty officer rating—most likely boatswain or quartermaster—and would long since have been there, probably at a level of first class and ready even to become a chief, since besides the ability to master a skill he is a natural leader of men. Then a strange thing happened, and one new to my Navy experience.

Porterfield one day requested an audience with me and stated calmly that he would prefer to remain a seaman. The reason given: He liked very much being a helmsman, steering the ship, which seamen do and thus at the point of becoming a petty officer an activity he would cease. It was a request so startling that I believe I would have rejected it on the spot but for one circumstance. We were on Barents duty at the time, and day after long day had been navigating waters as brutal as I had ever experienced. On watches with Porterfield, I had observed that there was something extraordinary about his helmsman's work—a touch, a way, an uncanny anticipation of, sensitivity to, what the ship was about to do, that seemed to put him in a class by himself. He totally loved that particular job—steering the ship—in a manner that seemed to reach into realms of the mystical, some might say spiritual. The request annoyed, even angered me. I told him what it was my duty to tell him, and what I felt to be true, that for a sailor to remain in a seaman's rating when everything about the Navy, and for his own welfare, had it that a man moved upward, was, for starters, plain stupid. "I know, sir," he said quietly. "I know that." And looked at me, saying no more. "I'll think about it," I said. "Meantime, for God's sake, you can stay a seaman." Neither of us ever brought the matter up again. There was one other rather odd aspect to Porterfield: For a man about to be ordained a minister of the Gospel suddenly to go into the Navy is an unusual thing.

There are few men I am more glad to have aboard than Seaman Porterfield. For reasons having nothing to do with his helmsman's skills. He has become a mainstay. When I think of the times ahead, I find myself not infrequently thinking of him, in an expectation of something from him far beyond his rating and his steersman's duties. There is about him the quality of an insidiously assuaging, easing, reassuring nature that affects the other men, brings them down to his own measured emotional temperature. There are people like that, rare in my experience, difficult of definition, whose very presence seems in some unexplained manner to calm men's thoughts and actions, the very air; just as there are others who seem, and just as curiously, to agitate all of these things from the moment they enter a room. His being of the former category has already in some almost abstruse way been of high value in these times; and I foresee will be even more so in those to come. A quiet unobtrusive humor, an attunement to human feelings and thoughts of the moment that seems as precise as that to the ship's helm, an unvoiced (for he never "preaches") but infectious assumption that all things will come right—and with all this, in Porterfield's case, a profound touch of the con.

Later that night I find myself standing by him at the lifeline midships, looking out at a tender waveless sea through which we glide without roll or pitch, sea and ship seeming caught up in some precise and sympathetic harmony with each other. Tonight's fantail music session was over and lights-out near. We both, as sailors will for no particular reason unless it be for some kind of reassurance, looked up at the ship's running lights. Still turned on at sunset as they had always been, eternal and silent voices of safety and of warning for any approaching ship, collision of ships at sea being the one occurrence never forgiven, never forgotten, marking both captains, and the vessels themselves, for the duration of their lives with the sea's scarlet letter: How remote the ancient law now seemed, gazing at that starboard green, those shipless waters. Still, each night, we put on the running lights, out of habit, out of a persisting hope.

We stood looking across the barren waters unfolding all around us to far horizons, shimmering under the stars; stood alongside, the bond between us of the sea seeming to transcend any difference of rank. We had chatted a bit. Then our eyes, as if on command, in the manner of sailors before heading for sleep, jointly traced a parabola from the constellations down to the sea, as if bidding good-night to it, will see you tomorrow. I had half turned to go to my cabin when Porterfield spoke in the soft twang-drawl that always fell with an insinuating gentleness on the ear.

"Did you ever play poker, sir?"

"Poker? A little."

"It's a mighty fine game."

"Yes, I've heard."

I caught the mild throat-clearing. "Yes, sir, it's a very *relaxing* game."

It seemed we were to have a pre-slumber conversation about the many virtues of the game of poker. Not for a moment did any notion occur to me that it would be a casual one. Porterfield was a man of intentions.

"Very relaxing," he murmured. "I've been thinking, sir."

I was silent. He was perfectly capable of navigating his way through whatever it was.

"Wondering if the captain would mind if we started a little poker game, sir. A friendly game."

I looked up at the stars, by old habit, just to make sure that they were about their proper business and where they should be, always searching out one or another of them, simply by whim, to certify the matter. In this case, Betelgeuse. He was, I was reassured to see, on station. The stars never fail us.

"What would be the purpose of this game, Porterfield?" I asked, still studying Betelgeuse. The drill requires that any such request be given its due consideration, without unseemly haste. Not to do so would only lessen its importance and make nobody happy.

"Well, sir . . . poker is a mighty relaxing game, Captain."

"So you've said." My eyes came down from the constellations and rested on the hushed seascape. "Men certainly need to relax."

"Aye, sir," the helmsman intoned soberly. "Relaxation does wonders for men."

I thought to bring us away from these pious homilies with something more explicit. Besides, it was my turn.

"Did you play it at that seminary in Louisville?"

The helmsman was not thrown for a moment. "Sir, I'm glad you asked that," he said in solemn tones that suggested we had arrived at a juncture of profound import. "It makes the exact point I'm trying to make here, sir. We did have a little friendly game now and then, we students for the ministry. Generally on Saturday nights."

I turned and gave him an inquisitorial glance. He stood there tall and gawky in the moonlight. "Saturday nights? I should have thought you would have been burning the midnight oil, putting the finishing touches on your sermons. Saturday is right before Sunday."

"Aye, sir, that it is. Myself, I know I always preached a shade better the next day—the Lord's Day, that is—if I'd had a little poker game the night before. That's how soothing that game is. Made no difference whether I'd won or lost. Of course, winnings went into the collection plate the next day." He paused. He was a man scrupulous with facts. "Half did."

"That was very commendable."

"Actually the Scriptures only require a tenth."

"I'm sure the Lord thought half a very generous division."

"I hope so, sir," he said.

He waited while we studied the sea.

"Aye, sir," the steersman continued. "A mighty relaxing game. Nothing in the Bible against poker; leastways that I could ever find."

"I imagine you know your Bible, Porterfield."

"Well, sir, a man can always know it better. Did you ever find anything, Captain?"

"Find any what, Porterfield?"

"Anything in the Bible against poker."

"Not in the King James Version," I said.

"That's the one I use, too, sir. Shame all those counterfeits came along."

"I imagine you also know your poker."

"Just average, sir," Porterfield said. I had a feeling this would be far too modest an appraisal. I sensed a faraway look in his eyes. "But it's a mighty lovely game."

I gazed up at the heavens, back at the sea.

"The Bible—the King James Version, that is—might not have anything to say about poker," I said. "But *Navy Regulations* does. Strictly forbids gambling. Are you aware of that article, Porterfield?"

"Aye, sir," he said rather gloomily. I heard a cough. "Actually it's the *Manual of the Judge Advocate General,* article one thirty-four."

"Thank you for the correction, Porterfield."

We both waited, both listening, with the second set of seaman's ears, alert for anything out of the ordinary, heeding the gentle sureness of the ship sliding through the sea, the ship telling us by that sound that all was well with her. I had spoken as though the subject were closed. I heard the helmsman's voice again beside me.

"Sir?"

"Yes? What is it, Porterfield?"

"About the poker, sir."

"What, the poker?"

"I was wondering, sir. Wondering if it might be possible that, say, in special circumstances, a captain would have the power to, well, suspend, so to speak, a certain Navy regulation. If he had a good enough reason."

"Are you undertaking to instruct me in the powers of a ship's captain, Porterfield?"

"Oh, no, sir. I'd never attempt anything like that, sir. No indeed. I was but speaking theoretically, sir."

"Anyhow I doubt if we have any cards, considering that regulation."

I heard a mild cough. "Something curious has happened, sir. A diligent seaman has turned up a half dozen decks or so. I hardly know how they got aboard."

I waited but a second. "Yes. Quite a mystery, I'd say."

"Isn't it, sir?"

I spoke judiciously. "Speaking just *theoretically:* The reason would have to be very special. Did you have any in mind?"

He spoke gravely, in thoughtful reflection. "Well, sir. Very few things relieve a man's loneliness more, I've found, sir. Yes, sir. Nothing takes a man's mind off things the way poker does."

I gave Betelgeuse a final look.

"Permission granted," I said. "Where do you plan to have the game?"

"In the steering-gear room," the helmsman said promptly.

It was an out-of-the-way place, far aft and rather deep in the ship, just below the waterline; one also the helmsman would know well.

"Not a bad choice," I said. "Foresighted of you to have selected it before this little chat. Good night, Porterfield."

"Good night, Captain."

Yes, a respite, a balm, that conversation was, having to do less with poker than with sanity. I turned, strangely at peace with myself, to go to my cabin and sleep.

To Be Lonely

He was an Old Navy man. And, as I have said, the best pure seaman we had aboard.

"Well, sir, I guess I liked Pacific duty best. Most of these younger ones—now they favor the Med here. I can understand that. Good liberty ports. Tangiers. Villefranche. Naples." He paused in respectful tribute. "Naples—that may have been the best of them all, the way they saw it. The one place you could always get anything: Aye, that was Naples. Me, I've always been partial to the Pacific."

He stood beside me, a truly immense man, and with it the quiet voice of one who finds it unnecessary to bluster. No one could have been more a son of the sea.

"Not for the liberty ports," I said. Boatswain's Mate Preston never liked being far away from the ship. He would seek out the nearest bar. But he did not really approve of the shore.

"No, sir, not for them. Oh, now and then. Yokosuka. Hong Kong: definitely worth a look. But mostly some little spit of island. And them few and far between. Longer at sea. Maybe that was it. The ship had a lot of sea to get around in. Lot of maneuvering space out there."

I smiled in the dark. "Yes. The Pacific was never short on maneuvering space, Boats."

I decided to venture it, just barely to touch down on its shores, to open the door a crack. I felt, in his way, he was trying to tell me something; something important.

"Some men found it lonely," I said.

He seemed to reflect a moment. "Captain, I figure if a man's a real Navy man . . . Well, sir, probably why he went to sea in the first place was to be lonely. If you want to look at it in a certain way."

It was a sober thought but I knew what he meant. The sea has no greater gift than that of solitude, which is at once a man's greatest friend and his greatest enemy. I said something that would make him go on.

"The only reason I can figure for a man going into the Navy," he said, "is to get away from all those shore people. And the Pacific was the best for that. That's for sure."

"You've got a point, Boats. You can certainly get away from shore people in the Pacific."

"That's what I figure, sir."

Boatswain's Mate Preston straightened his huge figure and looked out into the night of the Mediterranean. It looked pretty big itself, and lonely enough, the limitless waters unfolding all around us to far horizons where stars hanging low seemed to reach down fervently to touch the sea.

"Aye, sir," he said. "It's even bigger out there."

He would be the last to proffer an uninvited suggestion to his captain. But then he said: "Lots of islands out there. Probably some they didn't even get around to." Waited again, added: "For one reason or another."

A profound startlement held me still: the imparted knowledge of how far the crew's talk, their speculations, had taken them in considering another course; perhaps he was informing me that the Pacific might not arouse all that much opposition, or at least that it also had its adherents, its converts.

I decided it was time to change the subject.

"Hurley," I said. "Is he about ready?" For his coxswain exams I meant.

"Anytime, sir. He'll make a good boatswain. A good seaman. He's a Navy man."

Than that he could say no more.

Ballet

"In my eighteen years at sea I've known Navy people to come from just about any background you can think of. You're my first ballet officer. Your service record."

Lieutenant (jg) Rollins, I had always felt, got as much pure enjoyment, contentment if you will, out of her job—anti-submarine warfare officer—and out of the sea and shipboard life itself as any hand aboard.

"Well, it was this way . . ."

She looked up at the stars, back at the long plain of the night sea.

"I knew I was good. But I also came to know at some point that I would never go all the way: prima ballerina in a first-rate company. Pretty close but—if it's something like ballet, unless you can be at the very top, I decided it was foolish to go on. If there's any harder work I've not heard of it. And a short career. A woman is finished at, oh, age thirty-three. Only the top can justify that. I decided to check out."

"Was a Navy recruiting officer hanging around the stage door when you did?"

"Not quite. The idea of 'first' in *something* had got to be important to me. Silly, but there it was. The Navy—*noblesse oblige*—had just opened up this . . ." She indicated the stretching waters. ". . . to women. I decided to be one of the first to go to sea. And by God, I made it. How about that, Captain?"

"I congratulate the Navy."

She waited, as if uncertain whether to do so; then, as though impulsively, added something that rather startled me.

"Also I had decided I never wanted to get married. Being at sea was a good way to have that pass you by; no fuss in dodging it all the time like ashore."

It was not an excessive piece of vanity, the implication that she would have had to stave off a good deal of hassling. In terms of what are called pure feminine good looks, Rollins would probably have won any such contest on the *Nathan James*. To ask her for the reason for that decision would, of course, have been out of the question and I became aware that she would never give it to me voluntarily.

"In a way like myself," I said. "The sea had all the answers. And so here we are."

"Aye, sir. Here we are."

Weather

"They are bearing up rather amazingly well in my view." He spoke the word quietly: "Fortitude. I've never seen more."

We stood by the lifeline, somewhat forward of the after missile launcher; gazed across an acquiescent sea, manifestly about to change, full of intent. I could hear the first low muttering of the wind through the halyards and see swarthy clouds beginning to pass across the restless stars. Above and beyond us, the faint light thrown out by the masthead and range lights alone broke the ship's darkness. Near the midwatch, the weather decks deserted, ourselves out of earshot of all, we seemed nonetheless to speak in claustral whispers.

"I expected it of them." These were essential precursory probings, as we both knew. "But you're right. Bearing up better than anyone could have expected or had a right to expect."

As I have recounted elsewhere, we had worked out our own discrete ritual, the chaplain and I. I looked upward. The stars were leaving us fast, scampering for hiding places, abandoning us to the dark and somber vault of the night, the fog-mist beginning to envelop us. We heard the sea commence a low muffled roar as it received the riding ship. I recited the opening chord of the ritual now.

"I think I know real trouble when I see it. I don't think we are there, in any immediate sense."

"If we're talking about how long they will . . . wait." He stopped there and a silence hung.

I moved at once into an extra state of vigilance. To the multiple intonations of his voice I was attuned as to a complex cipher. In it now was something of presentiment, almost of apprehension, tinged slightly I felt even with fear. Therefore something to be heeded, since he was the least panicky of men, the last to raise false alarms.

"Tom," he said now, "I would put it this way." Even his rare, permitted use of my first name served to put me on notice, heighten my own aroused foreboding. "The sooner they know the better. It will only build. The men—I am talking about the spread of a kind of anxiousness. Rooted I believe in a feeling of uncertainty."

Coming from him, that was a rather major warning. Playing, I think, for time for the purpose of extracting more, even something quite specific, I spoke rather sidelong into it.

"I have never had more difficulty determining what is in their minds." He could be that much of a confessor. I waited, then said it. "I need to have them with me."

He seemed much surprised. "Oh, I think they are."

"I don't mean that. I mean with me whatever I decide."

Another reason for caution being that mentioned matter, the lethalness of words aboard ship, actually able to abet what one fears; to speak of certain things aboard ship can be the first step toward bringing them into being. He was silent for a moment, gazing at the stalking sea, which we were beginning to feel under our feet in the rise and fall of the weather deck. Both of us, with the instinct of sailors, looked up and saw the swarming clouds commencing to coalesce to form one black mass, sullen and huge, the last star extinguished; both anchoring ourselves more to the deck, feet reflexively spreading, planted, a bit more . . . "With me whatever I decide," I had said.

"Yes, I see the difference." I could feel in the dark his careful seriousness, his actual change of tone, a distant, almost delicate hint of reproach. "Naturally you will explain everything to them. When the time comes. The course . . . whatever it shall be . . . They peculiarly need a considerable measure of . . . explanation."

"Explanation?" A strange impatience flared through me. "The Frenchman? That Russian sub commander? Our own failures—nothing whatever received?"

With a twist of the shoulder I indicated our communications antennas, the wind now singing through the arrays under aroused seas.

"What remains to be explained, for God's sake?"

I felt from him a kind of intellectual shrug, as before things as they are as opposed to what one wished them to be.

"It may be a case of the unconvincible. They may have to see the nailprints, the wound in the side. Not strange, considering."

"We can't afford that kind of indulgence." A certain hardness came abruptly into my voice. Speaking more softly I said a vain thing. "Whatever it takes, I think I stand well with them there . . . in areas of persuasion . . ."

I was really not looking for confirmation of that self-ascribed attribute and he would know that I was not. His silence on the matter—neither of us was disposed to waste time affirming the other's vanities, either might mildly dispute a declared one if he so felt—was proof enough of that. One wanted to say outright, What if the decision should be to turn our backs on it forever . . . ? One could not. It would be to let predicted results dictate the decision; an abdication of everything a ship's captain was; cowardly, in fact. Still I knew that they were waters I had to test, as a ship on trial runs, a shakedown cruise. A captain must not back away from such matters; his only course is to seize them. I decided the time had come to put it as plainly as I dared.

"I need to have them *want* it that way. My choice to be their choice."

His eyes ranged from the high and coursing black clouds, now moved along more insistently by a freshening wind, to the dark sea which was beginning to respond in kind, its great mass sending waves surging to meet the oncoming heavens. Through their sound came from that voice a cautionary chord, softly spoken, in its way as bold as anything it had ever said to me as captain, its importance being a clear conveyance that what I had just spoken of as desirable was by no means to be taken for granted; there came a condition, distinct and unforgiving; rather hard in the way it fell on the air, his voice shading off into a tone close to insistence.

"It follows—it presumes—that your choice be the right one. Beyond any mistake. They must feel, know to an absolute, there is no other."

As if to temper this implicit admonition—it had in it even a touch of the threat—to balance it with comfort, he spoke again, the words falling soft but penetrating on the night.

"Some of them look to the Lord. But they all look to you, Captain."

I felt, along with a touch of wryness, a distant, perhaps hasty balm at that simple declaration. He had spoken to heal, to fortify. While making clear the remorseless fact that nothing was unconditional in our circumstances, he had as much as said he would go a very long way with me, to every possible limit be on my side, actively so, with ship's company. Help. Perhaps he had perceived more than had I that that was what I was asking for all along. Now, without the asking, he had offered it to me, a gift, freely given.

"Chaplain, I hope the Lord understands the respective weights you assign to the two of us—Him and this poor mortal sailor—in these matters."

His reply came in that same wry tone: "He has a tendency to understand. Especially, I sometimes think, all poor mortal sailors."

"I want them with me. But a sea captain: He cannot simply go with the majority. Even now. I would say especially now. I am not here for that."

He did the strange thing of touching my arm lightly, a lenitive gesture, his unseen hand coming out of the darkness. He was not one to go around touching people. I was not one to invite it. The touch may have had something to do with what happened next—unleashing it. I spoke, abruptly, in the way one sometimes does, not knowing you are going to say something until you hear it yourself; the words seeming to break through the dark mantle of the night toward his unseen being, perhaps without this merciful tempting opaqueness, never to have been uttered.

"Father . . ." I rarely called him that. "I have the responsibility of 305 souls. Their security, their welfare, their survival. Do you imagine I ever stop thinking about that?"

Darkness or not, I wished instantly I had not said it. It sounded a weakness, as though I were soliciting solace, pimping for sympathy. My voice over-earnest, even to myself, in it almost a pleading tone that I loathed. It was true that there was no one else aboard to whom I could speak my thoughts, and this not the first time I had spoken frankly with him; all the same there was a vast difference now. Previous times had concerned such matters as problems of one or another of ship's company, mine never among them. Sometimes concerned ideas in general, far from the Navy. Here now for the first time I seemed to have stepped squarely myself into his confession box. I was immediately anxious to get out of it, and as alacritously as possible. Then I became aware with a shock that I was returning the touch he had given me; but where his had been gentle, almost brushing, my hand was pressing hard into the flesh of his arm— hard enough another man would have cried out. I had not even realized what I was doing. I instantly let my hand drop limply on the lifeline. Then his very next words made me regret again, almost alarmingly so, that I had given voice to my personal anguish. The last thing we had time or maneuvering room for was the slightest shred of self-pity; certainly not from the officers; least of all from the captain.

"A heavy burden . . . Sometimes . . ." His voice emerged from the night as from gentle, inward origins; hesitated as though carefully framing words. "Sometimes I wonder if it's too much of a burden for any one man. I mean now . . ."

I turned sharply; looked at him—his dark shape; and he stopped again. Now and then I caught myself perhaps too vigilant for any sign, not of disloyalty so much, but of even the appearance of questioning, any remote or imagined intimation that in present circumstances there might be another and better way than the long-established one of a sovereign captain. For a moment I felt we had moved, all ahead full this time, into the most perilous of waters: the possibility of doubtings abroad on the ship. But no, he was speaking only in sympathy, in compassion; responding to my expressed need. He meant nothing directed at my leadership, my command. Of that I felt certain. He was not one to pussyfoot. If he had something to say he said it. Would do so even in that extreme matter, if ever it came to that. No one, not even his captain, could intimidate him, silence him, where he felt it his duty to speak. All the same I wanted to ask, *Have you heard anything in that place of yours, that confession box, concerning that subject?* Heard . . . dangerous unrest, even the stirrings of insurgence . . . anything close to these? I leaned toward his shape in the dark. Aware of the intenseness of listening there just by me; and of my own, alert for a murmur, a word from him. And heard only the hoarse sea, the ululant wind, no sound otherwise, not a whisper, only the hush from the waiting shipmate alongside. Then finally heard the words come from his lips, barely audible above the sounds of the elements.

"God will show us a way." He waited then, that declaration a mere litany to me, a recessional signaling parting, little more than a noise, falling scarcely heard upon the ear.

Felt certain, I said, that he was not calling into question a system itself, a captain's suzerainty. No, that is not quite the full truth. Doubt, thin slivers of it, remained . . .

I looked across the sea, unmistakably asserting itself now, ready yet again, lest, chatting away, we tend to take it for granted, to remind us of its regnant presence, its utter freedom to do as it pleased, our bodies now rising and falling as the ship, quick to take heed, began to meet her, sea and ship commencing once again their ancient and zealous fray. To attend this oncoming display, a fine obscuring mist, carrying with it a decided chill, began to impregnate the air. I had the feeling that there was something more clamoring to be said; from him; perhaps from myself. Waiting for him, should he so decide, I glanced forward to the bridge—all okay, the dim light of the ship's lights upon the deck house and rigging seemed to certify; back into the black void where the sea lay. Suddenly: "When we get where we are going. Wherever that is to be . . ." His voice faded off, swallowed up in the rising sound of sea and wind. I thought perhaps there were words following that I had missed, obliterated by the voice of the elements. I started to ask; did not; lost on the sea, the wind.

I looked up into the tenebrous firmament, seeming to rest like a weight on the ship's mainmast, the running lights now barely visible, the turgid hold of the night now complete; again turned toward where I knew him to be. In the enclosing opacity of the night, our chilled bodies beginning to feel the vibration of the ship as she pitched into the ascending sea, only two disembodied voices lowered to a barely audible quietude yet somehow full of every urgency, every doubt: words seeming dangerous, words seeming our sole hope. I felt a hush even within the climbing sounds of the elements, a corner of silence in which we stood all anticipant. I could feel the sea now riding hard under me, heard the undertone . . . as though another spoke, of my own voice, ". . . where we are going. If we are to be saved."

Then heard only the firmness and the gentleness, the duties of the office now paramount: there are times when even a captain can be given instruction.

"Tom, I do not have on my collar. But let us remember that not to hope is a sin."

I spoke almost brutally. "Then I stand without sin. I am hope itself."

"You are. For us all. Under God."

"God?" I said. It was as though the very word irritated, almost angered me. "Is He still around?"

"*Deus absconditus,*" he said gently, countering the anger. "At the most."

"What?"

"The God who went missing. Perhaps He went away for a while. If so, I feel confident He'll be back."

The fog-mist had enveloped the ship so that we were no longer able even to see the waters, only to hear their gathering roar and the smart flapping of the halyards before a freshening wind; feel the ship confidently penetrating this blind vale, leading us, all-trusting, believing above all else in the ship, with her into the night. Could scarcely see even the shape of each other, though standing but a foot apart. The deck coming up strongly now under our feet; one had to steady oneself. Gazing into blackness, as if undertaking to determine what might lie beyond it, we seemed to pierce through it with one of those single thoughts that can occur in ways we know not. Quite naturally, almost offhand, I heard myself to say, "What do you think, Father?" and his voice, equally soft and clear through a moment's pause in that duet of sea and wind, "There are others. There have to be others." "But surely not back there—not back home," I said, half-statement, half-question. The duet resumed: If he made answer, I did not hear it.

I could see the first wave come surging out of the mists and, breaking hard across the bow, board the ship, the ship responding with a plunging pitch a quantum deeper than anything before, throwing us with a certain force against each other. It was somewhere in that coming physically together that it came, or seemed to come. I thought, startling me, I heard him say—could not be sure because he normally no more would ask me a direct question about such a matter than I would him about what was said in his confession box—not sure, either, because of that clamor of the elements—seeming to come more a murmur than a question, "Have you decided the course?" And thought myself to respond, for the third time in a form of address I rarely used with him, "Yes, Father, I have."

We brought ourselves apart. Then distinctly, the words this time deliberately unmistakable, as though to get with all alacrity away from that abruptly touched-on matter: "We're in for some weather," I said. "I best have a look on the bridge."

I disappeared into the mist forward, guided only by the pale glow of the running lights and the sure knowledge of a seaman for his ship. Then I knew. I had been in his confession box myself, all along. Feeling clinging to me fresh doubts, presentiments undefined, something in me still uneasy less at what he had said than what he had chosen to leave unsaid; myself, too; for if he had secrets I did as well; yet there seeming no choice for now but that brutal and merciless one of leaving the air filled with unspoken and unspeakable thoughts. I recalled his words: "When we get where we are going. Wherever that is to be . . ." They seemed to ring in the night, herald of all that was ominous, unknown, to hover above the ship, over the last soul aboard, like a dark following cloud not to be shaken off however far the ship penetrated the night, clinging cruelly to her, and to demand something more: not to stop there . . .

The voice of the sea had assumed a deeper, more commanding tone and now another joined in: the rolling of distant thunder, hanging long beyond the veiled sky; now coming closer in, low and elongated, marching hard upon us; then an immense coruscation of lightning, scarring the heavens from zenith to sea, the following thunder breaking shatteringly almost directly on top of us, the ship trembling under it; once more a staccato series of lightning displays that seemed to illumine as day the entire vastness of the sea naked to the farthest horizon save for a lone and spectral ship riding through its cresting waves, bound only her captain coming to know where, and even so only were he permitted the rights of his command position, only if the men came along with his decision, his intentions for ship and ship's company. The relumined heavens lighting my way up the ladder to the bridge, I seemed to reach down into the utmost ends of my soul to see what fortitude of my own, what will and resolve, might be found there. The storm was coming on.

.6.

CONFRONTATION

It was as though my nights of prowling, of making myself accessible, had at last paid off; not in the way I would have chosen; finding not what I had hoped to find, though half-expected to; rather, what I dreaded most.

At least I am made aware, alerted. That is something.

All that day long we had glassed the beach. Not a sign of life. Not a human being. Not an animal. Nothing even worth picking up in our scavenging, not so much as a second wheelbarrow—an item, incidentally, almost obsessively desired by Delaney. "Very few things more important than a wheelbarrow, sir," the gunner's mate–farmer had informed me in his arcane way. A brief foray in the boat by Selmon showed prohibitive readings for any stay.

Then on this another of my nights of roaming with the intent of making myself available to all, I found myself standing along the lifeline next to Lieutenant Commander Chatham. No random encounter: I felt clearly, from the first, that he had sought me out here, having taken note of what was by now a nightly custom; having picked his moment. None about, due both to the lateness and to a gathering weather that hung heavy in a somehow portentous darkness; more of that heavy weather that seemed increasingly to come suddenly down on us in great contrast to the earlier prevailing stilled heavens, stilled seas.

We were without stars. Emerging from an opaque cloud cover a mild wind had come up, and one could feel under one's feet the slow preludial pitch of the ship, these life signs of sea and elements almost a welcome thing after the long silences over mirroring waters. The ship seemed to like the change, riding eagerly through the shallow troughs. Characteristically for Chatham, never one for small talk, he came right to the point.

"Captain, I had a little chat the other day with the engineering officer."

"Yes, Mr. Chatham?"

"We started talking how by cutting speed to, say, eight knots, we would take considerably less off our remaining available cruising time; it started me thinking about the idea of going just there and back."

I was instantly alerted. Normally I would have spoken sharply concerning the circumspection of a Navy officer's staying out of matters that were not his province, and in that area to await his captain's request as to an opinion. These days I gave a wider rein. I was not so stupid as to attempt to control men's thoughts, or even their talking with one another. After all, the amount of running time we had remaining was hardly confidential information. The very fact that he had spoken to such a matter was itself startling enough, unsolicited advice to her captain by subordinate officers a distinctly unusual thing on a man-of-war. Much more so was the possibility, coming immediately to mind, that he was speaking not just for himself, the likelihood even that had to be considered that he would not have done so unless he had a fair number of the crew behind him. This was the very last thing I should ask him. If true, it would certify his unauthorized role of spokesman for, leadership of, a part—how many?—of ship's company, with a particular right to be heard; an inadmissible thing, none more so aboard ship. I must not grant him that. And it was by no means certain. Chatham was capable of speaking only for Chatham. Even so, he must have had to work up a certain boldness to broach the subject. Caution set in. I remained noncommittal. If he so wished, let him push on. No help in that respect would he get from me. He waited as if gathering his inner resources to do so, then began to speak. Normally with a rather rasping timbre to it, his voice now came also with a certain growing insistence that I did not like. ". . . And if we came straight back . . ."

"We would still have lost propulsion time." I finished that sentence for him with a sharpness I had not intended. Certainly no one knew the figures more precisely than did I, the fuel loss at various speeds having been calculated with the greatest precision. "Valuable time. Perhaps crucial time. We've been over all this, Mr. Chatham. You have spoken with the engineering officer. Have you also spoken with Girard?"

"Why, no, sir, I have not."

"Since you have started these inquiries, you might wish to do so." I could not conceal all the sternness at what he was doing and I heard it now in my voice. "You might ask for the figures on the time remaining—I mean pursuing the course you refer to—we would have in her department. I'm talking about eating days, Mr. Chatham."

"Captain, I was only . . ." In his voice was something much less of apology than a kind of resentful defensiveness, the barest touch even of truculence.

"I know, Mr. Chatham." I tried to speak more softly. I could not see his features in the dark but I knew that he was quite aware that he had ventured into the most fragile of waters.

"Mr. Chatham," I said . . . and then waited.

Far off the night's first thunder rolled across the sky, merged with the sea's ascendant tone. Abruptly I had a sense of something projected from the body alongside me into my own, shortcutting the avenues of speech or even conscious thought. Something clearly menacing, drawn near; I stood in new environs, overt questioning, hanging in the air a sense of machination, of maneuverance, touching on complicity. Then, as suddenly and in complete contradiction, perhaps because the verifiable ground for such thoughts were of the thinnest, I wondered if what I was really hearing from within him was a cry of private distress, a supplication for help. An officer taken in a moment with a malady which came without either warning or symptoms. Presented with an untoward manifestation from any of ship's company, an occurrence of growing frequency to the point it had ceased to be a phenomenon, one's mind stretched these days to include the widest spectrum of utterly opposing causes before settling on one or on none at all, cause remaining irremediably shrouded. The thing then disappearing as quickly as it had emerged. In this manner for a strange moment I felt in myself a disorientation, not knowing whether I was dealing with the rebellious, or, quite the opposite, with someone in some desperate need that he was incapable of articulating directly. Or with some unknown third or fourth thing.

Great columns of that soundless night lightning that we had been experiencing began to play hugely over the southern sky to starboard, altogether marvelous and continuing; revealing the commencement of long rolling waves across the naked seascape, a blossoming of whitecaps on the blackness of the waters, the distant desert to starboard in its undulating geometry. I wished extremely to turn and look him square in the face in its light but did not, fearful of the stark obviousness of such a thing. I looked across the ship's bow. It was beginning to plunge more deeply into the troughs, slower in coming up. A sudden pitch threw us for a moment unexpectedly against each other. An absolutely unexperienced sensation shot through me—the contact of his body against mine seemed an unpleasant thing, one almost of distaste, this feeling itself so astonishing to me in respect to a shipmate that it seemed at once to constitute a warning, as of some dangerous bias toward a particular officer when there was nothing of any real substance, other than words, I could lay against him.

Perhaps in consideration of these speculations, ambivalences, a softer tone was the response called for. Certainly he had identified an amount of hostility in me toward his approach, likely to enhance rather than pacify the air of disquiet. Fearful of suspecting what was not there, I decided to reprimand him no further, not to build up alienation: To come through we would need not that but brotherhood. We had no more deadly enemy than divisiveness: true always of a ship, with its closely lived existence, in our circumstance greatly compounded. Men had a right to know they would be told, and presently. Surely they had sensed that anyway, indeed informed so by myself. But let him spread the word afresh. He seemed to have become adept at that. I spoke with quiet clarity, not untempered with firmness, striving for a balance between not diminishing him and yet squaring him away.

"Mr. Chatham," I said, *"we cannot do both.* Do you understand that?"

"I understand what you say, sir."

I fought back the flash of anger, at the obstinacy, the impertinence, of this answer. I had heard enough. It was not the time to get into it, nor would any time be with a single officer. When the moment came, it would be a thing to be shared with the last and lowliest rating in ship's company, all equals at that point. To discuss it further in this privacy was not only unseemly behavior for a captain, not the way to do things; it would also only confer on the CSO a special authority that I had not the slightest intention of recognizing. It should be stopped at once. This time I spoke with a manifest severity. Even so I went further than a captain normally did, or ought to do, to accommodate, in such a revelation to himself alone; along with some home truths.

"Mr. Chatham, here is the straight dope. The answer to what you're wondering is that I have not as yet made up my mind. I have neither resolved upon nor ruled out the course you suggest," going that far even. "When I come to a decision, I'll let you—and all hands—know. It will be soon. Is all that understood?"

"Yes, sir. It's understood." Still a slightly sullen note. Never mind. He had got the word. Then, just as I had thought the matter finished, it hit me squarely in the face.

"Captain, we want to participate in the decision."

I turned on him in as strong an anger as I had ever felt, or shown, since becoming a ship's captain.

" 'Participate'? 'We'?"

So it had gone this far. I waited a moment for the thing to settle in me, that inward hardness which, long since, entirely reflexive by now, had become my armament in extreme confrontation, every idea of indulgence toward this officer vanished.

"Listen well, Mr. Chatham." I could hear my own voice, quiet, cold, in the sudden hush, the deadly taut atmosphere, as if even the sea herself, always curious as to such developments in her domain, had paused to listen. "I intend for there to be not the slightest misunderstanding. As to 'participate.' This ship will continue to have a captain. He will reach his decisions as Navy ship's captains do. With such counsel from ship's officers as he feels needed, receiving it in the way it is always offered: when he asks for it. As to the 'we': I do not wish to know their names. But you may take that word back to them. The affairs of the ship will continue to be conducted in the manner just described. If all that is clear then let us speak no more of it. Do you understand me?"

Out of the dark the simply monotonic, the voice of the subordinate returned, still sounding no more than the requisite. "As you say, sir. I understand you."

"Good night, Mr. Chatham."

"Good night, Captain."

Dismissed, he disappeared into the darkness forward.

I stayed awhile, the extra heartbeat receding before the assurance of the ship under me taking on the rising waters. Now the elements began to unfold for my pleasure a modest, unthreatening display of weather, nothing for her to worry about, the ship dipping into the deepening valleys of the sea, each time with a faint shudder that moved up through her keel, up through the spaces of the ship to the weather decks, up through my legs, my body. I could hear above and forward the wind slapping the halyards and see the glow of the running lights leading us on into the night. The rhythmic sound of the ship's foghorn reaching down from the bridge—the routineness of the precaution, as if beyond the mists there was another ship closing on us, stabbing me like a physical pain. And suddenly I knew. Knew as surely as I stood there looking at the throbbing, lightning-illuminated sea, that Chatham was implicated. Deceit has almost a scent to it. No, not just that. Factiousness. Even the Jesuit had hinted as much. And putting all the signals together, an immense foreboding seized me; some disturbing and threatening element had come aboard, involving the CSO in some inexplicable manner. And the further thought, sending an icy chill crawling up and down my spine: If Chatham had been bold enough to approach me thus, argue with me as to the possibility of the impossible, what had he been saying to the others? Implanting hope for a place where all hope was gone? Prodding their thinking and their desires toward the most perilous and heartbreaking of expectations concerning their very home? Cruel this was.

Big foaming seas had begun to come out of the blackness, the ship responding each time with a tremor, readily conforming, adjusting, my face wetted by the salt spray, seeming to clear my mind to see into the truth of things in this solipsistic darkness: the ship more and more becoming split into opposing camps; the shores of the Mediterranean continuing to signal us their refusal to offer safe habitation, the hard consequent fact that, barring still possible changes in that respect, at Suez we would have to commit ourselves, never looking back, to one of the two choices available as to course; despite anything that Chatham had put about or that any others of ship's company might have led themselves independently to believe, that we were compelled to do one, fuel and food supplies dictating we could not do both—any seaman apprentice who used his head could figure that one out. Those who could not were simply identifying wish with fact: This tendency I accepted as natural in men and was one reason, among others, that it had never occurred to me seriously to consider any such notion as putting the matter to a vote.

I had long since come to terms with the possibility, even probability, that in the case of one of the two courses, should I decide on it, the loyalty to myself of the most faithful and unswerving of men might well be put to the severest test. Refusal, if I should issue it despite whatever opposition, to obey a lawful order. An effort even to take the ship. Nothing could be ruled out. In my mind I could even understand it, told the awful finality of what the men would have to be told. Men informed they would never see home again: Who could predict how it would take them? An understanding which did not for one moment admit the possibility of allowing it to succeed. My resolve lay in the confidence in my ability to control it well before it reached any such state; to reason, to persuade, drawing on the trust I felt resided in them toward their captain; the decision set forth to them in that firm mastery which traditionally had brought obedience from sailors in the direst of circumstances, ships being able to function in no other known manner; yet knowing that simply to command, to give an order, was no longer enough. I must compel belief from them by what came down to an absolute moral assurance on my part (the Jesuit was right in that): my way at least offering hope, if against odds; the other guaranteeing disaster, no odds at all. Our fate had always seemed to me to rest absolutely on our remaining united, a band of brothers. Nothing in my thinking took into account that the lines would be rigidly drawn, certainly not to the extent of either group having a leader, and he an officer. That brought a sense of authentic fear, of a foreboding greatly enhanced that it should be this particular officer; the last officer I should wish to discover at that work, for the simple reason that, as I have remarked, short only of the captain he is the most powerful officer aboard. Combat systems officer. As such, the most potentially dangerous of officers in circumstances, if remote, still not at all hard to imagine as possibilities in our near future. I was allowed to hope that the admonitions just delivered would have effect, stop in its tracks a movement already clearly underway; I would be an idiot to count on it.

I heard the ship under me, its very sound seeming to remind me of the true seat of my concern: the ship herself. The fact that we ourselves were such a stupendously dangerous device, racked up in magazines not far below where I stood 44 Tomahawks, each carrying a 200-kiloton nuclear warhead, a capability of destructiveness even I had really never attempted to comprehend; this infinite instrument able to go anywhere, do anything, now beyond any control other than that of the people aboard her. Yes, the truth was this: All of my anxiety, my dread, immense and profound, lay in not wanting another to gain dominion over this force, least of all an officer like Chatham, trusting no one but myself with such power. There it was.

From the rising sea I could feel now and then a tossed-off spray touching my face; refreshing, freeing up, it seemed, the full faculties I now brought to bear as I undertook quietly to assess the circumstance, even allowing myself to stretch it to its extreme limits. I was positioned by the lifeline aft, a matter of feet away from the after missile launcher. Due perhaps in part to its proximity, I had for the first time a thought that sent through me a wave of shock quite unlike any I had ever experienced in regard to the ship and the people on it, or any one of them, relating to a matter I have touched on, my growing concern over the fact that Chatham held, jointly with myself, the key to the missiles themselves, and to the devices that would send them off . . . the mind halted, made a movement, opened a door, permitting something quite terrible to enter, an errant and wild thought of what might happen if they should fall into the hands of one bent—for whatever reason or cause, fancied or real enemies, madness, revenge upon the human race itself or what might be left of it if you took the ship across the seas looking for these remnants . . . Perhaps the thought itself was the truly mad thing; but perhaps not, one often hardly knew of late, the rational and the aberrant sometimes seeming separated by a line thin as a human hair: The mind had presented only what was after all factually, insofar as we had knowledge of it, a largely accomplished matter. What remained might be viewed as merely a mopping-up operation . . . of the species . . . Chatham, for instance—I had not the slightest doubt of this—would have blown that Russian sub out of the water . . . All doors now opened, I even remembered once, in some random wardroom conversation, his saying, "I am glad to be a member of the generation that will see the last of the human race," a remark taken so unseriously at the time, viewed by all who heard as intended as shock treatment—perhaps Chatham angry at some mechanical problem aboard ship in his complex charges, the missiles, all of this long forgotten. Now suddenly even that surely ridiculous remark came back to repeat itself to me—preposterous that I should think of it just now; not able for a moment to bring myself to believe he, any man, could believe that literally. Still, the mind, recalling it, filled with a kind of distortion, a madness of its own . . .

The mind stepped back from the horror, slammed the door: but not before imbedding in me an idea untainted by the slightest doubt, cold as truth could be, felt now infinitely more sharply, frighteningly, than before: I would not want the missiles . . . weaponry I had even considered jettisoning, an impossibility without the collaboration of his key, no way even to get them off the ship without it, something he was certain never to give; his more than touch of arrogance I had long felt could itself be traced to his feeling of proprietorship as to the missiles . . . I would not want them under the governance of Lieutenant Commander Chatham. After the initial brutal impact of the idea, with surely its excesses, this I judged not excessive at all. Though I tried to put it away. To no avail: It was to hang on, never to leave me, try as I did to make it do so. Rather to increase: myself to come in rather a short time almost to wish for some act on his part (Was it this? Was I actually hoping he would undertake to lead a party against my choice as to course?) that would justify my separating him from his key: the fact of our keys canceling each other, one impotent without the other, somehow seeming no longer adequate protection—if I was considering going after his, it was not a difficult step to imagine his contemplating going after mine; the first time, too, for that terrible thought.

The mind halted, came to a full stop; aware that such imaginings, whatever their portion of truth, themselves could become the true danger. I looked up at the heavens. The clouds had opened up a small space, just sufficient to permit a handful of brave stars to gaze tremulously down, their abrupt appearance, sparkling as a cluster of diamonds on a black field, immediately somehow lifting my spirits. In their glow I reminded myself that we had not given up all hope on the Mediterranean. Some time back Selmon, in view of the absence of life on the beaches, had suggested a land foray of a kind not yet undertaken to establish perhaps conclusively the facts there, one way or the other. Involving a not inconsiderable personal risk, hence a risk for the ship, in his being such an indispensable officer, which had made me wish to think it over and to postpone decision. Now I decided to turn him loose on it tomorrow. It was something we had to know.

With the conversation with the CSO I ceased my nightly rovings and returned to the traditional calm austerity, and a certain remoteness, of a ship's captain. Just as well. Applicable to the ships that traverse the great oceans, there stands a small handful of rules, known to all mariners from times the most ancient, so validated by the centuries, on vessels of every description, ship's companies of every origin, as to be immutable. Among these is that which states that the concept that some favorable result is to be achieved by a ship's captain's efforts to draw closer to his men through so-called familiarity, by an effort to diminish the distance between them which the all-knowing sea herself has long ago decreed, is but the most naïve of myths, in fact dangerous in the first magnitude to the ship's very functioning, not least to the welfare of the men themselves, and the captain who attempts it a fool. If anything, the law held more firmly in our circumstance than ever. Men are to be commanded; and to be loved.

As stated, I had no intention of majority rule in the matter, not the remotest thought of instituting some shipboard seagoing plebiscitary system; the whole notion foolish in the extreme, perilous as a thing could be. But now, considering the possibility that I may have gone too far in my estimate of his potential for bringing disaster upon us; considering above all that unforgiving precept that a ship's captain, in his sovereignty, his power, in the absence of the normal checks and balances that restrain men, carries in him by these very essentials of his position more capacity for being wrong than perhaps in any trade men follow and therefore must never forget that he may be . . . reminding myself of these verities, very soon I found myself actually having a look at Chatham's proposal. Of allowing ship's company to make this one decision on the moral idea that they had a right to decide something so irreversible as to their own future lives. For the first time since assuming command of this ship, I considered in all seriousness letting them do so. Nothing could have been more strange, the very act, the mechanics of it, so contrary to the world of ships and of sea life. How in the name of heaven would you go about it—call for a showing of hands, with the majority to rule? Even the visualizing of it made it seem a ludicrous thing: sailors raising their hands while the captain counts them as in some sort of town meeting voting whether they wished to do this instead of that. Its only virtue—and a compelling one—appeared to be that it was the one certain way of forestalling any possible revolt in the crew: They could hardly object to a course chosen by themselves. But on further consideration, even this supposed advantage appeared to have its inbuilt fallacy.

What if the vote were close? You would then have a ship split against itself. I was far from sure ship's company would even *want* to make the decision: Among other things it would force each hand to declare himself before his shipmates, the divisiveness then a known and permanent thing, brought starkly out in the open. Shipmates thereafter working alongside one another knowing that there existed a profound disagreement among themselves as to the most fundamental of matters: where the ship was taking them. A ship divided on such an issue: I could taste, as surely as I could tell the movements of stars, her pernicious fruits. Bitterness, rancor, dripping so into that incessant immensity of tasks, navigation, engineering, and the rest of it that constitute proper shiphandling, as to threaten the ship at every turn in a world that has always been constructed on the principle of unquestioned one-man rule: orders, commands, decisively given by the captain and obeyed unhesitatingly by all others aboard, men and officers alike. This at a time that called for men working together to the utmost, shipmates toward a goal desperate enough of achievement even so.

As I continued to think on the matter, so many other objections presented themselves as to seem unending. To be allowed to make this decision might make them wish to make further ones; control of the ship and the course she should take slipping through the captain's hands, and at the very moment, fuel and food headed inexorably toward the zero point, that we commenced our most perilous times. A ship soon to be without a rudder. I would not myself wish to be on such a vessel even as the lowliest seaman; would flee from her as from a death ship.

And the final and greatest argument of all: They might make the wrong decision, based on false sentiments, unrealistic hopes; based on the wish that matters were a certain way, rather than on what they were; feeling confident I, the captain, could and would in the end turn away from such lures; much less certain that a diverse body of men given such authority would do the same.

No. I would make this decision as I made all others; fully aware that that method also was not without risk; it not being inconceivable that those against whose preference the decision fell might go so far as to rise up. I did not believe so. But whether it should happen or not: No weight must the prospect be granted. For a sea captain, that a course having been chosen by him as in his view the sole right one, has really no choice but to march into it; simply put, do the duty and take the burden that are lawfully his alone to carry out, his alone to bear.

.7.

THE ANIMALS

Each day, it seems, I gain respect for his knowledge. No radar, no sonar, none of the ship's supremely sophisticated devices for forecasting an enemy's approach are of the slightest account here. The fineness of his judgments, telling us where we can go and where we cannot, defining what we can do at a place and for how long, what we can pick up in our foragings and what we must leave be, however useful to our future . . . Lieutenant (jg) Selmon is showing himself an officer of very high professionalism. His vocation is the new priesthood. We do nothing without first obtaining his approval—his blessing. Even the distance off we cruise—inshore or actually out of sight of all land—is determined by his calculations.

Remembering the time, seeming so far back now, when quite a number of the learned felt they could predict with fair accuracy what would happen: The truth now stands clear that they had known virtually nothing of what they were talking about. In actual practice the nature of radioactive fallout turns out to be a matter of infinite, ever-changing complexities, of obscurity and treachery, of chimeras and realities, and the everlasting, mind-devouring difficulty of determining one from the other. A great deal, perhaps the major part of it, having to do with the winds,

301

with currents of air—these, as any sailor knows, being the most permutable, undivinable of forces even in normal conditions, the importance of this fact tyrannically multiplied now that they have become the transportation system of our foe. The winds dictate now, deciding where the deadly substances shall go, and how much of them, and where they shall not; all of this deviable and unpredictable in the entire, the fancies, the mercuriality, the conceits of these deities of the atmosphere determining in great measure our every act and intention, what place it is not safe to be at all, what place it is safe to be for one hour, and what place for four. All of them at times existent in a narrow range of geography, sometimes a matter of only miles apart, and their individual statuses as to safety and peril constantly varying with the arrival of new atmospheric cargo, or even departure of the old, as the winds may decide. The one characteristic they have in common is that there is some contamination everywhere, enough so that no land we have yet approached permits us an indefinite stay, all proffering a hospitality measured at the most in hours. Every day we stand in to scan and test the shore and then return to sea where we wash down the ship with the system designed to seek out and send overboard whatever particles she may have attracted. It works well, Selmon's radiac shows. But even at sea we constantly run into "pockets" of the toxicant (perhaps brought there by winds, then stalled by sudden windlessness)— the radiac is always manned, as much so as are the ship's helm, her radar, her sonar—and have to scoot out of them and once more wash the ship down.

Since our actions and our future are confined within those limits dictated by the field of Selmon's experience and his knowledge, I have a kind of continuing dialogue with him, undertaking myself to master to a degree the fiendish subtleties of this new dimension, a fourth now added to the ancient triad wherein life has dwelt and had its being since time began—earth, sea, sky. Now this sovereign newcomer, more fickle by far than any of the others, moving about, settling here, not settling there, almost whimsically one would say if the game were less deadly, its nature less feral, inflicting all with disconcertion, confoundment; and infinitely more stealthy than any of the elements sailors have heretofore had to deal with in its impregnability to all of man's customary warning devices—you cannot see, taste, smell, hear, touch it. That clandestine characteristic indeed constituting its most terrible threat, the men having to learn, a fact that in itself leads to an active and continuing disorientation, that the testimony of their senses is here worthless, the only guide of any reliability being Selmon's instruments. There have been one or two occasions when, gone ashore for some purpose on some perfectly lovely day of blue and sunlit skies, of sweetest air, to all evidences, I have had to speak sharply to men to make them reembark in the boat when Selmon murmured the ritualistic phrase he has adopted: "It's time, Captain." He has become like some oracle—half seer, half sorcerer—we cannot do without; anymore than the ship can dispense with her gyro-compass.

This new dimension: None aboard has penetrated to and come to terms with its almost spiritual meaning, if one may use such a term, so deeply as himself. His dispassionate calm, his—I must say, almost serene acquiescence in the fact of it: It is as though he has quietly not just acceded to but embraced this new order as having become in the nature of things, simply recognizing that to fuss or grieve or to rail against it is on the order of railing in previous times against the inconstancy of the sea or the capriciousness of the elements. There is one constant: the farther we are from land, the more out at sea, the lower the radiation count. Out there we have seen dolphins play, following alongside our ship. Also the deeper we move into the land the higher the readings. The latter had been established near Carthage where Selmon for that very purpose— a permission I granted reluctantly (and on the very next day following my night's talk by the lifeline with Lieutenant Commander Chatham), for I had come absolutely to comprehend that I could let no harm befall this officer—had marched straight inland as far as a mile, the rem count rising steadily until he knew he must go no farther. Later, behind the closed doors of my cabin, we had discussed this circumstance, this finding, and its implications for us; his first repeating to me at my request the readings he had encountered, nothing we had run into being anything like that high; figures which kept me silent for a while before saying it.

"It suggests that the continent is gone, all of it."

There seemed a stillness about, a calm not to be explained except perhaps by that other fact of how far we had come, in our beings, in our souls, knowing acceptance itself—of whatever probable reality—to be the very price tag of our survival. Clear explanation, too, a kind of parenthesis, now brought of why we had not seen human beings even on the beaches— the land so close behind rendered impossible to get through. I could hear Selmon's softly pitched voice.

"There is no way to know or to find out, Captain; not absolutely. But we know this: the larger the land mass, the greater the contamination. And its corollary: the greater the distance from the sea, the higher the level. With that immense mass far away from any sea, and with a mere mile from the shore become unacceptable, and climbing steadily . . . Close to a certainty, sir."

There is a curious thing, scarcely given to our comprehension of it, having to do with the unlimited capacity of the mind itself. If one is living in virtual entirety in the purlieus of unknowns, certainties of whatever kind can, in some bizarre and unknowable manner, have their comfort, especially if accompanied by a practical side, however final. Just as absence of knowledge paralyzes, this corollary: To know is to be able to act. With food supplies ever-diminishing, with each day one less of propulsion power for the ship, we had no time to throw away. If the message now was, move along, get on with it . . . That, in its brutal way, was something. Though perhaps not quite yet: Selmon was speaking, his words quietly, insistently, breaking through my thoughts.

"Sir, I think we should continue to take an occasional beach reading clear to Suez. Shouldn't require all that much time. It is just possible— somewhere down the line between here and there. Some place that for some not very logical reason escaped. Some fluke . . ." The words trailed off in their sense of the unlikelihood, the remoteness of the idea. "At the same time it might be prudent perhaps to begin to think further ahead . . . geographically, that is . . ."

His voice ceased—it took me a moment to realize. I sat looking at him, thoughtful.

"It went up—steadily—as you went inland?"

Somehow I needed the fact restated and certified. "Affirmative, sir. No backing off at any point. Even the rate was even. It was like a thermometer registering some rising fever. A very obvious correlation. I could see the ruins—in the distance. I had to stop."

I spoke an aside. "Still there?"

"No visible change, sir." He had mentioned before he went in that he had seen Carthage, on a holiday, not a half dozen years ago, and hoped to make it there this time. His counter meter had not permitted him to do so.

We spoke in studious, uncompulsive tones, in a manner meditative, our minds set to reassessments in this new light; the taking of fresh compass bearings for a ship blocked in its present course by impenetrable minefields. I was thinking of those inexorable laws of mathematics here applied of which he had just spoken, of land masses, of distances from the shores of seas. I had already, scarcely aware of the transition, the mental crossover, begun to look ahead, to put the Mediterranean behind me. Then—it was the first time—a thought took shape, an hypothesis.

"The one consistency appears to be that: the farther from land, the more out at sea, the less the contamination. Now you have added: the farther into the land, the higher. Might these taken together suggest an island as possibly having the best chance to escape it entirely? A particular sort of island. Not very large—and provided, most important, it be surrounded by vast spaces of water?"

I could see his mind carefully evaluating; he then spoke as if having reached a careful preliminary position.

"Based on the finding over there, and our knowledge of the substance's behavior to date, it would seem to be a strong candidate," he said. "Yes. A piece of land far from all other land, no part of it distant from the sea—also, as you say, the place itself situated in the most immense body of protective water possible." He paused a beat. "The problem: if such a thing can be found that meets other requirements."

I shrugged, deliberately, and spoke offhandedly. "Of course, we are speaking theoretically. It was only a thought, and a premature one. We are certainly not searching for any island. However high on that one list, it would almost be guaranteed to be woefully far down on the other— those requirements you mention."

A warning signal went off in a captain's soul. I decided we had gone far enough with this. It was the first time the idea of an island had been broached. Beyond this exploratory stage, I felt it was much too early at present to take it further. It was hazardous territory: the immense difficulties such a life would bring in its train; worse, for now, the certain hostility of ship's people to any such proposition, isolating them on some island in nowhere. Best not to test it further now, to let the notion—it was hardly more than that—retreat into our minds; rest there, a kind of possible fail-safe, if it should come to that.

"A wild thought probably," I said. "And Mr. Selmon?"

"Sir?"

"You are not to speak to the crew of this, any member of it. Any talk of islands. Is that understood?"

"Understood, sir."

"I don't think it'll ever come to that. Another thing. I see no reason to broadcast your findings—over there. Would serve no useful purpose. And might well add to the difficulties—mental, emotional . . . They have enough to handle. No need at all to hit down on them with that kind of news." I moved my tone of voice up a notch. "Clear?"

"Clear. I understand fully, sir."

The truth was, I was saving it. I looked quietly at him. "Meanwhile, I take your suggestion: We will stop now and then between here and Suez. Places you deem the best bets, if anything like that appears. It would be nice to be wrong, to find one of those freaks, flukes, you speak of."

"It would indeed, sir. In my view, we shouldn't give over all expectations there. Some place that by a twist lucked out: I would not rule it out. We have seen other aberrations. Nor would I place high odds there."

"I shall be careful not to do so."

He smiled thinly. We sat, silent, lingering for a few moments, pensive, contemplating, both of us, the knowledge he had brought back; undertaking, I believe, to get deeper into it, finding that not an easy thing; acceptance, I think, for the reasons given, being achieved much more readily than comprehension. I felt an unaccountable need in him to say something more before he left, so did not dismiss him. He made a slight movement.

"Africa," he said. He spoke the name of the continent barely aloud, as though to himself, as one speaks of the bygone, the dead.

"Yes, Mr. Selmon?"

"Odd, sir. I was thinking of the animals. Not to put them first. But rather that we have become accustomed almost to what happened to the people. London. Those beaches in Italy. And of course everything north of there. Paris. Grenoble . . . very pretty place. I competed once in the European games at the University of Grenoble—gymnastics."

"Did you?" I said.

The sudden personal note constituted almost rambling for him. "Sorry, sir." He waited a moment, collecting himself. "It's only that we have become used to . . . to hardly expecting that anything *but* that would happen to the people . . ."

"I understand," I said, for I did.

"So one thinks of the zebras and the lions, the giraffes and the elephants . . ." Poignant fell his voice, and strangely gentle . . . "The animals may still be alive. In fact, probably are, most of them. Not for so very long, I shouldn't imagine . . . though again we have no certainties. But for the present still around, down inside there. We know that."

"Are you saying that the animals will live longer than men?"

"Oh, yes, sir. Of course not a great deal so. And even among themselves, varying quite considerably."

Something jumped up, alert, in me. He went on to explain that for some reason nobody had ever been able definitively to determine or account for, virtually all other members of the animal kingdom stood superior to man in the amount of radiation they could absorb. Sufficient amounts, of course, would take any of them in time but all both endured eventually lethal doses longer and could survive unharmed doses that would affect deleteriously their alleged better on evolution's ladder. He continued in a mood contemplative, almost of a nostalgic character, a temperament in which I had not before seen him, an officer as he was entirely professional, to the point, given to excluding all extraneous matters. I found myself listening with a special intentness as he continued to educate me.

"They did these animal radiation tests at a place out in West Texas. Amarillo, Texas—it was the end of civilization," he commented. Selmon was from Boston. "The Wild West. They were a damned sight more secret than they ever needed to be—but then everything was. Secrecy was a disease. They picked up our whole class and planted us down there for a full month. Just so we could see it for ourselves. They didn't, couldn't, try it on everything. Rhinoceros, for example. Lions. Wildebeest. Not many of those in Texas. But almost every domesticated, or semi-domesticated, you could think of. Pigs. Sheep. Cattle of assorted breeds—to find out whether there were differences in the amounts a Hereford, a Charolais, a Santa Gertrudis, or a Brahmin could take—they actually tested, compared those four. Do you know what animal of all turned out to have the highest tolerance?"

"No idea."

"Prairie dogs. Plenty of those around Amarillo, Texas."

"Prairie dogs? How odd. Anyone find out why?"

"Not the foggiest. One speculation—a frivolous one basically—was that they spent so much time underground."

"Amarillo, Texas," I mused absently. "I believe that's where they put the things together. Place called Pantax. Any connection between the location of that industry and the animal tests being conducted there?"

"As a matter of fact there was. The radioactive ingredients being so conveniently at hand for the exposures."

"Prairie dogs," I reflected. "Who would ever have thought. Something rather profound in that if I could think what it is."

Again he smiled thinly. "I always felt so, sir."

"It would be interesting to know how giraffes fare in comparison with prairie dogs."

"Yes, too bad we never learned. No giraffes in Amarillo, Texas."

My choice would have been to find a couple of cows, along with a not very large bull, but I felt certain that, however these ranked on the radiation ladder, they would never make it on the nautical ladder, aboard ship: certainly not on a destroyer. Cows would insist on larger and more commodious vessels. If not cows, why not goats? They would suit my purpose just as well. Somehow I had the feeling, with no shred of evidence or knowledge to back it up, that they would also make better sailors. I had checked the matter with Selmon. Were goats among those tested? Oh, yes. Plenty of goats in Texas. How did they rank? They had done quite well in the experiments, coming out at the higher levels of tolerance. I pressed my inquiry. If we found living goats would it be safe to take a couple aboard? Yes, provided they had not already reached unacceptable levels. What about their milk? The probabilities were these: Their milk would not be safe to drink immediately. But as their radiation levels diminished, in time it should be perfectly so. All these responses he gave me readily in conversational tones. Another thing that I appreciated in Selmon was his invincible lack of surprise at any matter put by myself to him and his absence of all nosiness, meddlesomeness. Of course, lieutenants (jg) are not given to interrogating their captains, and I was aware that inwardly he might be teeming with surprise and questions, wondering intently what we might be wanting with goats. Or maybe he had even guessed—he was, as I have said, a man of percipience.

I had high hopes of finding them, especially after Selmon's disquisition on their absorption capacity. I had traveled extensively in the Mediterranean during my two-year stint of shore duty at the NATO command in Naples, making dedicated use of that assignment to explore at the Navy's expense every nook and corner of a sea I loved above all others. People are not generally aware of the numbers of the islands of the Mediterranean. Of course, everyone knows of the celebrated ones— Malta, Sicily, the Greek islands—but how many know of Gorgona, of Ponziane, of Ustica, of Pelagie, Lampione, and Lampedusa? There are scores of such islands popping up here and there on the blue plain of that sea, islands that few outsiders ever touch; sparsely populated for the most part, a fair number unpopulated at all, at least by human beings. Most of them decidedly hilly and rocky; it may be due to these topographical characteristics, actually favored by him, that there is no life so indigenous to the islands of the Mediterranean as the goat. He is everywhere, in every variety. And has been there, as we know from reading the ancient Greeks—the goat, I always felt, was clearly the favorite animal of men like Pindar and Hesiod—more or less always. Indeed, the animal of the gods. Present and accounted for in how many friezes, in how many tapestries I had seen with my own eyes—at Patmos, at Rhodes, and a dozen other Greek gardens: Were not goats the one animal always certain to be around chewing the grass on Parnassus' slopes? In view of what Selmon had said, the Amarillo findings, they must be somewhere, on some island or another. If we wanted them we should have goats. I wanted them. Two. The Mediterranean, if indeed we were forced to put it behind us, cross it off, could well be our last chance to procure an animal that might turn out to be not just an asset but an urgent need in our future existence.

As we moved across the sea I ordered specific course changes that would bring us into waters I knew to have islands set in them. From the moment we had entered the Mediterranean I had ringed the ship with lookouts, as I have noted elsewhere—we were looking for other ships, for life ashore—equipped, each lookout, with 7x50 binoculars and with a sound-powered phone to communicate instantly to the bridge anything he raised. In addition the Big Eyes was now constantly manned. I shared my new intention only to the necessary degree, merely alerting all lookouts now to keep a sharp eye out for goats on all islands we passed. To these I always brought us close inshore. And one day one of the lookouts sang out, "Goats on the starboard bow."

We had steered, staying well off, by the island of Sicily, standing in the distance like nothing so much as a black sore festering in the blue sea. One wished it could sink into it, rather to leave nothing than this, and thus be put out of its misery; remembering, in my case, from NATO duty in Naples, from firsthand inspection, how the island was loaded with missiles. It happened on Isola di Linosa, lying about a third of the way between Africa and Sicily, and we took a boat in with a small party I had carefully selected. Very rugged hills covered with flourishing green grass and flowers of assorted colors, rising closely above a strip of powdery white beach of negligible depth. Nobody in sight. It was a pretty day, a gentle warmth flowing down from a sky where a few white billows of fat cumulus rode lazily against the azure. We could see the ship standing patiently out, gray-blue and immobile, sole lord of a gray-blue sea glittering in the still sunshine. A lookout had spotted them somewhere up there. Presently came from the heights their distinctive bleating sound. We looked up. A small herd of them, perhaps a dozen in number, had approached and stood just above us, their heads poked out in a leaning-over position, gazing straight down with a Parnassian hauteur and a contained curiosity at these visitors who had invaded what they seemed to regard as their private property. Then, dismissing us as of no interest, unimportant mortals, they pulled their heads back, bent, and began the serious business of munching the grass, in their digestive course following the green patches down the hill nearer to us, sure-footed on the steepish incline, ignoring us wholly. We stood conferring on the sand.

"Gunner," I said, "do you think you could wrestle down a couple of those goats?"

"Well, sir," Delaney said thoughtfully. "I've wrestled down goats before. But goats are a very tough animal, Captain."

I looked at the huge Preston whom I had purposively brought along, as I had Delaney. "Then perhaps you should take Preston here with you. See if you can bring back two."

"Two, sir?"

"A female and a male goat. I would appreciate that."

A certain look of enigma held Delaney's face. Then something like the remote glimmering of a comprehension—I could not be sure.

"Aye, sir. A nanny and a billy," he gently corrected my goat terminology.

The gunner's mate turned and picked four short lines out of the boat.

"Preston," he said with the authority of his Missouri farm boy's background, "bear in mind that goats are a very independent animal. They're nobody's patsies."

The boatswain's mate stood immense and impassive, as if it were beneath his dignity to counter any suggestion that he might have difficulty dealing with a goat. Delaney continued in educatory tones.

"What they are partial to is being scratched between the ears—not too hard. A goat takes that as a very friendly sign. Just keep scratching him there and you should be all right. I'll do the tying while you do the holding—and the scratching. Got that, Boats? *Between* the ears."

"Shall we get on with carrying out the captain's order?" the boatswain's mate said evenly. "Before they take off while we're going to school about them?"

"Right. Let's shove off."

The gunner's mate carrying the lines, the two men ascended the hill. The goats, hearing their approach, turned slowly and gazed at them, only lifting their heads from their munching, retreating not a step. Delaney and Preston came beside them. The gunner's mate appeared to be sizing up each member of the goat-family herd, making his selection. I had the clear feeling that he had at least vaguely discerned my intention and was looking for the finest specimens.

Then it was as if the two men had disappeared among the goats. A certain amount of bleating and *baa*-ing drifted down to us on the beach. Presently the two sailors were coming down the hill, picking their way with their burdens through the rocks. Delaney was carrying the smaller— manifestly the nanny—around his neck. Preston had the other, larger one in his arms. The hooves of both animals were secured in a fairly loose but adequate fashion, using double half-hitches. They made it to the beach where we approached and stood studying them. They were not your garden-variety goat. They were stunningly beautiful animals, with long silky hair that seemed to be a complete spectrum, lovingly blended in patterned patchwork, as if by some seamstress of angel's gifts, of the color brown: tan hairs, ochre hairs, chocolate, terra-cotta, coffee, sienna, mahogany, copper, umber, chestnut, Titian, all combining to form a rich and luxuriant pastiche of deep softness. Even in the sailors' arms the animals had the nobility of bearing of a born aristocracy, a natural imperiousness. They seemed to have stepped out of some ancient tapestry of priceless provenance.

"Mr. Selmon?"

The j.g. unsheathed and commenced to run his radiac over the goats while Delaney and Preston each continued studiously and with a wise gentleness to scratch his particular ward in the approved manner, between the ears. We watched in silence, hearing the low clicking sounds of the counter's emissions. The goats kept opening and closing their eyes, dreamily. As Selmon proceeded with his examination they turned their heads and observed him over their shoulders with melancholy and suspicious expressions. Selmon went over them meticulously, across their flanks, proceeding then to their necks. There he paused and looked intently at his meter. Then he ran the counter gently over their long-haired coats once more and back to their necks; again he paused and examined the meter. We waited for his verdict, watching him.

"Captain, we're not intending to eat these goats, are we?" he asked.

"Certainly not, Mr. Selmon."

"Then they're okay, sir," he said. "Nothing to worry about. What they have will soon disappear."

I felt an unaccountable sense of triumph, as of an important victory; the more so that of these we had had few. We stood then admiring the goats, which had passed muster and appeared tolerably content in the arms of the two sailors.

"Look at her," Delaney said proudly of his. "Just look at those tits, Captain."

Had he guessed? I was certain not. "It's time, Captain." I turned, startled in my appraisal of the animals, to see Selmon looking at his radiac.

We loaded them into the boat, where they kicked a little, not very seriously, then, as Delaney and Preston steadied them in a kind of rocking motion, settled down, seeming not to mind too much the short sea journey to the ship. We got them up the Jacob's ladder, where the gunner and the boatswain's mate set them down on the quarterdeck. They planted their legs sturdily while the two sailors kept a half-holding, half-stroking hand on them. They looked studiously around at the ship's ambience and *baa*-ed a little. Then remained peaceful, apparently convinced they were in not unfriendly hands, while sailors gathered to admire them where they stood now at ease, displaying themselves in a kind of holding of court, heads lifted in their natural haughtiness, above those ravishing coats, as if to say, "Look how perfectly beautiful we are."

"Do goats get seasick, Delaney?" I asked him.

"Well, sir, to tell the truth I don't rightly know. I've had plenty of goats," he said. "But I've never taken them to sea. But a goat is a very tough animal."

"Yes, you've told me."

"We can always give them seasick pills," the gunner's mate said.

"Let's billet them amidships," I said.

"A good idea, sir."

Shipfitter Travis went to work immediately building a pen for our two passengers. Doing our best for the goats, we situated this enclosure amidships, the least likely part of a vessel to induce seasickness. At first Gunner's Mate Delaney assumed responsibility for their welfare. Then, as his garden duties grew, he asked around and discovered that Signalman Third Bixby, the farm girl from Iowa, knew more even than himself about goats; in her opinion, considerably more. "I *raised* goats. They require very special care," she said, and took them firmly off Delaney's hands, feeding them various fodders we pick up along the way after Selmon has put his imprimatur on these gatherings with his counter, now and then giving those gorgeous coats a brush, walking them back and forth on the weather decks. They quickly got their sea legs, and soon followed her, without a leash, agilely up ladders, these perhaps seeming child's play after their accustomed cliffs. "Goats are smart," Bixby informed me one day when I came across the three of them on a stroll and was afforded a short progress report. "Sheep are dumb. A sheep would probably just have walked overboard long ago, not even knowing he was doing it." Ship's company seems glad to have aboard, safe and sound, at least two of the animals of the world. Their presence is a kind of comfort.

.8.

A SIGNAL FROM BOSWORTH

Years since it had become obvious what the initial objective of both sides would be: that at least the two had in common, mirror images of strategy. This was simply to take out, in the first minutes of any conflict, the command, control, communications, and intelligence network (C_3I) of the other. Otherwise known as "decapitation," another of that lexicon which came so obscenely to dominate and corrupt the effective language of the latter years of the century. (In the mindless vulgarity of the time, colorful phrases were evoked to picture the flawless beauty of these acts: "cut off the head of the Soviet chicken," as an instance, the authors of such metaphors smirking self-congratulatorily at their picturesqueness, as though speaking of some devilishly clever prank.) Decapitation: It was a relatively easy undertaking, though said by some to be easier for them than for us, due to their greater geography and dispersion. For them, the objective was to be achieved by launching simultaneously on Washington, D.C.; SAC Headquarters at Offutt Air Force Base, Omaha, Nebraska; the North American Aerospace Command (NORAD) in Cheyenne Mountain near Colorado Springs; three or four other backup places; and perhaps a dozen critical communications relay points including essential satellites, their locations all well known, their elimination a routine matter; to accomplish all of this requiring no more than thirty minutes at the extreme outside (if done entirely from their own territory), with a strong possibility that that figure could, with proper placement of launching platforms (submarines off American cities), be cut to fourteen minutes or even nine.

The idea was twofold and a genius of the manifest: (1) to remove the political-military leadership, the National Command Authority; and (2) aided by the Electromagnetic Pulse generated by a high-altitude burst, to leave remaining no means of communication through which to send retaliation orders even had there been anyone left to do so. Someone had speculated that the ideal time of all, the perfect time for the other side, would be when the President of the United States was delivering his annual State of the Union message, since on that occasion the entire American succession would be gathered in not just one city, Washington, D.C., but in a single room, the House of Representatives on Capitol Hill: fifteen constitutional successors to himself, from the Vice President clear through the Secretary of Housing and Urban Development and the Secretary of Transportation; present also would be the Joint Chiefs of Staff, who while not in the official succession would presumably be prepared if alive, the succession all dead, to take upon themselves, in the absence of any lawful provisions or authority, nonetheless to strike back in such a circumstance; parenthetically present also all members of both houses of the Congress. This wealth of potential usurpers to power gone, who then would anoint himself to give battle back? If he did how could he discover the various rituals—necessary ciphers, Go-Codes and the like—to accomplish a response? And if he did, how could he without any means of communication execute them? And if he found such means, would commanders on the other end follow instructions from this dubious and illegal source?

The whole proposition was so simple that it was everywhere taken for granted that whatever other ancillary strategies there might be, this was certain to be the principal one employed by whoever moved first. By the process of deductive reasoning, our having received no orders from anyone, in any place, one could come to no other conclusion than that this was precisely what had happened, that is to say, removal of all National Command Authority, along with the extermination of means of communications by both direct and EMP forces (though not at the State of the Union, that being always in January). One overwhelming imponderable remained: How had retaliation (if that, instead of first-strike, was indeed what it was) been achieved? Only two theories appeared plausible:

first, that the authorities themselves had had sufficiently lightning reflexes to execute response even as the incoming missiles were upon them; or that, had these reflexes been found wanting, someone not on the above list but sufficiently highly placed to have access to the stipulated "rituals" had taken it upon himself in those crucial minutes, even seconds, that remained, to get off one general order before being obliterated along with all communications; thus achieving mutual decapitation. An hypothesis, whichever of the two starter mechanisms actually employed, supported by our own orders to launch having come from TSP (Trinity Security Procedures), both that designation and the ciphers containing the orders being held under the ultimate classification, known at the starting end by an irreducible handful of highest authorities, the ciphers changed daily and reserved exclusively for one of two purposes: to give orders to launch, to give orders not to launch; further supported by the cessation of all communications not long after our launchings.

To these various conclusions, their general tone supported both by the reports picked up by the Russian submarine commander and by the *Bonne-fille*'s radioman, the uninhabitability of Africa, established tentatively by our own shore incursions and conclusively, it appeared, by Lieutenant (jg) Selmon's deeper one, added the final building block that installed in firm place my resolve not to take the ship to America; further, I had reached the sanguine determination that, abetted by such overwhelming evidence from such a variety of independent sources, I could now safely and with comparative ease win the men over to this inevitable position.

Then the signal from Bosworth arrived. A signal from that same origin and in that same encryption that had not reached us since that morning, seeming now so infinitely long ago though actually but six weeks, when it had instructed us to launch our Tomahawks high into the cold blue skies of the Barents Sea. From NCA: National Command Authority. Sent in TSP: Trinity Security Procedures.

From the beginning and continuing to the present moment, nothing had commanded more of our dedication—never, in truth, infringed by hopelessness, by disheartenment—than our efforts to bring forth responses from our communications system. I need hardly speak of its prodigious sophistication or belabor the technical aspects of its electronics, highly classified, unknown to the civilian world, even to whose highest experts its talents would have been wondrous . . . even to myself, accustomed to devices, tools, beyond the frontiers, still a marvel of capability, awesome.

Manned constantly, in rotation on every frequency, with special attention to the channels known officially as Survivable Very Low Frequency Communications System, which had been brought to a level of performance that had seemed, beforehand, able to pick up whispers from the remotest places and to break through or around every known type of interference or defense, whether created by man or the elements. Originally pursued by the Navy, as I believe I have mentioned elsewhere, specifically to deal with what had been one of the most dangerous and frightening of problems—the difficulty in reaching a submerged nuclear-armed submarine in, let us say, the Sea of Okhotsk, for purposes, for example, of instructing it to unleash its payload—or, conversely, not to unleash it—these channels, as refined, exquisitely perfected I should put it, by Navy persistence, breakthroughs in the art, had become the least fallible method for long-distance communications the insistent genius of man had yet devised.

It was on one of these that it came through.

The signal was sent at 1700, no one remarking then the precision of the time, no reason to do so. It came in with full audibility, free of distortion, clear and clean. The frequency was 26.125 kHz, which our confidential VLF manual readily identified as belonging to a global Navy Communications Center situated in Bosworth, Missouri, used primarily we knew to communicate with those same submerged U.S. ballistic-missile submarines. The message when broken reading in entirety:

FLASH 171700Z
FM: NCA
TO: ALL SHIPS
BT
ANY SHIP, REPEAT ANY SHIP, REPLY
IMMEDIATELY
URGENT
ANY SHIP, REPEAT ANY SHIP, REPLY
IMMEDIATELY
URGENT
BT

We immediately replied; received no answer in return. From that moment we continued to reply without cease, eliciting no response at any time other than a repetition of the original message. This had a peculiarity. Starting with that first time, it came, the message itself never varying, like the voice of some oracle of idiosyncratic, perhaps even purposeful habits chosen for a reason it did not deign to disclose, or perhaps even was unable to do so, perhaps even hopeful that we could figure out why, always on the hour and only on the hour. I was glad that in composing our reply, a captain's caution at work, I had withheld two elements: our exact longitude-latitude position—the general area the receiver would know by our transmission; and our precise identification as a guided missile destroyer, contenting myself only with what seemed needful, an unnamed U.S. Navy vessel; strictly instructing Bainbridge, our communications officer, not to go further in these revelations unless otherwise ordered by myself. It was after all more than the sender had done: He had not even said who he was, notwithstanding that our replies continued to ask him this question in particular.

I stepped out onto the starboard bridge wing and looked across the water to the shoreline of north Africa, along which we had been running our slow parallel course, moving eastward toward Suez. I scanned it first with the naked eye, then through Big Eyes; nothing moved, even the branches of trees behind the beaches motionless; a continent becalmed; lying silent under still skies across which echelons of cumulo-nimbus drifted indifferently; the great mass of land seeming almost menacing in her death throes, the sentence Selmon had pronounced on her, this hardly a metaphor, the continent being or in the process of becoming infinitely hostile to man, to the animals, unaccepting of them—I felt a shudder go through me; turned away to look at the blue plain of the Mediterranean stretching away to the eastern horizon, the sea seeming forever alive. Below me I could see lookouts circling the ship, together holding captive the 360 degrees of the compass and anything that might appear on it. I looked up. The faintest tremor of wind stirred the halyards, was gone, the flag and commissioning pennant silent again after that brief flutter. I knew then. Despite the peace of all elements I could scent weather in the air; could just make out the underlayers of olive hue, unerring signposts, beginning to form like belt bands on the enlarging clouds. I turned and made my way below and into the wardroom where the gathered officers started to rise.

"As you were."

As they all settled in, I turned promptly to my immediate right.

"Please proceed, Mr. Bainbridge."

Lieutenant Whitney Bainbridge was nearly bald, with a circle of strawberry hair giving a tonsurelike effect that made him look a member of some monastic order; he had an innocent, slightly feminine manner

317

which I personally found rather appealing; he was of the Catholic faith and had six children back in Lafayette, Indiana, where he had settled in after Purdue; his mind seemed always to be concentrating on something, perhaps esoteric code groups. He was perhaps the closest thing to a wizard (short possibly of Selmon) we had aboard, communications-electronics having become so vastly both more complex and more crucial since my early days in destroyers, having become a branch of warfare itself; so specialized that Bainbridge was by definition of his field—and of our condition, his person embodying our sole potential contact with the outside world—always attentively listened to. The incoming transmissions, each taped, had been meticulously scrutinized, analyzed, repeatedly so, for irregularities in rhythm, pitch, infinitesimal differences in pauses between code groups. Bainbridge repeated now for all to hear what we had discovered; it was not entirely a blank, a zero; there was something at least; actually something of possibly the first importance, the seeming clues, however, only raising more questions than they answered.

"The critical aspects are these. First, it purports to be from National Command Authority. That this may actually be the case is given validity by the fact that they're using TSP ciphers—in combination with Navy codes. Second, whoever is sending it knows Navy methods—the form of the message tells us that. Third—and this is the part that as communications officer gets to me more than anything else—in the three days we've been receiving it they have used a new code each day, starting precisely at zero zero zero zero, ending precisely at twenty-four hundred and exactly then starting another new code. Now since there are no more secrets . . ."

He looked over at me and I nodded. "Since there are no more secrets I can say this. All Navy codes are changed on a daily basis. Every twenty-four hours you have to place a *new* code in the electronic devices we use to transmit and receive radio messages—that's why the system is essentially unbreakable; crypto change cycles. What all this means in this Bosworth business is that whoever is doing this: one, he has exact knowledge of top-secret Navy procedures; two, he has access to top-secret Navy codes; and three—and this is the most important single element to these messages, as I mentioned—whoever he is, he possesses the Trinity Security Procedures."

Again he looked at me interrogatively. I nodded approval. Aboard the *James* only Bainbridge, myself, and the combat systems officer, Chatham, even knew of its existence. There being no need any longer for this selectivity, he tossed out the fact rather offhandedly to the officers at large.

"Of course it was always the single most highly classified series of ciphers of all. It's what we used launching Tomahawk. On the sending end, fewer people had it than had anything."

The communications officer paused and we sat a moment in somber comprehension of this litany of facts and suggestions and what their meaning might be.

"The exactness of the repeated message?" I said.

"Yes, sir. Of course we've been using perforated tape or computer generated message transmission for quite a while now. Where someone wanted to repeat something. The only possible area of variability is the timing of the messages, and even this can be done by a computer—in fact, is done that way in submarines."

"But as to the Bosworth signal specifically, Mr. Bainbridge?" I said, a bit impatiently.

"Sir, the invariability in pulse rhythm makes it almost certainly an automated transmission. No change whatsoever we can detect, one transmission from another—not even the minute, unavoidable alterations that manual transmission of the same message would reflect. An opinion fortified by the exactness of the hourly transmission times."

He hesitated, looked at me, and said, almost as if to make certain I had not forgot it:

"The one thing we do know, there is no doubt as to the geographical source."

His voice carried the suggestion of a bias in favor of the sender, of a willingness to believe. I looked at him carefully.

"Yes, I know, Mr. Bainbridge. And the sender himself, the agent?" My voice suddenly sounding hard to my ear, inquisitorial, cross-examining. "His identity? Nationality? Any hints in those directions?"

"None we have discovered, Captain. Other than what he claims to be. Fortified of course, as I noted, by his possession of Trinity Security Procedures."

He looked back expectantly at me, just waiting.

"As to TSP," I said. "By now, anybody could have come into possession of it."

"I suppose so," Bainbridge said rather distantly; again just waited.

"It could be a trap," I said, a little impatiently, wanting him to say more.

"Yes, sir. It could be. I've even wondered if it could somehow be connected with the Russian submarine."

"We've been getting regular reports from them," I said, astonished.

"I know. The idea is ridiculous, isn't it? It only shows . . ." He hesitated, as though floundering, sighed heavily. "It could be almost anything."

And stopped. I looked at him. It was just that, nothing more; one felt annoyed at these generalities, hence a bit annoyed at Bainbridge himself. But in truth there seemed nothing more to be said: thoughts, all analysis, run up against—so far, at least—an unyielding, impenetrable wall. It needed surely still to be continually tested since even such barriers can with persistence and resolve, with ingenuity, be breached—we had done so before; of course, an officer like Bainbridge, who possessed all of these qualities, would not stop doing that; he didn't need to be told. And yet, seeming an instance above all to be probed relentlessly, one felt a hesitancy in the face of this one, a smell of danger even in the trying, as if it meant us harm—a sense activating itself subconsciously, viscerally, beginning with the withholding of the ship's latitude-longitude position and of our precise identity I had ordered . . . A feeling somehow that utmost peril lay an inch behind that wall, that message. A message sticking a splinter of doubt into the conclusion on which all our actions hereto had been based and upon which, as above noted, I had decided finally to act, set our course. Selmon's African findings having been conveyed to the officers and, coming on top of the reports furnished by the Russian submarine commander, with the possible exception of Lieutenant Commander Chatham seeming at last to convince any waverers that such was substantially the fate as well of the place we had called home. Myself ready to announce my decision to the crew. And now this remote new element, possibly altering everything, and yet surely ephemeral, insubstantive, just because the sound bore all the aspects of a recording, a tape, as opposed to that from a being with life still in him. It was true that a mystery remained, embodied in a single question: What force then had activated it? A question one knew to a certainty now thrust itself into each soul present. It was not odd that the inability to answer this question should not act to convince us of its opposite: a living human being somehow behind that transmitting device. We had lived too long with mysteries, by the dozen, by the score, to be much impressed by them; less, fooled. Enigmas, never solved, had become a part of our lives, routine. To this was added a pragmatic vein: We had too much experience with what preset lifeless computers could do.

And yet, I say, a doubt had been inserted into our equations of high probabilities . . . of certainties as most of us by now held them to be. Fragile as a thread, this particular doubt, considering its geographical source, the first from there, wove itself sinisterly, tantalizingly, into our thoughts, our consciousnesses, our beings, where one from another part of the globe might on such suspect evidence have been dropped with alacrity, dismissed out of hand. And slowly but unmistakably from around the table I could feel it growing as a cell splits and multiplies. Leaving us finally with one last question to eat into our souls: Was that thread's name that one unmeasurable force, half mythic, half intensely real, which never ceased at once both to threaten us and to keep us going—was its name only hope? Of wanting to believe the presence of substance, of anything; when so much experience, so must intelligence subjected to the most rigorous analysis by men formidably gifted at such tasks, had taught us only emptiness was there? Surely we had by now become too—immunized, hardened?—for such luxuries. Nonetheless, this troubled palpable feeling of uncertainty, however hesitant, had infiltrated the souls present, the very air of the wardroom itself. Yes, myself. Adulterated with that inexplicable fear—one could reach out and touch this. Without knowing why, I could feel that the transmission, even the pursuit of its perplexity, its secret, represented, as I have suggested, a danger of a high magnitude; a devil's temptation; it was as though each time we replied the danger came nearer, that this was the very intent of the hourly incoming signal, that each exchange of transmissions brought that uncertain force, perhaps was intended to, zeroing in on us, and with hostile intent . . .

One felt a certain anger at these speculations; an anger at one's own fears; a feeling that our isolation had acted to make for fear's inbreeding; a danger of making cowards of us all, starting with the ship's captain; seeming an excessive timidity at best, where perhaps a tempered audacity was the quality called for. We were the last thing from being helpless; armed still, a 704-H ship, with a strength so vast as to give pause to any possible foe who might contemplate inflicting injury on us . . . The train of thought fed back on itself, collapsing in frustration, in irresolution, in something like dismay; the threat suggested in the transmission remaining. I turned back to Bainbridge—his seeming the one most inclined to push into it, the pointed reminder of where it came from, this advocacy itself mildly disturbing: due to the fact that he had been foremost of the "formidably gifted" men whose probings with his impressive array of devices, along with Selmon's interpretations both of them and of the two Russian-Frenchman reports, had helped teach us the actual conditions surely obtaining there. He spoke:

"Could we not at least give our identity, sir? If we were more forthcoming, perhaps . . ."

I interrupted that. "I would say where 'forthcoming' is concerned, it is up to them to set an example."

I looked directly at the communications officer, and some sudden doubt having to do with him flashed through me. We waited in the silence. I gazed idly out the port on a slightly arousing sea through which we moved on our slow speed. Then Bainbridge simply dropped the place-name softly into the hush.

"Bosworth, Missouri."

As said, it reverberated almost reverentially, as something iconlike; the words falling as into a stilled pool of water, rippling out in circles around the table, a quality almost hypnotic in it. I turned sharply to him.

"Mr. Bainbridge?"

"I don't know, sir. The evidence runs against it—the mechanical nature of the transmissions. But somebody had to put the tape in place . . . Aaron here . . . ," indicating Selmon, "mentioned the possibility of pockets which might get away free." He turned to the radiation officer, in his voice almost a pleading tone.

The astonishment at this was that Bainbridge's casting of doubt was at variance with his own previous opinions, an officer who had been as certain as any that nothing remained since his own beloved and almost godlike devices had raised nothing; coming from one whose opinions, judgments, in anything involving communications were, as stated, given the most special attention, this present reaction constituted a considerable breach. Finally Selmon answered, his dry tone at least forever unchanged; not a scrap of emotion there.

"That I did," he said. "Pockets. I wouldn't have picked the Global Communications Center at Bosworth for one of them that the Russians would leave in place. Obviously a bit of it left. I'd wager that everything that breathed in Bosworth went."

"The message then?" Bainbridge said. "*Someone's* breathing. And trying to tell us—tell anyone else that's left—something. Maybe trying to bring the remaining ones into touch with one another. Tell us where others are, where the safe places are . . ."

Hearing Bainbridge, a solid, calm officer, seemingly invulnerable to fancy, one realized how close beneath the surface it lay; a captain's alarm rising: With how many others might the case be the same? Selmon was unmoved.

"Then why don't they tell it, Commander?"

"I don't know," Bainbridge said, his voice seeming to collapse, half in frustration, half in anger—at what one could not say.

322

From up above I could hear the first swelling of the wind, reaching into us through the opened ports, see out them the commencement of long rolling waves on the revealed seascape, the first whitecaps blossoming on the blackening waters, the wind setting the sea into a cross-swell, the ship into a mild rolling motion. I had interpreted it as emotion. And yet: It seemed something more. It was as though Bainbridge sensed something in the transmissions that he was unable or unwilling to convey—perhaps his own fresh doubts had not coalesced into actual conclusion; that he felt onto something, at present elusive as a ghost, was still reaching out to grasp it, extract its secret; each time its escaping him just as he held it in his hands. He was simply too sound an officer, too profoundly knowledgeable in his field, for any captain to dismiss this as foolish wish. We waited in the heavy, brooding silence which seemed to rest in the most murky, darksome of waters, visibility nonexistent. It was time to open it up.

"Well, then?" Deliberately I turned first to the CSO. I had come to a determination: I would not permit that recent confrontation in the night by the lifeline to prejudice me against his opinions. He was no fool. Nobody could become combat systems officer on a DDG and be that. I should listen to him. Aside from these judicious and somewhat pious reasons, there was another motive, devious as could be, full of cunning: If matters fell that way, and I had in the end to move against him, I wanted him to have the minimum of excuses for his actions. I wanted this: that he had had his say and that not just I, but the other officers as well, had rejected it; I wanted to isolate him; make him without allies. It was a perilous game for any ship's captain to play. The CSO might in the process pick up allies himself. I felt it worth the risks; felt in any event that I had no choice.

"Mr. Chatham?" I said.

He shrugged. One knew at once: his position fixed, much strengthened now by that immense signal, whatever else you might say about it; his voice clipped, surer than ever, something of smugness in it.

"If we were wrong about Bosworth—not a soul here expected it—we could be wrong about a great deal else back there."

He let that opening settle for a moment, then came on.

"Earlier we haven't heard; ergo, nothing exists. Conveniently forgetting electromagnetic pulses knocking out all communications, any certain way of knowing. Simply no word: interpretation, nothing there. That has been the drill. Well, now we *have* heard." He marched steadily on, putting one in mind of a prosecuting attorney in a courtroom, and a decidedly clever one. "If the conclusions based on those first deductions were correct—with respect, sir, I never believed they were—this changes everything. That signal from Bosworth changes everything. I favor this ship doing what I've always favored this ship doing. After that signal, I don't see how anyone can come down on any other course. The fact it's as cryptic as could be makes no difference. There has to be some reason for that. We're never going to find it rattling around the Mediterranean. It has to be telling us something urgent, of the first importance. It's an NCA, for God's sake."

I listened quietly, attentively, pressing everything back. The wind freshening, reaching into us like a lamentation, a distinct pitch now added to the ship's roll. I could begin to hear the random tinkling of the spoons on the sides of coffee cups. Waiting a moment, in consideration of what had just been said, I then turned slightly in my chair.

"Mr. Selmon?"

"Well, sir, I suppose you could have the President of the United States—or at least the Chief of Naval Operations—or maybe a radioman third sitting there at Bosworth beeping out that signal. Come there, crawled there, God knows how, from God knows where. Whoever, if anybody, it is, not much in the way of brains left. Simply to keep repeating it. In fact that may explain it, be the clue. I'm thinking of those poor souls on the beaches. Maybe whoever it is in Bosworth has arrived at that condition. Sending out that mindless tape—no one who had the slightest power of reason remaining would do a thing like that. Maybe just telling us he's alive. That would be a thing he would do. Well, that's nice to hear."

What some might have seen as cold-bloodedness I believed was an immovable dedication to the evidence; almost a revulsion at what he considered dangerous fantasies. I looked out a port: skies blackening with clouds to match the changing color of the sea below. I heard Selmon go on.

"Aside from that, it doesn't alter a scratch our previous projections. If the objective is somehow to connect up with the human being, if there is one, or a thousand of them, holed up somehow in Bosworth, Missouri—though the reason for such an undertaking escapes me—how does anyone propose to get there? I don't suppose, sir, you want me to go through all the reasons again. I would have thought we had them memorized by now. But once more, sir. That land is fully, absolutely, contaminated; it will accept no human being; it is untraversable."

Chatham: "I consider that speculation; but let's say it's true. Then let us be absolutely certain on this one—by having a look. He's obviously not receiving our reply." He turned to Bainbridge. "Wouldn't you say so, Lieutenant?"

"It would seem self-evident."

One had to admire the closely reasoned argument the CSO was pursuing, as well as his subtle efforts to enlist allies as he went. He continued, pressing his advantage. "It's not just Bosworth, Captain. It couldn't be *just* Bosworth. That signal means there are almost to a certainty others not just in Bosworth—but other places back there, maybe many of them, maybe considerable numbers of people; unlucky enough not to have Bosworth's global communications and so unable to tell anybody. So *let's go find out;* at least get nearer to where maybe he can hear us. No, I'm not forgetting fuel. If the worst comes to the worst, and we truly can't get ashore, there have to be fallback places. Bermuda. Caribbean islands. Some place down there. We can at least be near— waiting it out perhaps while the place clears up sufficiently to receive reconnoitering parties. I'd like to lead the first one."

"There won't be," Selmon said flatly, as if he were correcting a pupil far out of his depth and not particularly bright anyhow—not one of the radiation officer's more attractive traits, part of that generally increasing loftiness of manner that was coming to characterize him. It could put anybody's back up, let alone Chatham, whose back went up pretty quickly as it was. He continued with something like weary patience. "We've gone into all this, but I'll say it again: The winds, their cargo—the pattern of winds west to east will have taken out the last one of those islands. That's flat; the last thing it is is hypothetical."

"Mr. Selmon . . ." Chatham, his voice barely concealing disdain. "I wish I was as certain about visible things as you are about invisible ones."

"Why, that's the difference in our fields, Henry." The radiation officer smiled distantly. His refusal to be made angry was one of his most formidable assets; the reaction of a slight but unmistakable condescension, as now, indeed sometimes prompting that emotion in others; his tone not much off the derisive with an officer considerably senior in rank to himself. "I'm sorry you don't understand that some fields of knowledge—example, yours, weapons—by their nature deal with matters that are visible; others also by their nature—example, mine, radiation—with matters that are not. That difference doesn't make either knowledge, or either field, the less viable."

"Mr. Selmon, do you *ever* consider the possibility that you may be wrong?"

"All the time, Henry. What I'm really concerned about here is this capacity for make-believe. Bermuda, Lord deliver us."

"Don't patronize me, Mr. Selmon."

"To what purpose would we go back there?" Selmon said, his habit being to ignore remarks of that sort except to bite back a bit, his voice a model of imperturbable rationality, his intent perhaps actually to provoke. "A little morbid curiosity?"

"*Morbid curiosity?* I have to call you on that, Mr. Selmon. I think it's a despicable word to use."

Chatham half rose from his chair. His face was a rage of purple.

"Now you listen to me, you superior prig. You call yourself a naval officer. You can't stand a deck watch. You couldn't begin to operate fire control. You couldn't conn one of our small boats. I doubt if you can take a sextant bearing . . ."

"I can count radiation," Selmon said quietly.

For a moment the CSO seemed about to leap across the table on Selmon. My hand hit the table, sending a jangling of saucers down the length of the table.

"*Knock it off.* Gentlemen," I said more gently.

Everyone had a shorter fuse these days, and it seemed to grow shorter by the day. I waited now for the temperature to lower; listened to another voice: that of the sea beginning to assert itself, accompanied by distant thunder advancing. One waited, in all patience, one tried to penetrate the meanings of sentences, of murmured sounds; of words; of silences . . . It was the reports furnished us by the Russian submarine commander that had fissured, if only to a limited degree, our unspoken pact not to talk about what had happened, not to dwell on it; fearful that once we entered that darkness it would swallow us up, destroy in time, possibly sooner than later, the mental and emotional faculties we so nonnegotiably required to see us through; feeling now we could at least probe the edges of it; more than that, now needing to do so, always with restraint, in order to make the decisions on which time was running out. I knew there were questions waiting to be asked around that table, knew their nature. I dreaded them as much as did the questioners themselves, yet knew they had to ask them before they could even hope to think of where their own views would come down. I made way for it.

"Anyone," I said. "Feel free to ask . . . anything . . ."

And so they began, as one knew they would, to inquire about their own hometowns, as if received knowledge might affect their personal preferences as to returning.

"Tulsa." It was young Jennings. "Mr. Selmon, I don't know why anyone would want to hit Tulsa."

"Very probably no one did, Mike," Selmon said.

"But you're saying . . . Assuming it wasn't hit . . . everything would be the same? The Galleria . . . Locust Park . . . the university . . . all of it would still be there?" Trailing off on a note half statement, half interrogation. "Just that there would be no people?"

"That's about the size of it, Mike," Selmon, who I am sure had never set foot in Tulsa, never heard of its mentioned charms, said gently. "Assuming, as you say, it didn't rate a missile." He hesitated, continued in uncharacteristically compassionate tones with the young officer, little more than a boy. "There may still be a few people—well, wandering around, scratching out."

"Just waiting for it? Waiting to die."

"Pretty much that," Selmon said softly. "People have different tolerances to radiation sickness. Not that it makes any difference in the end."

"Then I'd just as soon not see it. I don't want to see Tulsa," Jennings said almost fiercely.

We waited a moment, caught in that. "I'd say the luckiest ones were those with the lowest tolerances," Lieutenant Thurlow said reflectively.

"If I had a choice," Selmon said, "that would be mine in that situation."

"Of course, the luckiest ones of all," the navigator said, "were those smart enough to die immediately."

Some of those who came from great cities or from obvious targets hardly bothered to ask any questions at all. Ensign Martin, our assistant communications officer—her home was New York City—didn't say a word. Nor did Lieutenant Commander Coles, our operations officer, whose home was Norfolk; Lieutenant Polk, our weapons combat officer, who lived in Chevy Chase, Maryland, a suburb of Washington, D.C. It was as though they had with great effort, at immense cost in pain, erected walls around themselves and were not to be fooled or tricked into dropping these expert fortifications for no purpose at all save to let insufferable pain in. But most of our officers were from more distant places, from the small towns of America. As the exchanges went on, it became evident that a higher measure of hope resided in these. Selmon did little to encourage them. The principal difference in the large cities and the small towns appeared to be that those in the former went instantly for the most part while those in the smaller ones were able to hold on until the fallout from the larger cities had reached them. Almost a philosophical question arose

327

as to which were the more fortunate. Still, everyone seemed anxious to make a case for his own town.

"I'm sure everyone here has been made aware of the special glories of Big Spring, Texas," Lieutenant (jg) Rollins said. "I've tried earnestly to do that. What would you say . . ."

The deck officer's voice also trailed off. "Houston would have been a certain target," Selmon said quietly. "NASA."

"Big Spring's four hundred miles away," Rollins said, voice low, almost hopeful.

"Karen, I'm afraid that's as much as next door with that fallout. We've seen with our own eyes an almost analogous situation. For Houston, read Naples. For Big Spring, read Amalfi. Went sometime back, I'm afraid. Texas: caught between the massive fallout from Houston in the eastern part of the state and from another certain target in the western part, Amarillo—all our nuclear devices were assembled there. Texas may have been the first state to go in entirety. In fact, that projection was made years ago in some of the internal studies. No one ever said much to the Texans about it that I can recall. The odd thing about it was that at that very time people were talking about getting away from the crowded eastern states, the big cities, to have a better chance—and some doing just that. Moving to places like Texas."

"I get the picture," Rollins said shortly, not wanting to hear more. "A big joke on Texas, wasn't it?"

This went on for a while. The names of different states, different towns, cities, the names of home. Time seemed to stop as the names, some familiar, some not, fell around the table, a sense of nostalgia curiously combining all the antitheses, of affection and horror, of resignation and refusal to recognize what had happened, of acceptance and of denial of belief. The names falling hauntingly, cruelly, into the air, time forgotten, time remembered, while Selmon, with a gentleness and patience I had never seen in him, made his estimates, guesses, at the fate of each. It did not go along without his being challenged.

"You're not saying that everybody in the country is gone, are you, Mr. Selmon?" Lieutenant Bartlett pressed him.

"No, sir," Selmon said, his voice taking on more of his customary firmer tone. "I've never said that. I would be extremely surprised if that is the case." But he was not to be budged from his central holding. "What I am saying is this: that that is true for the great majority of the population; that most of those remaining are in varying conditions, all on the downside—exactly the same kind of variations we saw at Amalfi, all along the northern Mediterranean beaches, in other words beyond any help; and that the smallest segment of all is pretty much untouched up to this point, as least so far, may or may not remain unaffected—putting figures to it, this last group to be counted in the thousands at the most. That is the evidence."

"In the *thousands?* For the whole country?"

"In the thousands. And I personally wouldn't guarantee that figure."

Then Lieutenant Girard spoke up, her voice tranquil as ever yet seeming firmer than usual from one who generally knew her own mind.

"Mike's right. I don't *want* to see what it's like there. Those people on the beaches at Amalfi . . . I don't want to see them . . . in North Carolina . . . in Massachusetts . . . There are some things it is better not to see."

"Nonsense."

Startled, we looked down the table at the CSO. "We're all missing the point."

Lieutenant Commander Chatham spoke coldly, brutally, forcefully. "It's not a question of what we *want* to see. It's a question of needing to know. I mean absolutely know, the only way you can. We'll never be satisfied if we don't have a firsthand look. We could never live with ourselves."

I saw it at once as an immensely cogent and appropriate argument, its strength felt immediately, bringing us all still. The next I found less so.

"It's what the crew wants," he said.

"The *crew*, Mr. Chatham?" Myself now feeling a flash of anger, my voice taking on its first edge; anger and alarm. "I hadn't realized you've been polling the crew."

He seemed at least a trifle abashed. "Not polling, sir. It's a sense I have."

"A *sense*, Mr. Chatham? I also was unaware that you had taken to testing the *sense* of the crew." That warning in my voice, I decided not to pursue this little clash. "Let's get one thing straight. We're not discussing what the crew *wants*. We're discussing what's right for this ship to do."

"Then, Captain, only one course is. This ship has a responsibility to go find out. She has a duty to do so."

It was as if I were playing directly into his hands.

We waited in the merciless silence, in mute anguish at these thoughts of home, now first articulated, men torn, it seemed to me, as much as men could be, pulled two ways by forces each of which was so powerful that every soul around that table seemed in danger of being rended bodily apart. I turned then, no avoiding it, turned as always I must, as I was forever seeming to do, to Melville, the engineering officer, who had sat throughout silent as a shadow, letting the emotion play around him, taking no part, not even mentioning or inquiring about his own hometown of Charleston, refusing to move out of the one realm that was his, in which he kept himself isolated; waiting for us to come back to it, as he knew in the end we must; asked him and received the latest figures on our fuel reserves, depleted somewhat from the last calculations by our reconnoitering of the north African littoral. Inherent in all projections emergency reserve plus search time in the Pacific.

"Assuming straight home and back this time. Just to look. No reconnoitering." I felt a certain desperation in my voice. "There and back—to right here. Total cruising time?"

The words had seemed to come from myself with a volition all their own; words I had not wanted to speak; felt immediately I should not have, their only effect to raise false hope, to leave the door open a crack. Chatham's words stabbing my mind: *Responsibility. Duty.* Words sacred to a ship and to any sea captain. A flash of surprise crossed Melville's face which never showed surprise; from the "there and back" obviously. Then the quick comprehension: We could not traverse Cape Horn, a matter previously settled. Slowly his head rose from his clipboard; his large brown eyes with so much white in them looking dead-on into mine.

"Thirty-four days, sir. There and back. Twelve-knot steaming."

"Mr. Melville, take us through Suez. After the American trip."

"Aye, sir." Clipboard. A little longer at it, while we waited. I watched his hand move over it, the long black graceful fingers that made one think the word pianist. "Rough calculations here, sir. To Diego Garcia, thereabouts. Possibly beyond by a few hundred miles."

"Never reaching the Pacific?"

"Well, we might *reach* it, using up reserves. Nothing left to look around for something when we got there."

The cold known fact, stated, seemed to bring one's heart still. I remembered: effectively, fetching up beyond the Horn one way; at Diego Garcia now the other. Removing in reality what in my innermost soul, not yet so much as alluded to, I was coming more and more to judge was our only hope. I asked what did not need to be asked of a man like my engineering officer. Making it with respect, something he would understand.

"No chance for error there, sir?"

"Captain, whatever else is hypothesis, that is not. There's nothing hypothetical about our fuel supply." The tone half sardonic, half apologetic, as if it were somehow his fault. Through the ascending sound of the sea I heard him say: "If we went the other way first, coming back, transiting Suez . . . well, sir, we'd end up, for all actual purposes, bobbing up and down somewhere in the Indian Ocean."

The words, quietly as speech could be spoken, absolutely professional; the engineering officer's voice in its even cadence cast in those unedged Southern tones, this oddly making what he had to say the more deadly; the verdict falling knell-like in the silence of the wardroom. As if his end and sole obligation was not to favor or weigh but simply to present options to his captain; as if to say, I have performed my duty; now perform yours.

The sound of a rising wind, a gathering sea, came leaking through the ports; then from afar off, a single clap of thunder, like a siege gun. I sat, reflective, spoke in reflective tones, wanting that atmosphere for what I was about to say; wanting perhaps to point them gently toward that other hope.

"There have to be others. It is simply impossible that we are the only ones." Turning again to him whose evaluations would seem to be the most authoritative on that subject. "Mr. Selmon?"

His own voice fell softly, caught in the quiet tone of assessment which had descended upon the wardroom.

"It has to be so, sir. To think we are the only ones would in my view be irrational. We're just on the wrong part of the earth to find them. The Russian submarine, of course. Maybe a few others. But principally I would bet on the Pacific, that part of it in the southern hemisphere. The islands, I mean, not Australia, New Zealand, not any land masses—they all had targets, one kind of target or another, that one side or another had to take out. Islands that had nothing on them but a few people, too insignificant to merit extinction and clear of wind patterns passing over heavily targeted areas. Best bets of live human beings on those. In my view, a conclusion almost inescapable."

"Mr. Bainbridge?"

"I'd accept that but add that there are clusters of live human beings above the equator and in the other hemisphere. Of course I'm thinking of the Bosworth signals. If there are some there, likely there are some in other places."

"It's all possible." I sighed. "None of this is contradictory. Gatherings of people scattered around the globe. Some of them maybe in quite excellent health. Anyone disagree with that general assessment?"

I waited. No one spoke.

Abruptly, perhaps from feeling pushed against the wall, nowhere to turn, having to strike back myself, something hard and angered—by what I could not tell, perhaps only at the way things were—arose in me.

"Sure," I said. "Sure, there are probably a few people back home. In fact there're probably a number of these 'pockets' scattered God knows where." I spoke brutally. "We can't simply go up and down the earth, looking for them. Not in the light of what Mr. Melville has just told us. Did everyone hear him? And if everyone did, is anyone suggesting we start some sort of fucking treasure hunt to find as many of those pockets as we can before our fuel runs out and we end up wallowing in some sea somewhere?"

"No, Captain," Chatham said. "Only at home."

I regretted already that outburst. "Gentlemen, ladies, I apologize to all of you for my language."

I could hear the rain begin. *We would never be satisfied unless we had a look.* Yes, an immensely powerful argument. I had to give him that. But what would the price be? No man should be given that choice, no group of men. No, not even Navy men, in whose lexicon no words stood higher than the ones he had uttered. Duty. Responsibility. Then I heard Chatham, something insinuating and sly in his voice:

"Captain, there's something that hasn't been mentioned. The Bosworth NCA signal: It's as much as an order to go home. By that very designation. National Command Authority—the highest. Using TSP ciphers. In addition to that, *Navy* people are obviously sending it, doing the transmitting. *Navy* message form. *Navy* code security procedures—changed every twenty-four-hour day. Just as the *Navy* does."

He had come on stronger than I had ever known Chatham to do, and done so shrewdly, employing what seemed to be forceful evidence. Had come on also, I had to admit, with every sense of personal conviction in the right of what he was saying. But there was something more to come. A great deal more. He paused in the gathering silence, for all the world like the gunnery officer he was, waiting until his target came dead in the cross hairs. Then he let go.

"If we can't take orders from the Navy—not to mention the National Command Authority—from whom, in God's name, are we to take them? I don't think it's time for Navy ships, Navy officers, any Navy command whatsoever, to start disobeying Navy orders."

So here it was, at last. Slowly my eyes came back from looking at the sea to looking point-blank down the table at the CSO. I became aware that a peculiar tenseness had invaded the wardroom, penetrated the last one of the officers, their eyes, all of them, looking up the table at me, expectant; every officer as aware as I was myself of the implications in his words: the first open questioning of my authority; not direct, but a manifest testing of the waters. A silence unlike any other held sway with something of fear and shock in it, something absolutely ominous. No sound save that of the augmenting rain drilling down into that atmosphere. How clever that was of him to save it until the last, like a surprise witness. Myself knowing that it was the last possible choice of a moment to seek confrontation; knowing as well that I must not altogether let it pass. I listened to the rain.

"There's weather coming," I said. "We have but a few moments. As to your point, Mr. Chatham, naturally the captain of this ship will decide whom, if anyone, we are to obey. All others need be concerned only with obeying him."

"Of course, Captain. I meant only . . ."

I cut that off. "I think we've pursued the matter sufficiently for today, Mr. Chatham. You've made your various points."

Somehow then looking down the length of the wardroom table to where those two always sat, mute, the Jesuit at its very end, facing me, the doc to his left, thinking I never knew what with either. I should mention that in these officers' meetings, neither ever volunteered an opinion—each had to be explicitly asked for one; this not a peculiarity of theirs, rather the way of Navy chaplains, Navy doctors, their area of authority lying in healing, one physical the other spiritual, not in the decisions to be made as to the ship's course and action, these matters the Navy in its wisdom reserving for officers of the line. Nevertheless, seeking counsel wherever it might be found, something making me ask.

"Doc?"

"I'm not sure it makes sense," he said. "But I feel we have to go home."

"Commander Cavendish?"

He waited a moment, a man who by vocation and choice heard far more words than he spoke, these always offered with the least of portentousness. "Not much, Captain. It seems pretty clear: the question, I mean, not the answer. Mr. Chatham speaks of duty, of responsibility. They're the right words. I might suggest that we give more thought to what the fulfillment of those two really consists of, in our special circumstance . . ."

An immense scar of lightning flashed across the starboard port, the following thunder breaking directly above the ship, for a moment silencing all talk. *In our special circumstance.* The words striking into me with the quickness of the lightning flash, words entering me both as sword and as comforter . . . the weather had stopped him, or he had stopped anyhow. No time now to attend to them in any case. For suddenly I was paying heed to the ship. I looked now with intention through the ports upon a whitening sea; listened now not idly but with a seaman's ear: The roll accompanied by a deepening pitch as she moved into the troughs, the ship slower in coming up. I glanced at Chatham, at Bainbridge, attempting to assess my own assessment of these two curiously allied officers. Together they were a considerably potent force in shaping the opinion, the sense, of the ship. Their motivation to my mind as far apart as could be. Bainbridge: simply innocent hope. Chatham: *From whom are we to take orders.* And the other: *It's what the crew wants.* The two phrases seemed coupled, part of one thing, bringing altogether near the one terrible danger of all. Control of this ship: that was the missile officer's intent, the sea herself seemed to speak to me, telling me so; secretively reserving any answer to that other question: to do what with? Not just to take her home: Nothing could convince me the intent stopped there. *Control* of her, her immense striking power: That was his every purpose. I came away from this. I must have felt that their position had to be given its every shot; we could not turn our back on it; not yet. I had the deepest fear of the consequences should I do that. Added to all this, surely, that long and almost unbearable talk of home. Almost helplessly I turned to the communications officer.

"Mr. Bainbridge," I said. "Concerning Bosworth, Missouri, here it is. The wraps are off. You may identify ourselves, our position, tell them anything else you judge might elicit an intelligible response. Prepare and show me the messages. Starting right now. Get cracking."

Even as I rose, from down both sides of the wardroom table, the officers of the USS *Nathan James,* heads turned, half of them right, half left, all, including Bainbridge, looking at me with the one expression of startlement, as if it were the last decision they expected from me. Then the communications officer found his voice, a miraculous lift in it.

"Aye, sir. Immediately, Captain."

Almost as if synchronously, the elements let loose. A great blaze of lightning shot through the ports, filled the wardroom; the following thunder breaking close aboard. The ship shuddered through a sudden pitch, trembling and lurching as she moved into the valleys of the sea, the sound of wind and waves rising above the ventilation and machinery noise.

Then, tired of waiting, the torrents of rain exploded and began to hammer the ship. Jennings, the junior officer, moved quickly to close the ports without being told to do so.

"I think the ship needs us," I said, rising. "Let's batten down."

I listened to that plaintive sound, forever mysterious and poignant to sailors, of rain falling into the sea, quietly now, haunting as chords in a requiem; the mists hanging low in the water, visibility no more than a couple of ship's lengths; the ship seeming to move through a void of nothingness; now and then a low soughing of wind as from sentient beings emerging from the spectral darkness. I looked up: masthead and range lights barely penetrating the haze. I had stayed for the changing of the watch; stepped then from the pilot house onto the starboard bridge wing for this final captain's check, after the strong weather we had been through over the past hours, before making below for my bunk.

The day had seemed forever, the emotion of the wardroom lingering, heart still rended by what my officers had had to be put through, the thoughts of home from that stronghold box where they had so long resided in silent agony ever since the launching in the Barents now forced brutally into the open; each officer forced at last to think, in considering our decision, of his own hometown, what it might be like there, was anyone alive in any one of them, was one of these a wife, a daughter, a son . . . a father, mother, sisters, brothers . . . if so, what might be their condition . . . torment added upon torment until at last the intolerable memories, thoughts, feelings, the whole great horror was stuffed almost violently back into its locker. Not all achieving this success. Later, walking along the passageway in officers' country to my cabin, I had heard from behind two closed stateroom doors the sounds of sobbing; hesitated, hand almost coming up to knock softly; continued on. Chatham had spoken well into that awful tide of remembrance; his argument had every worth argument could have: We would never be satisfied until we had seen it with our own eyes. It was wisdom itself; the words, once uttered, became something like a commandment, engraved in stone, haunting the mind. As for myself, I had no one to go home to, not any longer, and quite often I had felt that this constituted my chief strength. I was not at all certain I would have possessed the courage of my own officers, having others—wives, children—back there and yet with every fortitude carrying on, fulfilling their duties. A wave of the most intense respect and affection for them held me for a moment in the night. Who could now blame them if they came down on Chatham's side? To go see with their own eyes;

even, as the Jesuit had said a time back, if it meant seeing the nail prints in the hands, the spear wound in the side. Who was I, lacking their motivation, their desire like the passion of the Lord, to oppose them? The thought seemed to lead directly to what the Jesuit had said this day.

It had happened so quickly, filtered even so through arriving weather, the sudden realization that the ship was signaling her need for us in her battle with the sea . . . so quickly that only blurred impressions remained as evidence. Said what he had said, stopped there. But I felt I heard it as much as if he had said it directly into my ears. Himself knowing that he did not need to do that in any detail, knowing that a mere signal would suffice; knowing the fact to be long deep as could be in me, buried beyond the reach of any Fathometer, any determination as to the matter lying after all across far seas, thoughts as to it easily postponable, other urgent decisions daily upon one . . . his knowing also, and this the intent of that signal lest by any chance I miss it, that now something vital to it had arrived—we could not do both, not fulfill both obligations, duties. That was what he was saying. The choice as to direction the ship would take for the first time forcing those other competing considerations up into realms of consciousness, terrible and impermissible thoughts, one wanted to scream to them to go away, thoughts not fair to thrust upon any man, least of all upon a ship's captain who did not want them, a mere mortal, who had crushing in upon him enough other insistences to test all his capabilities, this being the last ever to be one of them. Even the Jesuit, surely morally the bravest of men, pausing as in some sort of cowardice, and of fright, before them, the words unwilling to come off his tongue, managing only those two it seemed everyone was mouthing. Duty. Responsibility. And I knew: His concept of those two words had nothing whatever to do with Chatham's about going home. God's will, he might have added—though he seldom used such expressions—if something, the weather or his own fears, had not halted him from saying the other. *We have the means. Who else for sure that we know of does?* I would never have added that codicil of his, having ceased to believe in such words, such expressions as—God; in such phrases as "the higher purpose" I had heard him use, if only once or twice. They were not for me, not any longer; other than that, knowing, and for the first time, that the Jesuit's unspoken question was in all truth the real question I must now decide; not wives, children, brothers, sisters, at best their corpses perhaps to see, at worst replications of those half-living half-dead beings, creatures, wretches, no nomenclature as yet having been invented for them, their species being so new, first seen on the beaches of Amalfi; our just fate surely not to go see those now on the beaches of Virginia and the Carolinas, of Massachusetts and Maine; not to go back and in some form of suttee, throw ourselves on their funeral pyre. I remembered now that single time, when with a strange, seemingly offhand lightness that later I was to look upon as almost eerie, he had said, "Naturally these men are under my spiritual care . . ." A single beat of a pause: ". . . these women." From any ship's captain's point of view, ship's company being the correct designation, the last seeming utterly unnecessary, even offensive: Why *these women?* As though some new category, meriting an extra measure of that care; a distinction for the same eternal reason unacceptable. For a moment I forced the matter, despite my tremblings, into direct thought. Phraseology different, coming at it from polarly opposite bearings, Jesuit and myself, our objective: Could it have been more identical? Did it not have to be? The single consideration before which every other purpose, hope or desire had to give way? Was anything else thinkable? Any truth existent other than that nothing on earth be permitted to stand in the way of it, least of all the relatively inconsequential opinions or trifling desires of men that we go this way or that? Standing alone in the night, I knew it for the first time, in a kind of Damascene clarity, forced in that light myself to embrace it as our sole purpose; feeling the pale rain falling on me. And felt an absolute terror. Not believing any longer in God, it was as though I had become God myself. The final decision now almost easily made, as I suppose decisions are for God. I would give Bosworth until Suez, with our own new forthrightness, to tell us something besides gibberish: by that time also the southern shore of the Mediterranean having given us by then its own final answer as to habitability. If negative on both, assemble the men.

I turned out of the rain, passed through the pilot house, exchanged a pleasantry with Lieutenant Sedgwick, the OOD, and made my way below to my bunk; feeling utter calm, falling into instant sleep, the rain heard but as a soothing patter on the weather surfaces of the ship all around me.

.9.

THE DESERT

It all began with the R and R stop.

Now and then we stopped at a beach to get some exercise and to have what was best described simply as an outing. We badly needed outings. We had a certain amount of sports equipment: a half-dozen footballs; three volleyballs, I believe, and a net; a dozen softballs and a half-dozen bats. Touch football was the game of choice, having the virtue of accommodating any number of players and degrees of skill. Lieutenant (jg) Selmon always went ashore first to take his readings and to report back either that the place was unsuitable or that it was good for two to five hours as the case might be.

For some time now, finding a place had not been an easy thing. For a considerable stretch the coastline all along Algeria and Libya had exhibited a prohibitively high reading. I felt we rather desperately needed some R and R and proceeding on our ever-easterly course across the blue void of the Mediterranean we made frequent stops in search of a place for it. Finally down the coast, not too far away now from Tobruk, Selmon came back from one of his forays with the glad tiding that a touch football game of up to four hours would be acceptable on a stretch of white beach which we could see across the water. Vigorous exercise does wonders for sailors long shipbound, especially if it involves fun as opposed to the universally

338

loathed calisthenics. True sailors have astonishingly little need to stop on shore but all need to stop some, after which they are all—I have not known a single exception to this rule—delighted, rather relieved, to get back aboard their ship, their secure home. The boats were quickly lowered away and soon had ferried ashore all but a skeleton crew for this welcome diversion. Before long, goal lines had been emplaced in the form of a derelict and weathered windlass, let go from some long-ago ship, we found on the beach for one, and a large piece of whitened driftwood we found for the other. Two teams were loosely constructed along the general lines that divide a ship's company: those who work on the weather decks and those, such as the snipes, whose naval lives are spent deep in the ship, out of sight of wind and wave. With certain further arbitrary divisions of those who work between these two, the radiomen and messmen, for example, being assigned to the deck team and the combat information and weapons people to the snipes. Nonplayers constituting the cheering section and cheering section and players alternating from time to time as the desire struck them.

It was a pleasant if barren setting, suffused in peace and quietude, devoid of any evidence of incursions man may have one time made on it. The beach was of an exceptionally soft sand and white as bleached bones. I was struck by its almost immaculate cleanness, its virtual absence of kelp. One way it sloped down into a blue-green water of a particular clarity and, under still heavens, as untroubled as some lagoon. In the other direction it met the great desert; the endless sands unbroken, varied only in the majestic and corrugated dunes that rose to break its awesome and forbidding sameness like high waves breaking across a silent sea. It stretched away beyond us like a mighty sea itself, a sea of sand extending to the farthest horizon, in a solemn and immense loneliness, with a nobility and greatness of its own. The tawny desert sands, an indigo sea, the sky of paler blue: These three constituted entire the universe at this stop in geography, they and our ship standing consolingly off in the near distance. Even the one thought that troubled me whenever I left the ship scarcely touched my mind looking at her now. I had made it a practice not to be long from the ship at a time, out of a vague but always existent fear that some gathering, some quickly arranged cabal might seize her and take her on a destination that differed from that intended by myself, that she might sail off toward the western horizon before my very eyes. Today—feeling because so many of ship's company, including her CSO, were ashore that such an act was scarcely manageable—that fear lay far away, overwhelmed by a sense of ease I had not felt in weeks.

The afternoon did much to make the cares and concerns that were always with us recede if only for a few hours. The happy shouts of sailors disporting themselves filled the air, joyous yelps ringing out from the water and from the touch-football contest. The final score was an arguable thing, each side claiming the higher figure. It was near 1800 and I was engaged in the dilatory and soothing occupation of observing that remarkable display—one would go far to see it, for it is one of nature's most sublime profferings—of a huge scarlet sun preparing to set half over sea and half over desert when Lieutenant (jg) Selmon approached me and abruptly said it was time to go. I was startled at how quickly the time had slipped away, and had almost forgotten that there was someone like Selmon around to tell us when we had to break off. "Captain, it's time" was the phrase he had some time back settled on and employed now. It was as though he were some sort of plenipotentiary timekeeper from whose calls there was no appeal.

We started embarking in the boats to head out for the ship standing about a thousand yards offshore. I was thinking, with gratitude, how the faces of ship's company appeared more relaxed than I had seen them in some time. How little it took! How little really sailors asked! How little complained when compared with so many of the whining human race. I felt again in me that surge of affection, shielding, paternal. I was waiting to go in the last boat off the beach when I became aware of the imposing figure of Preston, the huge boatswain's mate, coming toward me. He was wearing cut-off dungarees and nothing else.

Now he stopped and just stood there in a strange silence. Then he said the name once, just that, nothing more, in that quiet, clear-toned voice of his which seemed less a contrast than a complement to his physical impressiveness, as if loudness were always unnecessary and inherently vulgar. Then said it again. I looked beyond him. The sea-desert sunset was commencing its daily act of farewell. Solarly speaking, it would have to be the right time of year to witness that feat and as I watched I was thinking that it was a fine gift, a blessing, perhaps even a favorable omen, that we just happened to have put in here at the right time.

"Yes? What about him?"

"I can't find him, Captain."

Instantly, somehow, I thought back on my recent conversation with him when, in the course of my late-hours prowling of the ship, I came across his lone figure standing by the lifeline, looking out across the dark waters at the desert, white in the nightfall; his musing as to whether men, or kings on camels, had crossed it drawn by the star toward Bethlehem— some talk, too, there had been about the future of the ship; but most of all that it had been he who had wanted to articulate the words of home; then suddenly remembering something about Moses wandering in the desert. Hurley his reverent disciple, Preston had been bringing him along for his rating, in that special relationship, both ferocious and loving, in which a Navy man possessed of a special and indispensable knowledge and experience, hard come by over long years at sea, takes on the job of passing all of it along to a young and eager, often apprehensive apprentice. The boatswain's mate's words were so perplexing that I believe I did not immediately comprehend him. I must have asked him what he meant.

"Just that, sir. He's gone."

"Gone? What do you mean, gone?"

One would have thought there was nowhere to go at that place. That was what made the word, what Preston was attempting to impart, so strange, almost incomprehensible. I turned and looked across the beach at the last boat, loaded to her gunwales with men, ready to cast off; waiting for me, in fact. I was aware of the men in the boat watching Preston and myself beyond them with expectant and wondering looks, almost as if they had sensed that something had gone wrong. I took a couple of steps closer to the boat and sighted along the faces of the men in it. I turned back to Preston.

"He must have gone in one of the other boats," I said.

The boatswain's mate was speaking, trying to explain how this could not be. "Negative, sir . . . We were together at first . . . He's a good runner . . . I blocked for him . . ." There was a pause before he went on. "He said something about getting in a swim . . . No, sir. He couldn't have gone. We would have gone in the same boat . . . He . . ." The big boatswain's mate hesitated . . . "Well, sir, he would have waited for me."

I looked at him and understood. Of course. Almost a matter of respect, of proper deference. The boy—he was not much more than that—was under the big man's wing. The word "gone" seemed to hammer at me in its slow-dawning twin meaning. For a moment it held me still, immobile in the initial glimmerings of foreboding. All of this time we were facing in the general direction of the sea and the waiting boat. I think we must have turned at the same moment and looked in the other direction. Then without knowing really how I had commenced doing so, or with any conscious intent or purpose, I found myself walking away from the water, across the beach, coming to the edge of it, stopping, gazing into the boundless waste of the great sands. We stood in silence, transfixed.

The huge scarlet ball started gently to lower itself impartially into both desert and sea, in an epiphany of immolation that stopped the heart,

341

now the bottom half of it already gone, the top half fast disappearing and as it did, spreading a tint of cinnabar scarlet everywhere over that total immensity of desert, sky, and sea, as if bestowing upon the entire universe a queenly benediction. Before our eyes as in some miraculous ritual the desert turned that startling and exquisite color like some gown with which the departing sun rays adorned it for approaching nightfall. The great red ball vanished. Almost instantly a coolness, a chill, entered the air, as suddenly as if some deity charged with regulating desert matters had flicked a switch. With the chill, and the oncoming dark, the desert took on a spectral air, a powerful stillness so transcendent and forbidding, so impenetrable in its ancient air of mystery, that one ceased in awe almost to breathe, much less dare speak; one felt a sense of active menace, as from a violent serenity; fear crept in.

I had come to its edge, refusing to believe any man would simply willfully disappear there, not a sailor, anymore than he would jump overboard from his ship into the sea. We stood gazing far away into it, into its complete hush where now came like a tremor and a lamentation a sudden, a long and mournful sigh as from an actual human voice that sent through one a chill greater than that of the air—a keening breath of wind sweeping as a phantom across that enormous solitude, bent on its business of sculpting the huge and ever changing dunes; then that awesome silence again. Stood until our unwilling eyes were pulled downward to the deep and clear footprints that violated the virgin sand. Footprints naked, unshod. Our eyes came slowly up, in unison, and followed them to where they led inward into the desert.

Without a word we began to pursue them, Preston alongside me in an entire silence, the sand muffling our steps, our eyes looking always downward at the continuing trespassing track, a left-footprint, a pace, a right-foot one, feeling the depths of the sand pulling at our shoes as they plunged into and obliterated the other naked footprints. Then stopped again while our eyes lifted slowly and followed the ungiving line which continued on as far as they would take us. We walked a little more, hoping in our foolishness to see somewhere ahead the end of them, not once speaking, just looking forever downward at the lonely necklace of encroachments. Stopped again; looked up once more; stood once more gazing in a kind of transfixation at the trail of invasive footprints leading on endlessly into that sand vastness otherwise unmarked, chaste, undefiled.

The desert was beginning to darken. I glanced up and saw the evening star make its appearance in the eastern sky. Venus, all lonely and majestic; seeming oversized, overbright, gazing down itself on the great sands, on us, and somewhere out there ahead on another. The whorled dunes sliding westward into the night, reaching up to the multitudes of stars now coming on. We stood motionless in the chill—how astonishingly cold the desert could be when night came on!—surrounded in an absolute hush which we did not break. Listening for a faint sound from beyond, a cry of distress, keeping our peace so as not to miss it. I felt I had never known such a sense of loneliness, no, not even on the most distant sea. Then suddenly loud and piercing yells began to break the stealthy stillness. Our own: which one of us came first I did not know, only that both of us stood there implanted in the sand, our hands cupped as megaphones to our mouths, shouting out his name over and over, first together and then, as if by arrangement, by turn, spelling each other, shouting at the tops of our lungs, until hoarseness began to overtake our voices. Only a vast silence flowed back to us in answer from the desert wastes.

"Why don't I go see, sir?"

I turned sharply to him. Everything in my captain's soul was brought to a state of intense alertness by the absurdity I had just heard.

"What? What did you say?"

"I could go look."

"No, you could not." I could hear the harshness in my voice, that captain's sharpness of absolutely forbidding something. "Boats." I spoke more softly. "There isn't time. We're up against our time limit right now. Mr. Selmon."

"Sir, what if I just . . ."

"Preston," I said, more sharply still.

I looked up at him in the fading light, at his largeness now taking on a silhouetted aspect which seemed to enhance that very image of vast strength. It radiated from him in an absolute promise of its validity, its availability. I suppose if it had come to such a foolish question as physically restraining him he could have brushed me aside with one blow, and nothing like a full one needed at that, from one of those massive arms. We stood in the sand as if rooted there, gazing into that void; the desert—it must have been the accelerating darkness, hurrying in upon us—seeming increasingly to surround us, its shrouded plain pressing in on us, almost as if to lure us onward, to say, You come along too, as though quite prepared and even hungry to swallow ourselves as well. Something so irresistible one felt oneself fighting against it, some powerful force beckoning us there shot through me, made me fear for ourselves, lest it pull us also into its mystery.

"Boats." I could hear my own voice distinct in the enhancing shadows, the tones of a quietened and urgent plea. My concern about the one who had vanished was now entirely gone. I thought only of the one who had not. The ship was not going to lose anyone else if I could help it; and she emphatically was not going to lose her best seaman. "Who knows how much of a lead he got? It could have been an hour. It could have been two hours . . . He's far away now." I reached over and touched his arm and said the word. "He's gone."

He looked at his captain. In the chilling gloom, I could not see into his eyes, only a great muteness, a sort of stricken dumbness on his face, seeming to envelop his huge and desolate figure. Then he looked out at the unending trail imprinted in the sands, on into the desert distance. He would not disobey his captain, everything he was spoke against that. And yet . . . For a moment I thought he was simply going to turn and march off, following wherever those footprints led him. I tightened my grip on his arm, down into the hard flesh, my fingers seeming no more than would have a child's to make a beginning on its circumference.

"Let's go back, Boats."

I could not be sure, so quietly did it come from him. He looked at me, then down again into that chain of footprints, and I thought I heard him murmur a single word: "Shipmate."

"Boats," I said, "they'll be waiting for us. The others. The boat. The boat has to get back to the ship. We have to get back to the ship."

I would never really know. It just may have been that one word that did it. To no one did it represent more—from no one need more. Or maybe a simple realization of the hopelessness of the thing, of its finality, out of reach now, of shipmates—of anything. He waited, still looking far off into that infinity of sands. Then his eyes came back and rested on me.

"Aye, Captain," he said. "They'll be waiting for us. We have to get back to the ship."

.10.

UNKNOWN TO GEOGRAPHY

The mind was obliged constantly to range ahead, groping, into all unknowns. In the event Bosworth produced nothing; in the event the Mediterranean should fail us, as now appeared almost a certainty. As we moved ever nearer Suez the process—intense, searching, rejecting nothing, giving punctilious consideration to all—was stepped up: What before appeared remote courses, distant and unlikely options, now came more distinctly into contention as this sea's promise fell away. So it was that I had ever more interrogatory talks with Lieutenant (jg) Selmon, who was sworn to secrecy, probing him for everything he knew on his subject: vaporization, incineration, fallout, contamination, radiation—whether of lands or of people. Especially lands I catechized him about. What most likely happened where? So much was guesswork, as I have noted, but general expectations, always subject to later, on-the-spot verification, could be attempted—indeed, we had no choice but to do so, then to exercise our most prudent judgment of the moment; then hope. Subject to such caveats, his feeling was that two places offered the most promise, these being the Indian Ocean and the South Pacific; that somewhere in all their immensity of waters lay the best bets of having escaped. For two reasons: the relative paucity of worthy targets in both; and, hugely important, because of the patterns of the planet's winds.

My hand moved, a finger extruded and settled itself on a dot in the very middle of the Indian Ocean.

"Diego Garcia," I said.

More than anything else, almost more than for an assured food supply, I longed for replacements of the cores of highly enriched uranium fuel on which our nuclear reactors ran. (Myself always having to bear in mind that the odds were stacked quite heavily against *Pushkin*'s quest on our behalf.) Lacking new fuel, we would simply come dead in the water in a matter of months. Every day's steaming told me with a certain ferocity—I heard it in the very movement of the ship through the sea, each wave she took as though counting down—how little time really remained to find something habitable; that without fresh fuel we might have to grab the first thing we raised, however unfavorable otherwise, and that when we did we should never be able to budge from it. Given the new rods, we could go on more or less forever—or at least five years. What a millennium that seemed! What a sense of freedom it would give us! What burdens lift. These obtained: We could vastly increase our range over the waters of the earth; prospect many more places for possible habitation; have a look just about everywhere; above all, do both things— see home and look elsewhere; not have to make the terrible choice that would otherwise be forced on us in not many days more—at Suez, with what effect among the crew no man could guess.

One matter stood much in our favor. Beginning with the *James* class of DDG's, nuclear-propelled ships were built around a much improved nuclear reactor, and one reduced in physical size. The size permitted two reactors in a ship such as ours but at the expense of core life. To compensate for this loss a technology involving serial replacement of fuel rods had been perfected, meaning that it was now possible to replace a limited number of rods at a time, thus continually extending the core life (eventually a "normal" refueling evolution would be required but the "serial" method significantly reduced its frequency). Accordingly, due to the improved design, remote nuclear support facilities containing replacement rods existed in a number of U.S. naval installations around the world, generally stored on board submarine tenders.

For our purposes I knew to a certainty of but two places where such tenders, storing such rods, were stationed.

"Diego Garcia," I repeated. "Nuclear rods. Plenty of them stored there. We know that. Mr. Bainbridge?"

We were in the chartroom, just aft of the pilot house, the door closed: Lieutenant Bainbridge, the communications officer; Thurlow, the navigation officer, present because of his large knowledge not just of his field but of geography as well; and of course Selmon. A shaded light shone like a stage spot from directly overhead down on the chart table and upon the Mercator projection laid out there.

"Of course, we've tried raising it many times, sir," the communications officer said. "As we have every place else."

It was one of the largest United States Navy bases in the world. We ourselves had replenished there and I remembered the facilities for everything, every possible kind of stores and in huge quantities. Enough food stockpiled, for instance, to feed vast fleets, to feed a ship's company of our size to the last days of even normally lived lives, and uncounted tons left over. No place on earth was more distant from America. It had been built for no other reason than that the distance between the Philippines and the Mediterranean was so great. Something in between was needed to care for fighting ships. In such manner did a Portuguese name, a piece of land otherwise unknown, unvisited, unimportant, become—the phrase was—a vital link. Vital links brought other things.

"Their long-range communications could be knocked out," I said without much conviction. "Mr. Selmon?"

"If they got those they got all the rest, I would imagine, sir."

My finger left that place, moved, slowly, on a westerly course, into another ocean, came down on another dot, on our last remaining chance for fuel.

"Guam," I said. "Also had a submarine tender stationed there. Storing nuclear rods."

Even as I named the island, something hopeless and unforgiving stirred in my memory. It was also a mammoth Navy base, second largest of them all across the seas. When Magellan found it, he had started something for future generations of sailors—American—that he could not have imagined. Over the years the island had become virtually a Navy principality, as Navy as Annapolis, the Chamorro people the most U.S. Navy body of human beings anywhere; working for the Navy; their men entering the Navy. The Navy-Chamorro symbiosis was a thing all its own. On another ship I had put in there many times. A people gentle, quite lovely, altogether intelligent, with a pretty island, much larger than most, that rose from green-on-azure waters unsurpassed in all the vast Pacific. On its acreage, what the Navy didn't have, the Air Force did. The long-range bombers. The missile-launching sites. I straightened up a bit, still letting my finger rest there. Things had to be said.

"Guam. That place was the biggest supply dump for hydrogen bombs, other nuclear armament, of any place outside the U.S.A."

"I've heard that, sir."

"It's true. I saw it."

"Did you, sir."

Selmon's voice was bright-toned, that of an apt pupil hearing his archaeology professor describing some historic dig he had been a part of. I remembered. Selmon at least seemed to want to hear it. And for this briefing, it needed to be put anyhow.

"They took a bunch of us nuclear captains there to see it. Racked up in those tunnels they cut into the hills, then concreted. All of them perfectly camouflaged—driving by, you'd see nothing but breadfruit trees. Then in the tunnels hundreds of those things. Thousands. They should have renamed Guam—Redundancy Island. Enough on that one island to blow up the universe, say six hundred times over. No island anywhere was anything like what Guam had become. Even more nuclear fuel waiting for us on Guam. We could pick up enough of it to go on forever . . ."

I stopped. In the realization, like a streak-through of horror, come and gone, that every word I said condemned Guam.

"So we can safely assume that Guam and Diego Garcia got scratched pretty early?"

"It would be a natural thing, sir," Selmon said. "I can't imagine them so stupid as not to get those two right off. The first wave of missiles, probably."

"Well, they weren't stupid," I said. "At least not in that way."

"No, sir. I don't think they were that kind of stupid," Selmon said wryly.

"The breadfruit trees," I said absently, as if I had not heard a word he said. "I never saw so many breadfruit trees either, as on Guam. It's a wonderful food. Quite interested me. A man could almost live off breadfruit . . ."

I stopped, shocked at my own meandering, and the silence hung. Selmon's voice came through the dark, a touch of alarm in it did I fancy? I felt he was looking curiously at his captain.

"Sir, I'd say to stay as far away from that place as possible. It's had it, sir."

I smiled distantly. "Don't worry, Mr. Selmon. We shall not go to Guam."

Our minds ceremonially interred Guam—more accurately, left it a seared hump rising from the Pacific blue. For a moment more: I remem-

bered good swimming at Guam, Tumon Bay, the water clear and sparkling a hundred feet down. I laughed abruptly, sensing that this startled
my officers, as well it might, a spectral laugh to my own ears.

"Gentlemen, I was just thinking. The very *first* bomb, that toy, the
Hiroshima one, took off from Tinian, sister Marianas island, right next
door to Guam, as we all know. I was just thinking something extremely
banal. The same thing perfected a thousandfold coming back to exterminate the place that first sent it off. Mr. Bainbridge."

"Sir?"

"The communications situation with Guam?"

"Same as Diego Garcia, sir. Often tried. Nothing raised."

I revved back, composed and analytical. "Then that is that."

Diego Garcia . . . Guam. They seemed our last bets for nuclear fuel
replenishment; the urgency of thinking of a reachable place that would
take us in so suddenly enhanced.

"Gentlemen, I would say we were looking for a place so useless,
worthless, good-for-nothing, far from anything that was anything, that
absolutely nobody could find any good and logical reason, or any reason
at all, to do away with it—in short, the dregs, or at least the ends, of the
earth. Would you agree, Mr. Selmon?"

"From a radiation standpoint, sir," the young officer said, "you
probably couldn't describe it better."

Now we bent over again, studying the Mercator projection Thurlow
had laid out of the Southern Hemisphere. We commenced looking for
tiny dots on vast reaches of ocean. Selmon had educated me: the smaller
the body of land, the more surrounded by water, the farther away from
any mainland, the greater the chances of habitability. Thus—if we should
find nothing else—minds searching with fierce diligence for that one
point of earth set somewhere in millions of square miles of ocean that
would receive us, sustain us: some last resort to fall back on if need be.
We peered at minute and faraway clusters in the two ocean vastnesses,
as if one might say, "Come here." The chart spoke not at all. I turned
to the navigator.

"Mr. Thurlow," I said, "I want you to prepare a list of every island
found on any chart of these regions, the list to have one restriction: to
qualify, it has to be distant from any conceivable target. Then find out
everything you can about it. From the hydrographic charts and studies in
our marine shelf. Also we've got the *Encyclopaedia Britannica*. The climate. What might grow there. The place mustn't have too many people.
And what people they do have, their nature and characteristics. Not of

a hostile enough character, or in numbers sufficient to overwhelm the ship. Whatever you can find. All you can find."

"I understand, sir. Captain?"

"Yes, Mr. Thurlow."

"The best place of all might be a place that is off the map. One completely unknown to geography. Some island listed nowhere. There are always such places. Places passed by. Uninhabited places. Some of them very possibly capable of supporting men; determined men." He waited a second, adding curiously, "And women. By definition, places that no one got around to simply because they were so out of the way—out of the mainstream. Of trade routes, commerce, of the normal sea-lanes—of no imaginable potential, strategic or tactical. And thus directly to our purpose. Not necessarily bad places in themselves." I heard a slight, sardonic laugh. "Grass grows on them, that is. Not at all necessarily sandspits."

We paused before this portrait. Lieutenant Thurlow: Some of his speculations I had found to my own mind remote, unrealistic; but others, ones no one else thought of or imagined, in the event turning out to be true. There was a considerable silence. Then Selmon, in tones of rather wry musing:

"You know what would probably be the best bet of all, sir?" Startling us, the radiation officer gave an abrupt laugh of his own—coming more seldom, more sardonic than Thurlow's, that of a man who saw life as it was. Selmon's hand reached out; hesitated, hovering over the chart like a blessing and a hope; then the forefinger poked out and landed on a larger place deep in the chart; as far down, in fact, as you could go.

"Antarctica. It just might be the one place to remain free of any fallout—now or forever."

Weirdly the adverb, one become strange to us, seemed to give back an echo. It required verification. I turned toward him.

"Did you say 'forever'?"

"It's possible, sir. Nothing certified on these things, as we know, but . . . I've been doing the calculations. There's quite a fair chance that it would have all dissipated before it reached there; using up itself on the rest of the earth; the main point being that the air flow into Antarctica from anywhere else is so small that there is nothing or very little the contamination could travel on."

"That's rather sweet to visualize, Mr. Selmon."

"Not so strange that it would come through. Really the one faraway place. The North Pole: it's actually quite close to places inhabited by man. Why, we know the Russians actually stationed ballistic-missile submarines right beneath the Arctic ice pack. The Arctic's got people. The Antarctic couldn't be more different. No people. Surrounded by the Pacific, Atlantic, Indian oceans coming together—separated from other continents by hundreds of miles of open sea, the place utterly remote. In the Arctic, ice starting at the seventieth parallel; the Antarctic the fiftieth. In fact the Arctic would have been one of the first places to go—those Russian subs if nothing else. Not a doubt that the Antarctic will be the last—if it goes at all."

"Quite within the realm of possibility," Bainbridge put in. "As a matter of fact, when I was stationed in the Pentagon—I suppose I can let the rest of you in on this now," he said, in a rare witticism for the communications officer, "I was put in a Navy section called PNW—for Post-Nuclear World. The very existence of the damn section was itself so classified that we had a joke about our studies being so top secret as to be stamped 'Burn Before Reading.' "

Bainbridge received with a smile the small ripple of laughter. "Anyhow, one idea given a very serious consideration was the positioning of something called a 'Mobile Continuity Force.' The idea was to create a task force of vessels built solely for the purpose and cram them with all imaginable survival gear and personnel . . . food, clothing, medicine, tents . . . doctors, nurses, mobile hospitals, ambulances . . . grain and vegetable seeds, fertilizers . . . Jeeps, landing craft, helicopters . . . standing ready to take all this to pockets of survivors who might just be around here and there in the United States. Plans even called for each ship's company being composed half of men, half of women: In case there was nobody left, they could procreate all by themselves. Having built this task force, the idea was to pick the place on earth most likely to survive all-out nuclear attack. There was no argument as to what that place was. The vessels were to be stationed in the South Polar Sea—however great the fallout everywhere else, contamination there being either of low intensity or nonexistent."

We all listened with fascination to this account of the communications officer's former duty. I softly put a question into the absolute silence.

"And what happened to that particular Pentagon plan, Mr. Bainbridge?"

"Well, Captain, the Joint Chiefs shot it down. Two reasons. In the event of that kind of attack the whole country, they figured, would be so contaminated that the ships couldn't get anywhere near it for a couple of hundred years or so. The other was that building and positioning those ships, so they reasoned, would signal to the Russians and everybody else that we believed we could survive a nuclear confrontation; contradicted the reigning philosophy of mutual assured destruction—that a nuclear war was unwinnable. While they were about it, they deep-sixed the whole damned section as being too dangerous just sitting around thinking up things like that and sent us all to sea."

"At least, Whitney," Thurlow put in, "there was the favorable result that otherwise we would never have had the pleasure of having you aboard."

"A very handsome compliment, Mr. Thurlow. I thank you very much."

We sat for a moment in silent contemplation of these revelations.

"Well, now," I said. "The South Polar Sea is still there. And so is Antarctica. If those predictions on which that fascinating contingency plan was based of a . . . What did you say that thing was called, Mr. Bainbridge?"

"Mobile Continuity Force, sir."

"Typical Navy nomenclature. If the predictions of low or noncontamination in fact hold . . ."

I paused in this fancy.

"There's just one drawback," Thurlow said. "For us personally, I mean. I doubt if men can live on nothing but fish."

"No, I suppose they couldn't," I said vaguely. The mind made a movement. Half the mind went off somewhere, to attend to something, I couldn't tell what. "I hear it's pretty cold there, too."

"Yes, sir. I just felt to mention it—Antarctica. Meantime, that place," Selmon said, "—assuming that good thing occurs—will have to remain in the hands of those that have it now."

"Those that have it now, Mr. Selmon?"

"Penguins and sea leopards, sir," the radiation officer said. "Especially penguins. Thousands of them. Tens of thousands. They have a good shot—just my opinion—of not being touched at all. To go right on living as if nothing had ever happened. Maybe—except for a few bugs around the earth—the only thing that will. Penguins may very well own the earth; presently if not already. What's left of it."

"Penguins and sea leopards," I said absently, my mind still preoccupied as though trying to identify an elusive object. "Imagine penguins and sea leopards outlasting the whole works. Well, probably they deserve to. Especially penguins. I don't think they ever hurt anybody."

"No, sir. They'll probably wonder—from time to time—why men don't come around anymore. Gawking at them and taking their pictures. Then they'll just shrug and go on like always. If penguins shrug."

All this was decidedly loquacious and nonscientific for Selmon, who generally stuck to the technical facts. His having let go, it seemed to encourage another county to be heard from; with that sanguine and ironic air it had.

"If penguins survive, it'll mean the new evolution can start that much further along," the voice said almost cheerfully, as if there was nothing without its bright side. "Instead of with one-cells. Puts everything a few million years further ahead, right? I wonder what'll evolve from penguins?"

That was Thurlow. "Yes. Well, now. Shall we get off the penguins and back to us?" I said.

That night I could not get Antarctica out of my mind. If Selmon's suppositions fell in . . . A very fat hypothesis to be sure. And yet. Was there some way? Some way, finding it true, we could possibly make it there? I started with known assets. We were a ship, from Barents duty, equipped formidably for cold latitudes, including Navy polar-weather clothing aboard in quantity, much else; not least, a ship's company deeply experienced in battling frigid zones at the other end of the earth, on one of the coldest of seas. But the Antarctic: That was a quantum step up in frigid zones. The elements would be our foes. No problem otherwise of hostile welcome I could foresee. They would certainly be willing to share it with us if I knew anything about penguins. I remembered once standing in front of a large refrigerated cage containing a half dozen of them at the National Zoological Park in Washington—myself just back, in fact, from picking up my orders at BUPERS for the *James,* happy as a boy at this command; completely certified, all the insistent imprimaturs fulfilled, to command such a ship as I now went to: a qualified mariner; an authenticated noncrazy, nor likely to become one; a couple of hours to kill before the flight down to Mayport, knowing no one in the city, therefore visiting the animals, who didn't require invitations, couldn't refuse me. The only time I'd ever seen penguins. Feeding time came. The man entered with a bucket of fish. Instead of hassling him and climbing over each other to get to the fish, the penguins simply arranged themselves in a neat semicircle in front of him, as though taking their places at table, and there waited, each, patiently and quietly, until the man held a fish over its mouth, which then came open and took it, mouth then closing immediately. Presently giving a little yak of a noise which sounded like "Thank you." No one shoving anybody else or trying to get another's fish. Manners, politeness, decorum, consideration: all obviously important to them, greed vulgar. I felt you could count on their compassion, their willingness to share. Was there any way at all, if it should come to that, to deal with the frigid temperatures? With the food problems? None occurred. And yet the mind simply wouldn't let go, give up, on any place that might have conferred on it that sublime distinction of Selmon's. "It just might be the one place to remain free—now and forever."

I stuck Antarctica in a corner of my mind.

.11.

DECISION

"**S**hipmates," I said, and told them at once, "you will remember that when I spoke to you in the Strait I told you of our hope that we would find a place in Africa, establish a temporary home, and keep trying to set up communications with America as to some place we might safely land there. Wait it out. I have to tell you now that Africa is not going to take us in."

I had deliberately brought the ship to rest off Suez. We could just see its mouth in the distance. It was the fairest of days, so windless the ship swung not a degree on her anchor, the fulgent sunlight shining down from an unclouded sky of palest blue upon that intense and darker blue of the Mediterranean, stretching serenely to all horizons, the dying continent lying in the distance astern. A deep peace seemed to pervade the air, the universe, to embrace all in an almost ceremonial stillness. Only the ship broke the vast and plaintive solitude. All of light, of beauty of day; yet, thinking of what I was about to do, it was as though I stood on the shore of a somber and darkling sea. Uncertain as to how they would receive it; aware of the chasm on which I was poised, great peril close as could be to the surface. I looked down across the figures of the men and women of the ship, crowded body to body into the spaces below where

I stood on the after missile launcher. They waited totally without sound or movement.

To one thing I had irrevocably made up my mind. It had now become necessary to assault them with the last cruel detail; both as to these new findings on that shore behind me and to those concerning home, the latter to some degree withheld, softened, the last time, in the Strait, when I had mounted the platform of the after missile launcher, as I had just now, and spoken to them. Then, though never dissimulating with them, I had tempered the brutality of giving them in explicit terms what had happened to their homes. Then I had spoken with compassion. Now in its stead a sense of ruthlessness lay upon me. This time they must not fail to understand. I had decided to have three officers address them, and in that order: Girard, to tell them about diminishing food supplies; Melville, the same as to fuel; and finally Selmon, as to conditions there. The first two making it clear to them that we simply had neither the fuel nor the food to do both things: to go home and to try to find a new home in the Pacific; Selmon to acquaint them beyond any possibility of misunderstanding with the evidence that there was little if anything to go home to. Girard and Melville had spoken. Now I said, "Mr. Selmon."

I had told him beforehand to withhold nothing, either as to America or Africa; to tell them unsparingly, yes, unmercifully. He now proceeded to do so. He stepped up and stood beside me on the platform. He began to talk, the facts seeming the more pitiless for the steady, stolid recitation he made of them, as if being so incontrovertible in their stark deadliness, they needed no tricks of persuasion. First he disposed of Africa, as he had with me, in a few brisk sentences. Then he directed their attention to that other mainland, commenced to take them piece by piece through the last harrowing detail, offering not an ounce of propitiation. He told them that at the very best we might see on the beaches of Massachusetts and Maryland, of Virginia, Florida, people such as we had seen on the beaches of Amalfi, other beaches in our sweep of the European side of the Mediterranean. Did they remember them? Well, the only difference in those at home, those who might still be alive, would be that these would be considerably further gone in both physical and mental deterioration than those unforgotten figures we had viewed there. The portrayal came on relentlessly. Another difference: We had been able to spend an hour or so on the Mediterranean beaches. But now we could not do that on any of the beaches that he had mentioned. Not on Cape Cod or Rehoboth. Not Cape Hatteras or the Carolinas. Not Charleston, our home port. Not Georgia, not Jekyll Island, which many of the men knew from being not far away. From Jacksonville to Key West, not Florida. "Any man who spent five minutes on any of those beaches . . ." He paused and added, "Any woman—could never have children again," he said as if he wanted a simple illustration to give them an idea, "even if he or she lived." Then that sort of intellectual shrug that had become so much a part of the radiation officer. "But, of course, at the levels obtaining he would be dead in a week, a few weeks at the outside if he should be so unlucky as to have an exceptionally high tolerance."

He held back nothing. Having dealt with matters that concerned one of our two options as to course he turned to the other, as I had further instructed him to do. Our best bets for finding a habitable place lying somewhere among the islands of the Pacific, giving them in considerable detail why that was so—the vast spaces, the comparative absence of worthy targets, the surrounding protection of large waters, the pattern of the earth's winds—all the reasons he and I, along with Thurlow and Bainbridge, had so meticulously explored that day in the chartroom, and the conclusions we had arrived at: All of this he set forth in the most calm and cogent terms, in a voice free of the slightest taint of emotion, concerned only with the evidentiary and the probable; radiating himself the composed air of one who knew absolutely what he was talking about; everything about him suggesting a man of incorruptible allegiance to a single purpose: Where does the truth lie? He carried immense conviction. His very manner, I think, making the reactions to the monstrousness of what they were being told come more slowly than they otherwise might have, but then coming the more certainly. As he spoke I watched their faces, impenetrable reflections passing across them like clouds as the dawning comprehension of what was being said to them made its inexorable, its ferocious inroads into all the fortifications of hope they had so assiduously erected. It was a masterly presentation.

When he had finished a great silence seized ship's company, so consummate that it seemed the very breathing of men could be heard. Selmon and I stood there waiting. Ship's company waiting. No one, it seemed, wanting to break the adamant stillness—perhaps not yet having the voice to do so. After what Selmon had said, and this itself on top of the naked statistics set forth just previously by Girard and Melville as to matters of food and ship's fuel, it seemed merciless what I had to do, like hitting a man when he was down. But it was for that very reason I knew I must proceed to do just that. To go after them while their defenses were breached, dealt such a blow. My part now to deliver the final one. I spoke into that silence.

"Shipmates."

I looked across the waters, down the littoral of the continent, Suez—which we had reconnoitered—just beyond. I turned back.

I looked down at their upturned, waiting faces, all attentive, with a certain fixity of gaze, in each case directed on their captain, all silent; faces each of which I knew so well, knew the man or woman behind each face; each to me so individually different, particularized, over that range of personalities, temperaments, idiosyncrasies, existent in seamen, in nature it had always seemed to me marked by a much wider spectrum of variability than in landsmen; each known by myself and to each other in that intimacy of relationship, in its intensity, its absolute dependence on one another, one and all, to be found nowhere else on earth, only a ship offering it—youthful faces; older faces; faces of men, of women, faces of those still little more than boys, girls: faces in which, thinning, the first reflections of reduced food rations were just beginning to be observable; all of these my own; every face raised toward mine.

One does not harangue sailors. I spoke as any captain of the smallest sense speaks to them; directly, without frills, never in a raised voice. Sailors will hardly hear words said any other way, or if they do will dismiss them; sailors desire it straight.

"Shipmates, a choice must be made. Between going home and setting course for the Pacific. That is absolute. We cannot go home, then if we find it impossible to live there, go to the Pacific. You have just heard: We simply haven't the fuel or the food to do both. It has to be one or the other. We cannot have it both ways."

I waited a moment, unnecessarily perhaps giving each step of information time to be precisely absorbed, beyond the least doubt as to clarity.

"As for home: All of you know that we have never stopped trying to reach it by every means of communication available to us. All of you by now are familiar with the Bosworth signal. What is it? As far as can be determined it is a recorded message being sent out at prescribed times by some sort of computer device, with no meaning whatsoever that anyone has been able to make out. We have given them our position, our identification, everything, asked them to explain. Nothing but that same incoherent message. But a few human beings in Bosworth, Missouri, and perhaps some other places of the country are no reason for us to go home. For one thing, it's as certain as anything can be that we could not get across the beaches and inland to where they are, if they are, and remain uncontaminated ourselves. In fact, as Mr. Selmon has said, radiation readings so high, anyone making that journey would probably die long before reaching them, especially since he'd have to walk to wherever they are."

Waiting again for the same reason; as well, before delivering the hardest part of all.

"But aside from these reasons, I must give you another for not going back: I don't think you want to see it. If we found people alive, we could not take them aboard this ship. The sicknesses they have would soon in all likelihood contaminate the last one of us. Could you go through that?" I found myself speaking harshly. "Not picking them up? Suppose, let us say at Charleston—because so many of us have homes there, that is probably where we would make for first—suppose we found living people and some of you had relatives among them—could you stand not picking them up, abandoning them? Something else: Should you decide to join them, jump ship, go down with them, do you think they would thank you for adding that to their misery? The last thing they would want would be for you to have to make that choice." I came down as hard as I knew how. "You would not want to see them, the way they are. But more important even than what you want is that if they, a few of them, are there and breathing, they would not want to see you. Do you understand that? You have heard Mr. Selmon. They would be like those people on the beaches of Amalfi. *They would not want to see you. They would not want you to see them,*" I repeated, the hardness for a moment overtaking me. I made my voice come softer. "You know what they would want? What they would say to you if they were here to say it? 'For God's sake, try to find a safe place for yourself.' That is what they would say. 'A place where you can live out your life, maybe do something, maybe start over . . .'"

I waited, reaching deep inside myself for strength to say it, feeling myself as much hearer as speaker of words, the sentence about to be pronounced being on myself as fully as on them—far more so, since if the course failed, I who had decided on it, who was promising so much, would be the chief criminal of all—words that began now to fall down over the men and seemed to drift out over the stilled and listening sea, she returning them like echoes of utter finality into our ears.

"Shipmates, we cannot go home. That is my decision. Not if we have remaining in us any will to live, any desire to survive. I take it that the last hand of us does. The ship is our country now. It is the only country we have. We have no other choice than to go through Suez. We are greatly fortunate that it is open. Since we have not enough fuel to go around the long way, by the Cape of Good Hope. Those of you who believe in God should consider that an immense gift. Those of you who do not should believe that this is a very lucky ship. We should all believe that in any case. We will use our fuel to transit Suez, proceed through the Indian Ocean, and commence our search where our best chances lie—among the islands of the Pacific."

I was aware of their faces turned up to me with expressions of silence I would never forget, their eyes held in a fixity even now of not fully realized recognition of what they were being told; faces simply looking up at me, as the bearer of this news, in the unbroken stillness, the hush as of eternity under the bright sunlight now streaming down and setting the Mediterranean blue around us all dazzling; the world, life itself, the contemplations of men, seeming frozen in time, as though all chronometers had stopped and awaited a signal, a rewinding, to resume their ceaseless countdown; the unrevealed look of profound and hidden suffering, of anguish too great to allow its escape; knowing that no words could breach that grotesque and unutterable misery, the horror irremediable, and so best kept within; eyes looking up at me, seeming full of a great light, trying to grasp the ungraspable. And all the time themselves saying not a word. It was as though I was looking at men congenitally mute; unable to speak. I waited for that sense of triumph to come in me— instead came something else . . . Abruptly I felt an acute sense of inner disturbance. The breathless silence seemed to press down on me more than would have a chorus of protests, a cacophony of objections, eating into my resolve; the silence seeming brutal, as if it were their turn to be so for the brutality they had just been put through. One wished they would speak; at the same time, not wanting questions, one hoped contradictorily that they would not. The total silence from them held. In the beginning reassuring, it now of a sudden seemed infinitely menacing. It had been easy. Too easy. Something was not right. To the last hand ship's company standing where they had stood through those agonizing minutes, or perched on ship's fixtures—all motionless as in a sculpture. It seemed as though with a conscious effort to make clear and firm my voice that I gave the order.

"Duty watch, make all preparations for getting underway. Mr. Thurlow."

"Aye, sir?"

"Make us on a direct course through Suez."

"Just a moment, Captain."

Lieutenant Commander Chatham had stepped forward.

"From whom, sir, does your authority now derive?"

.12.

THE PARTING

The men making room for him, he stood directly below me.

"If what you say is true, there is no government. There is no Navy that we know of. Who gives you the right to make these decisions? To decide the destinies of every one of us. By whose authority do you assume these powers for yourself?"

I felt no anger, was not even surprised at feeling none. It was almost as though I knew that this would have to come sooner or later. Felt rather something like relief at the inevitable having at last arrived, that whatever now happened it would not henceforth be hanging forever over me. It was to be settled, once and for all, one way or the other; knowing but one thing, that the ship would never be the same.

The words had fallen with a certain eloquence into that terrible quiescence, made so by a rational content even I could not deny: What indeed was now the source of my authority, my rule over these men? Words strengthened further by a case by no means without merit, indeed an entirely reasonable one—the Bosworth signal, the fact our own information was by nature far from absolute, urgent parts of it coming from what might be deemed suspect sources, dead Frenchman, recent-foe Russian; a case reasonable even to myself who had rejected it, bound to

361

seem so to many hands, their thoughts unceasingly riveted to loved ones, wives, children, cruel and unacceptable that they not be allowed to go determine for themselves their fates. Before such forces my own weapons suddenly seemed shadowy, ephemeral, wholly vulnerable, quite capable of being swept away like sea foam before the wind, in a single sudden moment of upheaval by resolute men with so simple and so great a motivation as turning the ship around. Against the first, the challenge to my authority, I had remaining only my own will and an ancient law of the sea having to do with a captain's unquestioned sovereignty off soundings; that and something others might rightly reduce to flagrant vanity and that even I viewed at times as but a prop to sustain me, a belief that only I could bring them through; against the second, my faith in Selmon's determinations, that only death and horror waited at the end of the course this officer standing below me would choose for the ship.

These assessments aside, all made by visceral rather than mental processes and in the time span of a blinker's flash, I felt that great current of raw fear, in nature unlike any previously known, in myself, equally in all who waited, a fear one could almost smell and perhaps idiosyncratic to what had happened with such swiftness: the unspoken cognition sensed to a certainty in every hand that, hardly realizing it, we, seamen all, had stepped across that line which is the most awesome and forbidding known to the world of the sea, by nature also with results no man could predict, that might in that hair-trigger air that had claimed each one of us the moment Chatham had spoken turn on something done, or even thought, in an instant's flare of emotion. Hence, nothing more insistent than to exercise the most precise control over my own, to present insofar as possible a calm demeanor, while I calculated whatever course might be available to me. To gain time the first urgency. For all these reasons surely with great intention speaking so, my voice came to my own ears almost weirdly softened, bell-like, even duly inquisitive, in the fervent stillness.

"What is it you want, Mr. Chatham?"

"Take the ship home, sir."

There was a movement, a surge among the men, at those words. Something felt rather than heard. That eerie, implacable silence: That was the scary part. The thought flashed through my mind like a warning buoy blinker set atop an underwater hazard on an unknown sea. *Did he have sufficient men to take the ship?* Followed instantly by an immense thankfulness for the decision I had made a while back to remove the small arms from this officer's control: that armory securely locked now, myself in possession of the key. I simply stood waiting on the missile launcher

362

platform, seeking clues as to their intention both in his own demeanor and that of the men, waiting to hear him out, voices carrying easily in the windless air, the stilled waters. For some reason I turned for a moment. Forward and high above me I could make out the ship's commissioning pennant limp on the halyards, above it the national ensign, equally so. I looked now directly at him. There was a fire in his eyes. Other than that an air of the utmost composure, suggesting an officer whose mind as to course was irrefragably made up, who had entered with every consciousness of his acts on a purpose he had every aim of achieving. His voice, not a tremor in it, reached me in tones of unqualified resolve, and those of an officer now become a leader of men.

"There is life back there. We know that more than ever now. The Bosworth signals told us that. Our people, our families are there. Some of them may still be alive. Some of that land—*our country*"—a sudden almost ferocity of expression, more normal speech then resumed—"is habitable. We want to go and find out these things. We intend to do so. We don't believe you have the lawful power to deny us that right. The ship is not yours, sir. Not any longer. No legal authority exists to give you that kind of power over us."

I felt the time had come, whatever else I did, to fulfill a patent duty. I spoke quietly, carefully, nonetheless in a captain's tone.

"Speaking of lawful powers and of legal authority, I must warn you, Mr. Chatham, that you are in the process of making a mutiny." I spoke over him to the men. "I give the same warning to whichever of you may be considering joining this officer in this affair. All of you are familiar with the punishments dealing with that activity as contained in the *Uniform Code of Military Justice.* They have been read to you from time to time as required." I turned back to him. "Mr. Chatham, I suggest very strongly that you abandon whatever it is you have in mind."

"It is too late for that." He spoke with his first touch of arrogance. "I say to you this final time, sir: We want this ship to come about and set a course for home."

Now, I thought. Nothing I could speak into that fast-ascending tension was going to be without risk. But the barest opening had been presented me, in the form of a single word. Now. Move into it now.

"We?" I said.

"A very considerable number of us. To my personal knowledge. And perhaps many others unwilling to speak out; or afraid to do so."

I could hear from among the men an almost keening murmur, something in it chillingly threatening, that seemed intended to support this spokesman, a strange, animallike sound; leaving me with the certainty that my time to act might be measured in minutes or less. I felt I had two things going for me. First, I did not believe he had in his camp as many men as his manner suggested; perhaps a score or so, no more. Second, I had somehow that captain's sense that these, while men dedicated totally to a purpose, their minds invincibly made up, had no explicit, worked-out plan for achieving it; if so, they would have executed it, quickly and conclusively, got their work done. Yes, they had talked, planned, even conspired. But as, for instance, to the actual taking of the ship: I felt to a certainty that, even if they had the numbers to justify the attempt—allowing, too, for the possibility that they might hope to sweep up in their cause those men, of whom I knew the ship had not a few, who were still wavering on the question of whether or not the ship should make for home, bring along in the unleashed emotions of the event, the fire spreading, even those entirely neutral hands—even so, I felt sure that they had left such matters to the conditions of the moment, even that moment now abruptly forced upon them by my announcement that we were proceeding through Suez; no time to devise such a plan. They were feeling their way. Nothing worked so well against a nonplan as a plan and an intention specific to a detail; now, in an instant's light of divination, mine took possession of me. I needed a moment. I felt immensely alone, a sense of utter pregnability. Suddenly, as though listening to another, I could hear my own voice ice-cold in the tense silence of the after-deck.

"To your personal knowledge, sir? Unwilling to speak out? Afraid to do so? You overflow with sources of intelligence, Mr. Chatham. One almost owes you a debt for educating a ship's captain in matters aboard his ship."

Perhaps it was that captain's inner voice that had seldom failed me, circumventing those processes of normal reasoning thought that surely would have said it was an absolutely unacceptable risk, to tell me now instead that it was my solitary hope, that none other was available; above all, telling me that if done at all it must be done at once, on the captain's own initiative, before this explosive atmosphere ignited into more deadly alternatives than the one I now intended. I felt no assurance whatever but that an attempt to seize the ship, however unplanned, might be made in some headlong moment, before men brought to this pitch could even know what they were doing . . . determined men governed only by extreme passions all too readily understood, noble as could be imagined, convinced rightly that, the ship now come to Suez, they were dead up against their last chance to make certain they would see their homeland, their families:

I could see their minds working; an attempt sure to be fiercely resisted by men of a counterview, or men only Navy-loyal to the ship and her captain, the consequences not bearing thinking of. I had to act before such events should occur, and do so decisively. I looked at the men. Something like a fever now visible in the faces of more of them than I wished to count, something tremulant, strained, about to give way, my time fast going. For one poised moment I felt the utter finality of it, the no turning back; then took the step I had made an oath to myself I would never take.

"A very considerable number? Very well. Let us find out how considerable."

I could feel time rushing in upon me, some cruel chronometer counting down, my eighteen years at sea seeming to pass before me in the fraction of a second, as though I might extract some helpful suggestion from that long servitude, below me three hundred shipmates nerve-taut, and suddenly it seemed my most precious asset was that I knew sailors. I could see their faces looking up at me, caught off guard, and, if I read them aright, caught also in their own uncertainty, foreboding, at some unexpected turn of events, its nature inexact to them. I felt a momentary lift. Gone quickly in the eerie silence then resumed, that profound and unnerving mute waiting, a stillness so intense that the smallest wash of a softened sea could be heard against the ship's sides and which seemed to conceal all the thoughts of men. Disregarding him, I spoke over the CSO to ship's company, in a captain's voice bent on making it straight and to the point, almost as if I were anxious to get it over with, to let them do whatever it was they wished to do; that I had no intention of standing in the way of it.

"Lieutenant Commander Chatham has spoken of 'lawful powers.' Asserting that I no longer have them over you. Perhaps he is right. One might think even in our circumstance—especially then, when every hand's very life depends on a good functioning of the ship—that a ship's captain possessed those powers until he did something or failed to do something that was a just cause for relieving him of them. What are those causes here? Negligence of duty? Cowardice in the face of the enemy? Incompetent seamanship? Dispensing illegal punishments on members of ship's company? These are some known causes for removing a captain from his command. So far as I can tell I am not accused of any of these. The charge against me appears to be that I have decided, after careful consultation with responsible officers, indeed after talking with many of you, not to take this ship home. For reasons which have been explained to you in the most persistent detail and which I do not propose to repeat here. That decision is the act for which I am to be relieved of my captaincy. As for 'legal authority,' Mr. Chatham does not say where that prerogative resides. He suggests that it is now in ship's company itself. Very well. Let it so be."

They had been taken as unawares as it seemed to me men could be. That much was clear; the startlement in their faces, this time appearing to linger, showed it. I pressed it home on them.

"Since that is what you seem to want, you may have a choice, one I will abide by. Before you make it, let every hand understand the following matters as you have never understood anything." I could hear my voice come hard. "One choice is this. I will remain your captain. If you so choose, you will have made the last choice you will ever make aboard this ship. I do not need to waste the time of sailors, of seamen, in giving reasons. Sailors know them. It would not work. Not on this ship. Not on any Navy ship. Since I do not claim perfection for myself, or infallibility, where doubts exist on any matter I will consult, ask for, consider advice, listen to anybody aboard this ship, as I have in this instance. I will continue to do so. And any man who has anything to say can come to me and say it. But, that done, decisions will then be made as they are always made on a Navy ship of the line. By the ship's captain. I intend to be obeyed. There will be no more talk as to 'lawful powers' and 'legal authority.' Understand also that by that choice, this ship will go through that canal you see off the starboard beam and will proceed on a course for the southern oceans and ultimately, if it should come to that, for the Pacific until we find some piece of land that will accept us, sustain us. That is the only course on which I will take you and the *Nathan James.* If you turn this ship about and make a course for home you will not do so under this captain. That is one choice."

I waited long enough only to let them fully grasp it.

"You have a second choice. It is that I cease from this day to be your captain. You may run this ship yourselves." My words came now scornfully, almost contemptuously. "By whatever method you may decide. Either by choosing your own captain. Or by any other method of operating a Navy ship that may occur or be invented by the more clever among you. And you may take this ship where you please."

I had finished.

"Are you men out of your minds?"

They turned as one in the direction of that voice. It was Boatswain's Mate Preston, towering over all. His voice, always so even-cadenced, that curious contrast to his massive figure, now took on a tone of fury, of its own contempt.

"You call yourselves sailors. Do you think you can run this ship without a captain? And do you think yourselves fit to choose one like some frigging shore election. Sailors! Where do I see sailors?"

"You got it all wrong, Boats," another voice came, whose I could not tell. "We don't care who the captain is. All we want is to go home."

It was as though a Babel had been released, other voices rising, the silence abruptly and rampantly broken, clamorous and opposing opinions erupting in an upheaval of heightening acrimony. I had had enough. My own voice came in a shout.

"Knock it off, all of you. *Right now.*" The silence returned, as complete as before. "There's been enough talk. Too much. Let's get on with it."

I came down harshly. "Those of you who want the ship to go home, step to the port side. Those of you who want her to go to the Pacific, to the starboard."

They remained motionless as statues. It was as though as sailors they were stunned equally by the strangeness and the enormity of what had suddenly been given them; something as foreign to them as could be; men accustomed to having their lives governed by a sure despotism, inured to a world of orders and commands, now told not just that they could resolve a matter themselves but one that would both utterly alter their present lives and the conduct of their affairs and determine forever their future lives. I spoke savagely.

"You heard me. That is what you wanted. In God's name, *move. Now.*"

It began, even so with what seemed an infinite slowness, the first men to move proceeding to the starboard side of the ship, presently some moving to the port; others appeared clearly to hesitate, as though undecided to which side to go. Myself not realizing it was over until I became aware that I was looking down a long clear space to the open sea, men in numbers ranged on either side of it.

"Mr. Thurlow."

"Sir?"

"Will you please count those on the port side of the ship."

"Aye, sir."

The navigator started walking along it. Then he had stepped back and stood looking up at me.

"One hundred and nine hands, sir."

Now for the first time I looked straight at the contingent congregated along the ship's port lifeline; eyes held helplessly there, in me room only for the profoundest shock. So there were so many as that set against the course I had decided on. A full third of ship's company! Their numbers, the fact that they were now gathered together in such an ominous separation from their shipmates across from them, severed by that gaping space, the very physical partition making clear to all the terrible divisiveness in ship's company . . . matters far worse than they had been before: Then, no one had really known the extent of it; now, the ship stood starkly, openly, visibly sundered. Chatham: he had won what he had set out to win: to show me, show us all, how split the ship was. I had fallen directly into his trap. I had not the least idea what he intended to do with his triumph. I became aware that he was speaking to me, his voice harder than before; those tones of something like arrogance returned, even of command.

"Captain, what we demand are boats. We want the gig and three lifeboats. They will accommodate us. To try to make it home."

At first I did not comprehend what he had said. Caught by an inexpectation, an astonishment; stupefied by what I had heard. Never for a moment having counted on this. Then, looking into his face, the face of a determined officer, unflinching, knowing the reality. That much planning, and to the last detail, they had done. "To try to make it home." It was that phrase that did it, the sorrowfulness, the heartbreak of it, suddenly slamming at me as I gazed now at the men arrayed along the port lifeline, studying individual faces, stared both in a kind of stunned dismay and an onslaught of agony, of pain, yes, of a kind of hopelessly poignant love for them, that their desire, their determination for home should have gone thus far. Chatham was right. There were things about my men I did not know. For a moment an overpowering compassion for them, a great pity, struck at my will; myself shaken, almost tottering on the launcher platform—wavering not just physically but in my resolve. Then a second horror hit me. I spoke as a seaman.

"How in God's name do you propose doing it?"

"Very simply." He spoke with a kind of arrogant defiance. "The gig will tow the lifeboats."

"My God," I said.

I could hear Chatham's voice coming at me, in it now tones of insistence, hard, pressing, the voice almost of a superior; that, and what he had to say, yanking me violently back.

"Well, Captain. Do we get the boats? Of course, you still have the choice of turning the ship around."

Suddenly I became aware that Lieutenant Girard had appeared from somewhere and had taken up a position squarely facing Chatham. From directly below me I could hear her.

"Mr. Chatham, this is an evil thing you're doing." Her voice cold and hard. "You're taking these people to their deaths."

"Stay out of this, Girard." Chatham's hardened voice was equally cold. "It's no affair of yours."

"The hell it isn't." I could feel the rage rising in her, the loathing for this officer. She spoke over him to the men on the port side, her voice not shrill but low, intent, carrying. "Are you mad, all of you? Do you have any idea what it will be like? Five thousand miles on the high seas in open boats. And that way—towed boats?"

I could hear a certain rustle of unease among the men. Her voice kept coming at them.

"Even if you make it back you'll be like those people at Amalfi damned quick. Have you forgotten them? Aren't there enough dead people? Are you so eager to join them? If you don't care for yourselves, don't you care for the idea that we need every live person we can hang on to?"

A terrible silence held for a moment. She turned her fury back on the CSO.

"You have no right. No right at all."

"Leave it, Miss Girard," I said.

I looked at the men on the port side who had reached that ghastly decision, their faces telling me this resolution was inflexible, not one of them moving from where they stood in the pitiless stillness, waiting only my reply as to whether I would now make possible the attempt. I looked then at those on the starboard side who had chosen the ship and as I did a knowledge that filled me with horror seized me: The hideous truth was, I had no other choice than that or the one Chatham had now reached such a point of arrogance, of insolence, as to offer me: Send them home in the boats or take them there in the ship. It was one or the other; conscious at the same instant of something brutally bitter: that he knew this full well, indeed that his every move had been dictated by that shrewd perception and the reasons it contained. There was no way in the world these two bodies of men could now abide on the same ship and ourselves go forward on the course I had chosen. The ship would simply not work; the ship herself would not allow it. The awful alternative was to cast men into open boats on a voyage across two great seas fraught with every peril . . . and not just any men: shipmates, men I had commanded, with whom I had been through so much, toward whom I had sworn the most solemn oaths of care and protection. Yet, as certain as the stars of night these same men, kept aboard, with their obsession nothing had been able to breach, would come back at us, perhaps having converted others to their cause, the ship at some point in her course torn apart, mortally so this time the greater rather than the lesser probability, by events far worse than what had happened this day. Our future at best full-laden with the gravest of incertitudes as we ventured now into a vast unknown, we would need every hand pulling together to have any chance at all of bringing the ship and ourselves to safe harbor. A ship with a crew so divided on a matter so fundamental as the ship's very course, her destination: It was lunacy. No captain with a shred of sanity left would ever take such a ship off soundings had he the slightest opportunity to alter matters; least of all the captain of a destroyer with its inescapable intimacy. Well, that opportunity had come. It would not do so again. I must not fail to seize it. (As for that sole other choice I had, bringing the ship 180 degrees about, heading home: Did I for one desperate moment consider it yet once more? I cannot say; if I did, it was only instantly, viciously, to suppress it.) Survival itself demanded it: a ship's company united, loyal to their captain, a loyalty but moments ago put to the severest test, that larger body of men by the starboard lifeline, wanting to go where he would take them. In a surge of savage ruthlessness I realized I wanted all others gone, off my ship; to the last hand.

I turned to him where he still stood, directly below me. I, thinking myself a judge of men and especially of sailors, knew now: I had always underestimated him, both as to his qualities of strength and as to other qualities less admirable. Only now did his achievement, and its execution, reach me in all its fullness. There had been something masterly, Machiavellian, about it. He had forced me skillfully into a position where I had to give him the boats—that, or take the ship home; he had seen into my mind better than I into his, seen there the unacceptability I would attach to keeping so many men on the ship who did not want to be there. He had to show me the numbers and I had even helped him do that. All the same I had helped myself; helped the ship: She would now be rid of men certain in time to endanger her. In that sense our purpose had been curiously identical, and each had realized his own. We were quits as it were. And as we looked now into each other's eyes, I had an absolute sense that we both knew all of these things to the last detail, and that each knew the other knew it. Knew also, in a final truth, something far worse, the terrible knowledge that would go with each of us to his last day on earth: that we two had been the authors of the dread decisions that had this day been made in the lives of men. A flapping in the halyards, a sudden freshening of sea breeze, startled me like a portent, a great chill seeming to pass through me; then all came silent again. I gave him my answer, quietly enough, if in a coldness that said the matter was decided.

"In response to your 'demand,' Mr. Chatham. Permission granted. You may have the boats."

I looked again at the men on the port side. In their faces there was something like rapture, as if they were already home, had simply obliterated any thought of the appalling passage intervening; this alleviated in others by a clear grimness as to what lay ahead. In all faces something beyond reaching, irredeemable: I knew, in an infinite anguish, that I had lost them. I looked again at their leader below me. In his eyes I saw triumph but also something else: that hard look of a sea officer already in the process of becoming a commander of men, a peculiar gleam, a look I knew well—for I possessed it myself. He wanted no doubts left.

"The boats to include the captain's gig?"

I spoke curtly. "Aye, Mr. Chatham. You shall have the captain's gig."

"Then we will be ready to cast off at first light."

I was startled at that. Twelve hours. Yes, they had planned it all.

"As you wish." Now I allowed myself a brutal note. "For now, sir, you will go immediately to your stateroom and bring me your launch key, all keys to weapons systems and spaces. Preston!"

"Sir!"

"You will accompany Mr. Chatham. You are to stay with him until he has brought the keys to me. Is that clear?"

"Aye, Captain. Very clear, sir."

The big boatswain's mate stepped smartly forward from the starboard lifeline and took up a position close to the officer, eager, I felt, to keep an eye on him. A look half smile, half scorn crossed Chatham's face.

"That was unnecessary, Captain."

"Perhaps so," I said. "But in this instance I felt it best to exercise my lawful powers."

Then I spoke to all. "Ship's company dismissed."

From their port and starboard sides the parted men now moved, mingling again.

Chatham's earnest desire for the captain's gig was understandable. It carried forty-three men. Draft 3'19" fully loaded, length 41'6¼", full load displacement 28,800 pounds, fuel capacity 180 gallons, two 250 hp diesel engines. Sturdy, seaworthy—men had crossed oceans in boats less so. Equipped with provisions including sextant and nautical tables, radar, full sails rigging when the fuel gave out . . . towing lifeboats decidedly would not help . . . a fearsome voyage it would be. Still I believed skilled seamen had a chance. All our boats were supplied with exactingly chosen survival gear: bailers, flashlights with extra batteries, desalter kits, fishing kits, food packets, first aid kits, drinking water, Very pistols, signaling mirrors, portable radios, shark repellents, floatable knives, hatchet, signaling whistle, hand pumps. During the few hours I saw personally to it that they were further equipped as much as they could be with additional stores, food, water, other items; including small arms, ammunition, drums of diesel fuel—the reason for the third boat being these extra stores—that would give this arduous voyage its best chance.

Next morning, the sun just pushing over the horizon, every hand stood topside as the gig and the lifeboats were lowered away, then were laced together, the gig in the lead, the three boats astern her on short lines one after the other, the tents which could be raised over them in hard weather now lowered. It was a luminous day, a great serenity lying upon the waters under stainless skies of azure, everywhere the almost translucent stillness that had held these last days. I stood on the quarterdeck as each of the 109 passed by me before stepping onto the platform of the accommodation ladder in the order in which Lieutenant Commander Chatham had directed them, this also meticulously worked out by himself to place hands with the desired skills in respective boats. Each pausing a moment as he came abreast of me, starting to salute until they sensed that I did not want that; I shook a hand, pressed a shoulder: a man I had known as closely as I felt men could passed on, together we passed out of each other's lives. My mind as I looked into their faces seeming like some endless kaleidoscope, unwinding back over my time with this man or that, fetching up an individual memory, something having to do with him. In every single case myself trying in that mind to discover, as he came before me, why that particular man was leaving, what had led him to his dread decision. Some even made sense. I found it almost weirdly natural that all three of the men who had married Norwegian girls back at our base in the Hardangerfjord went—Signalman First Brinton, Boatswain's Mate Second Hubbard, Chief Quartermaster Hewlett, remembered myself standing up as best man for each of them in the little church of St. Peter's-of-the-Sea, at Husnes, its steeple the last thing we saw standing out, the first returning from the Barents. I had somehow the feeling that they had vague, fanciful hopes of making it back to Norway—by what means I could not imagine, guessing that neither could they. More glad than not that Hewlitt was going. Other than Lieutenant Thurlow, he was the best navigator the *James* carried, would be invaluable to the voyage, perhaps crucial to its success. There were clear patterns I could understand. Most of those departing were men with families; wives, children. But then also a couple of women: one, Hospital Corpsman Lockridge, who had been closest of any of us to those wretched souls on the beaches at Amalfi and the other places along the littorals of Italy and France where we had stopped to render what little aid we could, herself giving direct physical help, bandages, medicines, where nothing could help, perhaps her sheer acts of emollience and care doing so for brief seconds to those spectral creatures looking at her out of sockets of eyes—myself, seeking any connection whatever, however tenuous, even farfetched, somehow tying that experience to her departure. It was all I could do to keep from asking some, *Why, why?* I asked none. There was no time, and the question would have been worse than senseless; yet unspoken and unspeakable thoughts heard between us in the remorseless silence. Ensign Jennings, the youngest officer aboard, a wife, a child he had never seen in Tulsa, Oklahoma, staying a moment in front of me; his lustrous eyes glaring like some bewildered son caught in events too large for him, in a mystery he could neither understand nor solve, into those of a father, as if I, whose relationship to him had not been unlike, might at this very last moment give him some answer; none to give, myself placing a hand on his shoulder, his moving on. Madness! I could only think as they passed by. Madness! And also silent, hoarded thoughts of a different kind, of the most immense thanksgiving as to the men who were not in that terrible line. Chief Delaney, the Missouri farm boy who seemed to know everything there was to know about growing things and who was so zealously tending the garden of seedlings he had started aboard that might one day make all the difference; Noisy Travis, the shipfitter, who one day might build us dwellings: these two men alone quite possibly indispensable to our survival. Others: Porterfield, our best helmsman and something else: if there was one man more than any other who had helped his shipmates to bear up, it was he—had almost willed some of them through after the launchings and down to now by some mysterious quality of the spirit he seemed to possess. It would have been sore to lose him. Thinking of times to come, I thanked God with all my heart that these, certain others, had chosen to stay with the ship.

Then the last hand was down, only their commander remaining, standing beside me on the quarterdeck. It was the first time since these happenings that we had been absolutely alone. For those of my ship's company leaving I had feelings such that only the application of the last measure of self-control I possessed had enabled me to see them pass by and step onto that accommodation ladder. For the officer who now stood before me: I felt I had never known until now what anger was. Not so much for the mutiny as such as for taking them into what now lay before them. Knowing it would be as senseless as the other, I did all I could to suppress it as well. Not with a full success. We spoke in a kind of chill formality.

"I wish it could have been different, Captain," he said.

"There was never any chance for that, Mr. Chatham. Once you started making demands of the captain of a Navy ship. Once you decided you knew best. I hope to God you know what you are doing, sir."

"Naturally I believe I do."

I had no patience with that; nor did I like his tone. I spoke with a cold rage. "I cannot forgive you for what you have done. I would have preferred to see you before a general court-martial had circumstances permitted. That is where you belong. Some of these men wanted to go on their own: That is true enough. But few enough I believe to cause the ship no harm. You did everything you could to encourage others. You misled them."

"Not in my view, sir. Who is to say which of us is right?"

I was done with it. I looked down at the boats in the stilled waters, at their passengers, back to him. I wanted him out of my presence, gone. I spoke with an infinite disdain.

"Now, sir, you will get off my ship."

He stepped onto the ladder platform, turned, facing upward, smartly saluted the national ensign high on the mainmast. The ancient Navy custom seeming a mockery; though I knew he did not intend it so, it was reflexive in him. Then he was moving down the ladder, stepping into the gig.

The little flotilla of gig and three lifeboats rode gently just behind the ship's stern, hardly bobbing on the resting sea. The fantail of the *James* stood filled with sailors looking a last time down into the faces of shipmates numbering some of life's closest friends. The men and the women in the boats looking up at us on the ship . . . it was almost more than the heart could bear. The Jesuit, standing on the very tip of the fantail, conducted a brief religious service, sprinkling holy water, saying a prayer over the boats and their passengers. "Our God and Ruler of the

374

Deep who alone knowest the hearts of men, alone knowest the truth and meaning of thy servants' decisions, guide these our shipmates on their long and difficult voyage over the great waters. Watch ever over them, give them calm seas and good passage. Great Navigator, bring them at last in thy everlasting mercy to safe harbor . . ."

Then simultaneously boats and ship were getting underway in opposite directions, the small and larger white wakes merging, hands of shipmates on both lifted in farewell. The *Nathan James* gathered way, proceeding slowly through the gently parting waters. All hands not on watch remained on the fantail, gazing as I did from the bridge wing at the four boats in column line, the gig towing the other three, moving away from us over a blue sea, glassy under the climbing sunlight, the stillness broken only by the quietened noises of gig and ship; the faces of all the occupants of the boats save only the coxswain at the helm of the gig seeming to me to the last turned toward the ship. Soon they were but specks on the vast and empty Mediterranean. Then they had vanished over the western horizon. I faced back, stepped into the pilot house.

"Right standard rudder," I spoke to the helmsman, Porterfield.

"Right standard rudder, aye, sir."

"Steady on course zero eight five."

"Steady on course zero eight five, sir . . . Checking zero nine zero magnetic."

I could see it up ahead. "Helmsman, take us through Suez."

"Through Suez, sir."

.BOOK V.

THROUGH THE
GATES OF
ACHERON

.1.

EDEN

Thurlow, Melville, Selmon. Navigation officer, engineering officer, radiation officer. It was with these three chiefly that I plotted our course with such care, probing long over charts spread out on the navigation table. It embraced three principal elements. The first was to take us on as direct a course as possible to the southern Pacific, where Selmon had calculated our best chances lay. Our course, as finally determined and refined in the light of all considerations, called for us to proceed N. by N.E. across the Arabian Sea as far north as Bombay; if finding nothing to turn about and make a S. by S.E. heading, reconnoitering the western littoral of the Indian subcontinent, and pass through the Laccadive Sea between the Maldives and Sri Lanka into the Indian Ocean; bending around Sri Lanka, east through Ten Degree Channel, then S.E. through the Andaman Sea and the Strait of Malacca, Malaysia, Kuala Lumpur and Singapore to port, Sumatra to our starboard, here crossing the equator; from the Strait of Malacca entering the Java Sea, Indonesia to our starboard, turning then on a course almost due east into the Flores Sea, the Celebes to the north, thence into the Timor Sea, past Cape Maria Van Diemen into the Arafura Sea, the great mass of Australia to our starboard, through Endeavour Strait and into the great ocean-sea of the Pacific. Such a course, while in no way definitive—we had not the fuel for more extensive explorations—should at least give us a fairly clear idea of conditions in Asia and the chances of habitability there by leading us past the named lands, while proceeding by the shortest route to the Pacific, should they all fail us.

We would, of course, allow for any detours along the way that seemed promising, approach various land areas both to determine if any contained living and viable communities of human beings, neither eradicated by direct hits nor contaminated unacceptably by fallout, and if so whether these might be of sufficiently hospitable nature to take us in; in the absence of such valid survivors, examining those areas to determine if any were, first of all, habitable as to contamination and if so able to support us through a natural fecundity of soil. We were not without hope in respect to these possibilities. Still, however, believing that our principal chances lay in the southern Pacific, and there in those areas "unknown to geography," to use Thurlow's phraseology. Allowing for the indicated side excursions, Melville now calculated that this procedure when completed would fetch us up at approximately 08° S. latitude and 164° E. longitude, where we felt with a reasonable certainty that, along with the above reasons, the long passage of fallout and hence its termination would have brought us to habitable regions. At that point, according to Melville's rigorously measured computations, aside from emergency reserve, we should have remaining on the reactor approximately two months of running time in which to find a suitable place. All of these projections were based strictly on proceeding at a speed not to exceed twelve knots. It was thus that we emerged from the Red Sea and entered the waters of the Arabian Sea. The above reckoning, I should mention, allowed further for a brief exploration of east Africa on the chance—quite remote, but not, according to Selmon, to be dismissed entirely—that some livable area might yet be found along that coastline. A strictly controlled reconnaisance: We must not expend an excessive amount of fuel on this not overly promising diversion. I determined that we would test the shores of Somalia and of Kenya only so far south as the equator, and, should we find nothing, come about and proceed promptly on the first phase of our course, a heading N. by N.E. bound for the Indian subcontinent.

This course decided, I gathered the remaining ship's company early of a morning on the fantail, and, having brought the ship to rest at a point about twenty miles off a place called on the charts Ras Mabber in Somalia, once again mounted the after missile launcher to tell them all of this in considerable detail.

As I waited to speak to them, I thought how we stood on the brink of a vast unknown, lonely figures about to embark on the most uncertain of voyages, all beyond a black void. Yet something passed upward from them and into my soul, real as the sea around us. A strange and unexpected thing had occurred. Our numbers reduced from 305 to 195, I sensed to that captain's certainty that succeeding the terrible events that had brought us to so much smaller a ship's company, something had taken place of a nature I could never have foreseen. Abetted by that general inner urgency that had become so a part of us—that knowledge that griefs, however great, could not long be lingered over by men in our circumstance, survival itself requiring all attention to the pressing daily demands—we seemed instead in a mysterious and wondrous catalysis to be more tightly drawn together and to one another. It was as though in the act of choosing the ship, of making, for whatever reasons, these perhaps themselves varying hand to hand, that choice, the very fact of each hand who stood below me having separately, individually, of his own free will, personally done so, we were more shipmates than ever. Bound inseverably to each other; each and all bound to the ship; seeming to clasp us together in a fresh resolve. A faith incompatible with reason, greater by far than the facts as we knew them justified, all ahead of us, the passage we were about to undertake, speaking of uncertainty, saving only the certainty of hardship and nameless peril. Vain enough, too, I was that, yes, I felt that the selection each hand had made embraced not just a personal choice of the ship but of myself their captain as well. That sovereignty, so powerful before, seeming thereby not just reaffirmed but conspicuously augmented; any remnant of doubt as to its validity there may have been vanished; as though whatever my decisions might now be, there would henceforth be no thought of questioning them. Ship's company, such as remained: They rested in my hands. They had made to me the great gift of their fate. Something deeper than earth knew cleaving us to each other. Its strength already put to the test. Watch and watch we now stood, with these reduced numbers. Four hours on, four off, around the clock, day after day; a shipboard test of men normally brutal; now, not a hint of complaining, of malingering. I doubted not the fears beneath; their suppressing them but made greater the courage.

I became aware of something else; something that came swelling on the air, like a field of force. In their faces something indomitable. For a moment—for the only time I could remember in all our odyssey except behind the closed door of my cabin, tears stood in my eyes; I fought them back: leaving something imparted from them to myself, my blood seeming to run freshly strong. A freshening of wind sounded its wailing sough, elegant as a flute, through the ship's halyards. Then all was stillness again.

"Shipmates," I said. "We face a future which I have to tell you is as uncertain as a future could be. The course we are about to undertake: It will not be easy; it will be harder than I can say; we will have to bear pain. It will test our endurance to the limits. We will learn what fortitude is. We will need the last hand pulling his best to make it through, and all pulling together. But we are not without assets. We are seamen. We know the sea. We have under us the ship. We are American sailors. That is another name for men of courage; men who do not whine and do not give up. We have been through much; we have stuck together. Have helped one another without thinking of it as help. We have been a good ship. It is that that has brought us thus far. If we hold fast to it, we can make it. Find a place, make a home for ourselves, yes, a good home. We have the skills to do it. But we will need more than that. A good ship is a band of brothers. There has never lived a blue-water sailor but knows that. We have been that also: band of brothers and sisters. That is our strength. Above all we must not give that up. I count on every hand to keep to it. To help any shipmate who may need help; to help the ship. More than that, the ship counts on it. We ourselves depend for our lives on it."

Their eyes looking up at me, that look of dauntless steadfastness, that heartrending yet stirring sailor's look I had never seen on the faces of other men of taking what might come reaching up to tear at my heart and soul, at everything that I was; yet nothing giving me more strength. Even as I related to them the grim facts, sparing none, it was as if they embraced them in their brotherhood, in their defiance. Even as I went over the course in the greatest detail, more so than I had ever done, giving all the reasons for it, they seemed borne down not a whit by the imparted knowledge of all the horizons that in all probability must be crossed, each full of unknown trials; none, even the final horizon, giving certain promise that we would find what we must find. I finished up.

"On slow revolutions we have the fuel to reach the Pacific, and enough remaining to give hope that we can find a place. We have food to get us there—though I have to tell you that rations must be reduced even further. We will work harder than we ever have. I expect every hand to do his part. Knowing that your shipmate is as tired as are you; his belly as hungry. No one knows what we will meet up with as we now start our voyage. It is possible—more than that it is likely—that we will encounter dangers far greater than any we have been through. We would hope to find others who would help us, take us in. There must be others out there, possibly willing to do so. But I can give no assurance as to that. If we do come across people, they may prove hostile to us. If it comes to that, we will make it alone. But we will make it. I aim to bring every man, every woman of us, through to safe harbor." I waited a moment. "One more thing. Above all we have each other. You have stood stronger, more steadfast than anyone would have a right to ask for. No one ever led a finer body of men and women. I have never been so proud in my life of anything as to be your captain."

Concluding, I asked the Jesuit to say a prayer for us. It was brief:

"Almighty God. Thou who watches over sailors, over all who venture on great waters, guide Thou now the *Nathan James*. Give her a true course through the seas which are Thine. Give us strength to meet adversity with perseverance, pain with faith. Keep us in our love for Thee, and for one another. Let us trust in Providence—and rely on ourselves. Remind us to care for the shipmate to our right, the one to our left; to help whosoever shall need help; as all of us, at one time or another, will. Grant us self-denial, constancy. Bring us through all trials, keep us from harm. O Lord Our God, Almighty Pilot, steer this ship safely over every horizon, to good haven. Amen."

I then asked Porterfield to lead us in one of his hymns, the men seeming to like these. He picked one of their favorites and presently the voices of the men and women rose, softly blending . . .

Amazing grace! how sweet the sound
That saved a wretch like me!
I once was lost, but now am found
Was blind, but now I see.

The notes came swelling on the air, in the sailor voices falling out over the Arabian Sea . . .

Through many dangers, toils and snares,
I have already come;
'Tis grace has brought me safe thus far,
And grace will lead me home . . .

I waited until the last strains had died away and only the brooding stillness held over the ship, across the waters.

I turned to my XO. "Mr. Thurlow, make all preparations for getting underway."

Soon I could hear the great anchor rise, the long drawn rumbling of iron links running through the hawsepipe seeming overloud in the solitude that lay all around us. Slowly then the ship began to part the stilled waters, bound on our first exploration, the 200 miles of the coastlines of Somalia and Kenya—not a mile farther—we had allotted ourselves; that, barring a not expected habitability, would be our last look at that continent.

For the record: Not even trusting myself with both, I now gave one of the two keys required to launch the missiles to Lieutenant Girard, at the same time designating her to succeed Chatham as combat systems officer, a billet for which she had qualified during shore duty, one presumably to be chiefly titular from now on, concerned principally with upkeep, ourselves unexpecting of either attacking or being attacked by anything or anybody; having also instructed her before Chatham's departure to obtain from him the combination to the safe in his cabin in which the key was kept and under no circumstance to reveal that combination even to her captain.

The diversion along the coasts of Somalia and Kenya was for the purpose, as indicated, of making a final determination as to Selmon's belief that Africa was gone. He had arrived at this projection as to a near certainty in the penetration he had made near Carthage, courageously taking his counter a mile inland and observing its readings steadily incline. This result itself had added another piece of evidence to a fact long known, that interiors of land masses were almost certain to be both more quickly and more heavily contaminated than littorals; a premise borne out in our own experience, most notably on the European side of the Mediterranean, by those pockets of human beings we had encountered along its shores, their having fled there for the precise reason that the lands behind them no longer tolerated human kind. For our final validation I chose an empty beach we came upon some 150 miles into our allotted maximum of 200, near a place called Lama in Kenya. There I led ashore a small party, this time Selmon not going alone, but accompanied, besides myself and Thurlow, by a shore party of eight, all of them being expert marksmen and armed variously with carbines, automatic rifles, and sub-machine guns; all under the charge of Gunner's Mate Delaney. As an index of habitability we hoped to encounter animals, the marksmen and their armament brought along not to dispatch any of these but to be used only if we were attacked. The party including also two of our biggest and strongest hands, Boatswain's Mate Preston and Machinist's Mate Brewster from the hole; also Bixby, along not as a signalman third but as one knowledgeable about animals, having been about to become a veterinarian when the Navy summoned her. As I believe I have mentioned elsewhere, Selmon had educated me in the fact that based on studies conducted during that part of his Radiation School Training spent near Amarillo, Texas, it had been established that as a rule animals possessed considerably higher tolerances than human beings, generally twice or more as much—over a period of forty-eight hours, 350 to 500 rads for man being considered the mean lethal dose as opposed to 1,000 for animals, these of course varying considerably animal to animal; while the Amarillo determinations included numerous species of domesticated animals, others such as elephants, lions, giraffes, hippopotami, not being prevalent in Texas, had not participated in the experiments, hence had tolerances unknown.

The beach at Lama, as we stepped out of the boat coxswained by Meyer with her hand Barker, yielded a reading on Selmon's instruments that appeared to dash any slender hopes we may have had as to habitability here. It allowed us but four hours ashore. The expectation being so low, the disappointment was not great. I decided to proceed inland for a bit anyhow in order to make my own test of the littoral-over-inland habitability theory—personal knowledge of it seeming perhaps useful in our future search. Thus we penetrated into the bush lying just beyond the beach, single file, moving through vegetation and trees thick enough but not so much so as to require the machete ministrations of Preston and Brewster, Selmon and myself at the lead, our armed squad of eight strung out behind. Rather dark, now and then opening into a small clearing where we stopped for Selmon to take a fresh reading; at the third such clearing, this:

"It goes up, Captain. Very slowly."

"But it goes up?"

"Oh, yes. It goes up."

"Can we try a little more?"

"No problem yet. Still, not too far I'd think."

"Frequent readings then."

"Aye, sir. Frequent readings."

The wild growth became thicker; Preston and Brewster, summoned forward to the lead, had to wield their machetes frequently now, their huge bodies making long slashing entries into it. Through these we emerged into another clearing.

The men having come up and gathered around so that we formed a cluster, we all stood still in the great beauty of it; grass so green and glistening it seemed to have been but recently sprinkled with dew, under our feet extending all the way across the clearing and guarded all around by a ring of great many-trunked trees, their long branches stretching protectively over it. Thurlow was the first to speak, in a quiet voice which fell upon the stillness.

"Those trees, sir. They're the baobab. They're supposed to be the oldest living thing on earth—twenty-five hundred years or so. The Africans say they're the tree where man was born. If civilization started in Africa, one might like to think it started right here."

Delaney, a religious man, embellished the idea.

"Aye, sir. A regular Garden of Eden."

"Right now . . ." Selmon was looking at his counter. "We'd better get out of Eden."

I had been here twice before—not the exact spot but similar ones in this same country. It all seemed familiar. And yet there was a difference, the nature of which I did not at first discern. Then I knew. It was the absence of sound. More than by any other characteristic, I had always associated Africa with sounds. Of millions of sounds of insects, the carrying sounds of birds, infinitely varying, of all the animals, of unnumbered thousands of living things, a marvelous cacophony, a great and mighty symphony of life itself. We heard nothing; not a single sound. Only a breathless silence, as if God—if indeed He did commence matters here— had created the setting of Eden but not yet got around to creating its fortunate inhabitants. And yet there seemed nothing peaceful in that arcane and transcendent quiescence; rather it seemed somehow a cruel stillness.

Then—it was as though my thoughts had been heard—from behind the bush and the trees on the far side of this clearing we were startled by a sound. A silence. Then another. Silences again. Then a number of sounds, differing all. I had always loved, immensely enjoyed, animals—had made those visits to Africa for that reason—and knew the sounds of most. These seemed to come from creatures I had never encountered. Sounds I had never heard. Something strange entered the air, invaded our souls, seemed to be felt among the men. A fear; a sudden caution; a foreboding.

"Let's have a look," I said. I spoke to Delaney. "Gunner, have the men put their pieces on ready."

"Aye, sir."

I heard the clicks as we proceeded cautiously across the clearing, where the bush began again. It was not thick here, no machete work necessary by Preston and Brewster. We had gone I would have judged a hundred yards when we broke again into a clearing far larger than any before, this one almost entirely occupied by what I knew as a wadi, a watering place for animals, surrounded again by stands of baobab trees. Ourselves coming again into a cluster, the source of the sounds stood before us.

The variety of them slammed overpoweringly at us. Perhaps fifty animals. Quickly I could make out a pair of lions. Three elephants. A giraffe. Some eland. Zebra, gazelle, wildebeest, kudu. I think it took us a little while to comprehend, overwhelmed as we at first were by the sight of so many different species, some of them natural predators of others so that it seemed strange for them to be gathered so peacefully together at one place. Then, as our eyes moved over them, something out of recent memory came to strike terribly at us. The animals seemed to have arrived at almost exactly the same state as had the human beings on the beaches of Amalfi. Chronologically this just about fit.

Some just lay, breathing hard, at the wadi's edge, patently in a dazed state, occasionally looking at us as through blurred vision. Some were obviously blind. The same stigmata we had seen before. From all, large chunks of flesh had fallen away as though they had been viciously clawed, remaining flesh hanging in tatters, and as with the human beings we had encountered, this process seemed ongoing as if more loss were continuing to take place before our eyes; their bodies decomposing, slow bleedings everywhere; their coats gone mangy, great festering sores where hair or hide had been. A huge elephant tried to get up, succeeded in taking a step or two, fell down again with a mighty crash that shook the forest; weirdly, the other animals hardly seeming to notice, to hear. A great lion spasmatically staggered about, apparently trying to get closer to the wadi, then collapsed, just as had the inhabitants of the Amalfi beach. Mostly they did not move at all, as if hoarding dwindling reserves of strength. Their faces—and this was almost the worst part of all, sending a chill of horror and of unspeakable desolation through us—even their faces seemed to carry expressions highly similar. Looks—I do not think one imagined this—of bewilderment and stupefaction, and for the same reason, the immense mystery and inexplicability of what had happened, was happening, to them. Actually not that many sounds from them: low moanings most of all, heavy breathings as if choking for air; if bewildered by their fate, seeming acceptant of it. I do not know why it should have seemed so astonishing, and in itself so devastating to us, that these symptoms covered almost the exact same spectrum as those of the human beings we had seen on those other beaches. It was certainly not that we felt more sorrow in respect to the animals than we had with the human beings. Perhaps in our sadness a little of this: that none of these species who were before us had had anything to do with what happened. We stood in absolute muteness, the only sounds those the animals made; the sounds of suffering. From high overhead a slight wind came up, sending a mournful note whispering through the baobab trees that surrounded the wadi. It was as if the trees were crying.

It was Gunner Delaney, the farm boy, one growing up with animals, who first spoke.

"Captain?"

I did not need to hear the question. I was about to give the order when Bixby saw two of them coming toward us. As they approached, unafraid, they seemed in astonishingly good health. Fine coats, unstigmatized bodies. Two lion cubs, each a foot long. Bixby sat on her haunches, examined them. I watched her, the thin light of the clearing falling across her auburn, liquescent hair, something of tranquillity in that supple girlish figure whose knowing hands—fast as could be on the blinker light—now felt over these small creatures, one then the other, tenderly, expertly.

"They look fine," she said. She looked up at me. "Captain?" She did not say it; she did not need to. The idea would have been to take them along, aboard ship, down the line to release them into some place habitable.

"Mr. Selmon," I said.

He knelt alongside. Bixby held first one then the other while he ran his counter over them. He also looked up at me.

"Much too high, Captain," he said. "We couldn't risk it."

Bixby set the last one down gently; stood away. They seemed to want to follow her. She picked them up, one in each hand, and carried them down by the wadi; returned.

"You may proceed, Gunner," I said.

The eight spread out. All expert marksmen. The shots crashed through the jungle. Volley after volley. Soon all sounds ceased. It had taken a little while. We had had barely enough ammunition for some of those great creatures. In the great stillness, seeming more so than ever in the lingering echoes of the shots, we could see the curlings of smoke rising over the wadi, moving in soundless languor upward through the baobab trees.

"Let's get out of here," I said savagely.

We left Eden.

We made our way, hurrying as much as the thick growth would permit, back through the bush. Once, pausing briefly for Preston and Brewster to do some machete work, I remarked to Selmon, "I hear no birds," and he replied, "Birds have the lowest tolerances of all. They would have been the first to go." Soon we were emerging onto the beach where Meyer and Barker stood at their boat, waiting. Beyond across blue waters we could see the ship riding at anchor. We boarded and headed toward her. All the way out we sat with our unvoiced thoughts. Back aboard I gave orders for the ship to make its course at once, N. by N.E. as previously determined. I stood on the bridge wing watching Africa fade behind us. A thought would not leave me. Why we had had the mercy to put those suffering ones out of their torment but not to afford the same favor to the human beings on the beaches at Amalfi, the other places. Had it been a failure of compassion? As I watched the dying continent recede forever across our white wake, I wondered if the situation recurred, if we found any more human beings in that state, whether we should extend to them the same kindness we had shown the animals? Then thought: What would it do to us?

Then Africa was no longer to be seen and we stood surrounded only by the Arabian Sea, moving slowly through gentle waters bound for our first destination, India.

That very night happening to be the date for *Pushkin*'s surfacing at 2300 Greenwich, I reached him with no difficulty, informing him of the finality of Africa's inhabitability, stating that we had transited Suez and were now standing east, giving him in detail our proposed course clear through to Pacific regions. He in reply telling us that he was skirting the Bay of Biscay and on a heading for the North Atlantic en route to the Norwegian Sea, thence to Karsavina and his mission, Thurlow bringing me the message, translating its Russian.

"Karsavina," I said.

"Aye, sir. Karsavina."

The word had become a beacon for us. Thurlow understanding all, our two hearts sailed with the Russian submarine far away, headed north, as the *James* pointed her bow toward far different, and faraway, waters.

.2.

A CHARRED WORLD

Proceeding at our creeping twelve knots, we had reached a point about forty miles off Bombay when the first intimation of the fate of the Indian subcontinent presented itself. We came on. Selmon standing at his repeater in the pilot house, giving frequent readings—eerily like a leadsman sounding out constant depth readings lest his boat hit shoals—I was still somewhat surprised when still fifteen miles away, he offered me a reading which left no alternative. Thurlow had the conn. I informed him.

"All engines stop." I heard him give the order to the lee helm and presently the ship came dead in a placid sea.

We stood at the bulwark of the starboard bridge wing staring in wonder and incredulity across the waters of the Arabian Sea with that brilliant aniline blue that characterizes them; observing both the place where we knew by navigational fixes the city of Bombay to be and the littorals extending on a N.W. by S.E. bearing both ways from it. Below me along the lifelines I was aware of many sailors joining in these observations, gazing dumbstruck at it as at something transmundane. A great stillness lay over all. No winds stirred heavens or waters and from the men and women themselves I heard not a sound or a sigh. I was aware of a signalman standing nearby crossing himself. It stood there in a terrible brooding silence. I think it was the very size of it, its overpowering immensity, that more than anything brought our minds and our souls stilled, in a nameless fear—a quiet terror, I believe I could call it—and of a new kind. The immensity, I mean, of that black and monstrous mantle. Grotesque, hideous, it blanketed the entire eastern horizon, extending vertically from sea level to as high as the heavens went; horizontally from as far as the eye took you on the N.W. bearing to as far as it took you on the S.E. one. The mantle was at once brutal and eloquent, the first in the sense of the horror it emanated, the second in the sense of its true power made known. There was something absolutely anarchic about it, and utterly barbarous. Looking at it, one felt one had never known until now what fear was; one felt an invisible paroxysm pass through one, a motionless trembling of the body.

Sailors all, we were no strangers to nature's great and humbling manifestations: the ferocious seas, the black howling nights of the Barents; dark massiveness of thunderclouds—we had seen these, many others. They seemed in memory casual things. This appeared in its hugeness, its dominion, an occupation force of the firmament itself. Something discarnate, otherworldly and mercilessly real, the very badge of the cataclysm. More black than gray, it gave the appearance of absolute opacity and seemed less gaseous than a solid and hard wall, impenetrable, permanent in character, as if it were here the earth came to an end. This part of the illusion at least was modified by looking through our Big Eyes which revealed the billowing, swirling nature of the mass, but further increased its emanation of ominous menace by a feature not seen by the naked eye: long lashings of lurid red flames licking now and then across its surface and through the pall, stabbing out from it like giant inflamed tongues. I raised up and looked again with the naked eye. Again that overpowering grossness of it, extending in a sinister shroud across half the visible sky, struck down upon us. Our silent and stopped ship seeming tiny, infinitesimal before it. The thing had an awful and tyrannical force to it. Even across this distance its smell carried, exhaling that absolute promise of infinite peril, virulent, harboring the new corruption, this no illusion, the knowledge of this weaponry it carried being the most frightening aspect of all to us—had it not spoken across fifteen miles of sea and, lest there be any misunderstanding, informed us of the very fact on Selmon's instruments? A fair warning: Approach me not; not one inch farther. If it said anything it said that, and with all arrogance, confident of strict obedience, for it spoke the truth. We had learned: We stood in quite proper terror before it. I don't know how long we just stood there watching it, appraising it. It was time for practical matters.

"Do you think they got a direct hit, Mr. Selmon?"

"God alone knows, Captain. No way to tell."

Selmon had long since educated us: Even if the missiles and the bombs had been dropped elsewhere, sufficient dust and soot would have been injected into the atmosphere and massive quantities of pollutants released in the form of NO_X, cyanides, vinyl chlorides, dioxins, furans, pyrotoxins—oh, yes, I had been a quick study as to the recondite terminology, it being absolutely urgent as to our own future—to inflict an equivalent punishment on lands and peoples quite far away and having nothing to do with the conflict, the winds transporting these toxins, shedding them, their radioactive fallout, and the attendant fires as they moved across land masses. We had once had a discussion, one I believe I could describe as philosophical in character, as to the two categories of victims: concluding that those killed immediately in target nations were more fortunate than those in countries which were in no way the object of direct attack by anyone, their inhabitants thereby enduring more lingering deaths from the process I have just described. We gazed at that thing across the blue waters.

"The winds have had more than enough time to bring it here," Selmon said in that detached voice which I had come to consider as one of the more important ingredients of our salvation in circumstances where alarm of manner could have started its own fires and ones which would have consumed ourselves quickly enough. "Still, there's no way to know to a certainty. Except ordinary reasoning telling you that no one had any reason to drop them on India."

"Pakistan possibly."

"That's true. I'd forgotten about that fuss. And vice versa."

First I, then Selmon, bent and looked again. Nothing but the tawdry sameness—the red flagellations across the solid black. We straightened up.

"I wonder if there's anyone alive in back of all that."

"Let's hope not," Selmon said. "But I'm afraid . . . there's not been that much time. Quite a number still somewhere in there I'd judge. I'm glad we don't have to see them, sir," he said as if in thanks to that vast obscuring black purdah.

I asked for a reading. He stepped into the pilot house and brought it back. It had gone up slightly even without our moving, up from the reading which itself had prohibited any further advance. I looked north where the curtain extended, if anything more massively.

"Well, Mr. Selmon. Would you agree we've reached our northern-most point? No further in that direction?"

"Aye, sir. It could only be worse. We should get below the equator, sir. The north has nothing for us." His tone had a rare urgency to it. "Except to harm us."

Knowing that when I gave the order the ship would have reached as far north as she would ever in all her life go, I waited a moment.

"Mr. Thurlow," I said then.

"Aye, sir."

"Bring her about. One hundred and fifty degrees. Down the coast-line. Fifteen miles off at all times. Unless Mr. Selmon allows us closer."

"One hundred and fifty degrees, aye, sir." And in a moment to the helmsman, Porterfield. "Right full rudder."

"Right full rudder, aye, sir."

"Steady on course one five zero."

"Steady on course one five zero, sir. Checking one five five magnetic . . ."

I could feel the ship make her wide half circle and come about, something both real and forever symbolic, forever poignant, about it. We who had come from, lived there, would never again venture into northern latitudes. All the way down we could come no closer than the designated fifteen miles. All the way down the coastline unrevealed, clothed in the same towering dark cerements, rising thousands of feet into the atmosphere and now and then through it the same gleamings of red flames. Passing through the Gulf of Mannar and approaching Colombo we could see across the waters the identical phenomena, the city invisible, the entire land embraced in the thick billowing smoke, and the whole of the nation of Sri Lanka seeming on fire. Bending on our course around it, we proceeded in the coming days across the lower reach of the Bay of Bengal, across Ten Degree Channel, and entering the Strait of Malacca, Sumatra to our starboard, Malaysia to our port, we passed where our readings told us Singapore to be, also enshrouded in the great black pillars. A hush had fallen over the earth; the only sounds the occasionally heard crackling of fires in the distance, like dark death rattles. Moving ever southerly, we coursed the eastern littorals of Sumatra, finding something fractionally different. Slight liftings of the pall to give brief glimpses of empty beaches, the forests behind them engulfed in smoke and flames as of long duration.

It was as if we had passed through the gates of Acheron to bear witness to the immolation of the planet, a whole world on fire, smoldering, a charred earth. We did not linger. I chafed at the necessity of keeping our running speed at twelve knots, would have preferred to open her up and flee past these places. It was not that we did not feel compassion, not that we had become hardened. No, it lay more within the mind's apparent ability, if sufficiently conditioned over a period of time, to accept almost anything as normal when verified by observation. At least it was at this state that we had now arrived. I was not surprised. Observing these cities, places, nations, consumed already or in the process of being consumed, become charnel houses, the very fact of there being nothing to be done about it, by us or anyone else, kept the emotions on a kind of hold, a certain sadness but no more. What else was there? One learned to ration compassion; to draw miserly on one's not-unlimited bank account of feelings. Rather, and this was not a brutal thing, there was a desire to put them behind us, to see what better lay ahead: What lay ahead could not—so we felt then—be worse. A man who learns when not to weep is a stronger man, and certainly a more effective one, for that knowledge. Indeed, under conditions so final, weeping itself would have seemed to constitute a kind of sin, a sacrilege; most of all for the reason of being so inadequate. Passing by, we looked, then looked away. Passing by, we did not weep.

And so we moved, a solitary ship coursing through the waters which have always been kind to ships, letting them pass; moved past these funeral pyres, the men seeming after a while scarcely to notice them; our ship, our minds, our beings pointed only ahead; after a while glad of every single mile which placed them in our wake. We did what we could. Everywhere we went we bombarded the nearby country with communications in its own language, on every available frequency. Our nautical library afforded a considerable amount of translation of essential navigational material and calls of all kinds—identification calls, distress calls, "I require assistance" calls, "Do you require assistance?" calls, every call possibly needed by men to send or receive—into every language used where ships went, which meant the entire globe. Nothing came back to us.

One of these was China. Reaching our nearest point to it, in the South China Sea, we had turned all our frequencies loose on her. Nothing. We had wondered what had happened to China. It was too far out of the way to go have a look, we had not the fuel to spare; not a drop for sightseeing. Nothing suggested it would be any different. Worse, Selmon felt.

"All that land mass," the radiation officer said, "the fallout coming directly at it, from right next door. Massive, unbelievably massive amounts of it—probably making what we've seen look like cloud puffs. They must have been among the first to go. By the same token, I suppose, a blessing of going quickly, very quickly—something rather comforting in that, isn't there, Captain? It wouldn't be too surprising if there wasn't a single Chinese left by now. Not in China anyhow."

"Yes. Well, I suppose we must take our comforts where we can find them."

"My thoughts exactly, sir."

Selmon had moved into a sphere of thinking which I sometimes envied, sometimes abhorred; knowing I was helplessly approaching the same sphere myself.

Sometimes we got glimpses through the pall, and in the case of one town, Maura in the Bangha Islands, a good deal more. It was a singular experience. Almost no smoke at all lay over it and Selmon's readings enabled us astonishingly to keep approaching until we had reached a point no more than five miles off, where they attained a level that made us stop the ship. The word had passed quickly throughout the ship and all hands came topside to stare at this wonder, the sailors lining the lifelines. It was a fishing port I knew from an earlier Navy cruise, myself an executive officer on another destroyer; the town well-known throughout the world of sailors, ships putting in there because of its exceptional natural harbor, deep and embraced in long and protective encircling promontories; become in consequence a refuge from storms, a place of replenishment, a liberty port familiar to all Asiatic hands. The town had a certain charming aspect I had observed in only a few other ports on earth: The sea opened directly into the town. Curaçao in the Caribbean was like that, where you stepped off the ship almost straight into the main-street shops with their Dutch aura. By a coincidence this island was also originally colonized by the Dutch and seemed noticeably like its Caribbean sister, in neatness, in charm. From the stopped ship, now well within the harbor, we could see with absolute clarity straight down the principal street, see the buildings and the shops, none over two stories, each well cared for, see where the street went up a hill, see the houses on both sides, see at the very top of the hill the Catholic church. Everything well kept, shipshape—and undisturbed. The town appeared utterly intact, ready for business, even a couple of bars I remembered. We could see the merchandise in the unshuttered windows of the shops. One expected people momentarily to emerge from the shops, others to enter the bars. Everything ready, waiting; waiting in fact to receive the sailors of the *Nathan James*. For one blind second, a fleeting forgetfulness as to the new nature of things, it occurred to me I should turn my attention to liberty parties for my ship's company, in extreme need of it, so long without it—in a breath of shock brought myself back to reality. Everything ready for such parties with only one difference from the time I had been here before: There were no people. That there were no live ones did not seem so strange as the fact that there were none of any kind. Not a body, a corpse, revealed anywhere under the sweepings of binoculars, of Big Eyes.

"How do you explain it, Mr. Selmon?" I said where we stood on the bridge wing, looking down and point-blank into the town.

"A fluke of the winds, I'd say, sir. They brought it. Then they moved on."

"But the people?"

He shrugged. "They managed to do something with themselves. When they found out what was happening to them I'd say. Just left, maybe. In their boats . . . I don't see any boats . . ."

His voice trailed away. He stepped inside, looked at his repeater, stepped back.

"Sir, I'd say just about five minutes more here."

I looked up the street; down on the hands lining the lifelines. They simply stood gazing at the town as at a curiosity. From high on the hill a shaft of sunlight flashed from the cross atop the church. I had once been to Mass there. I remembered that for the fact that they still did it in Latin, the priest either not having heard of Vatican II or ignoring it. It had been a kind of reassurance. I turned away.

"Take us out, Mr. Bartlett," I said smartly to the OOD.

We proceeded through the South China Sea, the black monsters in the heavens still visible far off, hanging on, as though tracking us. We knew, of course, that they would move on us when the waters got narrower within the ganglion of lands in which we would soon be trapped. We braced ourselves for them.

.3.

THE DARK AND
THE COLD

We first began to notice their approach one morning passing through the waters of the Sunda Islands in the Malay Archipelago, at approximately 01°10′ S. and 105°20′ W., our position having just been checked by myself with Thurlow in the chartroom. I had stepped out onto the bridge wing and looked up into a sky free of clouds in our immediate vicinity, the same black masses standing far off as they had been for days; had looked routinely at the bridge thermometer which recorded a temperature of 74° F. Presently, high in the sky, bearing N. by N.W. from the ship, I noticed casually a few clouds make their entrance into the virgin blue. They were altocumulus but instead of being their characteristic flocculent white bore long brown and even black stripings. I proceeded about the ship's business.

No day passes but that a mariner looks up at the sky fifty times, on one of possibly changing weather, many times that; that sky which tells so much to him who has eyes to see. Throughout the day the clouding increased, especially that altocumulus with its curious darkened aspect; more so now, full overcast never coming, the sun always shining down. So long accustomed to observing cloud formations, I had the peculiar sensation, making no sense as related to anything I had ever seen in the behavior of clouds, that the altocumulus had somehow been penetrated by some of that higher and distant black mass we had observed for such a considerable period now. It was as if strange combinations, mutations involving the very clouds, violating traditional performance, were underway in the heavens themselves. We had become accustomed to seeing new manifestations aplenty. Looking back, one was aware almost daily that the numerous prophets of events had missed entirely many of these; they had been as babes in forecasting what it would be like in actuality. (In fairness, one should add that the failure of their predictions fell principally on the underside; and that a number of them had spoken, using one of their favorite words to cover any possible oversights or failures to foresee, of unpredictable "synergisms.") This one I felt was improbable. Nevertheless worry, in a certain discernment as to what was happening, with it a foreboding that seemed rooted in reality, a curious expectation that had been in me all along, had begun to penetrate my consciousness. The following morning saw simply more of the same. Around midday rains fell on the ship, not particularly heavy, but steady for an hour or so. Then stopped. Clouds remaining over us. I was standing on the port bridge wing around 1430 studying these when Selmon stepped through the pilot house door and approached me.

"Captain?"

"Yes, Mr. Selmon."

"The clouds, sir. The rain."

The language seemed idiotic. I knew Selmon was not.

"Yes, what about them?"

"I've been taking readings from the rainfall. It's low-grade radioactive, sir."

I looked at him steadily; feeling no great surprise; deep inside me, prepared for it.

"Those are nuclear clouds, sir." He waited a moment, as if figuratively looking at a calendar. I had never known a man with a more systematic mind. "I'd say they're arriving just about on schedule."

It was almost as if he would have been disappointed had he made an error in his timetable.

We had learned long since: The winds were now become the true rulers of the universe. Indeed they had for some time, almost from the first, been dictating our actual course. They were the drivers of the high black mantles; of their progeny now descending on us. These had only been awaiting the whims of the winds. Now they came, prevailingly variant tenths of west, now due, now W. by N.W., now N.W. by W., not strong, Beauforts 2 and 3 usually, occasionally freshening to 5. They came bearing gifts. It was as if those singular clouds were pursuing us, that of course an illusion created by the fact that we were a solitary ship on the seas. As we proceeded S. by S.E., through the close waters, unavoidably on the short fuel-conserving course we were following being more and more surrounded by land, the skies fluctuated as to cloud cover. On some days more, some less, but whichever, all of them of that darker hue which to a mariner had always forecast rains. Only no rains fell. More significantly, this overcast becoming darker and by the day, seeming also to hover lower in the skies. And finally this happened: Even with no rain to parachute them down on the ship, Selmon began to pick up patches falling on her, minute at first, but not so much so as not to disclose to his instruments that they were radioactive. Now he constantly roamed the ship looking for them, obsessively. Increasingly, he had to look less diligently. Increasingly, he found not just patches but large swaths fastening themselves to ship's surfaces; to weather decks, to stanchions, to boats, to the five-inch gun, the Phalanx, the missile launchers. The clouds dropping sprinkles of fallout, precipitations not of raindrops, but of dust and soot. And steadily their radioactive content rose.

Then an observable change: Very thin hazes, of a mistlike aspect at first, had begun to form like a delicate membrane across the sun itself, sometimes for an hour or two, then for a half day or so before full sunlight returned. Each renewal longer and of a more umbrageous character, constituting finally a kind of penumbra, rather like a species of partial eclipse. We found ourselves keeping our running lights on longer as day approached, turning them on sooner as night came on. Then another thing happened. The thermometer began to record drops, also slight initially, never precipitous, still to levels not to be expected in these waters. Thurlow, our navigation and meteorological officer, began tentatively to force this to my attention. Then one morning I came on deck to find a palpable chill in the air, along with a sun more obscured than previously by what could only be described as a kind of luminous dust. I had a look at the bridge thermometer. It read 48° F. In what appeared an obvious companion to the cover of contaminated cloud, the drop in temperature continued over the following days, slowly but on a steady downcurve. I had Thurlow check tables in our nautical and meteorology library. No such lows had ever been recorded in these latitudes. We continued on course.

The sun could still be seen or at least where it was, more clearly at times than at others. One day looking up I could observe that at the moment it hung in its dusky cloak at the zenith. A twilight gloom prevailed now at noonday. A strange and absolute stillness seemed to weigh down on us, on the ship, as if the stealthy luminous dust had brought with it not just its tenebrous shield but this bodeful and ominous soundlessness as well, broken only by the mildest of winds bearing N. by N.W. and whispering intermittently across us in mournful notes. The substance reached down now to a point not far above the ship's masts, stopping short of the waters which stretched in a glassy motionless repose, mute like all else, to all horizons, these vertically foreshortened only by the lurking nigrescent shroud crouched above them. Stopping there, hanging, like an opaque window shade drawn to a precise level and no further, as if, having established a domain of obscuration vast and unchallenged over the heavens, it yet hesitated to take on the great sea itself.

At first, as we proceeded toward the Java Sea, the overcast still allowed leaks of sunlight through holes in the clouds. Soon, however, these were sealed and the overcast became solid. We had lost the sun. This was followed by a heavy, blackish layer of fog and haze consisting of roiling, turbid vapors that enshrouded the waters and rolled in swarthy, infinitely languid waves over the ship, obscuring even the lookouts for periods of time, as the ship made its creepingly slow encroachment into the noiseless veil, speed reduced to eight knots. Now at noonday one looked up and could barely see the gleam of the masthead light. I was much aware of a possible new danger of a high order, its first evidence appearing one morning when a huge hulk loomed up in the murk, the lookout Barker in the bow reporting on the sound-powered phone, "Ship dead ahead!" the officer of the deck Thurlow's instant "Hard right rudder," Porterfield's instant execution in putting the wheel over. Through the swirling vapors we could see our port side slide by this monster—we could almost have reached out and touched her—a tanker of over a thousand feet she must have been. She was but the first. I was not too surprised, aware of the fact that we were moving through what had been the most traveled East–West sea-lanes in the world. I left standing orders for the ship to keep slowed down to a bare steerageway and ringed the ship with lookouts, our visibility on occasion reduced to not much more than a ship's length even with our powerful searchlight aimed into the murk; myself keeping during this period to my chair on the starboard side of the bridge. I also further minutely instructed Porterfield and the other helmsmen. "You men. Steer like you never steered. Don't wait for the command. Steer by seaman's eye. If you see something, bring her over hard." And finally I set a watch on the open bridge, Bixby and other signalmen ringing the church-sized ship's bell, in a counterpoint with the foghorn, the two great alternating sounds blaring and tolling out spectrally over the ship and into the black haze entombing her. Porterfield during this stretch standing longer watches than anyone, saving us from collision more than once, having almost to be pulled away from the wheel when I could see his own exhaustion overtaking him. Still I was surprised at the numbers of the ships. Hulks of ships; every type of ship, it seemed, known to the seas; merchant vessels mostly, the occasional man-of-war, a couple of times a passenger liner. All looming suddenly, mute, darkened, out of the murk, they seemed to constitute some great ghostly fleet, of all flags, drifting rudderlessly as the waters took them. Far from any desire to approach them, much less board them, we were concentrating absolutely in avoiding them, not to ram them.

The sooty darkness becoming ever more impenetrable, the thermometer continued its steady fall. Thurlow's research showed 62° F. as the lowest recorded reading on present latitude. One day around noon I came on the bridge, turned the flashlight on the thermometer, and saw a reading of 27° F. A rain began to fall out of that opaque blackness. It seemed to pelt soot and dirt against the ship; thick, penetrating rain. Flashing the strong light around, I could see the raindrops seeming to freeze solid the moment they touched the ship, covering everything, gun mounts, even lifelines, and creating a freezing slush on the weather decks. I looked up and saw icing beginning to attach itself to the mast and top hamper. I turned and sighted aft, directing the light there. Thin stalactites hung from the deck gear and antennas. The ship was gradually being wrapped in a skin of ice. We were three degrees below the equator.

Fortunately the cold was the least of our worries in the practical sense. One circumstance of immeasurable good fortune came to assist us. We were a cold-weather ship, rigged for some of the most frigid waters earth held, the Barents; the ship herself fitted with sophisticated deicing devices, which we now commenced to use, and with the best cold-weather clothing the Navy had been able to devise. The latter we had some time back turned to, Girard's supply department breaking out the Arctic gear. It was a godsend. Most of all, a ship's company with much experience on deep-temperature seas; undisturbed by cold, by icing, knowing how to cope with them. Nor was there great surprise at this development. Again Selmon had prepared us. Sometimes I was alternately alarmed and irritated at the stolid, almost insouciant manner in which he had come to

401

accept these new manifestations as being now in the normal state of affairs.

And so, grotesque figures in our Arctics, we entered the equatorial waters of the Java Sea.

Something far more ominous than the cold came to attack us. This was Selmon's constant readings and the nature of their curve. For it was not long before they registered that the weather decks were unsafe for any period of time. Soon—by that time we were exactly, deliberately so, mid-sea between Jakarta on our starboard and Borneo on our port—they reached a level where it was dangerous to be topside at all.

Now, in brute force, that terrible substance began to lay siege to the ship herself. I instituted extreme measures. I sealed the ship and her personnel. All lookouts, all weather deck stations whatever stood down; all personnel kept below decks at all times, save only for the essential pilot house watch. Most fortunate of all, the *Nathan James,* considering the nature of her mission, had been constructed with just this possibility in mind; that is to say, that her fiercest enemy might turn out to be not the usual ones that threaten destroyers—submarines, mines, aircraft, other surface vessels armed with surface-to-surface missiles—but that other hostile force which was now attacking us. An overpressure system for protection against the ingress of CBR (chemical-biological-radiological) contamination; all incoming air filtered, more reliance placed on recirculating air inside the ship; internal air pressure maintained at a higher level than external pressure: the *Nathan James* class indeed being the first ships to have the complete system built in. Combined with the use of sealants which by deep research and experimentation had been brought to an extraordinary level of efficacy, these measures made the ship's interiors as impervious to outside contamination as is a submerged submarine to seawater; men could live below decks with complete safety so long as they did not venture onto the weather decks; a partial exception being the pilot house watch, working in a space where glass "windshields" were essential to the conning of the ship. But even in the pilot house, using the same sealants, along with other protectants such as triple-paning, the builders were able to achieve a very high degree of impermeability to radiation, if not quite the perfect protection possible below. In addition I made bridge watches as small as consistent with the ship's safety, also halving the length even of these to two hours in order to limit exposure; all bridge hands issued gas masks; all subject to a dosimeter reading from Selmon immediately on coming off watch; then to bathe immediately. They not the only ones for this latter precaution. The ship herself we washed down frequently; the ship immersed in high fountains of water from the special device created also for ships of our original mission; the ship quite literally having herself a bath, the strong streams of water reaching everywhere topside meant to carry away all foreign material; the effectiveness of the system much diminished due to the contamination of the sea, nevertheless it might help marginally.

Thus a strange and sealed ship, no hands in view except the few in the pilot house necessary to navigate the ship, day after day, night after night—the two barely distinguishable—we proceeded ghostlike through the miasmal gloom. By now no one needed to be persuaded as to the perils of radiation contamination, the nature of its affliction. Those poor souls on the beaches of Amalfi, those animals in the Kenya bush, had been our teachers. In the closed pilot house I would sometimes glance at Selmon standing at his repeater, which afforded readings of the outside; looking steadfastly at it. The only illumination that of it and the shining ovals of light cast by the binnacle, the engine-order telegraph, the gyrocompass. All of us become considerably thinner from reduced rations, there was something especially skeletal and disembodied about his naturally slight figure in that gloom. He was going virtually without sleep. Standing there now like some haggard hierophant before the altar, gazing reverentially into his hallowed reliquary; preparing, as some intermediary before a higher power, to cast from it his sacerdotal pronouncements, our sole chart and compass.

Sometimes then, myself, checking the gyrocompass, turning savagely, stepping out for the briefest look into the stillness, behind me the pilot house doors rolling shut on silent runners, and peering through the substance as though it might somehow be clearing. Standing on the bridge wing in the bone-chilling air, now to zero levels here five degrees south of the Equator, peering through the caliginous pall. The substance had a taste to it, there was something foul and corrosive in its breath—gritty, granular, a fetid, dirty thing, redolent with the taint of virulence, of death. Choking, stifling: One wanted terribly to cough but held back, fearing that if one started one would fall into uncontrollable spasms never to stop; the murky turmoil swirling back across the ship and around her mainmast, the swirls faintly illuminated by the red and green running lights shining from the ends of the bridge wings. Nothing visible. No sea, no sky, no horizon. It was as if we were back in the mists of time. We moved in an etheric stillness, a silence broken only by the soft swish of the slowed ship slicing through the waters into the tumult of vapors, which with instant avarice closed around us and held the ship in its embrace of feral, choking blackness, seeming a solid obstacle in her path so that the ship appeared to have to shove her way through it. It was as if we were approaching Hades' shores, had entered and were navigating the Styx itself, now and then hearing the deep moan of the wind from unseen skies above us, whispering through the halyards like laments from the dead.

No, for the hands—the great majority of ship's company—kept below decks, risks of a physical character which presented themselves during this long part of our passage while present were less of a threat than those of another kind. That greater risk came from a supernumerary who had boarded the *Nathan James* and who went by many names, came in many spectres, some of which were derangement, mental disorder, loss of reason, insanity.

I myself brought them regular reports from topside; had to tell them over and over again, their hopeful faces looking up at me, that there was no change, no lifting of that vicious gloom. Bear in mind that these were men accustomed to working in the pure ocean air. Now cooped up, sealed below decks, not permitted to venture topside. One became aware of a strain which seemed to draw our minds ever tighter as the days—all nights really—went on, the tension becoming something very like a chronic physical pain. Feeling, each of us, the mass of that unseen awful substance sitting down on the ship. I sensed some sinister emotion creeping into them; a feeling that we might never come out of it; that they were doomed forever in perpetual night to this existence, ending in—what? Men, even men of proven fortitude, have limits. It seemed an immense mystery. Despite all of Selmon's explications, making it clear to any rational mind, we could never fully understand it. Oh, yes, intellect could understand it; it was clear enough. Heart could not. Daily, the strain became more visible in some . . . the mess deck gradually becoming a little hell of its own. We lost any clear idea of time, the night-day synonymy contributing to this. Sometimes the screeching of the wind heard through our steel walls sounding like a threnody, seeming the sounds and sighs of evil conjurations creeping in upon us like some malevolence aimed only and explicitly at us—who else could they be after? We seemed at times like men being driven slowly, inexorably, to sanity's edge by this hideous force fastened upon us, in its unspeakable cruelty sucking our strength, our spirit, our very life's blood—most of all, our hope.

Of course, I made frequent short talks to them; not prolonged things;

sailors take inspiration from deeds, from comportment, more than from words; the best thing I could do for them was to suppress my own inner terrors, to present insofar as within my powers a steady countenance. I spoke honestly; maybe they gave me credit for that. Each time I descended from the bridge and that black world above into as dark a world—that other tense and insulated mental and emotional twilight world where they sat huddled, waiting—each time I came off that ladder, their faces looking up at me, the first times with hope, this gradually flickering out to become a kind of deadness of eyes as they awaited the same unchanging word from me . . . I could only report to them invariably that there was as yet no breach in conditions above. At first "everybody shall be safe" little speeches; knowing sailors too well to do too much of this; after a while giving up such phrases entirely, since they could not come from my true heart, something they would instantly know. Never presenting to them a face of despair—that equally not mirroring my feelings, not yet—but simply making my reports, giving them the straight dope. Their only word from the outside, these accounts, in that cavern they were as blind men; the only thing keeping men in that prison, their knowledge that topside lay death; quick death. Selmon's sensor readings: figures of which I made certain we kept them meticulously informed; by now every hand aboard having intimate knowledge as to rad tolerances, a kind of specialty added on to whatever each sailor's principal specialty happened to be.

As blind men: It was as though they had fallen into some bottomless black pit, the mess deck itself, in which there was no ladder to climb out of. Literally there was and some—overtaken suddenly with who could say what?—tried. I had foreseen this possibility and delegated Preston and Brewster, our two strongest hands—not to station themselves there obviously as guards, itself threatening as emphasizing our prisonlike aspect, but, one or the other, watch and watch, to keep always near that ladder in the event anyone should attempt escape. On one occasion, McPherson, a shipfitter first, himself a man of exceptional strength, moved steadily toward the ladder, Preston stepping athwart it.

"Out of my way, Boats."

"You don't want to go up there, mate." The big boatswain's mate spoke quietly.

The shipfitter started to move around Preston. The boatswain's mate shifted his body in exact response to block him. Then it happened. McPherson stepped back and made a charge; a really thunderous charge, quite exactly like a bull at his tormentor in the ring, a bull which could

405

stand no more, straight for Preston. As he reached him, the boatswain's mate's enormous hands came over and seized him, lifted his body clean, completely over his head—then simply dropped him to the deck, or rather lowered him, almost softly—not slamming him down—just dropping him. The shipfitter looked up at him; seemingly come to his senses.

"Just an idea, Boats."

"Sure," Preston said, yanking him up. "Anybody can have an idea, Mac. I have them all the time myself. Go have a cup of coffee."

Exceptional coping, yes, valor of a kind, also shining through. Lieutenant Girard spent the greater part of her time in the mess deck, where most of ship's company kept gathered, generally just quietly talking with one sailor or another. She was tough and she had a strong will—I had long been aware of those qualities, also of her sensibilities. But now this other side of her, this astonishing mansuetude. It was as though a fierce inner-kept obsession had seized her, a determination that we would beat that terrible force that was trying to take us under; putting in long brutal hours, seeming determined to pull this tottering man, that, through by her own sheer force of will, to will them through. Once I came upon her there, her arms around a man crying into her shoulder, her free hand slowly stroking his head until he quietened. One of those who came nearest to full collapse was Girard's own assistant, probably the person on the ship she was closest to, Storekeeper Talley, who practically worshiped Girard. It was almost as if Girard brought her through, by her love and her strength, and a kind of ferocious insistence to Talley that by God she was going to make it because Girard said so. Her ingenuity, her resourcefulness, in coming up with whatever might remotely assist our struggle. Reading aloud: That was her suggestion. How little one would have imagined that something so simple would have helped so much! Girard bringing books from our library in an astonishing variety, great novelists, poets, simple adventure stories, to all of which the crew would equally listen as intently as children. Readers including herself, the Jesuit, Porterfield.

Speaking of the last-named, speaking of fortitude . . . of valor. Porterfield, as a helmsman. But also: of hymns and poker. Presently he and his guitar (sometimes accompanied by Gunner's Mate Delaney on his fiddle; the gunner, by the way, being one of the more fortunate hands aboard in having a daily job to do: a plan he had brought to me almost immediately the murk began to form over us—the salvation of our precious storehouse of plants, by removing them from their exposure to outside air to a place deep in the ship, keeping up their lifeblood of

photosynthesis through ultraviolet lamps borrowed from sick bay) . . .
Porterfield on his guitar, I was saying, leading the men and women in
every kind of song anyone had heard of that he could play—the helmsman having an astonishing repertory. A lot of hill songs, folk songs of all
kind, but more than anything else hymns. Partly because Porterfield
knew so many of them and consequently through long years on the ship
so did the men. "How Firm a Foundation," "In the Garden," "The
Old Rugged Cross," "Rock of Ages." They seemed to have less to do
directly with religion as such than with the brotherhood of shipmates,
the act of singing together seeming an expression of it, to me little short
of a gallant one. At times, stepping into the mess deck, one had the
impression there was a permanent choir practice in progress. Not a bad
choir, the men's and women's voices, the singing soft, curiously soothing, healing; though not infrequently it was something like the rousing
"Beulah Land" . . .

> *I'm living on the mountain,*
> *underneath a cloudless sky,*
> *I'm drinking at the fountain,*
> *that never shall run dry;*
> *O yes! I'm feasting on the manna*
> *from a bountiful supply,*
> *For I am dwelling in Beulah Land.*

"I'll be damned," the Jesuit said once to me in my cabin when we
were going over our morale readings. "I never knew singing those damn
hymns would do so much good."

The men seemed also to find the reading aloud of Scripture from
time to time an assuasive thing, and Porterfield had a good reading voice
with its soft accent of the hills. Old favorite passages they seemed to want
most of all; you might step into the compartment to see his tall, lean figure
standing there amid the mess tables, the men looking up at him, listening
attentively from the Old Testament . . .

> The Lord is my shepherd; I shall not want. He maketh me to lie
> down in green pastures: he leadeth me beside the still waters. He re-
> storeth my soul: he leadeth me in the paths of righteousness for his
> name's sake . . .

Or from the New . . .

Though I speak with the tongues of men and of angels, and have not charity, I am become as sounding brass, or a tinkling cymbal.

And though I have the gift of prophecy, and understand all mysteries, and all knowledge; and though I have all faith, so that I could remove mountains, and have not charity, I am nothing . . .

In addition, with my permission, Porterfield brought into the open the poker game which, supposedly clandestinely but actually also with my permission, had long been operating in the remote confines of the steering gear room, leading to other simultaneous poker games as under Porterfield's tutelage more and more of the crew became interested in this pastime. At these times, stepping into the mess deck, one had the impression one had wandered into a Las Vegas gambling hall. Mostly it was Porterfield himself. Just being around the tall, bone-lean helmsman seemed to act to quiet men; I don't know why: some assurance he radiated that against all evidence all things would come right; in that respect he was like Girard. Maybe, in his case, those peaceful Kentuckian tones: People somehow felt safe when he was near, a sense of warmth, of security. I wanted to relieve him of his watch duties so that he could devote all his time to these matters. He wouldn't have it.

"Captain, if I couldn't take my turn at the wheel, I wouldn't be good at anything else. I'd probably go around the bend myself."

Boxing bouts even: the Jesuit taking on his various old sparring partners, and any new ones who cared to try—seeming a curiously efficacious outlet for who knows what emotions.

Even so, these measures were but anodyne; an emollience standing thinly between us and the depths. I felt the men sinking deeper into themselves. Some appeared simply dumbfounded by it all. Sometimes terror in their eyes. Faces liquescent with pain, with incomprehension. Some lapsing into torpor, a numbness of spirit; the first symptoms of aphasia, catatonia, beginning to attack some. A sense of holding back an immense pressure. Occasionally a man stupefied with fear, sobbing convulsively, suddenly breaking out into indecipherable noises—once I had to strike one of them across the face, yes, an officer, young Ensign Woodward, and with the men watching—I had no choice—it would have been dangerous to let him go on in front of them. They had the decency to look away. Once had to shake a woman sailor—Thornberg—by the shoulders, to stop her crying, rising suddenly, approaching hysteria, her collapsing then into my arms, where I held her until the sobbing faded away. One would come upon a man just sitting in profound reflection, as if trying to figure it all out; another in a deep corner of the crew's compartment, huddled unto himself, in a kind of white solitude, head bowed, muttering something incomprehensible, low incantations; men knotted over a mess table in attitudes of prayer; men with expressions of vacancy in their faces, sepulchral stares, yet with wary eyes, as if something were about to spring on them; faces in a rictus of agony; plaintive sounds issuing, emanations of repressed anguish, of ruthless misery, unnamable fears; a man counting his rosary beads over and over; now and then a man quietly crying; one's unintentional glance would trip on a man caught in the motions of nervous trembling, on his face the shock of terror, a touch of lunacy—one would look quickly away—somehow one knew by some kind instinct whether to do that or to go sit by him; a face twitching with the strain, both trembling hands used to raise a cup of coffee to the lips—in a pitiable attempt at some countervailing to these onslaughts, I had put the coffee ration back to two cups daily. Sometimes—and I came to consider this favorable—a bluejacket would simply go into a trance, become oblivious to anything and everything; favorable because it served as a kind of anesthesia to bring him through. We did what we could as one shipmate or another became afflicted. Talking to him if that seemed to help or just sitting close by; myself dropping into a seat alongside one of these, murmuring into his ear something whether useless or helpful I could scarce tell. We helped, or tried to help, yes, I would say with great tenderness helped one another, whichever needed help most at any given moment it came about as we, gathered around him, her, brought that shipmate through, coaxed, willed him through. Men stayed in the mess deck, seeming to huddle close to one another, afraid to go to their bunks, afraid to be alone, finally falling asleep in their emotional exhaustion, heads on mess tables. Not constant these various manifestations. Sometimes whole days of peace, of no one breaking out; but then always their sure recrudescence. Always one felt also the great inner fight underway; men and women who had been through too much to yield now, their immense will to live; holding on to mere existence with clawing hands.

There was one thing, strange as could be, as to which I speculated as operating in our favor, an element of assistance which I could not be certain of even as to its existence much less its degree. The women. Here I am not speaking of any active thing, such as Girard's labors, but of something else. In some undefinable way I had the feeling that . . . I felt very uncertain as to this until the doc independently in one of our frequent sessions of considering every measure possible, himself basically as sardonic a man as I had known, said something very quietly to me. "My own opinion is that the mere presence of the women is keeping quite a number from going over the edge." A return to his sharper tone, an indication that he did not wish to pursue this hypothesis. "Don't ask me to explain it." If true, and I felt now more and more that such was the case, it was—and remains to me—a mystery.

Still, of all that happened to us since the launching in the Barents, it was the one time I felt we stood on the very brim of the abyss. That deadly poison just outside the bulkheads seeming to enclose us, hug us ever more tightly to itself in a choking embrace, pressing down on us, as if in its fury of frustration that it could not get at our bodies, it would yet get at our minds. Fears real, fears imaginary: It became almost impossible to distinguish the one from the other, which was which—coming to feel dangerously at times that perhaps any distinction didn't matter. As our ordeal continued, the unknowingness was what got at us; lacking any ability to figure it out, to put together the seemingly endless parts of this demoniac thing, so that we could even combat it, deal with it; lacking any true knowledge as to the fullness of its capabilities. Men deducing that a force that could so facilely alter the very fundamentals of temperature as a mere playful side effect would in time just as carelessly do whatever it needed to do to finish us off by some means it had not yet revealed; in the meantime toying with us as a sadist toys with the sure victim, wanting to prolong its pleasure, our terror. Yes, it was just that, the fact that, monstrous and intolerable, it seemed an uncomfortable apparition: That was the worst part of it. Our ship loaded with an immensity of destructive power, with every conceivable weapon to obliterate any enemy . . . all of this worthless against present foe, reliance on these inconceivably puissant arms becoming as some kind of savage joke played on us. One felt a towering fury at how this could be; how it could have come to happen; worst of all, nothing to vent the fury on. Some came to look upon it as some avenging terror—the matter of guilt, the Jesuit had told me, arising seriously for the first time in these, the quaint and bone-chilling idea that we, the ship's company, the very ship herself were all reeking with blood and were at last being brought to justice for our contribution to the devastation of mankind. One sensed it more so each day, an unpredictable and terrifying combination of inner rage and total helplessness: The men trembled on the brink.

I knew well that it was only that shipmate brotherhood keeping us from foundering, but even it at times wavered before this onslaught. At times I feared we were but a step away from . . . not mutiny, but something quite different, something worse . . . anarchic extremities; what forms they would take unimaginable but certain to be terrible, merciless, perhaps dissolving, disintegrating us all. Once, as I was passing through the mess deck, a man stood up and blocked my way—Cantwell, a boatswain's mate and our sailmaker, brawny, muscled, normally as mild as a man could rightly be, almost excessively placid—began what appeared to be a kind of cursing out of me built around the general theme of my having gotten us into this; a breathless hush suddenly hovering in the compartment as the men looked on. I listened in silence to this tirade, looked at him, dead in the eyes, a kind of wildness there, could feel the hair-trigger atmosphere all around me. Waited until he at last wound down. "Are you finished? You're right about that, Cantwell," I said. "Well, then. I'll just have to try to get us out of it, won't I? You men. Carry on." Then another, worse time, when I stood on the ladder bringing them yet another of those by now uncounted reports of conditions topside—no change, no break whatsoever in the pall, I had once more to tell them—out of one of those ravaged faces upturned to me came a sullen voice. "Why didn't you let us go with Mr. Chatham?" followed by a low rumble that sounded like a supporting chorus. I waited, standing what ground I had, the steps of a ladder, a feeling of a certain menacing surge of men toward myself, bringing everything in me to bear not to fling such words back in their faces, or at least not to speak in anger, still hearing a certain edge in my voice. "Let you?" I said. "Who among you was kept from doing so?" Another voice: "Why didn't you take us back? We couldn't be any worse off than we are." "Couldn't you?" my voice harder. "You'd be dead by now. Would you prefer that?" I stepped on down the ladder. The men stood aside and let me through. The moment passing like that, no assurance it would the next time.

The doc, himself looking benumbed with exhaustion from being at almost continuous watch, brought me frequent reports. Once: "I've gone over every member of the crew, Skipper. Let me get across a few physical facts. Pulse rates as high as a hundred seventy-three per minute, as low as twenty-nine—in some, at times almost imperceptible. The action of the heart: That concerns me most of all. In many, it seems to have lost its regulating force. One moment, quick, the next, slow: in the same man. No medical knowledge I possess explains it. We're in new territory, Skipper. Frankly, I'm scared as hell."

"You've got a great deal of company, Doc."

"Nobody knows. Cooped up like that. That frigging stuff sitting down on top of us. Oh, I suppose one could supply all the usual textbook words. Paranoia. Hallucinations. Delusions. Everybody seeing things. I've seen a few myself. Hysteria now and then. They don't cover it. I don't know a word that does. All I can say is . . . they're perfectly capable of losing control of themselves at any moment . . . they're hanging on by their teeth, Skipper."

The fact of the matter is, we all became a little deranged, some more than a little. We never realized it at the time, of course, how close to the crossover we came. One never does at the time. Our minds tottered, as of a ship listing sixty or seventy degrees, on each plunge into tumultuous seas, pushing against the limits of her inclinometer and her ability to right herself before she continued her peril-filled rolls into the deep, capsized; our minds did exactly that. To what degree, in the case of the bridge watches, these attritions were caused by the inroads radiation had made into us, to what degree because of the "living conditions" below decks I cannot say. No one could. But as day followed day, with most of the crew sealed below, as we seemed to go further into these mental rolls, pushing ever further against our emotional inclinometer, I at times had the feeling that the next roll would tumble us on over beyond any possibility of righting ourselves. The doc was right. One and all, they were entirely capable of losing control of themselves before even they knew it. To their immense credit, I could sense, as I have said, the great effort that even the most affected ones were making to control themselves—not to go berserk, not to break out into sudden, unstoppable screaming. If one did it, I felt others might, as in a contagion. That suddenly, in that mess deck, some maelstrom, some loosening horror—the nature and dimensions of which one could scarcely conceive—men suddenly clawing at one another, unspeakable acts—could, set off by the slightest spark, break out beyond any man's control. Madness beckoned.

Even I. Yes, even my own mind wavered, came closer than I prefer to think. An instance: On the whole the women were bearing up better than the men. I could not understand it. The *James* and her class were the first vessels laid down and constructed from the beginning by the Navy with the direct intent of carrying "mixed crews." Present as a plank-owner during her precommissioning days in the Pascagoula shipyard, watching her take shape, I was fascinated, at times sardonically amused, by the manner in which the builders so astutely engineered this capability, fashioning a bulkhead extending from the second deck to the weather deck between the women's quarters and those of the men so that the former could not be entered save from above or through a secured escape scuttle. The sole normal ingress to the women's quarters being by a ladder situated just below the pilot house and hence far from hidden.

This security seeming to me almost excessive, so I thought watching it being built in. Even had a male sailor had the notion of making the attempt—this itself so ludicrous I could not imagine it—and arrived successfully below in those female purlieus, I used to think humorously . . . well, given the complement of thirty-two sailors, themselves exceptional representatives of their sex, trained in addition in all sorts of arts, not the least being self-defense—I would not choose to be that man. "Lucky to get out of there at all in possession of his balls," I remember the foreman during the ship's construction remarking to me.

As I was saying: On the whole the women to every outward appearance were calmer during our ordeal, not entirely free of the extremes of emotional reaction which now and then gripped some of the men, but, it appeared to me, more able to contain it, one or two exceptions. Observing this, I went so far, familiar with the widely held psychiatric idea that sexual accommodation often takes care of the problem of emotional disorder, its absence frequently causing it, as to have the horrible thought of suspecting them of solving the problem in their own way, in their sealed quarters which even I could not enter at will. I mention this only to illustrate how far my own mind at times deviated from any true course, if only briefly, quickly telling myself, as in this instance, that this was nonsense of the worst sort and of which I should be ashamed—and was—even to let the notion reach my mind; dangerous nonsense at that. Still, going so far in my fancy as actually to consider asking Girard about it. I must have been for that second almost literally out of my mind. As I say, all of us, in various ways, went a little mad. This was mine. Anyhow, the shock of recognition that I had even had such a thought brought me to my senses, informed me that the problem here was not whatever the women might be doing but my own chimeras. Thereafter, alert for any more of these that might come at me, ready, lacking clear evidence, to strike them down; probably nothing but my own sense of a ship's captain's mortal allegiance in such circumstances seeing myself through.

Parenthetically, the following: It was sometime during this passage through the dark and the cold that what would have seemed crushing, removing some last fine thread of hope, was made known to us—made known to me alone, I should say, and to Girard and Thurlow, no one else in ship's company knowing of the arrangement with the submarine captain, a matter for which I now felt inexpressibly grateful. We had managed a couple of exchanges, ourselves telling him we were proceeding through heavy contamination, his reply far more cheerful—his submergence protecting him, how I now envied him and his ship that capability—informing us that, reconnoitering the Russian coastline, following the Northern Sea Route from Murmansk through the Kara and Laptev seas, he was negotiating the East Siberian Sea, with no difficulty heading toward destination; my heart had lifted. Then sometime back—losing all identification of time, I cannot pin down the precise date—we had lost contact with *Pushkin*. Repeated efforts to raise her, both at the agreed times of her surfacing for that express purpose, and at other times as well: Nothing came back from her. She had simply vanished. At first attempting with myself the spurious consolation that it was all a transmission difficulty having to do with the elements we were passing through, then reminding myself mercilessly that this, of course, had nothing to do with it, I faced up to the probability that she had been lost at sea—on such a perilous voyage, in such times as these, the number of ways that could happen was without limitation—and that therefore what little nuclear fuel we possessed, with its slim hope of holding out until we found something habitable, was all we would ever have; we would make it on that or not make it at all. Crushing, I said, the realization that that hope, of the Russian's bringing us a fresh supply, had been so abruptly obliterated. Remembering a final time her last message, that she would reach Karsavina the following day, not naming that place, but the excitement, exuberance, the triumph, coming through: "Great hopes for Turgenev." Then, as a conscious act, I brutally expunged *Pushkin,* her captain and her crew and her mission, from my mind as if they had never been. I turned inward, back to my own ship, my own ship's company.

Back to my own: Nothing is more remarkable than man's capacity for survival. Yet I thought the tension in the mess deck, the prison sentence stretching out, no end in sight, was approaching some breaking point, some explosion; the very real question of how much longer the men could take it, building as seas build under high winds and low pressure. Then these problems became as nothing, as a common cold, before evolvements infinitely more perilous to us, to the ship.

We never did anything like taking a muster. Frankly, the idea never occurred to me. If now and then the thought touched my mind that I had not seen a particular man for a couple days or so, the obvious answer was that he had gone off to be by himself, perhaps to cloak his manifestations from his shipmates, perhaps feeling that he could best work through them alone. There are innumerable places on a ship where a man might with ease accomplish this concealment. Storage lockers, sail lockers, steering-gear room, a couple score other sites. I scarcely knew it at the time in the turmoil of all that was going on, vaguely aware from time to time that this face was missing, that one, not certain but what its owner had gone to hide out in his misery in some remote part of the ship. Then one day the idea began very slowly to penetrate my consciousness—perhaps itself deadened somewhat by exhaustion—that there appeared to be what I might term an accumulation of absences; a certain number of men not having been seen by me for a number of days. Horror has its own way of announcing itself; not infrequently in a sudden illumination, an empiercement of the mental process. I knew in one instantaneous moment. Men were slipping overboard. A ship has many exits into the seas through which she moves, a man can go over the side quite easily, not even be missed for a while, particularly in the circumstances then obtaining. I immediately took a muster and discovered we had lost fifteen hands. Worst of all, three of them were women. I got the doc, the Jesuit, Girard in my cabin, door closed. Feeling myself going swiftly back and forth over some terrible dissonance of emotions that ranged from rage to desolation, stopping it by every exercise of will I had remaining from then slipping over the edge into that panic which, one knew as one knew nothing else, would take us all with it; perhaps these same elements at work in the others, I could not tell, their own forces of inner suppression surely equally applied. The conversation was hesitant in the extreme. It was as though we were afraid of words, of trying to spell it out, probe it, fathom it, as if dealing with some dark mystery which if investigated too far would explode in our faces. The most frightening intimation we had as to at least part of what was in process was contained in a note left where the Jesuit would find it by Bellows, a missile technician, one of those who had gone over; the Jesuit going on to suggest why the contents of the note indicated it was not an isolated case, that at least some of the crew were deliberately getting through some hatch or another to come to the weather decks, to stand by intention in that lethal atmosphere, deliberately contaminating themselves—some, it was possible, doing this more than once, then finally simply going over into the waiting sea. We all sat for a bit in a kind of horrified stupefaction at the very hideousness of it. The Jesuit continued.

"I don't think I betray vows, not naming names, to say—yes, in confession"—he had never before made reference to that personal resource—"some of them—it's very difficult to put it, they didn't put it any too explicitly themselves, due to, well . . . guilt. Catching up with them. That burden having become too great for them. Doing a lot of reading of the Bible, most of them. Some . . . in some of them . . . a fair probability I'd say . . . an act of penance . . . atonement . . . seeking thereby some kind of redemption . . . Of course, I had no idea they would carry it that far . . . until Bellows' note . . . its allusion to that reason . . . after the fact . . ."

"Atonement!" I exploded the word; the concept itself seeming to unleash a kind of fury in me; perhaps near some sort of edge myself. "We've got enough to deal with without having to deal with *atonement.* For Christ's sake, Father."

A soft smile. "Captain, you have just pronounced almost the very words I responded with when they were made by hands. Except the last ones," he said gently.

"Perhaps they're reading the Bible too much," I said.

"Shall I forbid them to do so, Captain?"

"All right, Doc."

He had sat there like an undernourished Buddha. He hated religion and everything about it; quietly thought it was the greatest fraud ever perpetrated upon man; a close second, and what he considered its first cousin, a subdivision of his own profession, the whole field of psychiatry-psychoanalysis-psychology. He and the Jesuit were quite good friends.

"Well, I'm a doctor," he said. "Or try to be. I can't speak to the mumbo jumbo. I'd say they just arrived at the limits of their endurance. We all have one."

"The hell we do, Doc."

I waited, looking coldly around that circle. The doc shrugged. He was not being insubordinate. He simply knew that he, like the Jesuit, had a fairly long leash, by his captain's preference; a leash, however, not without limitations.

"Fact is, I don't think there's any way of knowing." He spoke dryly. "I take it everyone here is aware that, medically speaking, we're sailing in uncharted waters. What we do know compared with what we don't is like a thimble of sand to the beach. What it'll do to people."

"Can you speak some English, Doc?" I said.

"I'll try, Skipper." He took a breath. "Maybe something went wrong with their—well, mechanism. Something that may be happening just to them. Most things that happen to human beings happen to them vary-ingly—different tolerances, all of that. The other possibility exists, of course: Something that may be happening to all of us. And if it does, that it might take entirely different forms than—jumping ship."

We all simply stared at him. No one spoke. Wondering, myself, surely the others as well, who could deal with such forces? I thought I had one small idea at least, pitiful as it might seem against them. I turned to the Jesuit, in my voice something like supplication.

"Father, I'm going to ask you to break a sacred vow. Could you give

416

us the names of those who have told you, or in future tell you, anything to suggest they are thinking of going over the side—whether for reasons of 'guilt' or any other reason? So we can at least keep an eye on them?"

He found at once the fallacy in the proposal.

"Aside from breaking my sacred vows, as you say, I don't know how long it would work. These are canny men. Sooner or later they'd find out what I'm doing and the confession box would dry up."

I felt a captain's impatience with this, with any verbiage that would get in the way of action, of doing something; tried to suppress it; hearing my voice still coming with a kind of feverish urgency.

"During that 'later,'" I said, "maybe we'll have talked some out of going over. Don't you think the Lord will permit an exception to your regulations under the circumstances?" I could not keep it back. "Or do you think He has lost all interest in saving lives?"

Something snapped in me. Maybe Girard's presence the strong reminder; I had a sense of her simply staring at me, in a combination—could I have imagined this?—of personal concern for myself and a hard and unyielding admiration of what I was about. I turned savagely on the Jesuit as if forcing some ruthless catechism upon him.

"You call yourself a priest. Do you realize that of those fifteen, three of them were women? And do you realize how few women we're getting down to? And do you realize what that means?"

A shock seemed to fill the cabin. Then, voice unraised, a certain tone:

"You're right, of course. Under the circumstances there isn't time to ask Him about those exceptions to my vows. I'll do it on my own. Up the line if He asks, I'll tell Him I couldn't get through to Him, there was a busy signal. Probably the case anyhow these days."

He was a Jesuit.

I was about to dismiss them.

"Captain?"

"Yes, Miss Girard."

She had a baffled look; spoke slowly, with great deliberation.

"Those three women. Salinas, Kramer, Stoughton, I don't understand it. Of course, they were affected like all of us . . . but that they would do that: I still can't believe it. That's all I wanted to say."

I looked at her for a moment, started to pursue it, ask a question, decided not.

"That's it for now. Miss Girard, gentlemen."

Almost simultaneously, something totally unexpected, trusting as we did in the ship's inbuilt protective devices.

We had passed into the Flores Sea. One day I stepped once again

from the pilot house out into that terrible murk, the atmosphere like a
wall, opaque, impenetrable; the object of these occasional exercises to
determine if I could see any suggestion of its lifting. How I longed to see
a single star! Purpose also being to isolate myself with my thoughts, to try
desperately to come up with some way through, anything. The firmament
stood merciless, heartless, invisible: nothing, only the onslaught of those
same vile vapors, that throbbing shroud. Suddenly out of it a snow began
to fall. The thermometer—I had just checked it by flashlight—stood at
twelve degrees above zero Fahrenheit; we were off a place called Diji,
eight degrees below the equator. Sensing something strange, I held my
hand out, held it out for a minute or so until enough of the snow had
gathered in it; I turned my flashlight on that flattened palm. The snow
was black. I felt like weeping. Instead I stood awhile under it in the
absolute darkness, the snow thickening, hearing the faint wail of the wind
like a dirge. With a vicious movement I wiped the horrible stuff away on
my Arctics. I stepped back inside the pilot house, caught for a moment
in a spasmatic coughing, from that squalid substance and from some
unspeakable rage. I found Selmon staring straight at me; something almost hostile in his look.

"You shouldn't stay out that long," he said, quite sharply considering
that he was speaking to his captain.

There was something so unnatural in the rebuke that, coming closer
and seeing his hollowed face in the light of the repeater, pale as the
complexion of a ghost, his eyes seeming to glisten wildly, I knew with a
shock that alarm had at last reached that phlegmatic personality; a kind
of desperation I had never seen there seeming to ooze out of him; something of a dark terror on it; knowing the man, registering an instant fear
in myself.

"What is it?" I said.

"Captain, the bridge watch, all of them . . ." His voice, always steady,
seemed to tremble a little in its hoarseness, as if some ravaging chill
had seized him, or the substance itself had done so, and as if this itself
was evidence for the dread thing he was saying. "Every hand standing
watch here . . ." I became aware in a kind of horror that the present
watchstanders were watching us intently, listening, they themselves, out-
landish in their Arctics and gas masks, seeming bedazed with unspeakable
fatigue, or with something else too terrible to think of . . . "These
readings . . ." He looked down at his repeater, its dim glow reaching up
just enough to reveal his specterlike face. "They are approaching unacceptable levels. Sir."

■ ■ ■

They sat assembled in my cabin. Selmon, the doc, Thurlow, Melville, Girard.

"Captain, we have to get out of this," the doc said. "Those men going overboard . . ."

"We can forget them," Selmon said. He spoke brutally, in his voice a direct, relentless urgency I had never heard from him. "Let's talk about those still aboard. The men are accumulating too much of it."

He was speaking of the bridge watch. But that had been rotated among men able to stand any of its positions.

"We're talking about forty-five men," Thurlow said. "And we're talking about the only men who know how to navigate and conn this ship. Watch officers, quartermasters, helmsmen, lee helmsmen. One-fourth of ship's company."

"How much farther on present course, Mr. Melville?" I had alerted him to make calculations. He had his clipboard; he looked at it; spoke with his usual precision, his impervious courtliness.

"Three thousand one hundred miles, sir."

"Mr. Selmon?"

"The readings have been going up. Slowly, but steadily. We expected that. But the rate of the upcurve has increased—with it, the readings on all bridge watchstanders."

"Doc?"

"We've had some mild cases of illness, as you know, sir. All temporary. Whether they were due in fact to minor, passing radiation sickness or to something else, there's no way of telling. Everyone of them being a bridge watchstander suggests something. Effects becoming somewhat more severe. I wouldn't like to see any worse cases of it."

Selmon: "Three thousand more miles of it: On present course we'll be passing near large land masses, all we've met the most contaminated spaces of all. If that rate continues . . . We don't know enough about it. What men can absorb. Not that finely defined. But we know this: we'll soon be into levels . . . lives will be at risk . . . which ones we can't tell. Different tolerances as we also know. There's no way of telling—take Porterfield's tolerance—as opposed to Meyer's . . ." she had been standing lee-helm watches. "And I do know this. We're approaching margins we haven't seen before. Three thousand more miles through this . . ." he said again. Stopped, spoke in his old quiet formality. "High risk, sir. At least for all watchstanders; for forty-five hands." His voice dropped to an utter evenness, calm, this itself sending a chill through the cabin: "Everybody else below decks should make it."

The coldness of that, from the least of alarmists: He did not mention

419

that the forty-five included himself; included among others present Thurlow; myself. Doc and Melville, Girard, kept below, not at risk.

"The other course, Mr. Melville?"

"I've done the rough calculations, sir. It'll take a month, thereabouts, off our fuel supply."

"And off our food supplies as well," Girard said.

The course through the Timor and Arafura seas and then along the northern coast of Australia had been originally chosen, as mentioned, as being the shortest one into the Pacific, along with the attraction of taking us through normally inhabited areas where we might find uncontaminated lands and human beings who would take us in. The Australians, particularly, I had kept thinking of. Any hope as to the latter objective having diminished considerably in the light of recent explorations only seemed to increase the prudence of the first and holding to it, its intent being to use the minimum of fuel in order to have as much as possible remaining to search our most promising prospects for habitability. Even going the short route, Melville had calculated that, arriving at our destination, we would have but two months remaining for that purpose. This we had viewed as an irreducible minimum. Now the other course, the one to take us out of the radioactivity threat, would halve that to one; diminish our search period desperately; to the peril point. Forty-five men. It was a terrible choice to have to make. To lose the fuel that might enable us to find a home; to arrive at that home with possibly so many of the crew lost, gone. A fourth of ship's company. And the very men, as Thurlow had pointed out, who navigated the ship. But not just that. Myself. Selmon. Thurlow, who would normally succeed me. Who would succeed Thurlow? Who could replace Selmon? For that matter, myself. So great had my vanity become, I was not confident that any other could bring them through. I found myself reaching into the darkest depths.

"Let's do it," I said. "Let's get out of here. We'll have to take our chances with the fuel."

At daybreak—one still in the gloom—Thurlow, Selmon, Melville and I stood by the chart table and plotted the new course. Taking the first breach in the Lesser Sunda Islands, our first chance to remove ourselves from these land-choked waters, we executed it by passing through the Selat Alor into the Indian Ocean. I opened us up, the overcast pursuing us for a period of slightly over twenty-four fours. Selmon took his new readings; very low, they allowed the men who had been imprisoned below decks to be released, brought topside, as men released from a dungeon.

Then one morning we came on deck, all of ship's company—only the engineroom watch below—and stood watching the huge vermilion ball rise majestically from waters of brilliant blue; as of a phenomenon we had never seen before; stood gazing in wonder, in a great hush, as it began its ancient transit across clear and windless skies of a softer azure; forgotten men brought here by an act of deliverance; sailors brought back to their own sure home, into the great security of the sea, the waters of salvation.

.4.

EXILE

Moving out into the Indian Ocean across the Wharton Basin, as far as could be from any land, we stood S. by S.W., proceeding across Broken Ridge straight down the hundredth longitude. Sailors accustomed at times to be as indifferent to the sea as a landsman might be of his backyard, the great ocean seemed now to us to be invested with magic properties. We were like men seeing for the first time the great beauty of the planet, what a lovely place earth was. Emerging from the long darkness and cold, released most of all out of that foul and pestilential air we had breathed so long into the full and magnanimous sunshine, the pure ocean air, we were men reprieved. We had come home, our natural home; and turned to the restorative sea for healing. How fortunate were we to be sailors! Standing, as sailors seldom do, simply gazing across the great blue blaze of it, the immense cleanness of the open sea we had almost forgotten, stretching in an undefiled plain to all horizons: What pure joy for a seaman to see a horizon! Looking up into that other azure, at that softly delicate sky of low latitudes. Everywhere on the weather decks, men and women who had seen neither sun nor stars for weeks basked with voluptuous torpor in the first, transcendent days, under the blessed rays corpse-colored bodies, shed of their Barents Arctics, beginning to take on tans, remaining thin, on short rations, nonetheless looking infinitely better to one another—we could hardly have looked worse; at night, bewitched by the second, reluctant to go below where prison had been, many brought mattresses topside to sleep under the great constellations, the stars, so long gone into hiding, now in their splendor seeming to hang low in the sky, seeming purposively, with intent to render succor, to ring the ship in radiant comfort, a tiara of them perched atop the ship's mainmast. In the wonder of the cloudless skies, the caressing westerlies we soon encountered, familiar Venus sitting on the dark edge of the horizon, visible now to them not only many additional stars known to sailors, but others most of the crew had never set eyes on, stars, constellations, which held court only in southern climes: the great Southern Cross, Phoenix, Carina, Musca, bright Canopus.

As sailors, we gloried in this world of a new sea, in differences unknown to those who had never taken ship below the planet's great dividing line, the equatorial barrier. Not just unviewed constellations but everything about it seemed changed: stars coursing around the Pole clockwise, the opposite to their northern-latitudes habits; the very winds blowing counterclockwise instead of clockwise as on north parallels. Thurlow and others knowing, of course, that the phenomena stayed the same, merely the observer's point of view changing; an example, the moon looking upside down, the moon's north pole being always north, but seen from the Northern Hemisphere it being at the moon's top while from the Southern Hemisphere being at the bottom. The navigator took delight in explaining these simple matters to those of ship's company unfamiliar with them. Most of all it was the sheer exhilaration, the ineffable bliss, of breathing uncontaminated air, and the purest air earth holds—that of the open sea. One found oneself consciously taking deep breaths of it. To save every possible drop of fuel, I cut our forward speed to eight knots, making us seem barely to move through the stilled seas parting ever so gently for the ship.

Sometimes, proceeding through that sweet ocean vastness, standing on the bridge wing and looking aft down the length of the ship at men on watch going about their work, men off watch lying somnolently in the sun, my thoughts stood relaxed, a contentment, something like exultation in me observing them. I had always, perhaps from living among sailors nearly all my life, had a higher opinion than some of the capacity of men as to courage, as to kindness, as to selflessness so profound as to be scarcely explicable. Looking down at them now, these opinions could not have been but greatly fortified. How well they had held up! In a sense they had never been more tested, either of these two groups, and which had been more so it would have been difficult for me to say. The pilot house watch, standing brutal watch shifts, navigating the ship through that awful murk, knowing, each man, each woman, that as they did so they were steadily absorbing into their bodies amounts of radiation, never knowing when its accumulation might reach a point to bring on a terrible sickness, or worse; never flinching from their duties, not one hand backing away from it, begging off, refusing duty. Or that greater portion of ship's company which, while protected from these onslaughts, had had to live for those weeks in that prison below decks, hardly knowing where their ship was taking them, no assurance that they would ever come out of it. Both seemed to me to belong in those higher realms of fortitude, one might say valor.

Never truly removing itself from that corner of my mind it had permanently reserved, ceaselessly emitted the off-and-on signal of a buoy off soundings warning ships of some treacherous unseen hazard, telling me that even once into freer waters we had precious little fuel left for any search for habitable space before we should come forever dead in the sea. Our course had been arrived at after the most meticulous consultations with Thurlow and Melville, the indispensable Selmon, of course, always participating in these discussions, held, as considerations dictated, sometimes in my cabin, sometimes poring over charts in the chart room. We had determined to proceed at the strictest speed I have described straight down the longitude until we reached the fortieth parallel, and there to turn due east, following then a course which would take us well off Australia to our port, operating on the assumption that it had suffered the same fate as all land masses we had encountered. Bearing always in mind that should events prove us happily wrong in this assessment we would, of course, turn back north to explore the southern littorals of the great nation-continent. Barring that unexpected development we would continue to stay well out, soon turn on a N. by N.E. course, pass through the Tasman Sea over Lord Howe Rise and make a final starboard turn which would lead us the last hundred miles into the vast reaches of the southern Pacific where all our hopes lay. Melville, continuing constantly to calculate and recalculate, was able one day to proffer me something precise that could not have been more welcome.

"Captain, I have a piece of good news from the engineering department," he said.

"I don't believe it."

He grinned sheepishly. "This eight-knot speed of ours— well, sir, I figure if we keep to it, by the time we depart Tasmanian waters we will have added two weeks to our fuel reserve as previously calculated under twelve knots."

We were gathered around the chart table during the midwatch—the four mentioned officers—in the darkness of the chart room, the only light that shining down on the spread-out chart of the region, our heads in darkness. I looked where Melville was.

"Well," I said. "Well, now."

"Yes, sir," Melville said. I could not see his soft smile; I knew it was there.

"So we have six weeks to make our search." I felt the enormous lift in all of us. Knowing at the same time that we were taking too much hope from this, still feeling that any hopes at all were best seized on. "I don't know why that should seem so much better than four weeks. But it does."

"It does that, sir," Thurlow, his dividers poised in his hands, said.

"We shall certainly keep strictly at eight knots," I said.

"Every mile at that speed helps." the engineer said.

"That it does. And we'll keep her there. So long as these seas hold." Only they made it possible; rougher waters, we would have to increase speed to keep steerageway. "See to it, Mr. Thurlow."

"Aye, sir," he said. "Willingly, Captain."

Perhaps overanxious, all of us, to grab onto the least improvement in our prospects. Nevertheless, refusing even to consider the danger that we were becoming hope's fools, that night I turned into my bunk feeling more borne up in spirit than in any time I could recall. I even resumed the reading, that precious nightly thirty-minute pleasure reading, stretching back for years, almost to the beginning of my life on ships, given up of late from the sheer exhaustion that had always reached me by that time when we were making our passage through the dark and the cold. The book was *My Ántonia.* I read with satisfaction, forgetting, as in former times, all problems, all vicissitudes past and future. At the end of the half hour, marking my place, laying the book aside, shutting off the overhead light. I lay awake for a bit, feeling a comfort and a satisfaction in the awareness of the barely moving ship, its diminished sound reaching up to me through her engine room, the fuel that speed was saving us, increasing our Pacific chances; fell asleep. I was next aware of a strong hand shaking me. Unmistakably I knew it as Preston's. I don't think he was even aware, or ever would be, of the unnecessarily excessive force he applied to the objective of awakening one as boatswain of the watch; always immediately apologetic, as now, when one indicated the fact, my "It's all right, Preston. I'm awake." The instant stopping, withdrawal of the hand, the "Sorry, Captain."

"What is it, Boats?"

"It's Bixby, sir. Signalman third."

"I know Bixby's rating," I said irritably. "What about her?"

"Mr. Thurlow"—he would be the OOD—"says you better come, Captain."

Fear—alarm—arriving out of the exceptional indistinctness of this message, I swung my legs out of my bunk and engaged the reflexive quick routine of an act performed ten thousand times, on a score of seas, of getting on trousers, shoes, shirt, when some officer of the deck had felt it prudent, for any one of countless reasons, to awaken his captain. I looked at my watch. It read 0245.

I could just make out first light beginning to appear through the twin ports of my cabin. The doc was there. Girard. Thurlow. They had all been up the night.

"How's she making out, Doc?" I said. She was in sick bay.

"She's going to be okay, Captain. Shock mostly." His eyes were strangely quiet, meditative. "Minor bruises. Put up quite a fight, I'd say."

I turned to Thurlow. I had picked him to do the questioning of the crew. "Any word?"

"Negative, sir," Thurlow said. "Half the men, so far. Nothing. We'll have been through the other half by late morning."

"Keep at it," I said. "Whatever it takes . . ." I paused, looked around that circle of officers . . . "We'll find out who did it."

"That we will, sir," Thurlow said grimly. He more than anyone seemed to reflect what was in myself. I had wanted him particularly for the questioning; he would be good at it, ruthless.

They left and I sat awhile in my cabin, doing nothing. Just sitting. I thought about Bixby; an unaffectedness perhaps given her by that Iowa farm where she had grown up. I remembered talking with her that night by the lifeline. The sailor's uniform seemed but to enhance the unsullied aura of her young being, her body girlish and slim; a special gentleness seeming to come through, later feeling this more seeing her care of the two goats we had picked up, something both comical and strict in it; remembered her hands gently evaluating the lion cubs. Yet a good toughness about her I had felt. During all we had been through she had borne up as well as any, not a whimper, at least none I had seen or heard of;

any kept inside. We had talked about how she became a sailor. The Navy was lucky; but nineteen, very young, very intelligent to have made signalman third so early. I remembered how with mock humor she had mentioned as of a great distinction her hometown of Odebolt, Iowa, as being "the popcorn capital of the world." I had a choice of tears or cold rage; found in myself only the latter.

And so I sat, a long time, listening to the buzz of the bell clock attached to the bulkhead above my desk, listening to time but not reading it; glancing at the gyro-repeater, also placed there but not seeing where it was taking us. I felt that strange stillness of mind such as sometimes, perhaps peculiarly then, comes to one in the face of the unspeakable, the unacceptable. Accompanied now by something cold and savage and of boundless sorrow. How terrible had been the chill in me, hearing of it! It was unlike anything else. Unlike the human beings on the beaches of Amalfi; unlike the animals in the Kenya bush; unlike those hands going overboard in the dark and the cold. One person. It made no sense. But there it was. Those had been purgatories not brought on by ourselves, at least not directly. But there was something beyond that. I suppose deep in me I knew why. Not wanting, not willing, to get into that, even in my innermost soul. Nonetheless knowing there that, the horror of the act sufficient in itself, shipmate to shipmate, that it should be a woman, one of but twenty-seven . . . this vastly deepening it. There came over me a terrible resolve. There was once a legend among men who followed the sea that every ship had a Jonah, or a potential Jonah, the metaphor broadly defined as anyone whose presence aboard might bring extreme harm to a ship, and I had known many an old seaman who believed that. I was not one of them. And yet my resolve seemed as theirs. We had a monster aboard this ship, loose among us. Nothing that had happened aboard the ship since I first took command of her—excepting only Chatham's leading 109 hands off the ship—had anything like this effect on me, including the myriad travails we had been through. They, after all, were tests for sailors. This was the opposite of that. This hideous act: It seemed to profane those tests, to mock them; to profane fortitude, to mock valor, the courage of ship's company in surviving them. To mock, with brutal scorn, something even greater: the sailor's code, stretching back over ancient seas, held inviolate, sacred, in ten thousands of ships; among countless seamen; saying: One protected shipmates as brothers, now sisters too; one did not harm them. To do so was the ultimate defilement of everything a sailor was; that the sea meant.

We waited for Bixby. She herself had been as if the act had deprived her of speech. Two days passed. We made our turn at the fortieth parallel, proceeding due east at our languorous eight knots on the course which would take us off Australia. I think I had made up my mind from the first instant of being told. I knew what I would do. I was waiting for Bixby. But nothing came from her. For the first time a terrible thought struck at me: Perhaps she did not know. We might never know who it was; he might remain among decent men; continue, the act not repeated, to the end to be an accepted part of ship's company. The thought was unendurable; filled me with revulsion. Never knowing which out of all the faces one saw daily it was, all suspect. I rejected the idea, brutally. But its real possibility made the waiting the more horrible. No one of the four talking to her—the doc, Girard, the Jesuit, myself—at any point thus far had tried to pry the information out of her. All attended only to her care. She had suffered a mild concussion, perhaps a contributory factor to her silence. But one felt it was something beyond that. One day, alone with the doc, I asked viciously, "Was she a virgin?"

He seemed almost shocked at the question; perhaps only shocked at the savage tone in which I had asked it, seeing what was happening in me.

"Oh, yes," he said quietly. "She was that, Captain."

Thurlow stayed at it, questioning all hands, requestioning. I could sense in him the absolute outrage, Navy-proud, that such a man calling himself a Navy sailor should be on a ship he was on. I came to admire him for his tenacity. "Whatever it takes," I repeated to him. "Understood, sir," he said with a cruel, wolfish look I had never seen in him. "Fully understood." He would not let go; keeping to it as the ship parted the waters at that ridiculously slow speed, something funereal seeming now to hang over the ship, poisoning the joy that had been ours on coming into these free waters. Men and women, shipmates, seeming to go silently about their tasks. But also something good, stirring my soul. No break whatsoever as between them, I was reassured to see. The act seemed under the code of ships, of sailors, to be outside anything that might pertain to whether a shipmate was a man or a woman.

Two more days we continued. Reaching meridian 137. In another seventy-two hours the south tip of Australia would be off our port bow, our course taking us within forty miles of her. From there the appearance or absence of the familiar shroud of black murk would determine whether we would stay off or approach any closer to reconnoiter. The choice would not be ours. It would be that of Selmon's instruments: They would say yes or they would say no. Bixby's silence continued unbroken. I picked

Girard to try, asked her to probe on the edges, not to press. I sensed her willingness, eagerness, to do a little more than that—her feeling that Bixby had a duty to tell, and now.

"I think she's blacked it out, sir," she reported back to me. "I confess I pressed pretty hard. Do you want me to press harder?"

She seemed more ready to do so than was I.

"No," I said. "We'll wait."

All of ship's company questioned, questioned again. Nothing. Then I returned to my cabin that night after checking the mid-watch. I had lingered awhile on the bridge wing, trying to gain sustenance from the night of great beauty, the ship proceeding through still seas, under multitudes of stars regnant in a cloudless sky; eyes resting longishly on the Southern Cross, still seeming strange to see it there, standing like some new queen of the night. Nothing helped. Something seemed to have stained, fouled the ship, ship's company; as long as he remained aboard, each of us feeling that stain on us; the ship herself seeming disturbed at having him aboard, wanting to cast him off. The very thought of such a creature being on my ship: It would not let me alone; tore at me, ate at me, in a kind of pure fury. I went below to my cabin. My hand was on the cabin door when I saw a slip of paper sticking out from under it, only blank paper up. I opened the door, picked it up, closed the door, deliberately not looking. Knowing. I sat down at my desk and turned it over in the lamplight. It held a single name, a last name. Did not even give his rating. It was almost as if he deserved none, was no longer a Navy man. I breathed a deep sigh of unspeakable relief.

It was over within the hour. I summoned Thurlow to my cabin, gave him the piece of paper. He was the man for it. He was soon back. He had had to awaken him; took the man to his own stateroom before confronting him. He spoke quietly to me.

"He did it, Captain. He came right across." I could imagine. I didn't ask what devices Thurlow had used. I didn't care. He spoke with that wolflike expression. "Shall I place him under arrest, sir?" It seemed a rhetorical question.

"No," I said. "It isn't necessary. The questioning was absolutely private? No one else knows?"

"Affirmative to both, sir."

"Keep it that way. Leave it for now. And—thank you, Mr. Thurlow."

He looked at me curiously, arose, stood there waiting.

"Good night, Mr. Thurlow."

"Good night, Captain."

I kept to my cabin nearly all of the following day, the ship slowly approaching Australian waters. My mind was quiet. I tried with some success to expel from it all emotion; of anger, of rage, yes, of anything resembling revenge. I tried to think only of the ship. What was best for the ship. I had almost ceased to think of *him*, as a person. Only the ship counted. Next morning, now but twenty-four hours from Australian sightings, I summoned to my cabin the following officers: Thurlow, Girard, doc, the chaplain. Announced my decision. They waited in longish silence. Then the Jesuit.

"Captain, you can't do that. You have to come up with some other punishment."

Everything was quiet; voices; all. The sound of a slowed-down ship moving through a quietened sea but a murmur through the ports.

"No," I said, in those tones.

The Jesuit went on quietly; yet summoning, I knew, all his formidable powers of argument.

"How many of us are left, sir? We have lost so many. For that matter, how many known human beings—whole human beings—are there left anywhere? Not enough known about that that we can afford to dispose willfully, intentionally, of a single one."

None of it reached me. On the contrary, I felt a kind of savage coldness in my ability to answer that with my own cogency.

"Why, that's all the more reason, Chaplain. Anyone that much of a danger to whatever ones remain."

He tried again. "The psychological stress he went through, Captain—during the sealed-up time . . ."

His voice faded off.

"I know," I said, hardly hiding the contempt in my voice. "We've all been under psychological stress, haven't we, Chaplain?"

The tenseness now of a sudden felt in the cabin, the Jesuit trying a final tack; something more bold by far than he had ever said to me.

"With all respect, sir. Do you have that power? Without a court-martial. Without anything?"

This was the easiest of all. Ordinarily I would have come down on that hard, even with him, this questioning of my authority. Now I simply looked at him, feeling the great gulf between us; simply wanting it over.

"I'm assuming it, Chaplain."

"Captain, I would urge you with all the force in me not to do it. I dissent strongly from it."

"Your dissent is noted, sir." I was tired of this; for the first time in all our relationship tired of him. I seemed to want to cut this off, and to do so brutally; said without knowing I was saying it, "Chaplain, if we let things happen to the women, we won't have to worry about having around those human beings you speak of, will we?"

I waited a moment, to give anyone else who so wished a chance to speak; I would not ask them. None did. I thought for a moment Girard was about to; didn't. I turned to the navigator.

"The first land we pass, Mr. Thurlow. That's all. Miss Girard, gentlemen."

Twenty-four hours later, we raised Australia in the distance; the sight of the great vertigo of billowing smoke and soot obscuring it no surprise, seeming to us by now altogether normal. We continued past it, staying well out. I examined the charts and discovered that as we made our turn into the Tasman Sea, we would pass a small place called Three Hummock Island; not far off the mainland and therefore requiring us to pass well off with its area certain to be equally contaminated. I conferred with Selmon, informed him of my plan, enquired as to its risk. He received the information without emotion, as if it were not his affair, his duties lay elsewhere; pondered.

"We would have to test as we proceed into it, Captain. The probabilities are, if it is done quickly—very quickly—just in and out—the ship, ship's company, should suffer no harm."

At 0800 next morning we stood ten miles off, the island enshrouded in the same sooty vapors that entombed the nearby mainland. Selmon at my side, warning me of ascending readings but thus far tolerable, I had ordered all hands, women excepted, topside. They stood in the murk, along the port lifeline, watching in silence. Number 2 boat lowered, the Jacob's ladder dropped, going down the ladder the following: Selmon; the chaplain; the man under a double armed guard; Preston and Brewster carrying two large boxes; myself. All except the prisoner wearing gas masks. The boat moved through the murk and the gloom, the ship's riding lights soon lost to us. Presently we bumped ashore on a gravelly beach. It was darker than twilight, the air infinitely sooty, filthy. The place itself seemed like some blackish and rotting corpse of a piece of earth, ravaged, feral to an absolute, emanating an utter hostility to anything, plant, animal, that breathed.

"What's the reading, Mr. Selmon?"

He held a flashlight to his counter meter. We had never stood in such high readings.

"We should leave immediately, sir."

"Release him," I said.

The men did so. The Jesuit quickly did his rituals; the liturgy, the rather distinct words of the priest, the murmured responses, both voices swallowed up in the gloom.

"Let's embark," I said the moment he had finished. To Meyer: "Open her up, Coxswain."

As the boat started up and moved quickly out, for an instant we could just make out through the murk the dim shape of his form standing there, presumably watching us. He stood between the two large containers Preston and Brewster had fetched from the boat and set ashore: food rations for four weeks, the maximum time estimated by Selmon. We could not see the .45 caliber service pistol I had also left him. I thought I saw him raise his hand as if to say good-bye but in the miasmic vapors could not be sure. Otherwise he did not move. We turned and did not look back again. Soon we were being guided in by the riding lights of the ship. The men, also wearing gas masks, were still standing at the lifelines. Yes, I had ordered all hands there, excusing only the women, to witness punishment, as in olden days of ships. And for the same reason. I looked at my watch. We had been gone twenty-one minutes. I spoke to the officer of the deck.

"Mr. Sedgwick, dismiss the men. Get us underway at once. Straight out to sea."

We stood off the island, came back into clear waters and resumed our N. by N.E. course well out into the Tasman Sea, crossed over Lord Howe Rise, made our starboard turn at Cape Maria Van Diemen, passed due east across the Kermadec Trench and as dawn broke entered the widest of oceans; believing in all hope that surely somewhere in all its vast reaches there was a place for us—a hope tempered by the stern and sobering knowledge that we had but six weeks to find it. In the end using up the major portion of our allotted time until that moment, under God's grace, first light of a day in the fifth week, that Billy Barker, standing lookout watch on the bridge wing, sang out something that brought still the hearts of all within the sound of his voice.

"Birds off the starboard bow."

.BOOK VI.

THE LAST WOMEN

.1.

THE SETTLEMENT

The sea belongs not to man, but to itself. It is in that that it is most unlike the land. The land can be regarded as man's in that it has been given him to do with as he pleases. For better or for worse he can rightly be called its master. Over the period of his existence man has subdued, improved, mutilated, ravished, rearranged, conquered the lands of the earth, altering them to his purpose. Over that same period he has not conquered in any real sense so much as a thimbleful of the sea. The sea has never known anything resembling a master, least of all man. The sea, when in a charitable mood, has let man use it, pass through its domains and dominions that connect the lands belonging to him. In its less charitable moods it has attacked him, overwhelmed him, destroyed him, eaten him and his ships alive. In either case the sea has remained as it was, unaffected, unchanged by man, as if he were a minnow. The greatest wisdom shown in the creation of the planet was that which deeded seven-tenths of it to the sea, leaving but three-tenths to the desires and whims of man. The only argument one might have with this decision is that perhaps man—avaricious, aggressive, dangerous as he is—was given an excess portion. For his own sake he might have come out better if all the earth had been made water, with, reserved for man, a single island perhaps the size of New Jersey perched in the middle of it. It was even possible that—with isolated exceptions here and there—this alteration in the original plan had effectively been executed; and—who can say?—intentionally so, by the original Architect, who, having seen the flaws and failure of His first plan, decided intelligently to throw it out and to try another, begin all over. It is the sea that is eternal.

Now dawn moved at its thousand-miles-per-hour pace across the earth, under the profound obscuration unseen by the greater portion of it, but at some point over the Pacific breaking free to shine down upon a particle of land in the vastness of waters and upon a settlement set high upon cliffs of Pompeiian red. Below the cliffs, in the lee of the shore, half a cable's length out in fifty fathoms of water, a lean gray ship, beautiful to see, rode to her anchors. She was the guided missile destroyer USS *Nathan James* and her company was in the midst of moving from ship to settlement, as boats going back and forth told.

It was a remarkably handsome settlement, neatly laid out, well-built and shipshape, as might be expected of anything put together by Navy craftsmen; obviously nearing completion. Its centerpiece was a building much longer and larger than any of the others: mess hall, study hall, and general assembly hall for matters that ship's company would need from time to time to discuss. This structure and the area around it formed a natural dividing line on one side of which were four dormitory-sized dwellings. On the other side, spaced among the tall, guardsmanlike trees so that the essential beauty of the place was preserved, arranged so as to be out of sight not only of these dwellings but of each other, sat twenty-six small structures.

One other feature was immediately noticeable in the settlement. Not far from the cliff's edge a watchtower rose high above all else, above the island itself, so that it commanded across the dense green a 360-degree view to all horizons of the endless, empty Pacific. On the tower platform was emplaced Big Eyes, brought there from the ship, and manned twenty-four hours around by a two-man watch of lookout and messenger. Such constant vigil might seem excessive. It is instinctive in a man-of-war, in its people; and thus also in this circumstance—the island vulnerable on all sides.

Our community is flourishing beyond all expectations. Most important of all, as to food, we are eating not only abundantly but well, very well indeed. The Farm on the other side of the island now yields fructuously under the direction of Gunner's Mate Amos Delaney, the Missouri farm boy, the vegetables as they ripen and as we need them ferried by boat around the island and hoisted up the cliffs to our mess hall. (A foot-path has also been hacked through the bush between farm and settlement.) The island itself is providing its interesting additions to the daily fare. Reconnoitering the island, Delaney has turned up breadfruit, plantains, wild yams, taro plants, ti roots, these edibles under the wizardry of our cook Palatti coming out surprisingly delicious. But perhaps chief bounty of all is the prodigal fishing grounds which seem to surround the island, particularly on the leeward side below and out from the high cliffs. Suspended from these now are two strong ladders down which our fishermen, under the charge of Boatswain's Mate Angus Silva, the New Bedford trawlerman, go each morning to the boats berthed at the foot of the cliffs, go early, go in the dark, often, so fecund are the grounds, return quite early with the harvest of differing and highly palatable fish—albacore, mackerel, swordfish, rock cod. Men can do worse than dine daily on fish and vegetables caught or picked but hours before eating. Delaney's farming and Silva's fishing detail, along with the watch on the Lookout Tower and the skeleton crew aboard ship, are excused from work on the settlement, on which all others, under the astute guidance of Noisy Travis, our carpenter, are engaged. Today he and I gave it a fairly final once-over.

"I guess it'll do," he said, surprisingly loquaciously for him.

We had paused amid the larger buildings. They gave off an air of sturdiness and strength. We had already inspected the other ones invisible from here among the trees. They also were stalwartly built and, in their relative smallness, to my eye there was something curiously comely about them as if a special care and attention by the builders had touched their lines.

"It'll very much do, Noisy," I said. "How much longer?"

"One week, Cap'n."

And I knew it would be exactly that, no more, no less. Two weeks ahead of schedule.

It is impossible to exaggerate how proud I am of the settlement, which means passionately proud of the men and women who have put it together. Proud of their workmanship and their dawn-to-dusk working hours which they themselves had insisted on. Of course, they have had goals to work toward.

■ ■ ■

In respect to the two matters I had foreseen might present the greatest difficulties to face us, the situation is this:

As to governance: At the moment we began to build on the island I gathered ship's company in its usual assembly place on the after deck and addressing them from the usual place, the after missile launcher, announced my decision: We would continue under the traditional system of Navy and shipboard governance, that is to say, one-man rule by the ship's captain, until such time—estimated at three months—that the settlement should be completed. That accomplished, we would gather in one of those buildings, the assembly hall, and as our first order of business ship's company itself would decide under what system we were thereafter to be ruled. Deep inside me I have alternated between a determination to hold on to the captain's sovereignty as the only method that will work, and a longing to be relieved once and for all of the fearful burden; to lay it down and be merely one among others of ship's company.

As to the matter of the women, as reported earlier in these pages, I had made, after considerable agonizing—in the end all caveats coming up hard against the question and stopping there, "What is the alternative?"—the decision to leave absolutely and exclusively to them the matter as to what the arrangements would be in respect to themselves and the men; had directed them to conduct their discussions of the matter in totally secret sessions in which all men, myself included, would be excluded from participation of any kind; had informed them that their decision would then become in every sense law, unalterable even by their captain and to be enforced by him with the authority of matters covered by general court-martial; and finally had ordered them to have their decision—their terms—completed, ready to be put into execution also by the time the settlement should be completed. But one of these terms necessarily agreed upon by themselves and activated even as the building of the settlement commenced: the twenty-six separate structures, so widely scattered among the tall trees.

.2.

A WALK WITH
THE JESUIT

"**D**o you believe there are people out there, Captain. Others?"
"There have to be, Father."

We had left the settlement not long after first light, moving along the clear-running stream above the waterfall, to either side of it the tender early sunlight flashing down through the high trees, the island never more fresh than at this hour of awakening. The green that lay everywhere ranging from a deep emerald to an almost-white lime, all of it glistening, speaking of vigorous life, its uncontaminated exuberance washed daily by the island's gentle one-o'clock shower. The soprano call of small birds heard down through the branches, now and then a swift tinkling of leaves as one of these, in a flash of red or yellow or bright blue, decided to move from one tree to another, or to skip down for a drink of water from the stream, feet away from us, absolutely unafraid. All of these presentations matters of pure delight but surely to none more so than to men of the sea to whom their immense and never-ceasing variegation struck almost childlike, intoxicant ravishments after the oneness of the sea. Not far in on either side the bush thick, impenetrable. Then a kind of break, unexplained, as though made by man but obviously not, appearing after a while, a steep grassy clearing that led upward and which we followed; for sailors the sheer novelty of land-climbing exhilarating, and as we moved,

439

hearing from the N. by N.W. course we were making the first sounds of
our former home; now came swelling on the air that amalgam of sea scent
and the island's fragrance, beginning sweetly to enfold us. Pushing upward
then, coming out at last on the majestic cliffs that formed the entire
western side of the island and on one of its highest points.

We stood a moment looking all around in the dazzling stillness that
held everywhere. Here commanded across the dense green a circumferential view to all horizons of the Pacific, rolling endlessly away in the great
solitude, holding fast the imprisoned island on all points of the compass,
the island lying prone and serene in the grasp of the sea. Even the fact
that you could see the entire island from here seemed to accentuate our
loneliness, our incarceration. The settlement, or any other sign of man's
presence, hidden from where we stood. Straight down, the stately cliffs
made an awesome free fall to great jagged rocks interposed here and there
only by an apron of white beach. On the lee side the sun, still low on the
horizon, turned into one gleaming, almost blinding immensity the sea
spread out far below us, whispering to the shore the sole sound of any kind
in a mute world. Suddenly the silence was broken by a flight of birds,
cawing discordantly, sea birds not land birds, some species of white tern,
taking flight not far down the cliff from some home of theirs, whether
disturbed by us or simply heading out anyhow, as they did now, for their
early morning fishing—just like Silva, I thought—we could not tell. We
watched their long gliding flights as they caught an air current and swept
in effortless, near-motionless flight down toward the blue.

"Let's rest here," I said.

"Amen," the Jesuit said, though I was gasping more than himself
from the steep climb, my calf muscles trembling. We sat on the rocky
ledge, no more than feet away from its sheer drop. Looking southward and
away and down the coastline and far below we could just make out the
configuration of the *Nathan James,* double-anchored in her bay, alone on
a shipless sea.

"Maybe I should take up boxing," I said. "You're hardly breathing."

The Jesuit still worked out daily with one or more of the men who,
principally through him, had become interested in this sport. No one kept
in better shape—and yet of late there had been a certain wanness in his
face that had begun to concern me, the fact of his effortlessness in the
climb seeming to negate it.

"Anytime, Captain," he said. "Be glad to instruct. No charge for
lessons in your case."

"On second thought, no thank you." I had seen the way he had come home with his punches on men much larger than himself. He laughed quietly. We settled in on the rock, cross-legged, looking far out, trying to find a horizon. In this early morning it was hard to distinguish sea from sky; sat watching the limitless sheet of blue stretching away in the transcendent stillness, the very firmament seeming to stand before us in all its irredeemable blankness, emptiness. Gazing at the vast seascape, ominous in its self-confident might, its hauteur, impregnable, as if to say only I have survived; the timeless, the mocking, contemptuous sea.

"Do you think there's any chance they're alive, Tom?" I said. I thought of them now not so much as mutineers but as poor lost souls: lost shipmates. Nevertheless I sometimes wondered.

"Something makes me believe so. I don't know why. It doesn't make sense. Even if they made it in open boats across that great distance, what was waiting for them on the shore . . . The level of the contamination . . . Yes, I know how desire can cloak reason; listening to the heart, not the mind: One is trained not to do so. And yet . . . And yet . . . somehow that feeling that they came to some safe harbor, somewhere."

"God knows I hope you are right. But I cannot share your belief."

We both, as if that was enough for the dreadful memory, the forever unburied thoughts, came away from it. I looked across the sea as if trying to see through its very horizon.

"But . . . aside from them. There have to be others."

Every time I sat and looked out at those great waters, it did not fail to happen. Pervading everything, a terrible and brooding enigma; what was really out there, beyond them . . . did we really know? If alone, one stopped this manner of thinking before it got too far, knowing somehow the infinite peril of too much of it. With another, the Jesuit most particularly, one felt safe in pursuing the matter, at least for a while.

"Why have to be?" he asked.

"A feeling part of the mind: It doesn't make sense that we should be the only ones. Part of the spirit: There simply have to be people somewhere besides ourselves. Also a sailor's instinct. Maybe a sea captain's instinct. The emptiness of that sea doesn't seem right."

It was remarkable how one subconsciously kept looking for a ship to appear from over the horizon, hull down she would be from this great height, a sailor's sense of absolute unnaturalness that that immensity of waters—to a sailor existing for that sole purpose, to carry ships—should be forever blank, a void. I murmured something of the sort now.

"No ships. That's the one thing I can't get used to. I never will. Someday a ship will come over that horizon."

"One may well do so," he said quietly, feeling my emotion, himself a sailor, too.

"I don't really think so," I said. "But I prefer to. I have an idea the sea feels unnatural herself without them; misses them." I laughed shortly. "Feels it's been deserted, abandoned; asks, where are the ships?"

He waited, then I heard as though an exhalation, a question, as were most of these, as much to himself as to me.

"If they're out there at all . . . where?"

"From what the Russian submarine captain told us—and from Selmon's deductions—they all shape up about equally. Equally bad. Maybe a few unreachable pockets . . . South America . . . home." The pain any articulation of the last word carried had come mercifully to be dulled somewhat though not perhaps ever to be fully obliterated. "Short of those . . . possibilities . . . the Russian's reports had that finality about them."

I remembered that I had told no one, not even the Jesuit—no one save Girard and Thurlow—of that deal with the Russian captain. His quest to find us fuel in the wastes of Siberia seeming now increasingly hopeless from the first. We had heard from him quite regularly up to the time he was approaching the depot at Karsavina. That had been five months ago. Then the messages had ceased—just like that. All our efforts to raise him on the agreed frequency fruitless: We had sent him repeated messages that we had found a habitable island, were building thereon, awaiting his coming, and had received no reply. Nevertheless I had included in the settlement plans an extra dormitory, explaining it away by mentioning that we would doubtless need it ourselves in the future. The possibilities of what had happened to the *Pushkin* were endless: ship's company run out of food, starvation, mutiny from these, other deteriorating conditions aboard the submarine . . . One's mind could go on. I had all but given up expecting ever to see her again. Not an unmixed failure. The absorption of her crew into our community, as substantially promised by me in return for the fuel, part of the deal, would surely have been a staggering undertaking, fraught with peril and pitfalls every step of the way. On the other hand, her not coming meant that we would never leave this island. Once I had speculated with myself whether I wished more than all else for her to come or, equally, not to do so; that long deep-black shape to appear against the blue horizon, representing whether menace or salvation I knew not; with the long cessation of any reports, some time since even this exercise dissolved as entirely hypothetical. I heard my own mirthless laugh.

442

"Except the penguins," I said.

"The penguins?"

"Antarctica. Selmon still thinks it may have got away. Complete uncontamination. Proceeding as if nothing ever happened. Bliss all around. Odd to think there may be more penguins now than anything else on earth."

"They may have company. Just possibly. You knew about the Antarctica Pact, of course? Twelve nations, I believe, all agreeing not to exploit the place—just explore it. Altogether about 1,500 men, a few women, down there, scientific types, during their summer season—which was when things went. Matter of fact I had a friend from Georgetown a part of it, a fellow priest though down there as something else. A geologist specializing in ice formations. I'd hear from him. I've wondered a time or two—if the continent is in fact habitable—whether he's still alive."

"Yes, I'm familiar with that project. God knows what happened to those people."

That continent of cold seemed another planet as we looked out over this tropical infinity of turquoise, appearing to render our voices soft so as not to disturb the world lying in radiant silence; this and the great emptiness filling one with an overpowering, almost unbearable sense of loneliness, relieved in each only by the shipmate presence of the other; remaining, a sense of solipsism, as if we were the only two on earth.

"Still . . . I find the idea settling in more every day, Tom," I said. "The idea that we are the only ones, nothing beyond that horizon there. As I say, I don't believe it, not intellectually. But the longer I'm on this island, the more it seems to be so in my heart. It's probably that even if there are other people, we'll never see them. Actually that—acceptance, is it?—makes it easier. That old blessing of finality, nothing you can do about something so you turn to what you have and say to yourself, 'Let's have a look here and see what we can make of it.' We've got a lot to start with. The Farm working out so well—what the island itself adds to that. All those fish out there. No shortage of food. A damned healthy, helpful place, this island we've come to. When I think what far worse places we could have come out on . . . We've been blessed. So my mind now runs this way: This island will most likely be our home for the remainder of our lives—all one hundred and seventy-eight of us. We'll never step foot off it. So let's get on with life here. Do the very best we can with it. Who knows—if we're up to it, we might make something pretty good of it."

"If we're up to it," his voice came in a soft echo; then another tone of his I knew, of firmness, of resolve. "Well, we'll just have to make damned certain we are."

A plaintive silence, a stillness of unspoken and unspeakable thoughts, palpable and merciless, something irremediable . . . suddenly as if vaulted from it one felt a lift out of all this, a surge of possibilities bursting into the mind, of great expectations . . .

"We have a chance to start over," I said simply. "And not to fuck it up this time."

"Aye, that's it," the Jesuit said, a tinge of high excitement, rare for him, coming through; not short of a kind of fervent zeal. "How many collections of—men, women—have ever been given that chance? Starting over . . . even the very words. It may be God's greatest gift to man."

I could hear my own voice, a gentleness of tone as quiet as the reiterative whisper of the sea far below.

"We've got every shot, God knows. Mainly this ship's company. Not just their skills, though we would never have made it without those. But the kind of men and women they are. The way they've turned to, from the beginning. The Farm. Building the settlement: I feel a sense of accomplishment in the men—they feel it too. When I think what they've been through. My love for them—it is like a pain sometimes." I opened the door a bit. "The only love I have ever had. Whatever happens, there is nothing in life I would have traded it for."

He respected that with his silence. We were quiet a moment, the sea now seeming sweet stretching before us, its voice on the shore itself somehow a reassuring, healing thing.

"So fine a company of men, so good a place we've come to . . . we have every chance men could ask for. If we can make it through this one thing . . ."

From long habit I could sense his waiting, his sure sense not to interrupt. He was simply standing by, with no sense of impatience or hurry, to see where he might help—even if it were to disagree, oppose a thought, a plan, a policy I had in mind. His absolute unhesitation in doing so a major part of the gift he brought a ship's captain. But directed always to the good of ship's company as well, with all of my own intensity, my sole star guide: their safety, their well-being. That common devotion binding us; sometimes not agreeing as to where the star pointed . . . A slight fear at the reminding myself of this fact moving through me now; fore-feeling his probable opposition as to some of the matters I was about to spring on him; perhaps overanticipating this in the light of that undertaking that had come so to torment me, now that it was right on top of us. I gazed out into the immense solitude of the waters.

"As to whether there are others. Had we best not forget it? Keep up the ship's communications watch, of course. Otherwise . . . for one thing, to continue these speculations, in any way to encourage ship's company to do so . . . would only make for disquiet. Of that I feel certain. Rather we had best act as if we were . . . in the absence of other evidence, act, conduct ourselves, as if we were the only ones . . ."

Across the sky had begun to move shoals of white clouds that were nearly pink, high voluptuous cumulus of an extraordinary loveliness against the pristine blue, and we sat simply watching their movement, infinitely languid, somehow seeming to announce to us that though the sea might be wiped clean of ships, the sky still had its own mighty fleets; taking in their beauty, taken with the thoughts that had just been expressed; myself reflecting the while on the man beside me. His mind was as fine a tool as I had known. A Jesuitical-Navy mind! What a force that twain made, I had often thought, not without a kind of wry humor. An extraordinary mind to begin with, forged and repeatedly tested under two of the most unforgiving disciplines known to man, each labyrinthine in its complexity, replete with subtleties, with sometimes cruel nuances, that no outsider could ever hope to understand. Navy from youth myself, I once in a while felt that from knowing him so intimately, the experience of seeing his mind at work, I had also added the Jesuitical aspect to my own armory, so that our minds were two evenly matched forces—an illusion, I realized; I could never hope to equal that aspect of his. As I have recorded elsewhere, he was the only person I could talk with in absolute forthrightness. Knowing as I now prepared to do so that the tentative, possible "solutions" I had worked out might well find in him their strongest adversary; none more formidable given his influence with the men, the moral authority that during his time on the ship had long flowed to him, increasingly so, not so much from his title as from the kind of man he was, a man tolerant, even expectant, almost wryly amused, as to human failings but inflexible where principle—as he saw it—was involved. And speaking of power: now, with what was to be upon us, Lieutenant Girard, the leader of the women, moving up to equal, perhaps to surpass, the priest. His own power in a way seeming locked in some sort of indistinct contest with that burgeoning power of hers, my sense of the two forces seeming to be headed on some uncertain collision course.

"Their health," I said. "Physically I have never seen them looking better. The to-be-expected minor interferences. Hardy"—he was a seaman apprentice in Delaney's farm crew—"cut himself pretty savagely on one of those grappling-iron plows the other day. Shanley"—he was an electronics warfare technician in Silva's fishing detail—"same thing out on the coral, though not so badly. Otherwise, the ship's people: fit as they've never been. The doc is astonished—but not surprised really. The men are eating well. Fresh fish. Fresh vegetables. They're working hard on the settlement. They're getting in all that swimming, volleyball, touch football, in their off hours. Cigarettes have run out. No liquor. Christ, a man can't help being in good shape."

I laughed shortly. "You know what the doc said to me? 'Captain, if there were other Navy ships around and we had some sort of fleet fitness competition, the *Nathan James* would win sailing away. And if we had a fleet-wide Atlantic City "good-looking contest," our ship's company— our men, our women—the others would just take one look and give up. We're coming to have a company of Greek gods and goddesses on our hands, Captain.' Isn't that fancy language for the doc?"

The Jesuit smiled. "A bit overdone, perhaps. I don't see Preston especially enjoying being called a Greek god. Or Noisy Travis. But I take the doc's point." He spoke quietly. "When I look back on those half-alive creatures we were when we came out of that passage in the Sunda Sea—as a lad I always imagined hell as being something like that—into the Indian Ocean . . . the angels must have been riding on our topmasts, sir."

"Let us trust they still are. If there are tropical angels." I took a breath. "So much for the physical side of ship's company. Otherwise . . ."

I lingered, hearing that sole sea sound, reflecting on the past weeks: On the whole, the ship's company appeared well content. If beneath this one sensed the expectancy, one felt no unbridled urgency on their part; now that the women themselves were fashioning the details of a plan to be announced and execution of it to commence at the completion of the settlement—all this they had been told—the men seemed not just to accept but almost to embrace this order as to precedences, the idea that it was imperative other undertakings be attended to first; preeminently, that a settlement be established as the first essential to our well-being, to our survival. They could expect—aye, look forward to—the other thing, but they understood full well that in their own best interests this order was but fitting: first to get the community working. And we were achieving that. Far from there being the slightest sense of rapacity in the air, the men waited not just with patience but with respect. A distinct sense of a special consideration in the air operating from the men toward their women shipmates; and—if I did not misread it, an immense percipience on their part—a realization which translated into sympathy for the great difficulty the women were even now facing in trying to work out something, solve a problem filled with such infinite complexities. Along with an extra solicitation for their welfare. Delaney, for instance, coming to me one day, concerned. "Captain, don't you think you should take the women out of the fields?" "I don't see the slightest reason why, Gunner, but I'll check and get back to you." Referring the matter to Lieutenant Girard, her confirming my reading. "Why, that's very thoughtful of Delaney, sir. But it's nonsense. What would the women do with themselves?" I summed up the essence of this assessment now to the Jesuit. He was in substantial agreement.

"The men themselves," I said. "Something like a feeling of contentment."

It was a question. He waited a moment. I could sense his own independent evaluation at work. Then: "Reassured as to the way things progress. Contentment may be a little too strong a word."

"Then of expectation, you mean? Of waiting for it?"

"Yes, that says it. They know it will be soon. They wait."

"For the word from the women?"

"Yes. But I think they wait in trust for the most part. And a certain perplexity. Wondering themselves how it could possibly be worked out."

"And some trepidation?" I was prying on the lid of his confession box; he would know that, and knowing, protect it; but afford me that which violated no confidence, and filled in blanks of dangerous ignorance.

"Trepidation? Oh, yes. For everybody."

"Perfectly natural."

"Perfectly natural." The Jesuit gave a low laugh. "Preston said something to me." With the name I knew we were outside the confession box. " 'Father, it's going to be almost like incest—a man's own shipmates.' He was entirely serious; concerned."

I smiled wryly. "I think when the time comes most of the men will bring themselves to overcome such sentiments."

"Affirmative," the Jesuit said again.

I turned a little toward him on our parapet perch on the sea cliffs. I needed to get it out of the way, that one thing that had haunted me so; fearful of its augustness, its presumptuousness; yet it would not leave me; here beside me the only man I could say it to.

"Listen to me, Father." Deliberately, given the subject matter I was about to broach, employing that form of address. "I need to say something before we go any further. Not as to the fact of doing it. But as to another consideration."

Again he waited, attentive only to my needs, and I said it, trying to present it as might any naval officer making a report, in the prescribed manner drilled into naval officers from midshipman days, straight, emotionless, but certain hard facts to be taken into account before reaching a vital, perhaps fateful decision as to course, which these facts directly bore on.

"However great we look, as the doc says, and actually truly healthy, no one knows what may have happened to us. All that contamination we went through. Changes not affecting our own health, now or—we hope—in the future. Something else: We may or may not be capable of reproducing ourselves. Some of us may be sterile. All of us may be sterile. And if we, or some of us, are not—can reproduce, some of those may be flawed as to the kind of children resulting, others not. All of us may be flawed in that way; none of us may be. The doc says that. Selmon says that. There is no way to tell as to any of these matters. No way to tell the whole from the sick—genetically speaking. No way to hide from the fact. So it concerns me. Do you understand?"

"Oh, yes. I understand. I understand the circumstance and I understand your concern."

"I've been trying to come to my own understanding as to it—to the position we must take. I am still doing so." I paused. "Father, let me give you one point of view . . . a kind of theological argument, you might say. Bear in mind that I'm an amateur in these matters of reasoning, logic, compared with yourself."

He smiled. "That kind of statement always makes me want to grab my pocket to see if my wallet's missing. Please proceed."

I reached now to that quieter, more philosophical manner, tone, that flowed customarily between us, bound us in a kind of rhythm; two men quietly exploring a difficulty, a problem: seeing how far it might take them down the road to some form of solution. Now trying to reach him on his own grounds. Somehow, as I began, more intensely aware even than before of the great emptiness of the sea stretching before us, of the stillness of the green island all around.

"It goes this way. God intended to wrap it up. Otherwise, given the fact He has all that power, as you religious ones are forever assuring us, why did He let it happen? Could it be that He decided He made an error back when? That man didn't work out, that he is a biological and evolutionary freak; that unlike any other to inhabit it only disturbs the earth, does harm to it; that he must simply disappear, and let evolution start over and see if it can come out better next time. So that to try to continue ourselves is only standing in the way of God's intent, so far as we know pretty well accomplished except for ourselves—maybe a few others out there somewhere; in that sense such acts almost a defiance of God's will. Consequently, our first responsibility is not to reproduce ourselves, even if we can; on the contrary, it is to make certain above all that we do not do so. In order to accord with His expressed and obvious purpose."

I stopped, conscious of what a long and laborious speech it had been; nevertheless knowing that I had to say what had for so long been in me, burning there in a way not without its torments. I sensed his soft smile. I had entered his territory and its pursuit obviously interested him; gripped him.

"A pretty argument," he said. "I see a good deal of cogency in it. It has one flaw, of course. Man hasn't been done away with. We are here."

"Are we? Men and women who, in the first place, do not know if they can reproduce at all. Secondly, that if they do, do not know but what the result will be mutagenic babies. I hardly call that being here in the sense of whole human beings alive on the earth."

"But those are mere conjectures, Captain. You said yourself that the doc doesn't *know*, Selmon doesn't *know*. They're just throwing dice. We may be flawed. We may not be flawed. Quoting yourself, we don't have the faintest idea. Even if only one man of us is not, one woman of us is not, then God has not done away with the human race."

"Do you wish to take that chance of mutated babies to care for? On this island?" I said brutally. "Or worse: create a mutated race?"

I heard a certain upward movement in his tone, a detectable rise in the temperature of our dialogue.

"Captain, we have taken many chances. If there is any matter where there is no choice it is this one. If there is the slightest possibility that we have life in us . . . we simply must find out."

"It's quite possible that the only way we are ever going to discover the answer is for every man to screw every woman." I meant, probably—a stupid idea—to shock him. And I could not help repeating the other argument. "And I say again, it's whether we should, whether we deserve to be continued."

He seemed to have had enough at least of that one.

"Deserve? Are you God?" he said viciously.

It had come suddenly. For a moment a tense impasse held between us. We stepped back from it as from a chasm; fearful, equally both of us, of dangerous emotion. Serious rift between us greatly inexpedient on my part, his influence with the men. Though this tolerance had its limits, not yet reached. I quieted down, felt him doing the same. He waited a moment. Then turned from looking at the sea to looking at me, a certain quiet fixity of gaze in those deep-set, anthracitic eyes; that face I had always thought with its curious mixture of spirituality and sensuality. His voice was quiet again, no attempt at being persuasive but rather as though stating a home truth or two.

"Do you realize what a fluke it is, Captain, that we have women aboard? God put them here for a purpose. The most important purpose of all."

I always had profound reservations about people who enlisted the Almighty on their side, with no visible permission on His part. In fact one of the things I liked best about the Jesuit was that this was a practice he almost never engaged in. Until lately, when he had begun, to me an ominous, almost sinister sign, to drop the name of the Divine now and then into our dialogue, as if that Being were automatically in his corner in all matters. There was nothing I suspected more in human intercourse. He said now:

"It is not by accident that we have women aboard."

I came away from it; feeling that to pursue what God had in mind when the most pressing concerns were coming right down on top of me was a waste of precious time . . . Besides, there suddenly occurred to me another way to resolve this matter . . . another source whose decision and province it more rightly was than that of either of us.

"Let us leave that matter aside." I waited a moment. "In letting the women decide, as planned, the nature of the arrangements, some usual restrictions as to the matter of sexual practices will quite possibly go by the board." I turned and looked straight at him, feeling an almost malicious pleasure in confronting him with that. "If you—or God—has objections in that area, I would like to hear them stated now."

His smile actually soft; part the ridiculousness of my thinking he was in any way to be shocked; part his invincibly resourceful way of dealing with anger: Don't even recognize its presence. He spoke with an almost impudent delight.

"The Church is marvelously adaptable, Captain, even versatile. Hence its endurance. So was our Lord. It was He who spoke of the ox in the ditch on the Sabbath."

I could play that, too. I had not been a missionary's son for nothing. "Also I hear there is neither marriage nor giving in marriage in heaven. Mark 12:25."

He gave me a half-arch glance. "Have we arrived in heaven?"

He went on quickly to something that obviously had been on his own mind. "Captain, I have to say this. There are some—there are more than a few who . . . knowing that whatever the arrangements, they will have to be . . . let us say, different . . . are beginning to question the morality of it."

"The morality?" The word shot out of me.

I knew at once I had been given access to his confession box—no names . . . thus okay . . . valuable information . . . his trying to prepare me. I led him on.

"Did you say the *morality?*"

"To the extent some might choose to abstain altogether."

The idea was instantly disturbing; the implications all too clear. The idea of a divisiveness wherein one portion of ship's company, themselves forgoing, looked upon another portion of it as engaging in immoral practices. Nothing could be more dangerous to our community.

"I don't like it," I said. "It would be absolutely unacceptable."

"Maybe I can do something there," he said quietly. That was a gift.

"It would be greatly desired if you could."

Something told me not to pursue it, to let it rest exactly there. I turned away from it.

"As you know, Girard and the women will presently come up with . . . whatever they come up with." I had sensed, as noted, a certain rising tension between himself and that officer . . . its source uncertain to me, but my speculations defining it as something rather precisely having to do with what was in progress at this very moment between ourselves: the women. Girard's influence with them, over them: the priest's influence with them. I felt I needed to know more as to the reality of such a possible conflict. Furthermore, a reminder might be in order that there were other forces at work, perhaps as strong as his own, in this area we had been discussing. Maybe as well a touch of baiting in my intention. "How lucky we are to have Lieutenant Girard. A smart, capable officer. Sometimes, forgetting gender, I think the smartest we've got aboard."

He said nothing. I said, "Or do you disagree?"

"Oh, no. Doubtless an accurate evaluation. Captain, may I say something?"

We were somewhat back again, fortunately—if not completely so—to our more customary, emotion-excluding tone of discussion. "Could I stop you?"

He grinned. "Just this. Lieutenant Girard is all you say and probably a good deal more. She is a great asset to this ship's company. Her gifts are numerous. I'd say she's quite aware of them—not at all necessarily a negative quality; in fact, on the whole I think a favorable one: Modesty is a much overrated attribute. Unless I'm badly mistaken, she has another. I risk the sin of redundancy in telling you something you surely already know. She has a hunger for power."

"Quite possibly true. With the undertakings that are about to come to pass, that could work to our advantage—maybe make all the difference. Assuming her decisions and judgments are the right ones, the best ones— I lean heavily to the side that they will be just that—she can lead the women to her will. And, of course, if she—or they—venture into areas not their prerogative: I am still captain of this ship."

Somehow, perhaps because of that last expression, it came then, my entering his confession box as I knew all along I would at some point do. Speaking with the quietness one does then, half to myself, half to him.

"Starting over," I said. "I have no illusions, Father. However good a ship's company, this is something new, different. Something men and women, at least men and women of this kind, have not tried. Only a fool would predict what will happen. I've lived all my life with sailors. I wouldn't choose any other men in the world above them. One doesn't have to sanctify them but I know for a fact that sailors have more caring for the man alongside than . . . well, than any other collection of people I've ever run into or heard about. Will that hold on land? Will it hold with the women business? Aye, there is my concern, Father. And it seems—well, that only the question of the women stands between us and every chance at making a good life on this island. And that, now, we're about to begin. The men—the women . . ."

I paused, sea-listening, went on. Came to the point that was the chief author of my anguish.

" 'The men will be better for having the women.' There is a trap in the truism. Whatever the women come up with, given the mathematics of our situation, the men are not going to have them at will; any time they want it. Far from it. At the very best a tough rationing system."

It was almost as if this problem had not occurred to him, something I did not for a moment believe.

"Any priest knows that full-time celibacy is far easier than not-often-enough fornication."

He gave a mordant laugh. "Sex!" he suddenly exclaimed. "Everything connected with it. Causes more problems, people spend more time thinking, worrying, agonizing over it than all the rest of the woes of man put together. Of all the verbosity I've listened to in confession . . . nothing so drives people—men, women—off the rails. The presence of it, the absence of it: Which of those two did more so I never could decide. If it were not heresy to suggest, I would sometimes think God had begun to doze, was excessively fatigued, hadn't worked it out properly, when he put that part in place . . . Forgive the homily, Captain. But Christ, how sick I used to get hearing it sitting in that box! Strictly in confidence, this."

"I shall keep my vows not to tell anybody." I sat, amused, and something else: speculating that that outpouring might well be a halyard signal of his own not fully vanquished carnality. I returned to course.

"Men are possessive of their women," I said. "There's my great fear."

"It's not the men I'm worried about."

I turned to him. "Then you're worried about something. What is it?"

He looked out to sea, speaking as he did, myself sharply surprised at the rather hard, wheel-over degree turn our dialogue now took, a matter obviously for some time of urgent concern to him; his more formal tones.

"You won't mind, sir, if I repeat what I remarked to you awhile back; and amplify a little? 'You regard women too highly,' I put it then. In what you say I perceive that I may have been in error." He gave a nonchalant shrug. I recognized that circuitous gentleness which he quite often employed with me, invariably undergirding a most firmly held point. "Also I may not have been sufficiently precise then. What I meant to say was that I thought you may fail to recognize their capabilities when possessed of power—true of all of us human creatures to be sure. Accented in their own special ways in the case of women. Women aren't very polite."

So it was that; I could not have understood better what he, to be sure in his Jesuitical way, was getting at. I returned his own tone.

"What an interesting way to put it. Yes, I recall those helpful strictures. What you said is the case. You were perfectly right. I've been at sea most of my life, as I pointed out. I don't know women, that's true. I couldn't be more aware of that regrettable deficiency in my character. But I think I know human beings reasonably well; not from possessing any especially percipient powers myself, but simply from being longtime a sailor and a sea captain; shipboard life I've always felt exposes every strength and every weakness present in a man in a way no other life does. You will forgive these banal reflections, Chaplain, while I'm sure agreeing with them." I found myself actually enjoying this wonderful speech. "And if you'll allow a novice's observation, I'm not at all convinced there are all that many differences, aside from the obvious one. In fact I have grave doubts as to some of those that have been for so long alleged. I remember one in Henry James, otherwise a great favorite of mine. You familiar with James, Chaplain?"

"Intimately."

"James says somewhere, 'A woman in any situation is an incalculable factor.' Pronunciamentos like that—so facile, so fashionable for so long, many of them propagated I have a notion by women themselves: I am deeply suspicious of them. Take that one, for instance: I have seen no evidence of it. I haven't found it so, differences, in sailors—women sailors; almost indistinguishable from men sailors, I would say, in our ship's company at least, in all the qualities that count: dependability in doing a job, courage, thoughtfulness as to shipmates, their sailor's word good as any man's."

"Do you know what you're overlooking, Captain?"

"No. But I'm sure you are about to tell me."

"The women will presently cease to be sailors. They will commence being women."

The cawing of the birds, returning from sea, fussing stridently at us for daring to park so near their nests, startled us, silencing all else, all human intercourse. Just as well. The truth was, I not just understood his presentiments, his forebodings, and where they were directed; I in considerable part harbored them myself. I was fearful, perhaps in a way only another sea captain could have understood, that to admit these conjectures into the realm of potential validity would be to increase the likelihood of bringing them about; myself absolutely convinced that above all the women must be given every chance. We had come very near. I was grateful to the birds. I started to stand up.

"Time to climb down. Oh, by the way. As to that other matter . . . the question of reproduction," I said, as simply as that. "I've decided. That also I will leave to the women."

His answer, so assured, surprised me. "Captain, I shall be perfectly content with that. Tom."

Something in his voice. He had turned facing me.

"I think the time has come to tell you something that might not show up in my service record. Have you ever wondered how I got here?"

His tone was quiet, unemotional. I said: "As a matter of fact I have. Now and then."

He gave a small, wry laugh. "Because of what we've been talking about. The women. One woman in fact. A student of mine, of all banal things. The Church knows how to handle such matters. Put temptation beyond reach."

I spoke as quietly. "How odd. The thought had crossed my mind a couple of times. I don't know why. Perhaps . . . men who like women and whom women like: I always thought you could tell."

He laughed softly again. "I don't know about that. The irony, of course, was that the impressment to the fleet was arranged before there were women on ships. The Navy played a trick on the Church."

"I'm immensely glad. Tom, I don't have the slightest idea why you're telling me this. It doesn't make a particle of difference in anything, of course. Besides, celibacy in priests: I never had a strong position on that."

"I had. I have."

I decided to put it straight. "Will you participate in whatever the arrangement turns out to be?"

"Not in a thousand years. Can we get along now?"

As we rose, he suddenly seemed to wobble on his feet, teetering straight in the direction of the cliff's edge, feet away. My arm flung out, seizing him around the waist. I had a glimpse over his body of the huge jagged rocks seeming to reach up to us from their clusters far below . . . yanked him back, our two bodies collapsing together closer than I would have liked to the cliff's edge. We crawled back, myself half pulling him. We straightened up.

"My God, Tom. Are you all right?"

I was shaking; he seemed as calm as if celebrating Mass.

"I'm fine. I don't know what that was. A sudden dizziness. Maybe we sat too long."

This was ridiculous: He was in much too good shape to have been affected by that.

"You haven't been ill, have you?"

"Nonsense. I'm the best man on this island."

"I'm going to check with the doc."

"Feel free to do so," he said, almost curtly.

I looked out and over that prodigious drop; scary. "Christ, we could have both gone over." I glanced down at the rocks. "Not even a chance to swim away. There are better ways to go."

He laughed shortly. "Sorry, Captain. I wouldn't have wanted to take you with me. I feel very bad about this. All the same, thanks for grabbing me."

The thing was, he didn't seem to feel bad at all. He seemed to find it almost comical. I was more than irritated.

"I guess there are tropical angels," I said. "Let's go down."

As we came down the hill the island's gentle rain made its daily appearance and we stood under the trees and waited for it to finish. I had not realized we had been so long away.

"I wonder if He's made up His mind."

He had spoken as if to himself. I turned sharply in the eerie shadows, uncertain of what I had heard.

"What?"

"Assuming the women go along—I feel perfectly confident as to that, Captain, you'll see . . . women want babies . . . I was thinking of the problem you mentioned . . . Whether we are in truth to be the last . . . or . . ." Light and shadow seemed to flicker across his face in the darksome surroundings where we stood . . . It was almost as though those embowered shadows had become a chapel, freeing him up to use religious terminology he felt it would be excessively pious to employ outside of churchly walls . . . "if we have others present in us . . . That will be the true and only test, won't it . . . of what we've been talking about . . . your most interesting proposition, hypothesis . . . whether man was a mistake or not . . . Yes, I wonder if He's made up His mind. Whether to give us a second chance."

For a moment I somehow connected all of this with the incident on the cliff's edge which at this moment seemed to take on a mystery of its own in my mind, something extraordinarily peculiar about it. I looked at his face as best I could make it out in this darkness at midday and could just discern his distant smile and—if I was not mistaken as to any appraisals in these moments—a curious—an astonishing—zeal, close to fervor, that made me feel a quiver of foreboding. Then, to my infinite gratitude, the twenty minutes—they had seemed far longer—were up, the rain had finished for the day, the bright sunlight returned, all dappled down through the trees, setting the drops of water glistening like pearls on the virescent leaves. I felt a decided shakiness inside, as though I had returned from another world. We stepped out of the trees into the sunlight and made our way back to the settlement.

All of these things I pondered. Not least, the near miss on the high cliffs. It was almost as if something had pulled him toward the cliff's edge, almost pushed him. Dismissing that as instant nonsense. Not least of the dangers that continued to confront one these days, I reflected, reading things into things.

.3.

THE KEYS

I felt the hand shaking me, was instantly aware and alert. I recognized the lookout messenger Dillon. Behind her through the open door I could see the earliest blush of first light.

"Sir. Billy believes he's raised a ship on the horizon."

I scrambled into trousers and shoes. Moving fast out of the cabin, passing Dillon, following close behind me, now beginning to run, scrambling up the high ladder to stand alongside Barker. The last stars paled in the sky, taking their leave, and first light, borne on a pink glow that spread across the horizon, was just beginning to announce a new day over the vast and, to the naked eye, empty sea. Barker's long lean form was still bent to the Big Eyes and by the way he was moving the instrument within a close, small arc, I was made aware that whatever it was he had seen, he did not of a certainty see it now. Still scanning over that arc he spoke.

"Bearing zero eight five, she was, Captain."

He stood aside and I bent and came hard on to that fix. I looked for some time more; then swung the instrument each way, tracking twenty degrees or more in either direction. Came back to zero eight five bearing, looked some more. Then straightened up.

"Was," I said.

"Zero eight five, sir," Barker repeated firmly. "No mistaking. A ship."

I had never known him to be in error on such a matter. He might not always be able to identify the object but if he saw something on the sea, something was there. I stood a moment watching him, looking up into those eyes with all their unblemished frankness, then turning to look out over the island's treetops in that direction. I could make out the morning star, oddly itself on the approximate bearing on which Barker had fixed his sighting. The sun was beginning to climb the sky, bringing daylight to the unsurprised sea. Meantime he bent and looked again through the oversize binoculars.

"All right, Billy," I said.

He straightened up.

"What did she look like?" I said.

"Sir, I had her in range about a minute." He paused. I spoke with a touch of impatience.

"Yes, yes."

"First light. It was hard to see clear. But she was there. I swear it, Captain. Smack against the horizon line."

"You don't have to swear it, son," I said softly. "Just tell me."

"I would have said maybe a destroyer, like us. But a fair size longer. Definitely not a merchantman. I could make out guns—maybe they were missile launchers. At that distance . . ." Yes, at that distance you could probably not make out the difference . . . "man-of-war. No doubt about that. Then she was gone. Maybe she dived."

"Dived?"

"A sub. Maybe she was a submarine."

Something jumped in me.

"Captain, I *know*. There was a ship there."

"Yes, Billy," I said quietly. "Well, she isn't there now."

I started to climb down; turned.

"Anything about color . . . shade?"

"Color, sir? Well, of course, any ship looks pretty dark on the horizon. If anything, I'd say she looked, well, more than usual anyhow . . . black. Very black."

I turned back and climbed down.

If it had been anyone else I would have dismissed it as a mirage. We were big on mirages these days. Particularly of ships. Most of us, myself included, had imagined at one time or another that we had seen ships out there, far on the horizon. Seaman Barker had never had one such false sighting while on Lookout Tower duty.

And so I reflected. Subs know they can be least seen at first and last light—classically, for that reason, that is when they launch torpedoes. One wishing not to be seen would have his best chance then. She might not have figured eyes like Barker's.

I think it was Barker's sighting, whether actual or hallucinatory, that forced the matter to my mind: It was not inconceivable that the time might arrive when we should have to protect ourselves, this lovely uncontaminated island, which offered so much in the way of fecundity and habitability and to which we were adding so distinctively by our own efforts; it was just possible we might have to defend it against others who might raise it on the horizon, take a look at these exceeding virtues, and desire to have it for themselves. It was a finite chance. But nothing is more drilled into a naval officer than to prepare oneself and one's ship for the event he is most certain will never happen. This in turn made it now seem almost incredible to me that I had not only done nothing about but had almost forgotten something else: the two keys that were necessary to accomplish the launching of the missiles. I now found it a shocking thing that I had left my key in a place I would go days on end without visiting— the captain's cabin aboard the *Nathan James*. To be sure, in what would seem to be a secure place, a safe to which only I had the combination. Still, it was a matter of the most fundamental naval doctrine that the key, given the power of these weapons, never be in a location which its custodian did not inhabit on almost a continuous basis. I had been guilty of gross neglect of duty—if there had been anyone there to execute it, palpably a court-martial offense. All of this would surely be true as well of the other key, now in the custody of Lieutenant Girard, our CSO since Lieutenant Commander Chatham's departure; her key, I knew, kept in Chatham's old safe there, only herself holding the combination.

Now the matter suddenly became urgent in my mind: It must be corrected at once. That same day of the sighting I called Girard to my cliffside cabin; explained the situation.

"I want it set straight today, by both of us. And something else."

I explained my feeling that Barker's sighting, real or not, raised a concern of possible attack from the sea, in which immediate action would be required. We now kept a very minimum of crew aboard.

"I want a gunnery crew aboard ship. A small one—but continuous, permanent. Enough to man the five-inch gun, the Harpoon, and the

Phalanx in a GQ situation while the rest of us are getting in the boats and boarding ship. How many men?"

She figured for a moment. "Fourteen would be able to take action, open fire, while the others got aboard."

"Then see to it. Take the necessary men from the Farm, fishing, carpentry details."

"Aye, sir. Will do at once."

"Something else. We're also going to need some kind of General Quarters alarm system here on the island. Bring the launch GQ system off the ship and set it up for battery operation. Install it on The Tower. Everyone in the settlement area could hear it, if we need to get aboard ship fast, get the ship underway. Leaves only the Farm across the island. The sound wouldn't reach there. We'll have to use lifeboat radios from the ship. Send one to the Farm, mount the other on the Tower. Keep a radio watch on the Farm."

"That would work," Girard said.

"I'll get Thurlow on it. Now. About the missile keys. I want each of us to visit the ship today, each remove his key, put it somewhere on the island very close at hand. Since we have no 'safes' here, neither of us to tell the other where that place is."

"Of course, sir," she said, understanding immediately. "I'll see to it." She had risen to go do so when I detained her.

"Miss Girard?"

"Sir?"

Even before Barker's sighting had suggested the present unacceptable location of the keys—weeks ago, in fact—another matter respecting them had occurred to me which I also put away in the concentration on island business in what now seemed clearly an additional negligence of duty. Now it, too, had come surging up in my mind as a matter equally urgent to that of the keys themselves. While we were on the subject, it seemed the time to attend to it as well.

"If anything should happen to me—or to you . . . or to both of us . . . we should have backups . . . Otherwise, if somehow they were needed, the missiles would just be sitting there . . . no one able to launch them . . . The missiles would be locked in . . . forever . . . Are there two persons you and I could both trust? One for each key . . . one person each of us could tell where on the island, what exact place, his key is; how to get at it if that unforeseen thing happened . . . to myself, to you, to both of us. Each of them, of course, like ourselves, not to tell the other the location of the key in his charge. So that neither could get to both keys. Same

arrangement as between ourselves. Each, without any reservation whatever, trustworthy; no problem in keeping his mouth shut."

"That's a big transfer of power, Captain." She seemed to have a
doubt.

"So it is. But the alternative is worse. Missiles frozen in."

That phrase seemed to get through. She reflected a bit.

"I suppose we have to do it," she said, still not at all eager.

We both pondered.

"Thurlow," I said. "A natural, as exec. The other?"

"Delaney? A missile chief."

"A natural choice. Thurlow and Delaney then?"

"Fine with me, Captain."

"You have a preference?"

"Not much. Delaney."

"Then I'll take Thurlow." It seemed a random thing. "I want the
three of you to run through the launch drill. Next couple of days."

"Aye, sir. I'll lay it on."

She rose to go. "I'll see to the gunnery watch. Right now, if that's
all, I think I'll go to the ship, get my key, put it—someplace."

"I'll go with you."

Together, we took a boat out. I went to my cabin, she to Chatham's
old stateroom; each got his key, we came back. She went about her
business, I mine. Myself first hiding my key in what I felt was an appropriate place, herself I knew doing the same. I sent for Thurlow, set him to
the job of removing the launch GQ and two of the lifeboat radios from
the ship to the Lookout Tower and establishing a continuous radio watch
between the Tower and the Farm. Next I summoned Delaney and Thurlow, together, to my cabin ashore, and having explained the circumstance,
that the secret as to the location of the respective keys was to be that of
each alone, neither telling the other, under the same terms as existed
between myself and Girard, sent Delaney to seek her out and to be told
the location of her key, Thurlow remaining behind. I took him outside
and showed him where I had hidden my key, near my cabin. After a bit
we all came back. I wanted it got absolutely straight: no one else in ship's
company to know the slightest thing about this transaction. Girard and
Thurlow left. I kept Delaney back to tell him about the gunnery crew I
had ordered Girard to set up aboard ship.

"Would you like to go back to that duty, Gunner—or stay with the
Farm? You've got it running so well I think they could manage without you."

461

He grinned. "Not a doubt in the world about that, Captain." He seemed to ponder the choice. "Well, sir, now that you mention it, I have kind of missed the gunnery and the ship, looking after the missiles. If it's all the same to you I think I'd like to be back aboard for a spell."

"I'll tell Lieutenant Girard," I said.

We lingered, comfortable with each other, looking out at the sea.

"Those damn things," I suddenly said. "Those bloody useless things. Sometimes it seems like we're spending our lives caring for them, doesn't it?"

"Well, Captain, if it were my choice . . . May I be frank, sir?"

"Chief, I seem to remember you always have been."

"Sir, I would have deactivated them and sent them to the Greenland Ice Cap long ago."

I simply stared at him, startled by a memory. Once I had considered doing exactly that, back in the Mediterranean; stopped either by a captain's inbuilt resistance to that act of castration, conditions elsewhere not so well known then as now; stopped also by the awareness that it would have been the last thing the then CSO Chatham, without whose consent and cooperation there was no way the missiles could be removed physically from the ship, would ever have agreed to. But now we had a new CSO. I was just as certain that, although in my mind holding the same right of refusal as had always existed under the dual-key system, she would do whatever I decided in the matter; indeed, its being by no means uncertain but that she exactly shared Delaney's opinion. For the moment I stalled.

"There might be someone on the Greenland Ice Cap," I said.

"Just a manner of speaking, sir." He grinned again. "Let me study on it and see if I can come up with another place. Maybe Kingdom Come, as we say in the Ozarks."

.4.

THE ARRANGEMENT

I had had my separate quarters placed nearest the sea of any of the structures, extending from it a small porch or deck one could almost think of as the bridge of a ship, looking as it did almost straight down into the sea and from this vaulting clifftop vast to the horizon. Looking almost straight down also on the *Nathan James,* which I had brought for anchorage to this safer, leeward side of the island. On occasion the presence of the ship had come curiously to frighten me—an enigma seeming somehow connected with her power, her missiles, only twelve of the original number expended, though why this attribute, her having always possessed it, should suddenly become a source of disturbance in the mind baffled me. In any case this experience was rare. More often, to look down at her strengthened me, as now; perhaps as embodiment of all we had been through, survived; visible testimony, therefore, that we could survive anything that fate, never giving up, might still have in store for us. Looking at the ship, I thought again how God or that very two-handed fate, as one might have it, had shone on her ship's company. I could not have imagined that things should have gone so well for us.

Perhaps I was summoning these thoughts to fortify myself now that we had come at last to the brink of a great unknown, the issues harboring the highest prospects of peril: the matter of the women; the matter of governance. How were the men to share the women? How was ship's company to govern themselves? The former in particular: Its resolution, or the failure of one, I had come to feel, would in the end make us rise or fall, fail or succeed, turn this island into a working and satisfying community, even just possibly a fragment of paradise; or, tearing our ship's company apart, turn it into . . . it did not bear thinking about.

I looked once more across the sea, a slight haze blurring the horizon; an impregnable void, I sometimes thought, an uncrossable barrier; the sea up a little today, its voice heard lunging against the shore far below. I could see thin strips of foam here and there, replicas of the cirrus clouds which streaked the blue above; a slight and benevolent wind driving them across the crests of languorous waves; a certain throbbing of the waters felt; the wind playing a murmuring song in the leaves of the tall trees, on the island green all around me. Both ways, up and down the island, the sunlight struck the red cliffs in a dazzling splendor. I looked down at the ship. I could see her communications antennas high on the mainmast, the radio shack still on the twenty-four-hour manned watch, kept with all the old regularity, never abandoned; so long since it had picked up anything of any kind, even the Russian submarine sometime back vanished from its various bands.

It was the day on which she was to bring me the women's decision, their terms. I stepped inside.

Waiting for her to come, my thoughts coalesced around her and the women, and the crucial matter of what their relationship to the men in ship's company was to be. During our time on the island, even as we sat there in our old way, going over supply and morale matters in general, in our accustomed fashion, as time moved, as we awaited the decision of the women, due on completion of the settlement, it was as though my sovereign authority was being subtracted from me in the exact same measure as hers increased. I think we both must have been conscious of a single fact more than of any other, the one fact that neither of us would ever so much as allude to in its inexorability but which seemed to permeate not just us but the settlement itself, ever augmenting, in a profound suffusion which in the sure sense of the most fundamental change about to manifest itself took on the aspect of something in equal parts obsessively awaited, mysteriously feared: the power the women were coming to have over us.

It was impossible for me not to feel a certain amount of resentment at this, however inevitable the fact, unreasonable as it might be in the circumstance of there being no fault of the women in trying to obtain power. I even sometimes thought, quite irrationally, how dare they do this, bring in their femaleness? But of course they had not brought in anything. They didn't have to. It was there, that power, just by their being here. Though surely with their supreme if unexpressed cognition of what in the end rules the lives of men. Power simply from the fact of being female and in desperate supply; above all—when that phrase crept through the staunchest of barriers one erected against the very idea from the fact of its awareness tending somehow to bring on the most terrifying of emotions—of just possibly being, insofar as we knew, the last women; the reminder of the phrase seeming to invoke a feeling so totally antipodal as to send an invisible tremor through one's whole being; that far from being objects of resentment they must now be lodestars of the most extreme care, the fiercest protection; that perhaps we were to fall on our knees and worship these creatures; as if God had been discarded, substituted for by women.

Knowing that to allow such thoughts into consciousness—even if they were based on rational considerations—itself would tend to distort, warp, even immobilize the new relationships we were even now undertaking to install, my mind descended, to preserve its balance, even its reason, from these lofty heights, to wondering, speculating almost idly, sitting there waiting for her: What was the thinking of the women? Surely they had to like the power. Not to do so would be to violate human nature, more specifically certainly womanly nature, even I, no authority, literally a beginner in the subject, at least that much knew. Yes, my mind let itself—made itself—descend almost brutally from these elevated postulations to come down to earth. Speaking sexually, did they look forward to that one aspect that was inevitable whatever the arrangement turned out to be, or were they seized with the most solemn trepidations, even horror? Were they overcome with delight at the prospect of such vast power, or dreading that sure price of the fulfillment of it? The fact that I had not the slightest idea of the answers to these presumably all-vital questions telling me how little I was into the minds of women; how abysmal my ignorance as to their inner drives, their mainsprings, their true needs, requirements; and most appallingly of all, as to the extent in which these might vary, woman to woman. Should I ask of her at least some of these questions, the more specific and, suddenly now, surely urgent and enormously practical ones? Certainly not, I told myself at once. It was the last thing I should so much as dream of doing. Assuredly not those questions, and probably not any other. I should stay out of it, according to my original intention, which I now viewed as immeasurably wise, let them work it out to the finest detail, not so much as touch it.

Nevertheless, one question especially had nagged at me from the moment the Jesuit had first raised it in our dialogue by the cliffside: his report that some of ship's company were beginning to have "moral" reservations as to the arrangement now being devised, correctly certain that whatever it turned out to be in its details, it would have profound and fundamental differences to anything they had known. Myself hugely aware, as of an extreme navigational peril seen dead ahead of a ship, that any serious division of the settlement into "moral" and "immoral" groups would be fraught with the most dread possibilities . . . I had wished to get from her the information as to whether any women were included in those having such caveats. I dared not ask even that, such a question perhaps more than any other certain to be considered by her a breach of my promise, my decision, to leave the matter to them, the women. I must stick to course: Unless she herself brought these considerations up . . . asked for advice . . . presented mere suggestions as concerned arrangements . . . perhaps I should stay out of it even then.

In fact, she had come to me, not a few days back, and then, without my asking for it, and indeed surprised, almost startled, to hear her doing so, began to give me an interim report.

The truth was, besides all the sundry philosophical reasons just given, I did not really want to hear what discussions the women were having; what various, perhaps myriad alternative plans they were considering, evaluating. She appeared to feel differently—up to a point. To want to discuss it within limits—her limits. Perhaps simply to get another, and a man's, thinking, as I had so often hers in transposed situations. When she spoke it was almost as if our roles had been reversed, that she was the captain and I a trusted subordinate to whom she was accustomed to turn as a sounding-board for various ideas under her authoritarian consideration. She spoke to the subject abruptly—no preparation, no leading up to it, no transition. But also as matter-of-factly as if she were discussing some routine, if important, decision as to any other matter involving ship's company—daily inspections, liberty rotation. Calm, seamanlike as could be, she was into it before I could stop her.

"I think as many plans have been suggested as there are women," she said, in the tones of a naval briefing. "Our discussions are very free. We are getting close. We are considering every possible . . ." She hesitated. ". . . Arrangement. There are difficulties . . . One woman says she will have no part of it."

"Her name?" It shot out of me.

"Coxswain Meyer."

"Any special reason?"

"Billy. Seaman Barker. They want themselves for themselves."

"I understand."

"Well, I don't. It's completely unacceptable, of course." She spoke forcefully, the aura of authority palpable around her. "If we're to allow such a thing we might as well forget the whole business we're trying to work out. It's difficult enough without that." Her voice turned sardonic— and instructive. "I'm afraid falling in love is going to be the first thing forbidden. If we allow one . . . none of this will work."

All this concerned the women, and that part of it I had of my own volition surrendered as far as any control was concerned: all left to them. Yet, before I could stop myself, sheer curiosity barreled me along.

"Does any one woman have the option to refuse to participate at all?"

"We are deliberating that principle. Of course I have explained to them quite diligently that if one does so, it means that . . . that many more . . . for the rest of them . . . One suggestion was . . ."

"Lieutenant," I said rather sharply, coming to my senses, appalled that I had let myself get this far into it. "I do not want to hear another word."

A rather pleasing thought had suddenly occurred to me. It was not a new principle. Responsibility. I as captain lived under it incessantly. It was high time they realized there were two sides to this business of power. I spoke distinctly.

"You—the women—are to decide all these questions among yourselves. As previously arranged."

"Aye, sir. I was only answering the captain's questions." Quite briskly.

I took the reproof. "I was in error to ask them. I will not do so again. Do not tell me about it. Tell me only what you have decided—when."

"Aye, sir. We will meet your deadline."

"Four days?"

"Four days, sir."

"If you require more time I can extend."

"Four days will be adequate, sir. We will have our decision within four days. We are very near already."

467

Just before she went, seeming an afterthought:

"Oh, by the way, sir. No word on the Russians?"

"Not for six months now." I repeated what I had already kept her informed of, bringing her up to date after we emerged from the dark and the cold. "Not since that point off Karsavina. As you know, repeated attempts to raise them on the arranged frequency—and on many others. No replies. Lost at sea, presumably . . . we'll never know."

"And yet you're having that extra dormitory built. It would just about house *Pushkin*'s ship's company."

She missed nothing. I smiled. "Just in case. Nothing lost. If not the Russians, the space shouldn't go wasted."

Not missing that, either.

"How farsighted," she said briefly, returned: "Other than—one would hope they are not lost . . . but as to coming here . . . Just as well, I suppose. It would have complicated matters."

Unspoken the phrase, "especially for the women." Their never having been specified in my talks with the Russian captain as part of the agreement—its being equally obvious that they could scarcely not be. I hesitated a moment, uncertain of whether to say it; then, despite its vast uncertainty, its perhaps irrational premise, I felt I had a moral obligation to do so, her being privy to the arrangement with the Russian commander; also important to say it in that I needed someone to say it to, for a response to a perhaps bizarre idea, specifically, to test it.

"You know that ship Billy thought he sighted?"

The word of that had spread quickly through the settlement.

"Yes, sir?"

"I even had the idea it might have been the Russian."

"My God. Doing what?"

"Who knows? Approaching just enough to have a look at us. Disappears. Dives. For the time being. All this at first light, his best chance of not being seen while seeing us. Reconnoitering us."

She looked astonished. "Why would he do that?"

"I don't know. One gets ideas. Perhaps he has in mind to sink the *James*. Easy to do with her just sitting there, skeleton crew aboard. You don't have to look at me as if I'd gone round the bend, Miss Girard."

"No, sir. I'm just trying to grasp the idea."

"I don't really believe it," I said quietly, "in case you're worried about me. But we can't afford . . . in our situation . . . to disbelieve anything until we're shown otherwise, can we? If there's anything we've learned, it's that."

"Aye, sir, there's a truth." I could sense her actually coming around more at least to the possibility, however remote . . . examining it.

"When I was on the Tower I had a moment's thought of sending the ship to search for him. Decided no. It would leave the island undefended. He could just come in."

"And do what?"

"As to that . . . one can only speculate: Here's a working, functioning island. The only known habitable space. The Farm, the settlement, good fishing. All the needs of man. All ready for someone to move in."

"But, sir, as I understood the deal, we promised to share all of this with him anyway—in exchange for the fuel."

"What if he couldn't get the fuel, and he came anyway? He might then think we wouldn't share. Or: Why share if you can have it all? This island's also got women. These are all mere conjectures, Miss Girard. Normal paranoia for a ship's captain. I'll see you in four days."

As she began, and even as I attended with all my faculties to what she had come to say, in some separate part of my mind I began a process that in all of our many sessions together had never truly occurred: I observed her. Objectively so, almost as I might appraise a painting in some gallery. Aspects, some of which I naturally had been unavoidably aware of, as would have the most unobservant of persons, but now taking on manifest forms as I actively assessed them as discrete facets of her personality, her being; her mental and especially physical self (a painting being a physical thing). She conveyed a remarkably felicitous physical presence; she was cool and gleaming. A narrow, lanky racehorse figure; yet, I suspected what the French call *fausse maigre*. A distinctive "carriage," her movements fluid, untight, near metrical; incapable, one felt, of a sudden or jerky motion or gesture, of being surprised into something she would not purpose; an almost lyrical body, supple, lithe, at thoughtless ease with itself, reflexively responding as she wished; an actual tool of her inner intentions. One does not often see that, in man or woman. And in the manner in which I am speaking of it, that is, of utter unconscious naturalness, a quality I believe virtually impossible to teach; one has it or not. Emerging from her officer's hat and just touching the top of the epauletted white blouse was a pleasing plumage, blond-brown hair with the shining peanut-butter layers that bespeak the real thing as opposed to something out of a bottle. There was a cleanness about her, one having nothing to do with soap and water; clean-limbed, with her fairness of skin, the high, clean-wrought cheekbones, the clean lights in her hair. Above all one felt about her, like a barrier aura, that withheldness, a mystery of allurement that suggested endless discoveries to be made, if one could only break through it, some of them possibly of the most oppositive nature, not necessarily excluding a thriving bitchiness. One simply did not have the slightest degree of certainty what she was in that territory.

I observed these things now, as it were in a single comprehension, a flash, a moment, and wondered that I had not especially noticed any of them before. But of course I knew. One's subconscious, embedded in it an avalanche of Navy directives, dictated that aboard ship such attributes not be lingered over; in all things a captain must set an example. But more important, the intimacy of life on ships of a destroyer size soon creates a curious eye-of-the-beholder view of one's shipmates. One ceases actually to be aware of their physical aspects, certainly of those commonly associated with such terms as homeliness or ugliness or handsomeness (Billy Barker an example there) and comes instead to define these qualities in terms of the character, the goodness or otherwise, dependability and the like, inner worth as opposed to outward aspect, of the shipmate under consideration. This perspective, of course, exists to a degree on land but is magnified a thousandfold aboard ship, perhaps because every hand's well-being, and quite possibly life itself, depends on that shipmate in view. Lieutenant Girard's body had occupied no more of my thoughts than had that of Noisy Travis. My view had centered on how good a supply and morale officer the one was and how good a shipfitter the other. An old personal belief of mine may have explained further my present objective scrutiny and a certain esthetic pleasure I derived from it. As far back as I could remember, to me the primary beauties of life were three: the sea, the stars in their courses, and women. I judged this trinity to be God's finest handiwork, preeminent among His gifts to mankind, standing alone and unrivaled. I never put them in any order.

There rested in her lap an envelope the nature if not the particulars of what it contained I of course knew. Oddly, she seemed first to want to talk of other things, to lead up to that particular subject the envelope represented in all its cruciality and long-awaitedness rather than crudely to spring it; I curiously felt that the "random" matters she touched on first might not be that at all but rather have critical bearing on the main subject, if there existed a man discerning enough to see, perhaps even to master, such nuances. Through the opened side of my cabin we had a full 180-degree view of the Pacific, in the eternal emptiness it always presented us now quietened again to stand flawless and serene to that horizon beyond which the rest of the world lay. To watch it was almost helplessly to be drawn to thoughts both of what that world might be like now, and what it once was; to contemplations of the most immensely varying nature, one day to another; varying even more if one were with a shipmate.

"Paris," she said, looking across that sea, at that horizon, and as it were beyond it. Her voice with its low pitch fell as pleasingly on the ear as in any other matter, random or otherwise, that she might feel a desire to comment on, again the unfailing "naturalness" of her manner itself seeming in a kind of marvelous way to make any subject an entirely normal one to be discussing. "I'm glad I had Paris. That third school year there. I'm glad for every city I saw. Sorry for every city I missed. Now that they're not there anymore. Venice. I regret very much that I never saw Venice. Wasn't that a stupid thing? I resent not having done so. I envy you all those years in the Navy. You must have seen them all."

"Well, not quite all . . ." She had that strange gift, one I had run across but two or three times in my life in other personalities, of imposing her own mood on others, unresentedly so, if anything a pleasant procedure; I found myself doing exactly what she was doing, the cities, places, ports I had known beginning to run through my mind as of pictures out of some old book, historical in nature, cities and places of some ancient civilization, long since vanished.

"I'd like to hear the names of some of them—the ones you saw," she said, a tone close to playful in her voice, as if we had embarked on some game that might prove instructive; or if not that, interesting; even perhaps necessary, for a reason yet mysterious to me. So going along with her, I began to play it.

"Well now, let me see. Port cities, of course, most of them. Or cities not far from ports, close enough for a day, sometimes an overnight of liberty. No particular order, but as they come . . . Alexandria, Athens, Algiers, Constantinople, Tokyo—up from Yokosuka, the Navy base— Bombay, Djakarta, Shanghai . . . Naples, of course, landlocked there for a couple years, therefore seeing everything Italian . . . Palermo, Cagliari, Florence, Siena, your Venice . . ."

"My God, how I am jealous of you. It's not fair."

"Seattle."

She laughed shortly; in no way a put-down of that city; in fact, the opposite, to take the edge off the introduction of the places of home.

"Did you ever see Seattle?" I said.

"No. How was it?"

"Beautiful place. Especially to any sailor. Water everywhere. Even from above. Rained all the time. Heaven if you like salmon. I do."

"You saw so much! It seems I saw so little." Her body turned slightly more toward me—an awareness in myself of that movement. "Did you ever have the feeling—toward the last there, I mean—that you were doing things for the last time?"

The question startled me for the almost eerie precision of its accuracy. "Why, yes, I did. Exactly that. I think that started . . . well, about two years before it actually happened. How would you know?"

"I suppose because I had it. I remember, it didn't seem anything special, even unusual. That was the horrible part of it. It seemed perfectly natural, that feeling. I suppose one just accepted it. If you can't do anything about something, that would seem the smart thing to do." She laughed a little. "It should at least have made me hurry up more. I did—but not enough. I remember the last time I was walking across the Alexandre III bridge in Paris and I thought, I will never see that bridge again, never cross it again. On that same day, the Louvre, thinking: I will never see those pictures again. I felt that I was doing things for the last time. That I would never be doing this again. And having nothing to do with the fact I was leaving, going home. Normally I would be back. When I got back to New York . . . the same thing. I would look at people going into a restaurant just as if everything was going to last forever . . . into Bloomingdale's . . . people walking down Fifth Avenue on a pretty October day just as if it would always be there . . . the city, the avenue itself . . . and I would think, I am seeing these things for the last time . . . and these people, they will never be doing those things again. That certain knowledge that there was very little time left in the world."

The softly falling words, heard against the plangent metronome of the sea touching the shore far below—her voice had in it now a tone almost of sweetness, of some kind of music, however touched by a sense of infinite poignancy—came to me spectrally only because they were such punctilious representations of my own thoughts as they had been then, not really actively recalled until now; not at all aware, as one would not have been, or ever really wondering about it, whether such thoughts had been in others; a curiously singular sense of relief to discover now that they had been; that one had not been alone in having had them, though why this should have mattered I could not know. Somehow though, having the effect of drawing us more closely together in a way we had not before, a way of two human beings to whom this mental process had happened simply from the fact of both being that;

of the same kind; fellow members of the species. I felt oddly a kind of smile on my face.

"Strange. My feelings could not have been more exactly those you describe. I can remember going into San Francisco, sitting at a sidewalk café down by the wharves, saying to myself quite the same thing: 'I am doing this for the last time. Having this glass of wine. Watching those people walk by. I will never be doing this again. Nor will they.'"

"I never even saw San Francisco. It makes me feel guilty almost! But then—I was just too late. For so many places."

Then it was over. She turned away from the view, and as it were from the view of all cities, places, that might once have lived, existed, beyond that horizon. It was as if she had shut a door on the past—that that had been quite enough time for it, that we had perhaps the luxury for an occasional glimpse into it, as now, but that an excess of it was not to be allowed. To live in the past had become infinitely dangerous. As she turned back facing me I was aware of the remarkable pebble gray of her eyes and of her face suddenly lighting up as with some pleasure, some newly found joy or discovery that, having brought the other, she was anxious to bring me it.

"I was just thinking, Captain. It may well turn out that the most important cargo of all we brought out is those nine hundred and eighty-five books in ship's library. Do you realize that we have all of Shakespeare? *All* of him." Her eyes brightened like a girl's scanning a bounty of glorious gifts just conveyed her on some special occasion of her life. "All the tragedies. All the comedies. The sonnets. The histories."

"The fact relaxes me. He would have been anyone's first choice to make it out."

"*And* . . . we have one or more of"—those eyes lighting up— "Dickens, Conrad, Hardy, Eliot, Blake, Stevenson, Yeats, Thackeray, the Brontë sisters . . . Also, I'm glad, P. C. Wren, Dorothy Sayers, C. P. Snow . . ."

"Only Englishmen?"

". . . Gide, Balzac, Camus, Proust . . . Some Simenon . . ."

"No Russians?"

"Dostoevski, Tolstoy, Turgenev, Chekhov . . ."

"We're Americans."

"Faulkner, Melville, Twain, Emerson, Cather, Flannery O'Connor, both Jameses, Bret Harte . . . I don't think you've given me proper credit." She spoke almost peevishly. "I chose most of them myself, as I told you, in case you don't remember. You weren't very impressed at the time."

"I am now. I'll have to think up some award for you."

Her face lighted up. "And the *Encyclopaedia Britannica.*" She gave a sigh of awe and pride, this time as if offering me, and all ship's company, a gift beyond price. "The complete set. Aardvark to Zulu."

"That may turn out to be the most important of all. After Shakespeare."

"Yes," she said. "After Shakespeare."

She took a deep breath from all of this; talked now with excitement. "What's more, the men are reading. I've never seen people doing so much reading. Not in school, not anywhere. My father . . . well, he was a newspaper editor in a very small town in North Carolina . . . and we read everything. It's like that now with the men. Talley has given them the straight dope. They are to treat every book like it was the Gutenberg Bible. Give it the most tender handling, wrinkle or turn down no pages, use book marks she gives them . . . She examines each one when they bring it back, and gives them unvarnished hell if there's a scratch, a mark . . . Also we've got music tapes. Not so extensive but we've got three hundred and sixteen. Mozart, Bach, Beethoven, Handel, Verdi . . . They all made it!" She paused for breath. "Not to mention some pretty handsome rock, country and western . . . When not reading they do a lot of listening. Talley herself—I don't think she'd ever *heard* of Mozart. Now she listens to him practically all day. Think of all we brought out, Captain! All who made it. Aren't we lucky!"

"What are you reading now?"

"Nathanael West."

"I'm glad he made it."

"All of him did. All four in one volume."

"Let me have him when you finish."

"Will do. One other thing. We've got those thirty thousand sheets of bond paper you've put off-limits. I had an idea that at some point we might want to start, every one of ship's company, putting down whatever we remember . . . anything, everything. Also—more important maybe— everything anyone knows about some skill—all the knowledge every single one of us has. Isn't that what you had in mind for all that paper?"

"It was." I was astonished at the exactitude with which she was into my mind. "Let's start it as soon as the settlement is finished. But in a very controlled fashion: to conserve paper. We'll go into it up the line. Do it in the main hall. Couple hours a day of men off duty. Noisy on carpentry, Silva on fishing, Thurlow on celestial navigation, yourself on literature . . . Get it all down. Sheets rationed very carefully. Taken back after that two hours."

"Will do, sir. I'll set up a plan . . . Excuse all these diversions, sir."

"They're not that. They're . . . they couldn't be more important. Having those books, those tapes . . . those blank sheets of paper." Her own excitement reflected in myself.

"Aye, sir. They couldn't be more important. Now then . . ."

Absently her fingers moved over the envelope in her lap.

There was a touch of what I have already made reference to: that she had become captain and I the subordinate sitting across from her and awaiting her wishes, her orders, her commands. No change in her demeanor to suggest this—perhaps a certain added firmness in her tone, a detectable sense of authority, of being in control of the direction the conversation took, these but marginally increased from what had always been her self-confident manner. There was no insubordination. If anything she seemed to "sir" and "Captain" me more than usual. But I felt the vibrations of power, of prerogative, as if coming off her, reflected from her very skin. Having expected a direct proceeding now to the presumably decided question of the women, to the envelope still in her lap (I could scarcely keep my eyes off it), I was surprised at the turn she now took.

"Captain, I would like to discuss with you the question of the governance."

"The governance? Why, it's settled. Ship's company will decide as to that. When the settlement is completed. As promised by me."

"I know about the promise, sir. May I speak?"

I shrugged at the rhetorical question and she began, seeming to me to proceed with a quiet carefulness, scrupulousness, that was unusually intensified even in her, whose habit this was.

"Something's started again with the crew: men with thoughts aimed at home. Bigelow"—a missile technician—"asked Ears the other day to send a message to one of his children on her birthday. Started . . . then stopped. Shook his head. He cried a little. Now and then a number cry a little."

"I would assume that. I have cried a little myself."

"Jorgans"—a machinist's mate—"has started writing a letter once a week to his wife; delivers it to Talley as postal clerk when we had one—she takes it, just as she used to do. A number are beginning to speak of back there in the present tense again . . . their home towns, their families. You can walk around the island and see a man here and there just sitting on the cliffside looking across the sea to where it is, or was . . ."

"I don't consider these—manifestations—anything other than what one would expect."

"As to whether they're—resigned—to spending the rest of their lives here . . . I don't believe they consciously have faced up to that possibility— very few of them. They're putting that thought off."

"Yes, I sense that. Perfectly natural. Even favorable. So we can get on with what has to be done. The Farm. Building the settlement. By the way." I spoke with a certain asperity. "As to 'possibility.' 'Certainty' would be a nearer word. I would hope most of them are beginning to understand that."

I waited with some impatience: She seemed to me to be speaking of obvious phenomena, of a kind I myself well knew; the impatience restrained by the knowledge that she was an officer who never wasted time, invariably there being a purpose, most often an important even crucial one, in her procedures. She began then to speak in that slightly educatory tone she had at such moments, much familiar to me from our countless discussions of morale matters, of how the men were doing, speaking quietly but with that concentrating directness I recognized when she felt an issue was at hand of a troubling, perhaps even dangerous nature if let alone, time to head it off.

"Captain, I have to say this. I don't think many of them have reached your degree of finality—acceptance, certainty, as you put it—that they will never leave this island. However, I would also say . . . they're slowly getting there, most of them. Seeing these very permanent looking buildings go up, for one thing. I think given time most of them will come around; accept the island—as their home." She seemed to be framing her words to convey some critical exactness. "Except for a certain number. I'm not entirely sure those will ever come to terms with the island."

Again, I did not consider what she said in any way unusual; could not understand the anxiousness she obviously felt.

"I would expect it to take a rather long time for some," I said idly. "Perhaps the rest of their lives for a few."

"But in that number I'm speaking about—well, the thoughts are very much alive. Not working toward coming to terms with the island. Working toward: well, going home."

Somehow the phrase instantly irritated me. "Going home? Still? My God." I could feel myself giving a decidedly brutal note to the word. "What home? I thought that was settled. That God-awful time when Chatham and his people cast off in those boats in the Mediterranean. These people you're talking about now. They were given the chance to leave. They chose to stay with the ship."

"Men have second thoughts, Captain," she said, mildly, but almost instructionally. "Some wish now they had gone in the boats."

476

I came down from it. I shrugged as though we were dealing with an emotional rather than a realistic matter; a distorted state of mind of a few men given to imaginings, changeable in time perhaps, in any case not to be acted upon by those afflicted with it; objects of pity, solicitousness—and of help—these poor souls should be, certainly not of anger in their world of almost eerie fantasy: we had not come close to picking up anything; even those vastly puzzling Bosworth signals long since ceased, seas back; all of this, along with all that other mountain of validations, to any mind which had not entirely abandoned rationality certifying as would a coroner's certificate the death of the place she had just spoken of as home. Long since my mind had turned inflexible on the subject. Inwardly having much less tolerance than at one time with views so opposite to the overwhelming evidence, I nevertheless spoke quietly, considerately, even compassionately, as though dealing with the irrational; in it, however, a captain's unmistakable tone, of matters now become nonnegotiable; in fact, nondiscussable; of matters he had had enough of.

"You're doubtless right, Miss Girard. Men change their minds. And once they do . . . I suppose we should resign ourselves to the fact that there are always bound to be a few nothing will ever convince—short of our getting back on the ship, casting off, taking that course we're not going to take, can't take; and never will—long since decided, that matter. So long as they don't make actual trouble . . ." I could hear my voice adamant . . . "I'll leave them alone; with their illusions; I understand them; I even understand what they feel. Men have a right to illusions, especially those. But as to any serious consideration of that foolishness, madness. I'm not prepared to go into that affair again. It's finished. It was settled off Suez. Going home, as they put it. As they fully understood. That the choice not to go back was for once and all." I spoke rather sharply. "I take it you remember that was made clear to the last hand, Miss Girard."

"Indeed I do, sir. And have reminded of it those hands we're talking about."

I sighed, backed off again. "But I'll let them be. They seem harmless enough. Aberrants."

I could feel her compulsion to say more; a certain familiar determination hovering around her mouth. I had run out of time as to this subject. I wanted an end to it.

"All right, Lieutenant," I said shortly. "Let's have it."

"I'm not sure they're all that harmless, sir. If I may put the matter directly, I think you may underrate their tenacity, their sense of purpose."

It was as though she were giving me a lesson in the dangers of naïveté; even in basic logic. She continued as if to set me straight, indeed herself speaking rather trenchantly.

"I believe it's also wise to remember, sir, that they don't consider themselves—this group of men I'm talking about—either foolish or mad or even aberrant; nor present the behavior of such men; indeed, quite the opposite; and that this present equanimity is not any final guarantee that they'll remain forever passively content with—their illusions. They're in dead earnest. I would put it this way: They're biding their time."

The phrase, coming from the least of alarmists, felt suddenly threatening in the hushed air; to no one more so than a ship's captain who had gone through the business of rebellious men, was absolutely determined beyond anything else not to let any possible vestige of a similar uprising get a start, the mistake he had made once. It was not one any ship's captain was likely to make twice.

"Biding their time?" My voice abruptly taking on the tones of a sea captain confronted with unallowable behavior.

"If the governance should change. Majority rule. Believing then that they might change the minds of the others. The matter actually brought to a vote. Sir, I think they're waiting for the question of the governance to come up."

"But not to stay on the island—what other choice is there?"

"There is that."

She looked down at the ship. Something froze in me. I was afraid to speak. I looked out at the waters, down myself at the ship. Asked, almost off-handedly. "They would take the ship? How many men are we talking about, Lieutenant?"

"Twenty at least. As high as twice that."

I said it factually: "Forty out of one hundred and seventy-eight." I looked across at her. "I now appreciate your concern, Miss Girard."

I waited a moment. "I have a question which may strike you as curious."

"I am here to answer all questions, sir."

"I am glad to hear it." I looked straight into her eyes. "This one is, among those wishing to go back, are there any women?"

She looked me straight back. I thought I saw a flash of something like amusement in her eyes; it could have been something quite different.

"Negative, sir. Not a single one."

She immediately picked up: "I've often wondered if it was wise, sir." Her own voice altering slightly to take on that tone of persuasion I also knew as a sign of having herself reached a strongly held conviction on some matter she considered urgent, now the time to go to bat for it using all her finely honed talents in such circumstances. "More than ever I find myself coming to the determination that the Navy way is still the best for everyone. In fact, the necessary way. At least for some time to come. Certainly that it's too early for any change."

"It's not a question of whether the Navy way is still the best way, Miss Girard. The point is that they have to be given the choice. For the men to be ruled now in any manner other than one they choose themselves . . . I can think of no greater incentive to trouble." I shrugged. "Who knows? They're Navy men. They may choose the Navy way themselves."

"With all respect, sir, I don't think we can afford the risk that they will choose something else. Not yet . . ." Her voice seeming to bear in on me, a tone admonitory in it, almost a lecturing quality. She looked at me dead on. "I have to put it straight to you, Captain."

"Please do so."

Her words came at me, hard and clean-cut, bent now on convincement.

"I don't think you have the right just to give it up like that. If that time is to come, it's not here now. In fact the time could not be worse. I think it's your duty to *want* to continue in the old way, the Navy way, the way they're used to."

Suddenly I gave myself a lapse I would have thought I would never have permitted myself.

"I'm not running for office, Miss Girard."

At once I felt a sense of self-revulsion; felt I was soliciting, almost begging for fealty, for flattery; almost that she, seeing so, was slyly supplying these things. Felt a sense of falseness in the air.

"Don't misunderstand me, Miss Girard. I like being a ship's captain. Commanding, yes, ruling the men, my word final; yes, I like that. I'm less certain that I have any desire to be monarch of this island."

I should have stopped there. Instead, like some abject politician, overcome by his own self-importance, his sure sense of his indispensability, that men could hardly get along without him, preying avariciously on anything that would feed this feeling, I proceeded.

"Those who want to go home," I said. It was as if I were seeking some excuse, some justification, somehow to reverse my position, hold on to my captain's sovereignty. "What would they do if they achieved power? Seize the ship? Cast off—for home?"

"I don't think they're that rash. Or even for other reasons that they

479

would actually do it. Not abandon their shipmates to the island. No." She waited, again seeming to search for precision, to come as near as possible to exactly what she felt would happen. "Something like this: They would work—the word might be proselytize—to make their opinion the majority one. Then I think they might say to the others: 'We're taking the ship home. That is what most of ship's company now wants to do. You may remain on the island—or you may come with us. It's your choice.' They would be at least that fair."

The very word in that context made me angry, the mockery of it.

"Some fairness. Considering what they'd be taking them into."

"Remember that they—the ones I'm talking about—believe differently as to that. They think they would find something back there. Some place that would take them in—be habitable. And there is the fuel to go there. They all know it."

"Fuel." I spoke brutally. "The ship: we would need her for our very lives—if ever we should be forced out of here, have to find another place. If radiation hits this island. Not likely now, Selmon says. But still in the realm of possibility. They must know that. We would be trapped. Those who remain. They would place those in the most mortal danger." I turned to her, feeling utter calm. "Simply this. It will not be allowed."

I became aware of something in her eyes which seemed to mirror my own resolve; then something else that rather sent a chill up my spine: in them, too, that certain glow, that unmistakable sense of having won out, a sense of something like personal triumph. I was baffled. And one other thing: It was as though she looked straight into my eyes and saw what she saw.

She had stood up, was holding something out to me.

"Very good, sir. I simply wanted to get your agreement."

She handed over the envelope. And was gone.

I stepped out on my porch-bridge, for some unexplainable reason wanting a clearer view of the ship; simply quietly regarding her where she stood self-confidently aware of her beauty, her many and diverse talents; yet now something poignant about her, containing as she did a fatal flaw, as from a terrible illness: her low supply of fuel, emasculating her of her highest gift of all, which was to go as she pleased across all waters, starting with the greatest ocean-sea on earth now stretching in such ardent invitation beyond her, seeming rapturously to woo the ship. I appraised, a helpless professional habit, sea and sky as to sign of weather—of anything. The twin azures both now unstained, resting as if for oncoming night in an exquisite languor. I stepped back inside, opened the envelope, took out the single sheet of paper, and read the single-spaced type:

The Women's Conditions

The following arrangement will take effect upon the completion of the building of the settlement; the first, itself as a condition to all other conditions, having been built into the settlement.

1. Each woman will have separate and individual quarters, belonging as exclusively to herself, and to be as sacrosanct and inviolate as any private residence.

2. The men will be divided as equally as may be possible among the women, who alone will determine the method for accomplishing this division, including which man will be assigned to which woman. In the event of incompatibility, a man may thereafter be transferred, at the women's sole discretion, to another group and another woman. Such transfer shall be made not more than one time.

3. Each man will be granted a week on a rotation basis in which he may come to his assigned woman's quarters. The rotation will be chosen by the men by lot. In explanation: The time frame of one week has been selected for the reason that in the event of a pregnancy, the women do not deem it to be in the welfare of the community that any person, including the woman herself, should know the identity of the father; thus no man may claim the child as his.

    The above arrangement will not commence until two weeks have passed. During that time each woman's men may visit her on a basis of three per week. Thereafter, the one-man-per-week arrangement will go into effect.

4. The women will avoid demonstrating partiality for one man over another. In identical fashion, no possessiveness, no proprietorship or control of any nature whatsoever as to the woman is to be tolerated on the part of the men, nor jealousy of any kind. Any manifestation of these elements will be grounds for shifting the man to another group and another woman, or for suspending or excluding the guilty man altogether from these arrangements, as the women shall decide.

5. Any man or woman, finding himself or herself unable to participate in these arrangements, may choose not to do so, and no obloquy shall attach to the person reaching such a decision. However, a man and a woman cannot opt out in order that they may be solely and

481

exclusively together. Once any shipmate, man or woman, ceases to participate that person becomes a celibate.

6.   Since these arrangements are in every respect new and untested in our experience, the above conditions may be altered as time goes on, and at any point they choose, on the vote of all the women, solely at their discretion. However, all planning to enter into the arrangement should know that the women anticipate that any changes that might be made will be minor or procedural in nature and that all the fundamental precepts herein set forth will permanently obtain.

7.   As a final condition, the settlement's governance shall continue as on the ship for a period of at least six months, the reason being to make certain that the above provisions are backed by the full weight of Navy authority, rule, and discipline. At the end of six months, these arrangements having worked to their satisfaction, the women will not oppose any alternative system of governance which a majority of ship's company may choose; provided that that system, whatever it may be, agrees to the full incorporation and carrying over of all the provisions in this document.

The document was signed by all twenty-six women.

I sat there looking at the paper but not seeing it. In a little while I reread the provisions. The document was well drawn, everything anticipated, tucked in neatly. The second paragraph of Provision Three I found particularly admirable on the part of the women, demonstrating both that they knew their mathematics and that they were women of compassion, of benevolence, considering the long months of deprivation that had now existed, its meaning being that every man in ship's company would have been accommodated at the end of two weeks, otherwise that worthy attainment being for some more like six.

I reread once more Provision Seven. Yes, they understood its nature: power. Lieutenant Girard: that enormously brilliant comprehension that the area of women-men relationships, the territory of sexual practices, we were about to enter was fraught with such profound hazards of itself, in truth no one having any clear idea as to how these matters would work (sexual behavior at its simplest unpredictable as to outcome, this incertitude vastly, infinitely, multiplied in these arrangements), that to add that of an undetermined governance which might—as a random example— overturn all these carefully reasoned provisions was an unacceptable risk; she and the women in their profound shrewdness (in their own domain), insisting on the Navy governance which had always safeguarded them, knowing it would continue to do so with whatever measures might be required. Knowing also, to an absolute, I was vain enough to discern, that they had this flawless protection in present ship's captain. I shook my head, felt a sardonic smile at the astonishing adroitness—for here was the genius stroke—with which she had led me into the position the women wanted, quite slyly using her sure instinct that it was what I myself also wanted; sure even to the extent of writing it in beforehand. I had been had. But then I wanted to be had. The fact that the reasons for my remaining so as given in that tour de force of persuasion were quite distinct from the one set forth in the "conditions" in no way adding up to her having dissimulated, to having "tricked" me: She was far too intelligent not to have felt that foolish to attempt. The truth was simple enough: She believed, with equal passion, equal urgency, in both circumstances as absolutely requiring a continuation, at least for now, of the existing system of a captain's sovereignty. If the one residing in her area of responsibility—the women—perhaps loomed somewhat larger in her mind, as I suspected, that is but to cavil; it is only human to pay first allegiance to one's own interests. Nothing in this lessened by that other hard truth: I simply would not tolerate anything that approached the terrible time we had gone through before; that part of it, even the remote possibility of such a thing, a true service she had rendered me, alerting me; doing me the favor of granting me the perfect means of putting off any question of the governance, yes, for two reasons of the greatest cogency; only one of them, the insistence by the women on it, for their own reasons, needed to satisfy the men. There would be no trouble there. They would accept almost any terms the women laid down. And in myself not the slightest doubt that she had thought all of this through precisely: her knowing to an absolute there was no way it would fail to work with me; in that exchange she had held me in her hand; even my satisfaction a part of that.

None of this served to make her saintly in my eyes, rather to make her immensely artful, and blessedly wise; and yes, infinitely cunning. Otherwise: Suspicion, once let in the door, will hardly ever let itself out again. I could not help wondering what other motives, as yet unrevealed, awaited execution in Lieutenant Girard's mind; having to admit, again with a felt wry smile, that she was showing herself in all respects, so far at least, quite a master in her own exercise of sovereignty. The question to myself being: Did she have a still larger intention? Power is like a breeder reactor: the exercise of it irrefragably creating the need, sometimes urgent, for ever more forceful forms of it.

Finally I reread the entire document yet again, objectively dissecting it virtually word by word. I thought it just might work. Yes, altogether an admirable job. The Jesuit was right. They had ceased to be sailors. They had commenced to be women.

.5.

WORSHIP OF WOMEN

It is sometimes not appreciated by landsmen that sailors tend to be not only conservative but of a religious bent. This has been true since earliest times, and so much has been written on the subject, and the whys and wherefores of it, that I need not add to that considerable literature here. I will speak only to the question insofar as it concerned us, which was, as previously alluded to, that some of ship's company had what could only be described as religious or moral considerations as to the course we were about to undertake. It was the element—my attention first drawn to it in the dialogue with the Jesuit on the clifftop—that was very much on my mind as we gathered finally to celebrate the completion of the settlement, the day on which Lieutenant Girard would announce the "Arrangement," as I had begun to think of it, and on which those who chose not to be part of it would be allowed to stand aside. I was not at all sure but that their number might be considerable; the implications of such a division profoundly horrifying to me.

It was a gallant day, the kindly light of early morning radiant in cerulescent skies, the sunshine slanting through the tall trees and onto the large Main Hall where all ship's company save for the Lookout Tower

485

watch and the thinnest watch aboard ship (and these spelled so that all could participate) were gathered. Through the opened sides a faint and palliative westerly breeze came whispering off the sea far below and over the participants. The ceremony marking the completion was not, in some respects, unlike that held when a ship is commissioned; however, with certain other features added. A quiet sort of affair, as if deliberately containing, within the immenseness of emotion, that sense of victory, yes, triumph, that we had come through, all the fine shipshape structures around us testifying to the fact; a sense not of arrogance but of humility. A sense, too, of thanksgiving, as New World pilgrims might have gathered on shores of long ago, our prospects, I judged, more promising than had been theirs. So many elements, by God's grace or by our own fortune, operating in our behalf: a new home blessed with favorable year-round weather, with parturient soil; an island thus far in all respects forthcoming, the bounty of the sea to feed us; ourselves to care for one another. The valiant ship that had brought us to this safe harbor and visible just below seemed herself a participant in the ceremony (how worthily so!), her single break in the aching infinity of sea nonetheless also marking our isolation, our imprisonment, knowing as every hand did the desperately low fuel supply remaining on her, all this bringing a sense of loneliness but even that seeming to bind us the more indissolubly. Further, never articulated, naming them, travails we had been through binding us as only travails can, and finally, and most of all, the future binding us. A hymn accompanied by Delaney's fiddle, "Lead On, O King Eternal." Lieutenant Girard had come to me with the word that the men wanted to name the island. Porterfield, she said, had suggested Deliverance Island and they seemed to like that. I had made it so and it was announced now. Toward the end of the ceremony, the words of Psalm 139 read by Porterfield falling sweet and clear over us, seeming a declaration of accomplished fact . . .

> If I take the wings of the morning, and dwell in the uttermost
> parts of the sea;
> Even there shall thy hand lead me, and thy right hand shall
> hold me.

And yet, with all this sense of a band of brothers and sisters, a tension tangible to myself hung in the air . . . doubts as to what we were about to undertake. And most of all in myself, above-mentioned, the very real fear that enough might say no to the whole thing, for the stated reasons, with the most devastating consequences: establishing within our ship's company and our settlement two groups, one supposedly "moral," the other supposedly engaged in "immoral" practices. I was not at all sure we could survive that particular species of divisiveness.

Then came the Jesuit's homily.

Men and women both, they all looked up to the platform where he was standing and as he proceeded, I was witness to something extraordinary. Into those faces as he spoke came a slowly arriving . . . expectation, wonder—I do not wish to overstate this, but at times something very much like awe, as though they were being given a glimpse onto strange shores, the precise nature of which no man could predict but shores certain to be abundant with new and inexperienced behavior, conditions, yes, codes. And alloyed with all of this wonder, itself almost childlike in nature, just touching the faces through it, a sense of fear and of uncertainty, yes, the barest smattering of terror, but seeming of that kind also childlike, as children possess a fear of the dark—yet overridden, it seemed, as happens with children, by that beckoning of them into its surprises, its mysteries.

To reproduce the text of his speech would be to no purpose, for the reason that any literal interpretation of it might well obscure rather than reveal its real design. This, too, as with anything with him, all of intention—he seemed not to do, say anything, that was not of a purpose, absolutely clear one felt to himself if not by any means always, at least instantly, to his hearers. But now and then a phrase, a sentence, like a true compass pointed the way, to my mind unmistakably, provided guideposts to what was ahead; for today, I became aware, he had a very large intention; indeed, as he saw it, the largest. Always in those soft, assuasive tones. Of course, he had so much going for him to be able to accomplish all of this, this capture, as it were, of themselves. Ship's company believed in him in a special way. If he said something was wrong, it was wrong; if he said something was right it was right. Part of the strength of it being that it was not something he abused: indeed his tolerance as to human weakness being as far-embracing as I had known in his profession. And not one ounce of proselytism on his part; not the slightest effort to be "popular." That influence—power would be a better word . . . just flowed to him, a trust, a belief in—such as flows with all inevitability to the intelligent and to the strong and the cunning, and most of all to the resolute, to one with an absolutely fixed purpose, in circumstances such as were ours; for in the end perhaps all men are sheep, and only one shepherd. And this, also mentioned before, at this particular moment of the utmost importance: a power much abetted by the fact that into his ears in recent times had poured the pains, the anguishes, the guilts and the desires, the secret wishes and longings—perhaps these above all, the nature of the speech suggested, along with the reservations, the deeply held doubts of a "moral" nature—of such a large portion of ship's company. He knew more than anyone what they wanted, knew they were waiting to be told, and that whatever misgivings might remain, only his imprimatur would remove them, if anything could; in fact, was the one thing that might effect that accomplishment urgent above all else if—yes, if his intention were to have any real chance at all. A phrase, a sentence, I say, sometimes—the present speech—homily a better word, though not especially at all of a religious character, but surely that—the best homilies being those that while carrying manifestly little weight of religious content in fact harbor the most. First taking care of one particular problem, absolutely essential to dispose of if his intention were ever to be given the chance to become reality . . . "Our duty not to the people back home— they are no longer in a position to be fit objects for duty, and especially so from their loved ones . . ." How I cherished him for that, for coming down so flatly against the course that Lieutenant Girard had assured me a good number of them were contemplating, even to the point of considering means to effectuate it. In fact, that was clearly one of his two principal purposes; to make them understand that "home" was now, right here. (He was leading, building up with such consummate skill, to the other and larger purpose.) Rather, he left hanging for a moment in the air, a duty to something else. The odd part being that having said to whom duty was not owed by ship's company he did not go on to say at once to whom it was owed. I am certain the word "God" was not once spoken. He seemed peculiarly not to want to identify too—bluntly? too heavy-weighted? too vulgarly even?—the proper object of our duty; no reference whatsoever made as yet in that regard. Maybe he wanted each to seize on the concept first . . . as if it were his or her own; nothing could be more Jesuitical than that. To me—and not because of any special acuity of my own but due solely to my having been made privy to his mind and its workings—it was nonetheless as clear as the cloudless skies that hung sweetly above us on that momentous day; clear also the fact that what he was saying was that nothing in the world was by comparison of the least importance. And least of all—reiterating the theme as in a symphonic work—any desire they may have had to return to a country, or what was left of it, where not only could they do no good whatsoever, not the slightest, but . . . He managed to convey that such an act, for men—and women—in our circumstances, would have been monstrous and that—and now he drew closer—we had but one true course, given the constitution, the makeup, of our ship's company; that we did not so much as have the right to consider any other. The providential fact of our having both women and men aboard itself dictated our choice; in fact, that given that particular and rare condition, we had no choice. We were a "mixed" crew by a higher intent, as he had said to me: so that we could fulfill a function, man's highest—his first duty of all. And finally this: It was time for that distinction, hitherto in all our relations shipboard forbidden, to be made, declared, shouted out, gloried in, for us like a ship to come about, strike a directly opposite course. Never even by allusion so far, perhaps saving it, giving voice to that other word but seeming to me, as clear as pennants on the ship's halyards flashing their silent messages, to declare that no loyalty whatsoever existed save there. For what he was truly saying was that not only was there no sin in the procedures they were about to undertake, but that sin lay in the opposite course; that both the men and the women had an obligation to undertake them, that indeed they were to be looked upon as being done in the name of the highest power. Yes, that was it: It was their duty, their responsibility—words sacred to Navy people—their *mission* to do so. Did he actually use those words? I could scarcely say, so mesmerically, so convincingly did his words move over us, enter our souls. As much as saying that if sin were to be spoken of, or morality, it consisted in rejecting this incomparable bounty of having women present that had been our special dispensation, making of us a chosen people, that being all to a purpose. A moral duty: to continue the species first created by that highest power in the morning of time. Nor can I say to this moment whether he used a phrase so explicit. I think not. But nothing could have been more clearly understood.

And so it was. In the blessed and noble name of that endeavor he had given his blessing to the exceptional sexual practices, the trial and error of numerous combinations of men and women, on which our ship's company were about to embark. When he stopped, finished with this avatar of oblique clarity, and a stillness unlike any before, different in character if not in degree from any I had ever experienced, the subdued sea from below the cliffs sounding suddenly like an overloud drumbeat—a stillness seeming active and alive with the slowly awakening understanding on the part of ship's company of what had just been said to them . . . when he finished and simply stopped, I felt a sense of something like exhilaration. If there had been any doubt remaining as to these practices before the Jesuit's speech there was none after it (or almost none, as we were shortly to learn). He clinched it. He had given them his, therefore God's, blessing, and without ever using the latter's name. When he had concluded and they stood speechless looking up at him with that wonder in their faces I knew . . . In those faces not the slightest hint of lasciviousness, light-years from anything like leering, lust, concupiscence, that whole litany of the covetousness of the flesh. I do not wish to be misunderstood here. Neither was there in them the remotest hint of what has been called religious fervor, as scary in itself as the other. There was simply calm acceptance in the most practical sense, of the simplest, sailorlike nature. In what they were about to undertake they were doing no wrong. That was all they had asked for, that reassurance, and the Jesuit had given it to them. I knew we were on our way.

To conclude the ceremonies, Lieutenant Girard stepped forward and in as equable a voice as if she were announcing ship's orders of the day, read the text of "The Women's Conditions"; asked ship's company if any wished to stand aside and not participate. I felt I was holding my breath. One by one, seven men only stood up, including Seaman Barker. I gave a vast inward sigh of relief. And one woman only, Coxswain Meyer. (This of course, by the women's terms, while indicating that they had finally decided to let any woman, as well as any man, decide not to participate, granting Barker and Meyer nothing beyond the continued freedom to dispense with sexual activity altogether, most sternly as between themselves.) Thereupon, again as calmly as if she were reading out watch bills, read the assignments of the various men to the various women of ship's company . . . "To Storekeeper Talley . . . Machinist's Mate Brewster . . ." The readings proceeding like a most proper liturgy. "To Signalman Bixby . . . Lieutenant Bainbridge . . . To Radioman Parkland . . ."

Few men, as I have elsewhere suggested, are more directly acquainted with the effects of sexual deprivation than are ship's captains. Any captain can readily apostrophize to an interested listener the sharp difference, tangible in the very air, between a ship's company which has been six weeks at sea and that same company after three days of liberty in a port such as Naples, New York, or New Orleans, to name but three beguiling cities where that availability has never been in short supply to the seamen stepping foot on their piers. This is far from being an unimportant matter to the efficacy of a ship. Men thus accommodated make for a decidedly better functioning, if occasion arises, gallant ship than men who are not;

more dutiful in their shipboard tasks, less apt in their edginess to make perhaps crucial errors. I would be certain that centuries before psychology "discovered" that the privation under discussion is a primary cause of neurosis, uncounted thousands of sea captains starting before the time of Homer, and without benefit of the terminology, had routinely reached the identical finding.

Now having under my command a ship's company which had undergone such deprivation now going on to eleven months, I was in no way surprised at the dramatic change that occurred as the Arrangement proceeded. In those weeks that followed, a kind of deliciousness reigned in our settlement. A kind of new peace. Properly to understand these matters, one has to remember that the participants had long been shipmates and through as difficult tribulations of the sea as one could readily imagine had been brought to a closeness extraordinary even for that calling. And the fact was this: Without in any way disturbing that bond, they became something else altogether, something as it were grafted onto it: became men and women. This accomplishment was in no way fortuitous. Indeed I believe it was that previous relationship that made it work. At least so far. Jealousy, possessiveness, the feared disturbances that might attend the required mathematics—if these were to arrive at some future date, they had not thus far done so, certainly not in any ostensible way. Another less lofty reason surely coming into play as well: The men had been informed by the very terms of the Arrangement that any expression of these attributes would be grounds for the culprit's expulsion from the Arrangement altogether; he would become a man without a woman. Powerful restraint, this; the women not only having all the power in themselves; all the provisions they had laid down being backed up as well by the full power of Navy authority—represented in myself.

Still, I believe it was the higher concern that was the driving force: the idea that we were all unalterably in this together exactly as we had been for so long in everything and would continue to be for the remainder of our lives, insofar as we could see the future; that we were as attached to one another as is one cell to another in the body's own arrangement, that to cause harm to another was to inflict it on oneself; that a serious deviation in one of us from that dedication, that fixed standard of conduct, in which after all as Navy men and women we were so ingrained, could initiate a terrible tide surge through the entire community, with unforeseen results. I think every hand felt to the deepest part of the soul that individual responsibility. We were brothers; sisters. The subdivision now allowed of being also men, women: It did not disturb the other. The case was just the opposite; it was precisely that bond that made possible with this ship's company what might have had but a finite chance of working with another assortment of human beings. This new thing became but a delight, a very great one, added to the previous idiosyncratic relationship. And if I had to mention one factor above all that was its secret, I would say without hesitation: gentleness. It was accompanied by, embraced in, a great gentleness. Evidenced to myself by, among other signs, the striking fact that the men did not talk about it. I never heard a word from them as to what went on in the cottages, none of that prurient discourse which is not unknown among men having had their experiences with women, most of it also containing sure overtones of vanity. None whatsoever of that. I did not find this strange. It was portion of that respect—that infinite gratitude to them—yes, that something like the worship of women that now pervaded the settlement, in its quiet sort of way; for doing what they were doing; and simply for being what they were: women.

One saw an unmistakable new ease in the faces of the sailors, men and women both, the visible reflection of an inner quietening-down, a newfound and deep-reaching harmony, as they went about their regular duties, whether in the Farm detail under Gunner Delaney or the fishing detail under Boatswain's Mate Silva (both of these men, as it happened, assigned to Operations Specialist Dillon), or the settlement-upkeep detail under Noisy Travis (himself, though, one of the seven abstainers). Men were better, women were better. One felt something else with the women: their absolute sense of being in control. Far from objecting to it, the men appeared to feel that this suzerainty was not only proper: It was the only way the thing would have stood a chance of working.

In addition to my own observations as to these matters I had another source in a position to know to the most precise degree the actual state of affairs: Lieutenant Girard, the leader of the women. In our regular weekly session on supply and morale matters, the subject assuredly falling in the latter category, she reported to me in general terms developments in this area. (We had learned, I should add, in fact did so instinctively, to treat the subject with the calm, seamanlike matter-of-factness with which we dealt with all others, this impulse springing from her particularly in this instance, than for which approach there was nothing I could have been more grateful.) Such as after the Arrangement had been in operation about a month:

"There have been only those two transfers of men from one woman to another," she said one day. This was under the "incompatibility" clause of the Arrangement. "Frankly, I would have expected more."

As before, I was careful to stay out of all this in any detail. I would not have dreamed of asking for names. I left everything concerned with it to her and through her to the women. She had now become absolute commander of the women, their loyalty insofar as they were women transferred to her in a sovereignty as total as my own general sovereignty; perhaps, given that added instinctual women's loyalty to one another that I believe I noted at one point . . . given this to start with and build on, perhaps even more so. In fact, I wished to hear about it as little as possible, though there was no way as ship's captain I could allow myself to be closed off completely from so urgent a matter. I believe she knew this, and accordingly kept the references brief, simply the usual reports as to how matters were progressing. I did interject a word now and then, even the glancing question.

"The morale?"

"It has never been better, sir."

The subject never overtly mentioned now, nonetheless that sense of expectancy hung in the air—it would have been impossible for it not to do so. It would have been unthinkable to broach the matter, to pose specific inquiries; still one waited; knew furthermore that everyone in ship's company, every participant, man and woman, equally waited. Even Bixby making a point of reporting to me as a supposedly unrelated matter the fact that our goats, now doubled to four from their original two and both of them nannies, were in thriving health. One could not ask questions about it. One did not need to do so. The moment it happened Girard would tell me. Nor would she wait for our weekly meeting. She would come to me at once.

As to that inerrable sense of sexual fulfillment all about, manifest as the tall trees, that makes men so different, I must reemphasize the Jesuit's role. What he had done was effectively to remove the monster guilt, which otherwise at the least would have tainted many of those relationships in the twenty-four cottages, indeed made many impossible. It was ship's company coming around to his own view, as I have earlier suggested, that expelled whatever hesitations there may have been about the arrangements (save for the abstaining seven)—and there had been many of these, and probably more in the men even than in the women. (I would be the last to deny that some of our people were quite ready to be converted, some even not requiring such in the least, but many more still at first holding back, uncertain as to the proposed methods, and from what have always been considered the highest of motives.) It was a remarkable personal triumph. He had infused the settlement with his belief, constituting an absolute sanctioning, that not only was there nothing wrong with these procedures but that they embodied the most upright and essential conduct, amounting to nothing less than a clear obligation. Having become persuaded as to that, they could put it out of their minds and have fun. Few fulfillments in life are so rewarding as knowing that the act you are performing is not only one of the highest satisfaction but is also in the glory of a cause and one's duty in the bargain. Not that I believe the Navy men and women, being the quite down-to-earth human beings they were, dwelt on these matters as they went about their pleasures in the cottages. It was rather that what might have been an inhibiting factor was obliterated from their minds so that they could proceed to do what women and men like to do when left alone. I recalled the doc's term employed by him sometime before the activation of the Arrangement: the "intermittent neuroses" with which he described many of ship's company as being from time to time affected. These to all appearances had entirely disappeared, the doc himself so informing me in his wry, somewhat cynical manner: "Now I wonder why?"

And so the weeks went by. With all the beneficences, I am obliged to report that one event occurred to jar us for a time out of them. One woman—Susan Dillon—disappeared from the settlement. The most thorough search of the island, all hands turned out to reconnoiter it inch by inch, turned up nothing. I think all of us in our secret souls presumed—no one, at least insofar as I knew, ever once mentioning this speculation—that she had found herself unable to cope with the Arrangement.

Another thought entered my mind, troubling me. She was an operations specialist, one of the air trackers who monitored our Tomahawks to touchdown at Orel. Like anyone who made it in that job she was a very smart sailor. It occurred to me that she was the second of those, and the only other woman who did that piece of work, to disappear; the other one, Emily Austin, having done so some months back, not long after we came to the island. I pondered. I had another passing thought: Dillon's lovers included Silva, the doc, Selmon, Delaney, Preston.

We were well into the third month of the Arrangement when Lieutenant Girard informed me almost routinely that the women had decided upon and put into effect a change in one of the terms, a kind of codicil added to the original list. Article 2, I believe it was, this stating that no man would be moved from his assigned woman to another more than once, and this for reasons only of incompatibility, and then only at the women's discretion. That day she put the matter to me thus:

"Captain, the women have decided to shift the men around more. From one woman to another. In effect, a rather complete changing about in that respect."

She did not give me the reason. She had no need to do so. I felt pass through from her to me the first distant intimation of concern since the Arrangement commenced. She continued in those emotionless briefing tones.

"Actually, rather simply done. One woman's group moving to another woman; that woman receiving another's; and so on."

"I get the picture," I said, noncommittally, having no desire to hear further details.

"With this new procedure, within a certain time every woman will have been with every man."

"The women want that?"

I had made a dreadful mistake in asking that, and knew it instantly; a stupid and terrible mistake. It had just popped out. I saw something like anger flash from her eyes. Then she waited, not wanting to speak out of that; considerate of myself. When she said it, did so in the most matter-of-fact if quite brisk way.

"All the women want is babies, sir."

"Of course. Forgive my lapse in perception."

Her eyes rested on me in what I felt actually to be a kindly expression.

"I remain very hopeful," she said.

So it was that meantime all hands, men and women both, continued so, rather immensely better for the availability of one another that was by now so fully established as to have become an entirely normal part of the functioning of our community. As I said at the outset, all this came as no surprise. Ship's captains know about these things. There was only one person in the settlement who was not better. The ship's captain.

Inevitably there would drift to me emanations of the most erotic goings-on in those cottages set among the trees. At first enjoying a kind of vicarious happiness in the fact that my ship's company were at last accommodated with the one important thing that had been missing in their increasingly fulfilled lives on the island, this feeling began after a while to transmute itself, by the slowest of degrees and only over a period of time, into something quite different. Like all the men around me I had been able to block out the idea of that emollience with considerable success over the many months of our adversities: besides, we were intensely occupied with matters of survival, which is perhaps the one force

495

that can turn the focus of men away from such a fundamental drive. But now no perils pressed us, no enemies loomed on the horizon, hunger had fled into the distance, we were home free on what was turning more and more into quite a rewarding island, and all these thoughts that normally occupy the mind of an unfulfilled man returned. In my instance, to have these matters proceeding but a few steps away . . . it became difficult. Very difficult. Something intolerable about it. And there was not a thing in the world I could do about it.

To no Navy man will this need explaining. It would simply not have worked for the ship's captain to participate exactly as the other men participated: as one of five or six men—I sometimes lost track of the exact figure—assigned to a given woman. Nothing in it would have worked. There is no law of the sea more ancient, more unforgiving, than the one that proclaims that "fraternization" between a captain and those whom he commands is among the deadliest of traps the life of a ship presents him, however noble the intent, leading ineluctably to a slow diminution of the ship's captain's authority and sovereignty, and thereby eventually to the gravest of consequences, not excepting the putting of the ship herself at hazard. Lonely as he is, even in normal circumstances, a ship's captain is sometimes sorely beset by the temptation to step across that rigid line the sea, knowing all, in its wisdom long ago drew. To do so is folly; the captain who succumbs to it certain to reap, not respect and friendship, but their opposites. It simply does not work with a ship's company, a canon so absolute that no intelligent ship's captain questions it. And this—this ultimate fraternization as it were: It simply could not be. And so it was that I increasingly found myself living in a kind of erotic hell: envisionings, increasing in the particularities of their persecuting vividness, as to all the things going on in the cottages; quite explicit, almost photographic images of the women of my ship's company . . . yes, of Meyer, of Talley, of Garber, of Alice Bixby. At first hard to objectify them as being women as opposed to sailors . . . Then, realizing they were now the former in every sense and to a degree consummate . . . A torment seized me. The names paraded incessantly through my mind . . . the names of the women I had known only as sailors under my command. Then one day the name Lieutenant Girard. And I stopped.

I had almost forgotten: She was the sole woman, save for Meyer, not participating in the Arrangement, just as I was the sole man (except for the seven voluntary abstainers). It was a decision that half-surprised me and half-seemed almost as logical as my own: that as leader of the women, she could not participate, any more than could I as captain of the ship. For exactly the same reason that I could not be one of several men assigned to a woman, she could not be one of the women to whom several men were assigned. For she, too, now held something like a sovereign power, as to the women, and thereby to a large degree over the men. We never discussed it. But each of us feeling I am certain that these roles of ours—commanders—were indispensable to the continued well-being of the settlement, and each knowing that our respective positions of leadership, of authority, of power, of command, would be unacceptably jeopardized by participation.

Girard. Lieutenant Girard. Never using her first name. I had almost forgotten what it was.

At first the very having of the idea profoundly shocked me, and I dropped it instantly. The complications such a relationship would unloose, both as between ourselves and between each of us and ship's company, were so obvious and so almost unlimited in nature that they scarcely need listing. After a while the idea returned. Again, I immediately put it away. It was only to return again, with more force; to be rejected again. This cycle continued, the periods between when I was not thinking of it shortened, the consciousness of the proceedings in the cottages pressing me to the point of agony. I forced my mind to calm, to reason things out; thereby in time reaching a rationale and a conviction that ran somewhat as follows.

I myself needed this to survive, at least survive with all my faculties intact; if I did not survive, the settlement, the island, the ship's company, all that we had accomplished: All this would at the very least find itself at risk. This vanity of a ship's captain, and most particularly of myself, to which I have made occasional reference, may or may not have been based in reality. There may well have been others who could have stepped forward and taken my place and matters to have continued as propitiously as they now were. But that is not the point. The point is that I did not at all *know*—and there was no way to know—that this desirable thing would have eventuated. What I did know was that under my command, we had come through the most testing of events; that under it, the island was functioning as well as does a good ship properly commanded; more, that we were beginning to make not just an acceptable home for ourselves but rather—yes, a good home in which one could sense a growing well-being, seeming ever more to approach a feeling of love for this place. I felt I had had a great deal to do with these achievements. But I was human. Above all I came to feel not just that I had to have a woman but that I had to have this particular one; partly because of what she was, partly because of the fact that the above-delineated strictures concerning fraternization would not be breached in so doing, she being no other man's woman. I was taking no woman from anyone, for if Girard were not to be with me she could be with nobody.

These cogent reasons for taking the fateful step amplified with no difficulty, and began pressing my mind in almost constant iteration. I had to have a woman and no one else to have her. And it had to be one woman, Girard. I had to have Girard and have her alone. By the exact same token, she had to have me, and me alone: There was no one else she could have. The logic seemed impeccable: I took another step in the desired direction. I came to feel that that was owed me, that it was not an excessive reward for having led ship's company through all our terrible hardships from the Barents to this tiny particle sticking up in the great ocean-sea of the Pacific. After all, every other man had a woman. Why was I, who had brought us all to safe harbor, to be the only one denied this solace? By the end of these reasoned processes, proceeding step by step in orderly fashion, I had convinced myself that it would actually be wrong for this thing not to happen.

Having reached this impregnable position, even armed with this library of rationality, I yet knew this: I could not announce my decision to my own ship's company. They might understand and they might not; themselves having to share the other women, why should anyone have a woman all to himself: It was not at all implausible that such a question should arise. Being unalterably determined now to proceed, I had no intention of testing these waters. There was only one problem remaining as to these matters, which I had come, the question itself already decided, to consider almost logistical in nature: It would have to be done clandestinely, somewhere on this tiny island. Precisely where I had not the slightest idea.

Having worked all of this out, having given myself all these wonderfully logical, even lofty reasons to proceed, something else abruptly occurred to me. My God, I thought, all along I had just been assuming things on her part—assuming compliance. Vanity indeed! She might not be in the slightest interested. Especially in myself. For all her being a superb, astute officer, absolutely cool under fire, and professionally congenial, there had always been something withheld, guarded, even forbidding, about Lieutenant Girard, as I have earlier related; something that seemed intentionally to communicate to whomsoever that her personal, inner life was her exclusive possession, strictly off-limits: keep away. It was not inconceivable that she might not even like it at all. I had heard of such women. How stupid I had been to make all these assumptions, almost to take for granted her own willingness! Surely the last woman with whom one should make such a mistake. Nevertheless I would try, at least tentatively explore, with prudence, with infinite caution, ready to draw back instantly if my fingers were so much as singed. There was no one else to try with. I would wait for the appropriate opportunity to make my move; thinking, how calculating, how transcendently devious, I was becoming; nothing in life, my thought was, furthering that quality more than that particular enterprise of supreme self-interest I was about to set my course on.

It happened then; their absence not being noticed until two days after the deed was accomplished, we had been able to calculate, the reason being that the off-days worked out under the watch system we had instituted fell in his case at that time, so that there was another watch on the Lookout Tower, himself not missed. Indeed they must have picked that time to do it, to give them that head start lest we decide to try to overtake them. As for her, her coxswain duties kept her moving about. No one noticed at first. Then Lieutenant Girard brought me the news. Missing also—Number 2 boat. Our boats now all rigged with sails, all coxswains having become adept at sail-powered boating. None more so than these two. We sat in my cabin overlooking the sea they must have hoped would be their highway to somewhere. God knew where.

"The little fools," Girard said; holding everything back.

"Your conscience should be clear, Lieutenant." I was making words. "The system—the Arrangement—would never have worked once any exception was made. You said that yourself. And it was true. It is true."

"Oh, my conscience is clear all right," she said. "But for them to take it to the point of . . . doing what they did."

"Poets and others built their stories around love of that kind—that would test it to that degree."

Her tone was brutal. "To the point of madness, you mean, Captain?"

"Yes, I suppose I do. Not literally. But they say that kind of love makes you do things other people might call crazy. I wouldn't know. Outside my experience. I wonder which suggested it."

"Why Meyer, of course. A selfish little bitch. Both of them. As if bodies were all that important."

Then something appeared to give way for a moment in her. She spoke very tentatively.

"I don't suppose we could take the *Nathan James*—make at least a brief search."

"Leave it, Lieutenant. We can't spare a drop of that fuel. Selfish indeed: how dare they take one of our boats. Takes us down to two." The hardness in my tone real enough. Perhaps, also, in both of us, meant to hold back tears; useless tears.

.6.

LIEUTENANT GIRARD

We had gone there I believe innocently enough. Though committed to its happening, or at least—bearing in mind the great unknown of her own feelings, committed to testing the matter at some point, how I did not know . . . I had not crudely planned it for this specific day. Rather, it being our regular weekly session on supply and morale and now gunnery and missile matters and also a beautiful day, I suggested we conduct business while taking a walk; we had done this before. We proceeded away from the settlement, no particular destination in mind, through the rain-washed foliage, on a course—perhaps something subconscious in that—I had never before taken, toward the northern, least explored part of the island, now moving mostly along the corridor made by the stream bed, that area being clear of the thick growth, the morning sun filtered in soft dazzling shafts through the trees, then after a while up a high hill, hardly knowing the distance we were putting between ourselves and the settlement, realizing with a certain interest and excitement that we were into land-territory certainly neither of us had explored before nor, I believe, had any other of ship's company. It was a considerable climb. On the ascent I marked on my part a notable agility in her lithe body moving upward ahead of me. At last topping the hill, we could see

501

the island narrowing quickly now to a point not far ahead, and we went along the comfortable ridge until we came to its very tip, could go no farther. We stood and looked all around.

Glittering uncounted fathoms down went the sunlight through the waters, translucent far below us, straight down the heights. The view was a lookout's dream. It was, we could now tell, the island's highest point. There was hardly a place on the island that did not boast its discrete perspective, but this seemed from the island's sharp narrowing here like a ship's prow—one felt a strong wind would have blown you right off it—and from the elevation, the prince of all views. The sea near circumferential, seeming to come straight at us in a vast plain of turquoise, almost as if we were not on land at all but on a tall ship, sails unfurled and breasting the waters. Turning, a haunting prospect across all the bursting green of the island, and most especially straight down both its shores. The singularity being that the contrasts between the two sides were simultaneously visible from here as surely at no other vantage point, so marked as to make it difficult to believe one was on the same island; one side presenting that familiar fierceness of aspect, the other a sonnet of gentleness. To the west, the high cliffs plunging straight to the sea and stretching as far southerly as the island itself, seeming unapproachable; to the east, the land softly sloping to the white-sand beach reaching to the end of the island on that side, indeed to the Farm on the southernmost tip; the Farm, faraway, we could not see from here; no more could we see the least sign of the settlement on the western shore. It was a place of infinite solitude, at once glorious and the loneliest place that ever was, so untouched as to speak of the beginnings of time, no sense of life anywhere, only the eternal sea and a precious green island, flung up it seemed to adorn the immensity of the waters. Standing there, virtually encircled by the great waters, we seemed the only two creatures in the universe. We did not speak; it was as though the place forbade it. Stood I think a rather long time, in the stillness; a sense of time stopped, ourselves some sort of permanent statuary planted on this peak, the invasion of a sense of phantasm, as if attempting to divine what we never could; consisting, it seemed to me, in this incomprehensible strangeness of our standing there, not as of this particular day, but standing there at all, the mystery reaching back in time to our own origins far away, as human beings, to childhood, to youth, to lands called Oklahoma and North Carolina, to places called Annapolis and Wellesley, these very names now seeming ancient artifacts: What in the world had ever brought us here? Why? Felt this in myself, felt I was by no means alone in feeling it; that rare certainty of a given thought of oneself's being known identically, simultaneously, to one's companion. Startled to hear actual speech: "Why don't we have a look down there?"

The westerly cliffs, perhaps influenced by the nearby eastern sandy shore, seemed less forbidding here, not nearly so steep as a bit further down . . . indeed, before I knew it she was starting down this declivity, myself following, until we stood on an apron of beach, as if the western shore wished to edify us with the fact that it too could have one of these, and of fine white sand as well, where we now stood; if not much of one in size. The sea slid in with a whisper. We turned and scanned the cliff just above us and she saw it.

"Look up there!" she said, a girlish excitement in her voice.

Her leading, we climbed up the rocks until we stood on the ledge, not high at all above the sea. It was as though it was a porch for the sea. And for the thing she had had a glimpse of below. The cave that opened immediately behind it.

I followed her into it, not much surprised at finding it there. Islands and caves: They went together in my mind; the dozens of islands of the Mediterranean I had visited during my Naples tour of shore duty. I could remember none absent of caves; some always underwater; more, such as this one presently turned out to be, belonging half to the land, half to the sea. It was low to the water. Evidence, in fact, that at high enough tides the sea actually entered the cave, and if high enough, put it entirely under water. Fresh encrustations, barnacles, on its walls. We explored eagerly around. High enough to stand up in, most of it, and quite roomy. Tides, too, further manifested by the smoothness of the floor of gray rock. We moved into it, the cave going deeply enough that we soon found ourselves in darkness, or near-darkness, and I wished for a flashlight. We came back out into the sunlight and sat down at its entrance, on the porchlike ledge, and looked at the sea, hearing its low throb on the cliff stretching to the southwest. The cave seemed to delight, to excite her, its discovery, to bring a flush to her cheeks. She was wearing Navy work clothes, dungarees, shirt, and had picked up one of the baseball-type caps that were used by the trackers at their computer screens to protect them from flashing images on missile-launch; fair hair emerging from underneath. We sat talking comfortably.

"That cave, for some strange reason. I get the feeling there have been people here," she said. "Sometimes when I'm walking through the forest, too. Almost as if there still are. People watching me from within all that darkness."

"Yes, I've had that too. Perfectly natural, I'd think. If kind of spooky. But I believe we're the first. We've seen no evidence."

A long and comfortable silence; no compulsion to fill the stillness with words; watching the sea, turning all argentine now under a climbing sun. By habit, when with her, no one aboard more identified in my mind with the well-being of ship's company than herself, keen to its changes, its nuances, alert as a ship's lookout for signs of danger, after a time my soft, almost routine probing.

"Well, Lieutenant. Do you think the men are becoming resigned to . . . that this is it, this island . . . that we're here to stay?"

She waited, careful and precise as always in these matters. "More so all the time, I'd say. Partly the island and its goodness. Partly, what other choice is there? Except of course for that small party of men we've talked about that hangs on to there being life, habitability, back there. I sometimes think even some of them are changing."

Then I was surprised. She asked me something of a kind she never had, our talk always excluding questions the least personal in nature; some of that breached of late. Quietly, the tones of reflection seeming to take us, now somehow natural, perhaps having something to do with where we were.

"Yourself? Are you content to live out your life here?"

"I'm getting there. Anytime I get a little restless, I remind myself of all that dark and cold we went through. That awful contamination. Just thinking of it, I sometimes breathe it. Then I feel very good to have the island."

And yet again, coming on in those same quiescent tones, the susurrant sea on the rocks its backdrop. I sometimes thought her voice was the best thing about her; I had never heard it shrill, heard it raised. I had heard it tough, coming down hard. Now a touch of conversational curiosity.

"What do you miss?"

"There isn't all that much to miss, for me."

She hesitated, as if uncertain as to my meaning. Then:

"You didn't have anyone?"

"Not really."

She seemed to pause a moment. "Didn't you ever miss that?"

This was different. She was coming very close to my own self.

"I used to—now and then. Now I'm damned glad. When I look at some of the others—wives, children. I think how much easier it is for me. They're the ones who have it rough. I've very grateful not to have anyone. All alone. And you?"

"There was someone. I'm sure there isn't anymore."

High up and far away, gossamer cirrus had begun to streak the skies. Now I did move away from it. "Mostly what I miss is the ship. Being at sea. All I ever had. All I ever wanted." I laughed shortly. "I wish we could take the *James* for some runs. Some very short runs I'd settle for, even just around the island. I miss her, miss that." I sighed. "We can't."

"The fuel, you mean."

"We daren't expend a drop. If we should ever be forced out of here . . . Very remote. Even Selmon says that. Whatever was going to happen has happened. So he judges. Still with qualifications. You know Selmon. So we still have to have that reserve." I looked out to the horizon. Earlier merging synchronously with the sea, it now had begun to establish its own distinct line. "Of course, what I would really like is to have a five-year-fueled ship under me and take her around the world—to see with my own eyes what happened."

"You have doubts as to that?"

"Not really. I come down on the idea that—at the most—there are a few scattered clusters of human beings—somewhere. I'd kind of like to see where—and if. Talk with them. To find out. When I knock off the mooning, mostly I know this: These few miles of island—we'll always be here."

"Yes," she said, like an echo of finality. "We'll always be here. I'd like to see us fifty years from now."

"A number of children running around. Grandchildren . . . Reminds me: That project, all hands, putting down everything they know or remember. How does it go?"

A quick interest felt from her like a spark. "We'll be starting it next week in the Main Hall. I've talked with a number of the men—the women. You can't believe how eager they are for it, excited. They got right with it. Its importance. The women will be doing most of the work. Classifying the material—subject matter—history, skills, the rest. We're getting all organized for it. It's going to be good. What a nice big project! They want very much to do it. Excited by what exactly they'll be putting down. They understand it. We're about to turn into a community of writers."

"It's for the children, of course."

"Yes, for the children."

We were using the word as if it were a sure thing when we knew there were problems; maybe, both of us, feeling that saying it would make it happen.

I hesitated. "The men, you said, feeling better about the island. It's the women have made all the difference." Hurried on from that lest she think I was fishing for details, was prying into an area we had agreed should be reserved for themselves, and for her. "But I felt it before that. The beginnings at least of an acceptance—to live out their lives on this island. The women, too?"

It was quite otherwise. She seemed almost to welcome the subject of the women.

"I would say the women most of all. Any talk of going back—it's almost disappeared with them. Of course, not a one of them had ties of marriage, or children. They're like you in that. And me," she added. "I've come to consider it fortunate they don't."

"I hadn't thought of that. Yes, indeed. Extremely fortunate."

"And, of course, they're a coping lot. They wouldn't have got to sea in the first place if they weren't. I used to resent it like hell the way the Navy made it so damn deliberately tough, for me, for every one of them. I look back and say, Thank God. It took a lot of—something—in a woman to tough her way out through that. They handle things. Like right now. The way they're handling what we always thought would be such a problem."

I was surprised, even astonished—not at this recitation of the women's qualities, save only that she knew long since how entirely I agreed with such a characterization—but at what seemed a readiness, even an eagerness, to speak with such a direct reference to a subject on which we had so carefully refrained from being remotely explicit. Perhaps again it was simply being away from the formalities of our usual morale-and-supply session in my cabin.

"No one thought so more than myself," I said. "I was never more glad to be wrong."

I would not probe further. It seemed to me we had gone quite far enough, certainly further than we had ever before ventured. She would continue or she would not. I felt almost that she was debating with herself whether or not to do so. A sense also of an almost irresistible desire on her part to talk about it. I kept silent, making sure to do nothing to encourage her. It would have to be her choice. She took off her baseball cap and shook her hair back, the slanting sunshine seeming quick and eager to catch its own clean lights.

"You'd have to say they're pretty resourceful," she said. "Wouldn't you?"

"Lieutenant, I'd have to say they were just about anything you want to call them."

She spoke now in tones of philosophy, as if come upon a subject which it might be exceptionally interesting to explore, and by no means

506

yet exhausted; dispassionately discoursing on some striking experiment in human relations.

"I sometimes wonder if having all those qualities that brought them to sea . . . I wonder if there could be any connection between those and possessing what I would call . . . well, let us say, a generally high sexual quotient."

"Sexual quotient? An interesting phrase. If I understand it, I am glad to hear they possess it. It must help. But I would be out of my depth to express an opinion, Lieutenant."

"You don't mind if I express one?" she said, the first faint touch of tartness, so I felt, in her voice, almost of impatience with such a dull conversationalist. "Everybody, of course, has a sexual quotient, quite like everyone has an intelligence quotient."

"You educate me, Lieutenant."

She wriggled around on the rock, changing position, coming to rest cross-legged.

"I think my theory has a certain validity. These women particularly seem to me distinctly to enjoy it."

This statement constituted such a quantum step beyond anything we had ever got near as to snap my wits all alert, looking within myself and closely pondering. Her tone itself seemed to change at least to a nuance, now in it something like a wry, faintly mocking gaiety, if I were any judge of speech tones. But I remained baffled, in my uncertainty continuing to take refuge in commonplaces.

"Again we are fortunate," I said. "Beyond words."

"Do you like Conrad?"

"Love him."

"Conrad is what made me go to sea as much as almost anything. It was his doing. I probably wouldn't be sitting here otherwise. He has a line somewhere, one I always considered very funny and I'm sure he didn't. 'Women have always been a sailor's chief distraction.' I remember bursting into laughter when I first read that. So nice, clean, unequivocal. A model of a simple declarative sentence. I wondered then why he used the word 'sailor.' I was still a landsman. I understand now." She spoke with a certain sportiveness, and as if intent on pursuing this rather recondite subject whether I so wished or not, indeed almost as though spurred on by my reluctance. "I wonder if it could be turned around now. 'Sailors have always been a woman's chief distraction.' These women seem not to have any problem dealing with what normally would be judged an oversupply. Wouldn't you think so, Captain?"

"About the women not having a problem?"

"No, dummy. About there being what would normally be considered an oversupply."

The appellation slipped right by me. "The fact would be unarguable, Lieutenant."

She had never remotely talked so much, or so specifically, about the women, come anywhere so near to their emotions and their feelings as to the task that had been set before them. And she had not finished.

"Women are a lot more explicit then men in these matters," she said. She tossed her hair again, a rather pert, self-delighting gesture; it put me in mind of the best colt I had ever had, as a boy, who loved doing that with its mane; he very much knew his own mind; maybe the gesture went with the quality. "I think most men would be shocked to hear women talk among themselves. Learn a thing or two."

I was suddenly aware of a new, tangible aura to her; some instinctive, sassy, lofty, unabashed yet curiously soft air of femininity and confidence; an air of total assurance, as if she knew who she was and what she had.

"Again you educate me, Lieutenant."

I watched the sea. It seemed to be making up a bit, my nose detecting the approach of wind. I was wondering how far the water entered the cave on the high tide. I had the impression that my silence, or the brevity of my replies, my lack of questions, my absence of at least expressed curiosity, irritated, almost exasperated, her and that she had made up her mind, by God, to do something about it.

"Screwing several men at a time—I don't mean *at a time*—with that frequency. Well—it's all right. Not all that big a deal. That comes through loud and clear. Isn't that interesting? I've asked myself whether that would have been the case with just any men." The tones of the academy had returned, inward-turned, reflective, as if making a serious study of the matters in which she was so intimately involved. "I don't think so. So perhaps I'm giving the women too much credit. Perhaps it's because it's these men; men they've known such a long time; men they *like.*" That tone abruptly left behind, another, which I could only describe as an amused bawdiness, appearing. I felt myself being outdistanced, scarcely able to keep up. "Anyhow, they *talk* about how each man is different and they *like* very much talking about it. How they go on and on! How the fucking is different. One man from another. Some of it can be pretty funny, even to themselves. Sometimes I've wished you could be there to hear, Captain. I mean, hear them talk about fucking different men. What a pretty sky—those cloud-strips."

I think by now I knew; even my own denseness as to the ways of women having its limits. Perhaps at first having the sliver of a stupid thought that this was all calculated to torment myself, realizing quickly that she would be the last person on earth to do just that—she would have been contemptuous of such an effort; aware that it was something else altogether. And I had actually considered as to how I might go about approaching her! Appalled at my imbecility, witlessness, seeming now little short of cretinism, at my forgetting the one thing at least I knew about women if patently I knew little else: They are in control, in these matters; they always are. Especially this one would be. Above all, overwhelmed with this one thought: What I had at first judged out of character for her: I could not have been more wrong. It was exactly what she would have done to get what she wanted; and if there was anything in character for her it was that: to get what she wanted. Having reached the point all along intended, she finished off.

"Of course, I get pretty randy myself sometimes listening to them. As a matter of fact . . ."

I had been looking rather fixedly at the sea, turned to say I knew not what, and realized she was no longer there. She had disappeared into the cave, into the darkness where I could not see her. I started to follow; waited. Had there been any doubt, I must have known then; known from the accelerated beat of my heart; from a trembling that seemed to go through all my body; from that anticipation, that annunciation, that is like no other, though long it had been since I had experienced it. Waited until from the cave, I heard from a person I could not see, the low words seeming to reach me as an echo pressed out from the cave walls. "Why don't you come in, Captain?"

Her body struck as though a representation on canvas, achieving that richness of tangible alabastrine flesh seemingly known only to the brush of an extraordinary painter, more lifelike than life itself, where she sat back, spread-out dungarees and shirt her pallet, hands clasped around her drawn-up knees, all her whiteness unbroken from her wheat-light hair until it reached that other small analogous bouquet just visible in the curved-in position, one aware of firm hard breasts, with nipples mauve against the white, erect simply from herself being looked at that way (in the painting, by the painter). She spoke very quietly, a faint resonance from the cave walls.

"If we start this, we'll never stop it," she said. "We'll never stop fucking."

There was something clean and brutal about the words as she said them, and hopelessly truthful.

"You should have thought of that before you took your clothes off,

Lieutenant. In fact, before you started talking about it. Don't talk to me about stopping anything," something in me desiring to give back that clean brutality of her own.

I took off my clothes and looked at her, as I was aware she was at me. A meticulous, almost dispassionate kind of scrutinizing one was aware of in her, hard and absolute in intent, one's own not unlike, a sense of unrestrained ravishment seeming to fill the cave. A body made to have love made to it. My own body trembling slightly in a wave of lust. I was sticking straight out, even to myself seeming impossibly, almost comically huge, oversized. She brought a hand up and touched for a moment, response a quick jumping, the thing with an intent quite all its own, hand moving to mine and drawing me down alongside her, atop the dungarees and the shirt—the brassiere and, myself quickly noticing these almost fondly, our dwindling supplies in such items, the mended panties. Then only the unleashed ravenousness. Her lips, her hair, beneath her arms, very slowly all around her breasts, her nipples; everywhere; aware as from a distance of a long low keening beginning to come from her. How good she tasted! First the scent of fresh apples, then as arousal grew, the cunt smell, to me so identical to the smell of the sea, not just between her legs (the roseate lips, the astonishing wetness flowing from her, pubic hair, thighs all dampened), but from her mouth, from everywhere, the modulation from the one scent to the other wild and dizzying. The unwithheld availability of that body still a kind of disbelief, the compulsive, selfish single purpose of a starved man. Welcomed between her thighs, her hands clawing, pressing my head into her, the long continuing moans merging like counterpoint with the rhythm of the sea touching the rocks, where I felt I might never have stopped my rituals of gluttony had those hands not pulled me away almost violently; onto her, into her, the long deep everlasting plunging to another medley of now fiercer sounds until screams broke against the cave walls, fell out over an unhearing sea.

In her arms I wept, herself stroking my hair, my face. Tears of release from terrible burdens, impossible loneliness.

Which of the two of us it was that first spoke that simple truth, and how much later, I do not know. In the long, now unhurrying times before it, we had done many things with each other; made love over and again until at last the raptness of satiation arrived. Perhaps it was said simultaneously (as two conspirators with the absolutely identical purpose will instinctively arrive at the identical instant at the identical conclusion). At least it was known simultaneously. As a fact nonnegotiable. If there was risk—and I don't believe either of us felt at first that there was that much, both of us confident of our own joint ingenuity to be able to hide it—the risk was one of those that come along in life that simply have to be accepted. This not all that difficult, a ship's captain being accustomed to these, a temper of the will toward the taking of risks; she, I knew long since, possessed of this same quality.

And so it was, not just that we first made love, but that we knew at once that we would continue to do so. Even falling back, in extremis, on the possibility that if the others found out they would not only accept it, but understand it; less sure of this conclusion than of the other, that we could not in any case, whether understanding or something very different were to be forthcoming from them, go on without having each other.

It was around then that Lieutenant (jg) Rollins, our ASWO, disappeared. This time it was as though everything in the settlement came to an abrupt halt. Again we made a meticulous search of the island, all hands participating. Again nothing turned up. This time we thought hard and long, all of us. A distinct sense of alertness began to take hold of the settlement. Gathered in my cabin: Girard, the doc, the Jesuit, Selmon, Thurlow. Myself remembering a talk with her on a night by the lifeline in the Mediterranean: how she had given up ballet on realizing that she would never go to the absolute top; gone into the Navy both to be among the first women to go to sea and to escape (she had exceptional physical beauty) hassling about marriage, which, for a reason she had not disclosed, she wished never to have.

Girard: "I hadn't noticed a thing. I think she'd been gone a couple days when we checked her cottage. She wasn't seeing men—her period."

Captain: "Father, I have to ask this. Rollins was a Catholic. Was she . . ."

The Jesuit anticipated the question. "Negative, sir. As to whether she had a problem dealing with the situation, I'd say the answer was a categorical no. I may be out of line both with my Maker and everyone else here but I think I'd better say it: I'd say she rather enjoyed it."

A kind of mild surprise not at this experience of a given woman but at the articulation of it, especially from that source.

Captain: "Doc?"

Doc: "Rollins? Nobody healthier, Skipper. Took quite a long swim every day as everyone knows. Probably the best swimmer we have."

Captain: "Drowning possible? Overextending?"

Doc: "Outside chance. Still, even very good swimmers . . ."

Captain: "Anything to add, Mr. Selmon?"

Selmon: "Nothing much, sir. I think most of us felt she was rather introspective." He gave a small laugh. "Not that that's necessarily a negative quality. I'm introspective myself. But I did see her now and then taking those long walks of hers up along the cliffs. All alone."

I looked once more around that circle of officers. We had got exactly nowhere. Yet something seemed to hang in the air that I could not put my finger on.

"That's all for now. Oh, Miss Girard."

"Sir?"

"For a starter, from now on I want you to have someone check every one of the women's cottages every day, and report to me that it's been done."

"I'll check them myself," she said, a grimness in her tone.

I was about to break it up when Thurlow spoke. "I agree with Mr. Selmon about the introspection part. I think something was bothering her. What, I don't have a clue."

For some reason I gave the navigator an extra look. Something . . . maybe it was only that he was one of her lovers.

.7.

THE CAVE

Two calm conspirators we had become and in almost ruthless planning—her seeming more ruthless as to it than myself—set about weaving our cocoon of deception. We would meet at this same place once a week; we dared not risk more. At a time to be varied. Finding our way there separately. Returning separately, my waiting a half hour by my watch after she had gone, taking a different route. It was a great conspiracy. We flirted with immeasurable risk. There was no helping it. Once, afterward, my head lying in her lap, I voiced mildly a concern of discovery.

"If they find out?" I said.

"Let them. We'll simply tell them we decided to have what they have."

"I'm not sure that explanation will go over very big. There's a difference. One on one, I believe it's called."

"Don't worry," she dismissed that. "Nothing's going to happen." She seemed to be consoling, reassuring me, at the same time a tone of warning—not for myself, but for absent others—in her voice. "If it does, just let me handle it. If they make a problem of it, I'll tell them they can't have it anymore. I and the women: we'll simply shut everything down. I promise you results."

I burst out laughing.

"What in the world are you laughing at, Captain?" We now used these forms of address mockingly.

"You, Lieutenant. You know, I believe you would."

She seemed astonished. "Sometimes I don't understand you at all. Of course I would. I don't like being messed with. Except by yourself. But why are we wasting all this time talking and fancifying when we should be fucking?"

She somehow made the words both comical and highly incitatory, and used them, not often, but as she pleased. The undiluted girlishness— the impudent, brazen womanness. Perhaps on my part something, too, of an amused delight in the unexpectedness of all this after our countless hours together in our naval relationship, where if I had heard one of those words in that other incarnation I so constantly dealt with, intimations in the slightest of such a great hidden female desire resident in her, I would probably have fainted dead away in shock; her also, I think, in that so precise knowingness which never missed a beat, entirely aware of all this in me; perhaps in part a consequent delight of her own in displaying these qualities. Above all, the lightness some secret wisdom of hers, the magic key, as if a somber undertaking was the last thing in the world lovemaking should be, that the fatal flaw of so much of it. Literally the first time in my life for this kind of prolonged physical relationship; I who had had no love save that of the sea; who had never given myself in this way to a woman: feeling myself launched now on some undiscovered and sweetest of all oceans, endless in the diversity of its delights, proceeding over ever-changing horizons, seeming to take possession of one's heart, mind and soul, all one was; shuddering in a kind of terror-struckness that I might have gone through life never knowing this. Perhaps I was learning but the most banal things, nonetheless to myself all-astonishing. Most of all the mysterious transforming power of good lovemaking as to every part of one's life: One sees the clouds in the sky differently, the very stars of night take on a new aspect. To be sure, a slavery of a kind, as I was well aware: judging myself quite independent as men go, now much dependent on her, reaching a point that I could not have imagined life without the times in the cave. Yet feeling it to be a fair exchange: lovemaking's slave recipient of lovemaking's gift available nowhere else; above all, a peace of a kind never known to me. Curious that peace's wellspring should be the most abandoned giving of our bodies to each other; physical sensations so intense that I had not known even of their existence; once found in a given woman, I could readily understand why men killed for them.

Learning, too, why women are not interchangeable, why if it is to be of the highest, it is to be of but one, the pure luck in finding her scary. The secret woman I had now discovered—the lightheartedness, the marvelous tenderness—and altogether the gloriously, avariciously wanton female . . . in her, none of this, I came to see, the least in conflict with that other shrewd, immensely proper, Navy-professional, rather fortressed woman I had known so long. Perhaps that is woman's ultimate specialness: to be both, one to the world, the other, although also to him, not so much to a man as to herself alone.

"How can one so young know so much?"

"Just a born gift, I suppose," she said airily. "Since I haven't done it all that much. Not with that many men. And not as many *times* with any as this. With you."

"How many?"

"How dare you ask such a thing. Actually . . ." Thinking. "One, two, three . . ." Thinking back. "Well, kind of three and a half. Not that it's any of your business."

"Is that all?"

"All. Altogether, Captain. Do you want the details?" Then pertly, insistently, "How many for you?"

"You'd be surprised. I've been most of my life at sea. As you know—ships."

"Yes, I know all about ships. What a con man you are. And I also know about ports."

"Not for me. Very, very little. I was too much of a coward."

"How *many?*" Very insistently. "You asked me and I told you. Fair's fair. I won't let you touch me there anymore unless you tell me. I won't let you put your cock in me ever again unless you tell me. At once. You like my saying those things?"

"Approximately six," I said.

"I'm certain you're lying. If not . . . Only six! For a man of your age."

"I'm aware of that great disparity. I very much regret that I'm not twenty years younger and that I have not had sixty women."

"I suppose I have to work with what I have. I can't really say why I'm so good at it," she said blithely. "There *is* a saying you haven't really fucked until you've done it with a North Carolina girl."

"A saying I imagine invented by a North Carolina girl."

"I have a saying of my own. Would you like to hear it? I don't feel I've been fucked properly unless I've been sucked first."

"In that case, as you were . . ."

We had long times in the cave. Sometimes after our lovemaking taking a nap, falling asleep with the scent of her hair against my face, waking to find her alongside, some priceless surprise gift, granting myself the luxury of studying her while she slept, as if to imprint her in me, almost as though should anything ever take her away I would have her remembered flesh; gazing on that exquisitely made body, its clean radiance heightened by lovemaking, its young freshness, slender and cool, now in sleep all languorous, innocent; incredulous that it should be there all accessible to me, her very skin luminous and gleaming, scented with itself; a great tide of desire returning, before bringing her awake by the gentlest touch, whatever might occur, lips brushing arising nipples, hand placed flat on her pubic hair—and then we were beginning all over again.

Never would I have imagined the intense sensuality that outward manner of her concealed; how little we know of others, especially, I would think, those of us who think we know so much. A cognate voracity, these rituals, anarchic, a species of lascivious adoration on both our parts, an elegance in her eroticism. A temper for exploration, finding corresponding preferences. For herself, the long and tantalizing devotion there until I felt I might go through the roof of the cave before came the engulfing, the explosion, the harvest of white entering her mouth, by no means finished, the greedy continuing. I was put in mind of a quite elegant cat. For my part, never so ravenous as when knelt between those white thighs with that wondrous adornment, commencing that prolonged homage, appropriation, that intemperance, tasting her inner thighs all dampish, that proximate and softest of all women's flesh where wet stray hairs now clung, face buried exultantly in the fullness of her pubic hair, conscious throughout of the muted sounds, the soft writhing, of intense felt pleasure, not until the wetness flowed out in such sweet-tasting offertory actually letting my tongue first touch that place, that cunt, I had come to worship, bringing a spasm, a sound animallike from her, accompanied always by that gesture of her urging hands on my head, the prodigal liquescence with its sea smell filling my mouth, smearing my face, a substance so wonderful I would bring it to her mouth that she might know what it was that so drove me wild, my moistened fingers, having momentarily entered her for that purpose, now sucked avidly by her. I could never have enough of it, not leaving off until herself, able to stand no more, pulled me away for that other urgent conjunction, those complementary vibrations, that high paroxysm. Collapsing afterward into each other's arms, our bodies endewed with all the various wetnesses of us both, with sweat, with her cunt, with the come from myself strewn like white filigree across her belly, over her face, from another time, perhaps an hour, a half hour before. Our bodies sticking against each other's, the wonderful and pungent, long-lost smells of sex permeating the cave.

Always afterward she held to me as tightly as it seemed one could, clutching at me, a ferocity of clinging, sometimes drawing slivers of blood; then, more softly, all quietened, nestling into me like a child or some young animal seeking refuge, myself holding her close, close as could be, as if to furnish all the shelter and reassurance she might ever need from whatever it was she might fear. Fear of loneliness surely, fear of uncertain years ahead on this distant shore, fear that if we let go of each, the other might somehow slip away; for all of these I, too, felt for myself, holding all that warmth of her, all loneliness, all restiveness, all despair, ceasing as I did.

All the while we had been unfolding to each other and it was at times like this I began to realize not just physically; some species of emotion I had never known: an overwhelming compulsion toward all of her; a tenderness in which lust came to be alloyed with a feeling almost spiritual of tremendous protectiveness toward her; a determination to see that no pain, no hurt should reach her. I thought then how much I liked her as a person; her mind as free of sophistry as a mind could be, garnished with a fine mischievousness; capable of cunning but not of meanness; perhaps overimpatient with rank stupidity, yet as caring a person as I had known through all our travails, sailors calmed by her very presence; her tough courageous grace; myself overtaken with that old and great apotheosis that truth and beauty were somehow indivisible, one; suddenly aware that I had never been as happy as I was at that moment. Awakening her then in some chosen way to make love again. This time . . . Only the sounds of the sea reaching us from outside the cave; our lovemaking conducted to the most widely varying accompaniments; sometimes the lowest of murmurings; sometimes, the sea making up, a wild crashing of the waves on the rocks below the ledge. Always followed, too, that lightness she had, perhaps to slide off from the intensity of what we had just done, a lightness for me as well as for herself.

"My Jesus. What did we ever do before this. I'm like an animal in heat. But every time."

"A very elevated sexual quotient. You may require several men. Perhaps you should join the Arrangement."

"I regret that my elevated position forbids that."

"Your position is not very elevated right now."

And like a young girl talking of lollipops: "What a nice way to be awakened. Are you permitted to keep a secret?"

"Anything said in this cave."

"That time—through the dark and the cold—the women. Starting at Bombay . . . down through the Sunda Sea. Stopped just like that, when we came out of it into the Indian Ocean, into the sunlight . . ."

"Well, I'll be damned. I once suspected. Thought I was a damned fool. All of the women?"

"All of them. I don't believe a single one of us had ever done it before."

"Yourself, too, then?"

"Oh, yes."

"Meyer, Bixby, Garber . . ."

"All. Every one." She waited a moment, a faintly poignant tone: "It was a comfort. Pulled us through."

"I'm very glad of it," I said.

"It wasn't bad. But it wasn't this."

The secret life established, back in the settlement our relationship was as it had always been. As in nothing else one has great faith, sometimes excessively so, in one's ability to dissimulate in these matters; even so, I felt that no other knew. We had one scare. Once Silva's fishing detail approached more northerly than I had ever known it to do, still a couple of miles away across the water, a dot resting on the ocean; we retreated into our cave. Soon the whaleboat came about, started southerly again. We did not again see it make any visible incursion that far. I never believed that she believed the reassurance she had expressed, that it would go anything like that easy for us if discovered. One of our conversations— she had given that rather self-mocking laugh she had—making mention of the Jesuit.

"Would you believe it? He had the nerve to suggest to me his unhappiness that I was not participating in the arrangement. Even made a comment about my having such a healthy young body."

I took a look along her. "He was right about that."

"If I hadn't been taught differently about those people when I was a child I'd have told him I would join the Arrangement when he did."

"I'll explain to him that it is not entirely going to waste."

She was more somber. "I'll be honest. If the women found out . . ." She took a deep breath. "They'd have such a case against me . . . well, I simply have no idea where I'd stand with them any longer."

I could see now real concern—deep, true concern. For myself I refused to think about it. One takes the risk: then to worry about it, one should never have taken it in the first place.

Great sex. Yes, just that, and that enough. And equally it came to be, the simple holding quite as good as anything else, perhaps the best part of all. Saying nothing for long times. Then a curiosity each of the other, as to details, particulars in the other's life, breaking quietly through; her head in the curve of my shoulder.

"What would you have done if it had never happened. And you'd never read Conrad?"

"Straight back to Berryville, North Carolina; to take over my father's newspaper. I was smeared with printer's ink from the time I was five; hanging around the place; working there from about nine. Setting type to start with. That was all I ever wanted."

"To be a small-town newspaper editor?"

"I'd have been a good one."

"I believe that."

"I don't know if there's anything better to be. That and going everywhere: I would always have done that. 'Faraway places with strange-sounding names.'"

"That's close to mine I'd say. Sea life. Not quite the same though. The sea more important than the places to me."

"But both: to go over the next horizon."

"Oh, yes. That was the most important part of all. To go over the next horizon."

I waited a moment. "One of them in the Navy being in your case . . . Well, you got what you always wanted. Combat systems officer."

"Not that it means anything anymore. But still I'm glad. I got the damned title if nothing else. Also to do my own refresher course aboard on them—the guns, the missiles. The missiles," she repeated, a meditative layer in her voice, as though trying to probe a riddle. "I'm like that goddamned Chatham in that. Always fussing around with them. Checking, rechecking, making sure everything's all right. Over and over again. God knows why." I knew she had been spending more time on the ship. "It's almost a relief after dealing with the women. At least the missiles don't talk back to you."

"They won't ever talk to anybody again, thank God."

She seemed pensive, as if that had raised a question. "So it makes one wonder what they're still doing there, doesn't it?" The other, rather bright tone back. "But they do get to you. I understand Chatham a little better now, I'll say that. That high and mighty air he always carried around. Sense of such a fantastic power they give you. One gets a bit . . . well, obsessed. *Très curieuse.* Third year in France. Children love firecrackers? They're never very far away in my mind. I still feel that key on a lanyard under my pillow every night in the cottage. Right through the pillow."

All this time I had been listening with only half an ear, much more attentive to something that had become a habit with me, a ritual esthetic, almost beautified in nature, that rather somber contemplation of her nude body as one might contemplate some painting of extraordinary beauty, in a rather analytical, dispassionate fashion, simply looking at it, not even dreaming that one could touch it, such an act being on the order of touching a Caravaggio in the Metropolitan, instant arrest by one of those alert-eyed guards always hanging so innocently about; the visualness become a supreme delight, the engrossed wonder at that great mystery of how here was the source of both an exaltation and a healing to be found nowhere else on earth, nothing remotely competing with it; in fact here what life was all about, I was coming to believe, anything else increasingly seeming a waste of time, or at best only time to be got through in order to get to what alone was important, this sight alongside me one would have thought reserved for the eyes of angels; all this, as I gazed, inspected, seeming absolutely apart from any carnality. I thought I may have missed her last words.

"What did you say?"

"Nothing." Bright tone now half-impudent. "Just about my key being under my pillow. That's where I keep it."

"You're not supposed to tell me that," I said, keeping my attentiveness and my concentration where they were. What long and lovely thighs, elegant, unflawed, all of a whiteness whose richness of texture seemed to reach into, tear at one's soul in a glory almost painful, and as tangibly as that in the great painting, crowned by a flaxen diadem.

"Delaney knows it's there. And Thurlow knows where yours is. Anyhow what difference does it make now? If none of us has gone bonkers by now, none of us is going to."

"I suppose you're right."

"Then turnabout." Sensed distantly in my other fixation, something almost teasing in her voice. "Where's yours?"

Now what unfailingly happened in this liturgy, the esthetic, intellectual contemplation beginning to give way, or rather to announce its imminent conjunction with something quite other. When that occurred, I had discovered, the very best about to be. The guards had left the room.

The impossible realization that one could actually . . . My fingers touched the inside of them, lightly as one might touch a bird's wing, hoping it would not fly away.

"In that breadfruit tree," I said, rather absently, as if answering a child's question. "Just outside my cabin."

She gave an abrupt laugh, itself like a child's laugh of delight: playing hide and seek.

"In a breadfruit tree. Just imagine. The tree of the knowledge of good and evil."

"What?"

"Nothing. Sunday School class."

Her voice came to me as from far away, strangely reflective. "Got the title. Got the control. One-half the control. We go halves? Just like this."

Dampish thighs now. "Shall we forget the other halves? Shall we do something about these halves?"

Beginning to taste, slowly upward, dampness ever increasing, upward toward its source, thighs parting, the wondrous scent for which it seemed almost I had come to live merging with its identical twin, the scent of the sea reaching me from just outside the cave. Then that cry from her, words I had ever yet to make out, head buried there, the cry itself like none other I had ever heard; audible testimony to the great mystery.

And then, another day, something that I think neither of us had counted on, something toward which I had no intention. No more did I believe had she.

That day she had spoken from that same position we liked afterward, my head in her lap, herself looking down at me.

"Confession time. You remember when we first did it?"

"You mean the time you seduced me?"

"I never noticed any great resistance. Never mind. Well, I did it because I simply had to have a man. Any man. And there was nobody else. You could have been King Kong's first cousin. That was then. Now I want you to try being honest. Was it that way for you too? Any woman?"

"Yes," I said helplessly.

"Then for both of us. That was then. Now I want you to listen. Are you listening?"

"I'm listening."

I almost dreaded what I knew was coming. She was holding my face now and she pressed my head into her breasts so that, I think, we would not be looking at each other when she said it.

"Well, that's all changed for me. Now I could not stand anybody

521

else, even to touch my wrist. What I'm saying is . . . I like being with you . . . I feel safe when you are near . . . I love you . . ." A small, wry and ironic laugh. "How about that, Captain?"

I felt tears that stood in my eyes emerge, all across her naked breasts as she held me ever so tightly to them; the tears telling her that it was so with me; even though it was the last thing I wanted, knowing the endless difficulties sure to follow. Of these too, she would have known as well, known also that I was instantly thinking of them. There was nothing we could hide from each other. Her voice coming from above me.

"You're so great at making decisions. Well, what do we do about that one, Captain? Because you know what? We've let happen to us the same thing that happened to Meyer and Barker. Only we wouldn't let them do anything about it. Where does that leave us?"

It was another of our days. Love suddenly grafted to lovemaking, an immense new territory instantly entered. Lovemaking vastly sweeter. But also: the cave which we had once thought ourselves so fortunate to find now seeming increasingly inadequate, not a fitting measure of what we had. So easily is man spoiled. What I wanted was to move into her cottage with her, to be with her every night, to go to bed with her, to wake up and reach out and find her. My mind took off: I wanted us to be married: Either the Jesuit or Porterfield would do to perform the ceremony; mind going that far. When I suggested all this to her, this time it was she who hesitated; for the first time, real caution making its appearance in her.

"Let's wait a little," she said, her mind taking a keen look at it, that other woman, that professional naval officer, astute, attendant to a difficult problem. "Let me think. Let's both of us think."

"Will the others allow it, do you mean?"

"That's part of it," she said carefully. "But something else also." She waited a moment. "Something like this: We don't own ourselves, do we? Not completely. Not at all really."

How long it had been so, that we could read each other before either spoke; and words spoken, only the fewest needed to lay bare the whole dilemma; risks so numerous, quite possibly dangerous ones. All of this I now reflected upon myself, taking her point, even as she put it into words.

"What we would lose with them. Giving ourselves something very, very special that they can never in their lives have. We can't do that. We just can't."

"No, we can't. What do we do then?"

"I don't know. The cave isn't enough anymore."

522

"It isn't enough. It doesn't begin to be enough."

"Let's wait. Let's think," she said again. Came back to that thing I knew had been troubling her so. "We wouldn't allow it for Meyer and Barker. How in God's name can we allow it for ourselves? What would they think? Ship's company."

"I'm not sure I give a damn."

"You can't mean that. All right then, what would *we* think." A bitter note touched her voice. "Shall we take a boat and go off like they did?"

Something new seemed all at once to approach, to hover over us, a moment of aching desperateness. It was almost as though two loves stood facing off to each other: my love for my ship's company; my love for her; both—I had to have both. Stood around us also, as it were gazing at us in reproach even as we made love, two young figures like ghosts: Meyer and Barker. Unspoken between us, guilt had entered that cave. Our taking what they were not permitted to take; already doing that. From outside I could hear, in one of its repertory of cadences, playing against the rocks on the incoming tide, that sea where they had gone. Then I heard another sound.

From far away it came, pealing, blaring over the island, its raucousness much diluted here, but its idiosyncratic pulse and timbre at once familiar to any sailor, its source as known to us as though we stood next to it: the launch General Quarters klaxon I had recently had installed on the high Lookout Tower to alert all hands, wherever on the island, to any danger that might approach us from the sea; or of other, unforeseeable emergency or peril. Sailor's sure knowledge: It is never sounded lightly; its call instantly heeded, whatever else in progress dropped, for it had but one meaning: Harm has come calling. Without a word we scrambled out of the cave and started climbing hard up the hill to the ridge that would take us back to the settlement. Cresting it, hearing the sound much more clamorously now, the pulsating blast-pause, blast-pause pouring out insistently over the trees, reaching everywhere, the sound louder with every step we took. We were running now. At a controlled pace, knowing the distance, rating ourselves. No thought of going separately, as was our custom, we moved across the ridge, down the hill and along the stream bed. We ran on, myself outdistancing her, entering the settlement, breathing heavily, the common in front of the main dwellings filling with hands, Thurlow marching directly toward me even as Lieutenant Girard came up behind. "Captain," he said, taking time only to give me the essential facts, myself telling off coxswains for two boats, bearers for stretchers; these, the doc, the Jesuit, Thurlow, Girard, Delaney, myself, moving rapidly down the ladders which descended from the settlement to the beach.

We sat in silence in the boats as they took us past the apron of beach, Thurlow beside me, Delaney facing us reporting that he had been studying the plants in that area when he spotted them far below; the boats bearing off northwesterly, parallel to the forbidding cliffs which constituted the shoreline; having proceeded some distance until we were standing directly off a distinctly higher cliff with the characteristic great jagged rocks below, these now immediately ahead of us. The coxswains took us in at dead slow; no place to beach, we debarked into the shoaling water, thigh-deep at first, wound our way through underwater rocks. By the time the water had dropped to our knees we could see the crumpled forms of them up above us, come to rest a certain distance back from the sea. We scrambled with some difficulty, helping one another, up the rocks and across them; were halted by the sight.

We stood a few feet away looking down in the terrible silence of all hands. The mutilation was horrible, the bodies broken, the faces all but obliterated. I recognized them chiefly by the differing colors of their hair, woman's hair. The doc stepped up, knelt, hands moving professionally. Not even needing a shake of the head. I was distantly aware of the Jesuit also kneeling there, of the Sign of the Cross, the murmur of Latin words over them. Then of Girard kneeling, running her fingers in a moment's caress through the hair of each, seeming to pause a moment to wrap a curl of Talley's around her finger. I reached down and pulled her away. Without being told to do so, three of the sailors took off their dungaree shirts and placed them over them. Storekeeper Talley; Radioman Amy Walcott—"Ears" to all; Lieutenant (jg) Rollins, anti-submarine warfare officer. No one spoke. No one said it. The men got the bodies onto the stretchers and, taking a considerable time to do it, we carried them over the rocks and managed them, wading, into the boats. No one said it. Not said then, but to be said very soon. Someone was killing off the women.

.8.

THE PLAN

We sat alone, Lieutenant Girard and I, in my cabin above the sea, those other customary formal selves of ours—not the woman and the man of the cave—that had dealt so long with problems of ship's company now presiding.

The days following the discoveries of the bodies of Talley, Walcott, and Rollins had brought over the settlement like darksome clouds many things, in varying portions, one or the other chiefly holding reign at various times, switching about: a great fear, an unutterable rage, a sense of just-suppressed panic, all tangible as are objects one touches. There had been tough sessions in this cabin, differing groups, combinations, present at different times as we drew upon every resource, every idea to get at it, that any hand might have: the doc, Thurlow, Selmon, the Jesuit, Girard, Porterfield, Bixby, Delaney, Preston . . . in time literally every member of ship's company included in one session or another—and not only for ideas, but for another immensely secretive reason of my own, that one of them being the killer, he might by some betraying gesture, some slip of word, give himself away; a minimum of hope there as to anyone so accomplished thus far in his own secrecy and stealth. A multiplicity of thoughts and explanations held forth. One even that they could have been suicides, women finding out that they were unable to do, or continue doing, what they were asked to do: a thought earlier brought up about Rollins now being applied to all three. The suggestion—from Selmon— had outraged Girard, who had turned fiercely on him. "Jesus-God, that seems to be the party line for all of these women. I won't have it." Backed by every single one of the remaining women, in unanimous agreement that there had been not the slightest indication of such a thing from any of the dead women. Even, in discreet sessions with Girard and myself only present, the men assigned to each of the three women and interviewed separately by the two of us further confirming—in discreet language— quite the opposite (in addition, she and I alert in particular for suspects in these). And finally, the doc not present at that session, still performing his autopsies, the matter settled at the next one where he was, in a brief exchange.

Doc: "Rollins had been on those rocks some time. Talley and Walcott more recently. All had been choked first."

Captain: "Enough so to die before they hit the rocks?"

Doc: "No way to tell."

An exchange which sent something unspoken but terrible moving through that quiet group of shipmates present.

Various measures proposed to deal with the immediate threat. One struck down fast at the very first meeting: The doc had raised the idea of moving all the women into the empty dormitory.

"You mean stop the Arrangement?" I had said.

"At least temporarily."

The Jesuit had exploded in a manner unexperienced from him, with an overt rage at the softly proffered proposal.

"What's going on in the cottages must continue. *Has to continue.*"

I turned. "Lieutenant Girard?"

We had all looked at her, some absolute air of authority in these matters holding us, compelling us toward her, whatever her decision might be; deferring to her at every turn.

"The chaplain is correct," she said coldly, and in the tones of command-giving. "To do what the doctor suggests would be to give in to whoever it is. Absolutely not."

Her having spoken, it was as if that was that. "Very well," I said. "The Arrangement will continue. Meantime, no woman to go alone on walks."

I was referring to the walks all of us from time to time took in our ceaseless fascination of exploring the island. "Every woman to be accompanied at all times by an armed man of ship's company. You will see to that, Mr. Thurlow."

Looking at the navigator I remembered those highly successful interrogations he had accomplished in the Bixby matter, this rather gentle officer able to get answers from men when something turned obdurate inside him; as had happened now.

"I want every man, every officer questioned, Alex," I said. "By yourself. And when you've gone through them all, start over again. As many times as may be necessary. Understood?"

"Aye, sir," he said with a sort of grim satisfaction. "Understood."

Thurlow's questioning of ship's company had turned up nothing. He kept at it. A tenseness had settled over our community. Something intolerable; an inner rage felt in oneself, one's shipmates. A sense of evil having taken up abode amid us. Nevertheless the outer life continuing as before. The settlement battened down . . . waiting.

All of this time I had felt something was gathering, taking shape in Girard, something she was holding back. Now, alone with me, the feeling came true, and the reason. The death of Talley in particular had changed her; though those of Walcott and Rollins also. It was just that the storekeeper had worked directly under her for as long as they both had been aboard the *Nathan James*. She was a different woman, the sense of a terrible ferocity—brutal, cold, inexorable, almost emotionless—felt just below the surface, sometimes sending a chill even through me; mother lion whose cubs were being snatched away, killed, slaughtered; companion with it, a terrible resolve, felt like a field of force from her, to get whoever it was. Altogether that most dangerous kind of heartbreak and violation, one that never sheds tears.

"Yes, I have a plan," she said, her voice coming as quietly as ever but a hardness in it that had not been there before. If she had been feminine before, she was now female, cruelly female. "First, I don't trust anyone. What I want to do . . . If we tell everybody in one of those sessions it will get out, alert him. Anyone could be the killer. The only way to do it is alone. Myself. I don't trust anyone else. No one."

"Let's have it," I said briskly.

She told it to me. I was appalled, suddenly rock-hard myself.

"You alone? Absolutely not," I said. "Far too much danger to yourself. I wouldn't consider it. Aside from that, I can't imagine whoever it is would show himself on that cliffside again."

She was relentless. "Maybe not. But maybe so. Arrogance goes with that kind of murder I would think. Or maybe killers do return to the scene of their crimes. Especially that kind of killer. The kind who's hungry for more." Her voice came at me like an attack. "We've got to do something, for God's sake. We've got to try anything. We can't just sit here."

"The other point remains." My voice meeting hers unbending. "We can't have you the next one. The answer is no."

She waited a moment, yielding not an inch; pushed then against the absolute rejection, right through it. Softly, insidiously, this time.

"Then you come along. You're a marksman, Captain. Like myself."

I sat silent. She leaned forward a little, moved craftily into that opening.

"Here's how we do it."

She laid it out, briskly, precisely; working out the plan to the finest detail; the tactics; the timing. I listened to it with great suspicion. Finally she sat back, not just unyielding—demanding.

"Do you come along? Or do I do it some night on my own?"

"You wouldn't dare. Not against my direct order."

"Captain, in this matter I don't give balls about your orders. You try me."

Something hard and cold as diamonds in her eyes, looking unflinchingly into mine.

"I've got to get him. That's the beginning and the end of it."

"I'll come along," I said.

.9.

EXECUTIONER

Moonlight fell across the cliffs that night. Full moonlight washed the cliffs, fell through the tall trees onto the main dwellings, farther on lanced through stilled branches onto the twenty-six smaller structures housing the women—five of these now vacant. Silence only answered the moon rays, all ship's company, the island itself, asleep. Or apparently so, though down the cliffs terns awakened in their nests to a quickened rustle in the bush, gave forth their clipped irascible sound at the intrusion, this not being repeated returned to whatever sleep it is that terns enjoy. Silence resumed as a solitary figure stepped from the bushes and stood free of all noisy foliage, stood upon the long naked smooth rock ledge high above the sea; the moonlight defining the figure clearly as that of a woman; wearing Navy dungarees; no cap or hat; moonlight so full as to pick up the very color of the wheat-light woman's hair.

She sat down upon the ledge, safely back from its plunging brink, hands clasped around drawn-up knees; sat as though in reverie, regarding the sea stretching in a vast glittering plain to distant horizons; moon and unnumbered constellations unloosed in a cloudless sky conspiring with the sea in an offertory of unutterable beauty, infinite loneliness; the woman's figure seeming all relaxed, calmly poised, whatever tense alertness actually

529

there cloistered. She had done this before. Four nights now, come to the ledge, sat upon it; as though waiting for someone; some unnamed one to come calling upon her; as a woman might wait for a lover.

The vigil kept again, after a while she got up, for some reason took a step or two nearer the edge, looked over the chasm as though pondering it, the awful drop onto the jagged moon-struck rocks far below upon which shipmates, sisters, had fallen and which seemed now to reach longingly high up to her, their shapes actually given a voice by the sea playing on them a metronomic low-pitched rhythm, the only sound in the silent night. She turned back toward the slope that led down from the heights, an air of disappointment conveyed at rendezvous not kept, departing, perhaps to come another time, perhaps to give up once and for all on her wanted visitor; had taken a dozen steps or so across the ledge. Saw him standing there, motionless in the moonlight, a silhouetted shape, perhaps thirty feet down the ledge. Seemed to take a breath, then come perfectly still, motionless as was he. Stood regarding him dispassionately across that space between them.

She must have known that rather delicate figure the very moment I myself did so; crouched in my guard post within the bushes, a fractional moment's time allotted for the terrible shock of recognition, of identification. Then, instantly, a refusal to accept: Perhaps he himself was out for a stroll on a night so glorious; some wild absurd mistake to imagine that he, a man above all committed to the sanctity of reason, could have committed such acts; that almost frail body surely not even physically capable of doing so, the choking the doc had mentioned; mind insidiously then flashing back to a service record, to a scene on another faraway sea of a young officer hoisting himself with such effortless ease as to elicit a captain's admiration aboard a French yacht full of the dead: *gymnast's hands, stationary-rings-specialty hands* . . . Mind then almost violently coming off of this, again rejecting; waiting for explanation, surely momentarily to come from him, from there: From within my own darkness the scene before me seeming as though cast in daylight by the brilliance of the moon; the long ledge gleaming, the two figures frozen in shadowy tableau, actors on a stage awaiting direction.

Then voices, low but crystalline clear in the windless night, the unearthly hush. His, first, as detached, yes, as reasonable as I had always known it to be in shrewdly explicating some perverse problem facing us, one only he could hope to solve, involving his recondite field; present even now that remote, self-confident tone which had unfailingly carried the assurance that he could deal with the situation, knew precisely what he was up to; now leavened with an almost courtly air; the words themselves, however oblique, ghastly certifying what one could not believe.

"Lieutenant Girard. I wouldn't have hoped for yourself."

Like a heart-quake, an instant of unbearable sadness and despair deeper than any known pain that the same young officer who stood there . . . without him and his skills, exercised often with heedless courage, seeking out the very air we could breathe, we would never have made it, none of us would be here. Then that was swept away by the urgency of concentration on the arranged tactics; body prepared to move instantly from those bushes; right hand reaching stealthily down to unfix the safety catch on the .45 caliber, hand remaining on the cool metal; waiting, unstirring, breathing itself kept down. With a relief seeing that he stood between the cliff's edge and herself, myself a good deal closer to her than was he. Calculating: not quite at point-blank range for such a close-up gun, I would prefer him a step or two closer. Then the words from her heard after a pause, as though at some remarkable wonder; identity not enough, some puzzle that she still wished to solve, riddle to unravel; her voice as low as his but no reasonableness at all in it, rather a vast perplexity, laced with a strange cruelty.

"You intend to get us all?"

If she wished to elicit, he seemed all ready to supply answers: an old habit. To supply even a history. I could almost feel the soft unseen smile. Then hear the familiar mild loftiness.

"Actually, the undertaking began in that passage through the dark and the cold. The three women . . ."

A catch of breath from her, the felt surprise.

"You mean . . . Salinas, Kramer, Stoughton." She said their names, shipmates long since gone, resurrecting their memories.

"They were the easiest. After all, men were going over the side with some frequency." His voice uninflected, routine . . . rational; entirely unreluctant at the revelations; even, now, the faintest touch of vanity in it. "I believe I can say that no one ever suspected."

"No one did." A kind of mordant bitterness in hers. Proceeding, as though wishing, for some reason unknown, to extract confession from him, perhaps to make sure of each beyond all doubt, a prosecutor not content with one count of murder, or with three, but wanting the last one.

"Then the first one of the island? Austin. What did you do with her?"

"I buried her in a cave," said matter-of-factly.

"Dillon?"

"Her also."

"You killed the woman you were sleeping with."

"What does that have to do with it? Just screwing."

"Then the three more here. Talley . . . Walcott . . . Rollins. Over this cliff," she said. The first dim savage intention in her voice. "Onto those rocks down there."

At that, as if for the first time affected by this orderly recall of the sequence of events, or by the reference to the immediacy of scene of the most recent ones, he took a couple of steps toward her. I rose slightly in the bush, myself as much at hair-trigger as the weapon where my hand rested. I was astonished to hear her, still standing her ground, continue this dialogue, in her voice now a tone of curiosity, lethal curiosity I was beginning to feel . . . Myself hesitating, somewhat baffled, beginning to be fearful for her safety. Then seeing perhaps her purpose, as he came to a halt: to make him do so. Perhaps, I thought, with the intention also of bringing him step by step nearer to me. Holding back, trusting in her decision as to the necessity of what she was up to. She, as if she vitally required further information still; he, as before, recovered quickly, quite willing to reply with impeccable elucidation to any questions she might have; her continuing the interrogation now, pressing harder, more relentlessly.

"Why, in God's name?"

He had stopped his advance, as if, as always, fascinated himself by any abstruse matter, challenging the intellect, any in the higher realm, and glad in particular that she had asked that question, as if justifiability was the easiest part of all.

"Plain enough." I could sense the shrug. "What we had seen. Seen on the beaches of Italy. Those creatures at Amalfi—seen what my own specialty had done to them. Africa. Seen in the Kenya bush. Seen India, seen black sooty skies, night at noonday . . . All that aggrandizement of horrors, don't you remember? The unendingness of it, the perfection of the job man had done! Done coldly, almost carelessly. Yes, I think that puts it accurately—or as much so as I can rightly convey." It was as if he were questioning himself, trying as always to accomplish his prided precision. "I simply came to know that anyone who had managed to do all that didn't have the slightest claim to continue. *Shouldn't* continue. Even for his own sake, don't you know? Something so elementally deviant, warped, in him; some deep, irreparable fissure in his psyche. Doesn't belong here. Not constructed quite right for this world. In all of creation the only evil thing. The only one to destroy for the sake of it. Much better for him to go. Give some other species a chance—couldn't possibly do worse. *Mutatis mutandis.*"

He spoke in tones of earnest persuasion, as if it were important to him to convince her of the inescapable logic of both his decision and his actions.

"The very fact I can do what I'm doing—murdering the innocent: Doesn't that tell you how hopelessly flawed man is? If you should ask me what one thing . . . pushed me over the edge, you would doubtless say? Made me see reason I would put it. I'm not entirely certain. Usually in these cases it's a little thing." I heard an actual laugh, one of self-amusement, falling eerie on that moonlit stage. "Maybe the exact moment was when I saw snow begin to fall on the equator."

In a way, in those elevated tones of his, it came out as a masterpiece of cogency, closely reasoned, imperviously rational: Someone had to take on this essential chore. Finished with a notation of the obvious.

"And of course the only possible way to achieve the objective, once defined, was to do away with the one means that could continue him."

"Like me?" spoken almost softly.

"Like you and the other twenty-nine—was it?—I started with. Unfortunately." The sentiment actually came through as heartfelt, honest regret at their necessary disposal.

"One by one. So that we are now only twenty-one. You have quite a few to go."

"Yes . . . yes." Abruptly a distinct tone of impatience had entered his voice, as if there being that many remaining it were necessary now to get on with the job, that they had given quite enough time to this colloquy, however fascinating to the mind the intellectual exercise.

He took a step forward. "But presently to be twenty . . ."

"You like to choke them first, don't you, Mr. Selmon?"

She said it brutally, as a taunt. From across the ledge the rage came almost tangibly from him, as though at the unfairness of this caviling at his use of tools that after all were indispensable to his purpose. Now slowly, steadily on he came. She did not move, not even to step back; holding her ground, as though wanting him to come on; welcoming him. A wild thought tearing suddenly at my mind, a ship's captain's thought, that while we must not lose her, or another one of them, was there any way not to lose him whose skills we might yet mortally require—a moment's idea that I might actually step forward onto that stage and reason with him. Then the insanity of the thought itself was obliterated as I emerged from the bush, knelt, took point-blank aim at the advancing shadow.

A gunshot, not my own, shattered the night air.

For a horrible moment I thought it had come from him. I looked quickly at her, with an immense relief saw her still standing there, saw moonlight glint as off something metallic, something she was holding. My eyes flashed back across the space between the two of them. The terns had awakened with a furious squawk into the night, this time exploding in a frenzy of white from their nests, beginning to swoop upward into the moonlight. He stopped, appeared to stagger, took another step toward her, even as she moved toward him, as she came on firing again and again in an orgasm of savagery, six shots bursting on the air until the clip was emptied; the body sometime during them seeming somehow caught in a convulsion of surprise, of total inexpectation, a spastic reflex appearing to jerk it upward, tremble it a moment on the cliff's edge, where it pitched forward as though in flight, plunged high over the cliffs.

I came up by her, at the moment feeling in all that torrent of emotions rushing through me principally a hard anger; looked down at the .45 caliber she was still holding.

"I didn't know you were carrying that." I spoke harshly. I was shaking. "You never told me. You should have done so. Something could have gone wrong."

She waited a moment, spoke in a quiet viciousness that sent a chill like ice crawling down my spine in the warm night.

"I wanted to do it myself."

A shrill sound reached us from below. We looked over into the chasm. Under the moonlight we could make out the crumpled shape splayed across the great jagged rocks quite as three other shipmates had been, a flight of white terns circling as though in bafflement high over it, their shrieks piercing the peaceful night.

She ejected the clip methodically and stuck it in the pocket of her dungarees. We turned and started down the slope to the settlement. We had not gone far, crossing under the shadows of some trees, when a vibration seemed to go through her, bringing her to a halt, her body caught suddenly in a paroxysm of trembling. I put my arm around her. She stood there a moment, the tremor beginning to subside. My arm still lightly there, we continued, coming out from under the trees and into the moonlight lighting our way.

.BOOK VII.

ASTARTE

.1.

ADVENT

had made up my mind to give him decent Navy burial, the same as his victims, anticipating perhaps a mild demurral in a few. I was surprised therefore at the depth of the opposition from Girard and from some of the other women. Girard faced me off with it in a session in my cabin the day after the event on the ledge under the moonlight, during which time Noisy Travis was building the coffin, the funeral service set for the following day. She came on hard.

"I can't believe it," she said. "Putting their killer right alongside them. Jesus-God, Captain, he *choked* those women to death—or near enough to it before he tossed them over the cliff onto those rocks. He's to lie right next to them?"

I tried first explaining. "Yes, he is, and let me tell you why. For seven months, no one aboard put himself at such risk to bring us through. The first man always to walk ashore—at how many dozens of beaches?—into radiation unknown when he did so. My definition for that is courage: uncommon valor, if you like. Something else. He is the one, more than anybody else, whose knowledge and skills determined why this island might be here, free of contamination, had a good chance of turning up. He found us the air we could breathe. We would never have made it without him." I came down hard enough myself. "I don't know what you have in mind, Miss Girard: taking him out to sea and feeding him to the sharks . . ."

"I wouldn't mind that," she butted in, unflinching.

"Well, I would. He went off the rails at the end but before that he damned well did as much as any hand to see that the ship didn't. Before that he was a hell of a Navy man. A Navy officer. I aim to see him given a proper Navy burial."

"You could do that," she said slyly, "by taking him out to sea on the *James*. No burial more Navy than that."

I was not about to fall for that, the act for him alone a pointed exclusion. I decided to use another reason, also valid.

"We can't spare a drop of fuel." I settled that.

The Jesuit had been present at that meeting; he had simply sat off to the side letting us go at it. She turned to him, seeking an ally.

"You see what I'm saying, don't you, Chaplain?" A hectoring tone. "And it's what most of the women feel. I haven't taken a poll on it—I thought that would be obscene. And frankly I had no idea the captain would take this position. Well, what do you say, Chaplain?"

I cut that off before he could answer.

"It isn't for the chaplain to say, Lieutenant. It isn't the chaplain's decision. It's mine."

"The women won't attend the funeral service."

I looked at her, something beginning to bristle in me. I tried to allow for her being overwrought, but I had to put a stop to this.

"Listen carefully, Miss Girard." I could hear that familiar tone of mine, a captain's voice, cold and hard when I had reached a decision and now expected all hands to shut up and obey it.

"They will not only attend it," I said. "They will behave themselves as Navy officers and bluejackets are expected to when the captain issues an order. You will pass that word. Is that fully understood, Lieutenant?"

There was not an ounce of willingness in her answer. But I knew she would obey and see that they did so.

"Understood. I will pass the word."

I dismissed her, curtly enough. "Now that that's settled, that's all for today, Miss Girard. The chaplain and I need to go over the Navy arrangements for the funeral. We needn't detain you."

She had snapped to her feet and turned to leave as fast as possible, before she did simply looking at me, eyes flashing, a kind of loathing in them, saying but the one word: "Sir."

So it was that Storekeeper Talley, Radioman Walcott, Lieutenant (jg) Rollins, alongside in their individual graves, and Lieutenant (jg) Selmon, in the fourth grave next to them, lie forever now on a plot atop the cliffside, a pretty spot overlooking the island one way, the sea the other.

The following month went a long way to get us back to a measure of normalcy in the settlement, the ineluctable reverberations of the awful deeds, however, but very slowly beginning to diminish in the face of the lifted restrictions: women able to go about unaccompanied by armed men, the island once again a free and safe place. I suppose it would never leave our memories, what had happened to make those cottages now stand empty in the woods. The cottages themselves were there to remind us, the small gardener's crew of men and women continuing to tend and maintain them, lest the bush reclaim them, along with the remaining occupied cottages. For my part I tended to avoid coming near them; so also I felt did most of the rest of ship's company.

So it was I sensed us beginning to put that horror behind us, as we had found it essential to our survival to put behind so many other horrors—Girard, surprisingly, with all her exceptional ability in the earlier ones to do so, having the greatest difficulty at it now of any of ship's company. The deaths of her sister shipmates, Talley's death in particular, seemed to have left a permanent scar deep in the soul, some inner change felt in her, myself deeply concerned. Meanwhile, in the cottages, that profound undertaking that Selmon had attempted to interrupt and bring to an end, and succeeded to the extent of making a considerable dent in our mathematical chances to accomplish it, continued, itself helping as much as anything to temper the immediate past, as we faced ahead to that most urgent of all considerations occupying the community: Would babies come?

It was an exceptionally pretty island day. It had rained the day before, the island entombed in a mist which cut off visibility to the Pacific to no more than a cable's length. Work ceasing for that day, the farming and fishing details kept in, the men mostly giving themselves over to that project Girard had initiated in the mess hall, and which continued to fascinate them to an astonishing absorbed degree, of everyone putting down everything possible as to whatever specialty he was knowledgeable in, or for that matter anything else he thought of importance or interest about man and his history, to pass on to those children we all so fervently hoped would soon announce their presence in the wombs of women. The sun had returned after its day off, shining down out of cloudless skies of azure. Delaney's people were back at the Farm. Silva's had gone off to their fishing, and one could look out over the island and see it all freshened by the rain, the greens in their wide spectrum seeming more vivid, a glorious sweetness in the island. Thurlow was in my cabin looking out over the sea, not much business to attend to, ourselves chatting on sundry topics as they might occur. We had begun to spend more time together, why I was not sure, other than that I was coming to find in him, and perhaps he in myself, an audience, a kindred soul, for any and whatever reflections that either of us might want to engage in.

"As a ship's captain," I said, "I can swear to you, Alex, that not the least of blessings of our situation is that I no longer have to make out those damned officer's fitness reports. Or go over those enlisted personnel evaluations. I never imagined that simply taking the paperwork out of a man's life would be such an ecstasy. Would it be an exaggeration to say that of all man's chains, paperwork more than any other kept him from . . . well, living?"

Thurlow laughed softly. "A defensible hypothesis, certainly. Now that you mention it, looking back I think people spent more time in shuffling papers than in any other single activity."

Our manner in these conversations had become one in equal parts badinage and seriousness. "And would you further agree," I continued, "that the greater portion of it was entirely dispensable; no one a mite worse off if, oh, say, nine-tenths of it had been simply jettisoned?"

"We've found it true here, that's for sure. I guess we're all becoming islanders, sir. It hasn't taken all that much time, has it?"

"No, it hasn't. I wake up thankful, go to sleep thankful, for that. I think that contentedness in the island, of having made such a good place of it—good to start with, of course—is one thing that makes the last hand of us long for success in the cottages." Long since we had been able to speak frankly, in plain language, in almost routine fashion, to that matter, almost as to any Navy operation in progress whose outcome was of vital interest to us. "To have someone to pass all this onto—pass on the island and what we've done to make it a home."

"Aye, there's nothing everyone—the men, the women—want more."

"To have children to hand things down to: Could it be that that's the chief source of man's happiness, well-being? Is there any stronger drive in man?"

"Especially this time," he said, a bit of the lightness gone.

"Aye. Especially this time, Alex." Myself reflecting his more sober tone. "To pass on whatever may be left on . . ."

I grinned, breaking that spell, too serious, a bit of grimness in it, that had suddenly come over us.

"Nature doesn't change, does it, Alex?" Himself a man much interested in the large permutations of existence, the planet itself, the stars, weather . . . and of course, man and his place in all of this.

"Aye, sir. If we could all just learn to heed Nature, follow the directions she points us to . . . most of our troubles surely would go away. And they're rather simple directions actually . . ."

Bixby, that day's messenger on the Lookout Tower, burst into the cabin. These sailors knew to knock, someone like Bixby especially.

"Captain," she said, steady enough but the most absolute urgency in her voice. "Porterfield on the tower. He's raised what he thinks is a ship. Far out . . ."

I was already on my way, sweeping past her, feeling her and Thurlow right behind me, running toward the Tower, scrambling up it. Porterfield raised up from Big Eyes.

"Bearing two five eight, sir."

I bent to it. At first only the vast nothingness of waters, the view to the horizon immense, nineteen miles from that Tower. We were long since accustomed to mirages—all of us had at one time or another seen something on some horizon that he thought was a ship, was not, not once. My eyes, fixing hard, then seeing her, on the very edge of the horizon line, just the shape of her, no other identification I could make out. Then her coming nearer, distinctly with the intent of closing the island. How fast she came on! I was about to give the order to Porterfield to sound the general alarm (the drill of action if ever occurred what was now occurring, a ship approaching, long since worked out, part of it being the quick manning of the *Nathan James* to go out and meet her in case she held hostile intentions toward us and our island) . . . about to order the GQ when I made out the long black configuration, possessed by no other ship I had ever known, and last seen what seemed an age ago on a distant sea; coming on, closing the island. As she did, the blinker light atop her sail area began to flash across the waters. Through the scope I read the letters one by one: *T-U-R-G-E-N-E-V.*

.2.

THE TWO CAPTAINS

The two vessels lying a scant half a cable's length apart below the cliff; our own ship, the *Nathan James,* with her sleek gray lines; *Pushkin,* a low, long black configuration, actually a hundred feet longer; each pulling not at all at her anchors, each mirrored in the glassy waters; ancient enemies of the sea, destroyer and submarine, now lying in neighborly proximity. A quietness lay over the scene, over what was happening, and that seamanlike orderliness and competence, excluding the least evidence of agitation, of wasted emotion and energy, which takes over when there is urgent business to be attended to. Coxswains bringing our boats alongside the submarine's low Jacob's ladder to offload *Pushkin*'s crew for the short trip ashore, our crewmen assisting each into the boat; presently each helped out, set ashore. I suppose more than by any other single aspect I was struck by what I would term the "naturalness" of the scene, in a way only another sailor would understand; there seemed the minimal of strangeness in it. But no mystery really in this. Sailors even of different nationality are closer than in perhaps any other trade men follow; normal barriers attenuated; by no means completely obliterated, but fewer to start with, and these more swiftly overcome. The explanation obvious: the mutuality of the sea and the sea life, the kind of men drawn to it and the

542

kind of men made by it; origins hardly entering. Sailors off whatever ships inwardly know each other when they meet; they are never strangers. They are brothers of the sea.

More important even was that other ancient law of the sea, indelible in every seaman, of proceeding instantly to the aid of other seamen in distress; the fact that the two ship's companies were coming together on land in no way lessening this iron commandment. These particular sailors had arrived frail, almost ghostlike figures, bodies depleted, not a few close to the edge. Our hearts went out to them, having been ourselves in not dissimilar condition not all that long ago. I will remember well that scene, watching it from the top of the cliff, when the Russian officers and sailors, scarcely a hundred in number, first climbed, step by slow, agonizing step, up the strong ladders we had fashioned for its ascent; in fact, in such weakened condition were many of the submariners that in each case one of our men went behind one of theirs on the climb, steadying him, helping him up the ladder, ready to catch him should he fall back. When they reached the top, the doc and the hospital corpsmen waiting to take in hand those who immediately needed their attention. The truth of the matter, as the Russian captain had explained to me, was that they were near the end of their tether; their food stores of any kind down to near-zero levels, themselves on just-short-of-starvation rations. We were eager to share the bounties of the island—the fresh vegetables, fresh fruit, fresh fish. What a joy it was to see the way in which these fellow sailors, without such fare virtually since the launchings, now some thirteen months ago, fell on these offerings. Men reprieved, they were, from the long imprisonment of their submarine. I believe they looked upon us as their saviors.

I waited several days for his ship's company, including himself, to get some strength into them before taking the Russian captain on a tour of the settlement. I led him past the central "common" building—mess-headquarters hall—past the men's dormitories, his murmuring his approbation of their construction qualities, through the guardsmanlike trees that ended at last at the waterfall, symbol of our priceless fresh water supply, where we stood awhile as I described to him the stream that, falling from it, led across the island to our Farm which I also described. I sensed in him the marvel at the setting itself that had struck me when I first saw it that day, seeming now so long ago, that Coxswain Meyer and Seaman Barker and I first set eyes upon it and only the great trees stood there. He listened with the most attentive care, scarcely ever interrupting even with a question, only an occasional "yes, yes" in his good English to certify that he was taking it all in, missing not the smallest detail; a superb listener, like every good ship's captain I had ever known; briefing him meticulously, in Navy fashion, on the assets of the island: how the Farm was producing abundantly, food supplies increased by the island itself, the excellent fishing grounds just offshore. (Routinely explaining, something as a seaman he would instantly understand, why, despite the difficulty of access presented by the cliffs, we had chosen to build the settlement on this leeward side of the island, hurricanes sure in time to hit the other, windward shore, in addition the cliffs themselves a fortress against violent weather; in fact, since *Pushkin* had arrived a vicious storm bearing Force 11 winds, just below hurricane strength, had attacked the island, battering it for close on to two days, great waves traveling high and white up the unyielding cliffs, Noisy's buildings, in which we had battened down to ride it out, holding up with hardly a whimper. I was almost glad of the storm, to show how well we had built.)

Naval officers both—more, Navy ship's captains—all of this was done in the most straightforward fashion. Not the slightest barrier to communication, either in the providing or the receiving of the storehouse of facts, information, so readily assimilated it seemed. It was as if I were briefing a superior, or perhaps the officer sent to relieve me in a routine change-of-command, on the salient aspects of the new command in which he would soon be completely involved. In naval fashion, too, he confined himself, as I say, almost altogether to listening, myself nonetheless continually aware of his sharp, appraising eyes, which seemed to miss nothing. Now and then a question, always to the point, asking a bit more information on this matter or that—e.g., would the Farm and the fishing grounds feed more? "Easily so, Captain. About a hundred more men I would say, with no strain." "Is that so, Captain?" "Happens," I said, "to be about the size of the company of *Pushkin,* if I'm not mistaken?" "Why, so it does, Captain." I could hardly believe that this was his oblique way of verifying that we intended to keep our side of the bargain, although it was true we had not once discussed it since his arrival; on my part, a waiting for physical recovery before proceeding to such matters; on his side, surely almost a question of manners not to ask—in any event I felt this exchange had reassured him. If he needed further confirmation, on passing the dormitories, myself indicating the one in which a good many of his ship's company were now recuperating, volunteering, "We built an extra one, Captain. Let's see. For about a hundred men, I believe." His stopping then, turning and looking me directly in the face, all-serious. "You ex-

pected us, Captain?" "When we built the dormitory we hadn't given up
. . . After a while . . . honestly, I cannot say that I did any more, Captain.
In fact I had lost hope. In any event I felt the space would one day be
usable. Naturally we would expect our community to grow." Neither
making any further allusion to what that remark might easily have led to.
We moved on.

Having come some distance we began to pass through the thickest
part of the forest, deliberately left so, still some way more before we came
upon the first of those dwellings so different from all others, so much
smaller, no other structure visible from it, and he stopped a moment in
admiration before it. "How well-built, Captain—how neat and well-
kept." That was all. Continuing through the trees, before long another
clearing, an identical house, identically isolated, this time a briefer pause
while he regarded it—thoughtfully, it seemed to me. Nothing else said.
In this fashion proceeding, my guiding us along a hacked-out path that
took us past four or five more of these dwellings, in each case none other
in sight, each seeming embowered protectively in its green and flowering
setting. Himself, of course, not remotely referring to the matter, my own
mind blocking it out, refusing to confront at the moment, putting off, the
question inherent in the cottages: Back in Gibraltar's waters, I had in
essence promised the Russian captain to take his people into the settlement, participating in everything—except the women. That subject had
never explicitly come up.

I had a destination and I led us on until finally we had left the
settlement behind, reentering the pure forest, moving along the stream
above the waterfall. Soft and slanting came the mote-laden sunlight
through the trees, combining with their branches to fashion flickering
patterns of shadow and light on the water with its clean-flowing *piano*
sound over its bed of small shiny rocks. From the thick growth on either
side of the stream the songs of birds, his stopping to listen in the ardent
green all around, with a wonder on his face perhaps possible only in one
over a year at sea. Finally, taking up again, before long moving up the
sharp climb, as we approached the crest alerted by that sound familiar
above all others to sailors, making top, standing at last on the long
prominence that sat high above the sea. It was the same cliffside where
the Jesuit and I had first gone and which, for its isolation, had become
a kind of sanctuary to me.

We stood looking at the endless waters, then as if by joint intention
far and away down the coastline at the two ships we commanded, much
diminished from here, nevertheless their differing configurations easily

discernible and from this far and high, almost aerial distance seeming tied up alongside. He looked then, head turning this way and that, at the island itself, visible in its entirety from here, the settlement some distance away, its every evidence hidden by the trees and the thick growth, the island seeming an untouched thing, virgin, in the sunlight flashing off its impossible greenness a fragrant refuge set in a blue sea.

"What a beautiful place. Captain?" he said.

"Sir?"

He gave an apologetic laugh. "Captain, that is the longest journey I have made on land since . . ." His mind seemed to travel backward over great distances in time. "Do you suppose we could sit? Rest a bit?"

He had still not regained his full stamina, though he had forborne to say so. It occurred to me how thoughtless I had been.

"Forgive me, Captain." My apology being: "It was the same for me at first. Land legs."

We sat on the long ledge of smooth rock which formed almost an overhang, the very sharp drop hundreds of feet straight down to the rocks and the sea.

"You don't have acrophobia?" I said.

"All submariners do." I had no idea whether he was putting me on. "Don't worry, Captain. I won't fall off. These cliffs—what an extraordinary color."

Somehow the great beauty itself had always seemed to me to make the place more lonely, that and the unobstructed vastness of the sea, the distant low sound of the water touching shore the only sound in an empty and hushed universe . . . again, looking far down and away, the very fact that only the two ships occupied such immense reaches further enhancing that loneliness. We sat awhile in unspoken but agreed silence, contemplating these vistas, each with his thoughts; resting after the climb.

I thought of him. He was a handsome man, in a sailor way. In his bearing, a touch of what a landsman might take as swagger but which I knew well as the mark of the sea captain's essential self-confidence, of his knowing exactly who he is. His voice was marked by that other prevailing characteristic of ship's captains: quiet-pitched, but with that certain tone in it. Thick hair as black as licorice, seeming the more so for his unusually fair skin. Eyes as blue as deep waters, a strong chin, a bony-sculpted face; the eyes seeming curiously to combine traits of gaiety and of melancholy; and, above all, of that other sailor trait, a quiet watchfulness. A suggestion of an active inner life, of a strong personality, no surprise there; command of men sitting easily on his shoulders—

strong shoulders, topping a very straight and lean six-foot frame, tight, hard, a grenadier of a man.

I judged his honor to be beyond question; his word to be absolute. None of this, of course, meant to define a man as in any way naïve or innocent. If ship's captains were that, ships would not sail, seas would not part, men would not obey without question; i.e., a man capable of cunning as opposed to deceit; of any kind of stratagem in the world that would serve his ship and his men, short of treachery. Yet another mark of a ship's captain suggested: a man unusually forbearing as to human weakness, correspondingly cold and hard, if need be ruthless, when crossed. Mirror images of each other, ship's captains? Perhaps. Any of the same profession would tend reflexively to trust him; by the same conditions of that profession, in dealing with him to be equally alert to protect the interests of his own people, his own ship's company. So it seemed to me we approached each other; open but vigilant; receptive as to ideas the other might present but carefully scrutinizing them. Trust: He appeared to have judged that to be indispensable from the first. I thought of how he could have used the fuel to bargain with me; to extract concessions of one kind or another (I hardly knew what they would be: the women, maybe). He had not. The transfer of the fuel to the *Nathan James* had already been made. Trust, openness. I must wherever possible reciprocate, save only for that one secret relationship toward him I felt I could never do the slightest thing about: that we had personally destroyed his home city of Orel. I broke the long silence.

"Captain," I said, "there are no words in my language to express our debt. That of my ship's company. For what you have brought us. The nuclear fuel. I can put it this way. We have come, all of us, to feel a gratitude to the island, for what it gives us—even simply for taking us in; for being habitable. Nevertheless, all of us—some more than others—have felt prisoners on it, with a ship almost empty of fuel. You have made free men of us."

"I understand," he said. "We need say nothing more of it. Besides, we are quits as to the matter of gifts. You have taken us in . . . we could not have lasted much longer . . . Let us put an end to this, Captain. There is an old saying of a Russian poet, 'A thought spoken is a lie.' "

Despite that lovely Russian expression, other words would still need to be spoken, and with all forthrightness. And in their simplicity I felt would be fully understood. Now we spoke of our experiences. His asking me, I told him of our passage through the dark and the cold. Then he related the story of what had happened during the long months when we thought he and *Pushkin* were lost. When he had finished I hardly knew which of our ordeals had been the worse.

"Once we saw our motherland," he said, "something like a madness took possession of us—I confess that to you, Captain."

What had happened was not just a meticulous but a weird and repetitive exploration of the enormous Russian coastline from Murmansk to Vladivostok, back and forth over the same course, the Northern Sea Route. This not once but a number of times. Including, lest they miss an available inch, up and around Norway and into the Baltic Sea, there approaching Latvian and Lithuanian towns. The reason for this excess was not unlike that which I sometimes had imagined might have overtaken us had we decided to return to our own country. Now that they were in native waters, off the cities and towns which were the homes of many of them, ship's company "begged, entreated—I had neither heart nor will to resist them"—that they do this endless inspection of wherever any part of Russia could be viewed, to determine if there was life there; when they found none, still not giving up, but insisting on going back again and again to see if any had appeared since their previous visit. "I myself got caught up in this mad business," he said. "It was as if nothing could convince us." A horror had followed. "We continued to investigate coastal towns. Never sighting one live human being. Sighting sometimes untouched towns. Makarova, I remember for one, Babrovskaye—there were others. All the houses, buildings still standing. Just nobody in sight. One of these was a place called Tobseda, the hometown of a *starshima*—petty officer— of mine named Suslova. We had surfaced some miles offshore. I had let Suslova look through some binoculars, see his town. There was not a scratch on it. I remember his lowering the glasses, still looking at the town, saying something like, 'They must all be asleep, Captain. There—see that house?—the red brick one halfway up the hill—that's my house. My wife, my child must be asleep in there.' It was around noontime. I knew it at that second. Readings where we were being dangerously high, I was about to give the order to submerge anyhow and tell him to get below. Before I could he had his shoes off and was gone overboard, started swimming to his town. I waited until I saw him step on the shore. He turned and waved back, then started into the town. I gave the order to dive."

He paused a beat. "What Suslova had done seemed to give the men ideas . . ." *Pushkin* had lost over a period of time eighteen men as she got near their towns. After that he had stopped surfacing anytime the ship was in swimming distance of the shore. His voice took on a tone that sent a chill up the spine. "What was odd was—I could even understand it. If your own town was right in front of you, and everything was still standing, the houses, the shops and all, it was almost irresistible not to go have a look. Something pulled you in there. I was glad Orel was inland. I might have done it myself. I knew then I had to get us out of there."

A tremor seemed to go through him—and through me. During one of their criss-crossings of the Northern Sea Route they had put into the secret nuclear fuel depot at Karsavina, found there the fuel he had anticipated finding (along with enough uncontaminated food in deep storage vaults to permit him to do exactly what he was doing, the repeated reconnoitering). Meantime he had received our message that we had found a habitable island. Now he used this to persuade his crew to give up this insane enterprise; explaining that we had discovered a place that would accept men, were awaiting them as promised. "Even so, it was all I could do to tear them away from Russia." No way to tell us the correspondingly immense news that he had the fuel and was coming. Earlier he had taken me aboard *Pushkin* and showed me precisely why that was. Navigating the sometimes narrow waters, his VLF antenna, which trailed a couple hundred feet in the submarine's wake, had been severed—a sunken ship, he had speculated, one of numerous derelicts now occupying both surface and undersurface of these choked sea-lanes; thereby immobilizing the channels on which alone we could communicate. Whatever had done it, it was as simple and awful as that.

"Russia." The name fell on the island air as he concluded his account. "A terrible place. You are fortunate, Captain, in never having had to take your men to their own country. Just seeing it . . . it came close to costing me my crew, my ship."

Then silence. Then something that seemed like a shudder, a trembling, but was not. An unspoken signal of desiring urgently to leave the past in that sense of any intelligent man's doing so, and especially if it be such a one as his and his ship's, in that the past is beyond man's changing, beyond his redemption; of wishing only to look ahead; the future being the only thing possibly subject to man's control, what might ours be? He looked out at the horizon.

"Do you believe there are people out there?"

It had become an immutable fact of our existence, sometimes extracting terrible tolls. Whenever I myself had come here and gazed out into that boundlessness of waters, the thought had never failed to occur; or if there were another with me, to occur to both of us. It had kept me from paying as many visits as I would have liked to this place which, save for that, had become a comfort to me. There was no getting away from it; the thought was imperishable, appearing to have established not just a permanent dwelling place in one's subconscious but to pop up, like one of those chronic itches brought on by certain stimuli, every time one sat, as now, simply gazing out to sea, as though that horizon plucked it forth and set it buzzing in one's head, attacking one, sometimes producing something one felt not all that distant from madness. The circumference so huge, as if all the universe lay directly before our eyes, nothing preventing our viewing it in every detail, what had happened, what was happening even now, except that terrible horizon of nothingness which took on the aspect of an immense and opaque, an impossibly cruel window blind. It seemed to taunt one in its sadism. If only it would rise, even for a moment, and give us a glimpse! I was in no way surprised that he had asked the identical question, looking out into the infinity of naked ocean, looking at the horizon and as it were over it—the question which would never go away, eternal as the sea itself—what was now beyond? Even the answer always the same, as in some unvarying responsive reading in a churchly ritual, out of the Book of Common Prayer.

"There have to be," I said.

Until now, the thought could only have been speculation hypothetical in the entire, impossible of verification; a helpless game of the mind one played, whether one wished to play it or not. Even now, trapped in this fixed liturgy, mind dulled by it, protectively so, it did not immediately occur to me that it could be more than a thought, burst free from that theorem-exploring category where it had so long resided. With an active jolt, realizing even as he said it that matters might well now be different, conjecture subject to actual authentication . . . even so, comprehending only in part . . . it was still, so fixed were the old ways, difficult to grasp as reality as opposed to phantasm.

"The fuel," he said. "What do you intend doing with it?"

I sat and looked at the sea, down the coastline at the tiny particles of the two ships, trying to shake the old thinking. I simply didn't know. I felt I would have to have time. A certain interval in which to permit the new conditions, new realities, to take hold. Perhaps the island was getting to me, beginning to exert its hold, its claim—had it not given us everything, held back nothing, nourished us? Life was coming to be quite good here, more so every day it sometimes seemed, settling into a pattern by no means without its attractions, its beguilements; something he might not understand: We had been here months, himself days. Unable to give any real answer to the question he had asked, I fell back on equivocation, on platitudes.

"I don't know. The idea hasn't settled in. It was always . . . the thought that of course we must find out—had to find out. If we could. We couldn't. That was that. So . . . it was very unreal . . ."

My own words fuzzy, his came much more focused, almost as if verbally shaking me, his tone close to sharp.

"It isn't unreal anymore, Captain."

"Understand, we had given up expecting you . . . and the fuel. Now . . . yes, we have the means to go looking. Now, thanks to yourself, we have . . ." It was as if I were saying the words not to him, who understood it, but to myself, who didn't quite and was now trying to make himself do so . . . "We have a ship which can do that. Go find out."

"We have two ships which can do that," he said.

Again, as if prompted to do so by a lookout's sighting, we simultaneously looked down the shore to where both of them lay anchored. Why that thought—of not one, but two ships available for the purpose—had not occurred to me seemed even more astonishing. I found myself appraising the submarine in the distance; her lines, something unusual about her.

"Captain, I have seen many submarines. Ours; some of yours. I have never seen one that size."

"She was the largest ever built," he said, the barest touch, not excessive, of pride. He seemed to be studying her thoughtfully himself, even as he concisely, routinely, furnished me her salient naval aspects. "Two propellor shafts. Two reactors, three hundred and sixty MW each. Five hundred and sixty-one feet overall, eighty-five-foot beam, displacement twenty-five thousand tons submerged. Twenty-six, eight-warhead, five hundred-kt SS-N-20 missiles."

I thought of the *Nathan James's* 8,200-ton displacement. Of our own missile power, relatively so small. I had always regarded us as a powerful ship; but compared with *Pushkin* . . .

"You make us seem a lifeboat," I said.

"Of course, two-thirds of that space is for the SS-N-20's. As you've seen . . ."

He had more to say of her. "Oh, yes, her speed. Since there are no secrets anymore, Captain," he said whimsically. "Forty knots."

"*Forty* knots. On the surface?"

"Submerged."

"Jesus Christ," I said. "Captain, you have impressed me."

"Good. I was trying to do just that."

I found myself continuing to study that long black shape strung out on sheltered waters. A distinct aspect . . .

"You find something else unusual in her, Captain?" he asked, almost, I felt, teasing me along.

"Yes, I do. I see now. The sail area. That stub sail. I have never seen another like that. And one other thing. The hull. Much more of a . . . of a high rise to it."

"Very clever, Captain. You are almost on to her real secret."

I thought a bit, continuing to analyze her. "I wish I could say I were. I am not."

It was rather as if we were playing some parlor game in which I was to say, "I give up." I didn't say that. But unable to pin it down, I might as well have done so.

"Well, sir, I will have to reveal all," he said with that same Attic wit, as if giving away closely held secrets. "And risk a court-martial. *Pushkin* was built explicitly for operation in the Arctic ice pack. The high-rise hull—the stub sail structure: Both were to permit us to break through the ice for missile launch. Forward diving planes—you can't see that from here—mounted on the bow so they could be retracted to prevent ice damage—submersibles of course normally having sail-mounted diving planes."

"How stupid of me not to have figured that out," I said.

"In fact, our permanent station was there—the Arctic."

I reflected how we might well have been near each other more than once on our station in the Barents, his transiting that sea to the Arctic; how he might have seen us through his periscope, how in turn he might have been one of the submarines that not infrequently turned up on our sonar gear.

"But when you launched . . .?"

"A fluke. We happened to be in the Atlantic, just off Brittany. On our way back at flank speed to the Arctic. We had been sent rather abruptly on a mission unusual for us—to the Mediterranean—to keep an eye on your *Theodore Roosevelt,* which had suddenly showed up. What a monster! Stuck our scope up a hundred times to have a look at her. Biggest *carrier* ever built. I used to think, her sitting there in the cross hairs of *Pushkin*'s scope—forgive me, Captain . . . I believe you have an expression—shooting fish in a barrel. We have one something like . . . a single torpedo . . . Strange, we've still got all of *those* aboard . . . nuclear-warhead C-533's . . . never expended a blessed one," he said in what seemed a peculiar aside; picked up again. "Anyhow, then we were relieved on station by one of our other subs—Sierra class, as you called them—we didn't need a submarine like *Pushkin* to do that job, if it became necessary—and ordered back to our proper duty—the Arctic."

He turned to me, as in a confiding manner, his voice exceptionally quiet.

"Captain, let me ask you something. Did you know it was going to happen sometime? Know to a certainty? I mean in the sense of knowing that the sun would rise tomorrow?"

It seemed an important point to him, why I could not tell. It was easy enough to answer.

"Yes," I said. "I knew that." I suddenly felt I understood what he was getting at and added: "I would imagine that everyone in our position—yours, mine . . . or something like it . . . knew it, don't you? Everybody . . . on both sides . . . who was out there looking down the other's throat." I thought back a moment, trying to recall, to be as accurate as possible, since the matter seemed to be of some concern to him. "So much so that we almost never talked about it . . . Right now, I can't recall a single conversation of that kind."

"Just so," he said, as if that were the answer he sought, for reasons known only to himself. "To men like us—both sides as you say—doing what we were doing, it was only a matter of when, wasn't it? One thing we were certain of—we'd never see the end of the century. Nobody so much as mentioning that"—an almost imperceptible shrug of the shoulders—"for the very good reason of: What in the world good would it have done? Who was there to hear?"

He shifted a little on the rock ledge. "I wanted to get your opinion because . . ." He paused, as if wishing to be exact with his words. "In a way, that was the strangest part of all. I used to wonder if that had ever happened before: the people in the uniforms, the naval, the military people, most of them—not wanting it. Certainly they had in times past: After all, it was their profession. Not this time. True on our side. Yours?"

"Practically nobody wanted it," I said. "Military or not." I had become thoughtful, concentrating, caught up in his own odd exercise of trying, apparently, to solve a baffling enigma. "And yet it was going to happen. To me that was the strangest part. It was almost as though these things were there—so they simply were going to be used."

He examined that thoughtfully in turn. "Had to be used maybe? It would have been too much of a waste not to use them?"

I found myself beginning to have something almost strange as an affection for this man. Felt something of the same sort happening in him as regards myself—such feelings can hardly exist one-way. Nikolai Bazarov his name was: I caught myself from addressing him by his Christian one. He, meantime, brought himself back, as from a reverie, or a trip into the otherworldly, to his factual account.

"We had got as far as off Brittany when everything happened."

"And being handy, you were ordered to take out our Spanish bases
. . . And Gibraltar a side effect."

"Precisely, Captain." He spoke in reflective tones, simply as if wanting to wind up the account in a neat, sailorlike fashion, one ship's captain
to another. "I don't know if your ships had fixed targets." My heart,
mindful of Orel, fearful he would ask that of the *Nathan James*, not
certain I would give a truthful reply, skipped a beat. "I expect so. In any
case ours did. I came to identify our squadron of Arctic submersibles not
so much with their actual names as with the American cities they were
variously assigned. This one, Washington. That one, Chicago. That one,
Houston. *Pushkin*'s happened to be New York." A soft, indefinable trace
of a smile. "I pretty much came to think of her as the *New York.*"

"New York?" I repeated inanely. Why that should have given me
such a turn I couldn't say. Someone had to have that assignment; then—
of course, the fact of the man who did being beside me. I listened to that
voice, a peculiar, almost musical note now in it.

"Odd thing: I always had a desire to visit New York. Of course, I
suppose everybody on earth did. The great city of our times. Like Rome
of old. Wished I could somehow get a leave, a week or so, have a good
look around before we ourselves . . ." He took a deep breath. "One got
some strange thoughts on a ship submerged up there in the Arctic
. . . One got strange thoughts in a submarine with our mission . . ."

"Not just on a submarine," I said, remembering some of ours in the
Barents.

"Where was I? Oh, yes. New York: We had to be very good to get
that mission. And I won't deny a certain pride in having been given it;
true of myself; of *Pushkin*'s company."

He waited in contemplation, in ponderment; I could see the parade
of things past trooping through his mind; a spectral feeling unaccountably
beginning to take hold of me.

"I spoke just now of how most of us—and on both sides you agreed—
who were out there possessed the least taste of all for what we knew was
going to be. Still, I am ashamed to tell you the feeling I had when I knew
the hour had at last come and that by the unlucky chance of where we
happened to be, our mission was downgraded to a couple of Spanish bases
instead of the honor of taking out your great city. I actually felt cheated.
For one small moment I had exactly that thought. Regret. What a terrible
thing to have had it at all."

I felt no shock whatsoever at that, and promptly told him so.

"A very natural feeling, Captain, to my way of thinking. Not to want it but if it was going to be . . . I would guess that to have been true of just about everyone commanding a ship with your assignment, with our assignment. Every one of us . . . ship's captains."

"Perhaps. But I tell you, things had happened to our minds, Captain."

He paused a moment. "We never learned to talk with each other, did we? How monstrous that was."

He looked out at the vast seascape. "At all events, our own regular Arctic station . . . Fourteen minutes: That was the distance we thought of New York as being. Our entire cargo of missiles navigationally always targeted on her. One of them would have done the job—we had allocated twenty of the SS-N-20's just to that one city. Redundancy. I know you did the same."

"Oh, yes. It was the governing word." Now myself falling into his rather relaxed analytical mood, as if examining, as he said, some historical curiosity. "Just about the most important word ever it became. The reason for so many; for always adding on."

"One of the poets from my city of Orel might have written—if he had been around to do so—that we succeeded in making the world redundant."

We waited in the silence.

"Dostoevski." He said the word with a singular reverence. It seemed to hang in the air. "Do you know the Grand Inquisitor scene in *Karamazov*?"

"Yes."

"The Inquisitor may have had a point. Man had too much freedom. Freedom to eliminate himself."

In his words there was an absolute absence of bitterness, of cynicism, virtually—except for that one instance—of emotion. I did not find this strange—something of the sort had come to be true of myself, of my ship's people. With some exceptions, a singular detachment—I had always connected it with the mind's concern as to holding on to its reason; mind knowing that men in our circumstance must hoard their bank accounts of emotion, frugally expend. In this respect himself having progressed to a point perhaps a step ahead of our own. He talked more like a calm and professional student of history, preoccupied less with the morality than the actuality of accomplished events, probing matters of fascinating scholarly interest. Nevertheless suddenly a quiet laugh, equally free of the slightest trace of the sardonic, reaching my ears, actually startling me and enhancing that sense of the phantasmal I felt.

"Where was I? Oh, yes. New York was obviously turned over to one of our sister ships. And we got the Spanish bases."

The account was complete. I was silent a moment, again looking down the coastline at the huge submarine in the distance, reflecting on her story, her fate, which at last had brought her here. I murmured a banality.

"So you still have left an Arctic submarine."

"Anchored here in the tropics." He sighed. "Ironic, isn't it?" He suddenly brightened. "I wish there was an ice pack around to show how easy it is for *Pushkin*," he said, again with that allowance of pride any captain has in his ship, in what she can do. "She loves ice packs."

"It's still a good piece away but I guess the closest place would be the Antarctic."

He grinned. "Ice is ice. Same as the Arctic as far as *Pushkin* is concerned. Shall we make a quick voyage there—at those forty knots—so that I may demonstrate her capabilities to you?"

"I'll take your word for it, Captain."

We turned away from that diversion. Waited, thoughtfully. Then, back to realities, presently I could hear him going on. Tones again conversational, even, straightforward—in short, the briefing tones of a trained and disciplined naval officer who has something to say and was now, temporarily sidetracked, coming to the point; yet, as he continued, at times strange hesitancies which at first baffled me until I made up my mind that, not just a briefing, he also was feeling his way as he went, as any good seaman would, knowing himself in unfamiliar waters, these including the people he was dealing with, and represented in myself. He was not into my mind yet. I think he was trying to get there, and that all of the otherwise rather inexplicable dialogue he had initiated was part of his method of doing so.

"I have a plan," he said, looking out at the horizon, the sea having darkened a fraction, its line clearer. "With your permission, I would like to set it forth, the principal lines of it, inviting you to disagree. May I proceed with that understanding?"

"Please do so, sir."

"We have two ships; each now able to go anywhere. *Nathan James:* five-year fuel supply. *Pushkin:* ten years. Go separately; go together. But we also have the island . . . a place. A place which you Americans . . ." It was the first time in this context that identification or distinction of any sort had been made and it came in all praise . . . "good seamen, found. Something habitable, a place free of contamination . . . and having found, have built something fine, built well, built as sailors build . . . have brought food from the earth, from the sea . . . labors so hard one can scarcely imagine them . . . yes, something fine, very fine . . . I see it, I sense it. No, have done something much more . . . Have started a way of life . . . a community, one which functions . . . That community, this island—that is the most precious thing of all. We must hold onto the island . . ." I became aware with a certain shock of the word "we" entering this monologue . . . "We must never give up the island . . ." The word "island" striking like an epiphany, but now with a new ring, as if it were no longer just ours in fee simple, but his as well . . . an astonishment in me at this sudden interjection of joint proprietorship from one so newly arrived, deciding it meant nothing, actually could be favorable in the sense of taking him and his people in, and perhaps after all he had purchased his share with the most valuable of coin, the fuel . . . "It must be held. A great treasure, greater even than the ships . . . one such blessed plot of earth . . . that accepts men . . . more, nurtures them. A place without price . . . And yet . . ."

It was a rather marvelous speech, not without eloquence, and no reason in the world for me to think it was anything other than heartfelt. Still, I felt it a time to keep silent, to wait for the proposal he said he had in mind. And now this thing of substance came, the words breaking into the vast silence that held everywhere, otherwise broken only by the metronomic collision of the sea and the great rocks far below; his voice reaching me in quiet, rather pleasingly assuasive cadences. He simply nodded at the horizon.

"I do not think we can escape the . . . necessity . . . the responsibility, I believe it fair to call it . . . of sending one of our two ships on a mission to find out. The ship—either ship now, as I say—has the fuel to go anywhere. How long the voyage will take . . ." Again his shoulders shrugged almost imperceptibly, as at an unimportant detail. "Three . . . six months perhaps. In any case something less, I would judge, than, say . . . a year. Either ship can carry enough provisions for that period, even a submarine—those missiles we shot off gave us some extra space. What we would do, you and I, is: chart a general course. The ship herself free to make alterations, course and destination changes, as she proceeds, based on her own findings. Based, too, on what she reports back to us, final decisions to be made here. It should be an interesting voyage." He smiled thinly, turning slightly to me. "Rediscovering the world. A Magellan, a Drake, a Bellingshausen, all over again. Eh, Captain?"

He had just named three circumnavigators of the globe. The last mentioned, a Russian naval officer, being also in my own opinion one of the greatest of Antarctic explorers, I could not resist the opportunity to show off.

"Fabian Gottlieb Von Bellingshausen," I said.

He turned to me. "Captain, you have impressed me."

"Good. I was trying to do just that."

"The world needs circumnavigating again." His glance found the horizon. "What a voyage to make now—to *see* what is out there!"

"Agreed, sir. Any seaman would jump at the chance."

"Precisely. Do you find any major objections so far, sir?"

"I would prefer you continue."

"Of course. As between the two vessels, it would seem obvious which should undertake that voyage. A matter surely hardly arguable. *Pushkin.* Far less exposure for the crew. Submerged, she could penetrate the deepest zones of radiation . . . we did so in . . . Russia. Any coastal city, anywhere. She could . . . just for example, having spoken of that city . . . come right into New York harbor. Stick her scope up. Find out what really happened, what it's like, or a pretty good firsthand idea. To your people. Of course we know what in substance we shall find there. That is hardly the point. It is that there is something to having seen for yourself—in a matter so urgent—what you already know. One is compelled to do so, have one's own look. There is something in a man that insists on that if it is at all possible—as it is now. Something especially in a seaman that says this must be done. I found that true for myself and my men as to Russia," he said matter-of-factly. "We knew what we would find. Still, we had to see with our own eyes. Terrible as it was, I know now it was an absolute necessity—for the mind. For one's soul."

He paused, rearranging himself a bit on the rock. I had a small worry that he had moved too near its edge. An odd thing occurred to me—he seemed to be trying to persuade me, almost as a bait, that we should have a look at our home as he had had at his, at its known devastation (supposedly taking a given number of us in *Pushkin*—I waited for that, as to its details); odd in that it seemed a strange sort of concern for him to have. It was time for me to insert something.

"Some of my ship's company believe they will find habitable land there, thriving people; a place they can stay."

"Good," he said calmly. "Those possessing such fantasies above all should be included in those who go in *Pushkin*. When they find out so differently, they can come back and tell the others. You will be rid of that problem."

It was as if he had disposed of a minor detail, speaking very much like a ship's captain instructing me in the handling of a vexing, if easily solved problem. Having done so, he continued at once from this aside; above all, his voice radiating a captain's certainty as to course.

"I would not dishonor it by calling it the satisfying of a curiosity, this look at one's home . . . that part is a duty. But the ship really goes for something else altogether. However great the necessity of the other, that is not the ship's principal mission. The ship has a far more important one than that. She goes looking for places with greater likelihood of having people. That's what she's really looking for—people. Human beings. Like ourselves."

He paused, reflectively. "There's a practical side to this. She might, let us say, find people to bring here, making certain first that they are uncontaminated—the radiation officer would see to that. Not many—the island is too small. A few people carefully chosen. We would be compelled to be selfish, selective . . . people chosen for their skills or for something else useful to this community. More women would help." That reference so quickly made, with no emphasis whatsoever, a mere example, his moving so immediately on that any particularity as to it was lost, if intended in the first place. I decided not. "That but one of many possibilities. All dependent on what the ship finds out there." The slightest nod of the head toward the unrevelatory horizon.

Abruptly he turned directly to me, his voice while full of conviction all equable up to now, modulating to something deeply earnest, insistent, even with a proselytizing note.

"But the true reason for sending the ship is not even the practical one in that purely selfish sense. The reason is . . . simply that we have to know. If there are other people than ourselves. That is what we have absolutely to find out, Captain. We have no choice. I cannot explain why. I do not think I need to do so."

Of course I understood all of that. But there was something else and I held in my hand the core of my astonishment. This time I stepped in with it.

"You want to take your ship off and do that?"

He smiled faintly. "Not exactly, Captain. The ship, yes. I have a plan there, too."

I was about to ask the next question, feeling for the first time in the air that foreboding sense that after all of these brotherly interchanges, something else—hard, barrier differences—was about to make its appearance, when deliberately before I could, he proceeded in almost a new voice, discursiveness vanished, replaced by short, clipped phrases as to a plan obviously workable, perhaps brilliant.

"Pushkin to make that voyage. Ship's company . . . say, two-thirds of it—by necessity consisting of our people . . . the particular skills known only by submariners. The other third brought ashore . . . taken into this community. Replaced, that one-third, by your own sailors . . . their skills as destroyer men, seamanship skills, radio communications skills for an instance, easily transferable to a submarine . . . no problem whatsoever there, a minimum of indoctrination . . . a Russian-American submarine at that point and thereafter . . . just as here an American-Russian community."

And he simply stopped. I sat quite overwhelmed by my impressions. More than by any other single one, at the fluent way he had taken over, as it were. His references to the island, to anything . . . as if they were now all jointly held, by my people, by his people, jointly owned, simply taking that for granted. He had a complete plan for everything, down to the finest detail: One-third of *Pushkin*'s crew put ashore, to be replaced by an equivalent number of our people . . . yes, it was almost as if he had taken charge. I could not—indeed at this point was not prepared to do anything . . . other than stall.

"An interesting arrangement. I would hate to see yourself leave, Captain." I said it almost as a formality.

An actual grin, a tone turned light. "But I would have no intention of doing so. My fine executive officer is qualified in all respects to command—as much as I may like to think otherwise, my own presence entirely unnecessary. *Pushkin* goes on an exploration to find out what there may be on the rest of the earth, beyond this island. May find nothing. The important matters will be here . . ." He paused, seemed again almost proprietarily to look around. "This island. Where we have something of a certainty . . . All the important matters will be proceeding here . . . After all, this is now the center of the universe." He smiled mischievously . . . "Wouldn't want to miss them. Why, I would not think of leaving here."

I was astonished. Since the "Magellan" voyage was almost irresistible to any sailor, especially to the captain of the ship which would make the voyage, why was he himself not going? Wonderments crowded my mind, yes, suspicions. To give voice to these . . . if there was one thing above all we must avoid, it was suspicion of any kind as to each other's motives. Once they got in . . . To assure that they did not, he had taken that first immense step himself—the immediate, voluntary transfer of the fuel I have mentioned, without first trying to extract concessions of any kind. I must not be the one to introduce misgivings as between us.

"I would not think of leaving here," he had said. A beat of a pause. I believe I suggested that there was no reason to suppose that his uprightness excluded cunning. "Unless you should not want me."

It was my turn. "Come off it, Captain."

"I thought I had rather good English. I don't think I know that expression."

"Of course you do. You do now."

He laughed outright. "Then I shall consider myself invited aboard. That is to say, if . . . if the plan goes with you. Naturally you will need time to consider . . . Of course, if you do not like my plan, you can take the *James* and all her ship's company, conduct all of these explorations yourself, leave the island to us in safekeeping—we'll keep it in good shape for you until you return."

He had looked at me, saying that. His eyes had a light in them, his face an expression to be sure of a certain mirth . . . still, I had the distinct feeling one could not be sure that if I had said, "Why, what a splendid arrangement; we'll see you in a year . . ." One could not be sure at all. Impressions, thoughts, feelings, many of them in conflict with one another, rushing in on me; a time to say nothing, make no commitment; to back off; establish, after the hardest and coolest appraisals, a position. Then I knew what my problem was. Through all of this onslaught came one overriding concern—two such sea captains as sat on this cliffside both being on a single island . . . each accustomed to sovereignty, himself of a strong personality, hardly a man inclined to passiveness . . . such a circumstance seemed to me fatally flawed . . . there could be trouble, built-in, inherent, inescapable . . . trouble . . . Frankly, I wished he would go with his ship. I could hardly order him to do so . . . if nothing else the fuel he had brought us restraining me, seeming to exclude that option. Indeed that seemed to be the problem: I could not order him to do anything. I spoke pleasantly.

"I will discuss it with my officers and ship's company of the *James,*" I said. "And let you know. Quite presently."

"I shall await your answer, Captain. Incidentally, if *Pushkin* goes, we will need a new VLF antenna for her to report her findings back to us."

It was as though he had anticipated every detail.

"That will be no problem."

I had half-risen to go.

"Captain?"

"Yes?"

He spoke offhandedly, as though he had simply forgotten to mention another detail.

"One thing is to be taken for granted, of course. I hardly need say this. But lest there be any mistake, let me state it clearly—in what I believe you call plain English. I have been too long a sailor not to know that there can be but one ship's captain. Surely you assumed this in all that I had to say. I simply want there to be not the slightest misunderstanding as to that. Remaining here, I submit myself without reservation to your command, Captain. And to whatever duties you may deem me fit for."

So at last, I thought, he was inside my mind. If I had not known it before, I knew it now: I was dealing with a formidable human being.

"The matter had not occurred to me," I said. "But I appreciate your stating it so definitively, Captain."

He had stood up. "I am very hungry," he said.

I stood alongside him, held his arm for a moment, why I cannot say, perhaps as though, subconsciously remembering the Jesuit, remembering also that he was still in recovery from his long ordeal on the submarine, I wished to remove him from the cliff's edge.

"Then let's go eat," I said.

Climbing down through the green, it was with a certain startlement that I realized he had not so much as come near to asking about the women, whether the participation of his ship's company in the settlement was to include participation in them as well. I wondered why he had not done so. That he took it for granted? Or, just the opposite, that he would not even ask, now or ever? Simply leave it up to us. Even as I had these thoughts, as we walked along the stream bed, from him came the most casually pitched question, seeming idly asked.

"Any effects of the radiation on your men you've noticed so far?"

Something quite awful passed through me. I continued my steps, steadied my voice.

"Nothing noticeable." I told a technical truth.

"I'm glad to hear it. That was my chief concern about you. Especially when you were telling me about the passage through that terrible winter. Naturally—as I've indicated—that was one advantage—maybe the chief one—a submariner would have over a surface-ship sailor."

It was Silva's crew who found them. Having taken his fishing detail off the northern part of the island, a vicinity which had been yielding with exceptional abundance of late, he sighted something come to rest against a tiny spot of sand, one of those that here and there interrupted the high rocky cliffs on the eastern side. Saw the boat, approached, saw then *Nathan James-2* painted on its upturned side. The boat itself heavily battered, the sail which had been rigged collapsed, as if having encountered vicious seas. Later, looking at it, I was to remember that strong storm that had hit the island. It was not until he had come still nearer that Silva saw what was lying across the deck. They had tied themselves in. He put out a line and towed what was left of the boat down the waters to the settlement. We would never know but I was to wonder. Had they found nothing, realized it was hopeless and headed back to the only refuge? The Jesuit conducted the funeral services, brief readings from the Scriptures in the Main Hall. All of ship's company then marched up the hill, following men bearing the two coffins Noisy Travis had fashioned, of very differing sizes, hers Preston alone carrying on his shoulder. Earlier Noisy had made a cross to place over Billy, of the same fine wood that had gone into the settlement buildings; then had come to see me in a quandary about Meyer.

"A Jewish girl, I believe," he said. "A Star of David, Captain?"

Meyer had been about as nonreligious as a person could be. I remembered that humorous scene by the lifeline when she had complained of Billy's going on a bit too much about it. I was certain she would not have wanted the Cross, little more the Star of David.

"We have to put something," Noisy said. "Can't have something over Billy's, not over hers. Wouldn't seem right, Cap'n. I knew her pretty well, sir. I reckon she wouldn't mind."

It was a remarkably long speech for the carpenter, and the only one involving an effort at persuasion, even insistence, I could recall ever having heard from him, its heartfeltness reaching through to me.

"You're right, Noisy. Make it a Star of David."

Our little cemetery stood on one of the island's highest points, over the green a vast circumferential view of the sea, reaching to all horizons. It was as if we were still aboard ship, committing their bodies to the deep. We stood there, all wearing whites instead of the dungarees that had become our uniform, as the Jesuit read the familiar words. A slight easterly breeze was blowing, rustling the pages in his breviary, his having to hold them down . . . *In sure hope of the Resurrection* . . . In sailor fashion, ship's company joined in its own requiem, Porterfield in his wisdom choosing not a hymn, in consideration of Meyer, but a song, in consideration of Billy, that for reasons unknown has long had an almost mystical meaning to sailors; one also he knew they both had liked. "Shenandoah." The voices, men's and women's, rising softly in the air, falling out over the peaceful sea.

Oh, Shenandoah, I love your daughter,
Away, you rolling river,
For her, I've crossed the stormy water,
Away, away, I'm bound away,
'Cross the wide Missouri . . .

They went down in the separate coffins; the burial ground itself one space, however, so that they lay side by side, under Noisy's two escutcheons, united at last, forever so, high above the immortal sea.

.3.

THURLOW'S WARNING

A ship will deteriorate if it just sits. An exercise run: the *Nathan James* needed that, and regularly, say every couple of weeks. Before, not daring to expend the fuel, we were now freed up to indulge this matter virtually essential if we were to preserve the ship. We had had three now. The ship casting off at first light, returning at last light. Standing out, going over the horizon, making turns, executing various drills, shiphandling, seamanship, gunnery, sonar tracking and a score more, keeping her at low speeds to conserve fuel even though she now had such ample reserves. For purposes of these maneuvers I had divided ship's company into "starboard" and "port" crews; each of about eighty-five hands, alternating in the biweekly run, one under myself, the other under my executive officer Thurlow, so that all hands could keep their shipboard skills up to the mark. It had turned out that the men actually looked forward to the cruises, to resume being sailors if only for a day. Men now farmers, yanked from their tilling; men now carpenters from their settlement-upkeep chores; fishermen from that detail; all to discover again that they were still seamen, sailors; boatswain's mates, radarmen, electrician's mates, signalmen, machinist's mates, gunner's mates, enginemen, and all the many other specialties, given a chance to turn once again to their old skills, the idea being if they should ever be needed again—if the ship should go somewhere—neither she nor her crew would have rusted away. Wholly unlikely that eventuality now seemed, unless—what each week appeared a more and more remote possibility, until it became in our minds an almost dismissible idea—radiation might yet move in, attack the island which by now had become such a possession of ours, an ever-growing satisfaction in it, in its livability, in what we had made of it—more and more feeling, not just a refuge, but like—home. We could not protect ourselves against that distant chance of contamination except, should it ever happen, to flee from it on the ship. The exercise also serving another need—to keep the men sharp in what also seemed improbable, some attack on the island by unknown other ships or persons suddenly appearing from over the horizon and seeing what they would see, understandably desirous of possessing for themselves this forthcoming island, and all we had added to it—Billy Barker's claimed sighting came to mind; the ship then being required to defend the island. As to the former contingency, I had had a conversation once or twice with Thurlow, who, after Selmon, being ship's company's most knowledgeable man in the field, had succeeded him as radiation officer, concerning the possibility of anything atmospheric ever driving us out of here. He was entirely reassuring—well, not quite entirely, having acquired from his predecessor that mind-set as to the always unpredictable character of that new element, though not confronting us, it seeming an incontestable truth that elsewhere it had become an ineradicable part of the earth; of its very anatomy.

"Even with the most farfetched aberration of the winds," he said one day as we sat chatting in my cliffside cabin, "anything that was going to reach here . . . it would seem to be valid that it would have long since done so. Except . . ." He glanced out at the vast Pacific, at those horizons over which, if anything ever arrived at all, it would come. "I can think of but one circumstance that could alter that projection."

"And that?" I said mildly. "Don't keep me in suspense, Mr. Thurlow."

"No, sir. The only thing that might threaten us would have to be if someone, somewhere, fired off more nuclear missiles, dropped more nuclear bombs."

"Now?" I said in astonishment. "Who in the world would launch them or drop them? And at or on whom?"

"I'm just speaking of a very finite thing, sir. Surely we've all learned by now that in this field it's difficult to speak in absolutes, absent evidentiary data."

He was getting as lofty and as circumlocutory as Selmon sometimes had been. Understandably, it went with a profession in which the capricious, the unforeseeable, was commonplace.

"Try speaking some English, please, Mr. Thurlow."

He smiled gently. "Well, sir, we don't *know* what else there is in the rest of the world, especially in every particular part of it, do we? I hold as much as ever to the belief, all data as conclusive as you can ever get to absoluteness, barring visible authentication, that everything is gone. Correct that. *Almost* everything. Most of us have always felt that there were pockets of people somewhere, haven't we? Still are."

"Yes. I feel that, too," I said, a bit impatiently. "Other people. We've covered that ground. Please come to whatever your point was, Lieutenant."

"Yes, sir. I was getting to that. Suppose one of those places was a little larger than what we call 'pockets' . . . Suppose it had some missiles . . . Suppose there was one such group somewhere else, similarly supplied . . . Suppose they let go at each other . . . given the record to date I'm sure they could find some reason to do so . . . and introduced a fresh new supply of rather large contamination into the atmosphere . . . suppose the winds, such efficient couriers as we've seen, transported it here . . ."

"Suppose," I said.

He stopped. I simply looked at him. He remained entirely unperturbed under that steady gaze.

"You asked me about absolutes, Captain. There just aren't any absolutes in these circumstances, are there, sir? And what I describe is no more than what happened before."

"Quite a scenario. You wouldn't care to quote odds?"

"Captain, I don't think we can permit ourselves that indulgence where radiation contamination is concerned, where the winds are concerned . . . if we've learned anything we've learned that. But I will say, if not infinitesimal—we've learned also not to call any conceivability infinitesimal when speaking of those two forces—I would judge remote. Quite remote. I would go so far as to say extremely remote."

"I'm extremely glad to hear it," I said.

"Sir, one thing."

"Yes, Mr. Thurlow?"

"Our own missiles. *James*'s missiles. Now added, *Pushkin*'s missiles. I was doing a few calculations the other day. I happen to have taken a look down at the two of them lying there so close together—must have started these mental exercises. What's still sitting in the holds of those two ships . . ."

He stopped, as if sorry already he had brought the subject up. It was my turn.

"Yes," I said. "Go on, Alex," a certain insistence in my voice.

"Well, sir, their supplies have been scarcely touched. The *James* has forty-four Tomahawks in her magazine—seven hundred and four H's in our old Hiroshima terms. *Pushkin* has twenty-four SS-N-20's with eight five-hundred-kt warheads per missile—she only had to expend two: seven thousand six hundred and eighty H's left. Together, both ships, a total of eight thousand three hundred and eighty-four H's." He had no notes before him and the figures emerged as tonelessly as a memory-perfect accountant reporting any routine inventory. "Do you understand what I mean, sir, by the possibility of there still being forces existent that could do it all over again—I mean recontaminate the earth's atmosphere, or certainly a considerable portion of it, almost as badly as those things did before? Why, sir, one could simply look over the cliffside and strike the word 'possibility.' These two ships alone could quite do the job."

Thurlow's voice, all of equanimity before, seemed to my ear just at the very last there to have mutated a notch into something carrying the unintended tones of urgency. The ships were sitting just below us. We could actually see them. An element absolutely new had entered the dialogue, its chatlike nature abruptly catalyzed by those ships into something as real as could be, and strangely scary. I looked at him in a different way.

"Are you getting at something, Mr. Thurlow?"

"Nothing, sir . . . except the fact that the very existence of those objects—whether ten thousand miles away or a cable's length—prevents me from ever being able to reach those absolutes you were mentioning. I take it you meant absolutes as to freedom of concern from precisely what it is they cause—when launched, of course."

"Who in God's name would launch them?"

"You mean ours?" He shrugged. "Nobody, I suppose. Their . . ." He hesitated, found the word. "Being means they could be launched. I believe you were asking me as to possibilities, sir."

It was a merited reproof of his captain, a lesson in the most elementary of logic.

"So I was, Mr. Thurlow. And you were entirely in line." Now I watched his eyes very carefully as I asked it. "You're not proposing any particular action for us to take?"

"Sir, that is not my field . . ."

I spoke more briskly. "I asked you a question, Mr. Thurlow. When I do that, I expect an answer. I'm telling you to make it your field."

"Well, sir, if you put it that way, I would prefer . . ." For a moment, the rarest thing in the world for this officer, he seemed to find himself unable to say what he wanted to say, as if sorry he had ever got into the matter in the first place, opened this Pandora's box, his reward for doing what he was paid to do, analyze, complete with the best data available, every contingency, near or distant—his reward for fulfilling as radiation officer this essential duty, he must surely have felt, being to be most unfairly put on the spot. So be it, he seemed to be saying—since they want it, I will let them have it.

"I would prefer that the missiles ceased to exist," he said. "Our ship. The Russian ship. Hugging our island."

Coming from Thurlow, such counsel was enough to pop one's spine straight up, while sending a trickle of chill down it. I addressed him now in a soft tone, full of some heartfelt undefined gratitude.

"I want to thank you, Mr. Thurlow. You have been very helpful."

"Yes, sir. I feared I might have stepped across the line, mine of supplying facts and projections and yours of decision-making, sir."

I kept my smile inward, assumed a bit of his own academic-lecture tone.

"You need never concern yourself with that danger, Mr. Thurlow. Ship's captains need all the help they can get and are in no way infallible."

He seemed to find it unnecessary, perhaps even unwise, to make any comment as to that observation. Lieutenant Thurlow was never an officer to be underestimated—and not just in his naval duties, but also in naval relationships.

Taking that as his signal of dismissal, he rose and left. When he had gone I stepped out on the deck that formed almost a bridge, looked straight down at the two ships, standing so near each other. I could see men moving around on both. It had always given me a sense of peace to do so, and of reassurance—they could take us away if ever need be. Now my eyes seemed to pierce their hulls and see what was inside them; my mind recalling Thurlow's rather ominous words, "hugging our island"; seeing into their magazines, their huge inventory of missiles, comprehending, as an absolutely new thought, incredibly never having had it before, that in the sense in which he had spoken they by their very nature constituted the most immense risk to anything you might care to name, anywhere; let alone to the place from which one could almost have spat on them. For the first time as I studied them, those two ships appeared to me not as sources of comfort, of peace of mind, whether as to getaway or defense, but actual threats; our very own ships seeming that to ourselves. It seemed wildly fanciful. Nevertheless I stood there for what must have been a long time, looking at them, pondering the possibility of the impossible.

Thurlow's conversation: That had been a couple weeks ago. I had thought and rethought the matter. It would be a tremendous step to take. But then . . . what possible good could there be in retaining them? If Thurlow's nightmare should somehow come true, in some unforeseeable manner . . . so farfetched also as to have to wedge itself into the resistant mind, yet its realization not at all to be absolutely excluded . . . an aggregation of armament of a virtually limitless capability, the literal disappearance of the island itself so trifling for it as to constitute but a minor side effect . . . What in God's name were they doing there . . . doing anywhere? They would never conceivably be wanted by us to destroy anything or anyone else. They were in no way defensive weaponry. We were loaded to the gunwales with other armament for that; the Harpoon, the five-inch, the Phalanx CIWS; the Russian ship, similarly so. A species of horror struck the mind: There could be but one possible use remaining for them: to destroy ourselves. Slowly, ineluctably, my mind proceeded toward the unthinkable, of not just getting rid of our own Tomahawks, but of persuading the Russian captain that he should do the same with his SS-N-20's.

Another consideration entered: If her captain said no as to *Pushkin*, would I proceed in any case to purge the *James* of her missiles? No reason not to do so. Yet I hesitated at that final step; the ingrained instinct of a man-of-war's captain, the feeling that if we jettisoned ours, he should do the same. I was foolishly anticipating. Why would he possibly say no? Finally I reached a determination. I would put it to him. Let us both dispose of these things . . . *James* and *Pushkin* both, and let our minds rest easy. And with that decision mine did. I waited only for the appropriate moment to broach the subject with *Pushkin*'s commander.

Then I forgot the matter in the satisfaction of gazing down at the *Nathan James*. The ship even looked better since her biweekly runs. What a pure joy it had been to take her out to sea again, remembering my having done so yesterday. I felt a little sad that it would be four weeks before I would do so again; next time, two weeks hence, being Thurlow's turn with his "port" crew.

.4.

LAST CHANCES

The integration of the Russian crew into the community went off smoothly. There were innumerable reasons why this should have been the case, and hardly any why it should not have. I mention some of the former in no particular order. As would have been true of any man-of-war, *Pushkin* brought with her a wide variety of skills. Her hospital corpsmen found ready duty in our Medical Department, all under the doc; of especial contribution was that her complement included a dentist, since ours did not, his also taking up a billet there, and familiar already with the mouths of about a score of *Nathan James*'s company from that exceedingly welcome service extended us by the Russian captain at Gibraltar. The submarine's carpenter's mate joined Noisy Travis's building upkeep crew. *Pushkin*'s company proved no exception to what has long been the case in the American Navy, a matter previously touched on, that an astonishing number of sailors come off farms. At least a score of the Russian sailors were of peasant stock and these were soon happily at work in the fields alongside our own men in Delaney's crew. A half-dozen, two of them ex-fishermen, joined Silva's fishing detail.

How alike are sailors of whatever national and other background! This was an essential ingredient of the ease with which the conjunction proceeded. But the chief reason was to be found elsewhere. I speak of that realization deep within, scarcely brought to consciousness, a tangible fright even at the idea of confronting it, that there existed at least the possibility that we were the only ones, seeming to mean that we must cling to one another whether we so wished or not: for there to be allowed any serious friction, for there to be admitted any force whatsoever that would harm this solely known community of men . . . such a liberty was simply not permitted us. We were all—irrevocably, to an absolute—simply too dependent on one another. It is my last intention in any way to portray us as saintly; it was not that at all. It was rather that our own existence was at stake, and men have a great desire to live. In his own way I believe every hand on the island, American or Russian, understood that transcendent fact and its unforgiving sequitur: There were too few of his own kind to allow that other, to tolerate any striking out at each other; for anything of the kind to get started, moreover, quite conceivably enhancing until it wiped out the last one of us.

Nothing could have so electrified our community as the news that the Russians had brought with them such a priceless gift, a supply of nuclear fuel sufficient to give the *Nathan James* five years of cruising time at fuel-conserving speeds. I want to emphasize that the hospitality, the entire helpfulness, exhibited by the American sailors to their debilitated fellow seamen was extended before the fact of the fuel was made known at a meeting which I called in the Main Hall so to inform them. However, this revelation vastly increased the already forthcoming and friendly attitude of ship's company toward the new arrivals. They, before, looking upon us as their saviors for the succor shown when they first raised the island in not far from extremis state, we now in turn viewed them as our own liberators. Our gratitude had no limits. When from the cliffside we looked down at the *Nathan James,* we saw no longer a dead ship but one alive as she had been of old, ready to take us anywhere.

Anywhere? That was the question: Where should she take us? Where should we take her?

More than anything, there was the relief, of an absolutely instantaneous character, that we were no longer prisoners of the island. The door had been unlocked. All the inmates had been reprieved, pardoned; they could leave whenever they pleased. That was the feeling that in a great exhilaration swept like a freshening sea breeze through ship's company. Looking out at the immense waters, they no longer seemed great walls enclosing us on every side, but rather free roadways now easily traversable.

The overwhelming fact of this new mobility of our ship seemed in the coming weeks completely to dominate our community. Men could think, talk, of little else. At first there were aspects of it that seemed almost comical, if in a bizarre kind of way—as if everybody were going to rush down the cliffside, jump aboard saying, "Let's shove off!" "Where?" "Anywhere." As though if the ship had the fuel to go, that being what a ship is for, to go places, there could not possibly be any thought of not going. This shading after a while into a more sobering, almost contemplative assessment of the real question confronting us: What specifically should we do about this enormous new circumstance of our existence? Where should we go? Should we go anywhere?

Inseparable from these considerations, the fact of the island staking its own claim. Its very habitability as an uncontaminated place, acceptant of men, when all others had refused us, at first endowing it with an almost sacred distinction, it had by now reached much beyond even that status to appear in our minds as a place sentient, actively helping these once forlorn and homeless sailors, presenting us with fructuous soil to grow our food, bountifully adding its own edible offerings, its waters supplying us with an abundance of fish. Otherwise, this life providing many other things. Everyone was quite healthy in the salubrious climate, men had work to do but not too much of it, off-duty the island itself was a green treasure to explore. The sweetness and serenity also awakening the inner life . . . a truly amazing amount of the reading of books . . . men's minds occupied by the project Lieutenant Girard had commenced in the Main Hall of two-hour sessions in which all hands, rationed sheets of bond paper from the supply we had been hoarding, were meticulously putting down all they knew, all they remembered—an enterprise which absorbed, even excited them to a degree I could not have predicted. The long sweet days . . . they had adapted, learning, for example, as all men sooner or later do in the tropics, to take naps in the heat of the day . . . a good life, including even, a kind of ultimate gift that had somehow been managed, yes, women, providing that sexual satisfaction which so strangely alone brings peace to men . . . to sailors . . . the Arrangement working out astonishingly well.

Perhaps only the sum of its parts, yet seeming something beyond that, another thing, mysterious and wondrous as could be, taking place to a certainty in myself and which I sensed to be underway as well in the greater part of ship's company . . . the getting of one's soul back in the very nature of our new life. Men, looking upon what they had, giving the matter more scrutiny, were doubtful as to course. They waited, in a kind of second reflection; it was good to have a fueled, mobile ship anchored there in the sheltered waters below the settlement. Still they paused, much less taken than before with the idea that this was any reason at all to abandon so good a thing as had been granted them in the person of this island.

There remained that relatively small portion of ship's company, previously described, who, holding their one fixation to the point of obsession, knew exactly what they wanted to do, had for some time, and now that—as they saw it—there could not possibly be any objections to doing so, more openly began to ask, why did we not all get aboard immediately, head for home, see with our own eyes what happened, if we found a habitable place reestablish our community there, if we did not, always being free to return to the island? On the surface, the case for this course seemed unarguable, correctly insistent. Closer examination revealed that it fell considerably short of answering every question. Ship's company had put a great deal of themselves into the island, including many months of often brutal labor, under violent tropical suns on the plateau where the Farm now stood, into the altogether handsome, ship-shape gathering of buildings constructed with such mighty dawn-to-dusk efforts, such infinite care (including, the women for their part surely were remembering, those lovely cottages for themselves). What was to happen to the island in the meantime—to the Farm, to the settlement itself, all the fine buildings? Left to themselves they would of a certainty deteriorate, the foliage, the thick island growth would reclaim them, make short work of them, swallow them up as if they had never been. Men like Delaney whose hand lay upon the Farm, the rocklike Porterfield, even the normally inarticulate Noisy Travis, whose great craftsmanship had been the principal author of our fine buildings, spoke up, urging shipmates to stop and think; in particular, some of the women, these generally considerably more outspoken even than before, probably across the board exceeding their male shipmates in this respect—women like Ensign Martin, never a passive violet, along with the previously less vocal Signalman Alice Bixby, informed the men quite crisply that they were out of their minds. What were they thinking of even to consider forsaking all of this?

A tentative solution was put forth: Leave the island, and all we had added to it, in the charge of *Pushkin*'s ship's company—if they would agree to that caretaker assignment. No reason in the world they would not, quite eagerly so one would imagine: such an attractive and instant living place presented them as a gift. But even here the men began to have thoughts; thoughts which strayed considerably from those beautiful sailor-brotherhood fundamentals I have so lovingly adumbrated. Someone was heard to ask: "Doing that, taking *James,* heading home, assuming the finding of nothing, coming back—what if the Russians should decide not to let us back on the island?" Not out of cruelty, surely they would show the returning *Nathan James* the identical welcome, if needed the compassion, the succor, we had rendered the *Pushkin* and her crew. But what if—it was Thurlow who asked this—we should come back heavily contaminated ourselves? Accumulating on top of levels absorbed in our passage from the Barents to our present island, what would be the effects of additional inroads, further invasions of our bodies, almost certain to be substantially increased on the proposed reconnoitering of our once-homeland. All of this was profoundly sobering, enough to frighten brave men. Levels that conceivably could take us into areas of a highly infectious nature, observable physical changes, no known treatment, certainly none possessed by us, so that the Russians, seeing us thus on our return, had no choice but to deny the island to the very men who had discovered it and created this functioning community, lest these, permitted ashore, destroy themselves, these new tenants, eradicate what known little was left of people and habitable place, our very return suggesting there were no others. What other option would there be but to turn us away—by force if necessary? *Pushkin* was a heavily armed vessel. After all, we ourselves had refused to take in those poor contaminated souls on the beaches of Italy and France. What if we should return like them, even if in somewhat lesser degree? Compassion which will wipe out one's own ship's company—we had never had any great difficulty in rejecting that definition of the word. Why should we expect more from the Russians than we had found ourselves able to attain to in that regard? Seen in this light, it appeared to a number of hands that the priceless fuel in point of fact did nothing for us: that we were as much as ever prisoners of the island.

All of these matters gave ship's company much to ponder. Myself, of course, as their captain, most of all. The problem was by no means so simple as it may have first appeared—boarding *Nathan James* and casting off. Other indistinct but somehow ominous considerations seemed to hover about as we debated—inwardly, outwardly—what our true course should be. Trepidations hung in the air, and the difficulty of separating the real from the imagined. One in particular of the interjections the Russian captain had made in our continuing dialogue stuck in my mind. At one point, perhaps exasperated with the idea that, after all he had personally witnessed and reported so meticulously to us, sane men could take their ship off into what he felt was absolutely unacceptable and unaccepting atmosphere beyond the seas, he burst out, "If you must go into all that contamination, Captain, at least do not take the women into it—to die, to be made sterile at best. At least leave the women—so that, if you find nothing, we can continue . . ." He stopped there, with an absolute abruptness, as if aghast at what he had been about to say, my mind finishing it for him. Perhaps he was just trying to shock us into not going. Nevertheless, that reference to the women—its startling nature greatly magnified by the fact of its being his first direct allusion of any kind to them—seemed almost a reference to the *possession* of them, appearing to me to have escaped unintentionally from him in a moment of anger, seeming further to suggest some sort of intent he had not hitherto disclosed, all of this planting seeds of disturbance in my mind . . . I then dismissed it. He had wanted only to shock us into our senses. That was all. "I have seen Russia," he had said. "How can you believe America will be any different?"

Thus it was that the Russian captain's offer to send his own ship instead—her submerging capabilities vastly reducing possibilities of contamination—appeared heaven's gift, perfect solution to these burdensome matters. I turned then to a close examination of which of the *James*'s company should fill the thirty-three billets allotted to us under his plan for *Pushkin*—to "rediscover the world," as he so appositely put it. And as I did so, something totally unexpected attacked me as it were: a tremendous desire to make that voyage myself. Yes, I found myself seriously considering it, seduced into the very idea of it. Of this personal matter, tearing me as it did, I must speak here a moment for its importance, not so much in the decision I finally made as for the elements, some hitherto deeply hidden, its consideration forced to the surface and which were later to have such profound effects on our fate.

The Magellan factor, as I had come to think of it, had an almost mesmeric appeal to any seaman; more, to any thinking human being: What was out there? What did the rest of the world look like now, consist of? And most of all: Were there various enclaves of fellow human beings—or more? And if so, where? It was an enormous pull to be one of those who would discover the answers to such questions. All of this abetted by that small hard knot in myself, who long since had accepted the overwhelming evidence of one's own country, our home, having become to all purposes nonexistent, that twisting thought so ingrained in ship's captains: Always consider the possibility that you may be wrong. Especially when you are absolutely certain you are right. A shudder going through me: What if considerable life still existed there? But completely apart from that, the voyage itself. I actually confronted a great temptation: to ask the Russian captain to let me sign on. I was in no way qualified to command a submarine, but I was a good seaman and I would be eager, I thought as I almost helplessly toyed with the idea, to go in any capacity on such a remarkable voyage.

Immediately occurring, the question, who would assume command of the *James*, of the island? The idea of my own indispensability: I bore no greater burden, and it had grown through all our ordeal—and all our triumphs, explicitly what we had created on the island. Perhaps it is man's ultimate curse. I even knew that, and its terrible dangers. And yet, knowing, even employing every effort to stand away from the question and look at objectively what could never be looked at objectively, I forever came up with the same answer, infused with vanity as much as a matter could be: I was not certain as to what would happen to ship's company, to the island, without me. I had been the only captain this ship, these people— and this island—had ever known. I was not certain what might befall this community, and all that it had achieved and represented, on my own departure, whether by a substitution of myself or by another system of governance; what disturbances, troubles, even disasters might ensue in a system unknown to them. But more than that, system retained, I saw no one to take my place; supreme vanity or not, that was the fact as I viewed it. Besides—and this may have been the most compelling reason of all— my mission here was not finished (including most particularly what was happening in those twenty very special cottages). And finally—I must have been as bewitched as Ulysses by the sirens by the Magellan "rediscover the world" magnet to forget the fact—the person who would succeed me in command of the island would almost inevitably have to be the Russian captain himself: He had had no problem in rejecting that enticement, in designating his executive officer to go, himself to stay behind. The question instantly arising again as to why; given the agreed-upon wonder of such a voyage, how not going on it, and especially as its captain, could possibly be considered . . . one could not ask him . . . Opening doors of mistrust which one chose not to enter, knowing the certainty of mistrust's deadly poisoning in our mutual community . . . still, again despite all my elevated excursions into the propinquity of sailors, and patently into how well such a circumstance had worked with us so far on the island, I was not prepared to trust the Russian captain—or anyone else—that far: ascent to the leadership of this island, this community of men and women.

And then, in its very soaring midst, this tide of vaingloriousness collapsed, fell apart, swept away by a matter I hardly dared admit: my relationship with Lieutenant Girard, something that had spread to all parts of my being, all that I was, changing everything, in a way so all-embracing as to seem to me only a woman can accomplish in the experiences of men. When I said I could not leave the island, what I meant was that I could not leave her; knowing but one thing: never, so long as I might live, would I permit anything to separate us. It was a secret I kept tightly in my own heart. As I had these thoughts, the realization occurring for the first time that, with her near, I was content to live out my life on this island; bringing everything in me still, bringing as it were a final peace, all sweet and wondrous, that I had not known, it seemed, since that day, now seeming part of ancient times, that our missiles first left the *Nathan James* and ascended high into the blue skies of the Barents, bent on their terrible mission. No. I could not accompany *Pushkin* on the Magellan voyage. That decision became absolute in my heart. Thus, the faintest residue of reluctance remaining, I put the thought forever away and turned to the urgent affair now fallen upon my ship's company as to whether they, variously, should remain on the island or take that almost mystical look at what we had once called home.

Specifically, what others of us should accompany *Pushkin.* In this instance, the proper course seemed almost self-evident.

Other than those already suggested, another of the several advantages offered by the proposed voyage was the fact that it would enable me to get rid of our "discontents," men who felt there was something to go home to, some in a rather passive way, others more actively. I remembered Lieutenant Girard's perception that these were waiting for the question of the governance to arise; if "majority rule," should ship's company elect this, their chances of taking the *Nathan James* on such a mission increased. But now they did not need to wait even for that uncertain condition. The Russian's arrival with nuclear fuel for us would seem, as I have said, to set the *James* free. I had other intentions. For one thing I felt if the *James* went, so would I have to. Everything in me as her captain, so a part of my life as to feel myself inseparable from her, rebelled at the thought of letting her go, of watching her sail off over the horizon. I did not think I could do it. Something in me also fearful that if others took her, they might never bring her back. Thus the Russian captain's proposal of sending *Pushkin* instead, along with its other bounties, resolved two of our major problems in my favor: the retention of the *James* here at the island; and, as I say, the giving these men what they so insatiably wanted, a chance to go back or at least have their look; his suggestion to constitute about one-third of the submarine's crew American fortuitously coinciding more or less closely with the number of those who fell into the category I have just described. I did not fail to seize on the opportunity.

I called a meeting of ship's company in the Main Hall, in which I explained in great detail the Russian captain's offer to send *Pushkin* on a voyage which would explicitly include exploration of the coastal areas of the United States, dwelling in much particular on the immense advantage of the submarine in protecting our men from what otherwise, going on the *James,* the same voyage, was certain to be intense and very likely unacceptable levels of radiation, far greater than anything we had so far undergone even in our worst passages.

"I am pleased to say," I told the hushed listeners, "that those of you who desire to take a look back home will now be able to do so. We have the Russians to thank for that. Although I know you think differently, you could never get near the coasts in the *Nathan James.* You will be able to do so in *Pushkin . . .* I believe that your 'looking' will be confined to what you can see through a submarine's periscope. Never mind. If you find differently, if the land is habitable, *Pushkin* will put all who so wish ashore. That is my agreement with her captain."

The case for *Pushkin* was so strong, that for sending *Nathan James* so weak, that the former course was entirely embraced, in the quiet manner of sailors who can recognize facts when they are calmly and straightforwardly presented to them. The only question remaining: Who would the thirty-three be?

"They will be volunteers," I concluded it. "If these exceed that number, lots will be drawn, within the submarine's own requirements as to skills."

The plan was adopted and I so reported to the Russian captain. In the three days allotted, forty-one men made known their desire to go. The excess number was small enough that, having no taste to have left behind on the island even eight hands who had no desire to be there, I persuaded the Russian captain to take them all and put ashore that many extra hands from his own crew.

I mention now with sadness the name of one officer who it was almost inevitable would be a part of *Pushkin*'s voyage. Lieutenant Alex Thurlow. To no one could the "Magellan" aspect of the voyage have held greater appeal. Its very idea excited him from the first—he *had* to go. I mentioned sometime back that besides being a navigator, Thurlow was a kind of "Vesalius" of the planet, in that same anatomical sense—its makeup, its peculiarities, its whimsicalities. Now it was unthinkable to him that he should not see the changes, however dread, that had taken place in his subject. But these were all selfish reasons. There were other reasons, of the most urgently prudent sort, why he must go. First, as I had told the Russian captain, "I have never known a navigator to equal him. That great gift is wasted on this island." And of course his fluent Russian would make him indispensable as a link between the two bodies of sailors and officers: that the greatest reason of all for his inclusion. Indeed the Russian captain was so delighted to get him that he designated him to be executive officer of the *Pushkin* on her voyage. Thurlow was overjoyed at the prospect; I much cast down—it had been a slow process but I had become as fond of him as of anyone in ship's company, perhaps more than any other. That mixture of blitheness and utter dependability; that curious otherworldly quality I had come to find so attractive; a man of grace; somehow making for a discrete relationship.

Preparations went forward. The forty-one chosen Americans in effect moved aboard the *Pushkin* and commenced the indoctrination which would transform them from destroyer men into submariners. During the coming weeks the Russian captain and I—along with his executive officer who would succeed to command, a strikingly younger officer than either of us but one who as I came to know him impressed me as both a first rate seaman and commander of men, Thurlow also always present—spent many hours in the submarine's chartroom plotting the course of the great voyage. Whether *Pushkin* would literally circumnavigate the globe remained to be seen, depending on her findings. It was likely that she would do so, inspecting principally southern latitudes on the theory that some of these might have escaped (though we had found quite the opposite in the equatorial regions of the Sunda Sea), with the promised side excursion to the United States of America, the Americans aboard ready to depart the ship there and remain should they find uncontaminated territory. Going forward simultaneously, the provisioning of the submarine. We removed from the *James* to the *Pushkin* all remaining imperishables of food stores. In addition we stuffed the freezers and the lockers of the submarine full of the island's own offerings, both from the Farm and those indigenous to the island itself; with quantities of frozen fish. Transferred one of the *James*'s VLF antennas to the submarine. Steadily *Pushkin,* standing there below the cliffs, approached the moment of weighing anchor and casting off on her "rediscovery of the world"; each time I looked down at her, a thin small seaman's regret remaining that

I was not going with her. Meantime, with the excellent food on which they now gorged, with the healthful work such as the Farm and fishing details, the Russians, so frail and ghostlike on their arrival, fattened up as it were quite rapidly, improved remarkably as to physical condition. Finally the submarine stood ready in all respects for sea. Her day of departure was set, a week hence. The excitement in those who were about to leave: Some even clung to the half-bizarre, half-poignant notion that they somehow would connect up with those former shipmates, 109 of them, that Lieutenant Commander Chatham had led off the ship in what now seemed the impossibly long ago.

It was at this time that Lieutenant Girard asked for an appointment with me.

Concurrent with these developments, another had proceeded as it were on parallel tracks. As the weeks went on, what had before been but a muted underlayer as to the Arrangement palpably altered; a distinct suspense entered the settlement, which seemed to wait now almost daily and more ostensibly for the news that it had happened; this, in turn, no news forthcoming, before long beginning to be further leavened by a certain apprehension. I began to detect a subtle change in the rather beatific state of affairs previously existent as between the men and the women. Fully as much in the men as in the women, perhaps more so, almost as if it was they who were at fault, had let the women down. By now the circle had been completed as it were, Girard so informing me. Each of the participating men had been at one time or another with each of the women (had "known," using the biblical term, each of the women). Hope did not vanish. Nature can be slow to pick her times. All understood that. Nevertheless, given the numbers, the opportunities, all the seemingly favorable mathematics of it, the many weeks that had passed . . . The Jesuit even went this far: He approached the seven men who had chosen to abstain. They had done so for differing reasons. One or two, that they had wives at home—yes, they actually stated that as reason; more, despite the Jesuit's having vetted everything, on moral or religious grounds; one at least, Porterfield, from whom due to his having been a seminarian pre-Navy, the last-named the expected reason, actually something else altogether, his putting it to me rather haltingly, almost with embarrassment. "It isn't a matter of religion. It's—well, sir . . ." He hesitated at the word. "Esthetic?" I supplied it. "Something like that I guess." To these the Jesuit now put it that they had an obligation, a duty, to participate, almost—not a habit of his—pleading with them, promising that if they would do so, they could then return to their state of abstention and no further entreaties would be put to them, or demands made of them. (All this he related to me.) They agreed, with considerable reluctance, and with one exception, Noisy Travis, an immovably stubborn man. Results negative. An interesting side effect: Of the six previous holdouts, two now saw their way clear to overcome their objections and enter as full-timers in the Arrangement.

Girard's demeanor in our sessions: just the beginnings of a kind of analytical anxiety, the suggestion of an eerie fear, not large thus far but seeming of a peculiarly virulent character, as though one were taking slow, helpless steps toward some precipice—some terrible nothingness. All this conveyed, felt by transference in myself, not in anything she said; rather in the very absence of reporting. Nothing to report. A presentiment making its appearance like a third person present as we discussed by now rather routine matters of supply and slight matters of morale, anything to keep us off that other paramount subject. This foreboding augmenting not just in us but in all hands. Soon a kind of dejection, almost gloom, as to results so far—absence of results, I should say—hung over the settlement, as though we were about to be confronted with a profound horror as to ourselves.

Our other lives: There was one difference between us. She felt the secrecy, if it was that, necessary, at least for the time being. I chafed at the deception: wanted our rendezvous moved to her own private dwelling, one she had along with the other women amid the trees. Wanted it done outright, everything in the open, ready to handle any problems that might arise, any objection as to our being the only two who were solely each other's, as opposed to the sharing required of all others, men and women alike. She had a point in that they might not know; therefore let us take time for reflection as to what was best. True, they had seen us appear suddenly that day, entering the settlement at a run, summoned by the GQ klaxon tolling the discovery of the bodies of the three women: At first we thought that had told them all; later came to believe they might have concluded that we had simply been on a reconnoitering of a rather unexplored part of the island, an "outing" such as others constantly took. It was difficult to say: oneself at the center of that kind of emotion that existed between us can be blind as to such observations; still I felt our relationship, if known, was unresented. Whether it was known or not, or resented or not, one had no choice but to continue it. Beyond that I went along, for now; we waited.

But without once discussing it, we knew one thing to an absolute:

the stern danger that lay in permitting anything of what was happening between us to enter into that other relationship that had stood so long, worked so well, myself captain, her morale officer and now especially leader of the women. That this presented no real difficulty I think derived from the fact that, the responsibility so deep-rooted in each of us, we could not have lived with ourselves had we let anything impair our duties to ship's company. We were careful to preserve formalities. Two persons each we had become; living two lives; kept entirely separate, our former roles remaining precisely as before, knowing we must not let that other new life touch the old one. So far it had worked.

When she came that day to my cabin by the cliffside, unusual for her to make a special appointment, ordinarily waiting for our regular weekly session, one knew beforehand that some point of reality had been reached—and one had a pretty good idea what it was. Still, nothing could have prepared me for the actual moment. Reporting to me that they had tried everything—every combination, she meant.

"I don't think it's going to happen," she said.

The words in their finality at first inexpressibly poignant; then it was as if a great darkness had settled over us. We sat in silence; a sense of utter desolation filling the air. One looked out over the waters and expected to see the darkness standing down to the earth. The complete and unexpected . . . yes, terror I felt. I must have blocked out its significances; one oddly coming at that moment to stab cruelly at me: that rather joyous enterprise in which ship's company was putting down on paper all that they knew or remembered; that, for one thing, could be promptly scuttled. A void. One felt one had fallen into a void, its nature while definable simply as the absence of a time frame known as the future yet one felt a failure, or a refusal, of the mind to reach through to any real comprehension of such a thing. One felt an unspeakable numbness; an unbeing. New, unprecedented emotions. Nonexistence reached down and touched us. Her words, breaking into my thoughts, startled me.

"Do you remember what Mr. Selmon once said, Captain?"

I looked at her as one looks for the first time with pity at another. Hope dying so hard. My own words taking on a certain hardness to snap her out of it.

"It doesn't apply, Lieutenant. The women will have been equally affected with the men."

"The doc," she said. "We got to talking. He told me about some research he knew about. He said he and Selmon had discussed it."

"Research?"

And she told me what it was. My response flat, the decision reflexive, only from the long-ingrained habit always to listen.

"We'll have the meeting tomorrow," I said. "At thirteen hundred hours." I named the officers. "See to it."

"Aye, sir. Thirteen hundred hours." She stood up to go. "Oh, by the way, Captain."

"Yes."

"I've decided to participate in the Arrangement."

Something happened in me that had never happened before. I just looked at her.

"How long have you been thinking about that?"

"It hasn't anything to do with us."

"The hell it hasn't."

"Not a goddamned thing. It's this: I won't allow any chance to be missed."

I was angry, shaking almost. Spoke hard.

"I suppose you won't have need for our weekly business in the cave?"

"What a child you are. I'll be there next Thursday as usual. For the 'business,' as you call it. Suit yourself whether you want to join me."

She turned and walked out.

Present at the meeting in my cliffside cabin: the doc, the Jesuit, Girard, Thurlow.

"As Selmon and I agreed, we know next to nothing on the subject. We of course do know," the doc said, "one thing. Within limits, different individuals, male or female, are affected differently even by identical doses. But there was a hint—a bare hint in some of the data that was beginning to emerge—of something else. Some of the studies were beginning to suggest that there was a finite chance that the reproductive capacities of women would not be so quickly, or so completely, altered as would those of men. Some very preliminary studies suggested this possibility. Nature and Darwin at work again, Father? Extra protection for the female of the species?"

"Please continue, Doctor," the Jesuit said crisply.

"For the most part, these investigations were conducted by a man named Rosenblatt—first name Hillel—working at Rockefeller University in New York. I got to know him when I was there—in that way was pretty close myself to what he was up to. Two or three other places in the country on to the same thing, trying to find out. Using guinea pigs and Norway rats, of course. Couldn't do that sort of thing on human beings. And even so they had reached only a very tentative hypothesis stage. Not nearly enough evidence to support a conclusion. Still . . ."

The Jesuit's zeal in the matter, large before, something we had become accustomed to, was now perfervid, as if he were a desperate man. Pressing the doc.

"I understand the individual variations. I have more of a problem with such a precise, across-the-board effect—with the women not being equally sterile. They underwent the same exposure."

"I don't understand it myself, Father. But then you and I, we are not geneticists, are we? And we have not done the experiments, have we? Rosenblatt and the others were. And they did."

The doc was not one to bring up a matter he felt had no validity at all—he would have seen that as reflecting on his professional integrity. He gave that familiar bland look of his: It had long seemed to me a kind of disclaimer that yet hid something he was inclined to believe; as though he were covering all his flanks, just in case.

"I do not know but what the women are sterile, the last one of them. I am merely mentioning some of the studies. You have to remember that the body of literature on this subject was like a thimbleful of water to the sea."

"Yes, yes, Doctor," the Jesuit said. He was impatient with such metaphors. I think he felt he was being patronized. "Let me get this straight. If your Rosenblatt and the others were right, there would be a possibility that the absence of fertilizations may be traceable entirely to the men—all of them thus far sterile. And that some of the women at least may still be able to reproduce—given fertile men to do it with."

"That's it, Father," the doc said imperviously. As a nonbeliever of any sort in anything religious, I think he took an impudent delight in so addressing the priest. "If Rosenblatt was indeed on to something."

"But even those studies were inconclusive?" I said, as if reminding.

"Very much so, Skipper," the doc said. "They were ongoing. Stopped by what stopped everything else. I remember reading Rosenblatt's last paper on the subject. Hypercautious, as those people always are. But there was something new, a conviction beginning to take hold that he might be on to something. Making clear that his hypothesis might apply only to some women, that the margins of advantage over men in this area might be small but still determinative ones—and flatly stating he had been unable thus far to isolate any reasons for the phenomenon, if existent. Rosenblatt—perhaps a little too much of a philosopher for such a good scientific investigator—apostrophizing, as I mentioned to the chaplain, that it might be Nature at work. Stepping in once more. Still making it very clear—nothing absolutely conclusive. Yet he seemed to be saying . . ."

"So we would still be throwing dice," I said.

"Perhaps slightly loaded dice, Skipper," the doc said. "Who knows how many times you would have to throw them . . . And even if there is substance in these conjectures . . . If it were one woman in a thousand that fell under Rosenblatt's hypothesis, our chances would be remote. If, on the other hand, it were one in—say twenty-one . . ."

I had to have it confirmed, once more. I turned to our new radiation officer.

"The Russian men, Mr. Thurlow?"

He said it flatly. "As to exposure to radiation: no comparison. Far less, sir. We tested the last one of them, as you know. To a certainty. Minimal."

"We have to try it," the Jesuit jumped in. "Captain, forty-one of the Russian men, as I understand the *Pushkin* plan, are to stay on the island, become a permanent part of the community?"

"That is correct."

"So there is no hurry as to them. But fifty-three will be leaving. What is that timing, sir?"

"Five days now."

"Then I respectfully suggest that the departure of *Pushkin* be delayed . . . what is the hurry for that anyhow? Keep those men here until we find out to a reasonable certainty . . . As to one or more of them; one or more of the women . . ." He turned and addressed himself directly to Lieutenant Girard. ". . . And that for that period of time, only they . . . while they are here, nobody else. Not the American men. Not the Russians who are to remain—we have them for later, if need be." He waited and added: "As a temporary arrangement. If the women will accept the Russian men."

One had almost a chilling sense as he spoke, the quick apprehension, the seizing on a plan, something almost ruthless about it; amazed at the meticulousness of his ardor, at the quick precision of his logistics.

"Miss Girard?" I deferred to her.

By now it was the absolute law of the settlement. Anything concerning the women was subject to their veto; if exercised, that ending the matter; no explanations required; all sovereign as to themselves.

"Accept the Russian men? We would welcome them," she said quietly, as we all looked at her in astonishment. In her tone a certain

586

contempt that stupid men, ourselves, had wasted all this time when the women had already decided the issue; almost as if she had let us run on, and then announced her decision, to make clear who was in charge in these matters.

"Then I'll speak with the Russian captain," I said. I could not help adding, looking at her, "With your permission, Lieutenant Girard."

"You have my permission, sir," she said. "Please do so at once."

I need to mention now, for a full understanding of this meeting, the fact that the Jesuit had come to me the day before it with a finding I had asked for after Girard's report. Throughout he had been monitoring the entire process with a zeal that, at first seeming startling, a man possessed, had by now come to appear wholly natural, as if somehow part of his spiritual domain. (No one, not incidentally, had got along better than the Jesuit with the Russians, he and the Russian captain in particular having become quite friendly. I think they understood each other. On the Jesuit's part, I had not the slightest doubt, to myself something almost grim in it, this: With the evidence as to the American sailors becoming ever more clear, he saw in the Russians . . . could he have predivined Selmon's hypothesis? No, it was rather that he was prepared to grab any possibility.) The settlement, we all knew, had been quietly devastated by the failure to achieve pregnancies. The women; the men, as mentioned, curiously almost more so, somehow blaming themselves. What the Jesuit, with his impeccable sources, had to tell me was this: There would be no trouble with the American men as respected the Russian men and the women.

"Our men won't object to the Russians trying," he had put it. "They are willing to—not have the women . . . Temporarily of course. As for the women: All they want is babies. That is all they have wanted all along. Whoever can give them that." He paused a moment, his eyes far away, seeming to combine at once a fervor and a fatalism. "The Russian men— they would seem to be our last chance."

I had my session with the Russian captain, who acceded promptly to the delay in *Pushkin*'s departure. And so it was that there began in the cottages set prettily among the tall guardsmanlike trees a determination as to whether, in Selmon's half-cynical phrase, "Submariners will be the new fathers of mankind; if there is to be mankind."

.5.

THE *NATHAN JAMES*

It was a day of a peculiar loveliness, that on which the *Nathan James*, carrying half of ship's company, cast off at first light for her biweekly run, the ever-sweetness of the island at that hour, its purity of air, the first notes of awakening birds, the island attended all around by the vastness of silent waters, the twin scents fusing . . . all seemed to reach with a deep-giving peace into one's soul. It was Thurlow's turn to go and as usual when that was the case, I stood on the cliffside, hearing reach up to me in that hushed universe the long low clangor of her anchor chains moving through the hawsepipes, the sun just making its first appearance over the horizon to create a carmine sea. Presently, the anchors secured, I could see her beginning to make her turn on waters mirroring the full elegance of her lines, pulling away from *Pushkin*. I could see some Russian sailors, each run now with about twenty aboard—the ones who were to remain on the island—learning destroyer skills chiefly under Thurlow's and Boatswain's Mate Preston's direction while the Americans departing on *Pushkin* learned submarine ones. Thurlow on the bridge wing raising his hand, myself lifting mine back to mark farewells of a single day. It tore at my heart to think that I would be losing that fine officer, that rather special friend he had become, to that other vessel at anchor just below me. On the starboard bridge wing, I spotted also Lieutenant Girard, making her first run, simply have been too occupied with the matter of the women to do so previously, coming to me the day before with the routine request that she now be permitted to do so. A necessity really; although her additional duty of combat systems officer relatively nominal now, still her reason for going entirely cogent. "I need to run through the drills with Delaney and the men." Then a wry smile. "I think I need it anyhow, Captain. An outing, as Preston says. I haven't been to sea for a while. I can think better out there," referring I knew to our own problem, to that subtle change that had taken place, though that life went on, the weekly visits to a remote cave: we never mentioned her other life. Continuing as we had, not knowing, not as yet even discussing, how things were going to come out with us. Permission for her to go on the *James* routinely granted by myself.

I watched the ship stand out, perpendicular now to the horizon, quietly, all-confidently, parting the stilled waters, seeming to admit her as an old friend, glad to have her back. It was a beautiful sight to me and one, I realized in a certain wry astonishment, her ship's captain had never had the privilege of witnessing until just recently; I had always been aboard. I watched until she had disappeared over the horizon, bidding good-bye to her for the dozen hours required by the sun in its infinite precision to make its transit across the sky and to sink once more into the western ocean—at which time I would be standing there again, always somehow excessively glad, almost relieved, to see her safe return; occasionally, in the interim between departure and homecoming, that apprehension, totally without reason or foundation, ridiculous in fact, nothing surely but any ship's captain's exorbitant sense of proprietorship in his ship, having seen her vanish over the horizon, that she might not come back.

Before stepping into my cabin I glanced up by habit at the Lookout Tower and could see the normal watch of three hands manning it; the principal lookout, Porterfield, standing at ease by the Big Eyes; Signalman Bixby at the portable radio to handle messages to and from the Farm across the island, a radioman now also always maintained there for anything it might have to say; a messenger, Seaman Garber. All of these precautions, I thought, surely inessential—day after day these watches kept, and of course nothing ever happening, nothing ever appearing on the blue immensity . . . I had recently begun to consider whether the time had come to stand them down—then Billy's sighting that day always came back to caution me that another ship, not necessarily of friendly intent, might appear on those great spaces of water that surrounded us; we might need every moment we could get. This reminding me of that other massive weaponry not needed for this purpose and which so concerned Thurlow, reminding me further that I had made a particular arrangement to speak tomorrow with the Russian captain concerning the disposal, jettisoning of these, in both ships.

During *James*'s one-day cruise, it was customary for ship and shore to keep in communication and from time to time that morning I stepped into the radio shack, not far from my cabin and manned today by Radioman Parkland, its limited facilities (the principal part of our communications equipment remaining on the ship) including a simple VHF ship-to-shore transmitter rigged specially for messages between the island and the *James*, and had routine conversations with her, the ship reporting the usual things. Today a smooth sea, skies entirely wind-free . . . the ship proceeding through her customary drills. I went about the day's business. I believe it was about mid-morning that it happened. I have spoken in these pages of that special sense given, it would seem, to ship's captains in respect to anything pertaining to their ships and their ship's companies—especially, when that is the case, of something seeming not quite right. This phenomenon—if it is to be called so, though it is not even that to me—is a simple truth of the sea, as familiar to any ship's captain as the elements of ocean and sky in which his ship moves, as the very deck under his feet. That sense came now. The effect of it is always curiously pacifying, in the meaning of bringing everything quiet and concentrated in oneself, as if one knew from long experience that the time was at hand when all one's faculties would be required, no space left for the slightest scrap of emotion, space only for utter coolness to allow reason, and only reason, to take charge, in a matter about to be made known, an imminent confrontation. I was aware of myself rising slowly, stepping outside the cabin and going to where I had hidden my key, required for launching the missiles. The key was not there. I took the few steps to the cliffside, looking out to the vast seascape. The horizon blank, the *Nathan James* somewhere beyond it. I returned to my cabin, told the yeoman to find the Russian captain for me, his quarters nearby. They were back quite presently. "Let's take a walk," I said to the Russian. We stepped a few paces along the cliffside, stood all alone, out of earshot of all. I told him the bare essentials of the situation; the same dual-key system operative on his own ship, his fully and instantly grasping it; told him further that the three other persons having access to the keys were all aboard *James*.

We walked, moving a little rapidly now, to the radio shack nearby and I sat down by Parkland in front of the ship-to-shore transmitter. A clear day for transmission, Thurlow's entirely distinct voice presently on the other end. Myself making all-certain to keep my own entirely normal, making of routine enquiries.

"The captain speaking, Mr. Thurlow."

"Aye, sir."

"How is the run?"

"Everything four-oh, Captain."

"Fine." Every shred of emotion, of anything unusual, kept out of my voice, there was still no way in which he was not going to think strange what I would presently have to tell him. There was no help for that.

"Mr. Thurlow, I want you to return to the island."

"Return to the island, sir?" The echoed phrase coming back to me, surprise to be sure, and as if not certain he had heard correctly.

"Return to the island," I said again, more sharply. "Do you understand me, Mr. Thurlow? At once."

"Aye, aye, sir. Understood."

I waited a moment.

"What is your position, Mr. Thurlow?" and he gave it. I made my second fateful decision.

"And Mr. Thurlow. Go to flank speed immediately. That means you'll be here in . . ." I calculated quickly. ". . . Just short of an hour."

"Flank speed?" he questioned again; this time wonderment, an elevated surprise in his voice. Fuel-conscious, we never now brought the ship to such speeds on these runs. It was time to get off.

"Flank speed, Mr. Thurlow." I spoke in that captain's tone which said, no more discussion. "Get underway at once."

"Aye, aye, sir. Return to the island. Flank speed."

The Russian captain and I stepped back outside, stood a few moments more gazing at the horizon. Thoughts rushing in on me now from every side, now that I had chosen my course of action and executed it; one of these, almost certainly imaginary, a feeling that in Thurlow's voice there had been a tone of constraint, of not speaking freely, of perhaps not being able to, the tone of a man with a pistol pointed at his head; dismissing that as sheer hallucination.

"Nothing to do but wait," I said. "We should sight her in . . ." I looked at my watch. "Not much more than a quarter hour . . . fifteen minutes . . ."

All I could think was: *Girard, Thurlow, Delaney.* The Russian captain and I stood like statues, looking out to sea, as the minutes ticked away our eyes straining ever more to the horizon. The repeated looking at my watch; of minutes, of seconds, become eternities. Something stirred in me. I stepped quickly back into the radio shack, told Parkland to raise the ship. I recognized the voice of the OOD, Lieutenant Sedgwick.

"The captain speaking, Mr. Sedgwick. Put Mr. Thurlow on the horn."

A fraction of a pause. "Sir, Mr. Thurlow is not available at the moment."

"What do you mean?" I said savagely. "Not available? Put Lieutenant Girard on."

"Sir, she's down in stores. I'll send a messenger right away."

My voice came cold. "Mr. Sedgwick, listen very carefully. Are you proceeding toward the island?"

The connection went dead.

"Get him back," I said to Parkland, sitting beside me. She tried; tried again, and still again. Nothing. Then I heard something strange. Not from the transmitter. From another source. I stepped out quickly onto the cliffside.

Far and away I could make out the long white wake left by the Tomahawk as it ascended into the pale blue sky of the Pacific, trailing its cone of fire. Then I saw it burst, a puff of smoke, not all that large. I knew it at once as a TLAM-C, armed with a conventional warhead—a Bullpup, 1,000 pounds of high explosives. As I watched—I could not see the ship—I saw another Tomahawk rising heavenward, leaving its signature tail, knowing as its booster rocket dropped off that this one was different. It was a TLAM-N, a Tomahawk carrying a 200-kiloton nuclear warhead, and as it disappeared over the horizon without explosion, I knew that it was unarmed.

I continued to watch the parade of missiles up into the blue. First a conventional Tomahawk benignly destructing itself. Followed by a nuclear one, discarding its rocket, harmlessly vanishing from sight. The sequence continued. Suddenly my vision was obliterated by a white light far, far brighter than any sun. Standing there for a few seconds literally as a blind man, before, sight returning, I saw from that same space a fireball, beginning to expand outward in all directions, and knew it instantly as a nuclear detonation. As I looked, another Tomahawk climbed the sky, following directly behind in the path of the exploded one, it also now bursting and throwing out its blinding light, my head reflexively turning to shield itself. In quick succession I could make out others ascending over that same vertical roadway, each exploding in its fireball to join the others in a vast conflagration of the heavens. Myself now vaguely aware that others of the settlement had come to join us and to watch what was happening high in the skies.

The Tomahawks bursting one after another like roses to form a giant bouquet, this now magnifying in seemingly exponential fashion to occupy half the sky, soon then swallowing up, smothering in its embrace, the sun itself, while leaving the image of its presence shining through, as though the white sun of day had itself been transmogrified into another species of rose deeper, almost bloodlike, in color. A great flocculent white, moving in immense and infinitely languid layers, then beginning to coagulate with the mass as if to form yet another, variegated, dual-colored; the inane thought occurring that though I had launched them in the Barents and had seen their subsequent manifestations halfway around the earth, I had never witnessed the spectacle of their detonations, our practice runs in peacetime having of necessity to be done with conventional warheads. Their immediate effect, as they joined one another in quick succession, was one as much beautiful as awesome, and altogether glorious, as if the heavens had somehow conspired to give man, ironically before annihilating him with what the sight contained, set against their pristine blue, a display the grandest yet seen by him, vast in its dimensions, magnificent in its texture; an uncertain amount of time passing which none could have had the faculty to compute, and neither of us did; then, in yet another transmutation, as we watched, men struck immobile, impotent, glory was gone, beauty was attacked and eradicated, the rose and white beginning to convert into great roiling waves of black, of a violent ugliness, a vile and loathsome deformity, these effectively sealing off the sun as though night were falling much ahead of schedule—I glanced reflexively, mindlessly, at my watch, as if I had made some error in calculating the passage of the day, that surely it must be a half-dozen hours later than I thought; reading the time of 1118 to tell me I had not. Time itself seemed to cease to be a measure of anything. Suddenly by some violent effort, wrenching myself almost convulsively out of my dumbstruckness, activating the cold, icy reflexes of a lifetime of sailor's response to peril, a ship's captain's knowledge instantly brought into play that the last thing to be dwelt on at the moment was why and how, nothing being more dangerous; not to think at all. I ran to the foot of the Lookout Tower and yelled up to the watch on the platform. Porterfield, lookout; Bixby, signalman; Garber, messenger.

"Porterfield, sound the General Alarm. Then glass for Silva. Bixby, raise the Farm detail to come immediately to the settlement."

As the klaxon commenced its piercing, honking sound, seeming to rise discordantly over the peaceful green of a mystified island, I saw sailors moving rapidly toward the Tower. The Russian captain and I both from our near-cliffside observation post then looking a moment at the distant skies filling with those great curling waves of blackness; the thought unspoken flashing through me, surely through him, that an old enemy, one which both of us knew all too well and had engaged in previous battles, had returned to confront us again, no discussion therefore needed between us as to its nature; knowing further that every sailor standing before us knew, in a terrible awareness, its identity, its lethalness; saving time, no need to explain anything to anybody. Around us came men, not running, but walking rapidly toward us, American and Russian sailors. I looked at him.

"Captain. *Pushkin?*"

"Yes. At once. Everybody aboard."

I spotted Preston, told him to find the boat details and to proceed down the ladder to prepare to take on the crew. I turned and shouted the order in English and almost simultaneously heard his Russian obviously saying the same to his own crew. The men of both of the nationalities now moving quickly to the cliffside ladders, and starting down them. First down, the Russian captain. In orderly fashion, the men and women simply forming a line at the ladders, the moment one had his foot on the first rung, the next stepping forward and commencing the steep descent himself. Looking down I could see the ladders occupied from top to bottom by solid chains of moving sailors. Hitting the beach, each moving rapidly to the boats already manned, including the lifeboats under oars, a loaded boat heading toward *Pushkin.* I looked and saw the first figure emerge from the first boat, start up the Jacob's ladder, from there down a deck hatch and, I knew, to the sail, even making out his form from the near distance, as the submarine captain, knowing also that his first command would be to make all preparations to get underway. I waited. Waited for the first man from the Farm to emerge from the bush. Message received, Bixby had called down to me, the Farm detail was on its way. Silva and his crew of three fishing today somewhere on the waters off the other side of the island: Porterfield telling me he could not pick him up with Big Eyes. "Keep trying," I said. The waiting for the Farm people while otherwise seeming another eternity somewhat lessened by the knowledge that their arrival would coincide, more or less, with the time required to ready the *Pushkin* for sea, a species of grasping comfort in the realization thereby that these extra men, mostly Americans, a few Russians, would not be the cause of any delay in the urgent need for the submarine to get underway as quickly as possible. I looked up at the sky, seeing in a flash of thought all apocalyptic, as if we had been given all the close calls we were ever to be allotted, our measure of them run out, that this time it was at last all coming to an end, the great menacing pall forming; yet even now a thin blue line of hope from the fact that a good deal of clean sea still stood between that black thing and the island, a kind of wild reassurance at how it seemed almost to be standing still, the winds in our favor, or rather virtually no wind at all, recognizing this immense stroke of fortune, perhaps salvation itself, giving us time to abandon the island, the pall powered not by the wind but by its own engine force, pushing outward in all directions to propel itself with consummate indolence to all points of the compass, not intent particularly on attacking the island, its merely being a part of everything in its path it would soon engulf.

Behind me in the bush I heard a rustle and turned to see the Farm detail beginning to emerge from the thick growth; thirty-odd men and women in all, breathing heavily from a swift pace. No orders needed by myself—they had eyes to see, too, and of a certainty from the Farm itself the skies had told them of something that had gone terribly wrong. Now they, too, proceeded swiftly to the ladders. I stood alone, looking around, a last check. The grounds, the buildings . . . Nobody anywhere. Glanced up at the high Lookout Tower. Porterfield, Bixby, Garber still manning their posts.

"Silva?" I called up.

Porterfield was still bent to Big Eyes. He had never stopped glassing. He raised up.

"He's nowhere, Captain."

It hit me like a terrible pain even as I said it.

"We'll have to leave them. The ship needs us. Come down. On the double. All of you."

Shooing them ahead of me, I followed them across the space and onto the rungs, the last four of us descending together, alongside, almost in a measured beat. We stepped off the ladders onto the sand, moving quickly to join the others in the last boat, this presently pulling alongside *Pushkin,* where the only safety lay, a strange and, to the American sailors, alien sort of vessel, alien not from being of another nationality, that of no importance at all now, but such an opposite type of ship from their own, in fact their ancient enemy (not the Russians but the type of vessel itself), they destroyer men, the last ones now boarding the submarine, Russian sailors standing at the top of the Jacob's ladder, directing them through the forward and aft hatchways. I swung up the ladder and went to the top of the sail, joining the Russian captain. I stood a moment looking up for the last time at the settlement atop the steep Pompeiian-red cliff. The island stood deserted; our neat buildings all silent; stood as if in poignant resignation, as if saying good-bye.

"Is everybody aboard, Captain?" he said.

"Everybody I could find, Captain." And I turned my back on the island.

He spoke into the bridge telephone, the *Pushkin* swung and stood out to sea. He must have ordered flank, the submarine soon racing through the waters and straight toward that huge black mantle to all appearances moving not so much as an inch. Presently he spoke again into the phone—one would know he was asking for a sounding. He took one more look at the shroud in the high sky; ordered the ship slowed; turned to me.

"Time to dive. Let's go below, Captain."

I started down the ladder, could feel him behind me, hear the hatch closing. We emerged into the submarine's control room. In a matter of a minute he had given the command and we headed down into the safety of the ocean depths.

"If the periscope sensor will permit," the Russian captain said, "we can surface. At best it will likely have to be brief."

I stood, the only American there, in the control room, before the extensive array of panels not unlike our own. I was listening more than watching, hearing the pings of the sonar bouncing off the *Nathan James*, shortening all the time. We were proceeding very slowly—eight knots, another gauge showed. I heard one of the Russian watch-standers speak, then the captain, to me.

"Range four miles. Bearing zero eight seven."

He gave a command and I could see the depth-gauge start the other way, feel the submarine slowly ascend, finally leveling off. Another command and I could hear the periscope move up under hydraulic pressure. He sighted through the eyepiece, turned to me.

"Have a look at your ship, Captain."

I bent and peered through. The *James* lay as dead in the water as if she were at anchor. She looked absolutely untouched, not a scratch, all beautiful. Not a soul could be seen on her decks. Then suddenly there was a certain quiver of the submarine—not all that great actually, steadying quickly; myself continuing to look through. She was no longer there. For a moment I thought something had gone wrong with my eyes. Then that something had happened to the periscope eyepiece, as though it had burst. The screen filling with a chaos of wildly flying obstacles. Then the screen came all clear again, nothing wrong with the periscope. I could see blue water very clearly and scattered everywhere across it a vast debris, and somehow the feeling of the most immense stillness I had ever known, and the instant, impossible knowledge: She had blown up; disintegrated. "No," I heard my own voice as from a distance. "No." I could feel my hands tighten on the hand grips as if I were holding onto life itself; something move through my body as of the very tremor of madness but lasting as briefly as a single scar of lightning lasts and then gone, any force of will I had applied to kill it all unconscious, reflexive. I gave the scope back to the captain and even as he was looking heard him say, "My God," then heard him repeat a similarly brief phrase in Russian, perhaps, curiously, the identical expression. He raised up. He seemed as pale as a man could possibly be, but then that had always been his complexion. I said, astonished to find my own mind working, my voice steady.

"Can we surface? For survivors?"

"Survivors?" He turned from the scope, looked at me, the idea that there could be any. Then he was turning back and reading the control-room repeater of the periscope-mounted radiation sensor.

"Tolerable," he said. "It's still in the skies. Taking its time drifting down. Of course, Captain."

He gave the command and presently I could feel the submarine begin to rise, then break free of the waters. I followed him up the ladder, feeling others behind me; emerged atop the conning tower.

Aware first of a great blackness, darker than the most starless night, covering, in full occupation of the heavens, but yet below it, stretching in great circumference, the sea unbroken to all horizons; then, eyes bearing on the near-scene, all around the submarine, beginning to surround and envelop it in a kind of huge separate lake of debris, what had been a ship. Seemingly thousands of pieces, some curious sense of realization in a far-off part of the mind, and of astonishment, of how small they all were, nothing of size anywhere, the naked testimony of a clear fact: The explosion must have been one of unimaginable violence. A profound quiescence hung like a requiem over the scene. I became aware that the submarine was making its way with infinite slowness, the most precise care, through it all, and of Russian lookouts and as many of our own crew as the submarine's curving spine could accommodate, these having come quickly topside, scanning everywhere, with binoculars, with the naked eye—both for shipmates; myself on that large roster of lookouts. Seeing only the incredible amount of detritus, pushing languidly against the submarine's hull. We commenced quartering the area.

Nothing.

We quartered once more; a third time. Unnumbered eyes zealously searching. Conscious always of that huge weight of blackness descending slowly toward us. Finally the Russian captain saying something into the bridge phone, listening a moment. He turned to me, on his face an unutterable poignancy.

"I'm sorry, sir. The readings . . . they are moving fast toward unacceptable levels. Very probably this is going to be the most contaminated place on earth, quite shortly. We've got to submerge and get out of here. I suggest South."

"Yes," I said, hearing myself as of another's voice. "South."

.BOOK VIII.

PUSHKIN

Vivid in my memory as the time it happened, three months back now, is that moment when the great submarine *Pushkin* rose from the ocean depths, breaking with ease through a covering of ice floes, and there burst upon our vision a place so strange as to be unlike anything else we had ever seen. Stretching away in front of us lay a world of the utmost grandeur, its immensity of white, and of astonishing blues and greens of the greatest delicacy, dazzling in the refracted brilliance of its light. A great stillness held everywhere, the only sound the swish of our ship on dead slow advancing southward, as she did the pageant, unimaginable, majestic, unfolding before mute sailors. Soon far in the distance, ascending out of the wilderness of ice, showed a great chain of white mountains connected by glistening glaciers; then, most awesome of all, filling the entire horizon, rose across the waters, straight out of the sea, the Great Ice Barrier, shimmering regally in the sunlight, thrusting to the south as far as the eye took one. We stood in to examine this wonder, the ship proceeding cautiously, for a spell taking us directly along the seemingly endless wall of solid ice, towering high above the ship, the universal hush broken by the swell of the sea pounding and roaring against it in cascades of spume; the face of the Barrier broken now and then with fabulous ice

601

caves of the purest bright blue. The Russian captain had not a moment's time to enjoy these marvels. Himself at the conn, he was taking the ship with extreme care between ostensibly minor icebergs whose underwater aspects we nevertheless could not know; glancing at him in his calm concentration, picking his way through the bergs, I thought, as a fellow ship's captain, how fortunate we were to have an experienced Arctic Circle mariner commanding.

Pushkin's course now away from the Barrier, we moved slowly through the stilled waters of the Ross Sea, broken by scattered ice floes. Ourselves able to see great distances due to the fact that the curvature of the earth here flattened out, this world of silence and solitude seemed to come the more overpoweringly at us; its scale, its vastness; its virginal purity, undefiled, mystical. Nothing could have prepared us for the feelings that now took possession of us. The strange white world, the whiteness relieved by the most haunting range of colors, colors one felt one had never before seen, luminous greens, a soft amethyst, faint magentas, lavenders, delicate jades, reflected off ice and glacier, pale blues splashing off alabastrine peaks, as we proceeded through it casting as it were a spell over us so that we gazed awestruck, hushed as itself, into its stillness, spoke words as few as those one might have murmured at High Mass in some mighty Gothic cathedral; a feeling weirdly enhanced even by the great stately snowy-white icebergs we encountered, as many as two-score counted at one time from the conning tower, from sapphire pedestals soaring like huge pillars over a hundred feet in height, reaching upward to support the vaulted ceiling of an azurine sky; a world radiant in a kind of ultimate and primeval mystery, surely never more so than to these refugee sailors breathing in the purest air earth had ever held, inexpressible gratitude conscious beyond anything else, its embodying our very redemption, of how that sublime aspect now stood more true than ever.

Presently, passing Cape Bird off our port bow, a lookout sang out and as we stood in a host of Adélie penguins waddled out onto the ice to greet us, standing there squawking, exuberantly flapping their flippers, in all health. This was the greatest sight of all for it told us something all glorious, that all was as it had always been in this white world and that they had never so much as heard of what had happened elsewhere on earth. Saying good-bye to them, we stood out again, proceeding around Ross Island, next day sighting fin whales spouting lustily, if more evidence were needed that the contamination had not reached here: this, of course, imparted to us even before by the readings on the submarine's sensors;

still it was wondrous to see the live evidence in the penguins and the whales.

Long curlings of plume-like vapors now identified our destination, rising languidly from the volcanic cone on its summit; Mount Erebus, two and a half miles high, directly beneath it McMurdo Sound, which we presently entered, a waterway forty miles across at the entrance and fifty miles long, sculpted out of ice; beyond, the vast ice plain running unbroken to the South Pole. McMurdo Station: From the first there was agreement that it was for this one place we should make course, and not just that it was an American naval installation. The Russian captain, myself, and a number of others aboard were acutely conscious of what for some years had been in progress on the white continent. As it happened, Chaplain Cavendish was able to fill in the blanks, knowing as much about it as anyone aboard, by way of a fellow Georgetown Jesuit—as I mentioned earlier—who had done a number of tours there, not as a priest but as an ice geologist. Twelve nations had remarkably somehow been able to enter into an agreement not to exploit Antarctica, only explore it; some 1,500 scientists, mostly men, a few women, of that number of nationalities, glaciologists, paleontologists, marine biologists, oceanographers, meteorologists, microbiologists, cartographers, atmospheric physicists, a score of other fields, pursued their discrete inquiries all over its vast space during the Antarctic summer, a fraction of that number staying on through the Antarctic winter; McMurdo Station the largest on the continent, the center of American logistic and scientific activity; a thousand souls, two-thirds of all the continent's population, stationed there. Two questions seized us. The first, were any of them there now? Our greatest curiosity lay in the answer to that question. Closely behind it, in the answer to another: The extent of the stores—food, medicines and the like—which would have been stockpiled for such large numbers of human beings. Back on the island, *Pushkin,* in preparation for her intended global voyage, had been stuffed to the last cubic inch of her available spaces with supplies of food—with present ship's company, about six months' worth, we now estimated. After that, no island any longer to return to, we depended entirely on the great unknown of what lay elsewhere on the earth—other than possibly here, no place giving any promise of filling bellies due to become empty in one-half year. Only Antarctica held out hope. Our curiosity—our vested interest—was great as to both questions. The first as much as the second; the longing to know that others of our kind were alive, actually to encounter them, was astonishingly strong in the last soul of us, American and Russian; a fervor, an obsession; it was as though their very existence would offer a comfort, a reassurance, so deeply sought, so sublime, as to be beyond the limits of language to express. To discover these and to find stores would be as if in one stroke, by one place, we had been granted the most immense spiritual reward and the most immense bodily one that could possibly be our good fortune.

To update the reader's calendar: Approximately two years had passed since the launchings. Meaning that they had occurred during the Antarctic summer when the continent would have supported its greatest concentration of people. These scattered over it, bent to their various scientific projects, it was reasonable to assume that something like the following may have happened: Hearing the news, they had all proceeded at once to the McMurdo Sound base; further news, more explicitly the possible absence of any news due to the communications blackout created by the Electromagnetic Pulse, convincing them of the prudence of passing the Antarctic winter there, awaiting developments; another summer come, the intelligence quite clear at this point that there was nothing in any of their dozen nations to which to return; rationally, they had settled in to wait, to winter over again; to ponder some course of action, their stockpile of stores affording them plenty of time to reach a decision as to one. This was our general speculation, awaiting on-site verification, which we now commenced.

As we slowly penetrated McMurdo Sound that morning, the submarine proceeding at dead slow, topside in the sail were the Russian captain, myself, two watch officers, and two lookouts training binoculars on the base up ahead. *Pushkin* pushing gently through waters the blue of some flawless gem, broken only by decorative particles of ice. Temperature 15° F., the bridge thermometer read, quite comfortably cold for former Barents sailors (ourselves) and former Arctic sailors (*Pushkin's* company), all now bundled cozily in this gear from the ship's stores. Across the water, below great snow mountains, we could begin to make out the installation, the slate-colored buildings of sundry sizes huddled on the shore, their mass sitting there intrusively, as any mark of man would of necessity in this chaste world, which he had altered so infinitely less than he had any other space on earth; beyond the settlement, the great continent seeming to go on forever in an epic white emptiness. In the spectral silence that lay over the scene, all of us glassing meticulously the considerable expanse of the base for a period of at least five minutes, the Russian captain at the longer-range telescope, no one saying a word during it. He straightened up.

"Will you please try, Captain?"

I bent, swept carefully the entire diameter of the base, larger and more detailed in the telescopic lens, swept each building, slowly, once, twice, three times. Stood up, looked at him.

"Nothing that moves," I said.

"Strange," he said, the tones equally of bafflement and of initial disappointment in his voice.

"Aye. Strange."

We stood thoughtfully, both regarding it now with the naked eye across the water.

"I would have expected something . . . somebody."

"Maybe they're inside." I gave that dim hope.

"They would have seen us." Steadily we were closing the base. "Nevertheless . . ."

He spoke to a messenger who ducked below, soon produced a loud hailer.

"All of them would know English. Only ours Russian. You do it, Captain."

The English words, booming out through the hailer in a startling volume, shattered the silent scene. Briefly I identified ourselves as friendly, as a Russian submarine with crew Russian and American (we were flying both ensigns): Was anybody there? The buildings stood mute, unresponsive, before this assault, no figures emerging from any one of them. I brought the hailer down.

"Well, we'll just have a look," the Russian said, the undertones of enigma clinging to his voice. "It doesn't make sense. We'll just look," he said again. "All right, Captain?"

"By all means. Let's look."

Ahead was an ice pier. The Russian captain gave an order through the bridge intercom and presently Russian sailors with mooring lines were on the hull. He nosed her in with a perfection of seamanship and soon she stood tied up alongside the pier.

Searching through that cluster of buildings—the party of about a dozen, both Russian and American sailors, led by the two captains—was like proceeding through some ghost town, the spooky effect heightened by the enclosing whiteness of the setting, by the fervent stillness that presided everywhere. Our slow progress, one kept on edge as by the imminent prospect of a figure—a naval officer, a lone scientist—emerging and explaining all. Nothing. Nobody.

"When it happened, they cleared out."

"They would have done better to stay where they were," I said.

"Aye."

We stepped outside, stood looking around in the white silence, still pondering.

"Those must be the storehouses," he said, indicating the two large, warehouse-looking structures set in the snow at the far edge of the cluster. We had gone then into one, then the other of them; come upon as overwhelming a sight as, save for live people, could have been presented us.

Stretching down row after long row stood hundreds of shelves filled with stores. Brought to a halt for a moment in our dumbstruckness, we then began to wander in speechless awe up and down the aisles. Everything was here. First of all, food in great quantities; principally in the large freeze-dried ration containers used on U.S. Navy ships, along with hundred-pound bags of assorted foods, flour, beans, sugar, rice; also in huge freezers, one or two of which we opened, filled with great sides of beef, other meats, hanging in splendid long ranks. Shelves also filled with medicines; vitamins; cold-weather clothing; much else. Everything it seemed needful for a considerable community to live in a decidedly civilized and undeprived fashion. Where necessary, the stores especially packed for these regions and temperatures, thus in perfect condition. (Preservation of food being no problem in Antarctica, some of us familiar with the polar-exploration accounts of food of previous expeditions half a century old found on it, perfectly preserved, entirely edible.) We came to a halt in an open space and stood, still not a word said, stood in marvel contemplating this fantastic prospect, trying to assimilate the two emotions following on the two discoveries and pulling us in different directions. The immense sadness at the absence of ones like ourselves, human beings, these being what we wished more than anything else to see. The immeasurable, welling-up thrill of all that stood before us and all it represented. Rather than being able to count on but six months of assured supply of stores, of food . . . well, if one had had to pull some wild figure out of a hat, one would have probably guessed what indeed our later precise inventories and calculations showed to be just about the case. Something like a two-year supply for a thousand souls. For a company of 159 of the *Pushkin,* approximately a twelve-year supply. It was almost too much for us to comprehend. Taken together with our ten-year fuel supply for the submarine, these seemed to lift terrible chains from around us, the life prospects of quite potentially doomed men extended in a stroke to uncounted years. Men fear nothing so much as the spectre of hunger. Now that most horrible of all foes seemed vanquished virtually forever.

The most enormous lifting of spirits took possession of us, something little short of an ecstasy on witnessing an epiphany—surely the long rows harboring all our needs deserved that appellation.

Thus at McMurdo Station we first stayed, virtually all of us moving ashore. Life has settled into a pleasant if quite vigorous rhythm. Mornings, starting early, we are aboard *Pushkin* for the meticulous indoctrination of the American sailors, including myself, including the women, by the Russian sailors, in the peculiarities of submarines, converting our destroyer skills into submarine skills; learning to be submariners, respective ratings working under their counterparts—enginemen with enginemen, helmsmen under helmsmen, and so on. Hard, exacting work, requiring the closest concentration. Fascinating work to most of us, if nothing else for destroyer men to learn so precisely how their great traditional foe functions. Most of all, the stern awareness that *Pushkin* is now all, that in her lies our salvation, that therefore we must know her intimate ways in order to keep her healthy, sound, safe; profoundly aware, deeply grateful, of the fact that in her, unlike the destroyer, by proceeding in the ocean depths, we can go anywhere in perfect safety; all this giving us a growing affection toward her. Afternoons are given over to something equally intensive, equally vital—language courses in which every single member of ship's company, American and Russian, is enrolled, each learning the other's language (the rather considerable library we also discovered at the base containing language-instruction books, materials, in not just these two but as well in the several other languages of the Antarctica Pact member nations): full four hours in the Mess Hall, occupying the entire afternoon; this mastery indispensable not just to our two peoples becoming one community, but to the two ship's companies becoming one, to the very safety of the submarine, watch-standers needing to understand and execute instantly commands given in either language.

Two afternoons a week are liberty time. R and R including excursions on the ice shelf on skis, among the stores at the base being large numbers of skis of all sizes, or, to a restricted degree, in some of the vehicles, motor toboggans and others, we have discovered garaged in another of the buildings, all hands under strictest orders not to venture beyond prescribed distances—a ferocious blizzard, a whiteout capable of appearance with absolutely no warning. The library is an excellent one, so that we have not lost Dickens, Shakespeare, Dostoevski, the Bible, others, as I had at first sadly thought. So that also off-watch: Insofar as the Americans are concerned, they continue their almost ferocity of reading of anything, everything, that had so strangely commenced on the island; an absolutely curious phenomenon, as if they were under an obsession to soak up all the knowledge available; an infectious thing, the Russian sailors, observing this, hastening with their English lessons (the library containing few Russian books) so that they may join the Americans in what seems like a treasure hunt. Evenings always, after the serving of an excellent supper from our new supply of variegated stores, the showing of one of the approximately 1,000 videocassettes we have found, nearly all of them American movies, on the base's enlarged viewing screen (accoutrements we decidedly intend to take aboard the submarine); also, much awaited, another discovery, a pure luxury that required an inordinate amount of time for the Russian captain and myself to reach a decision as to its use—a large cache of beer and liquor, immediately wisely put by himself under lock and key, beer now issued on a ration of one bottle per hand every other night, the liquor withheld entirely. To say we are living well is of course to understate the matter. (The only difficulty, at first, one of sleeping patterns, of circadian rhythms, adjusting to the twenty-four-hour daylight.) Altogether, taking to the place to the degree that some of ship's company now are beginning to look with a certain regret, even a touch of apprehension, on the idea of leaving it and returning to the more uncertain and emphatically less unconstricted life of the submarine, to the ocean depths.

For of course we have to leave; as to that, there is no choice at all; that Sound now navigable that we look out on will soon undergo a profound transformation, immobilized for ship passage by ice nine feet thick; have to take the *Pushkin* out before she is imprisoned. We knew that some ships had survived the experience of spending a winter in the irons of Antarctic ice; knew also that that same ice had crushed and devoured others like match wood; into which category *Pushkin* would fall is impossible to predict; the risk of its being the latter absolutely unacceptable, forever cutting off as it would any means of escape. Together, and in consultation with other officers, both Russian and American, the Russian captain and I have worked out a plan which we presented to all ship's company gathered in the Mess Hall. Its principal lines go as follows.

We will cast off on *Pushkin* before the ice closes in, before the onset of the long twenty-four-hour-dark Antarctic winter. For approximately eight months we will proceed on *Pushkin*'s originally designed "Magellan" mission of discovering what else there may be in the world, in especial whether there exist other human beings. The mission, with no island of our own to return to as in the original plan, now drastically altered as to

principal purpose: to determine whether there is another habitable, sustaining place somewhere on the planet and in a more temperate latitude
on which we can establish another community. Barring the finding of it,
we will return here for the Antarctic summer, settle in as now, again
embark on *Pushkin* when winter comes, continue our search in other
regions of the earth not previously reconnoitered. If necessary, repeating
the submarine-and-Antarctica living cycle until we find a place that will
accept us. That happening, we will undertake a series of voyages between
that place and this one, to cram the *Pushkin* full of the stores we have
discovered, to empty those two warehouses to the last item, as many trips
as may be required to transport their contents to our new home. If finding
nothing, as I say, return here anyhow as our home for the Antarctic
summer. That being as far as planning could now take us.

What the availability of this contamination-free place offers us is
beyond price; not a hand but is all aware of it. It is quite possible that for
virtually the entire eight months of each year on *Pushkin,* passing through
zones of irradiation unforgivingly lethal on surface, we will be forced to
remain submerged, never seeing the light of day. We can return here,
move ashore, and during the Antarctic summer, with its exact opposite
of twenty-four-hour daylight, breathe in the wonderful air and enjoy the
sunshine, generally refresh and recoup ourselves before returning once
again to the darkness of the underwater seas and our search. Also, of
course, replenishing our food and other stores from the bounty of the two
warehouses. In a way we will be living like hibernating bears, disappearing
into our caves of the deep ocean for the cold months, surfacing during
the summer months to fatten up again in the Antarctic day of McMurdo.

It is a prospect full of incertitudes but, realizing how far worse our
circumstance could have been, our hopes burn bright; trusting, the majority of us, in the belief that long before the ten years have elapsed, we will
have found somewhere on all the spaces of the earth our new home.

Meantime, a word as to our present home, the *Pushkin;* a remarkable
vessel. She has turned out to be all her captain claimed for her, as we
discovered on our passage here. Actually built for operations in the Arctic
ice pack with her high-rise hull and stub sail structure permitting her to
break through the ice for missile launch, her forward diving planes bow-
mounted, submersibles normally having sail-mounted diving planes, so
they can be retracted to prevent ice damage, she has proved herself equally
at home in Antarctic waters. How fortunate above all else, as I have noted,
are we to have her, otherwise also a chosen instrument for our now joint

company; her vast size of 561 feet, eighty-five-foot beam, her 25,000-ton displacement, her astonishing speed of forty knots submerged thrown in for good measure. And above all: In her we are safe; no radiation can reach us if we come into it; we need only dive.

Almost immediately we came aboard the Russian captain initiated changes. As starters, "officers' country" became "women's country," the officers' staterooms turned over to the women. By a charming coincidence we have almost exactly the same number of women now as there had been officers in the submarine's original company. Also the space available in the submarine has been incomparably enlarged, and by a single stroke. Now the most extraordinary, intensive conversion involving the major part of the interior of the *Pushkin* is taking place. Here is how it began.

We had completed about two-thirds of our 4,500-mile passage from the island to Antarctica when one day the Russian captain mentioned that he would like to see me in his cabin. He shut the door and we settled in. I knew something was up. Something in his face; a wry, almost anticipatory look. From the first there had been an unspoken agreement between us that all major decisions would be made jointly by the two of us. I waited.

"Captain, I think we're a bit cramped, don't you? For space, I mean."

"We can't complain. We feel so lucky to have you . . ."

"I know all of that." He waved his hand as if to cut off any expression of gratitude, which seemed only to embarrass him. "I've decided to get rid of them."

"Sir?"

"The missiles. They take up too much space." He spoke as of redundant ballast.

The hugeness of the submarine was in that sense deceiving. The great SS-N-20's, extending up through two decks, in fact accounted for two-thirds of all of *Pushkin*'s space. They were the real passengers, any people aboard essentially their servants.

"We'd have a lot more room if they were gone," he continued. "A little work by the metalsmiths, that remarkable carpenter of yours . . . what's his name?"

"Travis. Noisy Travis." He had already seen plenty of Noisy's handiwork on the island.

"They and a few more of the hands could turn all that space into quite acceptable living quarters. A great deal more privacy for everybody. Elbow room, you call it?"

"Elbow room we call it. That would be most favorable," I said, hardly able to take his intention in.

"You approve of the decision, Captain?" His eyes had a glint in them.

"Absolutely. Certainly we could use the space."

Not absent from my consciousness, my something like elation at this proposal, a tearing moment of what had happened to the *Nathan James*— maybe himself, too, thinking of that as an even more real reason to jettison than the one given. I would not ask. I was deliberately staying away from this aspect of the immense step he had chosen that would accomplish this desired thing. But he was not.

"Won't ever possibly need them." He spoke offhandedly.

"Won't ever possibly . . . need them," I agreed.

Our eyes came together, locked, saying all. A tremendous moment really. Then on his lips the barest hint of a smile—wonderfully, with it, a trace of mischievousness.

"I thought perhaps you might concur. We will consider it done."

It happened as simply as that. Next day we accomplished it. Without surfacing. I remember looking at the chart in the navigation room and noting that we had just entered the Antarctic Circle. The exploding mechanisms of the one hundred and ninety-two 500 kt warheads safed. Then one by one, the vehicles sent off, their castrated hulks entombed in the Pacific, to lie forever on its ocean floor for the fishes to be curious about. When it was over and we were standing in the launch control room, he turned to me, spoke quietly.

"Let's trust there are no more, Captain," he said. "Let's trust that's the last of them. Anywhere."

I remember how casual it all was, no heavy, ponderous thoughts. Then even what there was of that gone as he and I proceeded, altogether like some homeowner having had completed an addition to his house, anxious to see it, to where they had been and gazing in incredulity at the enormity of that now-vacant space, thinking only homeowner's thoughts, of how better, people no longer tripping over one another, things were going to be all around.

Initial work was commenced even as we were in passage to McMurdo. But it was the discoveries of tools, implements and materials here that opened up the full possibilities. Among the base's considerable inventory were supplies of seasoned timber, welding tools, even a black-smith's forge. Provided with these, a Russian-American crew of about thirty shipfitters, molders, machinist's mates is beginning to transform where once the great titans resided—adding staterooms, a larger crew's compartment needed for the joint companies, a library; above all, perhaps, infinitely better berthing compartment (one of my delicate, diplomatic chores had been to get across to the Russian captain, once he had made his decision to jettison the missiles, that American sailors were accustomed to far less spartan spaces than his vessel provided, including on our own submarines; he is a quick study, and now both American and Russian ratings will find these much improved). When we cast off again on our inaugural eight-month journey, with the *Pushkin's* living space more than trebled, a far more comfortable permanent home she will be for our submarine colony of seventy-four Russians and eighty-five Americans, the Americans including thirteen women, eight going down with the *James.* Considering how long we will be in her and how long, in every likelihood, submerged, a great blessing.

So it is that while we have no way of knowing what the future holds, we remain steadfast in hope. To those who have come through so much, hope comes quite easily. And, of course, not to hope is a sin. Soon we cast off on our voyage; penetrating, as we expect, into the most deadly of irradiated zones, hoping to find within them one or more contamination-free "pockets" of habitability, perhaps even with live human beings in it. We will certainly take a close look at, among other places, the United States of America.

The day we were to leave the Jesuit and I took a walk.

Already the days have begun to shorten, the long darkness approaches. We walked away from the base, the ice beginning to turn hard, crunching not at all under our feet, our destination Observation Hill, about 750 feet high and quite steep, our objective to get in some hard exercise before the approaching long months of confinement in the submarine and also to view the place itself a last time. We cleared the summit and stood a moment before the great wooden cross erected in memory of the English polar explorer Robert Falcon Scott and his four companions. It commanded McMurdo Sound on one side where they had lived in their hut, still present, visible from here; and the Great Ice Barrier on the other where they had died returning from their conquest of the Pole. We read the inscription from Tennyson's *Ulysses:* "To strive, to seek, to find, and not to yield." Rocks of all sizes were everywhere and we sat on one of the larger ones. I checked my watch. It was almost straight up midnight. Far below us, against the pier, stood *Pushkin,* tiny figures moving about, final preparations. She would cast off at exactly 0300.

Earlier there had been a cold wind but now it had died away and we sat in the great Antarctic silence, reluctant to break into it. The sun, low now in the sky, seemed to wish to create some ultimate effect of splendor before it departed for the long winter months, a vivid red enfolding the northern sky, a soft indigo the southern, a delicate pink the great range of the Transantarctica Mountains to the west, gleaming splashes of emerald and sapphire and of diaphanous blues rolling off the endless white peaks and precipices, snowfields and glaciers, in a stunning opalescence, everywhere the snow dazzling with reflected light, and all under a pale blue heaven. We sat in silence trying to comprehend the vastness and magnificence of this strange place, the remotest earth knew, its unutterable beauty. Looking out over it, I thought of the great cleanness and purity of the continent which even man had not been able to desecrate; stood in boundless admiration of it that it had resisted the contamination, valiantly held on to its pure and sacred air. It was like the sea in that. It stood victor: it and the timeless unconquerable sea stretching before us to the north; both noble, both incorruptible. We looked up. A lone skua bird, its great wings outspread, riding an air current, soared high above, then took a pass over us, flew away.

Our eyes following the circumference came upon McMurdo Sound, twilight blue, clear and sparkling in the near distance, leading northward on the course we were about to follow, mottled with the "young ice" that had begun to form, telling us that winter will be very soon, time to leave. As we sat looking at the prospect, still wondrous to us after all these months, other thoughts, memories, with myself and with him as well I knew, seemed to throng in upon us. I said it quietly.

"She was a good ship. Brought us through."

"Aye, she was that."

"I never knew a better one. Or a better ship's company."

For weeks afterward I had gone over it in my mind, a thousand times, every possibility, rational or irrational, logic or fantasy, having its moment . . . repeatedly attempting to discern what was behind those last words of the OOD, telling me the astonishing thing that Thurlow, commanding, was not immediately available . . . thinking of every conceivable thing that could have happened after that; the remotest connections taking their brutally tormenting turns in my mind, even Thurlow's Russian-speaking ability, knowing Russian seamen and officers were aboard: I went so far as to attempt to determine if I could discover anything in that. Zero, as with countless other speculations, conjectures, most of them as preposterous as that one, leading nowhere.

As to the physical facts, in one of those self-inquisitions I had kept my mind orderly enough to come up with a sequence of events that bordered on the rational, using that strange word from the point of view of the perpetrators. It went as follows: The intent being to jettison all missiles they—whoever "they" were—had commenced sending off the TLAM-C's, the conventional Tomahawks, once they had reached a safe place high in the skies detonating them with a signal from the ship. To jettison the nuclear Tomahawks, they had only to leave them nonarmed— the arming being done by the same keys that launched the missiles. This they had succeeded in doing. Then something had happened with only one missile. Quite possibly, because of an inexactitude in the programming by someone not so exquisitely honed in the highly refined skills required by the procedure, inadvertently arming this single Tomahawk. The missile exploding, it had thereupon sent its neutrons back to the nonarmed missile trailing it, exploding the fissionable material in its warhead, this one then doing the exact same thing to the missile behind it; the sequence continuing through all the nonarmed nuclear-warhead missiles that followed. These deductions, initially occurring, seemed to me the first ones of a clear reasoning and in my desperateness for explanation I seized on them, assorted doubts, vicious in character, continuing to stab at me. Too neat—it was all too neat. And yet it carried all logic. As far as the explosion on the ship was concerned, the violence of it almost dictated that it could have been only one thing. The VLS—the missile launcher, the cells containing the missiles—had blown up. One or both of them. Blown up from some kind of malfunction perhaps having to do with operations to which it was not accustomed. Blown up not from explosion of nuclear warheads which had to be armed to do so, but from the many conventional missiles in its magazines—Tomahawks, Standards, Harpoons—all lethal by any but nuclear standards. A malfunction.

These various conjectures helped—but stopped far short of bringing me any kind of peace. The suspicion that hovered over all three of those whose very images kept passing relentlessly through my mind, each having expressed at one time or another that preference, being so obvious as to make one suspicious of the theory itself: that one or all had meant only to jettison, do away with the missiles, that something then had gone monstrously wrong. That only one had decided actually to attempt that goal the more likely theory, that he could have secured the necessary cooperation of the one with the other key . . . the mind fiercely resisted. Myself at first driven to the very edge by the effort to sort out, to untangle what could never be solved, as in some impossible feat of marlinspike seamanship . . . Delaney knowing the location of Girard's key, Thurlow of mine, Girard also knowing the latter . . . it had taken me awhile to remember that, a seemingly distant memory which I realized I was perhaps keeping deliberately shrouded in uncertainty, in imprecision, an intentional failure to remember, lest itself move me across that line, of a conversation in the cave in which having told me the location of her key, she had asked me almost playfully the corresponding information as to mine; the idea having occurred these past weeks that what had seemed at the time so lighthearted and happenstance had in fact been deliberate and purposeful on her part; this idea so freighted with horror that I banished it as a threat to sanity, along with one even more terrible, that the murders of eight sister shipmates had in some inexplicable way pushed her to what she judged to be an act of atonement for what the ship had done long ago . . . such speculations spawning other memories of what had taken place in that cave between us, these rushing in savagely to attack me. I had trembled on the brink of the chasm. And something else. Herself helplessly a part of the enigma, each time it rose in my mind, so did she, many other times as well; and each time myself, crossing unknown frontiers of sorrow, seized with a pain so great I knew I would not survive if I continued to allow it such free access to my soul. Her, the gone ship, the gone shipmates, all of it.

I had decided that it would serve no purpose to tell anyone of my and Girard's backup arrangement, that Delaney had known the location of one missile-launch key, Thurlow of the other. So much was unknown, the knowledge might harm the memory of the innocent. But then, after all this time, I had determined on one possible exception to this vow of silence: the Jesuit, swearing him to secrecy. I had waited. Now I decided it was best for him to know; but more important, feeling that the act of telling him would somehow make possible what I so desperately desired: not to erase entirely the last shred of remembrance—I could not hope for that, did not even wish it; but to stop the interminable questioning in my soul, as acts of confession are said to do. And so, on this hillside in Antarctica I related the circumstances, most specifically as to who had had access to the keys, while he listened in a silence deep as that of the great white spaces that surrounded us.

"An accident," I said, ending the account, surprised at the something like harshness in my voice. "It had to have been an accident."

I felt I could live with that; not at all sure I could with anything else; suddenly aware that he, the most percipient of men, knew this to the finest degree of sensibility.

"I prefer to think it was an accident," I said more quietly.

"I understand, sir." He waited a moment. "The damned things were never safe."

Somehow—who can ever explain the simplicities of these mysteries?—it was as if some intolerable burden were lifted from me; that I turned away from it; indeed that we both did. Faced a new direction. As if to say so, that the matter was closed, that the past was gone as all pasts must and we need concern ourselves only with the future, he spoke of another thing, even his voice wonderfully changed, in it an altogether bright if quiet tone.

"It looks as if we made it, Captain," he said. "The babies."

Some of that extra space in *Pushkin* will be a nursery. Three of the women are now pregnant. Ensign Martin, Signalman Bixby, Seaman Thornberg. The doc reporting that they are coming along fine. Their children will be Russian-American, American-Russian: Take your choice. Selmon was right about that, too, as he was right about so much: The next fathers of mankind are to be submariners.

He would never say it so I did, not excessively irreverently or sacrilegiously, I felt; perhaps a certain wryness in my voice.

"You mean God is going to give us a second chance?"

He allowed himself a soft smile. "Remember you said that, Captain. Personally, I never presume to go around quoting Him. But it does look that way, doesn't it?"

Suddenly the profound Antarctic stillness was shattered by the three loud blasts of *Pushkin*'s foghorn: striking haunting and lonely over the great solitude of the world around us, seeming to roll and echo off the nearby whitened peaks. It was the two-hour signal before getting underway that had been arranged; summoning sailors to the sea.

"Time to climb down," I said, rising. "We don't want to be left behind."

"Great Christ no, sir," he said, quite vigorously, standing up alongside me. "It's going to be much too interesting a voyage to be left behind. Just imagine. To find out what's out there . . ."

His voice trailed away. We started down the hill and made our way toward *Pushkin,* her two ensigns fluttering in the cold wind that had begun to come off the ice cap, the ship ready to cast off on her voyage to rediscover the world . . . But that is another book.